THE ETERNAL KINGDOM

Ben Peek is the critically acclaimed author of *The Godless*, *Leviathan's Blood*, *The Eternal Kingdom* and three previous novels, *Black Sheep*, *Twenty-Six Lies/One Truth*, and *Above/Below*, co-written with Stephanie Campisi. He has also written a short story collection, *Dead Americans*. In addition to this, Peek is the creator of the psychogeography pamphlet *The Urban Sprawl Project*. With the artist Anna Brown, he created the autobiographical comic *Nowhere Near Savannah*. He lives in Sydney with his partner, the photographer Nikilyn Nevins, and their two cats, Capote and Harper.

www.theurbansprawlproject
@nosubstance

By Ben Peek

THE CHILDREN TRILOGY

The Godless

Leviathan's Blood

The Eternal Kingdom

THE ETERNAL KINGDOM

Book Three of the Children Trilogy

BEN PEEK

MACMILLAN

First published 2017 by Macmillan
an imprint of Pan Macmillan
20 New Wharf Road, London N1 9RR
Associated companies throughout the world
www.panmacmillan.com

ISBN 978-1-4472-5189-7

1 3 5 7 9 8 6 4 2

A CIP catalogue record for this book is available from the British Library.

Map artwork © David Atkinson 2014: handmademaps.com

Typeset in Spectrum MT 13/17 pt by Palimpsest Book Production Limited, Falkirk, Stirlingshire
Printed and bound by CPI Group (UK) Ltd, Croydon, CR0 4YY

For Nikilyn Nevins

Acknowledgements

Those to thank include John Jarrold, Bella Pagan, Julie Crisp, Neil Lang, Pete Wolverton, Irene Holickit, Kyla Ward and Tessa Kum. All the people who have supported the books through all the ways that they can have earned my undying gratitude, as well.

But above all these people is my partner, Nikilyn Nevins. There are no words to properly explain the support, patience and love she has provided during the long journey of these three books. Over the years I have written this trilogy there have been international moves, visas, deaths in the family, illness, rooms without windows, market stalls, photography, tattoos, biobanks, Spanish, the adventures of publishing, and two black cats, Harper and Capote, who moved in. It is impossible to explain how important she has been during this time, but the fact that I am here and haven't disintegrated into a host of self-destructive behaviours perhaps gives some indication of it.

THE ETERNAL KINGDOM

Kakar
Eakar
Nmia
Allitilana
Gogair
The Saan
Ooila
Illate
Sooia

Satera
Yeala
Kingdoms of Faaisha
Leera
The Plateau
Mireea
Yenaim
Balana
Hitna
Kanja
Wilate
Zoum
Zoatia
Faer
Tinalan

Histories

Written by ONAEDO

Year 1029

After the Leviathan died, after her blood turned the ocean black and poisonous, there were no gods for over ten thousand years.

In 1023, that changed. The people of Leera cannibalized their homes and, with the material, built catapults and towers, and laid siege to the city of Mireea. The Leeran people claimed that they were the Faithful of a new, yet unnamed god, but it was not until the Mireean people retreated to the Floating Cities of Yeflam that she appeared.

Six years after that event, most people think Se'Saera was named there, and the Breaking of Yeflam was the first display of her power. It is not uncommon for men and women to claim that, as Yeflam's stone floors were torn apart, a giant made from a storm arose and spoke her name. But that is not true. Se'Saera was named across the ocean, in the country Ooila, in the First Queen's kingdom. Nor was her name said by any creature or being of immense power. No, her name was spoken by the saboteur Bueralan Le, a man who had been exiled from Ooila for over a decade, and whom our new god sent there to draw one of history's monsters, Aela Ren, to him. Only a few know that Se'Saera's first act after she was named was not to destroy a city, but to take the soul of a dead man and place it in the womb of a woman Bueralan Le had befriended. This first act of the newly named god, the cartographer Samuel Orlan wrote days after, was a most revealing one.

But few spoke about what happened in Ooila.

Instead, people talked of Yeflam, of its destruction, and of the trial of **Zaifyr**, the immortal man known more infamously as Qian.

Lady Muriel Wagan brought Zaifyr to Yeflam in chains at the end of the Siege of Mireea. In Yeflam, the head of the Enclave, Aelyn Meah, met Zaifyr at the gates of her giant stone city, and tried to convince him to leave. The two called each other brother and sister, and considered each other family. But Zaifyr would not listen to his sister. He had come to Yeflam to convince the immortals in the Enclave to stand against the new god and to go to war against her before she became too powerful. In the Siege of Mireea, he had learned that Se'Saera kept the souls of the dead in the world, in an endless state of hunger and cold, to fuel her own power. She had to be struck down, he believed.

What he did not know – what he could not know – was that the new god had already reached out to Yeflam. With the help of the Keeper, Kaqua, she had turned many of the immortals to her cause.

Zaifyr was killed by Aelyn Meah in the Breaking of Yeflam. The storm giant so many remember was her creation. Once dead, Zaifyr fell from the sky, into the black ocean, and was lost beneath the poisonous waves of Leviathan's Blood.

There were others in Yeflam, figures who were important to history, men and women we must not forget.

The first of these was **Ayae**, the former apprentice to the great cartographer Samuel Orlan. She arrived in Yeflam with the refugees of Mireea. Because of her newly risen powers – at that point little more than the ability to control herself during a fall and to create fire – she was not sent to one of the barren islands beneath Yeflam, but allowed to live with two friends, Faise and Zineer. There she acted as an envoy between the Keepers' Enclave and the people of Mireea. If the task was not a poisoned one when it was given, it could only become one. Ayae's attempts to help the people she had grown up with were thwarted, her friends killed, and in her grief, she began to turn to stone. She was forced to confront the notion that if she did not learn to control her powers, they would change her in such ways that she would always be a slave to the divinity within her.

With the aid of Zaifyr and his oldest brother, Jae'le, Ayae found a balance. It did not come from books, but rather from Yeflam's descent into civil war. She found herself fighting to protect the people of Mireea and Yeflam from the Keepers and Se'Saera's own hideous soldiers. In that turmoil, Ayae did survive and, I would argue, flourish. She did what all great warriors have done in a time of need.

It is strange then, that in so few years, history has all but forgotten her.

It has not forgotten **Aned Heast**, however.

This former mercenary, a man who had lost not just his leg in battle but also his reputation, began the war against Se'Saera as Mireea's captain of the guard. In the Siege of Mireea, he paid an expensive price to force a stalemate onto General

Waalstan and the Leeran Army. It was one designed to give him time to rebuild the Mireean force. If he had stayed there, he might have still been known as the Captain of the Spine. However, a letter penned by a former soldier was delivered by a Hollow, a warrior from the Pacifist Tribes of the Plateau. There were no words on the letter, just an image, but it was an image that forced Aned Heast to return to the position he had held years before: Captain of Refuge.

What can be said about Refuge that has not already been said? How can I describe a group of soldiers who do not work for money, but who answer the cries of those most in need, and who have fought and died through the most terrible battles of history? The recounting of their deeds through previous volumes of *Histories* will have to suffice. It is enough to say here only that Aned Heast was not the first Captain of Refuge, but he was the last. Under him, Refuge had been broken in Illate by the Five Queens of Ooila. He had been one of the few to survive.

The letter that the Hollow, Kye Taaira, held demanded Heast's return. He left Yeflam at night and travelled over the crumbling Mountains of Ger, through the haunted city of Mireea, to find the witch of Refuge, Anemone. She lived in the small town of Maosa, a settlement ravaged by Se'Saera's soldiers. By the time Heast arrived, the old witch was dead, and in her place, her granddaughter stood, instead.

Yet it would be the two of them who rebuilt Refuge, the two of them who history would not easily forget.

Of **Bueralan Le**, the man who spoke a god's name, we can only wish kindness. After the loss of his soldiers in Ranan, after his own blood brother was slain by Se'Saera and his soul given to Bueralan, after he sailed to Ooila . . . after all the tragedies of those days, and the days that followed his naming of Se'Saera, we can only hope that peace will find the former saboteur.

After the Siege of Mireea, Bueralan returned to his homeland in the company of Samuel Orlan. The two were the only survivors of the ill-fated mission Muriel Wagan sent into Leera, but it did not leave them allies. Every Orlan has had his or her own game to play, and the eighty-second Samuel Orlan was no different. When he and Bueralan arrived in Ooila, the latter thought it was but a matter of time before the former would betray him. When Bueralan presented himself to the First Queen of Ooila, Zeala Fe, and begged for his exile to be lifted, he thought that moment had come. But it was Orlan's intervention that allowed him to be returned to his home.

What neither man realized was that Zeala Fe was in a difficult situation. She was dying in the fashion that only those with a protracted illness can, and her children had begun to plot against her. As if that was not enough, the stories of Aela Ren's arrival in Ooila grew, and Zeala Fe knew she would need all that she had if she were to survive. A desperate, exiled baron was a man she could easily manipulate to serve this goal.

Yet, for all of Zeala Fe's power, for all her cunning, she could not stand against the brute force of Aela Ren's power.

Ren was the servant of the god Wehwe, who had died during the War of the Gods. Driven mad by the loss of his master, Ren gathered the other men and women like him – the god-touched, as they were known – and began to purge the world. He believed that if there was no god, there was no truth, or absoluteness. The horrors he committed in Sooia because of this are many and well documented. When word of a new god reached him, he came to Ooila in search of the man who knew her name. Aela Ren knew that for a god to be real, its name must be said by another, and that name must echo through all living creatures.

I have only my sympathies to offer to Bueralan Le. I fear little else can be done for him.

Aelyn Meah visited Leviathan's End five years after the Battle of Ranan.

She was a diminished figure by then. Physically, she was tall and narrow, a sinewy white woman emotionally fed on regret and sorrow. The last was so palpable that it could be felt when she entered a room.

To the people who were not yet part of Se'Saera's Faithful, Aelyn Meah was known as the Betrayer, the Fool's Breath, and the Daughter of Lies. Over the last five years she has been hunted and attacked by people from all over the world. She has survived not through her own cunning, but through the will of our new god. Stories of Se'Saera striking down those who lift a hand against Aelyn Meah are not uncommon.

It is not a blessing, or even a kindness, that sees Se'Saera protect her. It is, ironically, a curse.

—Onaedo, *Histories, Year 1029*

Prologue

At the age of six, Eilona Wagan's mother told her stories about the gods.

It had been her father's idea. Eilona was a quiet child and, in an attempt to get her to interact with other children, he had taken her to an afternoon performance of Tall Tales, a popular children's performer in Mireea. When the two arrived at the tent, Eilona had been so overwhelmed by the size of the crowd that she had panicked and her father had been forced to take her back to the Keep. The sight did not go unnoticed, but despite the potential embarrassment, her father returned alone and purchased all of Tall Tales's books. One of Eilona's lasting memories of him was when he returned and told her that, if she loved the stories, she could have Tall Tales come and perform for a smaller group. She told him that she did not care and he, for his part, ignored her. He sat down on the floor next to her and read. The afternoon's sun sank while his deep voice shifted between a whisper and a shout, depending on whether the scene was one of solitude or of action. He introduced her to knights and maidens and to their worlds of horses and swords and gowns and evil wizards. He laid the book in his lap so that his long arms could stretch and flow during daring chases and sudden rescues. He even made the sounds of hooves thundering down roads and swords crashing into each other. By the time the moon had risen, he had enthralled her with the stories printed on the roughly cut pages. He had done such a good job that it became a ritual, and after he died, two years later, her mother continued it.

Her mother was a very different person to her father, however. Whereas he was tall, lean and dark-haired, her mother was solid and fleshy and changed her hair colour regularly. She turned it from red to black to brown and, occasionally, she mixed lurid bright blues and greens into it as well. After Eilona's father died, it remained a sombre dark brown for nearly a year, as if, in her grief, a part of her had stilled.

Unsurprisingly, there were no knights and no maidens in the stories her mother told. Instead, she spoke of creation. She spoke of how a giant god tamed the elements and became their jailer with his huge stone weapons and long, long set of chains. She spoke of how the God of Death wandered the roads, and how he met with the stone statues of the God of Life in the first and last light of the day to discuss who had been born and who had died. She read stories of how the continents had been made by the hands of a woman, and how the sky was given currents and pattern by a man. She spoke about how fire was given to humanity, not stolen as others said, and how the first creatures to live in the ocean were commanded by their god to tell the humans who hunted them their names, so that they knew who they hunted and would do so with respect.

Even at the age of six, Eilona knew her mother's stories were morals disguised as fictions. It did not surprise her. Her mother did not believe in a world of gilded cages or fanciful illusions and, with her father's mortality now an event in both their lives, her mother would not indulge in it even briefly. Every fantasy she told her daughter had to have a point and a lesson. But it was not until much later that Eilona realized how rare the tales her mother told her were, and how they revealed in her a more educated mind than she had ever suspected.

When Eilona first learned this, she was far away from Mireea. She was in Zoum, in a small mountain town named Pitak, where the campus of the University of Zanebien lined the mountains like a series of old, broken guard posts. The nation of Zoum was defined by its bankers, by the solitary men and women who were called to witness deals, to act as proxies in sales, and to ensure that the finances of the world were kept in order. Most bankers believed that their work was important because there was no natural order in the world, but many people would have been surprised to learn that in the University of Zanebien, economics was not what was studied. It was, instead, a domain for philosophy. It was there, in these small classrooms, that Eilona discovered how her mother had pieced together her god-inspired tales from books so old that they survived only in half-translated copies, in rare editions, or in largely oral traditions. It was just one of the many surprises the university held for her.

Another was the experience of how, with Eilona living abroad, she and her mother became closer. She would not say that they were intimate – Eilona could admit now that she left Mireea in disgrace and that the contact she and her mother had until she was twenty-two was strained – but each year she was away, she saw the references of her childhood unravel and felt herself draw closer to a greater understanding of her mother. When she finished her studies and was offered a job as a lecturer, she stayed, as much to further her knowledge of the woman with whom she had fought as a child and young adult, as to further her academic pursuits.

When her mother's letter had arrived three months ago, Eilona had been relieved. News had reached Pitak that Mireea had been destroyed by Leeran forces and she had sent out letters to learn the fate of her mother and stepfather. But no matter her gratitude at the confirmation that both were alive, Eilona greeted the sight of the woman who delivered it, Olcea, with a terrible certainty.

It is much worse than has been reported, she thought as she met the witch. *My stepfather is dead. My mother is crippled. A witch does not deliver good news.*

Yet the letter the other woman gave to her was three pages in length and contained nothing personal. Instead there was a set of instructions for Eilona to deliver to investors and bankers throughout Zoum. It was, she thought, a letter that would have been surprisingly cold, even when she and her mother had been at their most distant.

Olcea, who wore layers of thick black and grey, sat before her while she read. Her wrapped hands rested on the table, while at her feet sat a solid backpack.

'Is she well?' It was the first question Eilona asked. 'She is not injured?'

'Physically she's fine, but mentally?' The witch offered a slight shrug. 'Things are difficult in Yeflam.'

'Is that why she sent this?' Eilona had led them to an outdoor table made from white-painted wood. 'It is – if I do what she says here, she will not be able to provide for herself, much less a nation.'

'I have not read it.'

'But she told you about it?'

'In parts. It sounded as if she had bartered for something.'

'What would be worth this much? This will bankrupt her. It will leave her with nothing.'

'Your mother—' The witch cut her sentence short and sighed. 'Mireea is lost. The Leerans have destroyed it. Our home exists only in memory now.'

Eilona's memories were not such that she would miss Mireea. She began to fold the letter along its creases. 'But you still work for my mother?'

'I made my life on battlefields.' Olcea paused and, in that moment, Eilona saw the fatigue set deep into the other woman's dark skin, the grief that was at its core. 'I left before the first Leeran soldier arrived in Mireea. I am not proud of that, but I did. I had planned to go to Gogair to start a new life. I told myself that a slaver's town always has use for a woman like me. That is what fear will do to you, child. Fear will lead you to betray who you are and it will cost you the image that you hold of yourself. My fear guided me all the way to Yeflam before I stopped myself. It was there that I realized I had spent too much of my time working with orphans to work for a slaver. I was still living in Yeflam when your mother found me. She did not spare me her judgement when she asked me to deliver this letter. I agreed because she was right in that, not because I thought she was right in what she wrote you.'

The conversation ended and Eilona escorted Olcea past the hedges and out onto the street before returning to the table and the letter. There, she sat until the afternoon's sun began to rise. By then, she had reread the three-page letter, refolded it, unfolded it, and read it again.

She would do what her mother asked: there was no doubt of that, even though she disagreed. What she did not expect, however, was that in doing what her mother asked, she would feel a pull towards the Floating Cities of Yeflam and the ruins of her childhood home on the Spine of Ger. In the following days, as she travelled throughout Zoum, as she saw the bankers her mother named, the feeling increased. Like her, each of the men and women she met had a list of concerns about what was asked. Each asked to see her mother's letter personally. All of them told her that what her mother asked for was a mistake. One said that her mother must be in danger. Another that it had to have been written under duress. When the last banker asked her to return to her mother to verify what was written, Eilona agreed. At the end of the week, she took her place beside Olcea in an old cart pulled by a hulking black ox.

Laena watched her go. Her partner wanted to accompany her, but she was still recovering from an attack of pneumonia caught on an excavation site in Faer, where the remains of a pair of statues created by Ain, the God of Life, had been found. Besides, Eilona told her, after she kissed Laena goodbye, her mother would probably be in charge of Yeflam by the time she and Olcea reached it.

She hoped that it was true. After a week of travel, she had almost come to believe it.

Then the new god, Se'Saera, was named.

For Eilona, the knowledge came upon her gently, but not without strangeness. When the morning's sun rose, she discovered that she could not remember a time in her life when she did not know Se'Saera's name, even though she knew, intellectually, that she had not known it for more than a day. In addition, it was a name with little context. Eilona knew only that Se'Saera was a god. She knew nothing of the ethics, morals, or structures that defined a god, that had defined the old gods.

For Olcea, however, the experience was less pleasant. She was physically ill after the name came to her and when Eilona asked about it, when she tried to help, the witch pushed her away. It was as if she had seen in the god's name a horror that Eilona had not and her violent refusal to talk about it in the following two months did little to explain the experience.

Yet, despite the revelation of the new god, the most troubling news was of the destruction of Yeflam. It arrived in bits and pieces: from travellers, from papers, from conversations overheard in towns. The Keepers had begun a civil war, some claimed. The Keepers had been thrown out of Yeflam, said others. Eilona recorded what was said in the letters she penned to Laena. She wrote about hearing that her mother was alive. That half of Yeflam existed. That

Se'Saera had been in Yeflam. That a civil war had broken out. That a war between Leera and Yeflam had begun. The story Eilona could piece together made little sense. When the mountains of Zoum gave way to the green plains of Balana and Olcea led them to the coast, she knew only that the danger her mother faced was worse than any she had faced before.

'You will be able to send the letters to Laena in Zalhan,' the witch said, sitting opposite Eilona in the cold night, the shadows blending into her clothes. They were near the town and the smell of blood and salt was faint in the air. 'It does not have much, but it has a postmaster.'

'Bankers take the mail to Zoum,' Eilona said. 'Or private messengers, like you. Postmasters are not welcome.'

Olcea shook her head. 'Who would have thought the mail would be so sensitive?'

'Bankers,' she replied, but the joke, like all their jokes of late, felt flat.

In the morning, Zalhan presented itself as a small strip of a town in the distance. At first sight of it, Eilona felt as if she was approaching something ominous – a feeling she struggled to rid herself of as she drew closer. She tried to explain the sensation away as a simple response to being near the ocean after Se'Saera's arrival. After all, the smell of blood and salt was the smell of the Leviathan's death. And hadn't Olcea told her that the slavers' town was not known for its law-abiding captains? She had been very clear about that when she explained that it was here that the two women would find passage to the northern side of Yeflam.

'There are no guards,' Olcea murmured from beside her.

The gate, which was made from long pieces of white-painted wood that had chipped over the years, stood open and unattended.

The ox pulled the cart slowly into the town. A long main road – the only road – ran down to the dock, cutting Zalhan in half. On each side of the road were wooden buildings. Most of them were two storeys in height, but every now and then one reached three, and when it did, it did so as if it were a height that the structure knew it should not aspire towards. Each had been painted a variety of colours – blue, green, white, yellow and red – and, as the silence in the town continued, the colours lent an air of strange morbid festivity.

Eilona felt her dread increase. She could count over twenty buildings, but she could not see a single person on the street. Likewise, she could not see anyone on the wooden footpaths that linked the buildings together. Nor could she see the outline of a person through the windows. As the cart made its way down the road, it also became clear to her that she could not see any activity on the three ships moored at the end of the town. In fact, the only life that she could see belonged to the shadow of a large bird, flying high in the sky.

'Stay in the cart.' The witch pulled the ox to a halt and then reached behind for her solid pack. 'You'll be safe here.'

'Where are you going?' Her voice rushed out before she could stop it. 'The town is empty!'

Olcea shouldered the pack and stepped off the cart. When her feet touched the ground, she paused. 'There's blood on the windows,' she said, finally. 'And you can smell the rot.'

The building Olcea walked towards was two storeys high and had once been painted a dark green. The three suns had faded it to a pale lime and, on the outside, there was a sign that depicted a ship inside a whale's belly. Eilona could not make out the blood that the other woman spoke of, nor could she smell the rot, either. But as Olcea walked away from her and her sense of dread increased, Eilona left the cart. Once she touched the ground, she could suddenly smell the stench of decay. By the time she had taken two more steps, she could see the stains on the windows: dark smudges of handprints, as if someone had left them there while trying to open the window to escape.

Eilona caught up with the other woman as she climbed the steps of the inn. There was a buzzing sound now, and it grew when the witch opened the door.

The morning's sun illuminated only the entrance, as if it knew the horror that it would unveil if it went further. Its limited intrusion on the room revealed not just the edge of a bar and the corner of an overturned table, but thousands and thousands of thick, fat flies. As Eilona raised her hand to her mouth to stifle the smell of the room, Olcea took a step forwards. When she did, a pair of lamps in the ceiling caught alight with fire and the shadowy blanket that lay over the room began to evaporate. Two of the table's legs were revealed to be broken off. The table itself was cracked down the middle. Against it lay the body of a young woman, her head split open. Flies lifted and fell upon her like a shawl, crawling from her wounds, her mouth and ears. Beside her lay an old man who appeared to be sleeping, though by the angle of his neck and the flies that covered him, it was clear that he was not. Another man lay close to him. In his hand he held one of the table legs, the end a blunt, bloody mess that was also covered in flies. Another woman followed, and then another, and soon their bodies began to blend into each other as the density of the insects grew to such a level that the sex and identity of the dead was lost. All that remained was the horror of the massacre.

'A witch,' a woman's voice said from above them. It was a strange voice: old, but deep and commanding. It ran through Eilona like a sharp blade across a brittle spine. 'What kind of witch are you?'

'A poor one,' Olcea said quietly. Her face was still as she looked up the stairs, where the lamps revealed only a shadow. 'I can steal a bit of the dead for light, nothing more.'

'Ah, modesty.' The first of the stairs began to creak. 'But it is not necessary. In here, in this town, you should be who you are.'

'I am nobody.'

'I doubt that,' she said. 'Very few people lie to me.'

At the end of the stairs, the flies began to rise and buzz as a long staff hit the ground sharply. Then – as if they had been hushed – the sound of the insects began to subside. The woman who had spoken pushed through them and drew closer.

'What happened—' Olcea paused and Eilona saw that the hand around the leather strap of her pack was wet with blood. 'What happened here is none of our business. What you have done is—'

'What I pleased.' The woman drew closer, revealing herself to be of such an advanced age that it was impossible to determine just how old she was. Her brown skin was light, as if it had been hidden away from the three suns, but it was mapped with deep lines and creases. Her grey hair was short and thick and had once – not so long ago, Eilona believed – been shaved down to her skull. Eilona pressed her hand against her mouth and tried not to speak, tried not to ask how long the old woman had been sitting in this inn, how she had survived the massacre here, though she desperately wanted to. She could not understand how a woman of her age, a woman clearly of no means – she wore an old robe of black and white and an equally old homemade leather belt with a dozen pouches – had been untouched. 'But if it helps you sleep at night,' the woman continued, 'they were slavers. Not all, but some. They had been running flesh to and from Gogair's markets and bringing home a quiet profit.'

'Are you a witch?' Eilona said, before she could stop herself. 'Did they try to make a slave of you?'

'She could never be a slave,' Olcea said quickly. 'The girl means no insult, My Lady. She doesn't know who you are.'

'But you do.' The flies drifted away from the old woman, refusing to settle upon her clothes, even after she had stopped at the edge of the natural light in the inn. It was there that Eilona saw the scars around the woman's mouth. Scars made from a thread that had bound her lips together. 'I ask again, what kind of witch are you?'

The other woman hesitated. 'The kind your brother does not like,' she said, finally.

'My brother. . .' She turned to the massacre that lay behind her, to the rot and decay that she had sat in for hours, if not days. 'When I came to this town, I received a letter about him from my oldest brother. He told me that our brother was dead.' She made a small sound of disgust. 'I am not usually a violent woman. Of my brothers and sisters, I think only I can claim that as a truth, but not here. Not in this town. As I read my brother's letter, one of the men here said that the new god would bring them prosperity. He even lifted a glass to the idea.' The old woman turned from the scene she had been staring at, turned back to Olcea and Eilona. 'Tell me, witch, the man that you have bound to you, the man you carry on your shoulder – can he crew a ship across Leviathan's Blood?'

'Yes.' The word sounded as if it was torn from Olcea's throat. 'But I do not have the blood to last that long.'

'Take what you need from here.'

'I would rather—'

'*Take*,' the woman repeated, 'what you need from here.'

'I will need some time,' Olcea said, her voice suddenly submissive. 'A day at least.'

'There is no rush.' The old woman stepped past her, but paused at the door. 'At least, there is no rush today.'

Before the witch could stop her, Eilona followed the woman out of the inn. 'Wait,' she said. Behind her, the renewed buzz of the flies had begun to drown out her voice. '*Wait!*' She took a few quick strides until she was standing beside the old woman. 'You did not tell us your name.'

The woman did not reply. Instead, she lifted her gaze to the sky, and from it, the bird that Eilona had seen earlier began to descend.

'My name is Eilona Wagan,' she said, a touch of desperation in her voice.

The bird, a strange, white raven, the likes of which she had never seen before, settled upon the top of the woman's long ashen staff.

'I am called Tinh Tu,' the old woman said.

Devastation, Birth

What brought Aelyn Meah to Leviathan's End was the funeral for the last Witch of Refuge, Anemone.

News of her death in Nmia, as recorded in the previous chapter, spread quickly throughout the nations of Se'Saera, delivered by her Faithful. Celebrations were organized in all the major cities. It was under this guise that I allowed myself a sombre funeral for the last active force of resistance against Se'Saera.

I do not know how Aelyn Meah heard of it. She made the journey alone and made no mention of who had told her about it. The crew of the ship that brought her to Leviathan's End said only that she paid them a fortune. She stayed one night.

What you read here was recorded on that one night before the sun rose and she returned to her hidden home.

'I do not remember what happened after Qian died,' she said in response to my first question. She sat across from me for the entire night and was strangely honest with me. It was not until later that I realized that this was the first time anyone had asked her what had happened after she destroyed Yeflam. 'The death of my brother awoke within me such a despair that all I remember of those first days are storms,' she continued. 'Awful, shuddering storms that tore a nation apart.'

—Onaedo, *Histories, Year 1029*

1.

Ayae shared a tent on Yeflam's northern shore with Caeli. She had done so for close to four months, since Yeflam broke in half, and both she and Caeli had called the canvas box home without a clause for half that time. The two first named the tent 'home' after they erected it on the muddy shoreline, but the joke, made in storm-drenched exhaustion and fatalism, gave way to the reality of their lives. After a week, it was their home: they lived in it, just as thousands of others lived in the tent city that sprawled along the shore. Their small patch of land, halfway up the first hill that led within half an hour's walk to the road into the Mountains of Ger, was theirs. The world inside the canvas was the world they could change and alter as they pleased, and so they littered the interior with small personal touches: Caeli attached a silver chain to the top bar of the tent that swayed when tremors from the crumbling mountains announced themselves and Ayae sewed patches of red, black and white into their grey blankets. It wasn't much, but it was enough. Enough that, as Ayae sat at the edge of her bedroll, as she pulled the laces of her leather boots tight, as she buckled the hard, dark leather covers over the laces, she made sure that she did not leave a dirty trail across the fabric. Once she finished, her right hand dropped to her sheathed sword and, after she picked it up, she pushed through the tent's flap. The tie that she used to lace it shut was an old piece of cloth from Caeli's Mireean uniform.

Outside, the campfires illuminated thousands of canvas tents just like the one Ayae had left. From where she stood, the familiar sight of the camp left her less and less with the impression of a huge, burning beast that had been killed before the Floating Cities, and more with the feeling that she was gazing upon a community. She could still see the creature in the camp's shape, but it was only at night, when the dark hid the torn centre of Yeflam in Leviathan's Blood from her. It should have been the other way, she knew: the sight of the broken stone cities and the half-submerged wreckage that littered the ocean should have made her think of a giant monster that had risen from Leviathan's Blood and torn apart Nale, but it was only during night that she could envisage the fantasy. Beneath the broken suns, the destruction was normal, a part of her daily life, like the tremors from the Mountains of Ger and the struggle for clean water.

Ayae buckled the sword around her waist, no longer feeling its weight. She had worn it since the night that Yeflam had broken apart, since the cart she was in made its way from Ghaam to Neela and then into the muddy land. On that night, the rain had sheeted down, and there had been little order and less shelter. Around her, now, the fires of the camp darkened and lightened her red-brown leather armour as she walked past, but on the night Yeflam broke apart, on the night the cart came to a halt in the mud, there had been virtually no light. Fires had been nearly impossible to keep lit. Aelyn Meah's dark, lightning-lit storm giant had raged in fury in the centre of Yeflam, and they had feared that it would wade towards the shore, but it had not.

Ayae did not know why. She did not know then, and she did not know now, why the Keepers and the creatures that had emerged from the ocean did not swarm onto the shore. She did not know why they had not killed the people there.

What she knew was that, by morning, the storm giant was gone, and so were the Keepers of the Divine and Se'Saera's monsters.

In their wake, Ayae was numb. It was in such a state that she was summoned by the two people who would seek to claim Yeflam – or at least its shorelines. She had met them in the first tent to be erected. It was no more than canvas on wooden poles, but it seemed almost decadent when she stepped beneath it and approached Lian Alahn and Muriel Wagan.

The former was the head of the Traders' Union, a tall, white-skinned man who, in cold and precise tones, did little to win over Ayae. The latter was the ruler of Mireea, a nation that had been lost to the Leeran Army nearly a year ago. She was a middle-aged white woman who pushed out in fleshy smears.

The tent had no walls, and men and women could easily drift close enough to listen to the conversations. In the confusion, anger and fear that drove the morning after Yeflam had been broken apart, many did, yet both Alahn and Wagan pretended that they had no audience and offered Ayae a place to sit. They had no chairs, only a blanket that covered the ground, but she took it anyway. For refreshment, they offered only sombre condolences for the loss of her friend.

'It is Zaifyr's death that we wish to talk about,' Muriel Wagan had said, sitting opposite her, her unadorned hands folded before her. 'More specifically, his brothers, Jae'le and Eidan. It is said that they are still here.'

'They are searching for their brother,' she had replied.

'Is he—'

'They are searching for his body.'

She found the words difficult to say, then and now. For weeks, she awoke expecting to hear that he had emerged from the ocean.

She expected him to tell her this while he sat in her tent, his smile – that half-smile of his – on his face, his fingers touching the charms woven through his clothes and hair.

'Jae'le is the one searching for him,' Ayae had said to the two before her. 'He and Eidan have made a small camp by the shore. They will not leave until he has found him.'

'And Eidan?' Lady Wagan asked. 'What does he do?'

'Sleep, I imagine.' When she had left him, the stout man had lain beneath a thin blanket in a tent, his wounds tended to by the pitch-black shape of Anguish, Se'Saera's first creation, and first betrayer. 'He can barely walk.'

'Will those two Cursed fight for us?' Lian Alahn asked, suddenly. He used the insult for them that was popular in Yeflam. 'Will they be part of our struggle? Will they take up arms against their sister and this new god of hers, Se'Saera? Will they help us repair the damage that they have done? Will they take responsibility for what their kin has done?'

'You should ask them yourself.'

'I visited them this morning.'

She smiled faintly. 'I hope you did not speak to Jae'le in that tone, then.'

The leader of the Traders' Union straightened. 'He is not a god,' he said, his voice rising not for Ayae, but for those outside the tent. 'Just as Aelyn Meah was not a god, nor any of the Keepers. Se'Saera has made that clear to all of us and I will not be treated by any of the Cursed as if I was an inferior man.'

'Lian.' Muriel Wagan's voice had a quiet chill. 'Now is not the time.'

His mouth opened, but he swallowed his words. After a moment, he rose and walked out of the tent.

'People are afraid, Ayae,' the older woman said, after he had gone. 'They have lost a lot. The two brothers of Aelyn Meah have lost much, as well, but people are afraid of what they will do. There are no answers to what happened between the Keepers or Se'Saera. The ocean only washes up the bodies of their friends on the shore. There are stories that the Keepers carried Aelyn away, that the storm giant flung Se'Saera's creatures out into Leviathan's Blood. There are others that say they fought together. We are struggling to make sense of it all and people need to be reassured. I would give that to them, if I could. I would like to be able to tell people that they need not be afraid. That Jae'le and Eidan are not like the Keepers. I have not spoken with Jae'le, not yet. I haven't had the time. But Lian has, and his requests have fallen on deaf ears – due entirely to his behaviour, I am sure. I would appreciate it if you could speak to Jae'le.'

'And tell him what?'

'Do not tell him anything,' she said. 'Simply ask him to understand the fear around him.'

That was how she had become the unofficial spokeswoman for the two brothers, the face for a nation of three, if she included herself.

It was Eidan who had responded to the fear, first. In the months that followed, the months where nothing was heard from the Keepers or Se'Saera, and the camp became more and more defined until it lit the landscape she walked through now . . . in those months, it was Eidan who came out to interact with the people around him. He let his beard grow out to hide the healing scars that ran down his face – the black lines that could be seen like matted hair – but he could do very little about the limp that he walked with, or the curled, unusable state of his left hand. Yet, it was exactly those things that made him amenable to the people of the camp, and when he told them that he would begin to repair his creation, when he told them that he would fix Yeflam, not a single person questioned or doubted him.

The cart Ayae used to drive herself and Eidan into Yeflam was kept in the stables. The mercenary Kal Essa had been given the task of guarding the stores of food and the animals, and it was one of his men who greeted her when she entered the stalls. Jaysun – a tall, white young man – already had a horse attached to the cart and Ayae climbed into the driver's seat, took up the reins and released the brake.

No one questioned her as she rode through the camp. She was not an unfamiliar sight in the early hours of the morning, and would not be when, a short time later, she and Eidan rode onto the bridge into the empty streets of Yeflam's closest city, Neela. There, the roads led out into the black expanse where the ocean met the sky, the division between the two marked by the remains of a violence that no longer appalled her.

2.

For a moment, Bueralan Le thought that he was still in Ooila, that he lay in the night-lit remains of his mother's house, asleep beside the smouldering fire he had built.

He knew that he was not. He was on *Glafanr.* Recently, he had stood on the deck as the orange light from the afternoon's sun disintegrated along its boards. From high in the rigging, up in the crow's nest, he heard a lonely flute. Its music had followed him through dinner as he ate alone and it had stopped shortly before he climbed into the narrow bed he lay on now. He knew then, even as he allowed the memory to take hold, as he allowed himself to be taken back, that he had not ridden up the overgrown, muddy road to his mother's house. He knew that the light had not shone into his eyes. He knew that the pain he felt from the shift of the saddle as he rode was an old pain, a pain four months absent. The lack of strength in his good hand as he held the tattered leather of the bridle was no longer one he felt. The splints from his broken arm were gone. The tall grey horse that was now stabled beneath the decks of the ship no longer needed to take a slow, easy walk to the front door. It no longer had to stand patiently while he struggled to dismount. It no longer had to bear his weight as he straightened, the pain of his broken ribs sending sharp pangs throughout his chest as he did.

I should be dead. He might have said the words as he pushed the door open, or he might have said them to the horse, or he might not have spoken them aloud. With each step he took across the cracked tile floor, with each step he took past the debris – the corpses of butterflies mixed with the ash from the fire he had built – Bueralan repeated the words. *I should be dead.* Before the remains of the fire, he began to emphasize a word: *I* should *be dead.* That, he knew, would be right. That would be fair. He had been beaten in battle. He had met a better swordsman. Death was the price a mercenary paid when he or she met their better.

He was not a stranger to death. His professional life ensured that, but so did his personal. He had watched his mother die in that very house, a death different to the ones he became so intimate with later. Bueralan never forgot how, on the night she died, he had taken his mother's still hand and sat beside her. Her dark skin had been pale next to his and there was no warmth in her body. He would not say that she looked at peace – he would not say a single person who died looked at peace – but he knew that she was done with her physical pain.

His mother had made it clear that she did not want her soul kept in a glass bottle, that she did not want to be reborn at the expense of another. 'That is the greatest crime of our nation,' she had said. 'We take because we are afraid, and in doing so we punish those who have not yet drawn breath.' She was not afraid of death, she said. She was not afraid of what happened after, even though there were no gods to take her by the hand, to usher her to paradise. 'We must not be frightened of death,' she said, more than once. 'It is a natural state for all of us.'

The witches had told her that her spirit would linger in the world, but she had not been scared of that, not in the way others were.

As a child, Bueralan had been taught by others – by his father, by tutors – to fear death. They had said to him that if a witch did not claim him shortly after his death his future would be one of oblivion. As he grew older, he had not believed them: he saw how death had become an industry in Ooila, one motivated by greed and by power. His mother had been right when she said that. Yet, Bueralan learned, she had also been wrong. In death, you did suffer. In death, you were subjected to generations of hunger and cold, and the slow, but inevitable loss of your sense of self. That was the legacy of the War of the Gods. Even knowing that, as he did now, he remained his mother's son. Returning to Ooila had strengthened that bond. It had reminded him that an important part of death was to make way for another life. You were part of a cycle. All living beings were part of the cycle.

He had forgotten that when the new god Se'Saera handed him Zean's soul, when she had promised that he could be returned.

In his mother's home, the sword that he had carried from Leera had lain near the fireplace. It was a straight blade: simple in design, plain but solid in its make. It had been given to him by an old white man without shoes when he stepped out of the Mountain of Ger. Given to him before he knew that his friends were dead. Before he met Se'Saera. Before it became clear to him that he was no longer part of the cycle of life and death.

You are god-touched and you cannot die, Aela Ren had said. *Not until a god allows you.*

In the dark, stuffy room of the ship, with the sword beneath his narrow bed, Bueralan opened his eyes.

He should have died, but he had not. The god Ger had taken his mortality away in a final act that offered no explanation. Samuel Orlan had tried to tell him what had happened, but he had not understood it until the Innocent, Aela Ren, had broken his bones and left him lying on the ground. Not until he been left in an empty barn with his injuries, left knowing that his mortality was not his own, that the equality he shared with other men and women no longer existed in him. He shared a life now with men and women thousands of years old, and who, in their immortality, wore the faintest impression of the gods they once served. It had not been until he spent the night in the house of his mother that he had realized how what he had tried to do with Zean was what Ger had done to him.

In the bed across from him, he heard Zi Taela stir and cough and, quietly, he pushed himself to his feet.

3.

'Don't light the lamp,' she said. 'Please.'

'What if I open the window?' he asked, softly. 'It's still dark out.'

'A little fresh air would be nice.'

Bueralan navigated the small cabin – no more than two beds pushed against opposite walls, split by a tiny table – to the small shutter that lay between them. The dark slick of the ocean greeted him when he pulled it open, along with the smell of blood and salt. Stepping from the window, he allowed a line of moonlight to slip into the room. It was by that light he saw Taela. Her large, dark eyes dominated her slim face, but it was not until she pushed her black hair back that he met her troubled gaze. She sat at the edge of the bed and, when she straightened, he could see the curve of her light green shirt and the ominous line of her pregnancy beneath it. He thought that she was more pronounced than other women were at sixteen weeks and he had tried to tell himself that it was because Taela was a thin woman, built from long, slim limbs, with delicate shoulders and hips . . . but when he thought that, his mind always returned to the sight of Se'Saera's hand forcing itself into Taela's mouth, the soul of another man in her hand, the first act of a newly named god.

'You shouldn't stare,' she said. 'It's rude.'

'There's not enough light to know if I'm staring. You can't accuse me.'

'I just did.' A series of coughs burst from her. When the last had finished, she said, 'Is there water?'

It was on the table. The moonlight caught the white lines of his tattoos as he poured a cup for her, revealing straight, unbroken and unmarred black skin. 'How do you feel?'

'Fine.' She took the cup, drank deeply from the warm water. 'Okay,' she said, once she had finished. 'No, I feel awful.'

'Sick again?'

'No.'

'Then what?'

'I feel . . .' In the moonlight, her face looked fragile. At any moment, she could begin to crumble beneath an unseen but known weight. 'At times, I feel as if something is scratching at me,' she whispered. 'I can feel fingers against my stomach. Strong little fingers with sharp nails, trying to catch a piece of my flesh to tear a hole, to escape the prison it is in.'

'Zean wouldn't do that.' It was all he could think to say. 'If he's there—'

'What if he isn't?'

'He is.'

She lowered her head and, in doing so, folded into herself. 'I don't want this.'

'Zean wouldn't want it, either,' Bueralan said, quietly. 'I know that. When we reach land, we'll find a way to stop it. All of it.'

'He's your blood brother.'

He did not disagree.

'There's no way to stop it,' Taela whispered, folding her hands around the cup. '*She* won't let us stop it.'

She was Se'Saera. The god was not yet aware of all their conversations: they had discovered that she could only hear you if her name was used, but that knowledge that not been gained kindly. Se'Saera had stopped Taela's first attempt to abort the child in Cynama because the other woman cursed her beforehand. Bueralan had heard after it happened, after he had spent the night in his mother's house and ridden into Cynama. He and the tall grey had approached the devastated city in silence. The air was heavy with sulphur and smoke, and the canals that cut through the streets were full of sluggish lava. It would not be until later that he heard how Joqan, one of Aela Ren's god-touched soldiers, had coaxed the eruptions and fires out of the earth. Until then, he rode past the burned buildings and black paths with a numbed sense of horror. He saw no one on the streets, neither in terms of survivors nor one of Aela Ren's soldiers, and the absence of either chilled him despite the oppressive heat. He might have turned around and left the city, but the horse never hesitated in its ride to the centre of Cynama. It did not stop until it was outside the remains of the First Queen's Palace.

Samuel Orlan had stood alone before it. He was a small, bearded, roundish white man whose hair was coloured by greys and silvers and he wore the same stained clothes of brown and white that he had worn for the last week. As Bueralan's horse approached, he did not turn his attention from the once elaborate building.

'Where is Ren?' the saboteur asked.

'He is here.' Orlan tugged at his beard. 'They are all here, searching tunnels beneath the ruins. Taela is there as well. *She* took her. Do not say her name, I beg you.'

It would only be later that it was properly explained to him, but at the time, he shrugged and asked, 'Did they find the Queen, then?'

'No,' the other man replied. 'She's not here.'

'She escaped?'

'I would not think so.' Orlan's weathered blue eyes met his. 'But no one has found her body yet, so perhaps there is hope.'

'Hope is not something we should hold to.' He slid painfully from the saddle. 'We're nothing but prisoners, old man. Aela Ren told us both that when he collected us from that barn.'

The cartographer was silent for a moment, his fingers pulling tightly at the end of his beard once again. 'Do you see the stones on my left?' he said.

He meant the rubble of a broken pond. They were stained with dried blood, but he had seen other stains throughout the city. 'What of it?' he said.

'That is where Taela tried to abort her child. Ren and his soldiers camped in this square last night. He left me on the edge of it like a dog, but even still, I was woken up by a scream in the heart of the camp. A scream from here – Taela's scream as our new god dragged her out of the tent, her legs stained with blood.'

Bueralan closed his eyes and tried not to imagine it.

'She dragged Taela before Ren and his soldiers and told her that it did not matter what she used – be it a knife or herbs – she would be unable to harm the baby growing inside her.' His voice was heavy, weighed down by what he had seen. 'She said that Taela carried her first true creation. Nothing would stop the child from being born.'

In the small cabin, Bueralan took the cup from Taela's hands and, without a word, held her as she began to cry.

4.

'Turn left here,' Eidan said, lifting the lamp higher. 'At the corner.'

Ahead, the fence of the factory yard fell in a twisted crush of wire. Through it and over it lay the end of the building's front wall.

The debris forced Ayae to take the corner wide, but the black and brown horse followed the instruction placidly, and the rotted inside of the two-storey building soon revealed itself through a mixture of starlight and weak lamplight. It was different to the other buildings she and Eidan had passed: there was no scaffolding around it, no sense that anyone had begun to fortify the foundations that had been shifted months before. Instead, the factory looked naked and exposed, the cracked and broken walls somehow still upright, though she could clearly see the weight of the building sagging down the middle. But it was across the floor that most of the destruction had taken place: the forges had been shattered into shapeless masses before collapsing next to broken barrels, splintered handles and scattered piles of coal and wood. The damage lay beneath a ceiling of chains that had once been used to hold apparatuses, but which now fell in limp lines and broken knots.

As if to announce what had made the destruction, a shudder ran through the stone streets of Neela, and Ayae tightened her hands on the reins to keep the horse calm. The quake was different to the aftershocks that ran through the Mountains of Ger and into the camp. The latter had a pattern, an almost predictable series of tremors, whereas what ran through Neela was anything but. The tremors here were sharp and sudden, and every time she was on it, Ayae believed that it was possible the stone would break apart and send her tumbling into Leviathan's Blood.

Yet, the tremors that ran through the city now were not as bad as they had been over a month ago. The whole city had shaken beneath its tremors then, but Eidan's repairs had stopped that, and it now shook only in places. The worst of it was near the bridge that led into Mesi, and on into the largely residential city that was dominated by houses built tightly against one another. Eidan was confident that he could save both – 'The pillars of both are largely intact,' he explained – but he was not so certain about Ghaam, that city that followed Mesi. There, a generous slope to the stone roads and paths left everyone with the belief that it would soon plunge into Leviathan's Blood.

Before Ghaam had become too dangerous to stand on, Ayae had walked to the end of it. Her path had taken her to the very edge of the city to gaze into the shifting mass of Leviathan's Blood and the yawning expanse that existed between Ghaam and the next city, Guranatan. That side of Yeflam, Eidan said, was quite safe: the fall of Nale had primarily broken the northern side of the Floating Cities. Still, Ayae felt no comfort. She had relived her memories of the night Zaifyr died and tried to imagine what would have happened had she been able to reach him. No matter how she allowed the story to unfold, she could never convince herself of a different outcome. She would only have died beside him.

'Here,' Eidan said. 'Here will do nicely.'

She pulled up the cart's brake. 'How do you know that one of the pillars is here?'

'I feel every part of Yeflam, even those that have sunk.' Slowly, he climbed down. 'It is said Sil could feel the same in her creations, in the continents, just as I do Yeflam. She could hear them as I hear the pillars beneath me, telling me their weakness.' With the lamp held in his good hand, the stout man limped along the street, his soft, loose clothes looking like an assortment of rags. 'At least, that is what is said,' he said with a hint of self-mockery, 'and you know you can always trust what is said.'

Sil had been the God of the Earth. 'How can you be so sure your power is hers?' she asked, following him.

'You can find her remains in the tunnels that lead to the Saan. You will probably never know this, but it is a unique experience to stand before the remains of a god still with your power. Hate is not strong enough a word for what they feel towards you.'

'Zaifyr told me that if you stand before any god, you feel that.'

'It is not the same. I have often thought that the gods hate all living things. It is not a theory everyone shares, however.'

'Jae'le?' she asked.

'There are better things to ask Jae'le about,' Eidan said. 'Ask him if he has found Zaifyr yet, for example.'

'I don't want to ask.'

'I have noticed.' He paused and turned to her. 'Why is that?'

'It's morbid, Eidan.'

'Only now,' he said. 'Death used to be sacred. To think about it, to ponder it, was considered an intellectual field for philosophers. I remember reading in my youth a book that argued that it was only through death that the gods bestowed their pleasure and displeasure. I think of what that author wrote, lately. In the days when the gods stood among us, a funeral was an event for a town as much as it was for a family. Everyone came out to see what judgement was passed on the deceased. Decay was seen as punishment, youth as a reward. To be returned to a child was something else, however, for quite often the gods would return such a person to life, to live again, and in doing so, exile them from paradise.'

'Did you ever see that happen?'

'No. Only Jae'le and Zaifyr saw such things.'

In the broken remains of the factory, she heard a sound: a stone falling, as if it had dropped through a hole in a floor. 'Are we being watched?'

'By two men.' With his good foot, Eidan began to clear a space on the road, pushing dirt and stone away. 'But my original point was that we have honoured the dead differently throughout time. Jae'le and I are simply men from a different time.'

'You should learn to cry,' she said. 'Aren't tears enough?'

'For our brother?' He gave a small smile and shook his head. 'It would depend entirely on whose tears they were, I believe.'

'Then be angry.'

Indistinct sounds – words, she was sure – came from the building. 'My brother is angry,' he said. He lowered the lamp to the ground, but did not turn towards the sound. 'I cannot make out what they are saying. The building is too damaged for that, but I do not believe that they are friends of ours. They are on the second floor, arguing.'

He would have trouble climbing the broken stairs. 'I'll check it out,' Ayae said. 'But, Eidan, if only Jae'le is angry, what does that leave you?'

'Sad, mostly.' He sank into a sitting position, both his good hand and crippled hand flat on the ground. 'I had not thought to see our violence return.'

He meant Asila, of course.

Ayae stepped over a section of rubble and began to make her way to the factory. She was in clear sight of the two inside, but she did not hear anything, or see anyone, even as the light from Eidan's lamp began to fade. She did not think of the men in the building as she approached it. Instead, she thought of Asila. It was not surprising: for Eidan, Jae'le and Aelyn, for all of Zaifyr's family, Asila was always the point of return. They were obsessed with it, and their obsession had begun to lay itself in her. She had finally begun to understand that Zaifyr's family did not return to it because of the madness he had suffered, nor because of the horrors he had unleashed: no, they returned to it because of the battle with him, because of what it had revealed of themselves, and because of the small, crooked tower in the Eakar mountains in which they had been forced to imprison him for a thousand years.

In the aftermath of that, their family had broken, and the world they understood had fallen away.

In the months since Zaifyr had been killed by Aelyn, Ayae had come to see Yeflam as the perfect metaphor for how the immortals viewed themselves in the world. Unable to form a unified whole, they had become two distinct entities, divided by what they had learned about themselves at Asila, and divided again by the violence that they had done to each other in Yeflam. It would take decades to repair what had been done to the physical nation of Yeflam, if it could be repaired. Eidan had been quite clear that he might not be able to save the cities that had sunk into the ocean. When he spoke, Ayae knew, he was not just speaking about his creation.

At the entrance to the factory, she paused. It was dark, but she could still see the damage inside. It was in worse shape than she had at first thought.

The walls sagged and the floor above her tilted down, as if it was ready to break apart and fall on her. Chunks of plaster and wood from both had crashed to the ground, mixing with the debris that the forges and tools had made, leaving the impression that the building had begun to weep in on itself. Yet, even with the sense that the factory walls could collapse around her at any moment, Ayae took a step forwards, her boots finding purchase between broken bricks. Her hand curled around the hilt of her sword and, above her, the chains attached to the ceiling began to catch alight with small flames, one after the other finding purchase on the metal. Ayae did it without effort, with an ease that she had become more and more comfortable with since the night Yeflam broke apart. Beneath the light, she continued forwards, until she paused in the middle of the room as a harsh voice caught her attention—

The floor above her shook.

And shook again as the two men had begun to jump on it, trying to bring the floor down upon her.

Darting forwards, Ayae made her way swiftly through the debris, the ceiling shaking after her as she closed in on the shadowed steel staircase.

The speed by which she came up the stairs and into the room surprised the two men. While both were startled to see her, neither hesitated to rush her, despite the fact that they were unarmed. As they drew closer, Ayae saw that the men wore old clothes, clothes that had been lived in for the last four months and showed the wear of that time, as did their faces. The first to reach her – a white, middle-aged man with shaggy, greying hair – threw a wild punch that she was able to step around easily, while the second – a black man of similar age, but with a head of short black hair – threw himself at her.

He hit the ground hard, causing the building to shudder, and both Ayae and the white man nearly lost their footing.

Ayae knew that the real threat was not the two men before her, but from the weakness of the floor. She could feel it sag beneath her feet as she took a step forwards to sway beneath the white man's punch. Her right hand thrust out, palm flat into his stomach, but rather than hitting him with all her strength and launching him through the air, she held back, and he doubled over instead. Her left hand, following through, landed on the back of the man's head and he fell to the ground unconscious. With a quick step, she lashed out with her right boot, and kicked the black man in the side of the head as he tried to rise.

'Well done,' a voice said behind her.

5.

Eventually, Taela asked if Bueralan could leave her alone, just for a while.

He pulled the door shut gently and made his way along the corridor, the low ceiling forcing him to hunch as he did. He glanced behind him, once, just once, as he stood at the base of the stairs that led onto the deck of *Glafanr*, but the saboteur knew that he could do very little for Taela: her pain could not be shared. Se'Saera's violation of her had been terrible and intimate in nature, a rape by all definitions, and Bueralan knew he could do nothing to change this fact.

On the deck, the moonlit water lay in a smooth, black expanse, mirroring the wooden boards that he walked across.

Glafanr was a huge and ancient creature on Leviathan's Blood. Despite its size, it glided through the waves as if it were a sleeker, smaller ship, and there was no doubting the terror it would strike into anyone who saw it coming for them. Standing beneath its five masts, Bueralan felt dwarfed. From the thick masts, sails made from a deep crimson unfurled, flecks of black littered through them. At the very top of the centre masts were two crow's nests. It was from one of those that he had heard the sad melody of a flute earlier. No such music greeted him in the darkness as he passed beneath it now. Below the deck, behind narrow doors and in rooms that ran three levels deep before the hold opened up, Aela Ren and his army lay in their narrow beds, leaving the piloting of the ship to other hands.

'You don't sleep, Bueralan.' Se'Saera stood at *Glafanr*'s bow. She wore a simple gown of white that, along with her white skin and blonde hair, caught the moon's light and left her with an ethereal quality. 'Yet again.'

'The night is the best time to be awake,' he said. 'Wouldn't you agree?'

'I merely guide the ship at night,' she said. 'It is my gift to the men and women who sleep beneath us – who sleep as they have never slept before.'

The night that Bueralan had ridden out of Cynama, the night he had begun to ride towards Dynamos and the hulking shape of *Glafanr*, Samuel Orlan had told him that Ren and his soldiers had not slept since the War of the Gods. On the day Linae fell, the cartographer said, sleep had been taken from them. As the old man spoke, the sky above them had been tinged red, turned that colour by the fires that burned in the city, by the lava that had awakened before they left. In that light, the men and women around him of Ren's army looked gaunt and malnourished.

'Imagine the gift she gives them,' Orlan had said. 'The weight she lifts from them with a simple gesture.'

To the new god, Bueralan said now, 'You buy them cheaply.'

'I have not bought them at all.' Se'Saera's gaze left the black ocean and met his. 'They are the mortal instruments of gods. They were once figures of glory. They will be once again.'

'I don't wish for glory.'

'I know. I have treated you poorly, Bueralan. I do not apologize for it, but I do acknowledge it.' She turned away. 'I can see now that I rushed to consume everything around me. To consume the world of my parents. My Faithful were at times affected by this. But with a name, I have grown . . . more aware of the world. One day, you will understand this.'

This change in the god's personality still unsettled Bueralan. At first, he had greeted it with relief, but it was not until he rode out of Cynama that he realized how deeply it bothered him. When she first appeared – after he had said her name – she accused him of conspiring against her with others. She had been much like the child he had met in the cathedral in Ranan. There, he would have said that she hated him, that she held the death of her Mother Estalia against him, and saw conspiracies and enemies everywhere. But that had not been the case since he had said her name.

'We will find the wreckage of a ship tonight,' the god said to him. 'I saw it in a dream. An hour before dawn, the wreckage will appear to you and I. You and Aela will swim over to it. You will search for the First Queen.'

'The First Queen is dead. She did not survive your attack on Cynama.'

'You said that in my dream. You wore that sword Aela allowed you to reclaim and you held it tightly, as if you would use it.'

The sword still lay beneath his narrow bed. 'What did you say next?' he asked.

'I said that I agreed,' she said. 'But I do not. The First Queen still lives. You will find evidence of her escape on the wreckage we find.'

Bueralan's only relief from her change came from this, came from the fact that she did not consider herself a complete god.

He had discovered it by accident, having overheard the new god and Aela Ren in the remains of the First Queen's palace after he had entered the ruins. As the midday's sun rose high, Bueralan had walked down a set of broken stairs and into a massive web of passages and cellars. He told Orlan that he was going to look for Taela, but mostly he wanted to be away from the smoke and the smell of sulphur. After a short, painful walk, the dark passage around him shifted and earth rained over him as the foundations of the palace's remains threatened collapse, he considered turning back to the daylight.

It was then that he heard Se'Saera's voice.

'The paintings are of Mahga, of the Fifth Kingdom,' she was saying. 'They were commissioned to show its splendour. Its decadence.'

'Rivers that run with gold,' the Innocent replied. 'It is surely what the Five Queens sought to remake in their reign.'

'No.' It was Taela who spoke, her voice cracking, as if it struggled against itself and its use. 'No,' she repeated. 'Zeala Fe did not want to remake Mahga. She showed me these paintings. She spoke about how it was a mistake to try and recapture it. How we had to break away from it.'

'In this matter, she was correct.' Bueralan could not tell if Se'Saera's voice leaked through the cracks in the wall or if it drifted up the passage he stood in. But he remained still, afraid to move and lose the sound. 'Mahga was Eidan's kingdom. Few could rule as he did.'

'Eidan believed he was a god. His brothers and sisters shared that belief.' It was Ren who spoke then, his voice calm. 'They left their kingdoms once they realized they were not.'

'I have seen parts of it,' Se'Saera said. 'The past is strange to me. It feels to me as the present does now. Last night I dreamed that Eidan returned here even as he did not.'

'The gods saw all of time at once. It was not linear to them. It will not be linear to you, once you have gathered all the power of the gods to you.'

'I once considered him an ally, Aela. He turned on me and spoke against me in Yeflam.'

'What did he say?'

'He passed judgement on me. My parents had left a messenger to tell the world that I was not their child. He agreed with it.'

'Was the messenger one of us?' the Innocent asked.

'No, he was a cursed mortal. His name was Lor Jix.' Se'Saera said the name without emotion and it was there, at this moment, that Bueralan began to realize just how much she had changed. 'He had been a priest of my mother, the Leviathan.'

'Yet you are a god,' he said. 'It is not just your name or your presence. I see you gather the remains of the gods to you. You are them, even if they did not wish you to be. I was never told the reason why the gods went to war. My master, your father, did not share that with me. The same is true of all of us. But we were their mortal instruments. We can see the divine in the world. We saw it in the pretenders. We saw it in the unfortunates who could not control it. We have seen what has happened when the divine has been broken apart as it has. I cannot imagine that any priest, cursed or otherwise, could look upon the world and believe that it is better for what the gods have done.'

'Yet Lor Jix did,' she said. 'But it does not matter. I see now that my parents could not exist as I did. I see that they could not accept that. As you said, I am them. With enough time, I believe Eidan will understand this as well. Before he dies, he will ask for forgiveness from me.'

If Aela Ren replied, Bueralan did not hear it.

6.

Xrie stood casually on the stairs behind her, his right shoulder against the sagging wall. A slim man only slightly taller than Ayae, he was a combination of elegance and steeled resolve that lent him an air of command. He stood before her in dark leather and a dark red silk belt, both immaculately kept, demonstrating a certain fastidiousness in his personality that emerged more strongly in his organization of the Yeflam Guard. Before Xrie arrived in the Floating Cities, before he left his family and descended through the twisting mountain passes to the world outside his homeland, he had been known as the Blade Prince of the Saan, but in Yeflam, where Ayae had first met him, he had simply been called the Soldier. He had been a Keeper of the Enclave and the Captain of the Yeflam Guard and, in both, he had been loyal to Aelyn Meah. In those days he had dyed the ends of his brown hair blue and let the colour run through the silk that he wore; but now the dark red of the silk belt also streaked his hair in a violent denial of the people who had betrayed him months ago.

'Don't clap,' she said drily, responding to his earlier praise. 'The floor might give way.'

'I try not to talk too loudly in here.' He spoke softly as he walked up the stairs towards her. 'We've closed off a lot of the buildings to stop people moving into them, but factories like this are difficult. And dangerous.'

Xrie and the Yeflam Guard had organized the evacuation of the northern side of Yeflam the night Zaifyr died. If you spoke to any soldier who served under him at that time – any soldier who stood beneath the sheeting rain and struggled to erect tents and organize people and help loved ones find each other – you would hear only pride in their voices. They would speak of how Xrie had been selfless, how he had done what the other Keepers had not, and worked for them, for Yeflam. If you spoke to the people Xrie had saved, opinion was more divided. Some agreed with his soldiers, but there were others who still believed him to be Aelyn Meah's servant.

'This building is part of our regular sweep through Neela.' He glanced at the two unconscious men. 'I know them,' he said. 'Tan and Casa. They were some of the first to work on the bridge into Neela. I have not seen either for over two months.'

'Now you have,' she said.

'Not the way I wished.'

Ayae knelt beside the white man – Tan – and rolled him onto his back. His face might once have been handsome, but it was now drawn and pinched with hunger. As she grabbed the front of his shirt to begin lifting him, however, the thin fabric that he wore gave way and revealed the edge of a tattoo on his chest. She heard Xrie grunt in recognition as she pushed the filthy clothes aside to reveal the tattoo of a whole sun on his chest. The centre of it held smaller versions of the complete sun, flames within flames.

'Se'Saera's mark,' Xrie said. 'Over the heart, as always.'

She turned to Casa. 'Let's see if his friend also has it.'

'They never travel alone, Ayae.'

She knew that, but she reached for the shirt, regardless.

Shortly after, the two stood outside the factory. They had carried the unconscious men past where Eidan still sat, his eyes closed, and lowered them onto the back of the cart. As they did that, Xrie's soldiers emerged silently from the surrounding streets. They numbered ten, no more than a scouting unit, but each of them wore the dark red of their commander.

'They are better off dead than returning to the camp,' Xrie told her as he stared down at the two men. 'There will be no mercy for them.'

'There is little mercy for anyone,' she said.

'But it is worse for those with Se'Saera's mark.'

Ayae did not disagree. The first sightings of the tattoo had appeared after the storm had broken and when the camp had begun to take shape. Ayae had seen a young man dragged out into the dirt streets and lynched by his friends one morning, his body stripped to reveal the tattoo.

Similar stories arrived from across Leviathan's Blood. Without the Enclave, the Floating Cities of Yeflam had fallen under the control of individual governors. The correspondence that came – most of it through Lian Alahn's contacts – revealed a fractured nation. Barricades lined the bridges, new laws were enforced, and anyone not born in the 'new' nations of Yeflam was looked upon with suspicion. Ayae was not surprised that the camp had received no aid since it had been established on the shoreline.

Before her, Xrie motioned to one of his soldiers for some rope. With it in his hand, he took a step to the cart, but as his boot touched the edge, Casa sat up slowly, but with a strangeness that was immediately noticeable.

'Yeflam,' he said in the voice of a young woman. 'It saddens me to see it like this.'

Xrie took a step back, drawing his sword as he did. 'You are not welcome here, Se'Saera.'

'I am welcome everywhere in my world.' Casa's head tilted as he gazed at the soldiers, who had also unsheathed their weapons. A lopsided smile crossed his face, as if the sight amused him, but he said nothing to them. Instead, he turned to Ayae. 'Surely you welcome me here? You who have seen so much of this suffering world.'

She did not reach for her sword, though she wanted to do so. 'No.'

'No?' the possessed man echoed. 'You have spent much too much time with Eidan and his family.'

'What is it that you want, Se'Saera?' Eidan emerged from behind the cart, the lamp in his hand. He spoke casually, as if he alone had been unsurprised by her appearance. 'I have no time for your sermons.'

'I came to speak to you. I stand on the deck of *Glafanr* and I talk to another just as I talk to you. I am different, now that I am named. I have expanded. I am no longer the small figure you once knew.' Casa's arm rose awkwardly to hold a hand out to him. 'I have come to extend an offer in exchange for your return. To you, my betrayer. You, whom I swore to destroy. I offer you a chance for redemption.'

'I have no desire to die.'

'To give yourself to me before death is to save your soul.'

Eidan grunted. 'I have seen how you hoard souls to use their power.'

'So you deny me a second time?'

'And a third, if I need.'

Casa's arm did not lower and his nod of acceptance was awkward, as if the muscles of his neck had weakened. 'I will see your love soon.'

'Bid her good day for me,' Eidan said, placing the lamp on the ground.

'I will be in the company of Aela Ren when I meet her.' Se'Saera paused as a tremor passed through Casa's body, but at the mention of the Innocent's name, Ayae's hand fell to her sword. 'He and his god-touched soldiers serve me now. You will not be able to stand before them.'

'I do not fear the Innocent or his soldiers.'

Ayae, her hand tight around the hilt of her sword, did not share the sentiment.

A gurgling laugh escaped the possessed man. 'Why do you defy me, Eidan? I can remake this world once I am complete. I accept that my parents did not break themselves apart for love. It pained me to hear it in Yeflam, but I will preserve this nation for that reason. It was here that the failure of my parents became clear. Here that their messenger, Lor Jix, told the world that they tore themselves apart so I could not be whole.' The words began to sound from Casa's throat strangely, as if he could not properly carry the emotion that the god had. 'I will repair what they have done, Eidan. Do you not want to see that?'

'You forget.' He reached out with his good hand and curled Casa's finger backwards, snapping the bone. 'I have seen what you create.'

A snarl emerged from the possessed man's throat, but as it did, the skin there began to bubble and fold and then, suddenly, split in a gush of blood. A gagging sound followed, as Casa began to choke on his own blood. Before anyone could react, his head fell backwards as the bone in his neck let out a rotten crack. Eidan, still holding Casa's hand, found himself holding the limb alone as a similar sound announced its departure from the whole.

'These bodies are so weak.' Se'Saera's voice came from Tan, who rose from the back of the cart awkwardly, wet with the blood of his friend. 'I will fix that.'

'Your creations are flawed,' Eidan said, still holding the other man's hand. 'You make only pain and suffering.'

'You speak of those who failed me.'

'No, I speak of you,' he said. 'As I have lain in my tent healing, I have wondered what convinced me to serve you and then so easily break away. I have thought about what I have seen and what I have been shown. I have begun to believe that others have made it so that I have seen you for yourself.'

The tension that coiled through Tan's body suddenly left and he laughed a young woman's laugh: carefree and innocent. 'You cannot see the world as I can, Eidan. My thoughts are not what they once were. They are more complete. I dream of fate now. It is the most beautiful and complex sight to behold. I see how futures and pasts and presents overlap and cross. How they hide one another and then they reveal each other. It is amazing. Fate twists around us so much that every conversation is an echo of another. Even this moment has echoes. I see you reach for me. I see the Soldier cut deep into this man's head. In both, the little flame stands terrified by the mere mention of the Innocent. This is divinity. This is truth unfolding before me.

'But Eidan,' she said, 'I assure you, I promise you, that in all those fates you die.'

7.

When the heavy rain slowed to a slick drizzle, the Captain of Refuge readied his soldiers.

Heast had spent much of the night next to a thick tree, watching the Faaishan bushland and cleaning water and condensation from the spyglass he used. A lean, grey-haired man closer to sixty than to fifty, he was fit enough to climb the tree beside him for a better view of the Leeran soldiers he was watching, but he did not attempted it. His left leg, covered by worn leather pants, was a heavy, steel appendage bonded at his thigh. It bent and moved awkwardly and, in the dry, it made climbing a tree difficult; in the rain, it made it impossible. Because of that, Heast stood in the shadows of the tree and, with the moon hidden behind a grey slate of clouds, counted what he could of the sentries in the blurred mix of dark that was slick across the glass eye. Fortunately, not one of them had altered his established routine.

After a week of watching the camp, Heast knew the location of each of the fifty-three tents inside it. He had memorized the distance between the seven fire pits that made a line through the middle and counted the number of steps from the last fire to the roughly built stables at each end of the camp by watching dozens of trips made by soldiers he did not command. And he knew that there were a hundred and twenty-two horses packed tightly inside the two buildings that bookended the camp, eleven more than the number of Leeran soldiers in the camp. But he also knew that twelve beasts had been allocated into pairs to pull the six wagons that lay on their sides as makeshift walls – and he knew also that the one lone Leeran who had arrived without a horse had done so because he did not ride.

It was a sizeable force, but more importantly, it was the Leeran command post for the western conquest of the Kingdoms of Faaisha.

Quietly, he gave the order to prepare to his runner, Ralen, a young, olive-skinned boy of fourteen. As Heast began to fold up the spyglass, the boy melted into the bush.

A pair of scouts had found the camp after a Leeran raiding party had come to the empty town of Maosa. Heast had left the two women there just for that purpose and they had waited three months before the Leerans arrived. By the time the force arrived in Maosa, Heast had left, not just with the soldiers from the town, but also with all the men and women who had been bartenders and seamstresses and everything between. He had taken them into the dirty scrubland and set about forging them into a small army.

Into Refuge.

'They've begun to move, Captain.' Ralen spoke softly as he emerged from the dense bush. 'Corporal Isaap asked if the witch would be making fires so that they could see.'

'He knows there will be no fires.' Isaap was a soldier who had been, before Heast arrived in Maosa, a First Talon – a rank translated roughly to that of a captain. 'I will speak to him after.'

'I don't mean to get him into trouble,' the boy replied. 'He meant no disrespect, I am sure. He is just nervous. None of us have ever fought—'

'I have.' Heast's pale blue gaze met his. 'Trust in me, boy, and you will live.'

Ralen swallowed his words and nodded.

But they were not Refuge.

Not yet.

In all the incarnations of Refuge that had come before, in the one that Heast had first served in, and in the one he had led, the soldiers of Refuge had been defined by a certain assurance that the soldiers around him now did not have. For the most part, it was not their fault: the majority of them had not been soldiers professionally, and those who had, had been poorly trained, and their ranks defined by wealth and favours. Most of them, Heast knew, would never be anything like the soldiers who had served in Refuge before, and many would not have the chance to become that. How many would fall tonight, though, depended on one Leeran, Kilian.

He was one of Kye Taaira's ancestors: a long-dead soldier whose soul had been drawn out of the soil of the Plateau by the new god, Se'Saera, and placed inside a Leeran soldier. Taaira told him how Kilian had been imprisoned in the land thousands of years ago by the shamans of the Plateau and, upon his release, had been bonded to the body of a Leeran soldier. The tribesman – a large white man with brown and red hair and a thick beard – had sensed Kilian first, before Heast had seen him lumbering through the camp. The Ancestor, as he was known, was a tall figure, taller than most men and women had the right to be. If Heast had taken it upon himself to describe the warrior to another on paper, he would have written that he stretched outwards, as if the soul of the Leeran he had been bonded with had tried desperately to push the dead man from him at the last minute, but had succeeded only in smearing him further through his body. Because of that, Kilian could not wear armour properly and had taken to strapping bits and pieces about him, giving him the appearance of a teenager playing with a child's costume.

'Do not underestimate him.' Taaira had spoken to the soldiers after Heast had requested he did so. They viewed the tribesman with trepidation and repeated among themselves the belief that he did not have any blood in his body, that he was a man the shamans of the Plateau had rendered Hollow, both in fact and name. For his part, Kye Taaira, believing that he understood the nature of their fear of him, would speak to them with a certain briskness, as if he had experienced it before. 'When he was alive, Kilian was known as the Iron Soldier. It was said that he would not break under any circumstances: be it starvation, be it injury, be it loss or torture, he could endure it. It was said that when you joined the warlord, you were given a trial by Kilian to measure your worth. The trial was one of torture. It was designed to see at what point you would break. But rather than administer it, Kilian would endure it beside you. He would suffer every burn, every break, every humiliation, until either you broke or you came as close to death as he would allow.' Across his back, Taaira carried an old two-handed sword, a weapon that all the soldiers who stood before him had been ordered not to touch. 'Only the best of the soldiers did not break. Only those that Se'Saera has returned to life now passed his test. Only they hung near death on the racks and in the chains beside him. It was beside him that the worst of Zilt's army were made.'

The men and women listening to the tribesman had shuddered at his words.

For Heast, the real problem with the Ancestor was that he did not sleep. Each evening, he would retire to a tent that was too small for him and stare out from the pinned back flap, watching every movement the Leeran soldiers made. On the first night, Heast had thought that Kilian was watching for Taaira, or for him, but as the nights drew on, and the Leeran soldiers avoided his gaze, Heast began to put aside the thought.

To his left, a slight trill ran through the bush. Beside him, Ralen repeated the sound. He then heard it repeated to his right.

The sentries had been marked.

Heast took a deep breath and let out a short, sharp sound, different to the others.

He began moving immediately. Ahead of him, he could hear the rustle of bush, the sound of men and women – the sound of his soldiers, of Refuge – rising and rushing into the camp.

Heast knew that he would not be able to match their pace. His steel leg sank into the muddy ground with each step, and he was forced to drag it a little each time he pulled it out. But he did not allow himself to be concerned by that. If he had had two legs, he would still not have kept up with the youngest of his soldiers, not at his age. As he stalked towards the camp he listened for changes in sounds around him, for the first clang of a sword against another, for the first sound of a voice that was not one he recognized.

It was the latter that he heard before the other.

The cry of '*Soldiers!*' sounded from his right. A second word began, but Heast could not make it out before it was cut off abruptly.

'Ralen,' he said without turning. 'That will be Sergeant Bliq's unit. Spot them and report the situation to me. Quick now.'

As the boy began to run through the bush, the first of the camp's tents came into clear view before Heast.

It was at that time that he heard the sound of swords ringing against swords.

A small ditch lay in front the first tent and in it lay a Leeran soldier. With an approving eye, Heast noted that the throat had been cut while he had been held, face-first, into the mud. He did not spare the body more than a glance before he stepped from the ditch. He came out from beside the tent, glancing into its open flap to see the limbs of dead men before taking in the sight of the camp before him.

'Captain.' Ralen emerged from behind him, his breath ragged. 'Sergeant Bliq has the north side secure.'

'Go back to her.' Heast stared down to the southern end of the Leeran camp, to where the sound of fighting had become louder. 'Tell her she is to issue commands to finish securing the side and then to bring her unit to the south. Tell her the Ancestor is not yet dead.'

8.

The Ancestor lifted his rain-slicked face to the night sky and howled. The noise pierced the sound of battle as if he were a lone wolf who had been cornered, as if he were a beast calling out to others in his pack, to the soldiers who might still be alive in the camp.

The sound drew Heast along the muddy road. He had passed the Ancestor's tent just before and seen that the ceiling had been torn away. But it was in the tracks at the front, in the slippery prints of both boots and hands that a sudden push into a standing position was revealed, followed by a charge. The Ancestor had known that the attack was coming, and that left Heast troubled. Taaira would have led the assault on this part of the camp, so it was unlikely that one of his soldiers had given away the element of surprise. Yet, Heast knew that the tribesman would have found the tent empty when he arrived. At that point, he would have realized the danger, and the need to correct it quickly. In setting out after the Ancestor, he would have passed, as Heast did now, the bodies of three men and two women from Corporal Isaap's unit. They had been ferociously hacked open, the tracks telling how Kilian had thrown himself at them, leaving Heast surprised that the Corporal and the last of his two soldiers were not among the dead. He found them shortly after, when the rest of the camp revealed itself, the three soldiers with Kye Taaira.

Behind him, he heard Bliq and her unit running up the muddy road, but he did not turn from the sight before him.

The Ancestor was forcing his way to the stables at the end of the camp, carving a trail with sheer ferocity. In each of his large hands, he held a great axe, and he wielded both in long, deadly slashes that forced any who came close to him to duck and weave backwards. Taaira had gathered up the majority of small units that had surged to the south-eastern part of the camp under Heast's command and pushed them into a larger force – fifty, he counted – with Taaira in its centre. The glow of his old sword was visible to Heast even through the hardening rain, and the light of it made it clear that the tribesman could not find the space to strike at the Ancestor. The latter had gathered a small force of thirty Leerans around him in his charge and their discipline had given him the advantage.

Heast was not surprised. In pure numbers, he had three soldiers for every Leeran in the camp; but in terms of trained and seasoned fighters, he did not have the same dominance. There had been seventeen veterans left in Maosa when Heast took command, and another ten, like Isaap, who had been pushed into ranked positions they were not ready for yet. In many ways, he viewed his small army as a mirror of the Leeran force as a whole, which had been forged of the nation's military and its people. It had been brought together under a new god and the command of General Waalstan and, though Se'Saera had bonded her soldiers together through blood to strengthen them, the truth was that a year of steady fighting had eroded the distinction between the two groups, a difference Heast was easily aware of in his own.

'Sergeant Bliq.' He addressed the short, thickset, olive-skinned woman beside him. 'The Ancestor is making his way to the stable. If he gets there, he'll try to run to another outpost. Sergeant Qiyala has already recognized the danger and is drawing the southern units to her. I want you to reinforce the defensive line she is making there.'

'He'll turn.' She was one of the veterans: all his sergeants were. 'When he sees that, he'll simply turn. Let me grab the others and reinforce this side first.'

'When he turns,' Heast said evenly, 'I want you to charge him and break the Leerans that are supporting him.'

She grunted sourly. 'That'll leave you in the open, sir.'

'Do you understand the order I have given?'

'Yes, Captain,' she said, and began down the road, past the collapsed tents and dead men and women.

'Ralen.' Heast turned. 'Tell Anemone she is needed.'

The boy ran to the left, through the tents and into the bush, his eyes wide.

Heast had done as much with the men and women from Maosa as he could. By and large, he was satisfied by their progress, but without seasoned soldiers to fill their ranks, they would struggle against the Leerans. Worse, he would simply be unable to press hard against General Waalstan—

The Ancestor turned.

At the sight of Heast alone, Kilian charged. His large feet tore up the ground as he stretched out his arms, his axes extended like wet metal wings.

Behind the Ancestor, Bliq let out a loud cry and, supported by Qiyala, the two units surged forwards.

The Leeran soldiers took a step back to defend themselves, but could not organize enough of a defence before the swords of Heast's force crashed through in an ugly and brutal violence. Worse for the Leerans, the actions drew in the surrounding soldiers who had held the ring with Taaira and relieved the tribesman of the defensive act he had been maintaining. Rather than follow the soldiers into the battle, however, he began to chase down the Ancestor.

Heast dropped his hand to the hilt of his sword, but did not draw it.

The tribesman was struggling to close the gap between the two. For every two steps that the Ancestor took, he was forced to take four. It was clear that he would be unable to stop Kilian before he reached Heast. Yet the Captain of Refuge did not move.

In the centre of Kilian's elongated chest was the ghostly shape of a man. The shadowy figure was twisted and hunched, as if a great pain had been inflicted on him. Ignoring the bloodshot gaze of Kilian, Heast focused on the real face of the Ancestor and thought how small he appeared in comparison to the body he possessed, how tiny and cruel his appearance once. Lost in the sight of it, Heast did not flinch as the large man drew closer and closer and the first of his axes lifted to come crashing down—

Only to find that it would not.

Roaring, the Ancestor lifted his other axe, but that too was suddenly weighed down, as if a dozen hands had caught it and stilled it with all their strength.

'I have a witch,' Heast said calmly. 'She will hold you long enough for the Hollow to reach you.'

A moment later, Kye Taaira's heavy sword burst through the Ancestor's back.

9.

The wreckage appeared an hour before dawn, just as Se'Saera had said.

Beneath the last of the moonlight, it was not at first clear what had caused the ship to wreck. The rocky beach stretched around the broken hull like the jaws of a giant animal, itself torn apart by the act of destruction on the vessel. The imagery lingered in Bueralan's mind as he rowed through the choppy surf to the wreckage and grew stronger when, near to the broken hull, Aela Ren reached into the black water and pulled out a limb. It was a man's arm, brown-skinned and thick with fat and muscle quickly going to rot. In the pale light, the Innocent turned the limb over in his own brown, scarred hands without revulsion. As he did, Bueralan brought the small dinghy along the ship's shattered bow, turning around the broken edges to gaze at the front that had been torn out, as if by the teeth similar in size to the rocks that lay in the water before the hole.

It was in that wreckage that Ren lashed a rope to a beam to hold the dinghy in place. After he attached it, the small man disappeared into the dark of the hull, leaving Bueralan to pull the oars in and follow him. As the saboteur stepped onto the deck, a match sparked and a lamp that sat on the ground bloomed, the light slowly revealing the bodies of men and women across the broken deck.

Each had been torn apart, ripped as if they were but raw meat.

'*Mercy*,' Bueralan whispered.

'There is no mercy here.' The Innocent lifted the lamp, the scars along his arms running back and forth like lit wires. 'It is doubtful that there is mercy anywhere in the world, any more.'

Bueralan knelt beside one of the corpses, one close to the broken edge of the hull. There, he reached for the piece of silver that had caught his eye. '*Mercy* is the name of this ship.' He pulled the small badge from the blood-slicked collar and held it up. 'This is Captain Islan's mark. This is her ship. She docks in Leviathan's End.'

'Leviathan's End is not a nation,' the other man said. 'It has no fleets.'

'Captain Islan is a mercenary.' The badge had an empty flag beneath an undefined face. 'All mercenaries call Leviathan's End their home.'

'Not all do. You know that as well as I do. But tell me—' Ren's lamp shone over a black-skinned woman, her body encased in black-and-red armour – 'How did one of the First Queen's soldiers come to be here?'

Bueralan stared at her face, the bone crushed and, in places, ripped away.

'Do you know her?' the Innocent asked.

'No.' He turned the badge over in his fingers and rose to his feet. 'What could have torn off her face like that?'

'A human hand.'

Bueralan wanted to disagree. As he examined the other bodies, he saw indents in the armour that had been made by hand, grooves that his hands could fit into. Despite his thoughts of a giant monster, it was clear that no such creature had attacked *Mercy* and dragged it to the shore. It had not been such a far-fetched thought: there were creatures that lived in the depths of Leviathan's Blood that rose from the floor only to hunt the men and women who rode across its surface. It was not common, but when they did rise from the ocean bed to take a ship, they did so with long, clear tentacles that splintered hulls and decks. They crushed men and women and broke their bones as if they were nothing but a child's toy before pulling them down into the water along with the ship. Over a decade ago, on the north of Gogair, Bueralan had seen exactly that. For weeks after, lone bodies had washed up against the shore, each of them a study in pain, but a pain that was not kin to what he saw now.

'Three humans, to be exact.' Aela Ren shone the light further down the hull. 'Each of them clearly much stronger than a normal man or woman.'

'Like you?'

'Like us,' he corrected.

'You didn't answer my question.'

When he turned, the glare of the lamp caught his skin, and the scars along his face ignited. It was as if the lasting impression of trauma that his god, Wehwe, had inflicted upon him at his death had broken through. 'No. There are two men and one woman who are not with us,' he said. 'But the nature of the destruction is not theirs.'

Ahead, a part of the deck they stood on broke away, revealing the hold beneath. Both men approached the edge and, as Ren swung the lamp out far to light what was below, dozens of crates were revealed. Leviathan's Blood had flooded most of the hold, but in that inky dark water, none of the crates floated. On them was a soldier bent at a terrible angle, with wood both around and through him, as if he had been the cause of the break in the deck, as if he had been slammed into it, then through it, before he crashed against the crates and tore them open. The jagged edges revealed silver and gold bars, bars that no one had made an effort to even try and loot.

'Someone was fleeing,' Bueralan murmured.

'The First Queen was fleeing,' Aela Ren said. 'It could very well be that what Se'Saera saw in her dream was real.'

'She said that we would swim to the ship,' he said, unable to disagree with the other man fully, 'but we did not.'

'Quite true.' Above them, the top deck of the ship groaned. 'And she made no mention of those who caused this.'

The stairs that led onto *Mercy* were narrow and empty, and Bueralan followed the Innocent up them, his hand on the hilt of the sword the other had let him reclaim.

He was not sure what he expected to find at the end of the stairs, though he knew that there would be more dead. Indeed, the first thing that the light of Aela Ren's lamp shone across was the broken body of a sailor. But it was not the debris of men and women that drew Bueralan's gaze once the bloom of the lamp shone across the wide deck of *Mercy* like a piece of fallen sun. No, rather, it was the three figures that knelt on the deck, their heads bowed, and their arms folded across their chests that he turned towards.

Only one could be mistaken for human: two of them were so heavily deformed that Bueralan was surprised they were alive. Both wore water-soaked furs, indicating that they, at least, had swum onto the ship. The man to his right was the largest of the three, a huge, hulking figure: his flesh had split and been sewn back up with what appeared to be links of chain and wire. In contrast, the man to his left was leaner and taller, so much so that his skin was hollow and sunken, the outlines of his bones easily identifiable, as if he were a half-starved animal.

The last of the three had neither quality. Instead, he wore old leather armour, the design of it a layer of wrapping, with each individual length tightened around his white skin, turning it into a new, darker skin, one that shifted with him as he rose to his feet, as he held his leather-wrapped hands together and bowed his head.

He had short blond hair that took on an almost white quality in the night and sat atop a smooth and unblemished face.

'My Lord,' he said in a voice that was soft, yet without kindness. 'We await our god with one of the gifts she so desired. We await with it to beg forgiveness.'

It was then, as the man's gaze rose, that Bueralan saw the woman's body strung from one of *Mercy*'s masts.

10.

As the morning's sun began to rise, the slaughter of the Leeran horses began.

'I must admit, Captain, that I find these acts particularly distasteful.' As Kye Taaira spoke, his gaze followed two men walking to the southern stables. 'I should not find it difficult to reconcile, but I do. An hour ago I watched men and women die in battle. Some I knew, some I did not. But already, I know that it is not their faces I will remember from this day, but the silence of those animals as the blades strike deeply inside them.'

'The beasts have been bonded with the soldiers they serve.' Heast had given the job to men who had been butchers in Maosa. They had greeted the morning's work with a sombre acceptance, for which he was both grateful and understanding. 'If I could, I would have it another way: we need horses, and when we don't need horses, we need the money they bring. But Anemone insists that there is nothing else to be done. They'll simply starve if we leave them.'

'That is why I will remember them before the men and women,' the tribesman said. 'For in them, the offer of our new god is clear: servitude or death.'

'Or rebellion.'

'I do not think she offers that, Captain.'

Heast turned away from the stable as the two men entered, their butcher's blades drawn. 'It is the third option,' he said. 'The old gods understood that and if the new god does not, then she will soon enough.'

'I do not think that tonight has warranted such optimism.'

'No,' he admitted, 'it has not.'

Slowly, he made his way through the quiet camp. Heast had lost eleven soldiers in the raid, but in this, he considered himself fortunate. The potential for further deaths had been there. From the silence of the soldiers around him, their sombre salutes and muted conversations, everyone knew that they had been lucky. Individual acts had kept the casualties low and individual acts had ensured their victory. In the last months, Heast had drilled into his soldiers that an army had to be more than its individuals, that it had to be able to succeed, with or without them. 'In battle, each one of us must be able to step into the role of another. One death must not spell a weakness for us.' Before the raid, Heast had known that he had not achieved that: his position was too valuable, as was Anemone's and Taaira's.

Ahead, the largest tent in the camp sat darkly, waiting for both Heast and Taaira. Made from the same green fabric as the others around it, the tent was three times the size of those. Its roof was weighed down by water from the night's rain and a guard stood outside, though Heast doubted that the precaution was necessary. When he stood close to the tent, he had the impression of it having its own presence, as if the fabric that had been wrapped around the wooden structure kept the essence of a watchful eye.

Inside, the sensation increased uncomfortably.

'It is a dark room,' Anemone had said to him, when he first stepped in. 'Not just in the light that is here, but in the acts that have been done here. Grandmother says that the fewer people who enter, the better.'

He had nodded and the order, when given, had been easily obeyed.

The witch had remained in the tent alone while Heast made his inspection of the camp, and she did not rise when he and Taaira returned. Instead, she continued to work through the narrow boxes before her, having already gone through the items that had been laid out on the floor: the small boxes, the knives and the glass jars.

Heast had not expected to find the Anemone who sat before him in Maosa. He had arrived looking for the woman she called her grandmother, a woman who had had the name she now bore, and who had been old for all of Heast's life. Yet, when he had arrived, he had learned that the Anemone he had known had died. In her place stood the slim, olive-skinned girl who hid herself in oversized clothes and dyed her hair an unnatural red. She was Anemone now.

'What have you found?' he asked.

'There are receipts for Gogair coin in the ledger,' she replied, not raising her head from the sheets of paper in her hand. 'It details the number of people they have sold, but there are no names listed.'

'No, there would not be. They would be going to the markets.'

'They do, however, list the coordinates where the ships pick them up from.'

Across the tent from Heast, Taaira approached one of the jars before Anemone. It had a briny, yellow colour to it. Inside sat squashed orbs. 'Eyes,' he said, lifting it. 'Why would you keep eyes in a jar?'

Anemone raised her head. 'They sell their slaves blind,' she said flatly, 'because they have seen too much.'

A sad sigh escaped the tribesman.

'Do you have more information?' Heast bent awkwardly for the paper that held the coordinates. 'We're not close enough to the coast to be able to put a stop to this trade.'

'There is this.' She rose from the floor, her legs pushing her upright. She held out the collection of letters that she had been reading. 'These are written by the Marshal Faet Cohn.'

The paper was thick and expensive, and what had been written had been inscribed in the Faaishan language by a thick quill. 'The marshal who survived the sacking of Celp over half a year ago.' Heast read it slowly. 'He has a very unflattering description of me. He also has a very accurate description of the land and two of the sites we have used as camps.'

'The letter is dated two weeks ago yesterday,' Anemone said. 'If we had not constantly been on the move, we would have been found. We would have been slaughtered by the people we are trying to help – by my people!'

Heast began to fold up the letter.

'Are you not angry?' Her dark gaze met his searchingly. 'Captain, we are fighting their war. It must anger you as it does me.'

'I am not fighting their war,' he said. 'Neither are you. You are fighting my war. And in my war, this letter is nothing but currency.'

11.

It was not the First Queen of Ooila who hung from *Mercy*'s mast. The morning's sun revealed a face that was too young and too healthy to be her and the sombre duty of identifying the woman fell to Bueralan.

'Greena Fe.' He spoke as a small boat was lowered into the black water from the huge form of *Glafanr*. 'She was the First Queen's daughter. Her oldest daughter. This was her ship.'

'The dreams of our god are still flawed,' the Innocent said, standing beside him. 'Fate does not convey itself in the subtexts and promises of an unconscious mind. She will come to understand that as she experiences it more and more like her parents did. For them, fate was not a dream, but how they viewed the world. They saw all the possibilities, all the strands of possibility before them, and they would nudge and push events until one was realized and another destroyed. In a dream, there is no conscious choice. There is misunderstanding and absence. There is doubt where there should be none.'

What that meant in relation to the three creatures who were responsible for the destruction on *Mercy*, Bueralan did not know. No answers were forthcoming, either. The blond man – the normal man – had introduced himself as Zilt, but he had not elaborated on who he was, or how he knew that Se'Saera had wanted the ship, or why he was begging for forgiveness. Ren must have had the same questions, but he had not asked any. Instead, he had nodded at Zilt, accepting what he said and then, with his scarred hands on the hilts of his old swords, walked to the stern of *Mercy*, to where the ship's wheel stood empty. There, he had waited, unresponsive until the morning's sun had risen and the First Queen's daughter had been revealed.

'She will be bothered by the mistake, but not by the actions,' Bueralan said. 'She will look at all those who have died here and shrug.'

'Her parents would have done the same,' said Ren. 'Why should their child be any different?'

Bueralan did not know how to respond to that.

'You cannot lie to yourself,' the Innocent continued, his voice solemn. 'Servitude does not require you to believe that everything your master does is fair, or even kind, for often it is not. You are in error if you look for morals in a god, for your morals are made by those around you, by those who have raised you, and each of them is born from a mortal concern. No such thought occurs to a god. When you realize that, when you have lived long enough that your own morals are no longer understandable in the world, but are something that you hold to nonetheless, you will finally begin to comprehend the true nature of a god. You will see that mortal men and women change. That they seek to remake the work each generation. That they are but a small stain in an eternity. When you do, you will realize how precious the words of a god are. How they use those words to define the world around you, to give truth where there is none, and substance that no mortal can see.'

That certainty, Bueralan knew, was what drove Aela Ren. In the last four months, he had come to believe that the scarred man saw and recognized the destruction he was responsible for. He was not without self-reflection or awareness and he knew the ramifications of his actions: but for the Innocent, there was no act he could perform other than destruction. He saw a world in constant flux to the morals and wills of mortals, and he saw a world of chaos.

In Dynamos, before the plank to *Glafanr* had been lowered, but as it drifted into the strait of the port, Bueralan had walked the town's empty streets. Around him, the buildings stood tall but silent, as hollow as the old butterfly corpses that cracked beneath his boots. Without any goal in mind, he found himself at The Mocking Quarrel, the inn that he and Samuel Orlan had stayed in when they first arrived in Ooila. Inside, he walked up the stairs and past the rooms. Through the open doors, he saw unmade beds, open drawers, and other signs of a hasty exit.

When Bueralan returned to the ground floor, he found Samuel Orlan sitting at one of the centre tables, a pitcher of beer and a glass beside him.

'I realized,' the cartographer said, 'that I have not seen a butterfly alive for days.'

'No.' Bueralan picked up a glass from the bar. 'In Cynama, I thought the fires had driven them away. But here, I have seen only their husks.'

'They will not rise again,' he said. 'She has drawn Maita's power from the ground as she rode here, as if she were putting a comb through her hair.'

The saboteur was not surprised. He placed the glass on the table and unstrapped his sword, laying it before him.

'It is what Aela wanted us to see,' Orlan said, raising his gaze as he spoke. 'Remember when he came to us in that barn, after they had conquered Cynama? He could have left us there. She had no need for us. But he came back for us, so we could see what she has done. So we could bear witness to her birth. He called us his prisoners when he stepped through the door, but we misunderstood the nature of our prison. We have waited for a shackle and a cage but there is none. We are not prisoners in the way we know the word to be used. Such a prisoner is not allowed to hold a sword. He is not allowed to ride off and reclaim it before he returns to the city.'

'We should walk away, then.' Bueralan began to pour warm beer from the pitcher into his glass. 'If it is that simple, after all. So why don't we?'

'Because we are caged regardless.'

He sat down across from the other man. 'Yes, we are,' he said, after a moment.

'I did not expect a god to return in my lifetime.' The cartographer turned his gaze to his own still full glass. 'Every Samuel Orlan has feared that it would happen, but I did not think it would be me. I am too old for it now. I should be finding a successor. A new god should be a concern for the eighty-third Samuel Orlan. Or for the ninety-first, or the hundred-and-ninth. One of them should be witness to this, not me.'

'But it is you.'

'Yes, and everything I have done to try and stop her—'

'Has been useless.' Bueralan took a deep drink, a quarter of the tall glass. 'I've not been any better,' he said, after he had lowered the glass. 'I don't have a plan. I don't know how to stop this. I am still trying to find a way to do that. But I know that when that ship comes to port, I will walk up the plank and I will find a cabin in it. I can do nothing else after what was done to Taela and Zean. Ren knows that. That is why he let me go back to my mother's house that night. That is why he allows me to wear a sword. What he knows about you, I do not know. I imagine it's something similar.'

'He wants me to believe in her,' Orlan replied sourly. 'No, not believe. He wants me to know. He wants me to stand beside him and support her. He wants me to admit that the world is better with her. He wants you to acknowledge it as well.'

'What we think matters very little to him.'

'No, what we think does matter. What all god-touched men and women think has always mattered to Aela Ren. They are his family.'

'There's a thought,' Bueralan said, and drank more of the warm beer.

He and Orlan drank the rest of the pitcher and another one before the saboteur left. At the door of the inn, he had seen the old man return to the bar for a third, intent on drowning his thoughts. But he had not seen him again until the last of Aela Ren's soldiers boarded *Glafanr*. He had been in their midst, a drunk and forlorn figure who, after he had found a cabin, had retreated into himself. In the months that they had been at sea, Orlan had rarely left his cabin and had spoken only when the door was opened, and when a question was asked of him. Even then, he had only spoken in brief snatches.

Beside Bueralan, the Innocent watched not the arrival of his new god at the wreckage of *Mercy*, but the three figures who stood at the broken rail awaiting her.

A Small Flame

'Weeks later,' Aelyn Meah said, after I asked her when she became aware of what she had done. 'It consumed me once I realized it. I saw it not just in my dreams, but in my moments of solitude. At night, I would see the storm giant I created tearing Yeflam apart. In the middle of the day, I would see the waves rise to crash into the pillars. But then my family . . .' She paused on the word. 'But then the Keepers,' she resumed, the change well noted, 'would reach me. They would pull me down from the sky roughly and sedate me.'

She fell silent. She would often pause while we talked, to gather her thoughts. What she said was important to her, even though she knew that very few people would read what I wrote. *Histories* threaded through the hold of my ship in Leviathan's End, but few people came to read them.

'I tried to tell myself that I was not responsible for what I had done,' she said. 'I was well aware by then of the extent of Kaqua's control over the Keepers and me. But it was hard. When I woke in the Mountains of Ger he was beside me. In those weeks where I was consumed by my power, he cared for me. He made sure I did not hurt myself. He fed me. He changed my clothes and washed me. He was so much the friend he had always been that I fell easily into relying upon him. When I began to tell myself that I was not responsible, that it was in fact his fault, I would be filled with such self-loathing that I would consider killing myself. I tried more than once.

'Kaqua was always there to stop me, of course.'

—Onaedo, *Histories, Year 1029*

1.

The morning's sun rose with a violent edge as Ayae drove the cart and the two bodies out of Yeflam in silence.

After Se'Saera left Tan's body, he had not lasted long. He had coughed and, as he tried to rise, the flesh and muscle around his neck peeled open, revealing the bone behind his throat. His neck had broken moments later. Little could be done for him and, in silence, Ayae and the others watched him die. Xrie had broken it first. After Tan had become still, and as the blood seeped off the back of the wagon, he said to them that they should keep the knowledge of the Innocent to themselves. Ayae did not know if he meant to keep it a secret from Muriel Wagan or Lian Alahn, or just from the camp population in general, but she had nodded in agreement, regardless. She did not agree out of obedience to Xrie or to his rank as his soldiers had, and neither did she agree as Eidan had with a shrug, as if it were not of consequence what anyone in the camp knew. No, Ayae nodded because she could not trust herself to speak. Even now, as the horse pulled the cart over the stone bridge, her fear uncoiled through her, causing her heart to quicken, her skin to prickle, and fingers to tighten and release the reins without any conscious decision on her part.

Aela Ren. She almost said the words aloud, but did not. *The Innocent.*

Ayae told herself that what she felt was irrational. Ahead, the bridge dipped down into the camp. The sprawling tents and dying fires that sat before her were in no way similar to the camp she had spent her early years in. There were no huge, fire-scarred wooden barricades. There was no fear every time that the huge gates began to grind open. No whispers that followed the sound, no voices that murmured as if in prayer, wishing that the Innocent was to the south, to the south, to the south. No, there was none of that in the camp she rode into. And neither was she the child who had lived behind that wall, either. She was an adult now. A woman. She had stood on the Spine of Ger beside the mercenaries of Steel. She had killed men and women. She had watched her friends die. And she had stood in the centre of Yeflam against the god who was now the master of Aela Ren. She did not need to be afraid. She—

Eidan's crippled hand fell on her leg. 'Careful,' he said, quietly.

A crowd had begun to spread across the road before her, the front of it leading down to the shoreline. 'Thanks,' she said, pulling on the reins.

The horse pawed nervously at the ground while Xrie and his soldiers cleared a path for the cart. As they passed, Ayae saw a heavy-set white man standing on the side of the road talking to the Soldier, pointing to the east. She followed his hand and saw, emerging from the morning's sun, a huge-sailed ship. The light left it unformed, as if it drifted out of the brightness like a long-forgotten creature of the sun god, Sei.

Beside her, she heard Eidan murmur the word, 'Saan.'

'Saan?' Xrie began to move to the shore, leaving the two of them to drive to the stables without a word. 'How can you tell?' she asked.

'Only they have masts so big and boats so unwieldy.'

At the makeshift stables, she left the horse, cart and bodies with Jaysun. He did not wince at the sight of the two corpses when he lifted the blanket over them. He simply said that he would see to their disposal and let the cover fall back. After Ayae thanked him, she approached Eidan and asked him if he wanted to go to where the crowds had begun to swell, but he shook his head. 'I'm tired,' he said. 'Besides, this is politics that I have no interest in.'

She watched him make his slow, limping way through the near-empty paths of the tent city, before she headed towards the crowds.

In a certain way, she did not quite know what to make of Eidan, even after the time they had spent together. When Zaifyr had described him to her, he had said that he was methodical, and that he had a certain coldness, an almost clinical nature to him. Yet she found his attention to Yeflam to be in opposition to that. It was, Ayae believed, emotion that drove him, as if, by repairing the broken cities, and those that had sunk, he was proving his love for Aelyn. She had not heard him mention her – in fact, he did not refer to the Keepers at all – but it was clear that Aelyn's betrayal of not just him, but Yeflam as a whole, hurt him, and she could not help but think that his actions were a message to his absent sister.

As she drew closer to the shore, the press of people around her thickened and the noise of the camp rose. 'Do you think they are here to conquer us?' Ayae heard one man ask. She did not hear the reply. A woman beyond him said loudly, 'This would not have happened if we'd rebuilt the fleet.' 'The Soldier,' said an older man. 'The Soldier was born in the Saan.' That man turned to Ayae and apologized as she tried to move past him. At his use of her name, her passage became easier, and it was not long until Ayae found herself at the front of the crowd, behind a force made from the Yeflam Guard, the Mireean Guard and Kal Essa's Brotherhood.

The Saan ships were huge beasts that wallowed in the black ocean. The single vessel that had risen so prominently in the distance was but one of three. The other two were revealed once the massive white and yellow sails that had drawn the first ship into view of the shore had been lowered. As she watched them drop anchor, Ayae thought that they looked more like cargo ships than warships. She could imagine them crashing through waves in storms and labouring in still water when the wind fell away and only muscle could move them. It was an opinion she heard repeated behind her, but it was followed by a jibe about the Saan sinking before they made shore. It fell flat when a man said that the Saan were the cargo, the Saan and their swords.

How would you feel, Ayae thought after, *if you knew that the Innocent would be here soon?*

A pair of longboats detached themselves from the first Saan ship and approached the shore slowly, a white flag held high before them. When the colour became clear to the crowd, it was as if a breath that had been held was let out, though Ayae felt no such relief herself.

In Leviathan's Blood, a brown-skinned, handsome man in heavy, pitted leather dropped from the first boat. The armour that he wore was to protect him from the water that came up to his waist. A second man similarly attired jumped from the following boat. With the water around their waists, the two hooked rope harnesses to their armour and pulled the boats onto the shore, revealing two warriors adorned with copper bracelets and an older man in the first, and half a dozen similarly adorned warriors with a woman in the second.

The oldest of the men was the first to step upon the shore: a thick, solid man with sun-darkened brown skin and long, thick arms. Of all the warriors who stepped from the boat with swords at their sides, only he did not wear any of the copper rings on his arms. Instead, a single, small, dull gold ring pierced the left side of his bottom lip: it glinted like a golden tooth in a smile. Yet there was something humourless about the man, a trait accentuated by the razor shave that ran across his head and face. It left a series of straight, humourless lines of age to define his features. Features that disappeared as he knelt and lowered his head.

He remained like that until Xrie approached. Once he was within speaking distance of him, the older man rose his head. 'Uncle,' he said, the voice barely carrying to Ayae. Then, louder, he said, 'We have come to settle blood.'

'You cannot claim that here,' Xrie said. 'Yeflam does not share your blood.'

'We all share blood today.' As the warrior spoke, it became clear that he was reciting lines he had rehearsed in the traders' tongue. 'The borders of land must be put aside. A blow struck at Yeflam is a blow struck at the Saan. In the First Kingdom of Ooila such a blow was made. It lingers in us like the destruction we see in Leviathan's Blood. In the First Queen's Province, our wound was made by the Innocent, Aela Ren.' A ripple of whispers ran through the crowd and Ayae's hands curled into each other. 'Hau Dvir told us how the swords of our warriors did not hurt him, how the strength of our finest failed, and how the Innocent's only desire was to speak of a new god, to hear her name spoken so that we could all hear it.'

'Se'Saera.'

'Yes, Uncle.'

'Rise, Miat.' From the ocean, the second boat was brought onto the shore. A woman stepped from it. Xrie greeted her as if there was nothing unusual in her presence, though even Ayae knew that there was, for the women of the Saan are forbidden to travel, and then he turned to the soldiers behind him. 'Send word to Lady Wagan and Lord Alahn,' he said. 'Tell them that the Lord of the Saan has come to speak with them.'

2.

Until he led the tall grey into the hold of *Glafanr*, Bueralan had long considered the transportation of animals an act of cruelty, one that he tried to avoid. Over the years, he had stood on decks of vessels both large and small, and watched as horses were lowered into stalls not large enough for them to lie down in. It was a mercenary's joke that, no matter how poorly you were housed on a ship, your horse had it worse. Packed tightly against each other, the animals spent the voyage in a canvas sling for support. At its end, they were lifted out and dropped into the black water to swim to shore. Bueralan could still remember watching the horses of Sky, the first mercenary unit he served in, swimming frantically after such an event, and the horror he felt when fatigued horses sank and did not rise. In the years that followed, he had taken to selling his horse at the market on the shore and buying a new one when he landed. It was a choice that he did not have as he rode into Dyanos, and one that he doubted, anyway, he could have acted upon given all that he had shared with the tall grey.

'You still have not named him.' Aela Ren had stood beside Bueralan as the sling was fitted to the beast before he was lowered through the hold's entrance. They had still been in Ooila, then. 'I would tell you that you should, that all things should be named, but we have had that conversation.'

'We have,' he had replied, watching the tall grey sink into the ship.

After a moment, the Innocent said, 'Kaze will take good care of him. You need not worry for his fate on this voyage.'

After he had returned from the wreck of *Mercy*, Bueralan had climbed down the ladder that led to the bowels of *Glafanr*. Kaze sat, as she often did, at the end of the space that ran between the stalls in the hold, the booths laid out on either side of her, big enough for horses to both stand and lie down in. With her back to Bueralan, she revealed a long, narrow, dark-skinned body. She was not as dark as Bueralan, and her hair was tightly curled and verging on a ruddy red. Her long life had left her with little accent – like many of Aela Ren's soldiers – and the saboteur did not know where she had originally been born. For her part, Kaze did not offer the information: she, like all of the soldiers on *Glafanr,* identified herself as the servant of a god that no longer existed. That was their birthplace and their nationality. For Kaze, that was Linae, the Goddess of Fertility, the first of the gods that had died.

'He has been fed already.' Kaze spoke as he drew closer, not turning from the table. 'He has been brushed and walked, as well.'

'Maybe I came down to thank you.'

At that, the woman turned to him, her hazel eyes peering through a pair of thin wire frames. 'Because we are so social, yes?'

'Social creatures.'

Above them, in the rafters of the hold, a hammock had been slung. More than once, Bueralan had found Kaze lying in it and reading, having preferred the company of horses to that of her fellow immortals. 'Yes,' she said, blandly. 'You came to ask about Taela?'

He wasn't surprised. 'She is showing—'

'Much more than she should,' she finished. 'I know.'

'What does it mean?' Bueralan stopped before the tall grey and rubbed his hand along the horse's head. 'For Taela, that is.'

'You should convince her to let me see her.' Kaze rose from her seat. On the table she left the old bridle and bit she had been working on. 'I know only so much from a distance. Linae made it easier for me to help a child into the world, but I cannot work miracles.'

It still surprised Bueralan to hear the god-touched talk about their gods, to hear them speak about the gods as if they were still their servants and their servitude had never ended. He had, at first, thought of them as individuals similar to those who were 'cursed', a belief helped by Aela Ren and the soldier Joqan. Bueralan had seen Ren's strength and speed, but it had been the way that the latter coaxed the lava out beneath Ooila that had assured him of it. If the servant of Sil, the God of the Earth, could do that, then surely all the god-touched echoed the god that they served. But at sea, a different awareness had come to define itself. Joqan rode the waves poorly and was often seen on the deck of *Glafanr* with a faintly ill expression. He could not create fire, or cause the earth to rise up out of the black water, and it was not long before Bueralan realized that here lay the biggest difference between the god-touched and the men and women who were 'cursed' with a god's power. The god-touched had been chosen, and had been given strength and immortality, but their masters had kept everything but the faintest part of their divine dominion from their servants. It meant that the god-touched did not fear it. They knew it, they could even touch it and draw from it. But they could not to control and master it in the way that the 'cursed' could.

'But you know something, don't you?' he said.

'It isn't for you to hear. It is for her.'

'She doesn't want your help.'

'Of course not.' After Cynama, after Taela had failed to abort the child within her, Se'Saera had sent Kaze to examine her. 'But I have never lost a mother,' the god-touched woman said. She stopped before the grey and held out a slice of apple for the horse. 'You should tell her that.'

'What about a child?'

'No child, either.' She scratched the grey's nose after he finished the slice. 'But sometimes they are lost well before they are born.'

'Do you think that likely here?'

'You are like a father,' she said. 'Has anyone told you that?'

He let the barb slide past. 'Just tell me,' he said. 'She won't talk to you, anyway.'

Kaze was silent. She scratched the grey again. Then she said, 'A god's child is never lost. And it is never normal.'

'Have there been many?' Bueralan asked. 'Many children of gods?'

'The name is common, but no. It is rare. There was a very famous prophecy when I was a little girl that said that twins would be born, one to lead, one to fear. The two began a war that lasted a generation and, afterwards, women who were thought to be pregnant with twins were drowned. Baar did that. The God of War. His two children were said to be able to talk to him, and often claimed to be part of his own awareness. That is why they went to war.'

She spoke mildly, as if the details were benign, and not something awful. Bueralan saw again Se'Saera's hand thrust into Taela. Saw her push Zean's soul down her throat. He did not ask how a child could be made from such an action, but rather what kind of child. Would it be a representation of Se'Saera, a part of her, like the twins Kaze had just spoken of? And if those two had been a part of the God of War, what would Se'Saera's child reveal about her?

Would any of Zean be there?

'On the topic of the God of War, I see you met General Zilt,' Kaze said. She gave the grey one last scratch, and turned from it, to the other horses. 'He was one of Baar's favourites.'

'He's god-touched?' Bueralan asked, surprised. The God of War had the distinction of being one of only three gods whose servants were not onboard *Glafanr*.

'No, he is not like us.' She laughed, as if the thought had humour in it, as if the leader of soldiers who allowed themselves to become monsters was funny. 'No, Baar had soldiers that he watched. He was said to enjoy the way they fought. He would find a second when he found a first, for he was a god very much about balance. Hence the twin children. Zilt and his soldiers were the last of them. The very first tribesmen on the Plateau were the other side of that equation.'

'Maybe Zilt should return the Plateau, then. He did not win any favours when he explained what happened in Yeflam after our new god left.'

'I heard some of it. He said that he was driven away by a storm.'

Zilt had knelt before Se'Saera when he explained what had happened, a chastised servant, a man admitting a wrong. 'The Keepers washed him and his soldiers away, apparently,' Bueralan said. 'But that was not the part that struck me. It was after that. He said that the Keepers were in Leera, waiting for us. Waiting for her, waiting to pledge their loyalty.'

'We're all friends, are we?' Kaze shook her head. 'What did Aela say?'

'He didn't say anything.'

3.

The midday's sun was high above the trees and the humidity had a touch of death's odour in it. The Leeran camp looked like bones: the tents stripped of cloth, supplies and coin, while the dead had been rolled into a pile, their weapons and armour removed.

Heast stood just beyond the dead, near the middle of the Leeran camp, where he had entered it the night before. Before him, the bodies of his fallen lay in a wagon. Eleven soldiers: four women, seven men, each still dressed and covered in thin blankets from head to toe. Not one of them was a member of his precious veterans. Heast did not like to remind himself of that, but he would not deny the reality of it, either.

He had told Refuge that he would be heading to Vaeasa tonight. He did not lie to them: he told them what had been found in the tent. 'The Lords of Faaisha will not be happy to see me,' he said to them. 'Lord Jye Tuael will tolerate me, however. At least, he will to hear what I say. If he is as corrupt as his marshal, then Anemone and I will struggle to make it back. If he's not, we will return with weapons, armour and soldiers. While I'm gone, Sergeant Bliq and Sergeant Qiyala will have command. Kye Taaira will be their second. Listen to all three while I am gone.'

He had approached the wagon after he dismissed them.

There was no horse to pull it, but Corporal Isaap and the remains of his squad had asked for the task of pulling it through the scrub to their next camp. Heast had ordered them to go ahead to the ruins of Celp. He would meet them there later. The bodies would be buried well before then, he knew. He would have preferred for them to be burned, but he knew that that was not the Faaishan way. Still, he trusted that Bliq and Qiyala would keep the tracks and the graves hidden as they made their way to Celp. When it came to the burial, however, neither knew the words that were said over the dead soldiers of Refuge. It had been over two decades since Heast had said the words himself, but he would not allow the cart to leave without him saying them. The soldiers had given what they had for him, given it to Refuge, and it did not matter that what they had was not enough, that it was not moulded by years of war, of the industry of violence he had brought them into. They had given all they had and he asked for no less.

'Captain.' Corporal Isaap appeared beside him, a heavy rope over his shoulder. He was a lean man, no more than a boy, really, the dark beard along his olive skin a patchy stubble of thin hair. 'I'm not interrupting, am I?'

'No,' Heast said.

'It's just that you looked as if you were speaking.'

'Merely offering my thanks, Corporal. A captain can do only that at this point.'

Isaap lowered the rope to the ground. 'It was my mistake, sir.' He almost called him marshal. A lot of them did. 'I don't know how, but the Ancestor heard us. You should have chosen someone else for the job.'

Heast turned to him, turned away from the wagon. 'How long have you been a soldier?' he asked.

'A few months.' Isaap offer a wry smile. 'Just over a year, I guess. I was given my post last spring.'

'What were you before?'

'Rich.'

'And you gave that up, did you?'

'No, sir. My parents said I could be rich and respectful in the lord's army.' He ran a hand through his hair, fidgeting, embarrassed by what he had said. 'My parents did not want the family to stay in Maosa. They said that there was no fortune there, beyond what they had. No prestige. They said I should distinguish myself to bring the attention of the other lords to me. You know how parents are, sir.'

'Mine have been dead for a long time.' They had, at any rate, not been like that. 'But I know what you mean. Not so long ago, I had a sergeant whose father was a very rich man in Yeflam. His son lived in the shadow of that for a long time. He tried to step out of it for years. I thought that there could be something in him if he managed to do so.'

'Did he? Step out of it, that is.'

'No,' Heast said. 'In the end, he was nothing more than his father's son.'

Isaap nodded. 'I don't want to be like that,' he said. 'I don't want to be my father's son. I have not always understood that, but I do now. I see how he never took responsibility for where the family was. For his bad choices. For the way he treated people. I own my mistakes, sir. The people here are dead because of me. I made the mistake when we came out of the brush. I came in before the Hollow was in position and others paid the price. If you want to strip me of my rank because of that, I'll understand, sir. I'll work it back.'

Before the battle, Heast would have been prepared to do that. It was not that Isaap had asked for fire, or that he had let his nerves get the best of him. No, it was his continual failure to accept orders, his belief that he knew better, the inability to recognize that he had none of the skills he believed he had. He had been barely trained in the year he had been a soldier. He had one advantage over the others in Refuge and that was that he could wield his sword with a certain amount of skill. It was the reason that Heast had given Isaap the job of securing the tents around the Ancestor.

Before he gave his orders to Refuge, Sergeant Qiyala and Bliq had both spoken to him about Isaap. They had waited for him outside the tent where Anemone worked. Both the sergeants had told him that the soldiers who had survived beside Isaap had done so because of him. They said he reacted quickly to the sight of Kilian rising, that he kept them alive and had pulled the survivors around Taaira.

'When I was a corporal, I lost four soldiers. Four soldiers of Refuge.' Heast bent down and picked up the rope. 'I made a small mistake. I washed a pot in a stream. I was nervous and I thought it would keep me busy. But the food scraps flowed down and they gathered in the rocks downstream and a tracker saw it. I had just gotten back to the camp when we were swarmed. The sentry caught them as they came up on us, but we were never meant to see a fight there. It was bad terrain. But I survived. Myself and one other out of six. A couple of days later, I told the captain just what you told me. I said I'd work back my rank. At the time, the Captain of Refuge was Tisoc Denali. He was a big man, Denali. Had fists like stones. After I finished speaking, I kept waiting for him to punch me. To punish me for what I did.'

Isaap followed Heast as he made his way to the front of the cart. 'Did he?'

'No.' He dropped the rope on the seat of the cart, took one end. 'He said to me that you make a mistake and people die. Then he said you make the right choice and people die. Then he left me.'

'That doesn't sound helpful.'

'No?'

He shook his head.

Heast handed him the end of the rope. 'Everyone dies in Refuge,

Corporal. By sword, by fire, by will. That is what we say over the bodies of our soldiers when we bury them. That was what I was saying when you came upon me.' He held up his hand as Isaap tried to speak. 'You have made mistakes. I will not tell you otherwise. Indeed, you might lose your rank one day, but it is not today. Put aside your father's shadow and it will not be tomorrow. Now, you find half a dozen soldiers to help you pull this cart. I don't want you doing it by yourself. When you bury those in it, you say the words I told you. They were soldiers of Refuge, and I need you to be a soldier in Refuge, not just for them, but for everyone else who stands.'

He left him there, tying the rope to the wagon, half a story in his mind.

Captain Denali had said more to Heast, before he left the hut he was in. In truth, he had torn strips out of Heast for his failure, and rightfully so. He had done it with the one surviving member of the group present, and he had done it in a voice that was hard and sharp. At the end of it, Heast had offered to resign, to do more than earn his rank back. He had said he would leave Refuge. He did not know where he would go: he was not yet eighteen and his life for years had been the mercenary unit. All the world he had seen, he had seen with them.

After Heast had said those words, Denali took one step towards him, as if he would strike out at the young soldier. His dark eyes burned, as if the words Heast had just said were worse than the men he had lost. 'You die in Refuge,' he said in a low, furious voice, 'or Refuge kills you. That is all there is to your life now, Corporal.'

4.

The Lord of the Saan and the woman who had arrived with him were led to the biggest tent in the camp. Once inside, the warriors who had accompanied them took up positions around the tent, their faces impassive as they stared into the crowds around them.

Ayae had seen little of the procession. The crowd, like a large animal, had followed the arrivals. In its shift and turn, Xrie and the Saan were lost to Ayae, and she did not think that she would be able to see them again through the press of bodies. That, at least, was not new: crowds had always hidden the sights from her. Quietly, she slipped out of the back of the crowd and, with a few streams of people doing the same, she circled up the gentle slope of the mountain.

'I am surprised you are not there,' Sinae Al'tor said to her. He emerged from the flow of people below as she reached her tent. A well-dressed, handsome, olive-skinned man, he smiled as if they were friends and shared something in common. 'You could be inside the fabric walls of Lady Wagan and Lord Alahn's tent, hearing what is said, voicing your own opinion,' he continued. 'You have no need to find a vantage point to stare at the walls like the rest of us.'

'Don't you already know what is being said inside?' she asked.

'It disappoints me greatly to hear that.' He wore a white silk shirt and finely stitched black pants above polished boots with bright silver buckles. Ayae had heard a rumour that he had snuck onto

Ghaam to retrieve his wardrobe. 'I run a brothel. I know only the secrets that flesh tells me.'

It was for that reason alone that she did not like Sinae Al'tor.

She had met him in the brothel he had owned on the night Yeflam broke apart, when she had fought the Keeper, Eira. But it was within the first weeks of the camp's creation that she saw more of Sinae. During that time, he established a network of tents at the eastern edges of the camp where men and women could sell themselves. Since the camp had very little currency, Sinae established a complex system of barters and favours, a system that, as coin began to enter the camp, left him with an immediate wealth few could equal. Rumour had it that he used it to access the markets across Leviathan's Blood, in the surviving cities of Yeflam, and beyond. Whether he did or not, it was certainly true that those who worked for Sinae Al'tor ate better than anyone else in the camp.

'Still,' he said now, 'this will strengthen Lady Wagan's position in the camp. Miat Dvir will not have come all this way to help rebuild Yeflam.'

'The Saan are not known as builders.' From the milling groups of people, a blonde woman dressed in dark red pants, a black shirt and a long, expensive, black coat, looked at the two of them: Sinae's guard, Ayae knew. Seeing nothing of interest, she turned back to the crowd. 'He said that they had a blood feud with Se'Saera,' she added.

'The rumour is true, then.' He sounded faintly surprised. 'A number of the Saan were said to have been killed in Ooila by—'

'The Innocent.'

'You don't seem surprised?'

'I was born in Sooia.'

'The edges of Sooia are not Yeflam, my dear.'

She shrugged, but did not elaborate. Xrie's desire to keep the knowledge of Ren to themselves was no longer one that Ayae had to worry about, but she had no intention of telling Sinae what she had seen in Neela.

'Soon, people will want to flee,' the man beside her said quietly. 'More people than is usual, that is. There are people who ask every day for me to secure them passage across Leviathan's Blood. They offer coin, favours, their family members, even themselves. They are desperate men and women. But there are no passages to be had. They never believe me when I tell them that, but it is the truth. Armed soldiers sit guard at the edges of Yeflam's cities. They shoot anyone who is uninvited. Muriel Wagan and Lian Alahn do well to keep it quiet that we are not wanted anywhere but here.'

They did it mostly through their own politics, Ayae knew. It was an open secret in the camp that Muriel Wagan wanted to go over the Mountains of Ger, to chase down not just the Keepers who had broken Yeflam, but the Leerans who had destroyed Mireea. In opposition, Lian Alahn wanted to rebuild Yeflam. He wanted to repopulate Neela, Mesi and Ghaam, and to rebuild much of the navy that was lost. In those differences – in those everyday arguments that took place directly before them – it was easy for the people of the camp to forget the politics of the rest of Yeflam.

'Do you know much about Miat Dvir?' Sinae asked.

'No,' Ayae said.

'You will, soon. He will come to speak with you.' Ayae made a noise of dismissal, but he smiled. 'Oh, no. He will be here. He will approach you as a supplicant. He will view you as a subject – that is how the Saan view everyone – but he will bend a knee before you. He will ask for favours.'

'Doesn't everyone these days?' She tried to make it sound dismissive, a quip, but failed. 'He will go to Xrie, first.'

'But then he will come to you. He will realize that Xrie's loyalties are not with him, but more importantly, are not with the Saan. That is why he will come to you. When he comes to speak to you, remember that Miat Dvir wants to see the Saan expand their influence outside the dusty home they live in. He wants them to be a world power. He thinks that it can even be done in his lifetime. Until very recently, he planned to begin his expansion by moving into Ooila. It was quite a daring move, really. He sought to marry one of his own children to the First Queen's youngest daughter. He sent his war scout out and sank into the resentment that the daughter had developed over the years. I do not think he would have been successful, not ultimately. The First Queen of Ooila is much more ruthless than he is. Regardless of how you thought it would end, it was a move that was intended to be a statement to the rest of the world. A statement he intends to repeat again through the opportunity presented by Aela Ren.'

'Only a fool would think that,' Ayae said. 'A fool far away from anything the Innocent has done.'

'I do not disagree,' Sinae said. 'But he will be here, and he will come here in the belief that you can give him that opportunity.'

5.

The corridors of *Glafanr* carried the sound of the ocean, as if it were an inlet by which a river began, and Bueralan was no more than a tiny raft drifting along it.

He had grown accustomed to the strange sounds within the ship, though he still found himself rejecting the notion that it had once been a vessel for the dead. Ai Sela, who was the captain of the ship, said that it had appeared before her after the Wanderer died. She had been his servant, a tall, brown-skinned woman who had travelled one end of the world to the other before her god died, and who in the aftermath found herself chained to the command of the ship. It was she who said the ship was alive, that it responded to her moods and those of others, even though she did not believe it to be sentient.

Glafanr was old. The wood of its hull and its masts was engrained with a quality possessed by only the oldest of ships Bueralan had seen. Yet the fragility that he associated with an old ship was not present on *Glafanr*. The hallways that he walked through now felt different from any others he had been in. Over the years, for one reason or another, Bueralan had stood in half a dozen shipyards. He had watched the hulks of the old beasts pulled onto shore to be stripped and dismantled. In each yard, Bueralan felt a certain sadness in the air, but when, after heaving himself up a rope to the deck of a ship that would be dismantled, he had felt the weak deck beneath his feet and smelt the rot that had set deep within the frame, he understood the necessity. There was a mortality within ships and the yards were, if a ship survived life on the sea, its only end. But on *Glafanr*, the saboteur felt none of that weakness within its hold.

'Orlan,' Bueralan said, holding open the door to his cabin. 'There are locks for a reason.'

The cartographer stood alone at the far end of the room, next to the small window. Recently, he had shorn his silver-grey hair short around his head. Yet, he had only trimmed his beard, leaving the thick bristles to form a solid spade down to his chest. He still wore his fine vests, the current one a bold mix of orange and black. The latter colour dominated in his pants and boots, but the shirt beneath the vest was white, a solid, true white that was in contrast to the tanned skin of his face.

'What do you think you are doing?' Orlan asked, offering no greeting. 'You cannot convince any of these people to betray Ren.'

Gently, he closed the door. 'Where is Taela?'

'Zilt came for her.'

'Why?'

'Because *she* asked it of him.' Orlan left the window and stalked heavily over to him. 'They know what you're trying to do. Did you think they wouldn't?' Bueralan could not smell alcohol on his breath. He had not smelt it since the day he had come aboard drunk. 'They know you're looking for a weak link among them,' the old man finished. 'A man or woman you can exploit.'

'And if I am?' he said. 'You've seen them since Zilt and his soldiers came aboard. They don't like them.'

'Ren doesn't like them,' the other man corrected. 'Don't mistake his thoughts for their own.'

'Because they have shown themselves to be so independent?' He glanced around the small room. 'There's a bottle of wine in here, if you would like to share it?'

'No.'

'There's water.'

A sigh of defeat escaped the cartographer. 'I did not come here to drink,' he said, the anger leaving his voice. 'I came here to warn you.'

'Warn me?' He stepped past the other man towards the small dresser and its jug of water and mugs. 'You seem to think our situation could get worse.' Behind the dresser, wedged so it would not roll, was a dark bottle of wine. 'I don't see you with a plan to make it better and I know Taela doesn't have one, so if one of us isn't trying something, then all that she, you and I are doing, is watching this unfold.'

'It could get worse for Taela.'

'What, she could die?'

Orlan did not immediately respond and, in that silence, Bueralan began to pull the cork from the bottle.

'Aela Ren has held these men and women together for over seven hundred years,' the cartographer said finally. 'You will not turn one against him.'

'They're too old to be blindly loyal.'

'Blind loyalty is the gift of old age, Bueralan.'

With the cork free, he held the bottle by its throat. 'Let me tell you something about loyalty,' he said. 'Loyalty is only blind if you are distant. If you are close, all you see are the cracks. Every army is filled with fractures. Discipline and loyalty are what smoothes the breaks and makes the bond that everyone shares stronger. But the cracks never go away. That's what makes a career soldier so valuable. They're there for the belief. Their loyalty is to the men and women they serve with and to the ideal of what they serve. To break that, you need to have engaged in something so horrendous that it challenges all the discipline and loyalty, that it causes every fracture in the unit to rise to the surface and begin to spread out like a spider's web.'

'They are not a simple army,' Orlan said. 'These men and women were once the servants of the gods—'

'And they have been destroying their creation.'

Before Orlan could reply, the door opened and Taela stepped in. 'The two of you sound like an old married couple,' she said. 'Is that our wine?'

Bueralan bit back his argument and his frustration and said, 'You want some?'

'Please.'

'I thought you were with her,' the cartographer said, stepping aside as she made her way past him. 'Did something go wrong?'

'What could go right?' Taela sank onto her bed, taking the mug that Bueralan handed her. 'I don't know what she wanted. Usually, she talks to me until I can barely stand. When she does, she tells me the most awful things. She tells me what she has planned for humanity, for the world. At times, I think she is telling me just to gauge my emotions, as if she's never been around a person who didn't worship her, and doesn't quite know how they will respond to her.' Unconsciously or consciously, the woman who had once been the Voice of the Queen rubbed at the swell of her stomach and took a sip of the dark wine. 'But when I got there, she simply looked at me and thanked me for wearing the shirt that I am wearing. Then she said, "When you go back to your room, tell those two men that I am happy."'

'With what?' Bueralan asked.

'She didn't say.'

6.

Sinae Al'tor was not wrong.

The Lord of the Saan, Miat Dvir, visited Ayae three days after he had met with Muriel Wagan and Lian Alahn. Before that, the Saan disembarked from their huge ships and set up a camp next to the already established tents. They were all male but for the woman who had accompanied Dvir, and they shared their tents with one another, and trained against each other. They spoke the traders' tongue in various levels of proficiency, and in the three days, stories emerged of confusion, insults and, once, a fight which no one could properly explain. But those stories were small and isolated, and for the men and women from Yeflam and Mireea, life continued much as it had before the Saan ships appeared. They continued to work on the repair of Neela and still went out into the fields that had become an important part of their lives.

Ayae returned to Neela twice with Eidan. He showed little interest in the Saan, so much so that it was she who was forced to bring it up, in the dark hours of their morning. 'They are here for war,' he said, and shrugged. 'The Saan exist to fight. It has not always been the case, but it has been for some time.' Then, after a moment, he said, 'They will come to you. To you, before me and my brother. Do as you wish.' She had thanked him, drily, and he had told her that it was his pleasure. He was trying not to smile, but the scars in his face gave him away.

Other than Eidan, no one repeated Sinae's words to Ayae. Instead, she heard pieces of gossip, stories of what was said inside the tent, and what was said, after, in the individual tents of Muriel Wagan and Lian Alahn. Everyone agreed that the Saan were here for war. Some said that they told the Lady of the Ghosts that they wanted to go over the Mountains of Ger before the month finished. They wanted to set up camps before the summer rains arrived and they wanted the Mireeans and the Yeflam Guard to come with them. She, it was said, supported that. Lian Alahn did not, and was said to be withholding the Yeflam Guard until the Saan agreed to help rebuild Yeflam. Miat Dvir was alleged to have told him that he did not care what happened to the land in the ocean. The quote Ayae heard repeated around the camp claimed that the Lord of the Saan had said that Yeflam was not real. 'It was a lie that men and women had been allowed to live on.'

Ayae had asked Caeli about that, but the guard did not know about the exact words. 'He said nothing to make Alahn happy, though,' she admitted.

The two were sitting on old wooden chairs when the Lord of the Saan approached. Ayae had come back from Neela earlier and found Caeli inside their tent with two trays of breakfast cooling for both of them. They had just finished the warm bread and pieces of ham when Miat Dvir, in the company of the middle-aged woman from the landing, walked up to their tent. Behind them, a Saan warrior with copper rings around the lower half of both arms followed, a pair of chairs held in his grasp. At the Lord's indication, he set these down opposite the two women and, after Dvir and the woman sat, he took his place behind them.

'It is a pleasure to meet you, finally,' Miat said to Ayae, first. He turned and offered a brief nod to Caeli as well. 'If you will excuse me, I would prefer another to speak for me. I do not speak the traders' tongue well.' He spoke it well enough, Ayae thought, but said nothing. 'Not like Vyla,' he added, placing a heavy hand on the arm of the woman at his side.

Vyla had light brown skin and she was not tall, not like Caeli, but nor did she have the lean body of someone short, like Ayae. Rather, she had a fullness to her that was hidden in the folds of her yellow and orange dress. She had a handsome face, one that was strongly defined by her chin and nose, and her hair was hidden beneath a brown and white spotted scarf.

'I thank you both for your time,' Vyla said, her voice deep and strong. 'We will endeavour not to take too much of it up.'

'I should probably leave,' Caeli said, rising.

Miat spoke quickly. 'No,' Vyla said. 'My husband wishes for you to stay. It would be a great insult to the Blade Prince if you left your home because of us.'

Ayae could see the surprise on her friend's face. Her relationship with Xrie had been one she kept private, one not common knowledge in the camp. 'I don't want to cause a conflict,' the guard said, returning to her chair. 'Besides, it is very public out here.'

The Lord of the Saan spoke. 'We will not be long,' his wife said. 'Nor do we have anything to hide. Besides, both of you are Mireean, are you not?'

'I have a job with Lady Wagan,' Caeli said, her words chosen carefully. 'Ayae does not.'

Vyla Dvir turned to Ayae as her husband spoke. 'You do not?' she asked, her voice holding the faint surprise that his did. 'We were under the impression that you supported Muriel Wagan.'

Ayae shifted uncomfortably in her seat. 'I do,' she said.

'Then,' Vyla said, after Miat had spoken, 'if Mireea were to march on Se'Saera, you would march as well?'

'I am not a soldier.'

'But you are . . .'

'Cursed?' Ayae suggested.

A faint frown creased Vyla's brow. 'That is not a word we use,' she said. Miat had not spoken first this time. 'The word that we use in our language does not have an easy translation, sadly. Immortal, perhaps, is a suitable description? You are like our uncle. You are like the Blade Prince of the Saan. You cannot die.'

'I wouldn't go that far,' she said. 'But yes. I am like him.'

The Lord of the Saan spoke. 'And there are two others,' his wife said. 'Two men who have been alive for a long time?'

'They keep their own counsel.'

'But you speak for them?'

'They speak for themselves.'

There was a brief conversation between the two, before Vyla spoke again. 'You must forgive us,' she said, shifting forwards on her seat, bridging the space between Ayae and her just a little more. 'We were under the impression that you spoke for the two men, and Lady Wagan spoke for you. We have been led to believe that you would take part in our campaign in Leera should Lady Wagan agree to join us. We only wanted to confirm this.'

'Jae'le and Eidan make up their own minds.' *And me?* was the unasked question. 'But they will not be soldiers for you.'

Miat Dvir nodded before his wife translated the words to him. He had heard the distinction in Ayae's words clearly. At length, he spoke to Vyla. 'My husband wants to be very clear to you,' she said, when he paused. 'The Saan will not be remaining here long. We will be going over the Spine of Ger. We will be going to war. He has seen a lot of things in this camp since his arrival. He has seen a lot of division. He supposes that it is only natural. But he would not bring that to war. He wants to make it very clear to you that he would bring a unified vision. He would stop this threat, not just to the Saan, but to all of us, before it can grow into something as large as the devastation in Sooia, or an empire like the Five Kingdoms. He hopes that you can remember this, and that you can pass it on to others, as well.'

The Lord of the Saan stood once she had finished. He inclined his head once to Ayae, and again to Caeli, before his wife stood and the warrior behind them picked up both chairs.

After they had left, Caeli let out a low laugh. 'Not even Muriel speaks to Miat Dvir the way you just did.'

'If he wants to speak to Jae'le or Eidan, he can go see them.' She could hear the annoyance in her voice. 'And he can speak to me himself.'

At that, Caeli laughed aloud. 'Oh, look what we have become,' she said. 'We demand to be spoken to!' She laughed again. 'Do you know, that is the most I have heard him speak in the traders' tongue. He showed us a lot of respect. In all the other meetings, Vyla speaks for him from the start. I've heard him say hello and goodbye, but that's it. But what he said to you, he had practised. His wife would have taught him that before he came here. That is her job, after all. All the men of the Saan are illiterate. But you – you get paid the compliment and you don't even know it. You just complain that he didn't treat you like an equal.'

'Shut up.' Ayae slouched into her chair, trying to hide from her embarrassment. 'Besides, you heard him. He just wants me to kill his enemies for him.'

'Yes,' the guard said, her smile fading. 'Yes, he does.'

7.

Heast arrived in Vaeasa after the afternoon's sun had set. He posed as Anemone's servant, his hair darkened with a cheap dye complemented with a heavy lean on a staff that he did not need.

It was in the remains of a town half a day's walk from the Leeran camp that he applied the dye. While he ran his hand through his hair, Anemone told him about the town that they stood in. It had once been named Niez and, though it was now little more than black stones covered in moss, over eight hundred years ago it had been the home of the third Lord of Faaisha. He had been found in his bed two years after he took office, poisoned. 'Grandmother,' she said to him as she walked around the outline of the house, 'always believed that the assassination was a lesson to future lords. It was said that Lord Niez had wanted to stop the private ownership of land. He wanted land to be owned by the state so that the land taxes went straight to the nation, but in doing so, he threatened the power of those who owned much of the land. It was they who poisoned him. Grandmother described them as a single beast with many heads.'

'I've heard similar stories before,' Heast said.

She turned to him. 'Do you not fear it happening to you? That the Lords of Faaisha will band together against you?'

'No.' He pushed his hands into a pool of rain water and began to scrub them free of the dye. The black drifted off in long twists. 'I will not be welcomed by all the Lords of Faaisha. There will be no parade for us in the streets. But Tuael will not stand against us. He'll be more flexible than the other Lords.'

'And after?'

'After?' Heast shrugged. 'He'll blame us for anything that isn't good for him. Of course, that assumes we'll be successful. He may not have to bother denying what he knew about Refuge if we are killed by the Leerans.'

'How can you just accept that?' The young witch sounded surprised. 'Don't you want to be thanked for what you have done?'

'It is the way it is.' He did not say it with rancour or bitterness, for those, he knew, were the inflections of youth. 'Even the novels about mercenaries have that right.'

When Heast and Anemone arrived in Vaeasa two days later, they were guided to its gates by the torches that lined the angular walls, as if they were a beacon of hope and safety.

As with most cities in the Kingdoms of Faaisha, Vaeasa was a huge, walled creation that had grown as the population within it did. The thick, white stone walls were laid in straight lines and, in the paintings Heast had seen of it from above, they gave the city the appearance of an unbalanced star. The walls did not just stretch around it in a single line. Each decade of new expansion had given rise to a new wall outside the old, making the city bigger with every new generation. Because of that, the interior was divided by old, discoloured walls which segregated the poor from the rich.

To reach the main gate of Vaeasa, Heast and Anemone walked through three barricades and hundreds of armed guards. The purple-and-gold cloaks and chain and leather armour that they were forced to wear offered little relief to the night's thick humidity and it had made the soldiers irritable. It rendered the walk that Heast and Anemone made through the barricades of thick wood and barbed wire twice the length that it should have been as they were forced to wait at all three of the checkpoints before they were questioned.

'Where are you from?' The first who spoke to them was a young man, a year or two older than Anemone. He directed his questions to her and purposely did not focus on Heast. When she told him that she had come from Maosa, he said without pause, 'And the white man with you?'

'He worked for my grandmother,' the witch told the woman at the second checkpoint. She was a heavy-set, olive-skinned woman who was sweating profusely. 'He is a cripple she took pity on,' Anemone added.

'You will be responsible for him.' The guard glanced at the tattoos on Anemone's hands. 'It does not matter who you are already responsible for.'

'Can you speak for yourself?' It was the third guard who addressed Heast. He was an older man, a Third Talon, to judge from the gold marks sewn into the purple cloak that lay next to him. He had spared only a glance for Anemone before turning to Heast and, interrupting the witch, asked his question. 'Where are you from?'

'Gogair.' Heast met the man's gaze. 'Originally.'

'Originally?' the man repeated.

'He is a cripple my grandmother took pity on,' Anemone said. 'Nothing more.'

'Your hand is bleeding, girl.' The guard did not turn to her. 'Your grandmother should have taught you how to hide that better when talking to someone.'

'It has been a long walk to the gate,' Heast said, before she could answer.

'Things are slow, but in fairness, a lot of people come through here. A lot leave, as well. A friend of mine left with a Hollow months ago,' he said. 'My friend's name was Baeh Lok. You haven't met him on the road, have you?'

'He travels a different road now.'

'I thought as much.' The guard spat on the side of the barricade. 'You two better hurry through, now. There's more people coming. After you find a place to stay, you have a drink for my friend at The Undertow. It was his favourite bar. Maybe I'll see you there when the sun is up.'

8.

'Shouldn't you be sleeping?' Bueralan asked.

'I do not like it,' Aela Ren said. He stood in the middle of *Glafanr*'s deck, Leviathan's Blood spread around him in an endless, shifting darkness. Above, the stars and the moon appeared pale, as if they were part of another world, dwindling. 'I am unaccustomed to sleep. After all these years it feels like the embrace of emptiness. When I awake, I feel as if the world has tried to reorganize itself. As if a thousand possibilities have suddenly been removed. It is an unsettling experience.'

Bueralan, who had stood on *Mercy* with him and listened to him speak about Se'Saera, was surprised.

'Shouldn't you be enjoying that experience?' Taela said, as if reading his mind. 'You don't want your new god to think you disapprove, do you?'

'I do not fear Se'Saera knowing how I feel. In truth,' the Innocent said, 'it is right that I feel this way. I am a man who has lived a long life in a world that is slowly coming to an end.'

'You say the most reassuring things,' she said drily.

'I meant only that Se'Saera will rebuild this world.' He turned to her, the faded moonlight highlighting the scars along his face, allowing it, for a moment, to look as if his skull had revealed itself. 'But both you and Bueralan appear to have been raised with a similar belief that a god must act in kindness, that a god is kindness. No doubt it is because you were born into a world without divinity that allows you to believe such a thing. It is oddly touching, in a certain way. Like a child believing that their parents are perfect.'

'Just imagine if the world was built on benevolence and kindness.' Bueralan could not keep the cynicism from his voice. 'It would be nothing but endless suffering.'

'It would be someone's.' The ghost of a smile touched Ren's scarred lips. 'The two of you are not new to power. You have stood beside people who wield it. Who is it better for? I ask you. A soldier, a queen, or a slave?'

'A god is meant to be different.'

'You have never known a god, so how can you say such a thing? What if a god is naught but a divine power forming itself into a philosophy? Or an idea that is prevalent among mortals?' Around them, *Glafanr* pushed through a swell. 'I stood by my god Wehwe for thousands of years and I do not claim to know him intimately. I would not dare. To do so would be to suggest that divinity is something that I can know, but it is nothing of the kind.'

'Then why stand beside a god?' Taela asked. 'If it cannot be known, why would anyone offer it loyalty?'

'Again, you think of a god as you do a king, or a queen,' the Innocent said. 'Perhaps it is our fault that you do,' he added. 'It is the responsibility of all god-touched men and women to represent the gods. It was our task to translate what they were to everyone else. When the War of the Gods ended, we stopped doing that. I have upon occasion thought that we should have defined what a god *was* in those years after. It would have made it harder for the pretenders of the Five Kingdoms to come to power. Of course, we were in no condition to do that after the war. Still, it would make things easier now. Not just for all of the mortal men and women in the world, but for you, Taela. If we had stayed in the world, you would know that the Goddess of Fertility saw birth as one aspect of a child's arrival in the world. She concerned herself with parents, with conception, and with the rearing of the child itself.'

'Ren,' Bueralan began.

'Let him say it,' Taela said, a measured defiance in her voice. 'Let me hear it.'

'Kaze will be of great help you,' Aela Ren said, unconcerned by her tone. 'She was made to stand beside mothers. She will do all that she can for you.'

'No.'

There was no give in her voice.

Earlier, Bueralan had been awoken by the sound of Taela heaving, the smell of vomit tart in the cabin. Wordlessly, he had pushed himself up, poured a glass of water, and handed it to her. He had taken the wooden bucket to the window and tossed what was in it outside. It was the same bucket he had carried to the deck with Taela, after she had finished drinking, and said that she could do with some fresh air. She apologised for waking him while they walked through the corridor, but he said that he should thank her. He had been dreaming about the City of Ger, beneath Mireea, and the Temple of Ger. In his dream, he had stood above the glass covering. He had not seen a piece of Ger's skin, as he had when he had stood there before, but a huge eye. It had stared up at him in question, and the fact that he had no answer had been deeply unsettling to him. 'I'll try and throw up tomorrow night then,' Taela had said, as they walked up the stairs, onto the deck, where Aela Ren stood.

'I am trying to help you,' the Innocent was saying, now. 'I know you will not believe that. I know that I am a monster to you. But soon, we will reach the shore of Leera, and we will be in danger there. You will need assistance.'

'I've had enough assistance from you.' There was no mistaking her tone. 'From all of you. You all stood and watched me be raped by your new god.'

'And we would do it again,' he said.

Taela spat at him.

Bueralan tensed, but Ren simply wiped the spittle from his face. He did not seem angry, or amused. Instead, he watched Taela as she walked across the deck to the prow of *Glafanr*. 'Once we land,' the Innocent said to the saboteur, 'we will be at war. It will be a different war to the one that my soldiers and I fought in Sooia.'

Taela blended into the shadows of the ship, her body a faint outline. 'Because of Zilt and his soldiers?' Bueralan asked.

'Because they were once the God of War's favourites.'

'Kaze told me that earlier, but she did not say it would make a difference to anything once we landed.'

'Baar saw war as many things. He was like Linae and Wehwe, like all the other gods. He saw war as liberating, but also an act of oppression. He knew that mortals took up a blade for coin, and that they took it up because of morals. Much of Onaedo's time was spent campaigning against the propaganda that many a nation created about it.'

'Onaedo?' It surprised him to hear Ren mention the ruler of Leviathan's End. 'What does she have to do with this?'

'A long time ago, she asked Baar to help her show the dichotomy of war to men and women. In every generation she asked him to bless a soldier to destroy and a soldier to preserve. General Zilt was one of the last that Baar favoured. The other was a man by the name of Kues—'

'Who led the Tribes into the Plateau,' Bueralan finished. 'Are you saying that they will rise up against us?'

'No,' Aela Ren said. 'But Onaedo will know that Zilt has returned. She will have felt it. And she will bring balance to this conflict. On Leera, we will find ourselves challenged in ways we have not been before.'

9.

Ayae's embarrassment over what she'd said when meeting Miat Dvir followed her into her dreams.

In her dreams, she wrote a letter to the Lord of the Saan and apologized for her behaviour. In it, she said that she knew better. She had been Samuel Orlan's apprentice. On the first official day of her apprenticeship, he had told her how important it was to understand other cultures. He gave her a stack of books, books larger than she had ever read before, each of them filled with maps and with descriptions of cultures and leaders. He said to her that learning to speak as many languages as she could would be invaluable in her new world. 'You will make maps for everyone,' he said, 'and each customer will have a different demand, a different desire, and a different way of thanking you.' As she wrote, she could feel the paper beneath her hand so strongly that she knew it was thick and of a fine quality. The sturdy length of the quill was also fine. So much so that, after she awoke, she could still feel it in her hands.

Across from her, on her own roll, Caeli slept soundly. One foot had been thrust out from under the blanket and Ayae briefly considered dipping it into a bowl of water, or tying it to her boots in a small but petty revenge. Instead, she pulled on her clothes quietly and, with the sensation of the quill still in her fingers, stepped outside the tent. Beneath the firelit sky she pulled on her boots and laced them tightly, before she threaded the sheath of her sword in place. Making sure that the tent was shut, she made her way down to the stables, to where Jaysun waited. In the cart, she drove out to Eidan and Jae'le's small camp.

Eidan waited outside his tent, sitting on a large log that lay before a dead fire pit. He was dressed in the same loose clothes that he always wore and, from a distance, she was struck by how harmless he looked. She wondered if the Lord of the Saan had thought that. Surely he would have made an attempt to see both brothers, even if he had not yet talked to them. She could see Jae'le standing in the shallows of Leviathan's Blood and wondered what Dvir would have thought of him.

In Neela, Eidan checked the work that had been done on the city's buildings and roads. In the last few nights, a sudden surge of progress had been made, with close to half of Neela becoming a series of straight, complete lines as scaffolding was removed and rebuilt around other buildings. It seemed to Ayae that, if Eidan wished, many of the lamps that lined the streets could now be lit and people could be let in.

When she mentioned it to him, he shook his head. 'We don't want people on Neela yet,' he said. 'There are still a number of factories to be demolished.'

They were close to the bridge that connected Neela to Mesi. When they stopped before it, Eidan left the cart, but instead of approaching it, he paused and stared out into Leviathan's Blood, where the wreckage of the other cities lay beneath the water.

'Is something wrong?' Ayae asked.

'No.' He turned back to the bridge. 'But from here we will need new stone.'

Did he plan to drag it up from the ocean? He had once told her that he had dived deep into the ocean to lay the original foundations. 'The bridge doesn't look that damaged,' she said. She stepped out of the cart, approaching the stone arch.

Eidan followed her. 'Cracks run all the way through it, but the real problem is on the other end, on the second bridge that connects to Ghaam. Chunks of stone have been torn out there. I'll have to break the bridge between the two before we start work here.'

'Isn't that what is holding Ghaam in place?'

'Yes.'

She could imagine the sound of stone grinding against stone, could see the churning black water devouring it. 'When do you want to do that?'

'Within the week,' he said. 'Before the Saan leave.'

'Do you plan to leave with them?'

'Do I look as if I want to fight Aela Ren?' He chuckled and it was a low, dark sound, one that surprised her and appeared to contradict his earlier statement to Se'Saera. 'No, that will simply be when I am ready. We will have to tell Wagan and Alahn. They should let everyone in the camp know before it happens.'

Maybe he's just stating the obvious. Ayae found that easy to believe, but she was not sure that Eidan would admit to it being more than a joke. In many ways, he was no different to Zaifyr. In fact, both his brothers were, at times, very similar to him. They would pass off dangers with a shrug and little more. But in other ways, both Jae'le and Eidan were strikingly dissimilar to Zaifyr. He would have asked her what Miat Dvir said, for example, while Eidan's mention of the Saan was the first he had made since she picked him up from his camp. He gave no thought to it because the Saan did not interest him, either as a threat, or a friend. Zaifyr would have asked because it had happened to her, and she would have told him in order to share that experience.

'Come,' Eidan said, climbing up onto the cart. 'It is time to go back.'

'Already?' She was surprised: the morning's sun had not yet begun to rise. 'You don't want to go into Mesi, or work on the bridge?'

He frowned. 'Do you not feel it?'

'Feel?'

'Paper, in your hands.' He lifted up his good hand and rubbed his fingers together. 'An urge to write words you do not know?'

'I—' She paused. 'I had a dream about writing a letter.'

'And you thought nothing of it?'

'Should I?'

He nodded, but said nothing else. As Ayae drove the cart through the streets of Neela, broken stone gave way to the clean streets where work had been complete. Throughout the journey, Eidan stared out at Leviathan's Blood and the sensation of paper in Ayae's hands increased. After a while, she began to smell ink. If he had been Zaifyr, she would have pressed him, to find out who was sending her this vision, for more details, but he was not his brother, and she remained quiet. She knew it was an immortal like the two of them and she tried to recall what it was that she had experienced when she had been in the presence of the Keepers. Quite often, she had felt a rush of sensations, because she had rarely been around one by herself. Being in the presence of all of them had made it difficult to separate who was who, but she could remember the calm of Aelyn Meah and the coldness of Eira. It was not them that she felt, that was certain. She tried to remember Kaqua, and was confident that it was not he whom she felt, either. Jaysun was surprised to see the two of them when they returned. He did not ask why they were early, but Ayae knew he watched them intently as they made their way out of the stables to the western edge of the camp. There, the fires burned strongly, and the tents where Sinae

Al'tor kept his business were a small hub of men and women. The guards he employed took Jaysun's place as watchers as Eidan led her out of the camp and along the shoreline.

The sky was beginning to lighten when they reached the shore and Ayae could see a ship out there. Unlike the ships of the Saan, this one was much smaller, and much older.

'Who is it?' she asked, finally.

'My sister,' he said. 'Tinh Tu.'

10.

The Undertow was a small bar. It was wedged into a corner that had been formed when Vaeasa had expanded, decades earlier. Built from thick timber, it was a simple building with a sloping slate roof. Its door was made from heavy wood and was held open by a plump purple bag filled with sand. Inside were two moderate-sized rooms, divided not by a step, as in other bars Heast had seen, but by a long counter with a door's-width gap in it to allow people to pass between the two rooms. A fat middle-aged man with dark olive skin stood behind the counter, cleaning glasses. When Heast and Anemone entered, he glanced up once but with no interest. It was more attention than those around him paid: the chipped and nicked chairs and tables were half filled with soldiers, and not one of them raised their heads as the two walked past.

Heast found the guard in the shaded garden out back. There, a handful of soldiers sat quietly at tables around him and, like those inside, did not glance up as the new arrivals made their way to where the guard sat.

'Mind if I sit?'

'I was hoping that you'd be another fifteen or twenty.' Beneath the foliage of the tree, the guard looked older than he had on the gate, the lines across his face deeper. 'The night is a long shift.'

'I'd buy you another drink, but the one you have is already

bought, is it not?' Heast pulled back one of the chairs, while beside him, the witch took her seat. Earlier, he had told her that she did not have to come with him to The Undertow, but she had shaken her head in response. *No*, she had said, *you will need me*. Heast said now, 'What's your name?'

'Seon.' The guard stared at the half-filled, dirty glass in his hand. After a moment, he said, 'You're right, it is paid for.'

'And the guards?'

'Lord Tuael said nothing would fool you, Captain.'

Heast stretched out his steel leg but did not drop his hand to it. 'Where is he?'

'Across the road, waiting.' Seon stood and drained the glass in two long gulps. 'After I refill this, I'll walk across and he'll walk back. He's not real happy with you and he won't be so happy to hear that you brought your witch with you.'

'I have a name,' Anemone said evenly. 'I can tell it to you, if you want.'

'I already know it,' the guard said sourly.

The atmosphere in The Undertow changed after Seon stepped through the door. The pretence of being off-duty fell away and the half-dozen men and women who had been sitting across from Heast rose from their tables and chairs. They tightened the straps of their scabbards before reaching for their cloaks. Not one of them wore a sign of rank on their uniform, which Heast took to mean that they were all part of Lord Tuael's private guard.

'How many warlocks?' he asked casually.

'Four,' the witch replied. 'They are across the street with their lord.'

Heast had told her, before they entered the bar, that they would not be greeted warmly. He had told her that they would be met with a display of force and that they would be under threat from the moment they entered The Undertow. *That is why you will need me*, Anemone had said to him. *It is my job to protect the soldiers of Refuge.*

Heast heard the door at the front of the inn close, the key turning in the lock. A moment later, the Lord of Faaisha, Jye Tuael, stepped out of the bar and into the garden.

He was a handsome man who carried himself with a comfortable authority. He did not wear a sword, nor did he wear leather and chain. Instead, Tuael was dressed in simple, lightweight brown pants and a long-sleeved shirt of hand-spun green that bore no hint of sweat or stain upon it. With a carefully manicured hand that bore only one simple ring of gold, he took the chair that Seon had sat in and, without waiting to see if either Heast or Anemone would rise to honour his presence, sat. He looked at them both silently until, with a hint of self-deprecation, he said, 'It is a pleasure to see you again, Aned.'

'You look well,' Heast said.

'It is early in the day yet,' the Lord of Faaisha said. 'At the end, I may feel much older than I am. If I do, I will lay the blame squarely at your feet.'

'It was you who wrote to me.'

'Did I ask you to kill Kotan Iata and steal his soldiers?' He shook his head. 'The other Lords of Faaisha have been urging me to deal with you, despite the fact that we are in the middle of a war. They said that I have invited a second invasion by Muriel Wagan. Most of them didn't even like Iata, but he was holding out against the Leerans. Tell me that he at least raised a sword against you, Aned. That he threatened you. Give me something that I can take back to the Lords.'

'You have a traitor,' the Captain of Refuge said.

'I have at least half a dozen,' he said without pause. 'Come now: I did not like Iata, but you will hang from a gallows for what you have done if you—'

'Your traitor is a Marshal Faet Cohn.'

That, Heast saw, had not been expected.

'You have proof?' Lord Tuael asked, after a pause.

Slowly, Heast pulled the letters out from where he had stuffed them in his belt, careful not to startle the soldiers who watched the exchange between their lord and the foreign captain carefully. The ringed hand that took the parchment did not tremble and the gaze that read the lines did not lift from the words until the end.

'A lot of people have questioned what happened in Celp, but no one suspected him of losing the city because of simple greed.' Tuael began to fold the letter along its creased lines with slow movements of his index finger and thumb. 'All that we face right now, all that we struggle with, and he indulges in avarice. Some men simply do not understand the virtue of restraint.'

'Did you suspect him?' Heast said.

'Of this? No. I am even surprised. Do you know how rare it is for me to be surprised?' He let out a sigh, as if something had been drained from him. 'I knew Cohn pushed for the slave trade with Gogair to begin again. His family made their money in flesh two generations ago and the pot has long smelt sweet to him.'

'I'm surprised that he became a marshal, then.'

'Tactically, he is quite an interesting man, but personally, he struggles to acknowledge that the world has drifted away from what it once was. He does not see that people do not want slavery. He does not see that freedom has become a currency that they want to indulge in and that they are happy with any rule that allows them this. I would not have thought it before this moment, but it appears that Cohn is so divorced from reality that he cannot see one of the horrors of this war is to be sold in Gogair. If this was to get out, he would be torn apart – literally, I suspect.'

The *if* of the last sentence had not escaped Heast. 'He can't remain a marshal, surely?'

'No, he can't. But the question is, can I allow this to be made public?' The letter folded, Tuael laid it on the table before him. 'Cohn has his supporters, even after Celp. He did not become a marshal without them. They will stand beside him, especially if it is revealed that the captain who killed Kotan Iata delivered this.' A note of resignation entered Lord Tuael's voice. 'But I imagine that you already knew that. My father had the greatest respect for you, Aned. Years ago, when we first met, when you had ridden into Vaeasa as no more than a simple mercenary and I hired you, he took me aside. He knew who you were. He had heard of both you and Refuge. He told me that you were not a man to be treated as anything but an equal. My father said that! I know it means nothing to you, but he viewed no man as his equal. Yet, he said I was to treat you as one.'

Heast made no attempt to reply. Jye Tuael's father had been a man whose dreams had been of expansion, of owning the entire continent that the Kingdoms of Faaisha sat upon. He had known it was an impossible idea, but in the final years of his life, it had turned him bitter. In a meeting that Muriel had attended in Faaisha, two years after he had taken the position of Captain of the Spine, Heast had seen that resentment for himself. The meeting had been to introduce Muriel to Jye, who was succeeding his father, but the old man had asked for a private meeting with Heast. There, he had stared at him with eyes that had turned yellow with the final stages of his cancer and had spoken of campaigns he had not ordered, his bitterness sharpened by his closing death.

'I will do you the honour,' his son said, 'of assuming that you do not mean to reveal this in public.'

'A weak Faaisha does not help me,' Heast said. 'But I have need of a few things.'

He laughed. 'I am letting you live.'

'My life was never yours to take.'

'Look around you, Aned.' Behind him, the soldiers in the garden waited, their hands on their swords. 'Your life is the payment I offer.'

'Do you know what was drawn on that letter you sent me? Did Baeh Lok explain that to you before he left?' Heast still had the letter, hidden at the bottom of his pack in the hotel room. It was a letter with a simple badge drawn upon it, its background half red, half black, with a colourless globe of the world over it. 'You called for Refuge.'

'Yes, but there is no . . .' The Lord of Faaisha paused. 'The Captain and the witch,' he said softly. 'The sergeant said that to me, before I crossed the road. Seon. I thought it a peculiar phrasing and nothing more.' He turned to the young witch, as if seeing her for the first time. 'You do not look like your grandmother, Anemone. Tell me, are my warlocks still alive?'

'Yes,' she said.

'Do you fear them?'

'No.'

'I once offered your grandmother a position here,' Tuael said. 'Would you like to hear what I said to her?'

'I have heard what you said to her.' Anemone was polite, but within that politeness there was a coldness she did not bother to hide. 'I am the Witch of Refuge. There must always be a Witch of Refuge.'

'So there must.' He turned back to Heast. 'Am I to believe also that the men and women from Maosa are your soldiers?'

'Yes.'

'You make it difficult for them to return home.'

'They have no home,' the Captain of Refuge said. 'You and the other Lords abandoned them months ago. But they're still fighting for you. I am fighting for you, as well, and what we both need is coin. Coin is the price for what I brought you today.'

'I don't have the coin you need.'

'I have not even given you a number.'

'Any number is too high.' Tuael raised his hand before Heast could speak. 'Faaisha is at war. Our finances are tied to that. But I have something else that I can give you. Something that is very fitting, in a way. I can introduce you to a benefactor.'

'And who would that be?'

'The First Queen of Ooila,' he said. 'Zeala Fe.'

11.

Tinh Tu did not greet her brother with warmth.

Out on the ocean, the morning's sun rose and Ayae watched a dinghy push itself through the surf, the ship behind it rising and falling with the swell. Both the ship and the dinghy had once been painted a dark green, but the colour had faded beneath the three suns and the ocean had stripped the paint from the lower hulls away. It looked as if clawed hands had reached up from the water to pull the ship down. Combined with the faded black of its sail, the ship gave the impression of being derelict, a description that, had not the dinghy made its way towards the shore, would have been one Ayae used for it. Yet the dinghy rode the swell and as it drew closer, as the shapes of three people became clearer, Eidan wordlessly waded out into the ocean. By the time he reached the dingy the waves had soaked through the clothes he wore and exposed the dark lines of scar tissue that ran across half his body. He looked like a creature that had risen from Leviathan's Blood when he took hold of the boat and pulled it ashore.

At the front sat an old woman.

The smell of ink returned suddenly to Ayae. She could see Samuel Orlan's shop, could see the glass pots he had kept in the workroom. The lids were gummed with dried ink, and when she had to open one, she had to be careful, because the ink would not flow for a few moments, before it rushed out into the small wells she dipped quills and brushes into. As quickly as the memory came to her, it left, the smell evaporating with it as Eidan emerged from the water. With his good hand he dragged the boat onto the sand.

'Brother,' the old woman said, a white raven circling down from the sky as she spoke. 'Your new friend feels many things.'

'Her name is Ayae,' he said.

'Yes, it is.' Tinh Tu lifted a long, ash-wood staff up and stepped out of the boat. 'Is Jae'le still looking for him?' she asked as the raven drifted onto her shoulder.

'He is.'

'At least I have not missed that.' She looked back at the boat, at the two women who had ridden with her, and then turned to Ayae. 'Look after the witch in the boat,' she said, the deepness of her voice cracking, as if it were a voice she was not accustomed to using. 'She has done me a service. It would be a shame if she died.'

'You seem to think I owe you something,' Ayae said.

'You do.'

Ayae was about to ask what, if anything, she owed, when she heard her name spoken in a harsh whisper. The voice was a familiar one, but it was only when Eidan's sister stepped away from the boat that she saw Olcea. The older woman was struggling to rise. She leant heavily on the third woman and her face was drawn, the black skin around her eyes and cheeks wan and sunken, and the bandages around her hands stained with blood. The stains, Ayae saw, spread to the rest of her clothing, though those on her hands were freshest. Forgetting Eidan's sister, Ayae rushed towards Olcea. As she did, she heard Tinh Tu tell Eidan that she wanted to see Jae'le—

Then Ayae reached the boat.

'She piloted the ship.' The third woman spoke quietly, her white hand taking Olcea's left arm as Ayae took her right. 'From the coast of Balana.'

'Eilona?' Ayae asked, the name slipping out, despite herself. 'Eilona Wagan?'

The daughter of Muriel Wagan met her gaze. 'I'm sorry,' she said, 'but I don't know you.'

'Hien,' the witch whispered, her gaze directing them to the pack at her feet. 'Ayae, please, don't leave him.'

'No,' she said, 'of course not.' She picked up the solid bag, heavy with the weight of a rotting head, of what remained of Hien, the soldier Olcea had bound to her service years ago. Ayae was careful when she lifted it, careful of the thin blade in the strap that the witch used to cut her palms in times of danger. She slung it over her shoulder before she took hold of Olcea's arm again.

Eidan and Tinh Tu were ahead, the old woman keeping an easy pace with her injured brother. For a moment, Ayae saw the emotional connection that she had thought absent when Eidan waded out into Leviathan's Blood to draw the boat out of the water. She did not believe that the bond was as strong as the one between Eidan and Aelyn, or Zaifyr and Jae'le. Those bonds transcended the responsibilities and affections of family. In Tinh Tu, there was instead a cool reserve, a distance Ayae had seen in brothers and sisters whose lives took them in different directions, and whose lives left them with different experiences and mindsets.

'Do you know her?' Eilona asked as they began to walk. 'You spoke to her, as if you did.'

'No,' Ayae replied. 'I don't know her.'

'She is a frightening woman.'

'I imagine she is.'

'She told me that she had sewn her mouth shut. When I asked her why, she told me not to talk to her for the rest of the trip.' A tremor entered her voice and she coughed to clear it. 'And I didn't. I didn't say another word until I spoke to you.'

Ayae had not met Eilona before, but she knew of Muriel Wagan's daughter. When Eilona left, Ayae had been no more than an orphan girl who worked occasionally for a witch, but even she had heard of the things she had done, of the trade deals she had ruined, the people she had insulted. It had seemed to Ayae that each week there had been a new story about Eilona where her stepfather or her mother had to make amends for her behaviour. The last, she recalled, had been in relation to a dead guard, and another guard's family, but Ayae had been in Yeflam when it happened. When she returned, the news had mostly been about Eilona Wagan leaving Mireea.

She had returned when her stepfather was injured in Leera. Eilona arrived with her partner, and it was said, by the few who met her, that Lady Wagan's daughter had changed. She was more measured, more thoughtful, more like her mother. That did not stop people from accusing her of being callous and cold because she had not stayed to care for her stepfather, however.

At Muriel Wagan's tent, the three of them were met by Caeli, who greeted the daughter of the woman she protected coldly. Caeli wore a mix of dark leather and chain, and the long, straight sword on her hip moved with her body as if it were a limb. After she let the flap of the tent close, she cast a glance at Ayae, asking a question to which the other woman, holding more of Olcea's weight than she had done when she left the shore, could only offer a slight shake of her head. No, the movement said, she did not know why Eilona was here.

The inside of the tent was a busy mess and in the centre of it stood the Lady of the Ghosts. Her right boot was on a wooden chair and her hands were pulling the laces that held the leather together when they entered. The boot and its companion would be hidden beneath a fraying gown of dark brown and red. As Muriel lifted her head from her task, Ayae was surprised to see how much likeness she had with her daughter, even after the months of living in tents.

It was impossible to deny the mirrored squareness of their features, of the thickness of their bodies. The biggest difference between Lady Wagan and her daughter was that the former dyed her hair a dark brown, while the latter's was red.

The lines around Muriel's eyes and mouth deepened as she smiled at her daughter. Eilona, for her part, frowned at the sight of her mother. What the look signified was lost to Ayae as the silver-haired healer, Reila, came quickly over to see the witch she supported.

'Olcea.' Her careworn, white face mirrored the concern her murmur showed. 'What have you done to yourself?'

'She piloted a ship,' Eilona said, again. 'From Balana. She painted the deck with blood she collected from Zalhan.'

'That's a pirate town.' Kal Essa spoke, then. He stood on the other side of the tent, beyond the wooden chairs and the frayed rug with the piles of parchment on it. A short man, the left side of his face was scarred like a thick spider web. 'They sell flesh, if they sell anything.'

'They don't sell anything now.'

Essa began to speak again, but Lady Wagan lifted her hand slightly, stopping him. 'It doesn't matter right now,' she said. 'Reila?'

'I'll take care of her,' the healer said.

'Use this tent.' She turned, then, and spoke to her daughter. 'I'm pleased that you're here,' she said, a hint of warmth in her voice. 'I really am. But I have a meeting over breakfast with the Lord of the Saan that I have to attend.' She indicated the grey-haired, middle-aged white woman who stood beside Kal Essa. 'Captain Mills and Caeli are accompanying me. Would you like to join us?'

Eilona looked down at her dirt- and blood stained clothes. 'I am not dressed for that,' she said. 'But I could accompany you for some of the way. I have to ask you about some things – and tell you about others.'

After they had left, Ayae helped Reila move Olcea to the back of the tent. There she laid the exhausted woman down on a makeshift mattress. As she did, she was aware of Kal Essa coming up beside her. He stared down at the witch who, in getting comfortable, had drawn her pack to her and wrapped her arms around the solidness of Hien. 'I can send a couple of my boys round,' he said quietly. 'I won't say that they do pretty things, but if need be, they'll shed a bit of blood for her.'

'You know her?' Ayae asked.

'She was a war witch, once,' he said. 'Most of what she did was before my time, but I have heard a thing or two.'

'She needs rest, mostly,' Reila said, rising. 'Maybe a little more, but not yet. If she does need anything, I'll let you know.'

The cue to leave was not subtle, and both Ayae and the mercenary took it. Outside the tent, the camp bustled. With half a wave to Essa, Ayae took her leave from him and made her way towards the small camp Jae'le and Eidan kept.

Their camp was defined by its single small tent and empty campfire circle. Further past it, she could see Eidan and Tinh Tu standing on the shoreline, but it was not to them that her gaze immediately fell. Rather it was to the lean black figure who was emerging from the water.

And the body he held in his arms.

The Last Story of Asila

Aelyn Meah folded her hands together in her lap. 'Did you ever meet Kaqua?' she asked me.

Once, I told her.

There was a tone in my voice and she smiled knowingly at it. 'You did well to ensure that he did not return. I was not so lucky. I thought I knew better,' she said, melancholy in her voice. 'I told myself I would never allow myself to be used. I told Eidan he was foolish to suggest I might be. I drove him away with those words. He came back, but he circled, and never landed. It is only later, much later, that I berated myself. I should have known, I told myself. I should have.

'Kaqua worked with another's desires, mostly. Not sexual ones, though he could, if he wished. But not with me. He saw what I feared, what I was enticed by, and what my intellectual compulsions were. He wove a web of them around me.

'I am sure, if he was here, he would defend himself. He would tell us both that I had to provide him with the strands for him to work with, but that was part of his trick, part of the way he made you responsible for what he had done. He did not see that an emotion, however fleeting, was not automatically something you wanted to act upon. He refused to acknowledge that he could be responsible for the thoughts he found. He had no desire to take responsibility for what he did.

'I never wanted to kill my brother. I knew what a folly that would be. But Kaqua did not know that. He did not know what I did.

'He did not realize what my brother's death would mean.'

—Onaedo, *Histories, Year 1029*

1.

Ayae stood silently on the shoreline beside Eidan and Tinh Tu as Jae'le laid his brother on the sand, sinking to his bare knees before he released the dead weight.

She could not speak. She had not believed that he would find Zaifyr. Had not believed that there would be anything to find. For the last four months, Jae'le had stood on the edge of Leviathan's Blood: it did not matter if a part of the sun had risen and the sky was alight or if all three suns had fallen into the dark and the night sky met the water without seam. He had stood there, before the water, searching. He spoke rarely and refused all food and drink. He had placed his consciousness inside the creatures that lived in the depths of Leviathan's Blood, searching not just for Zaifyr, but for a beast that had the necessary strength and delicacy that would allow Jae'le to lift his brother's body gently from where it lay and bring it to the shore. Now, when he released the corpse of his brother, nothing in Jae'le's face expressed loss. Rather, Ayae saw only triumph.

In her mind, Ayae had been easily able to imagine the state of Zaifyr's body at the bottom of the ocean: the rotted skin, the discoloration in his face, and the bloat that ballooned his stomach. Yet, the horror she could so easily detail was not before her. Zaifyr looked as he did in life. With his green eyes open, he gazed up at

Ayae lifelessly as she stared down at him. His auburn hair was clumped in wet knots, the charms of bronze and silver he had threaded through his hair tangled among each other. Across the rest of him, the charms that had once adorned his living body were still tied to his corpse, some bent and broken. Only his clothes showed the rot that she had expected to see in his flesh. It was in stark contrast to his body, a pale, white-skinned body that she could not turn away from—

'It is just as it once was,' Tinh Tu said.

—and which served only to highlight the unnaturalness of what she saw. 'How is he like this?' Ayae asked, finding her voice. 'What has happened?'

'He has died,' the other woman said.

'But his body! This is not how a body looks after so long!'

'Do you plan to be hysterical, child?' she said, turning her dark gaze on Ayae. 'You would be exactly as I thought you to be, then.'

'*Enough.*' Jae'le rose from the sand, the word a command given harshly. 'She is not to blame for what has happened here, sister.'

'You have grown sentimental.' Tinh Tu did not turn from her. 'She is but another wedge that drives our family apart.'

'We were splintered before she was born,' Eidan said evenly. 'It is not her fault that we find ourselves here, again.'

'Again?' Ayae broke away from the old woman's gaze. 'Again here in Yeflam? Again before the Mountains of Ger?'

'Again,' he said, simply, 'in Asila.'

'But he is not—' She stopped herself. 'You did not kill Zaifyr in Asila.'

'We did.'

She tried to respond, but could not find any words.

'He inherited the Wanderer's divinity.' As Jae'le spoke, a small pitch-black figure, no bigger than a cat, wound around her legs, its touch chill against her skin. Ayae had not seen Anguish leave the small tent. 'When I was a child,' Jae'le continued, 'and when my brother was but a child as well, the Wanderer would walk the roads and paths of our world. He would be seen in villages and in towns and in cities reaching for the dead. He wore a black robe that hid all of his body, and when he arrived, you would see but moments of him, as if he were an image, flickering. It was said that the Wanderer took the dead into his own kingdom and that there they would be rewarded, punished, or forgotten. He was said to come for the gods themselves, but I do not believe that. We know that the gods were not normal beings like us. They had no souls. They have no souls.'

The chill on her leg ran through her body. 'But Zaifyr,' she said softly.

'Zaifyr is like you and I,' he said. 'For a long time, we believed otherwise, but it is not true. Our divinity is not our being. What is inside us now has reached an understanding with the immortal part of us that transcends flesh. I often think that when others like us are afflicted poorly, when their bodies turn to stone, or gills grow along their neck and they cannot breathe our air, it is not because of the divine power within them, but because their souls have rejected the divinity that has been offered.' He paused, letting his words sink in for a moment. 'Or perhaps it is something different. A century from now, I may think so. But what I will not go back on is the knowledge that we are not divine, that we are gods, because I know that we have a soul, that we are tied to our flesh.'

'In Zaifyr's case, the Wanderer's power holds tight to that soul, and when the bond is severed, when it is broken, it looks for him,' Tinh Tu said, the end of her staff beginning to make a line in the sand, the start of a map, of a continent that Ayae could not immediately place despite all the maps she had seen.

'So you could not kill him?' Ayae said.

'He could not die.'

The distinction was not lost on her. 'Why did Zaifyr never tell me this?'

'Because he does not know,' Anguish said suddenly, his closed eyes on the body before him. 'Is that not the truth?'

'Truth,' Tinh Tu repeated, lifting her staff from the sand, before bringing it down, once, then twice in the centre of her image. The sand flattened, the lines in it straightened, and Ayae was finally able to make it out, to understand what she had drawn. 'I despise that word,' she said, her staff rising again.

'Sister,' Eidan began.

'No,' she said, an edge in her voice. 'Let her experience it. Let her *know*.'

Her staff fell a third time on the image of Asila.

2.

Ayae was struck blind.

In panic, she felt herself stumble backwards, felt her hand drop to her sword, felt a curl of flame open inside her, ready to strike out in defence. But the ground began to fall away, the sand not sinking beneath her heels, but rather turning to emptiness, as if nothing was below her. She desperately tried to regain her footing, tried to find solid ground—

There is a road beneath your feet because there is a road beneath mine, Ayae. It is narrow. It has been made by children who play in a lake nearby and it is surrounded by trees that turn brown and skeletal as the hard winter begins to approach. Ayae could feel mud beneath her boots and she stumbled in surprise at its touch. Despite her bad footing, she continued to walk, even though she had no desire to do so. *You are not alone on this child's path.* Tinh Tu's words were hard and precise, a steady and sure narrator. *It is the path that my family and I walked a thousand years ago. A walk guided by a blue light. It is a single strange light that grows and grows until you come to the edge of the woods and you stand before Asila.*

The city lay before her unlike any she had seen before. Its shape and form followed the side of a large mountain. Halfway up the mountain, on a flat piece of land, a dark tower rose in a straight line. From it a long path wound its way down to the base of the mountain, ending where the sprawl of the city began, nestled against both the natural and unnatural creations that reached high into the sky. It was from the city that the light that had guided Ayae through the woods originated. It was not a natural light, but it swept through the streets of Asila with a certain softness, and she felt, for a moment, that comfort was offered by it. Yet the longer she gazed at it, the more the comfort began to turn into a great sadness, an emotion that was shared by the men and women who began to appear beside her.

Our brother's book had come to all our nations that season, Tinh Tu said. *The seventy-first Samuel Orlan had written to us before, to warn us, but in our arrogance we had ignored him. It was not until each of us held the book that we began to sense the madness that gripped Qian. It was then that we heard about the horrors that were taking place in Asila.*

Beside her, Jae'le stepped past Ayae and began to walk down the slope and into the city. He was different from the man she knew now. His face was full, he was clean-shaven, and his hair was shorter, the length of it tied back into a short tail at the top of his skull. At his waist he wore a pair of swords, the hilts an elaborate design of a fierce, taloned bird, the likes of which Ayae had never seen before. The leather armour he wore was beautiful. Strips of dark green leather had been woven into the stitching, the colour blending with the thick, green-feathered cloak he wore, the cloak he still wore. Jae'le was followed by Eidan. The stocky man wore a chain-mail vest made from dark metal, and though it reached up to his neck and over his impressive shoulders, it did not cover his thick arms. Instead, a leather shirt ran down to his wrists and ended where leather gloves began. Over his back he carried a huge, two-handed axe, the whole piece a construction of steel, rather than a mix of wood and metal. It must have weighed a ton, but Eidan bore it with no discomfort. Aelyn came after him. The armour that she wore was light, thickest at her chest, but around her arms it was only solid black cloth. Despite that, there was a severe quality to

Aelyn's appearance that surprised Ayae. Her hair had been cut against her skull, just as the rest of her body had been stripped of any fat, leaving nothing but muscle, blunt nails and a certain raw violence that surprised Ayae. Lastly, Tinh Tu emerged from behind her, holding the same ash staff that she held now on Yeflam's shoreline. She wore robes of the finest fabric, made with the finest needlework.

Ayae followed the four down the hill to the outskirts of Asila. The houses defined themselves in the glow of the blue light, but what struck her most strongly about each building that she passed was not the colour, but the stillness in each of them. It felt ingrained, as if it had become part of the brickwork and timber, as if it filled the open windows and opened the shutters and the doors. In those gaps, Ayae saw wilting plants, rotting food, and she smelt an odour of decay that soon began to choke the air around her.

The first haunt she saw was that of a boy, no older than eight or nine. He crouched on the side of road, a rotting arm held in his grasp, the flesh torn open by his teeth.

At the sight of him, Ayae thought of Fo and Bau in Mireea, of the haunts that had torn into the flesh of the two Keepers, ripping them apart as if they were of no consequence. Yet what caused the sadness in her to deepen was not her memory, but rather the half-starved, feral look on the haunt's face as he spotted the brothers and sisters walking down the road. With a swift motion, he scooped up the limb he had been eating and ran further into the city and into the heart of the blue light where Ayae knew, without a doubt, the main collection of the dead awaited.

The men and women beside her spread out as they continued towards the centre of Asila, yet, with no will of her own, Ayae remained beside Tinh Tu. Wordlessly, the old woman led her through empty buildings. Inside them, Ayae saw bodies in states of decay, the skin torn, the blood drained and the bones broken. Next to them lay spoiled food and broken plates and cups. Not one body looked as if it had been ready for what attacked it. In this way, each new street saw a new series of horrors unfold and each new street saw the sadness that emanated from the brothers and sisters grow. At the fourth, a sense of inevitability began to rise in each of them. Because she followed Tinh Tu's memories, the thought began with her, but she knew, also, that Jae'le, Eidan and Aelyn thought as their sister did. By the time the pale glow from the city centre wound like a low fog around their feet and circles upon circles of dead flushed with Zaifyr's power came into the sight, the four siblings had reached a terrible consensus.

For over ten thousand years, the dead had spoken to Zaifyr. For over ten thousand years they had whispered to him about the endless cold and about the hunger that accompanied it.

For over ten thousand years, they had asked him to stop it.

As the dead flushed with Zaifyr's power began to part, as they created a path for his brothers and sisters to walk into the centre of Asila, Ayae realized for the first time the depth of the horror that Zaifyr had lived with. She finally understood the burden that he had inherited and accepted as his own. She saw the awful tragedy of his life, of the immortal life that saw the fate of all mortal men and women, the life that knew that everyone he loved and did not love ended the same. She understood, too, how he was powerless to alleviate their horror without creating a fresh, new horror. She saw for the first time the strength that he had to have to live with that for as long as he had. The discipline it took not to allow it to overwhelm him, for it not to consume him. But as she followed Jae'le, Eidan, Aelyn and Tinh Tu towards the huge, empty temple where he sat, the temple that had been built for him by the men and women who believed him to be a god, she saw the loss of all that control, all that discipline, and the madness in Zaifyr's eyes. She saw that and knew that it had been inevitable. No one person could bear that burden. Only a god could hold such suffering and sadness within itself, could allow it to be the foundation of his or her divine being.

But none of them, she knew, was a god.

And that, Tinh Tu said softly to her, *is how we came to realize that our beloved brother had to die.*

3.

How would the Captain of Refuge greet the First Queen of Ooila, Zeala Fe?

The question kept Heast awake throughout the day, and when Anemone knocked on the door to his room after the last sun had set, he had not slept. He had not even tried.

Heast had returned to the inn where he and Anemone had rooms before the crowds began to fill the streets of Vaeasa. The inn, a two-storey, twisting construction that ran along an old wall and over it like a choking vine, was named A Private Folly. The owner was a dark-skinned man from Nmia, his wife a plump, olive-skinned woman from Faaisha. Neither looked to be the representation of a folly in purchase or service. They were a busy and industrious couple who did not pause when Heast and Anemone returned from The Undertow. They greeted them as they came out to serve the breakfast crowd and asked if they planned to eat. Both declined, then climbed the stairs. On the top floor, where the hotel began to run along the stone wall, the pair had two rooms, one next to each other. At the end of the hall, Heast offered a polite nod to Anemone before opening the door to his room. Once inside, he took two steps and stood in the centre silently. *The First Queen of Ooila.* He repeated the thought again. He ran his hand through his hair, staining his palm with the cheap black dye. Wordlessly, he found a wash basin and scrubbed out what he could. In the room's mirror, he estimated half had gone easily, while the other half would have to be grown out.

'You cannot be surprised,' he said to his reflection. He was not talking about the dye. His cold, blue eyes returned his stare without pity. 'You cannot afford surprise,' his reflection said to him.

Before Heast had left the garden, Jye Tuael told him that the Queen had arrived a month ago. She had slipped into the country hidden on an old spice trader, *Bounty*, the bowels of the ship holding her private guard, gold, and little else. When she arrived in Vaeasa, she immediately met with Tuael and told him stories about the new god, Se'Saera, and about the Innocent. Her tales slipped out of the private meetings he held later with the First Queen and the Lords of Faaisha and their marshals. The Lords had not known who had let slip the information – they suspected the Queen – but Faet Cohn's letter was enough to provide an answer. 'Not that it stops what people know on the streets,' Tuael admitted. 'The First Queen has not made it easy, either. She has not come here to hide. She has come here to continue her battle against the Innocent. Let people know, she says. She does not care if the kingdoms are crippled by fear. She cares only about her war. But I cannot give her what she wants. I cannot give her command of Faaishan soldiers. I cannot make her a marshal. I cannot let her roam Faaisha on her own vendetta. But you: I could give her you, the captain she helped break twenty-six years ago in Illate.'

Heast had thanked him drily.

In his room, he sat on the edge of his bed and remembered when Refuge had fallen in Illate. Zeala Fe had not been the First Queen, not then. She had been the Third Queen.

The revolution on Illate had begun under the old First Queen Natai Fe's reign. A festival had brought her across the strait between Ooila and Illate every year, and that year, the leaders of the Illate revolution had taken her hostage. They poisoned her guards while they slept. On the same night, Refuge shut down the ports, strangling access to the country. A lot of Illate was ugly mountain ranges and the passes were easily closed by rock-falls and cave-ins. The port was the only real entrance to the country and Refuge held it for just under a month before Zeala Fe broke through the barricade. Heast could still remember the day her forces stormed into the capital of Illate, the morning's sun glinting off the gold-edged, white armour her soldiers wore. That morning, it was as if a second sun had risen.

Refuge did not survive the day.

After the battle, Heast and seven survivors hid in small houses throughout Illate. They slept in attics, beneath floorboards, injured survivors in a nation of people who had been denied the end of a brutal slavery that saw their children taken from them. Decades later, Heast was humbled by the risks those people had taken for his soldiers. In the face of their own bitter disappointment, they had cared for the remnants of Refuge, a task made considerably more difficult for himself after his leg had been amputated.

Eventually, Heast ended in Doscلna, a small town in Gogair, where he was tended by the elderly Anemone. The witch organized the construction of his leg and supervised its crafting to the end of the broken bone. After that, he had spent months learning how to stand with it, how to walk with the weight. He could still remember the awkwardness of those first months. His leg had not had the strength, not at first, and he had been forced to build up his lower body. He worried about the bleeding as well, but that, Anemone told him, was a consequence of the way she had amputated it. The old witch had done that with her magic. 'I had to stop the rot,' she told him. 'But you'll carry the weakness of the flesh.' He had nodded when she told him that. He was attempting to walk without a crutch for the first time when she spoke. He was trying to live with what he had. What she said was just another part of that task.

That was why, by the time Anemone – the younger Anemone, the granddaughter of the old woman who survived Illate with him – knocked on the door, Heast knew that he would speak to Zeala Fe in the same way he would speak to any other queen. He would treat her as the Captain of Refuge treated all who would employ him.

'It is time, sir,' Anemone said, after he opened the door.

'I know.'

Outside, the streets were busy. Smoke from the walls curled into the dark sky, obscuring the stars, and crowds gathered in the streets outside bars and hotels and inns. They gathered in such numbers that, if Heast had not seen the barricades that lay outside Vaeasa, he would have said that there was no war taking place in the Kingdoms of Faaisha, no fear of rationing, no fear of being laid siege to. He knew that other kingdoms were not doing as well – Maosa was proof of that – and he gave Tuael his respect for managing to keep the calm and sense of normality in his capital that many leaders would have struggled to achieve.

'You hear that a marshal died today?' The words were spoken by a middle-aged man outside a bar that Heast and Anemone walked past. The man spoke to another middled-aged man, who said, 'Cohn. He took his own life—' At the corner, an elderly woman finished the sentence when she said, 'A rope.' 'It is said he was in deep mourning over his failures,' a young woman said; a young man added, 'Celp was a disaster.'

'The Lord did not wait long, did he?' Anemone said quietly, once they had past the last two.

'No,' Heast agreed. 'But at least he did not ask us to do it.'

'What would you have said, had he?'

'No. That work is for the lord. We are not assassins.'

'Not ever?'

'Not here.'

The estate the First Queen of Ooila lived on was near the centre of Vaeasa. Above it, the stars were a smoky smear and, outside its large, ornate black steel gate, stood two of Tuael's purple-cloaked guards. At the approach of Heast and Anemone, the one on the left opened the gate. Immaculate gardens led up to a large two-storey building made of stone and wood.

The grounds were quiet, eerily so, and Heast dropped his hand unconsciously to where his sword usually sat. No steel touched his flesh, however, and he curled his hand into a fist instead.

At the door to the house, a single guard waited. Her skin was a dark black, and her face was narrow. Like a cat, Heast thought suddenly, though he was not given to such comparisons. Yet, as he drew closer, and her tawny eyes watched both him and Anemone without concern, he thought his description apt. There was, in the soldier, something careful and intent about her, like a cat who watched from a secret perch as a stranger approached.

'Captain Heast,' she said, when he came to stand in front of her. 'Anemone.' She wore black armour made from chain and plate. When she bowed to them, flashes of red could be seen in the joints. 'My name is Captain Lehana. The First Queen of Ooila has been expecting both of you.'

4.

'Qian—'

'That is not my name.' In Asila, Zaifyr sat on a small stool, surrounded by the dead. 'It has never been my name,' he said.

'It is the name of my brother,' Tinh Tu replied.

'It is a lie.'

An image flashed before Ayae, a sliver of a memory. The inside of a small house dominated by shelves of books, by papers that stuck out of pages, laid across a beautiful table, documents held in place by scrolls both old and new. Some were rolled tightly, and others were spread flat. Jae'le sat across from Tinh Tu. He approached her house as warlord, a man who was drenched in the violence of victory, a man who told her that she was no different from him. But the words that Jae'le used were not what Ayae heard. Rather, she heard the words that Tinh Tu spoke to the man behind Jae'le, the white man adorned with charms who leant against her wall. *Your name?* she asked him. *Qian*, he replied. She could detect no lie. She could feel only truth. 'Qian,' Tinh Tu said again in Asila. '*Qian.*' The emphasis contained in his name held an urge, a suggestion, an attempt to latch onto the belief he had had when he stood in her home so long ago. 'Listen to me, please.'

'That is not my name.' He repeated the words. 'That is not who I am.'

'You can stop this,' she said. 'You can let these people go.'

'There is no place for them to go.'

We did not want to kill him, Tinh Tu said to Ayae, the scene paused. *We had arrived on the shore of Asila as gods who could remember the war between our parents and the devastation it brought our world. We had a responsibility not to repeat that horror. But Qian would never be able to remember the day fully. Parts of it, he would: the devastation, the desperation, but never his death. For him, the moment was always absent, always blank.*

It was Jae'le who struck first.

He moved with such speed that, if Ayae had not felt a sudden sickening lurch – as if more sand had given way beneath her feet – when the scene she was witnessing slowed, she was not sure that she would have seen the steps that he took, nor the sword that he drew. She knew only that she would have seen him stop, suddenly.

No more than an inch before Zaifyr, Jae'le was halted by a dozen ghosts. Their cold hands held not just him, but the two swords that he had drawn, and which were within touching distance of the charm-laced man. Before Ayae's gaze, the swords were forced back, and she thought for sure the bones in Jae'le's arms would splinter, but then he released the hilts, and his hands plunged into the ghosts. A ripple followed, and each of the ghosts he touched appeared to be made of flesh, to be alive, only for them to fall back, their bodies incorporeal, but with a wound knitting across their chest: a wound made by a hand.

'*No!*'

The shout came from Zaifyr, a cry of horror for what he had witnessed, and the ghosts that still held Jae'le launched their captive through the air – but even as Ayae watched Jae'le fall, she felt the ground begin to shudder. The mountain looming over Asila splintered, huge pieces of it falling to the ground. They tore through the ghosts as they plunged into the ground, guided like spears by Eidan. Above, the sky turned black and a loud rumble of thunder emerged. For a moment, Ayae thought that it sounded like a sound of disapproval from a god, of a giant being that would emerge from the black clouds that gathered. But the lightning that webbed along the clouds answered to the call of Aelyn on the ground, and the bolts, when they fell, burst through ghosts and houses, and started fires.

Ayae had never seen such a display. For every dead man and woman who had been filled with Zaifyr's power and was struck, another rose from the remains, the cold hands appearing at times from the ground, and at times from nothing but thin air. On these occasions, it was as if the dead waited behind a curtain and needed only the nod of another to step forward and announce their presence. They would then flicker, as if turned to flesh. Or they would burst apart, no matter whether they were flesh or not. Watching it all, Ayae found that she could not turn away. A part of her wanted to do so, but a larger part of her could not. It was not Tinh Tu who ensured that she could not turn away. No, before her was a display of such power that it surpassed anything that she had seen in Mireea, or in Yeflam, and she was both humbled to witness it and terrified by the boundaries it broke, not just of the weather, or the shape of the land, but of the very divide between life and death.

None of the men and women she watched was a god, yet Ayae could see how another would believe they were.

The ground lifted around her and splintered and, as it did, her understanding of how reality functioned, how the gods had existed, broke apart with it. For the last year, she had heard how the gods had not viewed the world in the way that mortals did, that time and fate wound around them, each and every strand a possibility, but it was not until she saw Jae'le, Aelyn, Eidan and Tinh Tu locked in battle with Zaifyr that she truly understood that. It was not until then that she realized that within her was a power that did not adhere to any rule because it formed rules. Yet Ayae also knew that she did not have the power to do that. The world was created not by the sliver of a god's power that was within her, or the power that she saw around her, but by the complete and full version of it. By the unified whole of a divine presence that did not react to the world that it lived in, but created it, nurtured it, shaped it, and did so until finally it decided that what it had made could be broken.

'Qian.' She heard Tinh Tu's voice faintly. 'Qian, the house. My house. The house I grew up in. That my parents had owned. That their parents had built. That small, simple house.' Ayae heard Tinh Tu's words of truth, could sense, for the first time, the power in them. 'Qian, you are standing in *that* house.'

Across from her, Zaifyr paused.

'Qian, you are not in Asila. You are in my house. There is no destruction around you, there is no dead, there is nothing but my books, my papers, and you and Jae'le.'

Behind him, Ayae saw Aelyn emerge from the broken remains of the temple, from the debris of the city as a whole. The quiet sadness that had led her through the streets was now gone, replaced by a violence so thorough and complete that it had destroyed not just the infrastructure of the city, but the mountain itself. The remains of it sat like a shattered crown around the battle, an arena for men and women who had been, until recently, more powerful than any king or queen. It was through that debris that Aelyn emerged, unarmed, behind her brother. Her footsteps fell quietly, surely, and her hard hands flexed as she drew nearer. For a moment, Ayae believed that she would reach Zaifyr, that her hands would find his neck, and she would break the bone, and that he would be killed by her—

But she did not kill him.

Tinh Tu's words were not enough. The whispered descriptions, the probing of his mind, were weak because they were based on his name, and her belief that it was his. But Zaifyr was no longer Qian, and Tinh Tu's hold on him was fragile.

The haunts that materialized behind Zaifyr, that caught Aelyn's hands, were thin and ugly. In their faces, Ayae could see such hunger, such need, that she knew – as they sought to consume Aelyn, to drain her of life – they did so for a brief moment of warmth and fullness.

Jae'le's swords drove through Zaifyr's back with such sureness and accuracy that they broke his spine in two places, forced him into the arms of his brother, who looked at him once and then drew a dagger across Zaifyr's throat.

5.

Heast and Anemone were led through the silent house by Captain Lehana.

It was not empty, as the silence might have suggested. Women sat or stood in the rooms that they walked past. In some, games were played. Pieces of stone and bone were moved without words. Cards were spread and collected without the slap of the shuffle. In other chambers, books were read, and food eaten, and drinks drunk, all in a silence that was without oppression.

A narrow staircase took Lehana, Heast and Anemone to the first floor. A pair of armoured soldiers stood at the top of it, and another pair, clad in black-and-red chain and plate, waited for the three at the end of the hall.

Behind the door were two women.

The first was a middle-aged black woman. It was clear at a glance that she did not have the martial training of the soldiers he'd seen around the house, and she did not bear armour. Instead, she wore a fine gown of green and yellow, the colour highlighting the brown streaks that ran through her short, black hair. When Heast and Anemone entered the room, the woman rose from her place at the only table in the room, the surface of which was covered in herbs and stones.

Zeala Fe was the room's other occupant. She lay propped up in a large bed set against the far wall, a small and sickly thin woman enrobed in browns and reds. Her skin was sunken against her bones, and her hair, no more than white wisps, had been slicked back against her skull, leaving her looking even more gaunt.

'Aned Heast,' the First Queen of Ooila said. Her eyes were bright and without a hint of confusion in them. 'It has been some time.'

'We've never met.' Behind him, Captain Lehana closed the door, securing the five of them in the room. She was the only one to bear a sword. 'But it has been some time since Illate,' he said. 'Long years for both us. Have they treated you or me better?'

She smiled without revealing her teeth. 'You have already met my captain,' she said, turning from the question. 'Allow me to introduce Safeen Re. She cares for me in these final days.'

'Captain.' The woman left the table and stopped at the end of the bed. 'My condolences on your recent loss,' she said to Anemone. 'Your grandmother was a great woman.'

'Thank you.' The young witch was silent for a moment. 'My grandmother,' she said, finally, 'wants me to ask why you are not prepared for the Queen's death.'

'I am prepared,' Safeen said.

'What she means,' Zeala Fe said, raising her voice to interrupt the two, 'is that I do not need my soul caught. I do not need it kept in a bottle.'

'An Ooilan queen does not die,' Heast said. 'Is that not the law?'

'Do you obey laws so well now?' She laughed, but the laugh turned into a cough. 'Bring me my cup,' she said to Safeen once she had recovered. Gently, almost reluctantly, the witch lifted a mug from beside the bed and held it out to her. The Queen took a small sip and grimaced. 'You are right, however,' she said to Heast. 'An Ooilan queen is meant to come back. She is to be reborn so that her daughters can raise her to rule so she can raise her daughters to rule. She is to ensure that prosperity and dignity remain, even though the price is terrible for her to return. But there is always a price for resurrection, is there not, Captain?'

'I have never been resurrected,' he said evenly.

'I disagree. Look at you now.'

'I am as I have always been.'

'Are you?'

Heast said nothing.

'Did you know that, after the battle, the Illate people brought us a body?' the Queen asked. 'A white man's body. The men who carried it to us, to the Queens, said that it was you. The man's face had been cut up, but a blue eye remained – so bright, even in death, that I can still remember its colour. It was, of course, quite unlike yours, now that I sit before you. But the man had a tattoo as well. It was the symbol of Refuge. A number of the soldiers had that, however. When I questioned it, the men who carried the body said that it was the rings that identified you. Silver rings on the left hand. Rings you do not wear, clearly.'

No, Heast almost said. He had never worn rings, just as he had never had the tattoo, either. He knew the man who had.

'It was months before we heard that you were alive. By then you were already in Gogair, beginning your resurrection. For a while, the other Queens feared that you would return and rain terrible destruction on us.'

'Other captains of Refuge have done that, but it has always been a folly,' he said. 'Besides, I had lost too much.'

'Yes. Eventually we learned that only eight of you survived. Still, some of the Queens kept their fear. They said that you were young. That was enough.'

'I always expected an assassin.' He gestured to the chair that sat next to the bed and, after Zeala Fe nodded, sat. 'Why was there never one?' he asked.

'I always assumed there were.' The Queen turned to Anemone. 'Did your grandmother kill any?'

'No,' the witch said. 'She says there were none.'

'How genuinely surprising.'

'Why didn't you send one?' Heast asked.

'I considered it. You forced me to invade Illate and I did not want that. For years, I had been pushing at the edges of the generational slavery Ooila had been involved in with the people there. The public were starting to lose their appetite for bonding their children with children they purchased in Illate. We were taking fewer and fewer of their men and women to work in farms and households.' She indicated to Safeen that she would like another drink from the cup and grimaced again after she had sipped. 'But it was exactly that that gave Illate the confidence to rebel,' she continued. 'Oh, I look back now and realize I should have reached out to the rulers of Illate, but hindsight is a deadly trap for a queen.' She met Heast's gaze. 'At the time,' she said, 'let us just say that punishing you for my mistake would not have appeased me.'

'Illate still doesn't have its independence,' he said, not turning away. 'I doubt that either of us will see it in our lifetimes.'

'Mine, certainly, but yours – well, it is possible that Refuge will one day ride back into that country.'

'Is that right?'

'Yes. It is, in fact, a demand of mine once this war is finished. I want to see the people of Illate given freedom with as little bloodshed as possible. That is the other half of the payment for what I will do for you.'

'Which is?'

'Finish your resurrection.'

6.

Leviathan's End appeared from the darkness as two giant, burning eyes and Bueralan's first thought was that he had come upon a scene of destruction.

In his memories he stood, not on the deck of *Glafanr*, but on the deck of the smaller, sleeker *Jao*, beside his blood brother Zean and the first mercenary captain he had served under, Serra Milai. Like Bueralan, the former had never been to Leviathan's End, but the latter, who was twice the age of the young men, was returning to what she called home. 'The only home a mercenary has' were her exact words. She said them when she first announced the trip and that she expected the two to accompany her. When she said it, Bueralan had shrugged off her words. He had heard Milai say them before: the banks of Zoum were the only home a mercenary had, a cheap bar in a friendly city was another of the sole friends she had, the kip she rolled out on a piece of grass or dirt a third. But the Captain of Water, her body solid with muscle, her skin a dark brown, had said it more than once about Leviathan's End during their journey. Each time, she said it without the sly humour Bueralan had grown to expect, the knowing wink meaning she had no real home, and never would.

Leviathan's End was built inside the skull of the god who had been a Leviathan. The town itself was the cause of the burning eyes inside the Leviathan's skull, illuminated by the lamps that lined the paths and ceilings inside. On the night the *Jao* approached, a frost had covered the deck and ice had collected in the edges of the sails, but Bueralan had been amazed when they entered the skull and found it warm. The heat came from the huge fires that hung from the roof of the skull, the massive pots of oil attached to thick rods bolted into place.

'Can you imagine,' Zean said quietly, as *Jao* nudged the dock, 'what kind of person would dare build a town here?'

The town itself was suspended high above the black water inside the dead god's head. Below it, white trees lined the water's edge, growing from the bone. They reached up with thick and barren limbs but, for all their height, the lowest point of the town, the curving hull of a great ship that had been pulled out of the ocean to fill the centre, was still well out of reach of the trees. From the hull, thick wooden platforms stretched, joined together by heavy rope bridges that left the strong impression that the town was a huge tree house.

'I do not need to imagine,' Serra Milai said. 'Soon enough, nor will you. Onaedo meets all the new mercenaries who come here.'

'Is that why you had us come?' Bueralan asked.

'It is one of the duties that a captain must perform.'

He would not understand until later that there were officials who would not hire you if you were not endorsed by Leviathan's End.

Before Water ended, before Serra Milai disappeared into a secret retirement, Bueralan would be promoted to her second. He would sit in the meetings where the lords and ladies and government officials would ask about their standing in Leviathan's Blood. Where the question would be asked of all the soldiers in the small unit Milai led. Once, when they were denied a job because they had a new member who had not yet been vetted by Onaedo, Bueralan asked Milai why she had not lied. She had simply shaken her head and said, 'Onaedo will know if you lie.'

A cage took Bueralan and the other two from the dock to the floor of Leviathan's End.

The sight that greeted them when they stepped out of the cage was equal to the strangeness of his entry. The ship's sail-free masts reached up so high that the top of the Leviathan's smooth skull was within its reach. It sat in the centre of the town so much like a tower, or a castle, that the suspended torches cast the ship's shadow in multiple directions across the streets and buildings below it. It gave the town the only uniform look it had, for the platforms that held the rest of Leviathan's End were filled with mismatched buildings, where no single design ethos, or culture, was dominant. On them, unpainted white wood was shaped in squares and rectangles, while painted wood had been formed into circles. Roofs that were straight, ridged and circular appeared without care of their neighbours, and the windows were of such a wide variety that Bueralan could not even begin to count the many shapes they took.

This lack of cohesion was matched by the men and women Bueralan and Zean passed. Bueralan saw women from Nmia, whose skin was darker than his, and who had long spears and swords. He saw men from Ooila with axes and others serving in a bar. And he saw people with the dusty brown colouring that was close to Zean's being served. There were women wearing matched pairs of swords dressed in dark, red-stained leather with skin and hair so pale he thought them ill. It was not until later that he learned they were from the Wastes in the south, well past any continent he had seen. He saw a man from the Saan, his copper bracelets on the lower half of his right arm, his left missing. He saw a woman from Sooia, and another from the Kingdoms of Faaisha. As Milai led him and Zean deeper into the suspended town, more people appeared before him, so many that he soon lost the ability to describe where they had each come from, and when they stopped before a great, open area with long tables and clerks, he no longer tried.

'This is the heart of Leviathan's End,' Milai said. 'Here is where you sign with a crew. Here is where your job is recorded. Here is where your reputation is kept.'

'On scraps of paper brought by birds?' Zean asked.

'Yes.'

Birds – hundreds and hundreds – sat on white-stained stands behind the clerks. Yet, despite the variety in all the species, not one fought with another.

'How much do you pay?'

The Captain of Water chuckled. 'You're a cynical man,' she told Bueralan's blood brother. 'I like that about you, but it is misplaced here. You do not bribe anyone in Leviathan's End. You will be remembered if you do. Your misconduct will be marked, and it will be marked next to who you have worked for, and how much you were paid, and if you distinguished yourself.' As she spoke, a clerk rose from his table and approached one of the newly landed birds. 'The two of you will need to list yourselves here.'

'If we don't?' Bueralan asked.

'You will. Because if you are not recorded here,' Milai said, 'you are not worth anything.'

7.

'I told you,' Heast said, 'I was not dead.'

'The Captain of Refuge was.' Zeala Fe took the cup of bitter mixture from Safeen and settled it on the blankets that covered her frail lap. 'Instead, there was a man who looked much like him,' she continued. 'But he denied the title that was his and worked many jobs, where he remained poor because he kept little of the money he earned. Most of his coin went to the families of those soldiers who had died in Illate under his command. Oh, the actions were well hidden. Debts cleared, educations paid for – no banker in Zoum would easily give up the man's information. Not this man, especially. But in the port of Wisal the man was brought to the attention of the Eyes of the Queen, and very little was hidden from her.' A faint steam rose from the top of her drink. The First Queen of Ooila looked at Heast. 'Did you know the Eyes of the Queen, by any chance? Her name was Ce Pueral.'

'I never met her. Not in Wisal. Not anywhere else.' He felt a flatness in himself, a coldness he did not bother to hide. 'I did hear of her later. She was said to be your right hand.'

'I preferred to call her my Eyes,' she said softly. 'A conceit as I grew more and more ill. My body became a series of titles that others inhabited. But that was later, long after Wisal. She was but a captain, then, and it was purely by chance that you became of interest to her. She had travelled to Wisal for other reasons.'

'Bueralan Le.' The saboteur had been a young soldier in Water, then. Heast had hired that force. 'Surely you had other exiles who became mercenaries?'

'But few like the Baron of Kein. He was the son of a friend, and my Eyes thought he was a blind spot of mine. She convinced me that he needed to be killed when she heard that he was working for you. I was quite surprised when she returned and told me that she had left him alive.' She sighed and shook her head. 'Ce Pueral was a great friend, but a greater woman, I think. She had instincts that a nation could trust. I wish she were here today to speak with you.'

'I doubt it,' Heast said, his voice still cold. 'I do not appreciate my private affairs being peeled open like a boiled egg.'

'Few of us do.' Her smile, or so it seemed to Heast, was strangely indulgent. 'Tell me, Captain, did so many years of penance for your soldiers make you happy?'

'I am not a man given to penance,' he said.

'No? Then what was it for?'

'Loyalty.'

Behind him, at the door, Captain Lehana shifted slightly and spoke, 'You sent your wages for twenty-six years to the families of your soldiers because they were loyal to you?'

The Captain of Refuge did not turn to the soldier. 'You have a Queen,' he said, 'so perhaps you do not understand this, but when you sell your sword, you are not paid in the fallow times. You are paid only when blood is shed. When your sword is drawn. When it is you or another. A soldier of Refuge can be unpaid, even then. That is the nature of what we do. But a soldier of Refuge is like any other soldier. He has parents, she has a partner, he has a child. Perhaps she has neither and it is simply debts that she carries. Whatever the burden, it is the captain's burden, once they have died.'

'But after Illate, you must have been crippled with debt,' the guard said, a hint of horror in her voice. 'You must—'

'Have had to work,' Heast finished.

'When Pueral told me, I was impressed,' the Queen said. When she spoke, she revealed missing teeth on the right side of her mouth. 'If politics had been different, I would have offered you a job. Instead, I will be content with being part of Refuge's return in my final days. No, say nothing, Captain. Listen to me: I do this not because of you, or for our shared history. I do this because my loyalty ensures that I do. But unlike you, my loyalty is not just to the women and men who held swords for me. It is for the people who owned shops. Who sold books. Who made bedsheets. Who looked to me to protect them and to bring them prosperity. My loyalty is to the men and women that the Innocent and his god killed when they came to Cynama.'

'The Innocent?'

'Is it too much that I ask?'

Am I afraid, do you mean? That was the unspoken implication, but Heast was not, not now. If he was to be afraid – and he admitted that he might be – it would be much later. It would be well after he left this room. 'There are rumours that he has left Sooia,' he said. 'You can hear them in the streets of Vaeasa – but I have heard those words said before in other cities.'

'I have allowed you to speak quite freely in here, but you will not call me a liar.' The First Queen's hands tightened around her mug. The strength with which she did it revealed her bones. 'Aela Ren *will* be here soon. I will not live to see it. Already I feel the touch of the dead around me. But there is life in me yet, and I will see that man hunted for what he has done to Ooila. I will see him broken for the casual cruelty he inflicted upon my nation. I will not abide a single man treating my people as if they were the husk of a butterfly to be crushed.'

'My Queen,' Safeen said, reaching for her. 'You must remain calm.'

'No, I will not hide from this man before me,' she said, her gaze boring into Heast. 'He must know exactly what I want. Let my desire take what remains of my strength. I have hidden for too long in this forsaken city. I have tried to play the politics of the Faaishan Lords but I do not have the time and I do not have the coldness for it. I cannot steer them towards the threat that approaches their shore, though I have tried to convince them of it. I have told them they need kill this Leeran general who so vexes them now. That he must be gone so they can prepare for a far worse danger. But they will not listen. The only way forward is the man who sits before me. The only option for me is Refuge.' She took a breath, long and deep. 'The Lords of Faaisha believe they made a mistake when they requested you, Captain,' she said, her anger still present in her voice. 'They claim that they did not know the symbol for Refuge. That the soldier who drew it was playing his own game. That may be true, but what they do not understand is the gift that has been given to them, and if they will not take it, then I will.'

Heast was silent. He believed that Tuael knew exactly what had been drawn. He did not believe that Baeh Lok would have agreed to it, otherwise. The old soldier had survived Illate, and he had not, in any of the years after, drawn the symbol once. When it arrived in Yeflam, it had arrived with his approval, a message to his captain, an acknowledgement that the situation was much worse than what could be dealt with by the Faaishan marshals.

But Lok, unlike Tuael, would have known that the Captain of Refuge would not have arrived alone.

'Others have died fighting the Innocent,' Heast said, finally. 'Other captains of Refuge, that is. Four have died in Sooia and they died with more seasoned soldiers than I currently have.'

'You will have mine,' Zeala Fe said. 'All the soldiers here will be yours after today. They will not go home. They will be the spine of your new Refuge.'

He shook his head. 'The Queen's Guard does not leave the Queen. Even I know that.'

'But I am dying.' She took another deep breath and laughed a little as she exhaled. 'You sit at my death bed and you listen to my final wishes.'

'The mug, Captain,' Anemone said.

'He already knows, child.' The Queen grasped her bitter mug and sipped from it. 'You can see it in his cold eyes.'

'How long did you have before tonight?' Heast asked.

'Very little. Safeen has said a week, perhaps two, but I think less. I am in constant pain and my body fails in ways that I have long feared. I can no longer lift myself from this bed. To even be in the position I am now, I had to be helped. But worse is happening with my memory. I need drugs just to remember whose shift it is to stand guard outside my door. What would another week bring me?'

'Death can rob us of our dignity,' he said. 'Better we take it within our own hands.'

'I am glad you understand.'

'I do.'

'And of what I ask?'

'The Captain of Refuge agrees,' he said.

'The witch of Refuge does as well,' Anemone said.

'And the soldier.' Lehana's voice was heavy with emotion. 'The soldier of Refuge agrees.'

8.

It was a day before Bueralan met Onaedo. He was summoned to her quarters by a well-dressed girl, no more than a child, really.

The girl led him onto the deck of the ship, but left him at the door to the captain's cabin. After Bueralan knocked, he was invited into a large room. Inside, the walls held beautiful, elaborate tapestries of wars that Bueralan could not properly identify. They were separated by swords, axes, spears, and half a dozen other weapons, some of them broken, but all of them used. Beneath the weapons and tapestries were wooden stands that held pieces of armour. Across them was a range of strips of cloth from sashes, vests, shirts and cloaks. Some, Bueralan saw, were stained with blood, or torn, some so old that the fabric was naught but fragile strands over an equally old chain vest, or around the waist of a suit of dented armour. At the base of some of the wooden stands books and scrolls lay, and they, like the armour and the cloth, were also old – until Onaedo's desk, where a small collection of new, slim books were stacked on the floor by the right corner.

'Fictions,' said the woman behind the table. 'The latest attempt by men and women who live by the sword to try to immortalize their deeds.'

She was a tall, muscular woman, one who left the large table she sat behind looking as if it were but modestly oversized. There was, in her face, a certain roundness that Bueralan identified with people born at the southern end of Ooila, but her skin, a solid, dark brown, was not the darker colour of those who were born there. Her hair was short and tied in small knots across her head. The knots had been dyed a pale blonde, the colour a contrast to the dark red of the shirt she wore, and the black of her pants. He saw the latter when she rose from her chair to shake his hand, before inviting him to sit.

'They're no different from the tapestries on your walls,' Bueralan said, after he had taken the chair. 'What is it that we're taught? All art is propaganda.'

'I don't imagine any of us are taught that,' Onaedo said easily. 'Maybe it is just what barons say, before they are exiled.'

'Mostly they don't say anything.'

'Is that right?'

He held up his little finger. 'Pinky swear.'

'I'll take your word for it.' She smiled, but very little humour reached her dark eyes. 'In the case of these particular tapestries, they do not tell the story of a battle, however. They are designs from before the War of the Gods, from what I understand. They're not originals, naturally. They are reproductions of tapestries that were kept in the temples of Baar, the God of War. It was said they were made by the god's most favoured disciple.' She shrugged, as if it did not matter what 'they' said. 'The tapestries detail a set of rules for soldiers. A code of conduct for the battlefield.'

Bueralan looked again at the ones closest to him. Able to take a long, hard look, he could see the workmanship, the intricacy of the hand-sewing. His gaze lingered on the closest one, the field of faded red drawing him to it. On that background, a genderless shadowed soldier stood before a series of cages filled with corpses. In a sequence across the red of the tapestry, the featureless soldier moved through the bodies, until, at the end, it slumped to its knees.

'Simple rules, really,' Onaedo said, while he gazed at it. 'Do not kill innocents. Do not destroy the villages that have nothing to do with your fight. Treat those you take as prisoner humanely. Do not maim them, do not torture them. In short, do not rob the living of their dignity because you can.'

He turned back to her. 'Simple rules,' he agreed. 'But I have heard of all of them broken.'

'You will see them broken, as well. War is a terrible thing and it inspires in us deeds that are terrible. But if you wish to be protected by Leviathan's End, you will do your best to abide by these rules.' As she spoke, Bueralan began to hear a history emerge in her voice, one that echoed her experience. It was clear that she had seen things he could only imagine. 'If you break these rules, the books here that hold your deeds will be held against you. Reach a certain point, and your book will be closed, and you will be considered an enemy of Leviathan's End. It is important that you fully understand what that means if you are to work in Captain Milai's Water. Saboteurs are asked to do things that no simple soldier will be asked.'

'But not for the same price.' His wit fell flat and he half shrugged. 'I have been told,' he said. 'The captain has told us the good and the bad.'

'There is a balance in war that must be kept,' she said, using words that the Innocent would echo, years later, on the deck of *Glafanr*. 'A mercenary's life is not an honourable one in itself. Few professions are, of course, but unlike bakers, or blacksmiths, ours can so easily become one from which all honour is drained. After all, we are the many faces of many masters. A cruel lord can pay us to raid a village, while a kind diplomat can pay us to protect a road. Neither reflects who we are.'

'Does Leviathan's End keep that balance, then?'

'Partly. Mostly, I want those without masters to keep their respect. Let the lord and lady use their soldiers to burn villages. Let them torture and burn their citizens. Let their horrors be their own.'

Bueralan indicated the tapestries around him. 'They all say this?'

'Yes.'

'It is strange that I have never heard of this before.'

'Few people ask about the tapestries,' Onaedo said. 'Few remember the gods and what they said. But in your particular case, I would say only that you have led a very different life to the one that you will be part of now. You have had a much fuller education than a child born to a mercenary has.'

He nodded. 'One last question, if we are done?'

'One last, then.'

'I have heard you're very old.'

'I am.'

'Is this code of yours about respect for the gods?'

The ruler of Leviathan's End laughed. It was a short laugh, without humour. 'I have no respect for the gods,' she said harshly. 'You would do well to put such a concept far from your mind, young man. The gods created this world we live in. I am not so old that I saw that, but I am old enough that I saw them betray us and break our world. All they deserve is oblivion.'

At the time, Bueralan had thought Onaedo's words evidence of a borderline madness, a fact that he mentioned to Zean, after his blood brother had had his meeting. Zean laughed when he said it. Of course she was mad, he said. You only have to look at this town to know that. The newly minted saboteur could not argue with that. He would not argue when he returned, years later, to register Dark, and when he returned with new mercenaries to have them enter their names in the books. But it was not until now, as *Glafanr* made its way through Leviathan's Blood, as it closed in on the shoreline of Leera, that Bueralan recalled that first meeting and understood the cause of that controlled madness.

But more than that: he understood, finally, the anger that had allowed Onaedo to build a town inside the skull of a god.

9.

When Eilona woke, the afternoon's sun was down, and the night surrounded her. Against the fabric of the tent she lay in, the campfires left a series of strange, undefined silhouettes against the walls. In the first moments of being awake, she saw the gods in their various forms, stretched out in long lines, only to be compacted suddenly, then broken apart, as if the war that had raged for so long still played itself out around her.

But there was only one god now, she knew.

Se'Saera: the new god, the undefined god, the god who announced herself to Eilona with gentleness, and with such violence to Olcea.

In Pitak, the University of Zanebien would be busy trying to find out what they could about Se'Saera. Her arrival was momentous. Eilona was in no doubt that the university would send people to all the major capitals, to catalogue the reactions of citizens from around the world and to begin studying what the new god was. A god, they would argue, was not only defined by what it did and what it said, but by the reaction of people to it. A woman with a background in the study of divinity could, Eilona knew, make her career at this moment . . . but that woman was not her.

Earlier, when Eilona had left her mother's tent, she had realized her mistake in coming to Yeflam. It was nothing Muriel Wagan said, or did, that led her daughter to believe that. In fact, her mother had greeted her warmly, even as Eilona struggled to hide her shock at the age that had etched itself across her since she had last seen her. No, it was the men and women who greeted her mother in the camp that met Eilona differently.

She had recognized a number of them immediately. Ila, a dark-skinned girl who had been a childhood acquaintance, was the first. She stood before a tent holding a child. When she saw Eilona, her lean face turned hard and she went inside. A short while later, her mother stopped a white man who had worked in the Mireean market and asked him how his eye was. A wide strip of black cloth covered the left side of his face, but his uncovered right looked past her mother to find her while he answered. Eilona didn't know his name, but she knew what he thought of her. Another white woman came up behind him while her mother talked. Her name was Togo. She had once been a tutor of Eilona. She had three children with her – two brown, one white – each holding supplies and, after she had greeted the Lady of the Ghosts, she greeted Eilona. The chill in the former tutor's voice lingered in the air long after she had disappeared into the tents.

Her mother made no mention of it, though she must have noticed.

'This third woman you arrived with,' she said, instead, as they walked through the camp. 'Was her name Tinh Tu?'

'Yes.' Eilona was not sure what she should say out in the open. 'You don't seem surprised.'

'I am not.' A large tent began to take shape in the camp. At the edges of it stood soldiers in red cloaks. 'She has family here.'

Eilona recalled the inn and the dead in it. 'She mentioned a brother who died. Was his name Qian, by any chance?'

'He was known as Zaifyr.' Muriel stopped and turned to her. 'What happened on the way here?'

'She took my voice away.' She could not hide the emotion when she spoke, could not hide the mix of fear and powerlessness that defined her journey to the shore of Yeflam. 'It was shortly after we left Zalhan. When she said her name, I knew who she was. Olcea had known before me. I think she had met her before. I wanted to ask her about the Five Kingdoms, about Se'Saera, but she told me not to ask. She told me not to speak. Those were her exact words.'

'And you couldn't?'

'No matter how much I tried, I could not.'

Her mother grunted. 'She sounds like Jae'le. I had hoped that she would be more like her sister. For all her faults, I understood Aelyn Meah.'

The head of the Keepers of the Divine, the absent ruler of Yeflam. Eilona said, 'I've heard—'

'You've heard right.' Her mother turned away and began walking down the path to the tent. 'No one knows where Aelyn is now, nor any of the other Keepers. At least it is a small blessing for us. You cannot imagine what it looked like when she fought her brother. What it will look like when her family find her. If it is revisited here, we won't survive an hour.'

'Surely you have little say in whether they come back or not. The Enclave are not as powerful as the five siblings, but they are more powerful than you.'

'I know. It is one of the reasons we need to be part of the Saan's push across the mountain. We need to take the battle to Leera. Se'Saera's attention is elsewhere for the moment, and that makes it the best time – the only time. If we push into Leera while she is spread across so many fronts we can take the eyes of the Keepers, the monsters and all the soldiers away from Yeflam. If we do it quickly enough, we may even be able to destroy her.'

'The new god?' It was, Eilona would think later, entirely fitting of her mother that she would decide to go to war with a god. 'We don't even know what she stands for.'

'She is a god of horror. Of violence and death.' As Muriel spoke, Eilona saw the weight that sat on her shoulders, the weight that was slowly dripping through her entire body. 'If we bow to her, she will take all that we have. If you do not believe me, give it time. You will see it soon enough.' The tent was close now, and her mother stopped, and turned to her again. 'I will speak with you later. I have to convince a selfish man that he has to send our forces into Leera. I have to make it clear to him that Miat Dvir and the Saan will not help him remake the cities of Yeflam. They will not help him rebuild a fleet. I have to show him the obvious. But after – after that, I will send for you and we will talk properly.'

She nodded and said that she understood.

Her mother touched her arm, gently. 'Thank you for coming,' she said. 'Caeli will find you a tent. It won't be pretty, but you'll be able to clean up and sleep in it.'

The Lady of the Ghosts left with Captain Mills at her side. Once the two entered the tent, Caeli turned to her, and it was there, in the company of her mother's guard, that Eilona realized she had made a mistake in coming to Yeflam.

Eilona had been young, confused about herself and about her place in the world when she had grown up in Mireea. She could offer no more of an excuse for what she had done than that. In the years since she had left, Eilona had often thought that, if she had not been the child of the Lady of the Spine, her actions would not have been worse than those of any other confused, angry child. But she was. The power she had was more than most saw in their entire lives. When she lashed out, she did it without understanding what would happen. Who would listen to her. Who would do what she said out of an attempt to earn favour, or to simply use her as an excuse to do something they wished. It was a knowledge that Eilona would never forget.

Caeli, she knew, would never forget, either.

10.

Jae'le laid the body of his brother gently on the ground, his movements echoing how he would place him a thousand years later on the shore of Leviathan's Blood.

Ayae had listened to Zaifyr retell the story of his fall in Asila only once. He had not spoken of it again. Yet, when he had described this moment to her – the moment not of his death, but his defeat – Zaifyr had believed that his brothers and sisters had stood over him with an air of satisfaction. In Tinh Tu's memory, however, there was only grief. The difference lay in the narrators: Zaifyr had never hesitated in admitting the horrors he was responsible for in Asila, but while he had acknowledged the necessity of what his family had done, he did not agree with their imprisonment of him. In that act, Ayae knew, Zaifyr believed that his family had betrayed the bond that existed between them. It was not so much the prison itself that caused this feeling, but the one thousand years of his incarceration that had followed. Zaifyr had never been able to forgive them that length of time, nor the authority over him they had assumed. For Tinh Tu, Zaifyr's defeat was cause only for grief, for him, and for the responsibility all four had been forced to accept. It was a responsibility that Ayae knew still existed and one that, she realized with a sudden clarity, had guided the actions of Zaifyr's brothers and sisters since his release from their prison.

'His wounds heal,' Jae'le said softly.

Ayae watched the flesh around Zaifyr's neck begin to knit together.

'Is he still alive?' asked Aelyn.

Gently, Jae'le felt for a pulse. 'No.' But as he spoke, his free hand fell to his sword.

How must it have felt to kill a man you had called your brother for over ten thousand years? The loss must have been immense, and Ayae did not believe that she would have been able to pick up a sword again, if she had been present. The devastation she had felt after she killed Faise was still in her. Yet in Jae'le, the only hesitation she saw was that he had not already brought the length of steel up and cut down hard into the mending cut in his brother's neck.

'How is this possible?' Eidan asked, his voice a whisper.

'I do not know,' Jae'le said.

'Brother.' Aelyn's voice was a hiss. 'Look—'

A flicker.

At first, Ayae thought she had imagined it, that what she saw was a shadow at the edge of her vision, a piece of dark that shifted for no reason: but it appeared again and again, and in each flicker, she began to make out an image. It was not a shadow, but rather a figure draped in a long, black robe. As if it were made from darkness, the robe fell over the figure's body like no clothing that Ayae had seen before. It drifted. It wavered. It moved forwards. It moved back. As the flickers grew quicker and quicker, until they were almost constant, it became clear it was not a robe, but rather that the dark folds and movements were its body, its shifts and stutters an attempt to reach outwards, to grasp what was before it with its hand, and draw it upwards.

'The Wanderer,' Jae'le said softly. 'But I do not sense him in the way I do other gods.'

Suddenly, a wet noise came from Zaifyr, and the image of the god disappeared.

The noise sounded again, a gasping breath taken, but one filtered through a choke, through a throat filled with blood.

Ayae turned to Zaifyr and saw that his eyes were open.

In their depths, she saw an awful anger, one fuelled by a terrible madness.

All of which ended, just as suddenly as it began, when Jae'le brought his sword down.

After a long, drawn-out moment, Eidan said, 'He begins to heal again.'

'The Wanderer,' Aelyn said, her voice sounding small and distant. 'He begins to appear again.'

'If we could see a haunt, a soul,' Jae'le said, 'would we see him reach for our brother's soul? Or is this something different altogether?'

The return of the Wanderer's flickering body had detached Ayae from what was taking place. Instead, she saw beyond Zaifyr's brothers and sisters, beyond their closed circle above his body. As if she were being offered an insight, she saw the complete devastation that surrounded her. She saw again the broken mountain and the fallen stone that lay across the streets. She saw the ground that had been destroyed by both the mountain and the lightning that struck it. She recalled the ghosts that had lined the now shattered streets and how they had been momentarily rendered to flesh, before being torn apart. She could still hear the whispers of a woman whose very words, she knew now, contained such power that she, perhaps more than any of her brothers and sisters, was the most deadly. And she heard again the smallness in Aelyn's voice, the powerlessness that was at the core of it, the helplessness that was shared by the people who stood around her.

'He cannot take him,' Jae'le said, finally. 'Whether the god is truly here, or if it is a sign of something else, it does not matter. Our brother is not his to take.'

'No,' Aelyn said. 'He is our responsibility.'

11.

Tinh Tu did not reveal to Ayae the conversations that took place after Aelyn's words. She did not allow her to hear how it was decided that a prison would be made. Instead, Ayae felt her eyes close, compelled to embrace the darkness they provided, though she was not tired. When she next opened them, she was standing on the deck of a ship that she did not know. It was long and sleek, but it sailed without a crew. The sails were full with wind and the decks empty but for a white raven at the helm. Ayae tried to take a step towards it, but she could not move. The head of the giant bird turned to her and its blue eyes held her. She went to speak, but instead her eyes once again closed and when she opened them next, she stood on a narrow trail in the Broken Mountains of Eakar.

She had only seen the mountains in old paintings. As an adult, Ayae's world was not much larger than the roads that connected the Spine of Ger to the Floating Cities of Yeflam. Beyond the journey she had made from Sooia when she was but a child, the only time Ayae had left the roads that she knew was when she and Illaan took a holiday to the Kingdoms of Faaisha. Yet, even had her world been larger, Eakar and its mountains would have remained a mystery to her. It was a barren land: the soil was so deeply tainted that no living creature could remain on it. Linae, the Goddess of Fertility, had done that to the land after she was struck down by Sei, the

God of Light. Until recently, Ayae had always believed that without Linae's blessings, the fertility had been stripped from the land. She had never thought to question the belief, not until she had heard Lor Jix's description of what had happened before the outbreak of the War of the Gods. The ancient dead, once a priest of the Leviathan, had said that the gods had gone to war not because of each other, but to deny the new god, Se'Saera, her birth.

In attempting that, the gods very nearly destroyed the world. For the first time since Zaifyr's trial the entirety of that realization began to unfold within Ayae. Beneath her feet, she could feel the soles of her boots weakening, as if the ground was trying to devour anything that walked on it. But for all that the sensation was not a pleasant one, it was not unique, either: for all her life Ayae walked over the damage the War of the Gods had created. She had lived most of her time on the cairn that Ger had built after he had fallen. She had grown up watching men and women set up small towns to dig for gold, for the fabled fortunes around his body. She had heard stories of betrayal and violence before she could properly speak the traders' tongue of the city. She had seen the black ocean regularly. She had seen ships pulled out of its water, the hulls stripped of paint, the wood in a slow rot and warping. She had read of butterflies in Ooila that rose into the sky every morning and died throughout the day. She had heard of people being suffocated by the insects' masses. She had seen huge paintings of Leviathan's End, the famed mercenary port that had been built in the Leviathan's skull, and from which bone-white trees grew without leaves. As she walked across the dead land of Eakar in Tinh Tu's memory, as she passed through villages defined by petrified bones and wood, Ayae realized she had never thought about the responsibility that the gods had to the world. She had never thought about the fact that the gods had not cared what happened to those who had spent generations worshipping them.

Their war had been an act of self-preservation, an act of pure selfishness that had left only devastation in its wake.

It was a thought that lingered as she arrived at the spot where the tower would be built.

Eidan held Zaifyr. The stocky man had carried his body through the Eakar Mountains and along the barren plains. It was to him that the task of designing the tower fell, and when he began, he did not set Zaifyr upon the ground. During the construction he passed Zaifyr to the others, but before the night fell, the body would return to him. Ayae saw the reason briefly, for one night, with a long, indrawn breath, Zaifyr returned to life, and the confusion that he felt in Eidan's grip offered more than enough time for one of the others to drive a knife deeply into him. This time, the image of the Wanderer did not appear.

The tower, once complete, did not rise into the sky in elegant spirals. No matter what Eidan said to his brother and sisters, no matter what he did with his hands or his power, the building refused to take the shape he had envisioned. Rather, it sagged and leant, small in both height and width, and fragile in its appearance.

Inside it was worse.

With her arms outstretched, Ayae could reach each wall with the tips of her fingers, and if she lay down on the dirt, if she lay on her back, she could not stretch herself out. It would offer less room to Zaifyr, and he would find no shelves, no food, no books, no stool, and not even a privy.

The crooked tower was no more than a cage.

It did not matter what we did, Tinh Tu said to her. *It did not matter what Eidan said to us, or how he made the bricks, or how he reinforced the bricks within, the tower would simply not support a second floor or a second room. You have watched him bring in stone from the broken mountains, hauling it with his great strength for hours without complaint. You have seen him spend hours making his mix. None of it worked. Not one thing he did could lift it above the sad, pathetic thing that you see now.*

'You left Zaifyr in this.' She heard her voice as if it were from a great distance. 'You left him in this for a thousand years.'

Until Jae'le released him.

'Jae'le.'

She felt her eyes open.

'Jae'le,' she said again. 'You gave the tower life.'

'Yes.' Behind Jae'le, the black water of Leviathan's Blood melded with the night's dirty star-scarred sky. The three suns had risen and fallen while Ayae witnessed what had happened in Asila, but she felt as if more than a day had passed. She felt as if weeks had passed. 'It could never have held him, not in such a state. At first, I gave a little of my power, but after a while, it was more. The soil beneath it returned to life and worms began to live in the bricks, the first keepers of the tower, the first of a small ecology to grow in the walls we made. But do you know what concerns me now, Ayae? It is not the choices we made then, nor even the sight of the Wanderer. No, it is the choice I made when I released Zaifyr. In these last few months, I have had long to think. I have thought of Eidan finding the *Wayfair* and of the god-touched man who told him of Lor Jix. Of Lor Jix himself at the trial, and the words that he used, words that had been rehearsed for a long time.'

'The gods and their influence,' Eidan murmured. 'I have thought of it as well.'

'You think that it is planned?' Tinh Tu asked.

'But Aelyn—' Ayae began.

'Aelyn knew what we know,' Jae'le said. 'She knew that she could not kill him.'

Before she could reply, Anguish laughed in his low, rasping voice. 'You are desperate.' He had climbed onto Zaifyr's body and squatted now on his chest, a dark, inky stain that the four had forgotten. 'To think that fate is at work for you, that it has somehow been pushed to aid you by all these gods that lie around you in a state of decay? Fate is not on your side, Jae'le. It is only on the side of its creation. The same creation that the gods went to war to destroy.' Gently, he laid his cold black hands on Zaifyr's chest. 'Your brother may not decay, but there is no breath in him, either. He has no soul.'

'You are right.' Jae'le's filed teeth were revealed as he smiled. 'But do we not have with us a man who can see what my brother sees? Who sees the dead as well as he did?'

'Only with my eyes open,' Anguish said.

'Then open them.'

'Se'Saera will know.'

'But she will not trust what you see,' Eidan said quietly. 'After all, you are but a deceit.'

12.

The morning's sun revealed the ragged length of the Leeran port of Gtara. The sunlight ran across the black water like lances as *Glafanr* closed in on its docks.

Bueralan stood alone at the bow of the ship, listening to the oars dip in and out of the water as it navigated past half a dozen other vessels. From his perch, the saboteur could gaze into the open holds of the other ships. From them, chains spilled out onto the decks as if they were metal digestive tracts. In a future world, he imagined, in another time line, the chains might be part of a clockwork construction, part of a giant and elaborate mechanism that powered the ships across the black ocean. In this world, however, in his world now, Bueralan knew that the chains belonged to slavers. When the ships left Gtara, the chains would be thrust back into the holds, and men, women and children would be attached to each joint. The crew would thrust the chains and the people into the dark below the decks where they would huddle inside for the months it took to cross Leviathan's Blood to Gogair.

Jao, the ship that had taken them to and from Leviathan's End, had once been used to carry slaves. Zean had known the moment that they stepped on it.

Bueralan had said—

'I haven't seen ships like this for a long time.' Kaze came up behind him now. She was dressed in dark leather pants and a dark, stained leather shirt that was studded with iron at the wrists and shoulders. In addition, she had a long sword on her hip, a weight she carried comfortably. 'I had almost hoped they had stopped being used.'

'But not the trade itself?' he asked.

'I am too old for that.' She took hold of *Glafanr*'s rail as water sprayed up. 'There is a great wealth to be made in the exploitation of others.'

Bueralan smiled ruefully.

'I know how it sounds,' the god-touched woman said. 'It would be easier for you if I said that I was lured to sleep by the sound of human misery, would it not?' She took off her glasses and, with a piece of cloth, began to clean them. 'Some days, I think it would be easier for me, as well. I would not have to ask if my guilt was mine, or if it was simply weakness and regret within me for all that I have done.'

He did not want to respond to her words, not now. 'I thought you were going to stay with the horses,' he said instead.

'Se'Saera wants us all on deck.' As she spoke, Bueralan saw Zilt emerge from below, his deformed soldiers with him. Taela and Se'Saera followed. 'She wants us all to be present when she meets the Keepers of the Divine,' Kaze added.

'I wouldn't have thought she needed a show of strength.' The last to emerge was Samuel Orlan.

'You heard what happened to Zilt.' She nodded ahead. 'Is that them at the end of the dock?'

The wooden planks were empty of men and women, just as the ships and chains were, until the dock touched the land. There, and only there, waited a group of men and women.

'Yes,' he said. 'I recognize some. The one in the multicoloured robes is called Kaqua.'

'Which one is Aelyn Meah?'

'I don't see her.'

Kaze made a sound of disapproval.

'You would make the same sound if she stood there,' Bueralan said.

'I imagine so.' She hooked her clean glasses back over her ears. 'Long ago I learned that her kind are worthless.'

Glafanr gently bumped against the dock and a heavy rope was thrown over the side. One of the god-touched soldiers followed it down, to tie it securely to the dock.

The gangway followed and, as it was lowered to the dock, Kaze touched Bueralan's arm. He had not responded to her last comment, and he thought, for a moment, that she was inviting him to do so; but instead she was, much like a tutor, directing him to the line that had formed behind her new god. At the head of the line was Aela Ren, but he did not stand beside Se'Saera. Zilt stood by her side, while behind him – and before Ren and the others – waited his two deformed soldiers. For a moment, Bueralan thought there was symbolism in it, but he soon corrected himself. Orlan was right: Ren needed a god to define him. From a god, he took certainty and absoluteness, a sense of place and definition that Bueralan had seen in Onaedo. To her, Baar was gone, and his absence was a betrayal, but in his absence she was still defined by him. In that, she offered a stark contrast to those around him, a sudden insight into the blind need of the Innocent and his soldiers, into the desire of Kaze to care for Taela, into Ai Sela's captaincy of a ship that needed no captain, and the others, whose names and faces he had learned over the last months at sea.

Wordlessly, Bueralan joined the line. He took his place behind Samuel Orlan and Taela, and he did so alone.

An Unfinished Divinity

'Once I was fit to move, Kaqua ordered the Keepers to a small town called Gtara in Leera. I do not remember much of how we got there. I believe we walked. But because of the attempts I had made on my own life, I had been heavily wrapped in Kaqua's will. I have only flashes of the journey: a swamp here, a pair of crows there. There was some conflict when we arrived, but not much.'

Had Kaqua been in contact with Se'Saera? I asked.

'To my mind it was constant,' Aelyn replied. 'He was not Faithful, but he would speak to her regularly.

'He was unwavering in his belief that the god would show him how to ascend from his mortal body.' Here, her tone changed. A quality close to embarrassment emerged. 'Even I believed it. Under Kaqua's influence, the desire to be completely divine had come to consume me. I remember, on the day Se'Saera arrived at Gtara, looking around me at the sudden, dirty world I where found myself, and thinking that when I was divine, I would repair all that I saw before me.'

—Onaedo, *Histories, Year 1029*

1.

It was the sight of Aelyn Meah that Bueralan could not turn away from in Gtara.

He was the last to step off *Glafanr*, the last to leave the recently rebuilt dock that ran into the port, but he was the first to look away from Se'Saera and the Keepers and see the woman who had once led them. He found her in the middle of the barbed-wire pens that sat in the centre of the town, surrounded by Faaishan men and women. Trees at the edge of the town had been felled to provide posts for the pens and they had an unfinished, rough quality that Aelyn could have hurled to the side easily, but did not. Instead, she sat in the middle of it, the mud of the pen around the torn trousers she wore, her face so still that the saboteur thought, at first, that she had been turned to stone.

He had seen Aelyn Meah half a dozen times before. Each time, it had been from afar, from a seat in the theatres where she gave her public lectures. The talks had been held in the twisting white building that the Keepers called the Enclave, which stood in Yeflam's capital, Nale. It was there that he had seen some of the other Keepers – Kaqua the Pauper, Mequisa the Bard and a handful of others – but he had not heard them speak. He had gone to hear her, to hear one of the people who had been responsible for the Five Kingdoms, and who had in turn been part of the creation of Ooila. Each time he heard her speak, he was impressed by her awareness of her place in the world, and the influence that she had in it.

He saw none of that now. She appeared to have been stripped of her sense of self, much in the way that the men and women soon to be sold as slaves had been stripped of their identities.

'Do you see these people?' Se'Saera said as she approached the pen. 'I was like them, once. I was blind to the world around me.'

'But no more?' It was Kaqua who spoke. He was a tall, sonorously voiced black man who wore a faded multicoloured robe. It had been he who had stepped forwards to greet Se'Saera when she arrived. He had bowed to the god and said, in his particularly strange voice, that he and the Keepers were pledged to Se'Saera's reign. 'Do you now see the whole world,' the Pauper continued, 'as your parents did?'

'Not completely,' the god admittedly easily. She listened to the Keeper's words with half an ear, it seemed. Once he had finished she had walked past him. 'I see the future in snippets, in pieces that I must put together into a whole.' The slavers who had taken over the town stood around her in silence. They were the rough men and women with no uniform dress, but who had been lined up against the houses of Gtara like children at a school, regardless. 'I know more of the present,' the god continued. 'Since my name was given to me, and to the world, I have heard the voices of many. I hear prayers. I hear curses. I hear conversations that are neither. In just the past week, for example, one of my Faithful was killed in Vaeasa. He was a man of some importance, but another man had him stripped naked, and strapped him to a chair. What followed had a certain instructional element in it, but was not pleasant. My name was used by both men for the three hours that the conversation took place. At the same time, I heard my name said in Yeflam, in Gogair and in Ooila. I even heard the prayers of my Faithful in battle. It has been a strange and exhilarating change in my existence.'

'I look forward to sharing such a life with you,' Kaqua said.

'I am sure that you do.' She reached out to one of the slaves, a young olive-skinned boy. He could not be any older than thirteen, Bueralan thought. 'But first, we have much to discuss. Have you done to Aelyn what you have done to the slavers?'

'She has been very agitated since her brother died. I have had to keep her subdued so that she did not harm herself. The slavers simply lacked a proper respect.'

'Respect,' she repeated, as if tasting the word. 'Is that why you gave up Yeflam? Why you drove away my general and his soldiers?'

'I am afraid that was Aelyn,' he said, the strange tone in his voice suddenly magnified. 'We could do little to stop her.'

'You promised your home to me.'

'Did you still want it?' he asked. 'After all, you ordered your creatures to attack. We thought that you might have changed your mind after what happened at the trial.'

'Why do you think you can question me?' Her tone was mild, but as she said it, Aela Ren and his soldiers began to spread out around the Keepers. 'You are not my equal,' Se'Saera said. 'Do not think that you are.'

'Of course not.' The note in the Pauper's voice seemed to skip a beat, Bueralan thought. 'It was simply an honest question asked by a loyal subject,' he said, returning to it. 'You would have the right to destroy it after what had happened to you.'

In the middle of the pen, Aelyn Meah raised her head.

'I do not wish to destroy Yeflam. If I did, the words of Lor Jix would be given authority and they would be used against me. But if Yeflam is mine, if it is one of the capitals of my Faithful, then the words must be no more than that. Your failure to see that has forced me to enlist others to repair what you did.' Se'Saera lifted the cloth from the boy's eyes. The sockets were damaged, as if he had, until recently, been clawing at the injuries. 'Do you not feel the need to apologize to me?'

'I do,' he said. 'The failure was ours, and mine in particular. I thought that I had a stronger control on Aelyn. I thought – as we all did – that her hatred for her brother was something she would not resist. But instead of strengthening my hold on her, it weakened it substantially. I believe it was due, in part, to the presence of Jae'le and Eidan. She has never stopped loving the latter, and when he sided against her, it challenged my control.'

'But she still killed Qian, yes?'

'She did.'

'He was the strongest of them.'

'They are all strong,' he said.

In the pen, the boy Se'Saera held gave a slight shudder. 'Shhh,' the god murmured, as a thin strand of black appeared. It ran in a taut line from one end of the socket to the other. It appeared first in the right eye, then in the left. 'I had a vision of Yeflam,' she said. 'It came to me before my name was first said. In it, my name was obscured, but was reaching to me. It felt as if it had been hidden for thousands and thousands of years but was now rising towards me. It came from deep within Leviathan's Blood, as if it was the heartbeat of the world, but I could not make it out clearly. It left a great apprehension in me. Now I think that it may have been fear. Fear because the ruins conveyed the idea that destruction was close to me, close to the truth of who I was.' The strand in each of the boy's empty eye sockets had begun to spread and grow while she spoke, until pitch-black orbs filled the vacant sockets. 'Tell me,' Se'Saera said, releasing the boy's head. 'Tell me, Kaqua, when Qian died, was he was plunged into Leviathan's Blood?'

'Yes,' he said quietly. 'We waited for some time to see if he surfaced.'

'You should have searched. Jae'le has done that every day for him.' Se'Saera ran her hand under the boy's chin, before tilting it up to her. 'I used to have eyes like the ones I gave you,' she said to him. 'I made them myself. They could see the world as I do, when I wished. They could see the dead. You will be able to do that now. You mustn't be frightened by them. They are here for me. They are mine and they will not hurt you. I told that to the eyes I made before, as well, but they were deceptive. I thought that there was only anguish in them, not betrayal. The mistake was mine. I was not yet as formed as I am now. What I created was not truly mine. That is why my eyes are mine and you will be the carrier of them. It will be only for a short time and then you will be free. That is my promise to you. Do you understand that.'

The boy nodded once, but did not speak.

'You will take my eyes to the Mountains of Ger. You will be looking for a man. My eyes will recognize him. One of General Zilt's soldiers will take you there and protect you.' She released the boy's chin and turned to the blond man. 'One who runs fast.'

Zilt turned and, as he did, there emerged from the trees around the town, from the trees that led deep into the marshes of Leera, just under three dozen hulking, deformed men and women. One left its position and approached. It had long, dark hair wrapped around four pieces of sharp metal that sat on top of its head. It bore no resemblance to any gender due to all its ritual scarring and piercing, but the haunt that stretched across its body in a distorted echo of the flesh was, Bueralan believed, female. Yet, as frighting as it appeared, it lifted the boy from the pen gently. After a slight bow to Zilt, and a deeper one to Se'Saera, it began to run from the town, holding the boy in its arms.

'Now.' Se'Saera lifted the wire loop that held the pen gate shut and entered. The blind slaves stepped from her path, as if they could see her, but it was Aelyn whom Bueralan watched. She met the god's approach with steady, sad eyes. 'You have been underestimated,' Se'Saera said. 'I can see that now. The years have allowed for familiarity to become contempt. It is a lesson that I will take as my own after today. But before then, tell me, Aelyn: did you know that your brother was not dead when he fell?'

'Please, Se'Saera, allow me to ask your questions,' the Pauper said, rushing after her into the slave pen. 'It is easier—'

Se'Saera's hand rose to silence him. 'Aelyn,' she repeated, not turning away from her. 'Did you know?'

'He cannot die,' she said, the words forcing themselves out.

The god's hand plunged into Kaqua's chest.

2.

Lord Elan Wagan, who had been the Lord of the Spine until, with a tragic sense of inevitability, he became the Lord of the Ghosts, did not acknowledge his stepdaughter.

He sat outside his small tent, folded into an old, but well-maintained wheelchair. In the fullness of his health, he had been a tall, handsome man, and the echoes of that still remained, even though his muscles had wasted to such an extent that the bones of his long limbs were revealed starkly. He no longer talked, though he did still make noises: Eilona heard him hum a tune she did not recognize and mutter words she could not identify. She did not know what caused him to make those sounds, or if he was responding to anything at all, for he did not react to the presence or absence of his carers. He took what was put in his hands and ate what was put in his mouth, but the black cloth across his empty eyes was always turned towards the sky, regardless. It might have been nothing more than his memories, Eilona thought as she sat beside him. If so, she hoped that the mix of keft and bjir he was given every two hours allowed him pleasant memories.

Her stepfather had been the first casualty of Se'Saera's War. Before anyone had known about the new god, Elan Wagan had responded to the raids on Mireea by riding to Leera. He returned blind and, with the loss of his eyes, he had lost his self as well. Eilona's mother sent her a letter when it happened and she returned, with Laena, to Mireea.

She had cried when she first saw him, but when he began to scream during the night, she realized that a part of her world had been removed. Her stepfather had always treated her as his daughter. He had never once seen her as anything else, and in her visits home he had done much to mend the relationship between Eilona and her mother.

She did not know what terrorized her stepfather at night. Neither did Reila. 'I suspect that his injuries were inflicted at night,' the small silver-haired healer explained to her in Mireea. 'If it is true, there is little I can do to help him. There are some actions a man can simply not return from.'

Eilona sat in her small, cramped office, the walls around her surrounded by jars and small plants. 'What took his eyes?' she asked.

'No knife or finger. They were not removed by any implement that I know of. It is as if he was simply born without them.'

Or, Eilona thought now, as if they were removed by a god.

Did Se'Saera tell him that when he first met her? The afternoon's sun was starting to set out on the ocean, the scudding clouds and light mingling over it like burn marks. How the Lord of the Spine met a god was, perhaps, the real question to ask. Eilona knew he would not have approached her with respect, but did Se'Saera appear when he entered? The god would have looked like a child then, or so Eilona had been told. She could imagine a child standing on a street, surrounded by the buildings the Leerans were stripping to build siege towers and catapults. Her stepfather would have ridden along a road surrounded by men and women pulling down houses, tearing up floors and breaking roofs apart. She could see him on the back of his horse, approaching the new god.

Eilona loved her stepfather, but she was not blind to his faults.

He was vain, but his vanity was not one born from his looks, or even his intellect, but rather his masculinity. Now that she was older, Eilona recognized that he had always defined a part of himself through his physical prowess. He had been a captain in the Mireean Guard before he and Muriel Wagan married and, after, he had attempted to be both lord and captain. In hindsight, Eilona could see how such a role was never tenable, but after her mother employed Aned Heast to be the Captain of the Spine – a title she made just for him – her stepfather had responded by spending a fortune on armour, weapons and honorary ranks.

'How is he today?' Muriel Wagan asked as she approached. She wore a dress made from green, red and black, the edges of its sleeves and hem frayed. 'I am told he had a good night's sleep.'

He had awoken only once, Eilona heard. 'I was told the same,' she said. 'He seems content. I think he likes the sun on his face.'

'He always has.'

Behind Muriel Wagan came Caeli. The guard did not spare a glance, or say hello to Eilona, but rather walked inside her father's tent.

'How did it go with the Saan and Lian Alahn?' she asked.

'Difficult.' Her mother kissed her stepfather's forehead as Caeli re-emerged with a chair. She set it wordlessly next to Eilona. 'But in three days, they will begin to go over the Mountain of Ger,' the Lady of the Ghosts said, taking the seat.

'That doesn't sound like a difficult conversation.'

'No, but Miat Dvir wanted a young woman to accompany him. After she told him no, things grew heated.'

Eilona was lost, but it was Caeli who answered. 'You had asked too much of Ayae already,' the guard said. 'She has her own mind. She was always going to use it sooner rather than later.'

'You weren't supposed to become friends with her,' Muriel Wagan said. There was no rancour in her voice when she spoke.

'You were meant to watch her and learn about her. You were supposed to help me with her.'

'I needed a new friend,' the guard replied blandly. 'Besides, I didn't push her towards Aelyn Meah, or her brothers—'

'Thank you.' Her interruption was sour. 'Anyway,' Eilona's mother said to her, 'managing that was the difficulty of the morning. It was made harder when my guard took her side.'

Her stepfather had never liked Caeli. It was there, Eilona knew, that the first seeds of what would see her leave Mireea had been planted.

Caeli was only a few years younger than her, but their childhoods had little in common. If Eilona had been raised in the heart of all the privilege that could be gained in Mireea, then Caeli had grown up in the veins that kept that luxury alive. Her parents had been bakers. When their daughter expressed an interest in becoming a mercenary, they sought out Aned Heast and asked him for advice. He had taken over Caeli's education and, under his tutelage, the teenage girl was taught swords, knives, horses and all the various other skills that one needed to survive the profession of war. Once she had finished her training, Heast assigned her as the personal guard to Eilona's mother.

Elan Wagan resisted and Eilona took his side, as much to spite her mother as to support him.

The event that led to Caeli's appointment was the death of Joerl. He had guarded Eilona's mother, father, stepfather and her, since her mother's first marriage. Joerl had been a huge, brown-bearded white man whose downfall began when he was caught selling information about trade to merchants. Her mother and stepfather had approached him about it but upon hearing the accusation, Joerl had announced his innocence publicly and called upon the Captain of the Spine to recant. Heast had not, of course, and Joerl's disgrace went from private to public, before it ended in the public shame of suicide.

'His wife found him.' Her stepfather was sitting alone in his office. Eilona had come to find him after hearing the news. His face, she remembered, had been one of grief. 'He had cut open his stomach with a dagger.' He took a deep, shuddering breath. 'I told him not to challenge Heast. I told him he would not show mercy. I said he was not a man like me. But he did not listen, and now we will have a young woman of Heast's choice thrust into our midst. A young spy to report to him.'

Caeli had moved into the Keep after the funeral. In hindsight, Eilona knew that everything she did came from within Eilona herself, and not the other woman, but that did not change what had happened. She spoke against Caeli's appointment in public. In the midst of it, she realized that what she was doing was no more than hurting someone. She could still remember the starkness of the moment when she recognized that, the hollowness of it. But it did not stop her. She spoke about Caeli to trade representatives, to friends of the family, to other soldiers. She attacked Caeli's family, her inexperience, her looks, everything that she could. She became so vitriolic that at one point her stepfather drew her aside and counselled her against what she was doing, but it was too late.

Caeli's parents were assaulted in their home. The two men who did it were part of a fringe group in Mireea, supporting a cause Eilona could not even remember. They were within a breath of killing Caeli's father, having tied her mother up, when the guard came home. One of the men survived long enough to tell Captain Heast why they had done it, for whom, and the public outcry that followed was one Eilona knew she deserved.

'Things will be changing,' her mother said, beside her, drawing her attention back to the now. Before them, fires were being lit in the camp. 'Xrie and the Yeflam Guard will be leaving with Dvir.

Captain Mills will also be going with half our force. I had to commit Kal Essa and the Brotherhood, as well. The force that remains here is to be led by Captain Oake. She is Xrie's second in the Yeflam Guard.'

'Why is she not going?' Eilona asked.

'Her right arm was badly broken in the evacuation of Yeflam. From what I understand, it hasn't completely healed.'

'She put off having the arm set properly,' Caeli said. 'Said that others had greater needs. A week after it was originally set, it had to be broken and reset again.'

'Unfortunately,' her mother continued, 'Oake has more loyalty to Lian Alahn than Xrie does. That may become an issue later, but at the moment it is not. Our immediate concern is to ensure that you arrive in the Spires of Alati without incident.'

The Spires was one of the remaining cities of Yeflam. It was a city primarily of universities and schools. 'Why would I be going there?' Eilona asked, not bothering to hide her surprise. 'I have things to do here. Mother, you and I haven't even discussed the letter you sent me in Pitak.'

Muriel Wagan gave a small wave of her hand, unconcerned. 'None of the bankers agreed to do it, did they?'

'No, but—' Eilona hesitated. 'You were signing significant amounts of capital over to Lian Alahn. I was told that it was land you had spent most of Mireea's capital buying. If the deal went through, you would be bankrupt.'

'I needed his support,' the Lady of the Ghosts said without pause. 'But if he asks, it would be best if you told him the bankers were working on the deeds.' She sighed. 'I know how it sounds. It sounds like every bad business practice I have argued against. I even know that if it goes through, Mireea will cease to exist – and Alahn will push for it to go through for that exact reason. It is why you must go to the Spires. You have to argue for us while people still remember who we are.'

'I'm not a negotiator, Mother.'

'You sell yourself short. You will be a fine envoy to see who will help us.'

'Help us do what?'

'Make a new home. All I need is a city. Just one city. From there I can resettle our people from the Spine of Ger. Once I have that, I will be able to cut my ties from Alahn and gain some autonomy. But to do that, I am going to need the support from the governance in the other cities. I have to convince them to support the idea that Yeflam can be a collection of city states, rather than one nation under one rule, as Alahn wants.'

'But—'

'No buts. There simply aren't buts. We have an opportunity here, that is all. If it slips past us, Mireea will cease to exist. We will lose who we are, if we do not succeed. I mean we, as well. Right now the number of people I can rely upon is small. I need you to do this for me. For your family. For Mireea.'

'How will I even get to the Spires?' she asked. 'I've heard they sink any boats from here.'

'Olcea will take you,' Muriel Wagan said. 'She will pilot that wreck you arrived on. Caeli will go with you, as well. She'll keep you safe in the Spires.'

Eilona resisted the urge to look at the guard, to measure the coldness in her gaze. 'Will I need to be kept safe?'

'Probably.' Her mother smiled, but there was something tired in it. 'After all, your contact in the city will be one of Lian Alahn's sons. After he fails to buy your loyalty, I expect he will try to kill you.'

3.

'Kill them,' Se'Saera said. 'But leave Aelyn Meah.'

Her arm was still in the chest of Kaqua, but it had gone so far through him that her hand reached out the other side, a gory trophy on display for all.

The image burned into Bueralan's mind as the world around him became impossibly bright. Blind, he took a step backwards and dropped to one knee. He could hear sounds around him: shouts, grunts, sharp snaps and, strangely, a melody. The latter tugged at him, but its pull was not consistent, as if the tune was slippery and elusive to the singer. When he opened his eyes, blotches of dark swam in front of him . . . but through them, he could see the shapes of people and could hear voices crying out. 'To the left,' a woman shouted. 'To the buildings,' she cried again. To a defensive position, Bueralan heard her unspoken command. There had been nineteen Keepers, but now that Kaqua was dead and Aelyn was unable to support them, there were only seventeen.

Something bit Bueralan's hand – the one that was pressed into the ground to help him keep balance – and, startled, he flicked his wrist; but as he did, he felt another bite. He blinked rapidly and rose. The song continued, but its call was even less compelling to him now, to such a point that he found it fading from his mind, a fact helped by the teeming mass on the ground, the ants and beetles that were emerging from the muddy ground in such numbers that the single step he took was as if he stood now on a new surface, one entirely alive.

A buzzing sound accompanied it. It came from high in the sky and Bueralan lifted his head to see a swarm of wasps descending.

'*Now!*' He heard the woman's voice again but this time he saw her: slim, black-haired, olive-skinned. She wore a dark red robe. 'Mequisa—'

Whatever she thought to say was lost beneath the screams of the slavers who began running towards the slave pen, their weapons drawn.

Bueralan's attention fell not on the new attackers, but on Se'Saera and Aelyn Meah, who remained in the pen. Kaqua's body had been thrown to the ground and his blood stained the white robe that the god wore. Yet she presented no threat to Aelyn. She appeared to be speaking to her as Aela Ren's soldiers began to counter-attack. The swarm started to break apart as it fell upon the god-touched. Everything slowed for Bueralan and he felt as if he was watching the battle unfold in still images.

He saw the Innocent dart forwards and plunge into the depths of the Keepers, Zilt at his side.

He saw Kaze turn towards Taela, the god-touched woman reaching out a hand for the other woman, who had fallen into the confused insects on the ground.

He saw Taela push it away, heave herself up.

He saw slavers crash into the spot where Samuel Orlan stood with the god-touched. He could not see the cartographer, but the slavers fell beneath the blades of Aela Ren's soldiers.

He saw the Innocent bear down on the black-haired woman, his old sword plunging deep into her stomach, a scream erupting as he did. But the scream did not come from her: instead, it burst from the mass of insects on the ground and in the sky.

Bueralan had never heard such a sound before. It echoed a human voice so much that he half expected the wasps to remake their swarm and to form into a figure. He saw Zilt leap into the air, a pair of knives appearing in his hands. With a twist, he brought both down into the skull of the woman . . . and as he did, the scream died. Another flash of light burst, but it was weaker than the first. When he opened his eyes, Bueralan found himself staring at Se'Saera and Aelyn, who had not moved from the pen. For a reason he could not quite articulate, Bueralan found the sight unsettling, and he turned, just as a sword came rushing at him.

He swept it aside easily and the bearded white Keeper in stained leathers who held the blade continued past him, as if he had not intended to kill Bueralan at all.

The man took two steps, then stopped.

Ahead of him, Zilt's creatures had come out of the forest and now formed a ring of horrific, mutilated flesh around the fighting.

There would be no escape through that, Bueralan knew, just as the Keeper realized it. Even as the Keeper turned back to Bueralan, the saboteur found himself hoping that the other man would take the risk. He did not want him to turn around, did not want him to raise his sword towards him, and to lunge.

Bueralan parried the attack easily. Beneath his feet, ants and beetles crunched, but he kept his gaze on the man before him, on the emptiness in his gaze.

It was a look Bueralan had seen before. A captain in a barracks had lifted her sword after she had returned to find her soldiers had deserted her, and that only saboteurs waited. A lord had marched out alone onto a battlefield. A teenage boy had picked up a crossbow and swung it on Bueralan the day an army invaded his town. Not a single one of them expected to live. Not one of them measured the life they had in anything but heartbeats and breaths. Yet, though they were reduced to such a limited time, not one of them contemplated surrender.

The Keeper moved quickly, pushing Bueralan backwards, pushing him into the people who were fighting behind him, into the battle that was quickly turning into a slaughter. The saboteur took three steps back, before he stepped to his left and slashed outwards with his sword. The Keeper's blade caught it, but as it did, Bueralan pushed on, and before the other man could pull free, he jabbed his free hand forwards. His fingers grabbed hold of the Keeper's leather jerkin and, with a sudden show of strength, Bueralan wrenched the man off balance and snapped his head forwards. He smashed into the nose of the Keeper.

It was not a pretty attack. It lacked the elegance, or the skill, that a blow from Aela Ren would have had. The brutality of it, however, caught the Keeper off-guard. He grunted, stumbled, and did not notice the second step that Bueralan took, the step that allowed the saboteur to drive his knee into the Keeper's groin. At that, the man wrenched himself from Bueralan's grasp, but as he did, his feet tangled, and he went face-first into the mud and insects. Bueralan's sword followed, plunging down into his back, cutting through the immortal man's spine with an ease that he would have not thought possible.

The Keeper tried to move, but Bueralan, his foot on the man's back, pulled his sword out and then, as if it were an axe, hammered it downwards.

4.

'Your signature is required at the bottom, beside the Queen's.'

'This is written in Ooilan,' Heast said, after he took the parchment. The delicately transcribed words were a mix of black and red letters that read from right to left. Some he could recognize, others he could not. 'I don't read the language well.'

Tjevi Minala, the middle-aged, brown-skinned banker from Zoum who sat across from him, gave a small bow. 'Of course,' he said, from deep in the emerald-coloured leather of his chair, 'my apologies.' Behind him, a large window overlooking Vaeasa was surrounded by shelves filled with ledgers, books, scrolls and folios. When Heast had entered, the small, neat man, whose comb-over was as elegant as any he had seen, had pulled a folder from the collection and had laid it out before him. 'I have had a translation prepared,' Minala said now. He handed over a sheet of paper to Heast this time. 'The translation was made by one of my employees, but it was approved by the late Zeala Fe. You will find that she signed both the original and the copy for you.'

The second sheet had the same, delicate penmanship as the first. The language, from what Heast had been able read of the Ooilan, matched the official tone.

'Does something bother you, Captain?' the banker asked.

'No,' he said, aware that he had barely shown an emotion. 'I just read that Safeen Re would be taking the Queen back to Ooila. I wondered if she would require the Queen's Guard to help with the journey.'

'I do not believe so, but if she did, I am afraid it would be quite impossible.' He paused and made an graceful wave of his hand. 'Forgive me, I have presumed that you knew the intimate details of an Ooilan queen's life. I try not to make such assumptions, but the history you two shared . . . I digress, I see. It is sufficient to say that should the Queen's Guard return with Ms Re, they would be expected to take their own lives. They would be expected to begin their next life alongside the Queen, to ensure her safety.'

Heast would have said that he knew a lot about the Ooilan Queens, but he was surprised that he did not know that. He would have much to learn about his new soldiers, it appeared. 'Everything seems in order,' he said, reaching for the quill in front of him. 'I do have another question, if you do not mind?'

'Certainly.'

'Why the paper and the parchment?'

The banker offered him a rueful smile that revealed a golden tooth. 'All official documents must be written on parchment, but for copies, I am offered some choice. As my life advances before me, I have found that I prefer the destruction of trees, rather than animals, for words. Many have told me it is a sign of a weak stomach.'

'I prefer paper, myself.' He handed the sheets back. 'It is my childhood, I suppose. Paper was more expensive then.'

'It was similarly so for mine, but the rise of paper mills has made it much cheaper. In fact, I heard one scholar suggest that the rise of your profession's fictions helped with that. They drove the demand that allows for more and more mills to be financed.'

'At least the books are good for something,' Heast said.

'I have always enjoyed them, myself. Are you not a fan?'

'No.'

'Perhaps I would feel the same, if others wrote books about bankers. Still.' Minala dug into his files and pulled out a small strip of cardboard. A piece of blue twine led to a brass key. He held it out to Heast and said, 'In the last weeks of her life, the Queen purchased a warehouse for you.'

'What is in it?' he asked, taking the key.

'Items that a man in your profession will appreciate,' the other man said. He paused and, for a moment, drummed his fingers on his folder. 'May I speak freely for a moment, Captain?' he asked.

Heast nodded his permission.

'I fear that you are currently under the impression that your arrival in Vaeasa was unexpected,' the banker said, 'but I do not believe it was. I was called by the Queen to her estate over a month ago. In the very first meeting I had with her, there was no doubt in her mind as to whom she would be leaving her wealth. I will freely admit that I was concerned about this on a professional level. My outpost here in Vaeasa is not the most decorated post for a banker, and I have had my disgraces before. I shall not bore you with the details, but they were enough that I did consider telling the Queen that I would not continue with the work. I was – and still am – sure that I am the first and only banker she approached, and at the time, I simply thought she would find another to replace me. One, perhaps, comfortable with new scandal. And yet, as if the spies in my office could sense my doubt and predict my choices, I was summoned the following day by the Lord of Faaisha himself. I was assured that the Captain of Refuge would soon be visiting Vaeasa. I was also told, by the Lord himself, that he would personally ensure my safety, should there be any fallout from the Queen's choices.'

'Did he put that in writing for you?' Heast asked.

'Alas' – Minala spread his hands – 'he did not.'

Slowly, the Captain of Refuge rose from the chair. 'You and I will just have to stand in the same field and wait to see if it is barren or fruitful, then.'

Outside the banker's office Anemone waited in a small, but beautifully furnished room. She waited until the two of them were outside before she asked what had happened. He told her about the contract. The narrow lane the banker's office was in fell behind them. Heast said that the neat penmanship had officially said what the First Queen of Ooila had said when they had met her: they were to kill the Innocent. Afterwards, they were to aid Illate in a non-violent revolution. There was no stipulation of time frame for the latter, but a failure to engage the Illate people in a meaningful way would end with the contract being terminated. The bankers of Zoum would have their people monitor that, he told Anemone, after she asked how anyone would know.

'The bankers?' she repeated.

'They have a huge network of men and women who perform a number of tasks for them,' he said. 'We'll probably never see who reports to them.'

Anemone was silent for a moment, digesting what he said. 'What I don't understand, is why the Queen is leaving you this money,' she said, after a moment. 'To do so must be a great insult to the other Queens.'

'It must,' Heast agreed.

The streets of Vaeasa unfolded around them, the afternoon's sun sitting behind dark clouds. There would be storms soon, the Captain of Refuge thought. Maybe before the shattered sun sank into darkness. The threat of bad weather was much like the questions Anemone had asked about the First Queen. He could see the storm of the answers approaching, but he was powerless against them. He knew that the remaining Queens of Ooila would see what Zeala Fe did and react in fury. The wealth she had bequeathed to Refuge was of such a scale that it would have consequences for her province in

Ooila. A province that, from what he understood, needed to be rebuilt. Without the money, the Queen who replaced Zeala Fe – whoever, or however that was managed – would find her province's finances in ruin. She would have to rely on the other Queens. She might even increase the pool of people she took from Illate to compensate for her losses.

Truthfully, Heast could only view what the First Queen had done as a gesture to her fellow monarchs, a final indelicate motion that left them with no illusions as to what she thought of them. With it, she had ensured that there would be no easy years for Heast and Refuge once this war had finished.

If, he corrected himself. The Kingdoms of Faaisha were turning into a world that was created from the word 'if' for him. Tuael had let it hang in the air when they had met, and it returned now. If the war could be finished. If he and Refuge could defeat not just General Waalstan, but the new god, Se'Saera, and her soldiers, led by Aela Ren, the Innocent.

The warehouse opened by the key Heast held was in the eastern half of Vaeasa, in a series of streets defined by square stone buildings whose doors had painted numbers on them. The roads that they flanked were wide, and along them moved carts, drawn by both horse and ox. Heast and Anemone made their way through the afternoon's bustle, passing carts loaded with building materials, food and armaments. Most of the doors the carts stopped before revealed long, shadowed worlds of solid shapes that hinted at the organized, catalogued world of a city that was prepared for not just a long war, but a siege as well. The warehouse that the key opened was beyond those, at the end of a road with little sunlight.

The padlock was thick, solid, but well oiled. It fell open and Heast cracked the door open. Like a bright burning eye, a partly shuttered lantern shone from within.

'Lord Tuael,' the Captain of Refuge said, easing through the door. 'I hope we haven't kept you waiting.'

'One day, I will see you surprised.' The Lord of Faaisha sat on the top of a square crate at the front of the warehouse, the lantern next to him. He held a book in his hand. 'I worked very hard to be here ahead of you,' he said, closing it and placing it in his lap.

'You've worked hard to be ahead of me since I arrived,' Heast said. Behind him, Anemone pulled the door shut. 'Is there more light in here?'

Tuael lifted his right hand and clicked his fingers. A moment later, a dozen lamps flared, their shutters drawn back to reveal the warehouse and the soldiers throughout. They numbered over thirty and they stood on crates, in carts and on the ground. Each of them was armed.

'You were expected,' Tuael said, a bored note in his voice. 'I wanted you to be here to advise the marshals against the Leerans. I did not think you would come, so I sent Lok to you. He surprised me when he drew the symbol of Refuge, but I thought it was a private code between the two of you. Refuge had ceased to exist nearly thirty years ago, after all. I certainly did not expect you to kill Iata, take his soldiers and rebuild Refuge before you came here.'

Heast pushed back the lid on one of the crates and found it filled with leather shirts, each of them dyed black. 'Is that why you gave me to the First Queen?'

'I had little choice. The other Lords could not accept you after you killed Iata. What message would that send to the people of Faaisha? they asked.'

'It would have been difficult to explain why your marshals were so incompetent.' Heast left the crate and began to walk towards a cart. Behind him, Anemone followed, while the Lord began to walk parallel to them along the crates. 'You could have saved the people in Maosa.'

'They lived a lot longer than we expected,' Tuael admitted. 'After Faet Cohn lost Celp, the other marshals argued that we should treat that part of the kingdom like a gangrenous limb. Cohn himself led the argument. It is not so difficult to see why, now.'

'Waalstan never had the soldiers to hold that much land. Not securely, at any rate. It is why he split his forces up and scattered them.'

'Whereas now he is too deeply embedded to push out easily. Whatever the past, that is the challenge we now face. In this regard, however, Marshal Cohn will provide us with some help.'

On the cart stood a soldier, one of the women Heast had seen in The Undertow. He motioned for her to grab one side of a crate.

'After Cohn's death,' Jye Tuael continued, 'I had my warlocks pick through his soul, and his estate. They're still doing that, but they've already pulled out a number of things. A blank copy of *The Eternal Kingdom* held a number of scraps of paper, for example. Coordinates, for the most part, to where various outposts lay.'

Inside the crate were a series of spears, each of them carefully packed, the ends wrapped in soft paper. Gently, Heast pulled back the edge of one, to reveal a steel tube attached to the end. It held, he knew, a mix of black powder and iron balls, the latter of which would burst out in a spray after the wick was lit. At the sight of it, the guard holding the lamp jerked back, and looked at the crates nearby, crates that she had stood calmly upon with a lantern.

Heast lifted one of the weapons.

'Tinalan fire lances,' the Lord of Faaisha said, impressed. 'The horror made by the Marble Royals. In the last five years they have become the world's new monster story. Have you seen one before?'

'A deserter from the Marble Palaces came through Mireea shortly after the lances became standard issue. For a few coins he would show you how it worked.' Heast turned the spear over in his hands, remembering the splintered boards into which he had unleashed pieces of metal, stone and glass. 'I wonder if Aela Ren and his soldiers have ever seen these in battle?'

'I believe the First Queen thought not.' Tuael tossed the book down from where he stood. 'These are the coordinates that we've managed to take from Cohn's notes. When you leave Vaeasa – when you leave Vaeasa by night with these weapons that Zeala Fe has left you – you would be best to start working through them. The marshals will be doing the same.'

'What happens if we run into each other?'

'Officially? You're being tolerated, but Cohn had friends.' He paused. 'Anemone?'

'Yes?' the witch replied, her tone, Heast thought, deceptively mild. 'What is it that I can do for you, Lord Tuael?'

'I offered you work before,' he said. 'I'll repeat the offer. My warlocks are breaking Cohn's spirit, but the task is hard, they tell me. The new god has a small awareness around it, and they constantly touch her. You and your grandmother would be a great assistance to them and to me.'

'As I said to you before, My Lord,' she said, while Heast gently returned the spear to the crate. 'I have other responsibilities.'

'Are they more important than the fate of Faaisha?'

'My Lord,' Anemone repeated, and this time, the insult of the two words was clear, 'I offer you and the other Lords of Faaisha no loyalty, because you have shown none to your people. I was raised in Maosa, your gangrenous limb. It was, I admit, a terrible place, but it need not have been. Not if you had recognized that it was part of your body. But you did not and because of that, I no longer recognize you, or any of the Lords, as being part of the body I exist within. Should you wish to contest that, should you wish to somehow bind me to your command because of some heritage of blood you think I have to you or this country, I can only say that my Lord does it at his own risk. I am no more or less than the Witch of Refuge now.'

5.

The Keepers of the Divine died in a battle that mirrored the one Bueralan fought. It was short, ugly and violent.

The saboteur did not raise his sword again. The Keepers could not reach cover and, without a defensive position, the numbers were against them. There was little for Bueralan to do but stand and watch. Watch them die as their powers failed to change the tide of the battle, as the god-touched tore into their ranks with a ferocity that was at times shocking.

'His name was Paelor,' Orlan said, as he approached. There was blood in the cartographer's beard, but the stain did not come from any injury he had received. Before he turned to Bueralan, he had dropped an axe among the bodies of the slavers. 'He was one of the younger Keepers,' the cartographer added.

'He tried to leave,' Bueralan said.

'They all should have done that.'

'I expected more of a fight from the Keepers of the Divine.'

'Against Ren and the god-touched?' Orlan scratched the dried blood in his beard. 'They are bad enough, but with Se'Saera here as well? They should have known better than to come to Gtara.'

Should they? Whatever lens the Keepers viewed the world through had been fragmented and cracked. Bueralan had always believed that it distorted their place in it and allowed them to believe that they were gods, a folly that was nakedly exposed now.

Raising his head, Bueralan gazed at Aelyn Meah. After the last of her Keepers fell, she had risen to her feet. She looked around the battlefield flatly, as if the reality of it was one that she had long suspected would come to pass. He half expected her to leave the pen she stood in, but she did not. Instead, Se'Saera left the slave pen and slowly approached each of the fallen Keepers.

No one spoke to her as she did this. It was as if they all understood that what they were witness to was an important ritual. Yet it was difficult for Bueralan to describe what that ritual was, for the new god did not touch, or reach out for the bodies in any way. She merely passed them, and in doing so, offered the faintest recognition of each of the dead.

After she had passed Bueralan and Orlan, the saboteur reached down and turned the Keeper over. He was drawn to the broken, bloody skull of Paelor, to a difference in the man's body that he could not quantify. It was difficult to describe, but it was clear to him that a quality Paelor had possessed was now absent. It was not as simple as the life of a man leaving him after he had died. Paelor was diminished beyond that, somehow. 'She took his power, didn't she?' Bueralan said as he rose. 'She is taking all their power.'

'She believes it is hers,' the cartographer said.

Ahead of him, Se'Saera headed back to the pen where Aelyn Meah waited. As if she had been summoned, Taela fell in beside her.

'Could they have actually been gods, then? I had always thought that they couldn't be,' Bueralan added quietly. 'I don't know why.'

'They were not like gods,' Orlan said. 'At least, they were not like the gods I read about. You will have to ask others we travel with for their recollections, and when you do, you will hear what I have heard and read. You will see how they lived a life, not as we do, of moments, but of time. It is in our new god, actually. She sees the fragments of time that we cannot. She sees the past, the present and the future, and she lives in those moments. She uses them to understand the world that we live in. No Keeper ever lived like that.'

He saw the god take Taela's arm in her own. 'Does that mean she doesn't have free will?' he asked.

'If you had asked these questions before we went to Ooila, we would be in a different place, now.'

'Would we?'

Orlan shrugged. 'I don't know,' he said. He added quietly, 'So much has changed.'

Divinity was not humanity. That much was clear to Bueralan. He had begun to suspect, as he watched Se'Saera and Taela approach Aelyn Meah, that to be divine was to be a vessel. It was to be a structure in which divinity could express itself. In many ways, it was akin to the power of royalty, or office, or rank: its ability to command was independent of the body that contained it, but it was the individual who held it that detailed its expression. Where that comparison failed was that the power of rule was a socially created one, enabled through generations of teaching. The power of the divine was, if not tangible, then actual, and was something that was gathered, much in the way that a farmer might harvest wheat or corn, and if that was the case, then it was possible that Se'Saera did not have as much freedom to express the power within her as the ruler of a nation, or the captain of a mercenary army.

But if Se'Saera had limited agency, then what of him? Bueralan had carried her name within himself. He did not know if it had been given to him when Ger had reached out to him in his sunken temple, nearly a year ago. To be god-touched, according to Orlan and Ren and the others whose company he was in, was to have your mortality hidden in time, to be safely secured until you had done enough of the god's work, or until it tired of you. Bueralan did not know what caused a god to be finished with his or her servant, but he knew that it was not a request that the god-touched made for him or herself.

'I had heard stories of you, Bueralan.' Lost in his thoughts, the saboteur had not seen Zilt's approach. Instead, he had been watching Se'Saera talk with Aelyn, watching Taela fall a step behind her, as she had done with the First Queen. Before him, the blond man nudged Paelor's body with the end of his boot. 'I had heard that you were something of a swordsman. A warrior. But this? This was ugly. Dirty, even.'

'I can't imagine that truly disappoints you,' he said.

'Do not think of me as a man who does not value skill. I strived for perfection in my last life and I strive for it now, in my new one.'

'And the thousands you killed before?' Orlan said cynically. 'They were just imperfect?'

'Racially, morally, religiously.' Zilt glanced at him. 'Much like you.'

'What about me?' the Innocent asked as he approached the three of them. 'Would you say the same?'

'No,' the other man said.

'But these men are my kin,' Ren continued. 'I am like them and they are like me. Should you view one as flawed, you must, therefore, view the other in the same light.'

'If I have offended you, I apologize.' Beyond him, in the pen, Bueralan's gaze was caught by a sudden movement. 'It was not my intent.'

'Taela—'

But he was too late: alone, unguarded, the woman who had been a Queen's Voice thrust a dagger into the neck of the new god.

The darkness that erupted from Se'Saera washed over not just Taela and Aelyn, but all those who stood in Gtara, as if it was suddenly enfolded in a whole sun of pitch blackness. Bueralan was one of the last to lose his sight, and because of that, he saw the shape that bloomed around Se'Saera, the body that was, itself, darkness.

He saw a horrific half-formed shape, a creation of nightmares, of a beast with more than one face. It was like nothing he had seen before.

But he knew what it was.

It was Se'Saera's true form.

6.

On the day that Ayae left the shore of Yeflam, a storm rushed in from Leviathan's Blood. It turned the camp into a series of muddy, churned-up lanes that mirrored her emotional state.

She struggled with her doubt, self-recrimination and frustration beneath the morning sun's leaked grey light. Out on the ocean, heavy clouds suggested another storm, but it did not stop people in the camp coming out and lining the makeshift streets to bid farewell to the men and women who would soon be led up the road to Mireea, through its ruins and onto the battlefields beyond. It was, Ayae thought, a sombre procession. The Mireean soldiers who joined Captain Mills at the edge of the camp were accompanied by their families and their friends. Men and women handed them tokens – trinkets, small carvings, pieces of cloth – when they passed. The soldiers who were part of the Yeflam Guard were similarly treated as they left the camp and lined up behind Xrie. Only Kal Essa's Brotherhood avoided it, but they had been mobilized in the early morning's rain and now waited alongside the larger force of the Saan.

'There was some talk of having a parade,' Caeli said, standing beside her. 'Alahn suggested it, but Xrie refused it. He said the war had already begun.'

Se'Saera's War. Ayae had heard the phrase used a week ago, after the announcement that the Mireean and Yeflam Guard would be joining the Saan. 'How many do you think will die?' she asked.

'A lot of them.'

Ayae winced, despite herself.

'You still made the right choice,' Caeli said.

'I'm not so sure,' she admitted, letting her frustration have voice. 'Jae'le and the others don't need me. Anguish will take them to Zaifyr. I can't help there. I can't help when they find him.'

'When they find his spirit, you mean.' The guard shrugged. 'From everything you've told me, they don't know what they're doing, either. Who knows what will happen when they find him?'

Jae'le had told her that the four of them – he, Eidan, Tinh Tu and Anguish – planned to follow the lines that led to Zaifyr.

'What lines?' Ayae had asked him.

'I am not sure how best to describe them. Anguish sees them,' he said. Jae'le had come into the camp the morning after Ayae had witnessed Tinh Tu's vision of what had happened in Asila. He had come to the tent that she and Caeli shared. Ayae had been so surprised by the sight of him in the early morning dark that she invited him inside. Caeli, who had also awoken at the sound of his approach, sat on her bedroll, her naked feet strangely obscene while Jae'le spoke. 'They are like thin cords. Anguish described them as frayed rope. Broken parts of a larger cord. He said that they lead from Zaifyr's body up into the mountains.'

'How can you trust what he tells you? Even Eidan calls him a deception.'

'You must trust that everything is happening for a reason. All the words we say, all the actions we take.'

'How do you know this cord is even attached to Zaifyr?' Ayae pressed. 'I have never heard him mention that when he sees the dead. How do you even know it is real?'

'As I said, you must trust.' In the dark of the tent, he was a collection of strange shadows, as if he was a man who had not yet been fully formed. 'If we do not have trust, we do not have a way forward.'

She did not yet know what the way was, and she said that to him.

'If we can find Zaifyr,' Jae'le explained, 'if we can return him to his body, we may well be able to stand against the new god much more easily. She is afraid of him, after all. I saw that clearly in Yeflam.'

'If and may . . .' She let the words fade. 'You don't know what state he will be in,' she said instead.

'No, I do not. I am not blind to that. It may be that my brother will need years to recover once we return him to flesh. It took centuries for him to return to himself mentally after Asila. I have not forgotten that he does not remember the worst of those days' events, either. It could be that he does not remember what has happened at all when he awakes. The circumstances of his death in Yeflam are very different from his death in Asila.'

'Yet, by the same logic, he might remember all of it,' Ayae said.

'He might,' the immortal man admitted. 'And it could be that we will bring him to life only to kill him again.'

'Maybe it is better to leave him.' It would be the most humane thing that they could do, she thought, but did not say it. 'I know when we die there is a half-life for us, but it could be that is best. For him, that is.'

'You do not believe that,' Jae'le said.

'What will you do if he needs . . .' Caeli, speaking for the first time, paused. She was, Ayae thought, struggling with the word centuries. Struggling with the concept of talking to people who were thousands of years old. 'What if he cannot fight Se'Saera straight away?'

'There is still my sister,' he said to her.

'Aelyn Meah?'

'Yes.'

'You would go to war with her, even though she stands beside the new god?'

'That is not what I mean,' Jae'le said. 'My sister knew that Zaifyr could not die. I do not believe she thought to kill him in Yeflam. Rather, I think she thought to die herself. I cannot assure you of this entirely, but Eidan tells me that Aelyn had been off centre for some time. It could be true that she thought to free herself from an influence she did not control. Tinh Tu tells me that she could control our sister. With enough time, she believes Kaqua could, as well. Aelyn will never admit to needing help, but by then we will know if she does or does not.'

His words were still in Ayae's mind when she was summoned by Muriel Wagan and Lian Alahn to a meeting later that day. The sky was clear when the messenger found her, but each step to the tent felt as if it was being taken through the muddy roads that greeted her departure. She felt nothing but frustration. It was, she admitted later to Caeli, a frustration that had been building for a while. Perhaps it was because of Jae'le's visit, because they had been talking about him so much, but Ayae could hear Zaifyr's words, from nearly a year ago. 'People work on your sympathy and you are asked for favours,' he had said. It had been shortly after her powers emerged. 'You are manipulated emotionally or intellectually.' He had been speaking of his own experiences, and of how he had come to view himself as a god. Shortly afterwards, Ayae had agreed to help Muriel Wagan and, in hindsight, realized her actions had been a rejection of his cynicism. But now, removed from her home, from the house she loved in Mireea, from the world she had crafted for herself, she could see the truth in his words. She was asked, she was manipulated, she was pushed and prodded. She felt as if her kindness was constantly taken advantage of, that the exchange was one-sided, and endless.

Inside, the large tent held more than just the Lady of the Ghosts and Lian Alahn and their two guards. A table dominated the middle of the room, its surface taken up by a flat and uninspired map of the continent, detailing the shore of Yeflam, the Mountains of Ger, the Plateau, Leera and the Kingdoms of Faaisha. There were markers on it, some made in ink, others made from small models of soldiers and buildings, but her attention skipped past the map quickly, to the men and women around it. Miat Dvir and his wife Vyla were closest to her. Xrie stood opposite them, while Captain Mills and Captain Oake, the white-haired soldier who was second to Xrie, stood on either side of him. Lastly, the Captain of the Brotherhood, Kal Essa, stood at the back of the table. Of all of them, she thought that he looked the least happy to be there.

'Ayae.' Muriel Wagan approached her and took her hand. 'Thank you for coming so swiftly.'

She was not asked immediately. At first, the Lady of the Ghosts said that she and Alahn had reached a consensus and decided to support Miat Dvir and the Saan and form a coalition against the Leerans. It would not be easy, Ayae was told. The Innocent would soon land on the Leeran shore with Se'Saera. He would join with the creatures that had attacked Yeflam. Alahn pointed to the map and explained how General Waalstan's forces appeared to be well dug in throughout Faaisha and gaining ground. He said that they planned to contact the Lords of Faaisha and try to coordinate their forces. Once he had finished speaking, Muriel Wagan took up the thread again, and said, 'We would like for you to accompany our forces. For you to help them.'

'No,' Ayae said, simply.

The silence that followed was no more than a pause.

'You are not being asked,' Lian Alahn said, first. 'You are being given an order.'

'I am not a soldier.' Ayae crossed her arms, aware that as she did, she gave the impression of being defensive. 'Besides,' she continued,

'Jae'le and his brother and sister are planning to head into the Mountains of Ger. I will be going with them.'

'Has Jae'le found Zaifyr, then?' Xrie asked. His question was followed, almost instantly, by Vyla Dvir, who said, 'Should they not accompany us?'

She took both questions. 'He has,' she said curtly. 'As for accompanying you, I don't think so. More than that, I don't think you would want that.' Ayae forced herself to straighten her arms. 'If Jae'le wanted to do so, he could take command of your forces within hours.'

'My husband,' Vyla said, after Miat whispered to her, 'does not think that is likely.'

'That is because you do not know who he is, not truly.'

'The Saan are loyal.'

'Ayae is right,' the Lady of the Ghosts said. She held up a hand to silence the others. 'It would be foolish for us to believe that Jae'le, or Eidan, would do anything that we ask. They are joined by their sister Tinh Tu now, and if I am to believe what I have been told about her, we should treat her as we treat them: with the utmost respect and at arm's length.' She turned from the people around the table to face Ayae. 'But you are not like them. You are not flooded with centuries of power. You are a woman raised on the back of Ger. You are someone who shares our hopes and desires, and it would be of great reassurance to me if you accompanied us into Leera. You would be a great help to our soldiers. To all our soldiers.'

'You are asking too much,' Caeli said, before Ayae could reply. The guard left her position in the far shadows of the tent to stand beside her. 'She is not a sword, or knife, or a bow. You cannot point her in a direction and expect her to solve whatever is there.'

'You overstep yourself.' Alahn left the table, a cold anger in his voice. 'Is this how you allow your employees to act, Lady Wagan?'

'Caeli?' the Lady of the Ghosts said.

'She is my friend,' the other woman said. 'If I must make a choice between my friend and my work, then I will make that choice, My Lady. But you have forgotten something very important: Ayae is not a soldier. She does not know our formations. She does not know how to command troops. She does not know how to read the landscape of a battlefield and react to it. Xrie does. So do Miat Dvir, Fyra Mills and Kal Essa. So do the soldiers under their command. You will need that more than you will need her when our forces come against the Innocent. What Captain Essa said to you before you sent for Ayae was right. She will not win a battle against a seasoned army. You should heed his advice.'

'His advice,' Alahn said stiffly, 'is simply to replace Ayae with Aned Heast.'

'You don't quote me right,' Essa said firmly. 'I said our priority should be to reach out to the Captain of Refuge.'

'Have we not captains enough to make decisions with?' Vyla Dvir said, the words that Miat Dvir whispered to her. 'We know the reputation of Captain Heast, even in the Saan, but it has been many years since Refuge has ridden into battle. We have no idea what kind of force he will have with him. It may be no better than his most recent battle – which, my husband would like to remind you, was a loss.'

'My uncle knows better than that,' Xrie said. He had remained silent while the others talked, his dark gaze flicking to those around the room, before he settled on Ayae. Now, he turned back to the map on the table. 'Caeli is correct. Ayae is not a solution to our problems, no more than I am. It does not diminish us greatly if she will not fight beside us. Indeed, it highlights the necessity for us to establish contact with the Faaishan marshals and the Captain of Refuge. We should revisit that topic now. The letters we had planned to alert the marshals to our presence in Faaisha will have to change, after all.'

Shortly after that, Lady Wagan dismissed her. Ayae left the tent with a sense of relief but, as she walked along the dirt paths, she was surprised by how much she felt that a constraint had been removed from her. The feeling persisted throughout the day, but that night she began to doubt what she said. Maybe, Ayae told herself, as news broke of the plan to invade Leera, as soldiers prepared to march within a week, she should have agreed. Yes, she admitted, she had become tired of being asked, of feeling as if she was being used, but the men and women she saw before her would be in battle against the Innocent. It awakened in her an old fear, but it was not a fear unique to her, she knew. Yes, she had Sooia, she had her childhood memories. But all the soldiers would have heard stories about him. She said as much to Caeli, one night, before they fell asleep.

'Do you think you would make a difference, when so many others haven't?' Ayae heard the guard shrug beneath her blanket. 'I was serious when I told them that you would not.'

'But what if I could?'

'You cannot make the impossible happen. You are better off going with Jae'le and the others. Whatever they find, it will catch Se'Saera's attention. When that happens, they will need all the help they can get.'

As a cart emerged on the muddy road before her, Ayae recalled Caeli's words. At its front was Jae'le, and beside him, Tinh Tu. A large white raven sat between the two of them. In the back, Ayae could see Eidan and a series of blankets and supplies, all carefully arranged to cover Zaifyr's body.

'It's time,' Caeli said.

Ayae reached down for her pack and for her sword. 'Keep yourself safe with Eilona Wagan.' When Caeli had told Ayae about her new duty, she had been unable to keep a thin strand of disgust out of her voice. 'You take care, all right?'

'You too,' the other woman said, before she hugged her, and walked with her to the cart that would take her back home.

7.

‘Is it such a burden you carry, Taela?’ In the darkness, Se’Saera’s voice came to Bueralan without a sense of direction. ‘Long ago,’ she said, ‘a woman told me that the greatest gift of her body was to bear life. The woman who told me this was named Estalia. She was, for a long time, a favourite of mine. She was one of the people who found me. In her youth she lost two children but bore a third. It was after the latter that she spoke of childbirth to me, for her son, her only son, was born ill. You could see the illness upon him immediately. He struggled to move: he could not turn himself, nor could he straighten his limbs properly. Estalia came to me to ask for help, but I could do little for him. I wanted to, but I simply could not undo what had been done. I remember looking at him in the cradle where he lay, thinking how, through no fault of his own, he was such a flawed creation. Humanity had been designed to be weak, I thought. It was my parents’ intention. They wanted it so, though I cannot tell you the reasons for it. Perhaps it was fear. Or compromise. Or perhaps, of all their creations, it was only humans that thrived so well. Fate was something that they sought to control, but which was independent of them. I still have no answers for why they allowed humans to be so weak, but on the day that Estalia stood before me with her child, I promised her that I would do away with humanity’s weakness. I would give their souls a vessel of strength. You bear the first of those, Taela. You are the mother of my promise. Is it so hard to be grateful for that?'

There was an oppressive nature to the darkness, a sensation that left Bueralan feeling, for the first time in his life, claustrophobic. He wanted to push it away, to break out, but for all that he was left with the sensation of being surrounded, he could find nothing to press against. It surprised him, then, when he heard Taela's voice so clearly:

'There should be a hell for you.'

'It would be only how I wanted it to be. Do you not understand that already?'

As if it were a cloth, the darkness slipped from Bueralan, and he found himself standing in Gtara. Beside him stood Ren and Orlan, while before him stood Zilt. Out of the four of them, it was only the blond man who was unconcerned by what had happened. He held Bueralan's gaze, and in his eyes the saboteur thought he saw a darkness akin to what had just washed over him.

'Do not think of me as a cruel being, Taela,' Se'Saera said, her voice receding from Bueralan, yet still audible to him. 'I am not. It is your mistake to think that. I simply am, I simply exist, and it is from me that all words and acts will soon take their definition. Until then, I know I will have to bear the languages that have grown in the absence of my parents – but it is that very language that gives you such a problem.'

He could see the god now. She stood in the slave pen, her white robes unstained. In her hands she held the remains of the dagger Taela had thrust into her.

Bueralan began to move towards her. His legs felt wobbly, and he saw that the experience of the darkness had left many of the god-touched men and women likewise confused, but each step he took saw the certainty return to them. Ahead of him, Taela lay against one of the poles that had been wrapped with barbed wire, her hands folded over her stomach. There was blood there, he saw, blood over her hands and shirt, and he thought briefly that the child within her had been killed. That Zean had been killed. A thin thread of relief mixed with his concern for Taela, but it became clear when he reached her that the blood came from her hands: that the knife Se'Saera held was but the hilt of it, for the blade had shattered and shards of metal had buried themselves in Taela's hands and arms.

Tears streaked Taela's face, but it was anger, not pain, that was the cause.

'How would you like to be thought of, then?' It was Aelyn Meah who spoke as Bueralan knelt before Taela. The Keeper's voice was rough, as if it had not been used for months. 'You raped this woman, did you not?'

'I gave her a child.'

Don't move, he told Taela. Don't move. His hands took hers, unfolded them, revealing shards of metal throughout.

'You did not answer my question,' the Keeper of the Divine said. 'How do you wish for us to think of you?'

'I am a creator. I am certainty. I am absoluteness.' Cloth was pressed into his hand. Bueralan turned, expecting to find Orlan, but found Kaze instead. 'You will see that soon enough. It will be after this child is born. You will look at him and you will see all that I offer you. You, Aelyn, will bow to me on that day. I have seen that. It is why I have spared you.'

'You have not spared me for that.'

Gently, Bueralan pulled out the first shard of metal from Taela's hand. He did it as carefully as he could, but he knew that tendons would be severed, that the extent of her injuries would leave her crippled for months, if not forever, if they did not find a healer.

'You cannot see fate,' Se'Saera said. 'You cannot know anything of what will come to pass.'

'I know my family is coming,' Aelyn Meah said.

'Yes,' the god said, and in her voice Bueralan heard an uncertainty that reminded him of the half-formed being he had seen, one that embodied both confidence and doubt. 'Yes, they are.'

8.

Zaifyr felt as if he was drowning.

He knew that he was not. He could no longer take a breath, could no longer use his lungs, but that did not stop the sensation. He felt the pressure within his chest as if it was real, as if it rose and fell with a breath he no longer took. It was, he decided, as if the ocean had lodged its tides and swells within his lungs and cursed him to feel its every change. At its worst, he would taste blood in the back of his throat, and with that blood he would taste salt, as well. It was when he experienced all three that he struggled the most, because it was then that the memories of his body would return most strongly. He had to remind himself that they were an echo of what had once been real. They were simply memories of his self, of his long, long life, before it had ended. Before Leviathan's Blood took what had been, ultimately, his mortal form.

He remembered little of what had happened before or after he hit the ocean. His last memory was of his decision not to kill his sister, Aelyn. But in the aftermath, there was an emptiness defined by the ocean's breath inside him, a chill in his very soul that he could not escape. The phantom sensations of his body were made worse by the sight of his physical body, which he saw first upon returning to awareness. He floated before him, his bones bent at odd angles, his clothes torn, his charms broken, his flesh ripped. It was nothing like the time he had awoken in Mireea and stared down at his body.

Then, Zaifyr had been alive, his soul anchored in the spirits of other dead men and women. A line had eventually developed between him and his body, as if it was the chain of an anchor that he could use to mark the way back to the surface. His real danger had been when he used the cord to return to his body. The dead around him had also seen it as a way for them to return to flesh, and they had threatened to swarm him. Now, the dead simply ignored him and focused on their own remains, lost in their own confusion.

Death had not welcomed Zaifyr any differently to any other man or woman. Like them, he felt confused, prone to moments of panic, sadness and anger. Unlike them, his sensations were also coupled with a sense of failure. He had been unable to help the dead. He had been unable to free them from the torture that they, and now he, endured. Whenever Zaifyr felt that, he felt a strong sense of injustice. The God of Death's power was within him . . . but, no matter how much he wanted to shout that, or argue it, he felt another part of him say that for all his power he had just been another mortal. He could not help himself and he could not help the dead around him. Why, then, should death be any different for him?

It shouldn't, of course.

It was after one such conversation with himself that the Captain of *Wayfair*, Lor Jix, appeared before him.

Zaifyr did not know how long had passed before the ancient dead found him. Nor did he know where the haunted captain had been. Time revealed itself poorly within the depths of the black ocean, but he suspected that Jix had waited and watched him until his mental state was better. Of course, it may have also been that, after Se'Saera had been named, a terrible event had befallen Lor Jix and his crew, which was why they had disappeared in the battle on Nale, just as the new god had as well.

'No,' the ancient dead said in his awful, waterlogged voice when Zaifyr asked. 'It is as I said to you: I am bound differently now.'

They talked without words, without mouths moving. 'How so?' he asked.

'Come with me.' Jix looked the same in death as he had in life: a bald, bearded man with one eye a solid colour, wearing tattered pants and a jacket. With his thick hand, he beckoned to Zaifyr. 'Let us leave here. I will show you.'

He was strangely horrified at the prospect. 'I can't leave my body.'

'Do not be like them, godling,' Jix said harshly. 'Do not disrespect your heritage.'

The ancient dead moved away from Zaifyr, his body caught half-way between swimming and walking, his actions suggesting that for all his disgust, he could not leave his mortal remains behind easily, either. *Where is your body kept?* Zaifyr asked himself. In the wreckage of *Wayfair*, he was sure. In that broken ship on the floor of Leviathan's Blood, safely locked in a coffin where both the lock and the hinges had rusted shut so solidly that no creature could break either open. But yet, as Zaifyr pushed away from his body with a backward glance, he felt a tremendous urge to return to it, as if something quite real bound him to it. Instead, he made his way after Lor Jix.

The Captain of *Wayfair* made his way out of Leviathan's Blood in silence. He ignored any attempt Zaifyr made to speak to him, even after they emerged from the water, like two survivors of a wreck.

The coast that the two strode upon was defined by greys and whites and chaos. There was a camp on the edges of Yeflam, and for a moment, Zaifyr could not understand why it was there. He thought he was in a different time and a different place – a place in the far, far future, or one in the very past, after the War of the Gods – until he turned and saw the wreckage of Yeflam.

Eidan had caused that, he reminded himself. Eidan had broken the pylon that held Nale and, in doing so, had destroyed the balance of the Floating Cities. His confusion gave way to a sense of relief. Only a short amount of time had passed.

Zaifyr followed Lor Jix through the camp. The Captain of *Wayfair* did not pause, did not talk or show any interest in what was around him. He strode through colourless fires and grey-skinned men and women. For his part, Zaifyr wondered if his brothers were in the camp. And Ayae? But Lor Jix gave him no time to stop.

Instead, the ancient dead led him beyond the camp and into the Mountains of Ger. Once they left the camp, Zaifyr asked again where they were going, and again, Jix ignored him.

The road they followed led up into Mireea and, soon, the ruined city appeared, defined in the greys and whites of the colourless daylight world Zaifyr inhabited. Its buildings were broken and sunken, and the roads – the once-renowned cobbled roads – were shattered, but it was not this that unsettled Zaifyr. No, the growing sense of apprehension that emerged within him came from the haunts on the walls of the city, in the ruined buildings, broken wooden walls and gaps in the roads. There were hundreds. Each of them watched him, as no other dead had, and each of them, he realized, was armed. They had swords and shields, and they looked, he thought, very much like an army.

Jix led him to the centre of Mireea, to where the markets were once held. It was there that two spirits waited.

The first was Queila Meina, the Captain of Steel, who had died fighting the two Keepers, Fo and Bau. She looked much as she had in life, tall, with short, dark hair and, as on the few times Zaifyr had seen her, she wore leather armour and a long sword at her side. She did not carry a shield like the other dead, but upon seeing her,

Zaifyr was reminded of how the shields the haunts carried were similar to those that the mercenary group Steel had used to much success, and he found that his apprehension gave way to a stronger sense of disquiet. It was an unease that grew when Meina turned to him and inclined her head slightly, as if greeting a commander, or a lord, and in doing so revealed the second figure in the square.

The Wanderer.

Cannibal Messages

'Se'Saera killed Kaqua. She then gave the order to her generals, to Aela Ren and Zilt, to kill the remaining Keepers of the Divine.' Aelyn's hands tightened visibly around each other. 'She ordered them to kill the people who had been my friends for over a thousand years. She did it as if they were bugs, as if they were so beneath her notice that she did not need to watch while they died. Instead, she talked to me. She talked casually, as if we were friends.'

The memory clearly bothered Aelyn Meah. She shifted in her seat, the silence almost thick enough to pull over her shoulders. I understood: the other Keepers were as much victims of Kaqua's manipulations as she was. Free of him, they might have made different choices. Or, they might not have. Regardless of what they might have done, Aelyn was left with the memory of her inability to defend her friends and, later, her failure to show adequate remorse. She has been accused of both in the years since the Massacre of Gtara took place. It has been a story that has followed her around as if it explained her failure not to those she ruled beside – not the Keepers who died – but to all of us.

Eventually, I was able to draw out of her what Se'Saera said:

'She told me that I would never be a god,' Aelyn said. 'They were her first words to me while the Keepers died. It was not very surprising, in truth. Se'Saera was no different to Kaqua in that regard. Being divine was all she thought about. But what did surprise me was when she said I was part of her future. She said that in all the fates she could see, I was alive, and while I lived, she would be a god. She then told me that I should rejoice, for when she was whole, the world would be healed.'

—Onaedo, *Histories, Year 1029*

1.

The Wanderer was a tall figure, but not so much so that he was inhuman in his height. Next to him, Zaifyr was but a head shorter.

The god looked much as he had in the stories Zaifyr had been told as a child: tall, gaunt and dressed in a long, flowing robe with the hood pulled low over his head. Beneath the hood was darkness, but Zaifyr did not expect anything different. The Wanderer's face only appeared when he pulled back his cowl. When he did that, he took on the appearance of someone the dead knew. As a child, Zaifyr's parents told him that the Wanderer did this as a comfort, and he had been surprised when he came upon his first depiction of the Wanderer's face as a smooth, fleshless skull years after they had died. The painting had been made after the War of the Gods, in the centuries where churches failed, governments fell and people tried to make sense of what had happened. The Wanderer's skull face had been part of a sequence in which all the gods appeared half alive and half dead, their divine bodies giving way to skeletons that weighed down the world. But the Wanderer who appeared before him now was the one from his childhood. The only difference was the staff he held in his gloved hands. It was made from wood and came up to the Wanderer's chin. The god's hands were folded around the middle, the end firmly planted in the ground.

'He does not move and he does not speak,' Queila Meina said. 'He appeared after the new god was given her name.'

'Se'Saera,' Zaifyr murmured as he walked around the god. The robes did not rustle or shift. 'Her name is Se'Saera.'

'I heard it. We all heard it,' the ghost of the Captain of Steel said. 'But I will not say it. It has the feel of—'

'Being tainted,' Lor Jix finished.

Zaifyr paused, glanced at the two of them. Neither had approached the god with him, but instead remained a dozen steps away, at the entrance of the square. Upon his approach, Meina had not said a word to him, but merely stepped aside, as if she had been waiting his arrival. Since then, both she and Jix had been joined by other ghosts. They reminded Zaifyr of Lor Jix's crew, who had appeared over Yeflam as a replica of *Wayfair*, a replica that had broken apart as they fell upon Se'Saera in an attempt to kill her.

'Is this where you were taken after she was named?' he asked Jix. 'When you disappeared from Yeflam?'

'Aye,' he said.

'Is your crew here as well?'

'No.' For the first time Zaifyr saw the ancient dead hesitate. 'They are gone,' he said, eventually. 'But not gone, as well.'

'He is lying,' Meina said, a note of disgust in her voice. 'If you trust him, you're a fool. This old bit of death is nothing but another's tool.' Beside her, Jix snarled and began to speak, but the Captain of Steel met his gaze, and he fell silent. 'We almost killed him when he appeared here,' she said. 'He roared at us, threatened us, and tried to command us, but I would not have that in life, and I will not have that in death.'

The last surprised Zaifyr. 'How could you kill what is already dead?'

'Whatever you did to us made us different.' There were nods from the ghosts behind her, a murmur of agreement. 'It was not apparent to us immediately, not until creatures like Jix began to enter the mountains. A soldier of mine followed one of them into the mountains and attacked it. We do not know where it went after it was killed. It was not here, surely, but where else can the dead go?'

'The afterlife? The gods created paradises and punishments,' Zaifyr began, thinking that, if the dead were 'killed', then they would enter the realms that the gods had made as a reward for those who had been loyal . . . but as he began to say that, a deep pain struck him. It began in his chest, as if his heart had stuttered back to life. He stumbled forwards, away from the still form of the Wanderer. The sensation of drowning returned to him suddenly, acutely, and he desperately wanted to take a breath: but he had no breath to take, no nose or mouth to draw in the air he needed, and no lungs to fill.

'Your chest,' Meina said, forcing him to look down, to see the greyness of his body, and to see, in it, a small line of red. 'What is that?' she asked.

'Life,' Lor Jix said.

As suddenly as it came upon him, the pain began to recede. 'No,' he said. 'You cannot—'

'Child.' The word came from the Wanderer, from a voice that echoed, as if there were both a male and a female voice speaking. 'Child.' The male spoke first, then the female, but when the Wanderer spoke next, the genders were reversed. 'I do not know your name, child,' the Wanderer said. 'I cannot see you clearly. You are so far along the lines of fate that I can see only glimpses of you. Are you the man from the mountains of Kakar? Or another? The parts of me in you will persist. They will bring you to this moment. But what, exactly, is this moment? The threads of fate are breaking down. I see death. I see life. You have been struck down in a city surrounded by the dead. Men and women surrounded you. They are your friends, your family. I am trying to leave this message for you, but the time is not right. Fate has been broken. You must be imprisoned. The abomination must rise. It must be later that I see you. It must be when you next die. When you fall into the black ocean. But is that you? Or is it another that I see?

'It does not matter, child. I leave this message for you. My task for you.

'Fate has begun to reassemble itself. It is trying to join, to become whole, to destroy all its possibilities and all its variety. It yearns to be singular, as it once was, before we first found it. It has forgotten how bleak it was. How poor the world it created was. But then, we should expect no less from fate. It is mindless. It is without sentience, intelligence or moral. It seeks to return us to a dark future, a time of despair, for no other reason than it must. It cannot recognize the path of nothingness it creates. It does not see the world defined by soot and grime that leads to destruction. It does not see that the abomination it has created is but a tool towards this end. It does not know the oblivion that awaits us all should it succeed.

'We, your gods – child, we who created you and nurtured you – have done all that we can to stop fate. We have spilled ourselves into the world to deprive the abomination's completion. We have been forced to destroy ourselves. But it must be done. The abomination must not be allowed to become whole. It lies now where it was spawned, in Heüala. It lies there against the walls that were constructed long, long ago, when fate first made us. In the holiest of places, in the most sanctified of existence, the abomination survives behind closed doors, while its vessel – its one finger in the world – seeks to gather our remains to complete itself. Destroy the vessel there and you destroy nothing, child. It must be struck down by you in Heüala.

'Yes, you, child, must strike it down. You must do it with this staff. You must break the gates to Heüala down and slay the horror that it is within.'

2.

Ranan was a city without walls.

The road to the capital of Leera turned into a gentle slope long before the city appeared, long before the marshland, the swamp crows and the ugly light-blocking trees of the Leeran marshes and bogs slipped away. Bueralan, who had come to Ranan twice before – once ten years earlier and once in what felt increasingly like a lifetime ago – did not notice the change until walls of stone began to appear around him. Such was the gentleness of the decline, the natural feeling of it that, even then, he was barely aware that he travelled into the earth. He thought the walls had been built and were part of a defensive structure. The revelation that the earth *itself* was the wall that an invader must breach occurred to him shortly before Ranan became clear. Before he saw the smooth stone towers, the square houses that sat in rows like tombs, and the cathedral that rose above them all: before then, Bueralan realized that he rode into deep fissures gouged into the earth. From their base, he rode up narrow tunnels into the city proper. He entered the streets in the dying light of the afternoon's sun, the last to do so, the reins of the grey looped around Taela, who sat before him, unable to ride a horse herself. Ahead, Se'Saera, the Innocent and the god-touched soldiers were a slow-moving broken line working towards the huge shape of the Ranan's cathedral. Zilt's monsters were fanned out in front of them like a pack of dogs who had returned home. They ran on legs and arms through the city, leaping on stone roofs and climbing towers, letting out cries that bordered on howls.

The cathedral lay in the centre of Ranan and was separated from the city by deep fissures. It gave the land it was built on the appearance that it sat on a mountain that had sunk into the ground, but which had weathered both time and the elements, and was now reasserting itself.

'When I was here last, I saw a single man rebuilding Ranan,' he said to Taela, as the grey's hooves struck the black stone road in rhythm. 'It is hard to believe that he did all of this.'

'It looks as if it has been forced upon the world,' she said softly.

'Ranan was originally a wooden city. The ground was flat and whole and it looked as if it had been drawn from the soil, as if it had grown from its depths. People used to say that the Leerans had found it when they settled the land.'

Taela said nothing and Bueralan did not tell her that he had last come to Ranan in search of his mercenary group, Dark. He did not say that, when he had entered the cathedral, he had found his friends dead. He did not explain how he found Orlan in the grasp of a creature he could not see. The grey made its way to the bridge that rose over the fissure and allowed him to enter the streets that led to the cathedral. If he had begun that story, he would have ended up telling her how Se'Saera had given him Zean's soul. How, from here, he had gone to Ooila.

A part of Taela had not left Gtara, Bueralan believed. Her bandaged hands did not allow her to grasp the reins of a horse, and so she had ridden with him, and with Samuel Orlan. Se'Saera had made it clear that no one was to heal her injuries and, in the first few days, they had had to help her eat, drink and with other bodily matters. Each day, Bueralan had felt an emptiness consume her and it had not subsided even when a small amount of use returned to her hands. He wanted to believe that it was passing, however, and he would occasionally catch her staring at the front of the line, where Se'Saera rode. Zilt and Ren rode beside her, and behind them, the Breath of Yeflam, Aelyn Meah followed. He wanted to glimpse in those stares the anger he had seen earlier, the emotion that had led her to stab the god, but any hope he had that she was returning, if not to normal, then to a sense of herself, was broken the night before they entered the fissures surrounding Ranan.

'Bueralan,' Taela whispered to him. She lay next to him, covered by a blanket he had laid across her. 'Bueralan,' she repeated.

He had not been asleep. 'Yes?'

She shifted closer to him and, without thinking, he opened his arms, and allowed her to draw against him. 'You should kill me.'

He tightened his arm around her.

'I can't stop this,' Taela continued in her soft voice. Her emotions were tiny and desperate in each word she spoke. 'I can't stop her. I can't – I tried but I just can't. I can't do anything, Bueralan. We could stop her, though. You could. You're like them. You could just – you could stop it.'

His hand stroked the back of her head, the white tattoos a pale netting over her. He could see again the figure in Ranan, the figure he knew that was Se'Saera, and he could see the darkness of it, the incomplete nature of its skin, the surety of its musculature, and he asked himself again what she could have been, what—

'Bueralan?' Taela whispered again.

'She wouldn't let you go,' he said, finally. 'She'd only find another way to hurt you.'

Taela did not move away. She stayed in his grasp until the morning's sun began to rise, until the camp began to move. He helped her onto the grey and sat quietly until they were on the streets of Ranan.

The cathedral had changed since he was last in it. The ground floor still opened up into a huge area where the Faithful could gather. Wooden pews sat in neat lines before an empty podium at the far end. The afternoon's light came through the windows that lined the room and flooded it in a dark burned orange. If it was a portent, Bueralan could not see one, and he led Taela to the stairs that went both up and down. It was on the next floor up that he found a room for him and Taela. Bueralan had considering taking one of the square houses in Ranan, outside the cathedral, but Zilt's monsters had strung themselves out across the roofs and he thought better of it.

Taela lay down on one of the beds without a word once he shut the door behind them. Her injured hands curled against her swollen stomach and Bueralan laid the other blanket over her. She was asleep by the time he left the room.

He went in search of Kaze, but could not find her in any of the rooms around him. In fact, he was surprised to see that the floor he was on was largely empty. The only other room occupied was the one Aelyn Meah rested in. She sat on the bed, alone, her legs crossed beneath her, her gaze on the wall across from her. He was surprised, but the emotion was part of a larger surprise, one that had begun in Gtara when she had accepted Se'Saera's order that she ride by the god's side. He did not know if the two spoke, or if Se'Saera had threatened her, but he recognized in her the emptiness that was consuming Taela. Perhaps, he thought, as he passed the room and continued to search for Kaze, that was explanation enough.

An eerie silence followed him up the next stairway, onto the next floor. There he found an empty library.

The shelves were bare, like limbs stripped of flesh. The sense of disquiet that filled Bueralan in the halls only grew as he walked among the shelves. There were dozens and dozens of shelves, each of them with an air of expectation, as if they were waiting not for the already written histories, philosophies or fictions to be placed there, but for those that would be made. There was no place for the world as it was to be recorded on these shelves. He had never before experienced that within a library, and he found that the more waiting shelves he passed, the more his disquiet turned into an open revulsion.

At the end of the room large windows allowed the orange light of the afternoon's sun to drift in. From here, Bueralan could gaze out on Ranan, at the flat roofs and towers, and at the monsters that stood like sentries, staring out into Leera, where the enemies of their god would surely come, to fail in the first chapters of her new world.

'Are you lost, by any chance?' Aela Ren asked from his left. Startled, Bueralan turned and found a series of desks and chairs, neatly arranged. The Innocent sat in the centre, a single book on the table before him. 'If you are looking for the others, they will be in their own spaces,' he continued, not looking up from the book. 'We are solitary men and women when we are able to be. We like to be alone.'

It was a gentle admonishment, one Bueralan ignored. 'Have you asked yourself why that is?'

'You can surely be more subtle.' The scarred man rose his head and sighed. 'A mortal life is one that defines itself by death. Because of that, it rushes along, and meaning is taken from the acts that one makes, rather than its meaning guiding the acts. But for the immortal, for those of us who served the gods, the meaning is everything. Such a search is even more important now that we stand beside Se'Saera. We must ask ourselves once again, who are we? How do we define ourselves? The answers are ones that will be found in solitude.'

The book, Bueralan saw as Ren closed it, was titled *The Eternal Kingdom*. 'And you?' he asked. 'Do you know yourself?'

'It is a question that I ask.'

'That is not an answer.'

'No.' He was silent for a moment, his scarred hand resting on the cover of the only book in the cathedral's library. 'What is in this book changes,' Ren said, finally. 'You pick it up and you open it and the words alter. A history where the gods killed each other for their child becomes the history of a new god, one made from the wreckage of the old gods. It is like when Se'Saera talks about her creations. Her first she distances herself from. She calls it a deception, says that it is not her first creation. The child within Taela is her first, true creation, now. As our god becomes more powerful, she rebuilds her understanding of the world and, as she does that, she rebuilds our place in it. Eventually, I think she will rebuild the world without figures like me.' He offered a faint smile. 'It is a relief.'

The admission surprised Bueralan, more than anything else he had seen, more than Ranan, or Aelyn Meah, or Zilt's monsters throughout the city. But before he could say anything, one of Aela Ren's soldiers rushed into the room.

'Ai Sela is here,' Joqan said before Bueralan or Ren could speak. 'She says that *Glafanr* has disappeared!'

3.

The Wanderer's message repeated. 'Child,' he said, after he had finished. 'Child,' she said without pause. 'I do not know your name, child.'

The words followed Zaifyr out of the market square as he put distance between himself and the god. Outside the market, by the remains of a burned shop, he stopped and tried to close himself off to everything around him. *Asila*, he thought. The Wanderer had left that message, having seen what would happen in Asila thousands of years before it had happened. He had seen Zaifyr struck down. *The Wanderer said I died.* Zaifyr could not recall that. He could recall Aelyn stepping forwards. The dead were around her. She could not see them. She thought she was safe, but she wasn't. Then the ground was breaking as Eidan's stone giant began to emerge. *I remember Jae'le striking me. I can remember* – but there was blankness after that. He could remember waking in the tower. It was like when he had awoken beneath Leviathan's Blood. He had lost time. He could not remember what happened after he fell. After Yeflam, he had awoken to the sight of himself floating in the water. After Asila, he had awoken in a small, crooked tower. The floor was made from earth. The walls ugly bare brick. He had enough space to lie down and enough to stand up. When the door cracked open, a thousand years later, the sun hurt his eyes.

The idea that he had died sat strangely. He was dead now and he could not recall being separated from his body. Would it not be more of a truth to say not that he died, but that he had been killed? Yes, Zaifyr realized, that felt true to him. Jae'le would have struck to kill. His brother would not pull his blow. He would not risk the others in his family. To mirror the dash of red in his chest – the dash that was now joined by dozens more, as if his organs were beginning to emerge bloodily – Zaifyr felt a streak of shame. He had seen the intent in Aelyn to kill him, and he had allowed, over the centuries, for that to fall to her alone. He had allowed his resentment to focus on her. It was no wonder she did not want to meet him, no wonder she had wanted to drive him from Yeflam.

Lor Jix approached with a look of command similar to his expression when he had found Zaifyr in Leviathan's Blood. 'It lies now where it was spawned, in Heüala,' he said, his voice not his own, but the dual-gendered voice of the Wanderer. Shocked, the ancient dead stopped. His surprise was so real, so unfeigned, that he tried to stop speaking. 'It lies there against the walls that were constructed long, long ago,' he said, speaking through the ghostly hand he had raised, 'when fate first made us. In the holiest of places, in the most sanctified of existence, it survives behind closed doors, while its vessel – its one finger in the world – seeks to gather our remains to complete itself. But destroy the vessel and you destroy nothing, child. The abomination must be struck down by you in Heüala.'

Heüala.

The City of the Dead.

In his youth, Zaifyr had seen dozens of depictions, each altering and changing to reflect the belief of the culture it was in. He saw paintings of Heüala as a simple square house, others where it was a huge, beautiful city of spires and domed buildings, and some where it was defined by the long, twisting lanes of water around it. Every culture had its own version, but what did not change was the idea that in this city the gods would grant you access to paradise, or punish you in purgatory, or send you back to relive your life. Here, your life was weighed – by scale, by judge, by animal, by whatever method each god decided upon – and here you were found worthy of a god's favour, or not.

Zaifyr had not heard the name Heüala for thousands of years. One of his first acts when he established Asila had been to redefine it as the City of the Dead. He did it at the suggestion of Tinh Tu. She told him and the others that if they wanted to take the place of the gods, they had to take their language as well. They had to own all that their parents had owned, she once said, before the five of them realized that the gods were not their parents, and they were not gods. She warned them that the change would not be instantaneous, but slow. It would take place over generations. As long as they were careful, as long as they managed what was kept in books, in language and in memory, they could make the words of the gods their own. They would take the mantle of a god in the eyes of those around them.

'Child.' Lor Jix continued to speak, unable to stop the voice of the Wanderer emerging from him. 'Child. I do not know your name, child. I cannot see you clearly. You are so far along the lines of fate that I can see only glimpses of you. Are you the man from the mountains of Kakar?'

From behind him, from within the remains of the burned-out shop – Orlan's shop, Zaifyr was startled to realize – another ghost appeared. 'Or another?' she said. 'The parts of me in you will persist. They will bring you to this moment, but what, exactly, is this moment?' The ghost left the shell of the building and stood next to Jix, her words joining his in perfect unison as they repeated the Wanderer's message to him again. 'The threads of fate are breaking down. I see death. I see life. You have been struck down in a city surrounded by the dead. Men and women surrounded you. They are your friends, your family. I am trying to leave this message for you, but the time is not right. That fate has been broken. You must be imprisoned. The abomination must rise. It must be later that I see you. It must be when you next die. When you fall into the black ocean. But is that you? Or is it another that I see?'

Would the Wanderer not stop? Zaifyr's chest laboured, as if it were struggling to take a very real breath, and he saw that the red streaks covered his chest. Would he soon see the tether that he had seen before, after Fo poisoned him? Would he have to follow it back into Leviathan's Blood, only to drown again? In frustration, he began to tell the Wanderer that he did not care, but instead, he said, 'It does not matter, child. I leave this message for you. My task for you.'

The words felt alien, ugly in his throat, but Zaifyr was not able to stop himself from saying more. Furious, his legs aching, Zaifyr made his way back to the market square, where the voice of the Wanderer had only grown, his and her words emerging from all of the dead that waited there, as if they were but puppets for the god's use. With the message turning into a chant, he strode towards the Wanderer, towards the staff that he held—

Then it was in his hand and, around him, the world was silent.

He felt a weight lifted from his chest, as if he had surfaced from the ocean, while before him, the Wanderer began to crumble. Small cracks appeared quickly across the god's figure, as if it were made from stone, and the black robe began to break – *the black robe*, he realized, seeing the colour of it for the first time. A moment later, he felt water running over his feet.

The stream he stood in ran ahead of him, twisting through the ruins of Mireea, past the white brick walls of The Pale House, over the yellow-brown cobblestones, past the grey stones that had been used to make the Spine of Ger. It flowed into the green and brown trees and continued down the mountains, leaving him with a view of a sun that was not splintered, but whole.

'What have you done?' Zaifyr turned to Queila Meina. She and her soldiers stood in the river as well. Each of them looked very much as they had in life, with their skin white, black, brown, and more. 'Zaifyr,' she said, her words emerging from her mouth, as if she had air to breathe and lungs to use. 'What has happened?'

4.

Ayae approached the ruins of Mireea on foot.

Half an hour before, as the afternoon's sun reached its zenith, as the shape of the city began to take shape, she had climbed out of the cart Jae'le drove. He said nothing, only offered her a glance, before returning to his own silent contemplations. In the back of the cart Tinh Tu, Eidan and Anguish said nothing to her, either, but it was the latter who continued to stare at her while the cart pulled ahead, his blind eyes unconcerned with what lay before him. Ayae had asked Anguish, two nights before, if he planned to open his eyes to search for Zaifyr's spirit, and he had chuckled, his laughter strange and not quite human. He had told her they had been open since they left the shore of Yeflam. More and more lines were appearing, he said, but if he was happy about this, Ayae could not tell. She could not tell if anyone was pleased to be drawing close to Mireea, in truth.

She was not. There was, she thought, as she stepped through the broken gates and onto the cobbled streets, an infinite sadness in what lay before her. She had heard it said that you could not return to the places of your childhood once you left them, or at least not return to them in the same way, and while a part of her could accept that, she struggled with the destruction. Alone, she made her way along a splintered road covered in the debris of fallen buildings and wooden walls, the latter part of the defence that Captain Heast had built in preparation for the Leeran siege. But it was not the debris that bothered her the most: it was the sense of neglect and abandonment, as if it had all been meaningless, as if what had been invested in it did not truly matter. But wasn't that true? After all, the buildings that sank into the ground fell into the caverns that held the ancient Cities of Ger, and all that had been held within them was now gone. The loss of culture was not unique, the death of cities, of nations, was cyclical, as if the world was forever devouring itself to create new permutations.

A tremor ran through the ground, but it was not the first Ayae had felt. Around her, the buildings shook a little and, after they had fallen silent, she decided to head not to the market square, where she assumed Jae'le and the others had headed, but down the broken paths to her house.

The trees that Captain Heast had cut back in preparation for the siege had, over the last year, begun to grow back. It would be years – decades, perhaps – before they took on the thick canopy that had once been over Mireea and had provided shade during the hottest days of the summer, but the sight of the slim branches and new foliage pleased Ayae. She thought that, even if no one else came to fill Mireea, then the trees and wildlife of the area would. They could join the ghosts she had not seen yet.

Ayae's house, indeed her neighbourhood, had suffered little in the quakes that had ravaged the Mountains of Ger. It appeared before her much as it had when she last saw it: square and simple, but with an overgrown garden and broken windows. At the door, she fished the key out of a pocket, and unlocked it.

Inside, she could smell rotten fruit, and there were seeds and animal faeces, though nothing overly large of the latter, thankfully. Just black pellets from small creatures that had slipped through the broken glass with their food. She could see tiny prints in dust across the counter and in the fireplace where she had cooked. Gently, she ran a finger along the back of her couch, and along the wall to her bedroom, where the unmade bed looked the same as when she had left it. What remained of her clothes hung in the wardrobe, and for a moment, she stood there and stared at them, her current leathers and heavy cloth a contrast to the linens, shirts, pants and dresses kept in there. It was another life, Ayae told herself, reaching for a black shirt she had once loved. She could not imagine a point in her life where she might wear it again.

A sound came from the living room and she released the shirt, closed the wardrobe door. Half a dozen steps later, she saw Tinh Tu easing herself onto one of her couches, a roll of paper in her lap. Her long staff leant across the arm and, as Ayae approached, she saw that the old woman was staring at a collection of drawings, nearly two years old. The first was of her ex-partner, Illaan.

'I did not know you were an artist,' Tinh Tu said. 'You have a good hand. You could have made a living out of it.'

'I was a cartographer,' she said. 'I was apprenticed to Samuel Orlan.'

Tinh Tu unrolled a second, revealing Zineer. 'Could you have been the next Samuel Orlan?'

'No, I would have just been . . .' her voice trailed off. 'Just myself,' she finished with a shrug. 'I'm sorry, I didn't mean to be gone for so long.'

'You do not need to explain yourself.' The old woman unrolled a third scroll and Faise stared over her shoulder at Ayae. 'I certainly wouldn't.' Tinh Tu offered half a self-deprecating smile. 'Still, my brothers did send me to find you. Anguish has disappeared.'

She imagined Eidan's concern and felt in herself a sudden apprehension, but could not find it replicated in any fashion in his sister. 'He ran away?'

'No, he disappeared. It happened when we entered the market

square. Eidan said that he was there one moment, but gone the next.'

'As simple as that?'

'Interesting, is it not?'

'Do you think there is more to it?' *That he was a deceit for us*, she wanted to say.

'I think he is where our brother is, myself. When Anguish returns, Zaifyr will likely be with him.'

For Tinh Tu, Ayae knew, the prospect of her brother's return was not a cause for celebration. What she had shown Ayae in Asila left the latter with no doubt that Tinh Tu viewed Zaifyr's return as one that would be difficult. Ayae suspected that the other woman believed he would be mad, and that because of that, they would be required to take him, as they had done a thousand years ago, to the tower in Eakar.

'Eidan would say that this house felt very much of you,' Tinh Tu said. 'My brother has long said that stone and wood hold memories, that they remember who has lived inside them. Perhaps it is why he goes around the world, rebuilding what has been broken, keeping the memories of history alive. Personally, I think he makes the mistake of believing that his own memories and his own relationships with cities are shared throughout the world. Life is much more temporary, like blooms of flowers in spring. Still, for those who live as long as we do, his words are worth listening to. After we have finished, I am sure he would help you rebuild this city, if you asked him.'

'Mireea?' Ayae was shocked. 'I just had a home here, nothing more,' she said. 'It is not mine.'

'It could all be yours.' She rolled the paper up tightly and rose from the chair. 'I do not think the people who lived here will return, if it helps. But you should not be afraid to take what it is that you want. You need not be trapped by who you are. You need not put aside all of who you once were in the world. You can still have your dreams and your futures.' In the broken window, the white raven settled itself with a flutter of wings. 'To be who you wish to be is the greatest struggle for men and women like us,' Tinh Tu said, the roughness of her voice slipping momentarily into something gentler, but not yet kind. 'We lose all that defined us when our power emerges and, over our lives, we are threatened with our loss again and again, as if we were the tree that bore the blooms of the season. But unlike the tree, we are not planted by another. We are not stationary. We decide where it is that we set our roots. We decide how we weather the seasons.'

In the doorway, Tinh Tu paused and looked out into the broken sun, into the regrowing trees. After a moment, she tapped her staff down. The move called the white raven to her. With it on her staff, she began to make her way back to where her dead brother waited.

5.

Zaifyr did not know how to answer Queila Meina's question. Like her, he did not know how to react to the rich colours of the world, did not know how to explain how they had come to pass, but in that confusion, he could offer her the name of one who might.

'Jix,' he said.

'You're guessing,' Meina retorted.

He was, but he left the stream he stood in without admitting it. He splashed the remains of the god's stone messenger and water onto the cobbled roads of Mireea where he paused, surprised at the sight around him.

Mireea was undamaged.

Buildings stood solidly beneath thick canopies which gave the city a pleasant, shadowed feel. Zaifyr felt the urge to take a breath, to taste what he knew would be clean air, but he could not. Like a dim echo, the sensation of drowning returned to him, as if his body was filled with water it could not void.

He found the Captain of *Wayfair* on a wooden bench outside the market square. Any thought Zaifyr had that Jix might be able to explain what had happened was tempered by the sight of him staring at his black-skinned hands. 'How long has it been?' Jix asked as he approached. 'I honestly cannot tell you. I have lost track of all the years that I waited in the wreckage of my ship.' The dead man's awful, drowned voice was gone, replaced now with a voice that was ruined by his emotions. 'I had not thought that I would be so moved by the sight of myself.'

'You knew this would happen,' Zaifyr said, while Meina and her soldiers fell in behind him. 'You knew the gods left messages here. You knew they had plans for us.'

Jix lifted his head, revealing only one eye, the right. The left, in opposition to how it appeared before, was empty. 'I only suspected.'

'You expect me to believe that?'

'I am just a soldier, godling. I am told little. I piece together what I do not know.'

'Then what has happened to us?' Zaifyr raised the staff and swung it over the reconstructed Mireea. 'What has happened here?'

'I believe we are in a different time, a different fate,' Jix said. 'Did you not hear what the Wanderer said? The gods have constructed a series of events that are tied to the fates the gods have built. Each of our acts sends us down the path of one or another. They cannot control us, so they gamble on outcomes. It is why the Leviathan told me to ensure that you and I killed the abomination before it was named.' He looked down at his hands again, at his faded uniform of blue and red. 'I would be bound differently if we failed, she told me, but I did not understand it fully then.'

'But you do now?' Meina asked, moving next to Zaifyr.

'Both of you asked about my crew,' he said. 'Look at the staff.'

At first, Zaifyr saw nothing. It was made from dark wood and looked like other staffs he had seen, as if it had been carved from a single piece; but then, in the whirls and slivers of cracks in its length, he saw a vague shimmer and felt a faint coldness against his hand, a chill similar to that of a haunt. With a growing sense of horror, Zaifyr realized that the shimmers moving throughout the length of wood were spirits. Dozens and dozens.

'My faith is strong, but yet . . .' Lor Jix said, a true sadness in his voice. 'Yet I would trade my place here beside you with any one of my crew.'

'You made a deal with a god,' a new voice said, a voice that sounded strange and deep from the small, inky black figure that appeared on the road, as if it had been plucked from the air. 'You are a vein in a life you do not understand,' Anguish said. 'Faith is but a seductive delusion here.'

It startled Zaifyr to see him, just as it did to realize that the creature stared at Jix and the others with large, open eyes. They were completely black and nearly indistinguishable from the closed lids that Zaifyr had seen before.

'Your family brought me here,' the creature said. 'I led them here in search of you.'

'The red that we saw,' Meina murmured. 'Jix said it was life. It was your life, Zaifyr.'

'You have only to let it find you.' Anguish offered an inky smile. 'But it seems you have other plans.'

'We are to go to Heüala,' Zaifyr said.

'The name means nothing to me.'

'It was where the gates of paradise were built,' Lor Jix said. He still sat on the bench, but he stared at the small figure before him intently. 'I remember you. You were at the abomination's trial. You are her creation.'

'I was her eyes,' Anguish said.

The ancient dead's hand shot out, grabbing him. 'Then she sees us!' he howled as Anguish squirmed in his fist, trying to escape his grasp, but unable to. 'She knows what the gods plan!'

Meina's sword fell lightly, edge first, on Jix's arm. 'Let him go,' she said softly. 'If you don't, I'll see if you bleed, or if you simply break apart, like the dead I've killed before.' There was no give in her voice, but Zaifyr did not know why she wanted to save Anguish.

He asked her that while the small, inky-black creature scurried along the edge of her sword, to her shoulder.

'Close your eyes,' she said to Anguish, before she answered him. 'Because he is here,' she said to Zaifyr. 'Is that that not enough? That old piece of death just told us that the gods had plans. He doesn't know how many, but he knows that when one fails, another begins. He said that right before this creature appeared. Is that not coincidence enough to keep him alive?' She slipped her sword into its scabbard. 'Perhaps even my words are part of their plan. Maybe they push fate in a way that the gods want, or need. Who are we to say? After all, we're all being used like tools. We're no more than that staff you hold.'

'Se'Saera will know where we go,' he said, not disagreeing with her.

'If she is in this city of the dead, she already knows.'

There was little else for him to say, after that. Jix, Zaifyr could see, was not happy, but the sense that he, along with the rest of them, was part of something they did not control was not one that he was prepared to argue against. In that logic, each action they took, each choice they made, placed them in a fate that the gods had made. It was possible that not killing Anguish would be terrible for all of them, but it was just as possible that it would not. They would not know until they reached Heüala.

Unconsciously, because he knew that it would not be there, Zaifyr's left hand felt for a thin copper charm on the wrist of his right. Yet, when his fingers touched the bent metal, he did not feel surprise, but rather a sense of ease. With each charm that appeared on him, wrapped on chains around his wrists and in his hair, he felt more and more himself. He felt a sense of agency return to him, as well. This he doubted: he had returned to the shallow stream the Wanderer had stood in with no conscious thought of his own.

His boot was flooded with water and, despite himself, he laughed.

Of all the things that would follow him into death, a pair of boots with holes in the soles seemed oddly fitting, in a small, darkly humorous way.

'It is no joke where we go,' Jix said from behind him. He had stepped into the stream as well, and shouldered past Zaifyr. 'Heüala is the most divine of cities,' the Captain of *Wayfair* continued. 'It is where we are all judged.'

'We should be so lucky,' Meina said, as she too stepped into the river, her soldiers following her. 'Lead the way, Zaifyr.'

'I am just going to follow,' he said.

'That will be fine as well.'

The shallow water ran out of Mireea, but when Zaifyr stepped beneath the Spine of Ger, the clear sky and whole sun disappeared. It was replaced by a sky of empty darkness and fields of dead, brown grass. Zaifyr would have said that the fields, which ran as if they were straight, and not part of a mountain, had been burned. But the ground around the stream was muddy, and the trees that grew further out drooped with half-dead yellow foliage above exposed roots.

He turned back in the direction he had come: but the soggy, burned-looking fields stretched as far as he could see and offered him no sight of either the Mountains of Ger or Mireea.

'It was as Jix said, a different world,' Meina said. 'A world where the gods felt it was safe to leave us messages.'

'A world we cannot return to,' Zaifyr added.

The stream continued, but the world around them did not change, not for a long time. Again, Zaifyr felt that the ability to tell time was taken from him. The sensation was heightened by the parts of scorched grass and sickly trees that could have been endless reproductions of the first ones that he had seen. Zaifyr found himself expecting to see a spirit in the fields, one of the long dead that the gods had sent to purgatory, for he was sure that that was what ran beside the shallow water that he and the others walked through. But he could see none, and had no sense of anything in the fields. *Could it be*, he asked himself, *that all the dead are truly trapped in the world?*

Ahead, a shape began to emerge, accompanied by the sound of a large, moving body of water. Within moments, a ship appeared as the lamps on its deck began to ignite, as if whoever was on board wanted it to be a beacon for them – though Zaifyr could not see anyone lighting the lamps.

The ship was unlike any he had seen before. It was huge and old, its folded sails a faded red. It appeared, Zaifyr thought, as he and the others approached, that the river had been designed for it, rather than the river dictating its design, though he could not explain what it was about the ship or the lonely dock that it sat against that allowed him to think that.

'The ship of the dead,' Lor Jix said in awe. '*Glafanr*.'

6.

Ai Sela sat on the wooden pews at the back of the cathedral. Despite what Ren had said to Bueralan earlier about the god-touched being solitary, they gathered around Sela in such a tight circle that at first the saboteur felt as if he was an intruder. It was not until Aela Ren broke through the ring that Bueralan saw the exhaustion and grief upon Sela that caused such concern in her fellow immortals.

Sela had run from Gtara to Ranan. She had been left in Gtara to watch *Glafanr* and, because she was not expected join them in Ranan, they had not left her a mount. He could still recall the sight of her when they left the town: she had stood in the centre of the town with a look of relief on her face that he envied. Sela had had a terrible job: she had the blind slaves to care for, and the bodies of the Keepers and the slavers to dispose of, but Bueralan understood why she would prefer to stay.

'It happened two days after you left,' Ai Sela said to the Innocent, pushing herself to her feet as he approached. 'I left *Glafanr* in the morning to check on the slaves. I had put them in the hulls of the other ships. It was not a long walk, but I did not think that the ship was under threat. What could threaten *Glafanr*?' She ran her hand through her dark hair, grabbing at it as she did. 'It happened once I stepped onto the dock. I felt the air behind me change, as if the wind blowing in off Leviathan's Blood had suddenly picked up because of a storm. But when I turned around, *Glafanr* was simply gone. There was a ripple in the water, and I thought – I thought that it had sunk. I dived in after it, but *Glafanr* wasn't there. Of course it hadn't sunk. Of course.'

It could not sink, Bueralan finished to himself. A swell of panic ran through the god-touched men and women around Sela as they whispered and talked to each other. Only he and Orlan – who had pushed through the crowd towards the end of her story – did not share it. Instead, the old man's blue-eyed gaze met his with a cool curiosity. Something, he knew, just as Bueralan knew, important had happened.

'I can tell you what befell *Glafanr*,' Se'Saera said from behind them. She stood at the podium and looked, Bueralan thought, to have aged since she had arrived in Ranan. She was still young, and still beautiful, but she had cast off the last of her childhood youth and now looked like a young woman. 'But truly, you should not look for answers among yourselves. I offer this only as advice to you all. Do not look into yourself. Look to me. I have answers for you.'

'I did not mean to offend,' Ai Sela said respectfully.

'You have not.' The god left the podium and walked towards them. '*Glafanr* has returned to the River of the Dead. It takes Zaifyr to Heüala.'

Bueralan felt a jolt of recognition at the first name – he remembered the charm-laced man standing next to him beneath Mireea – but was confused by the second. The murmurs around him did not help. He did know of a River of the Dead, but it was in Yeala and was named because of sealife that came up it to die. At its end rested a huge lake filled with bones, but he was sure that the long, twisting river was not the one that Se'Saera meant. 'I can feel him approaching,' the god continued. 'The river has no defined length, but it will take *Glafanr* a long time to reach the gates of Heüala with him upon it. He is accompanied by the ancient dead who threatened me in Yeflam, and by others, of which only one I know intimately. He is my eyes. My first creation and part of my first betrayal.' She paused, as if she could see the great ship now, travelling the waters of another world. Perhaps, Bueralan realized, she could. 'What you see here before you is but a small part of me. My parents carried me to Heüala before they began to sacrifice themselves in this world. I can be threatened there, but I am not afraid. I have seen Zaifyr's arrival. I have seen the staff that he will use to open the gates. My general will fall at the same time and you, Aela, will go to retrieve his body for me.

'But first,' she said, her attention returning to those before her in the cathedral. 'First you and your soldiers will ride to the south. You will find a force there made from the remnants of Mireea and Yeflam. They have been welded together by the Saan, who have come here because of what happened in Ooila.'

'They will be dealt with,' the Innocent said calmly.

'You should know that Eidan is with them,' she said. 'He is in the company of both Jae'le and Tinh Tu.'

He nodded, but there was a hint, Bueralan saw, of pleasure and violence in his gaze.

Se'Saera began to leave, but in mid-stride she stopped. 'Fate is not whole yet,' she said, not just to Ren, but to all the god-touched. She did not face them, but rather stared at the empty walls of her cathedral. 'I know some of you thought I would have been better served to find the remains of my parents throughout the world, but the pull to Ranan is too strong, too prevalent in all the futures I see. Here, our victory will be won, and you will all stand beside me after it. None of you will die. You will all be part of my world. You will be the faces of myself in the world. You will define me to both the Faithful and the faithless.' She turned to them, to all of them, including Bueralan and Orlan. 'But we should not be complacent.

There are dangers. We are not under threat, but the shape of the world I will create is. We cannot allow for that to be subverted.'

After she left, the Innocent turned to those around him and issued a short order to prepare to ride in the next few days. 'And you,' he said to Samuel Orlan, after he had given it, 'I will need you. I do not know the land that lies between here and Mireea well.'

The cartographer met the other man's gaze without flinching. 'If I'd rather stay?'

'Bueralan will stay to care for the girl,' he said.

'That's not what I meant,' he began, but before he could say more, Bueralan interrupted. 'Let Kaze stay to care for Taela,' he said.

It was not just Orlan who looked at him in surprise. 'Why would you want to come?' Ren asked.

He could lie, but the saboteur knew it would do him no good against this man. 'It isn't about me,' he said. 'Taela needs care that I can't give her. Kaze can do that. I'll fill her place in your little army while she does that.'

The Innocent had questions, but so did Orlan, and the other men and women in the cathedral. He could see Kaze at the back of the ground, the last of the light caught on her glasses, and he knew that she had questions as well. And they should: Bueralan had told the truth, but it was half a truth, one that hid another, and that other truth was that he had a plan. A sudden, desperate plan, one first born in the conversation he and Ren had had about Onaedo. One that – if he wanted to help Taela – he could not wait to begin.

After what seemed like an eternity, Aela Ren nodded, and the exchange was accepted without further comment.

7.

In the early hours of the morning, the Captain of Refuge left Vaeasa. Beneath a smoke-stained night sky, a line of heavy wagons and soldiers made their way out of the gates and headed east, towards the ruins of Celp.

Heast did not see the Lord of Faaisha again before he left, but after Lehana and her soldiers had arrived, before the wagons were pulled out of the warehouse, before the horses were placed into harnesses, Tuael sent a messenger. The young man arrived with a rolled map, one drawn in sketches of ink that would have made Samuel Orlan shudder for its simplicity. It marked out positions stretching from the north of Faaisha down to the south. The first was the Faaishan force that the marshals had brought together, the second the positions of the Leerans. They were marked in white and red, respectively, while a single black dot in the east marked Refuge. The position marked was the outpost Refuge had destroyed before Heast and Anemone had come to Vaeasa, and he took from that a small pleasure, for it meant that Bliq and Qiyala had managed to evade whatever trackers the marshals had left there while they made their way to Celp. Beyond that, however, the message was simple: the Lord of Faaisha and his marshals were going to push down into the collection of Leeran forces, and they wanted Refuge to push up, into them.

It was a simple, if brutal, battle plan, one that would be won through bodies, blood and sheer numbers. Heast would not have thought the Faaishans had the numbers for such a push, but the map had a small note pinned to the back of it, which explained that a combined force from Mireea and Yeflam were marching with the Saan over the Spine of Ger.

The Saan.

Surely Muriel had not hired them?

'The Innocent killed the war scout of the Dvir in Cynama,' Lehana told him, after they had left Vaeasa, after the torchlit walls that defined the world behind them had fallen away. She drove the fourth of the eight carts along the road, the reins loose in her hands, and a finely made bastard sword at her feet. 'It happened at a party that the Queen's youngest daughter gave. Yoala announced her engagement to a Saan prince moments before the Innocent arrived. He killed her, and he killed a number of Saan warriors after that.' She tightened the reins as the trail they followed wound through thick trees. 'He did not kill the Saan prince. He escaped, and the Queen sent him back to his father.'

Heast stretched his steel leg out to ease the muscles on his hip. 'I would not want the Saan as my enemies,' he said, 'but they are not the boon that you would think them to be on the battlefield.'

'Are they undisciplined?'

'No. They fight well with each other, but poorly alongside others. Most experienced captains will not sign on to fight beside them.'

'Does that mean we'll leave, then?' Lehana had, Heast was discovering, a dry, quick humour. 'I can go back to my bed, my husband, my gardens and my gold.'

'You would miss the excitement of using Tinalan fire lances,' he said. 'I was surprised to learn that the First Queen had access to them.'

'She didn't. Truthfully, the Queen did little of the work for what is in the carts. The majority of it was done by a representative of Leviathan's End.'

Heast was surprised.

'I didn't think you knew,' Lehana said, after she saw his face. 'It was a woman who arrived. What I remember most was her neatness, how all her clothes were tailored to fit her exactly. She had a very precise way of speaking Ooilan, as well. There was nothing wrong with how she spoke it, and in fact, it was its perfection that set it aside. No slang, no slips in pronunciation, nothing. Her name was Zlyv. She offered nothing in the way of a last name. When she did speak, she spoke to the Queen. She said that she had been sent on behalf of Leviathan's End, to provide for Captain Heast and Refuge. I could barely believe what I heard.'

Heast shared her feeling, even now. He could not remember any battle in which Onaedo had used her own considerable power to influence a conflict.

'The Queen had begun to stockpile weapons and armour,' Lehana continued, while one hand reached back, into the back of the cart. 'We had not arrived in Vaeasa unarmed, but the Queen and I had always believed that we would need more, but because of the war, it was hard to get much from within Faaisha to put aside. The warehouse you saw wasn't even a quarter full before Zlyv arrived. But by the end of the week it was as we saw it. The Queen sent me to oversee the deliveries. Leviathan's End did not name a price for what was delivered, and for a while we all thought that it was not what it seemed.' She pulled out a package wrapped in brown paper. 'But it was,' she said, handing the parcel to Heast. 'It was everything, and more.'

The paper slit easily. A square cloth badge fell out, followed by others. On each of them was an empty image of the world over a red and black background.

There was no letter.

Heast picked up one of the insignias of Refuge and turned it over in his hand. 'Newly made,' he said.

'What does that mean?'

He shrugged and changed the topic. 'I was told,' he said, 'that you cannot go home. That none of you can.'

If Lehana was surprised, she hid it well. 'A Queen's Guard lives and dies with her Queen. At least, that is the tradition. None of us here was ever a guard for the Queen before. In a previous life, I mean. Pueral made it clear to all of us when we were given the posting that we were being given it based on our actions, our reputations and our dedication. It was not a secret by the time I was given my post, but it was still controversial. The Queen's daughters were quite open in their belief that we would still die with the Queen, as the guards before had.'

Heast handed her one of the insignias. 'After we are done here, you and your soldiers will be given a choice. You can stay, or you can go.'

'After?' She smiled and there was, in her smile, a gentleness. 'Captain, we're all going to die here.'

'After,' he repeated. 'But first, who is your best sergeant? The one who trains your recruits and runs soldiers hard.'

'Ko Dtnaa,' she said without hesitation.

'When we camp, I'll show her how to use the fire lance. She'll have the responsibility of training the rest of you. When we reach Celp, she'll also have new soldiers to break in. She'll find them dedicated and hungry, but inexperienced.'

Lehana nodded. 'And me, sir? Refuge cannot have two captains.'

'You'll be my second,' he told the soldier who, until recently, had been Captain to the First Queen. 'If I die, Refuge is yours to command.'

8.

What surprised Ayae most about Anguish's disappearance was how calmly Eidan took it. When she returned to the market square with Tinh Tu, she expected to find him anxious, pacing the broken cobbled road, having failed to find the creature in his search of Mireea. It was how Eidan had reacted in Yeflam after Se'Saera's trial, and Ayae knew that he felt a responsibility for the other, a responsibility that had been born in Ranan, when he had stood beside the new god.

She was surprised, then, when she entered the square and found both Eidan and Jae'le sitting on a pair of empty barrels, talking among themselves. The afternoon's sun had set and, if Ayae had not known otherwise, if she had come across the pair on the streets of Mireea before it had been destroyed, she would have thought that the two were nothing more than two poor men who worked in the markets. She would have thought that they had come to the end of their day's work. It was a surprising thought for her: she had not, before then, viewed Eidan or Jae'le as anything but beings of immense power. But here, in their old clothes, patterned by scars and thinness, they looked as far from that as they could be.

'I do not think Anguish will be back,' Eidan said to her. 'I think the events that gave birth to him have seen him taken elsewhere. My sister's suggestion is most likely correct.'

'Events?' They meant fate, she knew. 'You cannot keep trusting things you cannot see.'

'It is not simply belief I have. I was there when Se'Saera made Anguish. I remember how she was at first pleased, but soon bothered by him, in some manner. She called him Anguish because of the pain he was in, but I do not think she was pleased by that. I wondered about that until she told me that some days he felt as if he was hers and on others as if he was someone else's. I have a similar feeling here in Mireea. It is in the stones and the buildings. It is familiar but not. Close but distant. Wherever the ghosts have gone, Anguish has gone as well.'

'You think the ghosts are gone?'

'Yes.'

'Zaifyr remains the same,' Jae'le said beside him. 'But without our guide, it leaves us in a very strange position.'

'It leaves us paralysed,' Tinh Tu told him sourly.

'It certainly leaves us waiting.'

'For the army that follows us?'

It would be another three days before the combined forces of Yeflam, Mireea and the Saan entered Mireea. Once Ayae had climbed into the back of the cart in the camp, Jae'le had urged the horses into a steady pace to put distance between them and the forces. She had expected to still be in Mireea when they arrived, and the easy nature of Jae'le's shrug suggested that he had always thought the same.

'They are of no concern to us,' he said. 'Let them come and go.'

The night deepened around them and they continued to talk. Past midnight, Ayae found herself starting to drift to sleep, and to stave it off, she rose and walked over to the cart. There, she lifted the edge of the blanket that lay across Zaifyr. The moon and the stars lit him well enough that she could see the clothes his brothers and sister had dressed him in before they left the camp. They had done it carefully: they had acquired new clothes, well made and expensive, a contrast to what they themselves wore. They had combed his hair and, where they could, refastened the charms that had still been on him. More than a few were missing, but it was this attention to detail that, each time she looked at him, touched her deeply. As much as Zaifyr could not let go of life, his family could not let go of him—

'Ayae,' Jae'le said quietly.

She saw the ghost immediately: it walked down the road, a middle-aged bearded man in a robe.

'Is he . . . ?'

'No,' Ayae said to him. 'He is not a ghost of Mireea.'

She knew that with certainty. She did not know all the people who had died in the siege a year ago, but the robe the ghost wore was not one that anyone in Mireea would have worn. It reminded her of Se'Saera's priests in Yeflam, the ones who had stood on the wooden crates and spoken to crowds who did not care for them.

When the ghost reached for Zaifyr, Ayae's hand dropped to her sword – only to feel Jae'le's grip stop her from drawing it. 'No,' he said softly. 'Let us watch, first. Let us follow.'

The ghost picked up Zaifyr and cradled him in his arms like a child. He did not appear to notice the four of them. Soon, he began to walk along the damaged road.

Ayae believed he was heading towards the sunken remains of The Pale House, but she did not say anything to the others. She feared that she would be wrong if she said it, that they would skip ahead and the ghost would drop into one of the gaps in the road and disappear into the caverns beneath Mireea. If he did that, they would struggle to find him, she was sure. But despite her thoughts, the ghost continued towards The Pale House. Its front doors were half submerged beneath the cobbled road.

'Do you think he is a priest?' Eidan asked. 'He looks like one of Se'Saera's. Perhaps he is one she left behind.'

'Look at the robe closely,' Tinh Tu said. 'There is a pattern in it.'

Ayae could not immediately see it. The white lines of the ghost, the lack of colour in its body, kept anything but the shape of its body from her, until, as the ghost climbed through a broken window, she saw the vaguest suggestion of chains woven into a long-lost fabric.

'Ger,' Jae'le said, as if he had been waiting for her to see it. 'He is a priest who served the Warden of the Elements. Much like Lor Jix served the Leviathan, I would imagine.'

An ancient dead, then. A soul cursed by its god never to enter paradise. Ayae followed Jae'le and Eidan through the window into the remains of a once well-furnished office. There, on the sloped floor, she turned to offer her aid to Tinh Tu, but the old woman, who was climbing through the window, saw her offered hand and gave it such a withering look that Ayae mumbled an apology before turning away. She slid past the overturned table, the scattered papers and quills and out of the door into the office. If Tinh Tu's two brothers had not already left the room, Ayae was sure that they would have laughed at her.

The two were already at the end of the hall, half a dozen steps behind the ghost. A spiral staircase led them downstairs into the lobby. There, split tiles and broken plaster defined the floor, but in the far corner was a collection of blankets and pillows. It looked to be recently made, the items taken from the rooms of The Pale House, rooms that had once cost a fortune for a night's stay.

It was to that makeshift bed that the ghost took Zaifyr's body and laid it down.

Once he had done that, he turned to face Ayae, Jae'le, Eidan and Tinh Tu, and this time, she could tell that the ghost saw each of them. In slender, flashing lights, other ghosts began to appear around the priest, some men, some women, each of them wearing similar robes. After a few moments, over two dozen ghosts stood there, each of them surrounding Zaifyr, as if to protect him from the men and women he called his family.

9.

Eilona approached the Spires of Alati on the old, creaking deck of the ship on which she and Olcea had come to Yeflam. Tinh Tu had called it *The Frozen Shackle*, but Eilona could find no mention of the ship's name, either on the hull, or in the closed ledger in the captain's cabin.

She had returned to the vessel on the dinghy that had delivered her to the camp. As it had done on that day, a ghost rowed the small boat out to the ship, and as before, Eilona's mind was unable to picture a man between the two oars, rowing steadily at the command of Olcea. She wondered if Caeli, sitting beside her, could see it. She tried not to stare at the guard and found herself, instead, gazing out over the black ocean. Once on deck, the memories of Eilona's silent journey on *The Frozen Shackle* with Tinh Tu returned. Olcea had almost died piloting the ship down the coast and, at the helm, the old wheel was still covered in dried blood.

A part of Eilona did not believe she should have agreed to her mother's plan. Earlier, she had watched the combined forces of the Mireean, Yeflam and Saan people march up the Mountains of Ger. She had planned to stand beside her mother in support while the soldiers left the camp, and she had even woken in the early hours of the morning to ensure that she was there. But, as she stood in front of her tent beneath the grey sky, she began to second-guess herself. She was sure the soldiers would not be happy to see her. At the entrance to the tent she told herself that it would be best to remain away. Besides, her mother did not need her. Eilona said that to herself at least half a dozen times that morning, but she did not believe it. Her mother was no longer the indomitable figure of her childhood.

'Ah, the prospect of battle,' Sinae Al'tor said, approaching her. He was neatly dressed in fine black, as if he were going to a funeral. A step behind him followed his beautiful blonde shadow. 'It is meant to fire the heart, inspire the mind, and seal all your doubts inside you, where they will not be allowed to find voice. Unless you are a cynic, of course, and then you wonder how many can return from war with the Innocent.'

'In Sooia, he was once buried beneath a mountain,' Eilona said. 'It was five hundred years ago. The desert still had its oasis then. The southern side of the country was flooded with refugees. There are old sketches of them. They carry everything they own on their backs. I remember reading about it in my first year at the University of Zanebien. For some reason, I had always thought that the Innocent's conquest was done in a day, or a week, not in centuries. But he was defeated. It was his first real loss, and for a decade afterwards the people of Sooia thought that he and his soldiers had been killed. But he wasn't dead. He crawled from the mountain that had buried him. He and all his soldiers emerged as if they had been asleep and returned to their war.'

'Your answer, then, is none?' He smiled, and she supposed that there was, in it, something sad. 'Then the question for us is, what will we do, after?'

'I'll return to Pitak. To my house, to my research, to Laena. Maybe I will help her. She will have a lot of writing about the god Ain to complete.'

'But that will be temporary, won't it? Se'Saera will continue to spread herself further and further through the world forced upon us by the Innocent. He will demand that we bow to her.'

'I don't imagine you bowing.'

He shrugged. 'If it was the choice between death and life, I would bow. I have seen the dead. I have seen them in ways that have frightened me like nothing else. Who would wish to court that? I ask you.'

Not her.

But more tellingly, Eilona thought that Sinae's words mirrored a realization she had about her mother.

Muriel Wagan had very little. Olcea had tried to tell her that when she had delivered the letter to her home, but it was not until Eilona arrived on the shore of Yeflam that she finally understood it. Her mother was the Lady of the Ghosts because she could no longer be the Lady of the Spine. She was a wealthy woman but if her debts to Lian Alahn were paid, she would no longer be that. Stripped of title and wealth, her mother would be a middle-aged woman kept by the few people who had faith in her. Oh, Eilona knew that she would carve out a life for herself within that. Muriel Wagan had not been the ruler of Mireea through a trick of birth. She had built up her fortunes and political alliances while the lord before her declined. When she had taken control, she had done so because she had been intelligent, canny and fearless. With time, those attributes would allow her mother to regain the money she had lost, but without Mireea, would it matter?

Her mother did not define herself through her child, her marriages, or even her friendships. Eilona was keenly aware – and had been since she was a child – that her mother defined herself through Mireea. Ultimately, that was why Eilona had agreed to go to the Spires of Alati, to be her mother's envoy. On the deck of *The Frozen Shackle*, invisible hands drew up the anchor. Leviathan's Blood shifted and rocked the boat, as if the first of an acidic humour had awoken, courtesy of Eilona's thoughts. The ocean had the right to laugh at her acting as a political envoy. She lacked the political cunning to deal with Lian Alahn's son, to negotiate with the men and women she met in the remains of Yeflam. She was simply an academic.

If her mother only had more. If only she had not been so diminished. If only Eilona did not feel a responsibility to her. If only she had not begun to feel as if she owed not just her mother, but Mireea, this act.

10.

Beneath the starlight, Aned Heast sat on the back of a stationary cart and sewed Refuge's insignia onto the arm of the heavy shirt he wore under his leather armour. It was his third shirt, but his final shirt. It marked the third cold camp that he had made since leaving Vaeasa. There would be another two, he suspected, before he and the others reached the camp of Refuge.

He had no complaints to make. The carts had made good time and Heast had spent most of the time talking to the soldiers who rode alongside him. He learned their names and listened to their histories. He had spent a night with Ko Dtnaa, packing and firing one of the lances. Heast's own limited experience with the weapon meant that the pair were learning it together. But it was a simple weapon for all its brutality, one that did not require the finesse of a sword, or the targeting of a crossbow. On the second night, Dtnaa began organizing the other soldiers into small groups to learn the weapon. Watching the soldiers, Heast had to admit that the First Queen and her Eyes had chosen well. In the absence of either, he was not surprised to learn that the soldiers were fiercely loyal to the newly minted Lieutenant Lehana. In the last few days that he had ridden beside them, he had listened to them talk, had seen how they interacted with each other, and had watched as they stowed the insignia of Refuge into their packs or pushed them into their pockets. They were Ooilan soldiers, still. They were the Queen's soldiers, not Refuge's, not yet. When they died, they would die in the old service they believed they were in.

It was entirely likely that they would die, as well.

How many armies had been raised against the Innocent? Hundreds? There was no way to know exactly. In Sooia, generations had fallen to Aela Ren, and each time, a new rival, a new hope, had risen from the survivors. In Sooia, Heast had once met a young woman whose hands had been horribly scarred by burns. She had been the head of one such hope. But when she asked Captain Denali to ride with him into the heart of the deserts in search of Aela Ren, the Captain had told her no. He said that she should instead look to resettling her people.

Heast could not tell the First Queen's Guard they would survive the upcoming war. They had already seen what the Innocent could do, and he would not lie to them. But he did not want any soldier to believe that she was going to die. Such thoughts made a soldier careless. Heast had seen it many times: when faced with the inevitability of death, a soldier forgot the lessons she had learned in the battles she had survived. She would take risks that she knew she should not take. It did not matter if she was part of the First Queen's Guard, or if she was from the back alleys of Gogair. Once she decided that her death was inevitable, she would search for that moment, and in doing so, she would take others with her.

'My grandmother always said you had fine needlework. I thought it was a metaphor for your skills with a sword.' Anemone approached him with a tin cup of water. 'It surprises me how literal she was.'

Heast took the cup. 'I have probably sewn more flesh together than cloth.'

The witch eased herself onto the cart next to him. 'I will forever think of you as a seamstress then, sir.' In the dark, the tattoos that showed beneath her collar and wrists lent her the illusion that she was, in part, made from darkness. 'Do you marvel at how easily they sleep around us?'

She meant Lehana and her soldiers. 'No,' he said.

'Some of them could have been at Illate. Or at their parents' houses. You would think it would make things harder.'

'Your grandmother was in Illate as well.' Heast set the cup down. 'Also, you should remember that Refuge lost.'

'It does not feel it tonight.'

No, he supposed it did not. 'We all have moments in our life where we must redefine who we are. What the soldiers around us go through is no different to what you went through in Vaeasa.'

'Or you after Illate.'

'Your grandmother tells you too much.'

Anemone smiled. 'She did not need to tell me that, Captain. I have watched the title settle on you since Maosa. It has been like watching a person pull on a shirt after winter. It fits, but it is tight. As the days wear on, as the rituals of the summer return, it fits more naturally.'

He thanked her, but was not sure that he believed her, not now. Before he left Vaeasa, he would have agreed with what Anemone said: he was becoming more the man he used to be, the man who had been the Captain of Refuge. But after Lehana had told him that Onaedo had organized the crates that they carried, he had begun to feel a strangeness about him, as if he was not entirely within control of what happened around him. It was a feeling of insignificance, unlike one he had felt before. He had felt that he was but a small part on a larger board – that was, after all, the nature of being a mercenary, and the way in which war felt to the individual – but he had before been able to see the board in its entirety. To be unable to see it, to feel as if something was being kept from him, but that he was still being pushed towards a final conflict, was not an experience he enjoyed. It was similar, Heast thought, to the games he and Samuel Orlan had played in Mireea. They had been the games of old men who knew too much and who had wanted to test what the other knew. Heast had often felt that the cartographer played the game on a different board to his, one larger than the one Heast saw, and quite often he felt that Orlan played a much more complex game than he did.

It was a thought that he could not resolve easily and, as the morning's sun rose, he put it aside as he had done every other morning. His immediate concern remained the soldiers around him. Before any of them rode out against the Innocent, he wanted to dull the certainty of their own deaths. He did not yet know how, but he had to give them a future, had to offer them a world that did not end with the Innocent.

When they came across tracks on the fifth day from of Vaeasa, he still did not have an answer to that question.

They were close to Celp and, instead of making camp for the night, they had pushed onwards in the dark. The tracks appeared as slivers of shadows and were made by horses, more than Heast could count, but one of Lehana's soldiers – a tall, slim black woman she called Fenna – said that it was three distinct groups, days apart. The second, she insisted, was the largest. She told him that the first and third groups were about a hundred each, but that the second was about three hundred strong, though not all were mounted. She stopped in the middle of her explanation when smoke began to drift across them from the east.

'Break open the crates,' Heast said. 'The Leerans have found Refuge.'

A Baptism of Fire

'It was a powerful statement,' Aelyn Meah said. 'It has also been proven true. Se'Saera has healed our world.'

None would deny that: a single sun shines above us. The weather has patterns that makes sense. The moon is gone. The ocean is no longer black. The mad coast is safe, a grand swamp no longer changes its paths, mountains that once floated do not, and rivers that strangled communities and were as still as ice now flow.

'All my life I had worked to fix the damage the War of the Gods had done. That was to be my divinity. That was to be my proof to the world that I was a god. How could I deny that to the world in another?' Aelyn asked me. 'If my life, my continual living, was part of what ensured a healthy, stable world, how could I do anything but live?'

—Onaedo, *Histories, Year 1029*

1.

The smoke revealed itself not to be isolated strands, but a thick, dark cloud, one that Heast and the First Queen's Guard prepared to ride into. It began to form around them while the carts were taken off the road, the horses unhitched and the crates unpacked.

'Leave the fire lances,' Heast ordered. The night's light was obscured by the smoke, but not enough so that he could not see the fires ahead in his spyglass. 'Bows only.'

Lehana, who stood on the back of the first cart, nodded with grim satisfaction when she heard him, but the soldiers who had moved towards her, who had come to collect the weapons she handed out, did not share her agreement. Heast understood that: they had looked at the tracks, had heard the conversation he and Fenna had had, and they had looked for themselves. They knew that the numbers ahead were not in their favour. Still it would be foolish to take the fire lances, Heast knew. In the worst of the heat, the black powder would be a threat. It would be waiting to catch the flames around them, waiting to explode on their hips, or in the long tube.

At his horse, the Captain of Refuge pulled out a faded black cloth from his pack. Before him, Anemone wrapped a white cloth around her nose and mouth, but Heast kept his in his hand while he grabbed the pommel of his saddle.

'Leerans,' he said, after he had pulled himself awkwardly up. 'Leerans aren't all like us,' he continued to the soldiers around him, to the soldiers who had begun to wrap dark red cloths around their faces after they had mounted. 'Some are. Leera had a small army. They were well trained, but Leera was not a nation with expansionist plans, and their military reflected that. They did not have the soldiers you will see here. Se'Saera made the force you see here when she emerged. When she began her war, she drew all the people of Leera to her and told them to break apart their towns. She told them to tear down their homes. She told them to destroy their history. She told them that they were her Faithful and that they did not need their old lives. The first of Se'Saera's soldiers filed their teeth into sharp ends and ate the flesh of the people they killed.'

At the carts, the former Captain of the Queen's Guard paused. She held the last of the bows in her hand.

'The Faithful have given up everything to fight for Se'Saera,' Heast said. 'For them, there is no home to go back to. There is no land to defend. There is just the word of their god. That is how they will fight when you meet them.

'If we meet them on open ground before Celp, we will meet them in a wedge. The point of our wedge will be Saelo, Beilase, Zvae and Oya.' He nodded to the four soldiers who, one by one, returned his nod. 'It may be that we won't need to do that. It may be that we will fight in Celp. We will have Anemone scouting as we ride, so we'll know before we hit the town. But what we can be assured of is that we will be fighting in a burned landscape. Your horses won't like it. You won't like it. Use the bows to clear what you can from a distance. The quicker we can find Refuge and finish this, the better.' Heast pointed to the imprints on the ground, the three groups Fenna had identified. 'I know that what is there is not a small force, but it doesn't matter. We leave no one behind.'

Lehana approached Heast, a bow and arrows in one hand, and a small, curling bone-and-brass horn in her other. She handed the latter to him. 'Fight the way you were trained to fight,' she said, after she turned from him. 'Remember who you are. Remember where you are from. That is how we will survive. How we will win.'

'One last thing,' Heast said. 'You might come across a warrior that we call an ancestor. It'll be bigger than you, it'll look deformed, and it may even have extra limbs. Se'Saera pulled these soldiers from the Plateau. They were the ancient spirits that were imprisoned there, but she has tied them to the bodies of her Faithful. They are bad news. If you see one, you let Anemone deal with it.' He paused. 'Any questions?'

There were not.

Heast wrapped the faded black cloth over his nose and mouth. As he did, Anemone began to unwind the strips of cloth that covered her scarred palms. She had slipped a knife into the edge of the saddle. If things went badly, or if the battle went on for long, her hands would lose their strength, would become slippery with blood, and she would be forced to wrap the reins around her arms and hope that the horse she rode did not bolt or try to throw her.

Heast turned to the thickening smoke and nudged his horse forwards, into it. Was it a Leeran trap, this fire? He doubted it. The tracks were too obvious, too rushed, and the fire too wild, too unconstrained.

The fire had been allowed to grow. Heast was certain of that. The red tint of the skyline revealed how established it was. What he didn't know was who had set it. If the fire was restricted to Celp, Heast could imagine the Leerans around the ruins, awaiting for Refuge to emerge; but the fire was not localized. In his spyglass he had seen it in trees, the tops burning wickedly. Did that mean Refuge had started the fire? If so, it would be an act of desperation, a suicide tactic, for it had destroyed any secure retreat that they could have made.

What would he find in the smoke? Would it be small parties, or a large force? Would he reach Celp and find a ragged, angry battle, with soldiers half suffocated, or already dead? Would—

The Captain of Refuge stopped his thoughts. He would not get ahead of himself. He would see what caused the fire and he would deal with it, just as he would deal with the Leerans.

2.

The path that Samuel Orlan charted through the empty landscape of Leera was one watched over by the dark shapes of swamp crows. They flocked in the hollow remains of towns and turned the branches of trees dark, like a hangman's noose, in the winter.

It was a lonely, unsettling world that Bueralan rode through, further emphasized by the silent company of the god-touched men and women around him. In the camps, they set their rolls away from each other and rarely spoke. Frequently, before sleep claimed him, Bueralan would turn to gaze at the shadowed shapes of the immortal men and women, and he would see figures who had been stripped of all their humanity. He recalled, in those moments, how he had been told that, in Sooia, the bones of the dead had been sown into into the soil, and he wondered if he had made the right choice in leaving Ranan.

At least once a day, both Bueralan and Samuel Orlan were presented with an opportunity to leave the Innocent and his soldiers. It did not matter if the morning's sun was high, the afternoon's just rising, or the midday's sun riding low. There simply came a moment when he and Orlan could stop their mounts, where they could turn and ride to the east. Bueralan never took the chances seriously, but on the third day out of Ranan, he thought that the cartographer meant to do that. He and Bueralan had drifted far enough from the Innocent and his soldiers that they were but a shadow in the distance.

Next to him, Orlan leant over in his saddle and spat into the grass. 'I hope whatever plan you've got is a good one,' he said.

'It's not,' Bueralan said. 'It's desperate and half formed.'

The other man nodded and, without another word, nudged his grey forwards and closed the distance between him and the others.

Later, on the third night's camp, Bueralan thought of telling Orlan what Ren had said to him about Onaedo, but he didn't. On the fourth, he almost returned to the earlier conversation that he and Orlan had had on *Glafanr*. He thought about repeating what Kaze had said. On the fifth night, he realized that he wouldn't. It was not that he did not trust the cartographer – such a question no longer remained between the two of them – but rather that he did not truly know what he was doing. All he knew was that he was involved in a last-minute, last-chance, desperate leap, and he did not know where he would truly land, and what he would have to do, once he did. He only knew that he could not remain inert within the tragedy unfolding around him.

That was why, before he left Ranan, Bueralan had visited Aelyn Meah.

He had done it after he said goodbye to Taela. She lay in their room, her stomach larger than it had been only a day before, but she said nothing to him after he explained to her that he would be gone for a few weeks and that Kaze would look after her. He crouched beside her, wanting to reach out with his hand, to hold her, to tell her that everything would be fine. But he couldn't.

When he left her, he walked into Aelyn's room. The door was open, and he did not knock. The Breath of Yeflam sat on the bed against the wall, her back against it, her legs folded beneath her. She wore clean white linen clothes, which made her look like a prisoner in a cell, despite the fact that she could have walked out of the room at any time. But there were prisons, Bueralan knew, not built out of walls and doors.

Aelyn did not say a word as Bueralan entered. She watched him as he opened the window and looked out at Ranan, at its dark splendour, at the horrific creatures that sat on the flat roofs.

'I have a favour to ask,' he said, turning to face her.

Aelyn was silent for a long time, so long that Bueralan thought he might have to continue the conversation without her involvement. 'What makes you think you can ask anything of me?' she asked, finally.

'Nothing.'

She waited.

'I would like you to watch the woman down the hall,' he continued. 'Her name is Zi Taela.'

'I will not stand guard over her, if that is what you are asking,' Aelyn said. A breeze drifted through the window. 'There are others to continue that crime against her.'

'I do not want you to stand guard,' Bueralan said. 'I want you to make sure no one hurts her more.'

The air fell still. 'The best way to do that is to take her away from here,' the sitting woman said. 'She will never be free while she is forced to stand beside her tormentor.'

'I know.'

'Do you?' Aelyn Meah unfolded her legs and rose. She was a slight woman next to Bueralan, but she had, within her, a grace, a sense of confidence, that was intimidating. 'I have had another man in my mind for nearly a thousand years. He was a friend before the whispers began, before the nudges and promises, and I suppose that is why I let it happen. I have so few friends I forgot that it is they who betray you most. But for a thousand years he was there. His control was gentle, but it was still control. He took all the dark thoughts I had, all my fears and resentments, and he twisted them in me, made me question, made me doubt, and made me betray who I was. Can you possibly imagine how that feels?'

'I can,' he said.

'Then don't leave her here. The only way you can help her is to take her away. She will never have any hope while she is here with—'

'Do not say her name,' Bueralan interrupted, fighting the urge to reach for her, to close his hand around her mouth. '*She* can hear her name.'

Aelyn tilted her head, surprised. Then she nodded and said, 'Take Taela away from here.'

'And where would she go? Where in the world will she be free if our new god continues to exist? Where will any of us be free? If you can name a place, do it, and I will take her there. I will take us all there.' He paused and when Aelyn said nothing, he continued. 'I don't want to see her hurt. That's all. That's all I am asking you.'

'I will watch her,' she said, turning back to her bed. 'But I cannot promise you that she won't be hurt again. Not here.'

He had left shortly after that. He had walked down the stairs and through the cathedral and out onto the streets of Ranan, where Se'Saera's creatures were rising from their perches. When he had saddled the tall grey and joined the Innocent and his soldiers, the monsters were swarming to the cathedral, answering Se'Saera's call. Whatever she wanted, Bueralan gave it no thought.

A day's ride ahead of him was an army. Orlan's path had led Ren and his soldiers to it, a fact that surprised Bueralan a little, for he had suspected that the cartographer would hesitate to do that. Orlan knew, just as he did, that the army from Mireea and Yeflam would break against the god-touched men and women. They would fail against these men and women no matter what skill they had, because the shadows of men and women who lingered in the camp around him could not die. Their mortality was hidden, locked in a history that had never happened, or that had passed before they had been born. They were men and women removed from a fate in which they could die and they would slaughter all who stood before them.

How, Bueralan asked himself, would he stop such people?

3.

The smoke thickened, the night became one of shadows, broken only by the violent red line that drew them onwards.

Fat flakes of ash floated through the air. With each step, Heast's horse kicked up more from the still warm ground and stained both it and him in the remains of the destruction that they rode through. Around them, the trees reached up with fragile nude branches, like tall, inhuman dancers that had been turned to stone and left as warning statues. On them, the dark shapes of soot-stained birds kept a gentle roost. In silence, they watched the Captain of Refuge and the First Queen's Guard make their slow way across the land.

They had been fortunate. The line of fire that had been heading towards the west, to where they had been riding from, had died in a ravine a few hundred yards back. The Kingdoms of Faaisha were dotted with its like, and many of the communities had stripped everything but dirt and rock in them to make a fire break. In the summer, the eastern side of the nation was periodically ignited by fires and for years, before the summer set in, many of the ravines were cleared of all but rocks and earth, to act as fire breaks. The ravine that they had ridden through had most likely been cleared by men and women from Celp a season ago, but they had done a good job. Not so much as a single sapling had grown to allow the fire to jump the gap. The lack of wind helped, as well. It meant that none of the cinders revealed beneath the steel shoes of the horses could be caught and thrown into live growth.

In the other direction, though, where the ruins of Celp lay, it was different. There the fire burned strongly.

Another ravine appeared, a camp's charred remains within it. Silently, Heast indicated to four of the Queen's Guard and, with Anemone beside him, rode down onto the ash-stained floor. He could have pushed ahead, he knew, put his heels into his horse and ridden for the ruins, but he was still bothered by the story of the fire, by what he would find there. The fact that Anemone had yet to find any of the Leerans only made him more intent not to rush ahead. He was sure that if he did, he would find himself arriving, not only with exhausted, smoke-stained mounts, but to take part in a battle he didn't understand. That Heast did not want.

The ravine's walls loomed around him. The ground was warmer than that outside and sweat began to run down his forehead and spine. Ahead lay ash-covered dirt, rock and cloth.

Fenna handed the last to him. She leant out of her saddle and speared the fabric with her sword. It broke apart in Heast's grasp, but the fragment he held did not seem familiar. Nor did the tents that appeared shortly after. They were the remains of frames now, broken and barely holding onto their shape. The cloth that had been burned away and the remains of blackened rolls and backpacks lay beneath, vague shapes barely suggestive of the forms they once had.

There were no bodies in any of them.

A dead campfire appeared next. The stones revealed its shape, yet it was not from here that the fire had started, nor was it from the next one Heast saw, further along, where a large cooking pot still sat, held by its blackened steel stand. The Captain of Refuge did not pause to examine it. After the tents, the packs, the campfires and now the pot, he knew it was a Leeran camp.

He had not seen any sign of mounts and, outside the ravine, asked Fenna if she had.

'No,' she said. 'Not here.'

Shortly after, against the charred husk of a tree, the origin of the fire was found.

Lehana found the remains of the first barrel. She had been drawn from their path by the odd set of burns on the blackened tree: one side of it was so cindered it looked as if the flames had been poured over it. At the base, she found metal hoops that had held the barrel together. In the tree, a soot-covered bird watched her stand in her stirrups and run her mailed hand to a scorched elbow of the tree, where an axe had further sharpened it to wedge a barrel into place. A barrel that had poured out oil as if it was water.

A short while later, Anemone found another.

When they found the third and fourth, the flames on the horizon began to intensify and the ruins of Celp began to make themselves known in a series of suggestive dark shadows. Like the first and second, both barrels had been wedged into a tree by someone cutting into the arm of a branch first, and then set there to pour out over the tree and ground.

It had been done by the Leerans, but Heast did not know why. It was not the most effective way to start a fire, but more disturbing was the fact that they had lit the barrels of oil behind them. In doing that, they had allowed the fire to box them in, allowed it to consume their camps, their supplies, their clothes.

It was suicidal. That was what it was. Heast could only imagine that they had done it because they were not confident they could defeat Refuge. It was flattering, but based on the number of Leerans they suspected, unrealistic. Even with Kye Taaira before them, Refuge was still green, especially in comparison to a force that had been in battle for a year now. The Leerans would have every right to feel confident that they would win a fight. It was clear also that they knew where Refuge was. That they had found his soldiers. With the element of surprise on their side, why would they create a battlefield that was as deadly to them as to Refuge?

One of the First Queen's Guard found the first body. She dismounted beside it and turned it over. A face, burned beyond recognition, greeted him.

'Leeran,' he said, pointing to the white teeth, to the filed ends that showed through the charred flesh. 'Must have been one to set the barrels. Splashed oil over himself and lit it anyway.'

'This is pretty fucked-up,' the soldier, Oya, said. 'In my professional opinion, sir.'

Heast did not disagree.

Ahead, the ruins of Celp became clearer, and the flames could be seen there, holding to the edges of the buildings, but of people – of anyone – there was no sign.

4.

Eilona entered the Spires of Alati in the chill company of Caeli and Lian Alahn's son, Nymar. Olcea remained on *The Frozen Shackle*. She sat in the middle of the bloodstained deck, her bag before her, her eyes closed. When Eilona asked if she would come, the witch had shaken her head. 'It is better if I stay here,' she said, without opening her eyes. 'That way no one will try and sink our ship. Or take it.'

The tall, narrow-faced Nymar had been waiting for them on the long dock that ran like a broken stone finger into Leviathan's Blood. He was well dressed, in a grey silk shirt and black linen pants but, as the dinghy drifted away from *The Frozen Shackle* and towards the docks, Eilona watched him shift and fidget. He continually turned to gaze at the carriage behind him, as if being outside its protective wooden sides caused him a huge amount of distress. When Eilona and Caeli walked up the dock to him, Nymar greeted them with a vague nod and distracted introduction, and she believed that the two of them would be returning to *The Frozen Shackle* before the night set the next day.

'I do not know what it is that Muriel Wagan told you before you left,' he said, after she had shaken his hand, after he turned to lead them to the waiting carriage. 'But you should forget it all now that you are here.'

Another person would respond quickly, and with humour, but she only said, 'My mother told me that we are to negotiate for the people in the camp.'

'There won't be much of that,' he said and opened the carriage door.

It was not until they entered the streets of Burata that Nymar's comment made sense. Eilona sat in the small, but plush carriage and gazed through the barred window at the families and tents that lined the streets. Burata was largely a commercial city – its placement at the western edge of Yeflam, where it was the first port of call for trade ships, ensured that – but the people who sat on the ground in front of the temporary shelters, or who stood on the stone streets, were not merchants. They were families, by and large, and they gazed at her with a hint of despair and pleading in their eyes. Eilona's mother had prepared her for the sight, but her description of it as a housing crisis barely touched what she saw now.

Caeli sat beside Eilona, her sheathed sword laid across her lap, the end of it pointed towards her. 'Are these survivors from the fallen cities?' she asked.

'Yes,' Nymar replied. 'Just under half of Yeflam was lost three months ago. It has been a struggle to deal with the refugees.'

'Refugees?' the guard repeated blandly. 'How can you be a refugee in Yeflam if you are from the nation itself?'

'Without the Keepers of the Enclave, there is no Yeflam. What we are now we define by our cities.'

'Burata is a Traders' Union city, isn't it?' Eilona said. 'A least six of the cities on the western side of Yeflam are controlled by your father.'

'I told you: you should forget what Muriel Wagan has said.' Nymar leant back, frustrated. 'My father has very little control over these cities. Benan Le'ta's running of the Traders' Union left it in a poor financial state, and after Nale my father found that the organization did not have the capital to consolidate his power. What parts of Yeflam we did control were due to the debts he was able to call in. Perhaps if your mother's considerable debts had been paid, it would be different, but I doubt it. He is simply too far away to have much pull here. Take for example the farmlands to the south. They had a strong harvest this year, and because of that, they are strong cities. Without Enilr and Toake we would have all starved.'

Eilona let his words float in the carriage, then fade.

Outside the barred window of the carriage, the Spires of Alati appeared. In the night's dark, the thousands of spires that gave the city its name looked like the pointed ends on the old helms of soldiers. When the sun rose, Eilona knew that the resemblance would not remain: the light would break away the shadows that lingered around the spires and the straight lines that saw the largest outreach the smallest would become more apparent. But as she approached, it was different. In the dark, it looked as if the soldiers would rise and begin to ransack the cities around it.

In the University of Zanebien, Eilona had read a diary that recorded Yeflam's construction. The author and artist was a woman by the name of Yelna Nysyl, and she had sat on the banks of what would be Yeflam's southern shore on the first days. She had been drawn to it because of the sight of a pair of stone giants in the ocean. Like others who had lived on the shoreline, she had come down to the water's black edge to watch them sink the heavy pylons of Yeflam into the seabed. Her first picture was of that and a small boat in the middle of the ocean, floating calmly beside the two. It was there that she believed the Keepers of the Enclave had first sat.

Thousands of people were displaced in the construction of Yeflam, Eilona knew. In Nysyl's book there were accounts and images of families fleeing the islands that lay beneath the soon to be built artificial nation. She wrote about how they came to the shores with very little. How they came into conflict with other communities. At the end of the first year of the islanders leaving their homes, the conflict between the two communities almost came to bloodshed. It had been stopped by the presence of the Keeper Kaqua, who had come to the shoreline alone, and who had spoken to all the communities, mediating a truce between them. He promised them all that they would have a new home, soon enough.

In the streets that the carriage passed, Eilona saw men and women in brown robes attending the people on the sides of the road. They came with food and clothing. She saw a number of them sitting before small grounds, and talking in what she thought was a reassuring manner. Idly, aware that the silence in the carriage had stretched since Nymar mentioned her mother's failure to pay her debts, Eilona mentioned what she saw to him.

'The priests of Se'Saera,' he said. 'The Faithful are one of the few groups we've been able to rely upon.'

5.

Two days before Zaifyr's body was stolen, Xrie visited Ayae.

The Soldier found her in The Pale House after the combined forces of Yeflam, Mireea and the Saan entered the ruins of Mireea and set up camp for the night. Ayae had not gone out to greet him, but Xrie, as if he had known where they were all the time, climbed through the window of The Pale House, walked through the slanted rooms and made his way down the spiral stairs to where she and Jae'le were with Zaifyr's body, where he had been laid by the ghosts. Yet, when Xrie stepped into the room he was surprised to see the back of the other man, not as if he was unexpected, but as if he had not sensed him at all.

'Aela Ren would have killed you by now,' Jae'le said, when the other did not speak.

'He is not here,' Xrie said, leaving the stairs. 'But thank you for your concern.'

The sitting man did not turn from the ghosts before him. 'He cannot die,' he said. 'You must not doubt that. You will not be able to defeat him as you have others.'

'May I ask how you know this?'

'Aela is a scarred man,' Jae'le continued, as if he had not heard the other man's question. 'It is how you will recognize him. Whenever someone has said, in the past, that they have seen him, the truth has always been evident in their descriptions. He is a man defined by wounds.'

Standing against the wall, Ayae felt her breath catch. Briefly, she felt as if she stood behind the battered, marked walls of her earliest memories.

'You speak as if you were friends with him,' Xrie said.

'I did not understand friendship when I knew him,' Jae'le said, his gaze on the figure the ghosts surrounded. 'But I knew him.'

'Did you try to kill him?'

'No. I knew he could not die.'

'How did you learn that?'

'Hide who you are from him,' the sitting man said. 'Hide it for as long as you can. Hide it so you can cripple him before he knows you. It is the only way.'

Xrie turned to Ayae, but she held up her hand. 'I have no advice about him, if you mean to ask,' she said.

The Soldier was shaking his head before she finished. 'No,' he said. 'I came here to see Eidan. I thought he was down here with you.'

He's on the roof, she said and led him out of the room. Eidan stood in the centre of the roof. The afternoon's sun highlighted the black scars on his face and arms. The more they healed, the more the scars began to resemble an elaborate form of scarification.

'It is a small force you bring,' Eidan said, gazing at the people spread out through the broken streets before him. Like his brother, he did not turn as Xrie and Ayae approached. 'Will it be enough to destroy a god?'

'There are more,' the Soldier said. 'But if you wish to help, we will not turn you away.'

At the edge of the building was one of Samuel Orlan's maps. Ayae remembered that she had seen it here with Captain Heast, nearly a year ago.

'Ayae answered for us,' Eidan said.

'I answered for myself.' The map had fallen on its side, before rolling over. The miniatures had been damaged, she saw. 'If you wish to answer differently, you should.'

'I do not have a different answer.' The stout man took the opposite edge of the table and, when she was ready, lifted the map. 'We have other duties.'

'To Zaifyr?' Xrie asked.

'Yes.'

'But not to Aelyn?'

'I do not have duties to Aelyn.'

'Do you not plan to help her, then?

'Is that why you have come to speak with me?' Eidan did not set the table down, but held it easily while Ayae examined it. She did not realize straight away that he held it in his crippled hand, but when she did, she saw how much it had healed since she had seen it last. 'You have surely spent enough time with Aelyn to know that she would only resent any attempt I made to help her.'

'She taught me that we have responsibilities,' he said. 'We hold the world in our hands, she said. We have the power to reshape it. We have a responsibility to it.'

'Did you ever hear her say we had a responsibility to her?'

'No.'

Ayae kicked the legs out from under the table, folding them beneath it. She lowered her end to the roof and took Eidan's.

'When I first met Aelyn, she could not read.' The stout man took a step back from the map and, in doing so, he allowed the afternoon's sun to highlight the broken mountains, the scratched Spine of Ger and the broken paint across it. 'I offered to teach her, but she declined. She said that she would teach herself. It took her twice as long as it would have if she'd had a teacher. But she taught herself. After she learned how to read, she taught herself philosophy, law, history. No topic was denied to her. She took all of that learning and put it into her creation of Yeala. She did not allow me to help her there, either. She built a city of beautiful spires and taught the people in it how to fly. She showed men and women how to make gliders and kites and, in those early years, ensured that the city's balloons rose and fell without any danger. When the first people brought a civil war against her, she took away their power of flight. When they resented that, she killed them. I was there, that day. I remember walking beside her through the near-empty streets, where the people who broke the law were forced to live. I offered to spare her the horror of killing her own citizens, but she said no. She said, *I do not need another's hand. I will never need another's hand. I love you, but I will never be beholden to you, or to another.* She all but rejected Yeflam when I made it for her, after she was forced to destroy her spires. But by then our love permitted gifts. It allowed for us to do things for one another. But to ride into Leera for her would be an insult.'

'She saved us from dying after Nale fell,' Xrie said. 'I have tried to make that clear to Alahn and others since then, but few listen.'

'Do you think they will listen when she is back?'

'They will fall quiet. They will not be able to challenge her.'

'But what if she destroyed Nale because she wanted to?' Eidan asked. 'You have decided that she could not have done that herself, but what if she did?' He approached Xrie and, when he spoke next, his voice was quiet. 'I love Aelyn. I have loved her for such a time that the time I have not is but a few scant years . . . but I know she is capable of this and more.'

'You did not hear Kaqua's voice,' the Soldier said stubbornly. 'It whispered in the Enclave. It was sweet and it was fearful. It made promises to you. It spoke to your dark desires. It spoke to your loves. For the longest time, I thought it a test between us, but now I know otherwise.'

'Tinh Tu will tell you that he never made anyone do something that they did not wish,' he said. 'She will tell you his power came from Wehwe and he used only the truth.'

'Perhaps she is describing herself.'

'No. Tinh Tu does not have the kindness of the Pauper.' He allowed himself a faint smile. 'If it helps you, my brother believes there may be a time when Aelyn will need our help. I do not agree, but I tell you this so you know that we have not abandoned her. No matter what happens, I do know that she will return to Yeflam one day. She may not stay there, and indeed, she may not let it stand, but she will return.'

A tremor ran through the building, as if to emphasize Eidan's point, and once it finished, Xrie did not pursue the topic.

Ayae could see his need for Aelyn, for the Enclave, for how Yeflam had once been. It was a starkly naked need and that surprised her. In Yeflam the Soldier had always been composed. But he had to be: as people accused him of being a traitor, of being weak, the security of those without a home had fallen to him. Here, on the Spine of Ger, he did not have that responsibility. Now he had been given a different task and, as he marched towards it, she realized it was not the choice he would have made. The knowledge uncurled in Ayae like a scroll as she watched him shake Eidan's good hand, then her own. He wanted Aelyn Meah back. He wanted to stand beside her. Despite all that had happened, all that Eidan had said, he needed to believe he served someone with integrity. He was a soldier. He was at the front of battle. He was the will of a nation. Ayae saw that clearly as he walked to the edge of the roof. With a single glance behind, Xrie dropped carefully to the cobbled road. There, Ayae watched him walk to the market square, where the combined forces had pitched tents and lodged inside the remains of buildings. In the dying light of the afternoon's sun, Ayae was suddenly struck by how abandoned Xrie was. She realized now that he was a man whose world had been ruined and who was desperately trying to repair it.

Two days later, Zaifyr's body was stolen.

6.

Glafanr was its own world, a ship of islands, of nations, of cities. It was not like any other ship that Zaifyr had stood upon before. He believed that it was alive, but not in a conscious way. It carried a life similar to the one that soil held: a life that was part of a system, that allowed for grass and trees to grow. It was a life that remained in the wood of the ship's frame, as if it had been trapped there by design. It was this quality, he thought, that allowed it to travel down the still River of the Dead.

After Zaifyr and the others had climbed the plank onto *Glafanr*'s deck, the ship left the strange dock it had nestled against. Lor Jix had rounded on them and demanded to know who had released it, but they had all still stood beneath its five masts equally confused, and his anger died as suddenly as it had emerged. Still holding the staff, Zaifyr approached the great empty wheel. At the back of the ship, he leant over the rail and gazed down into the River of the Dead. For a moment, he thought he could see haunts within the water: they rose and fell, slippery and silver, like fish. But each time he thought he saw one, he was suddenly unsure if he saw anything. He tried to reach out with his power and found that he had neither the experience of it uncoiling from him, nor the sensation of touching the dead. For a brief, surprised moment, Zaifyr thought that his power had deserted him, that it was gone, but the panic he felt did not last. It was not gone. It was still there. He had lived so long with it that, even in death, had it been gone, he would have known. He would have felt the absence.

Beneath the deck of *Glafanr*, Zaifyr entered a narrow corridor with rooms on either side. He found Meina and her soldiers examining them. Since Mireea, Zaifyr had come to the realization that the soldiers who followed Meina's commands were not all members of Steel. Some were from the Mireean Guard, others from the Brotherhood, the other mercenary group who had fought in the siege. Each of them, though, carried shields on their backs, and swords by their sides, and they answered to the tall, dark-haired mercenary, and not to him.

'This is the Innocent's ship,' Meina said to him, later. They were in the captain's cabin and she sat in one of the old chairs around the table. Anguish was perched on her shoulder like a dark, forbidden pet. 'It sat in a harbour in Sooia for hundreds of years. It was said that no one could get onto it. That anyone who did was killed by a guard of such horror that it devoured their body after it killed them. Or during.'

Zaifyr sat opposite her, behind the captain's desk. He had been drawn to it by the book that lay in the centre, a book that was chained to the table.

'He isn't listening,' Anguish muttered to her.

'The Innocent is not here. Neither is Ai Sela.' He ran his hand along the book, his fingers trying to lift the leather cover. 'It won't move,' he said. 'What's the point of a chain?'

'What do the pages say?' Meina asked.

'It is lists of names.'

'Whose names?'

Zaifyr met her gaze. 'Our names,' he said, simply.

'My name?' Anguish asked. 'Is that there as well?'

He turned the pages forwards and back, and told the creature no.

'But the pages are blank for so long,' he said, turning over more and more of the white sheets than the book could possibly hold. 'They keep going and going, as if no one—'

'Has been to Heüala since the War of the Gods,' Lor Jix finished, entering the cabin.

For the ancient dead, *Glafanr* was a divine artefact. His ability to stand upon it was a sacred, impossible realization after so many years at the bottom of Leviathan's Blood. After his anger had left him, he had become lost in the details of the ship. He had watched the faded red sails unroll and fill with air that none could feel or see with an almost childlike innocence about him. He had run his hands along the wooden rails, and as he did, it seemed to Zaifyr that he forgot those around him.

'There are no dates,' he said to Jix as he sat in the old chair next to Meina. 'But I imagine you are right.'

'Yet another sign that we were expected,' Meina said, distaste clear in her voice. 'It does not please me to think that what I thought of as my choices were, in fact, another's.'

'If that is what you think, then you misunderstand the relationship that mortals and gods have with each other,' Jix said. 'The gods do not control us. They do not now, and they did not when they stood among us. Otherwise, they would not have had the relationship that they do with us. They would never have sought our faith.' He paused and, in his silence, the Captain of *Wayfair* appeared to be reaching inside himself, searching for the thoughts he had held in life. 'All captains pledged their loyalty to the Leviathan when I was alive. They all entered her service. They heard her voice and understood her desires. They took her rewards and they feared her anger. It was a relationship that they entered with her. I was no different. I paid my dues. I said my prayers. But I was always aware that my decisions were my own, never more than when she asked me to take on the task that led me here. I knew I would be part of a thousand other choices that would lead to one fate being chosen over another.'

'That is what happened in Yeflam, isn't it?' Zaifyr asked. 'You and I made choices that saw a new god be named.'

'Why would they create that fate?' Meina asked.

'I would have thought that Se'Saera created it.'

'I could not tell you,' Jix said. 'But what I do know is that we are all the creations of fate. Be it god, be it mortal, we are all part of this world, we all share it. One of us may create the futures, the pasts and the presents, but only one of us can realize it.'

'Because fate is not linear.' Zaifyr glanced at the book before him, at the slim pages he could see, and the countless thousands that he could not. 'Where does that leave us?'

'Drifting down a river,' Meina said sourly. 'We go where it takes us.'

'We must trust in our faith,' Jix said, 'and in our fates.'

Anguish laughed. 'You trust what has done this? After what has already been done to you? You are a fool. I would prefer to trust myself.'

'Fate is primal. It can neither hear you, nor see you.'

'But it made the gods. It made Se'Saera.'

'And us,' Meina added. 'You said that yourself.'

'You look for reason where there is none. You look for a start where there is no end.' With a resigned look, Lor Jix glanced at all three of them. 'You have all lived for too long in a world where the gods lie at your feet. You think it gives you knowledge. You think it makes the world knowable. You have never known what it is like not to know. What it is like to trust and to believe. When we are in the holy city, you will understand this.'

Zaifyr let his hand run along the smooth pages. There were no quill marks, and he thought it strangely appropriate, given all that had happened. But when he reached Heüala, he would not be satisfied by that. He would want to know who had written on the page, and with what. He would want, he realized, simply to know. To know everything. To know what had been done and why. He would have no time for faith in the holy city.

7.

Jae'le's hand shook Ayae gently.

She had been dreaming of Sooia. She remembered standing on an empty, dusty street of the town she first remembered. She was not the child she had been, but the adult she was now, and her boots walked over stones her bare feet had. She could see no one: not on the street, nor in the rough huts, where the cloth doors had been pulled back. She could see the rough chairs and the darkened pans, signs of life, of culture. She wanted to walk up to them, to rest her hand on the frame and call inside. Surely someone would answer. She would speak in Jafila, though she had not spoken that language for well over fifteen years and had forgotten most of it. But there, in her dream, she knew it, knew it intimately. If she could just move, Ayae knew she would be able to speak. But she did not move. She remained in the street and the dirt began to shift around her feet and the walls of the town began to shake and—

Jae'le's hand was on her shoulder. 'He is gone,' he said softly into her ear. 'Zaifyr is gone.'

From where she lay, Ayae could stare directly at the empty mattresses where the ghosts had laid Zaifyr's body. It was empty and the ghosts had vanished.

'An old man took him,' he continued, his hand still on her shoulder, his voice still soft, as if he told her a secret. 'He came up through a break in the floor. The ghosts parted for him. He picked up Zaifyr and returned the way he had come.'

'You saw this?' she asked as Eidan and Tinh Tu walked around the mattresses. Had they seen it as well? Was she the only one who slept? 'You didn't try to stop him?' she asked, but she knew the answer.

'What could anyone do with him?' Jae'le's hands knitted together before him. 'A dead man cannot die again.'

'They could burn him.' She could not believe she said it. 'They could dismember him. They could—'

'Do nothing,' he finished. 'If the ocean did not destroy his flesh, he is as safe as he can be.'

Ayae quelled the panic she felt and pushed herself to her feet. She picked up her sheathed sword as she rose and, as she approached the mattresses, belted it around her waist. Behind the three mattresses, she could smell water. It came from the gap in the floor that the old man had climbed out of. Staring into it, she could make out the faint, broken hint of rubble, a dangerously sloped path that led into the caverns below Mireea.

'Was the old man like us?' Ayae asked.

'There are worse than us,' Tinh Tu said. 'He was one of the god-touched.'

'He is the man who told me Lor Jix's name,' Eidan added. 'He follows the river to the east.'

Towards the Black Lake. 'Assuming the rivers have not been diverted greatly,' Ayae said, 'he can follow that towards Leera.'

It was Eidan who descended into the hole first. He used both his hands, though she could see that the scarred one was still weak, and it gripped the edges harder in compensation. When he let go and dropped the few feet to the cave floor, his fingers left indentations. Ayae's gaze did not linger on the breaks in the tiles, however, for after he landed, the floor began to glow with phosphorescent light. A single set of footprints glowed on the ground. In that light, Tinh Tu followed. She dropped her staff down to Eidan first, then lowered herself as a woman much younger in physique might. Ayae half expected her white raven to follow, but it had not liked the inside of the foyer and had taken to roosting on the roof of The Pale House. It had made no appearance by the time that Ayae and Jae'le had dropped to the stone floor.

Lit by the phosphorescent footprints, Ayae gazed at the broken remains of stone buildings and streets that she stood in. A City of Ger, she realized. She walked along the streets that had long ago lost their distinction from the stone around it. The buildings looked like old heads, the skin shrunken to reveal the shape of the skull, and little else. In some, roofs had caved in and doors had broken. Among the broken stalagmites, Ayae could see some faint lights, lost beneath two slabs of rock that had collided with each other. The lights she could see, Ayae knew, had been used by the men and women who had lived in the caverns after the War of the Gods. The people had been faithful to Ger and had shunned the outside world to be near him.

The Cities of Ger had attracted treasure hunters and miners. Many were lost to the rivers that ran throughout the mountains and which were prone to flooding. Mireea drew its water from two of the largest rivers that ran through the mountain, but there were others, as well. Each one of them ran the length of the mountains until they burst out in a series of waterfalls over the Black Lake in Leera. The lake was so named because it drew its water from Leviathan's Blood and was the cause of the continual growth of swamps and bogs that plagued much of Leera and left it poorly suited for farmland.

Samuel Orlan had taken Ayae to the end of the Spine of Ger – to where the stone wall ended abruptly – to show her the Black Lake shortly after he took her on as an apprentice. She could still remember listening to him tell her about the poisoned water while staring in awe at the waterfalls pouring into the huge, still Black Lake. The horizon had been one long dark smudge where the ocean and sky met in the smell of copper and salt.

The footsteps of the man who had stolen Zaifyr led them through a second and third City of Ger. In the second, the crumbling, stone faces of the city were exposed to the clear night sky and looked to be gazing up at the stars in awe. Xrie and the combined forces had left the morning after he had spoken to Eidan, leaving Mireea quiet. Beyond it, the third city began, and there the lower halves of buildings from Mireea, of houses and factories, speared through breaks in the rock as if they had fallen from a great height. Ayae made her way past both silently, feeling as if she had entered a world that she did not recognize, one that had taken what she had known and loved and left only a world of sadness in its place.

After the third City of Ger, the path of the body-snatcher went deeper into the Mountains of Ger. He left the rivers, which surprised Ayae, but she did not say anything to the others. Instead, she followed the lighted prints as they made their way through narrow splits in the stone, across a wide bridge that had once spanned an empty expanse, but which now provided a smooth road over the jagged debris from a cave-in. The prints wound down narrow and wide tunnels. Paths split frequently and the steps went left, then right, then up a small incline, before going down a steep wall that the four had to climb down.

It was shortly after the wall that Eidan stopped. 'A quake is coming,' he said.

It was much stronger under the mountains: the walls around Ayae shook and stones and dirt broke free. The ground beneath her feet opened in hairline fractures, and she stepped away from them.

'That seemed worse,' Tinh Tu said, once the ground stilled. 'Worse than the others.'

'It was,' Eidan said. 'We do not want to be here much longer. A mountain range of this size is difficult to control, even for me.'

The footsteps led them into a new tunnel, one littered by soil and stone. The phosphorescent light, however, remained clear and steady until the tunnel began to branch into a new cavern. From there, a faint hint of smoke could be seen, clawing along the roof.

'He is up ahead,' the stout man said softly. 'He has started a fire. I believe he is waiting for us.'

Jae'le took a step past him, but Eidan's hand stilled him.

'Zaifyr is not there with him,' he said.

'Where is he?'

'I do not know. He came down the wall with him. The stones remember the weight of the two, but they cannot tell me where it changed, or if there was another here with him.'

In the pale light, Ayae could see the concern on Jae'le's face. She thought that he might say something, but instead he nodded and continued forwards.

The smoke thickened and, shortly before the narrow tunnel opened into a much larger room, a fire was visible. It was a small campfire, ringed by rocks. There was a woodpile behind the fire, on which the old man Jae'le had told her about sat. He was an old white man, a nest of bones, grey hair and tattered clothing. He was small and did not look as if he could lift the blocks of wood that he sat on, much less a body.

But it was not that the sight of him that caught Ayae's attention. It was not he who stole her breath.

Behind him was a splitting bone, but to describe it as such, to suggest that it was a bone, was to give it a sense of perspective and reality that Ayae did not believe it had. It was of such a size that it filled the entire cavern behind the old man, the edges disappearing into shadows and smoke before becoming lost in the stone.

Upon it was a painting.

It was a battle, one in a city that Ayae did not recognize, but which was defined by flat roofs. Across the roofs men and women and creatures fought, while around them rivers of fire burned, the flames leaping out of the ground as if it had fractured, much like the bone that it was painted on. In the centre of the painting was a great cathedral and the smoke from the fire was drawn towards it. It twisted around the building, taking on a form that resembled the seething, unformed shape Ayae had seen at Zaifyr's trial. Her attention did not linger on it, but was instead drawn to the foreground, to the images of herself, of Jae'le, Eidan, Tinh Tu and Aelyn Meah. Her face was turned towards her, and in her eyes, Ayae could see flames, and fear. Of the five, only she was turned away from the cathedral, towards the entrance of the cave. On one of the flat roofs close to the cathedral Jae'le fought with shadowed figures, while further down, Tinh Tu led a force. But it was to the right of her face that Ayae found her gaze drawn, to images of Eidan and Aelyn, to the sight of the latter cradling the former in her lap, while Eidan's blood pooled around them and into the shadows of the cave.

8.

The gates of Nymar Alahn's estate were surrounded by Yeflam's own refugees and, from the room that she was given, Eilona spent most of the night watching them.

She was out of her depth. The thought repeated in her head like the chorus of a song. It had begun when Nymar's carriage approached the estate gates and sombre grey-dressed guards had come out to clear the road. When people had not moved quickly enough, the guards used wooden batons. Eilona saw one woman hit across the face and when she turned away from the grisly sight, she had turned to Nymar, who stared straight ahead, as if by doing so he could deny what was taking place around him. He did not move or say a word until the carriage halted outside the doors of his main estate. There, he stepped out of the carriage first and barked at the guards, demanding to know why the people were still outside his home. It was on the tip of Eilona's tongue to tell him it was because they had nowhere else to go, but she refrained. Instead, she stood in the forecourt and listened and watched. After Nymar finished, he turned to Eilona and Caeli and, after a struggle to compose his face, led them into the estate. There a thin white man whose head was shaved took them up to their rooms for the night. The man, who did not introduce himself, said only that a light meal would soon be provided.

The meal remained still, largely untouched. It was cold meat and fruit. Eilona had picked at it, but otherwise left it. Instead, she watched the people on the street. She thought about how she could not do what her mother wanted, not here. She had spent years outside the real politics of countries: she had lived in the politics of academics, of the university's small world of intellectual positions, and even there she had largely kept to herself. She had certainly not kept up with the practice of politics.

Her mother had not helped, either. Despite what Nymar believed, Muriel Wagan had told her daughter very little about what to expect in the Spires of Alati. 'We have a few birds,' she said. 'We get a few letters. It isn't much. I suspect that Lian gets some extra messages from his son, but what we know is vague at best.' Eilona's mother had known about the people in the streets, but not how bad it was, or about the Faithful.

'They were in the cities before Yeflam broke,' Nymar said while she and Caeli were still in the carriage. 'Se'Saera came to Nale herself for the Keepers' trial of Qian. She did not have a name then, and for the most part, the Faithful were largely ignored. But after the storms they appeared on the streets, offering food and clothing to the refugees.' He shook his head. 'They have saved a lot of lives.'

'She was responsible for part of the attack on Yeflam,' Caeli said. 'Surely very few would be willing to accept anything from her?'

'The Enclave is responsible for the attack on Yeflam,' Nymar corrected her curtly. 'Please see that you are informed of the facts. The Enclave was a corrupt government. The people know this. That is why they are ready to embrace real and alternative government, why they are ready to be something other than Yeflam. Fortunately, we are helped in this by Aelyn Meah's chief steward, Faje Metura. He has been speaking quite publicly against the Keepers.'

'Why would he do that?' Eilona asked.

'He is an honest man. In fact, he is the spokesman for the Faithful.' The look on Eilona's face must have said what she thought, because Nymar added, 'You must treat him with respect. It was he who negotiated the peace that all the cities have, and who has looked after the refugees. What you see outside the windows would be much worse if not for him.'

'Perish the thought that you might take responsibility for your own people,' Caeli said, the evenness of her replying revealing a cold contempt.

Perhaps because of that, Nymar did not speak again until he left the carriage.

It might have surprised her mother's guard to learn that Eilona shared much of her opinion. A part of Eilona wanted to press the point Caeli made, to tell Nymar that his response to the crisis was a poor one, that he was shifting the responsibility for his fellow humans to another. But she didn't. Instead of thinking about how Nymar would respond, she thought of Caeli, of how the other woman would think that she was agreeing not out of common sentiment, but out of fear, or another emotion altogether. After all, Eilona was suddenly dependent on Caeli, not just on her skill with a sword, but on her experience of these situations. Without her, she would have to rely upon her old knowledge, the knowledge that had led her so poorly in the past.

Eilona was woken by her door opening.

The morning's sun cast the dark shadows of the spires into her room and she saw, in the tall, sharp lines, the helms of soldiers again. When she rose stiffly from the large chair in which she had fallen asleep, she saw Caeli.

'Breakfast will be up soon,' the guard said, the smell of cooking food drifting in behind her, before she shut the door. 'We probably won't get much time to talk after that.'

Eilona nodded slowly. For a moment, she found herself unable to speak. She wanted to bring up the carriage, but to do so would be to unearth more of the past: of what had been said, of the attack on Caeli's family, of – 'It's awful here,' she said, instead.

'The first thing to leave a human is kindness for another.' Caeli walked over to the window, to where the nearly full tray of food still sat. 'You weren't hungry?'

'Look out of the window. How can you eat while people starve on your doorstep?'

'I eat when I can,' the other woman said. 'It is what living in the camp teaches you.'

'I don't live in the camp.'

'Not yet.'

Eilona did not know how to respond. 'What did you want to talk about?'

'Everyone here is afraid,' Caeli said. 'I don't mean the people outside, I mean the people in here, with us. They're afraid of being punished. Afraid of being thrown out onto the streets. Nymar Alahn holds that threat like a blade above the heads of everyone here. The girl who brought me my food last night told me that.'

'If she was afraid, why did she talk to you?' The words twisted in her, came out with a tone she didn't want. 'Sorry,' she said hastily, 'that didn't come out right – I meant only if she's afraid, why talk to a stranger?'

'Because I have a sword, I imagine.' Caeli gave Eilona a chill glance. It spoke of their history, of their roles now, of how the former wanted nothing for it but to end. 'It changes how people look at you. You give someone a sword, and they become a saviour, or a villain. Or maybe the girl was just desperate. Either way, she spoke to me. She told me that Nymar has a copy of *The Eternal Kingdom* in his room. She assured me that he is Faithful. If that is true, it does not bode well for anything we have come here to do.'

There was a gentle knock on the door before Eilona could respond. A young white maid pushed in the food cart, the plates on it shifting spears and swords, the metal struts jangling like armour.

9.

The morning's sun cast a dark, bloody light over Celp.

Heast and the First Queen's Guard had found more bodies, each of them burned as the first had been, as they approached the ruins of the city. They had counted eighteen, but Heast believed there were more. At the edge of Celp, before the ruined gates, he halted their progression and pulled out his spyglass. Beyond the ruins, a long stretch of blackened land ran until it was lost in the smoke and the violent light. He could see half a dozen figures there. After he closed the spyglass, Heast raised his hand and had everyone fall in around him.

'Anemone,' he said. 'Find out where Refuge and the Leerans are in there.'

She nodded and around her, a shield without needing to be told to be a shield, Lehana and the First Queen's Guard waited. They were stained in ash, the red of their armour all but obscured after the ride to Celp, just as the colour of their horses had begun to disappear. Heast could hear some of the soldiers cough and spit, saw some reach for water, but otherwise they were composed. He was pleased to see that. It meant that they too knew what kind of battle awaited them in Celp.

The city had been heavily damaged when General Waalstan had laid siege to it shortly after his battle against Mireea. After his success, Heast had heard that he made camp in the ruins for a week and had spent the time beheading survivors and harvesting their bodies for flesh. Heast tended to not give much credence to stories like that, but when he had entered Celp after Maosa, he had found headless bodies hanging crucified in the streets. There was no sign of the cannibalism that others spoke of – the bodies were simply too decomposed – but Anemone had told him that it had indeed happened. He ordered the bodies and the crosses torn down and the men and women and children buried.

Heast had stayed in Celp for a week. In that time, he had walked stiffly through the ruined streets and outside the walls. He studied the scars in the ground where the siege engines had been laid and the damage done to the buildings. It had been a quick battle, in part, Heast thought at the time, because of poor decisions by Faet Cohn. He had left a section of the northern wall under-defended and it had allowed Waalstan to punch through easily. The Faithful had swarmed the streets while a badly organized retreat was sounded. It had not occurred to Heast then that Cohn had betrayed his duty: he had simply thought the marshal unprepared and stupid, but he admitted that it made more sense to him now.

'Grandmother,' Anemone said, 'says that the Leerans are through the streets to the south.'

'And Refuge?'

'Scattered throughout the south and west.' She paused, listening to another conversation that no one else could hear. 'They are being herded towards the centre,' she said.

'Towards the town hall?'

'The fire is strongest there.' The witch sounded troubled and unsure. 'Captain, Grandmother says that there are no ancestors here, but General Waalstan is.'

That surprised Heast. 'What else does she say?'

'She says that the soldiers are on fire.'

He silenced the sudden conversation around him and pointed to the north, to the broken wall that the Leerans had originally come through. After Anemone said the General's name, Heast felt suddenly exposed, though he knew logically that no one was watching. There was nowhere in the burning ruins by the gates to hide. Still, he had felt as if an eye had been cast over him. He could not shake the sensation, not even after he and the First Queen's Guard had ridden through the broken wall and into the blackened streets.

Burning buildings and bodies lay ahead of them. For a moment, what Heast saw was overlaid with the memory of Mireea in flames. He saw again the industrial area of the city that had been attacked from a tunnel the Leerans had made. Queila Meina and Steel had been using that part of the city as a camp and they had been forced to retreat through streets of burning buildings before he ordered the floor of the city to be exploded.

The sensation of being watched intensified with the memory. Heast dropped a hand to his sword, but he could see nothing alive ahead of him. There was only burning buildings. There was only burned bodies. The soldiers are on fire, Anemone had said, but surely that had been a mistake. Surely the old witch had simply been unable to distinguish the two. If she had been right, surely screams would fill Celp, not the sound of fires, cracking wood, of dim shouts and faint battles, and little else.

'Lehana.' Heast indicated to the right, to the road that ran beside the broken wall, where a Leeran body lay by itself, and the fire was at its weakest. 'There is a main road that ends a little down that way. It runs through the middle of Celp. I want you to take half of the force down there. Take our best archers, but leave me our best riders. Anemone, you go with her. Try and contact Refuge in the city. Tell them we will clear a path down the main street. We'll try and bring the Leerans who are at the edges down for you to have a clear shot at, Lehana. We'll be riding in pairs. Try not to shoot anyone who looks as if they were born in Faaisha.'

'Sir,' Lehana began, but stopped, the smoke causing her to cough. 'Captain,' she said again, 'maybe I should ride?'

He was anything but an elegant rider, he knew. 'Refuge won't respond to you, not yet,' Heast said. He turned his gaze to the soldiers around her. 'When you hear the horn, that is the signal to fall back. We'll group up and push forwards then.'

Lehana did not like it, but he was right. She would be just another soldier Refuge did not know and, in the smoke, in the fire, they would just as soon attack her and the First Queen's Guard as the Leerans. Heast could at least limit that by his presence. With a squaring of her shoulders, Lehana gathered her soldiers to her. Once done, she led them down the smoke-stained street to the right.

After they had disappeared, Heast pulled out his canteen. He took a drink of water that tasted of smoke and used it to dampen his clothes. It was not much – it would have been better to soak his clothes in a barrel of water – but it would help dull the heat of the fires in the streets before him. Around him, the soldiers who had remained followed his lead. None of them, he was sure, relished the idea of charging into the fire.

Oya came up beside him. The muscular soldier had an axe in one hand and a shield strapped over her other. 'I want you to know, sir, that you won me ten gold.'

He drew his sword. 'What did you bet on?'

'That you'd order us to do something crazy stupid before the week was out.'

He smiled beneath his mask. 'You stay with me on my left.'

The flames were hot and, as if they sensed him and the soldiers with him into the fire, they seemed to grow. They became larger, gained shape. Briefly, it looked as if they wanted to reach out.

After a moment, Heast ignored the flames as he rode along the street. His gaze switched to the buildings, to the broken windows and doors where fire leapt out, and then he looked back to the street, searching for life, or for a sign that someone was watching him. He saw nothing: the closest he came to it was a body lodged in one of the doorways, the flames like a blanket over it. He did not know if it was one of his or Leeran. A couple of seconds later another body appeared in the street, face-down. His horse cleared it easy, its steel hooves falling on the broken stones, each step a steady, well-trained beat.

Another two bodies followed. These, he saw, were not completely covered in flames, and he could see the white skin, the Leeran skin.

Ahead, the sounds of battle grew.

10.

The morning's sun ran through the thick foliage of the campsite and tinted Leera in a strange mix of orange and green. In its midst, at the head of the camp, stood Aela Ren with a tin cup of water in his hand. The mixed light ran across his scarred skin, his leather armour and the hilts of his old swords. It left him looking moulted, as if his skin was breaking apart and revealing the monk that he had once been, so long ago.

'She's afraid,' the Innocent said to Bueralan.

'Of course she is afraid.' He held his sheathed sword and belt in his hand and, as he spoke, began to wind it around his waist. 'She has been raped, she is pregnant with—' he stopped himself before he said *my friend*. 'She has every right to be afraid,' he said, pulling the belt tight. 'We've all that right.'

'I did not mean Zi Taela.' Ren stared ahead, at the glinting of sunlight on armour and swords, at the bustle of a camp in the distance. 'I meant *her*.'

'Her?' The saboteur was caught off-guard but did his best to hide it. 'Are we having private conversations now?'

'It may pain you to admit it, Bueralan, but you are one us. You are the servant of a god who no longer speaks. You may think of those around you poorly, you may think of them as madmen and killers, but no matter what you think, we are loyal to each other.

We are a unique nation.' Aela Ren paused and drank from his cup. 'Before we left, she called Zilt's soldiers to her. You saw them as I did when we rode out of Ranan. You saw them run across across the roofs like dogs to her. What you did not see was her cut the strings that held them in their mortal bodies. You did not see her return them to death.'

Bueralan did not ask how Ren knew. The Innocent had led them from Ranan, had ridden first into the tunnels, and into the fissures. He could not have seen what he described, but Bueralan did not doubt him.

'*Glafanr*'s disappearance unnerved her,' the Innocent continued, his tone still matter-of-fact. 'She did not foresee it. She said this to me before we left. She said that she needed an army in Heüala, that she could not allow Zaifyr and his companions to pass beyond the gate. Only Zilt and the soldier she sent with the boy will remain in this world. She has seen Zilt standing beside her in the future. The other is sometimes there, sometimes not. But Zilt is necessary, she said.'

'Why are you telling me this?' he asked.

'We take our meaning from the gods. Be it many, or one, we are defined by what they do, and we in turn define that for those around us.'

'But she acted out of fear?'

'Yes.'

'Does that mean we won't attack them?' He nodded towards the sharp flashes in the distance. 'Are we going to turn back to Ranan, or are you going to return to Sooia?'

'We will not turn,' Aela Ren said. 'We have been given a task and we will complete it.'

Bueralan made a frustrated noise. 'Then what does it matter if she acted in fear?'

'A god moves us like pieces to enact the events that that he or she sees. Before the war, when there were many, the fates a god made were often built from alliances, or from singular desires. They would use us to build that existence. They would sacrifice people, nations, and even servants like you and me, to build that. They did it because they saw an end that we could not. Our new god, our singular god, like us, cannot see an end, and that is why she has responded in fear.'

'Would you have been given pause if she responded differently?' Bueralan asked. 'If she had responded in anger, would we even be talking?'

'I would have still paused.' He turned the tin cup over and emptied the water. 'The question we must all ask ourselves is if her fear over Heüala highlights another's design? If her arrival is the signal that we have collapsed into one fate, one future, then have any seen its end? We know she hasn't, but what of the old gods, our gods? What if they have seen the world as it is? What if they are the designers of the world that we now stand in?'

'What if they are?' Bueralan asked.

'I have no answer.' Ren began to walk into the camp. 'If the old gods saw the fate that we head towards, then why did they not speak to us, and empower us to act for them?' Before him, the god-touched men and women had begun to assemble. They stood there, a collection of soldiers in armour and weapons that did not match, bound by something much larger, much fuller, than any soldier who fought them could imagine. 'For thousands of years, we have lived in a world without a god's definition. We have lived in a world without truth. We have watched as mortals create lies to stave off chaos. We have watched them insist on falsehood as if it were truth. But why? Why would the gods allow that? Why would they do that, if they saw a single fate that they would set themselves against?'

Bueralan did not respond. He could see, in the man beside him, the depths of his need, the depths of his servitude, and he could see how, without it, he had sought his own violent definition of the War of the Gods. In that way, Ren was a stark contrast to Samuel Orlan and Onaedo, who had abandoned their servitude. Orlan – the first Orlan, the one whose name had become a tool for a god – had killed himself rather than serve, but for Onaedo, the rejection of her role had occurred later, when the gods had failed her. Having stood beside Aela Ren and the other god-touched men and women, Bueralan understood that clearly, now. He could see the scars that the gods had left on both Orlan and Onaedo, just as the absence of the gods left similar marks on the Innocent and those who had joined him.

In another time, the saboteur in Bueralan – the part of him that searched for chinks in armour – might have thought he could pick at the edges of Aela Ren's needs. Bueralan would have thought he could build a path that would allow him to turn him, to flip him. But Aela Ren would not betray Se'Saera. Bueralan knew that. The god gave Ren meaning. She brought an end to the emptiness that had driven him into Sooia. There he had taken the last visions of the gods, the sight of their destruction, of their war, and focused it into his life. It was madness, of course, but Aela Ren's existence without gods was madness.

Samuel Orlan had known that, Bueralan realized. He had tried to tell him that when he came to the room he shared with Taela. He had tried to tell him that it was not just Ren who saw the world like that, but all the god-touched men and women. Orlan had tried to tell him that what Bueralan saw in Kaze – what he saw in her desire to help Taela – was not a break he could exploit, but simply who she was when her god stood beside her. It was the same part of her that saw her take part in the genocide that had gripped Sooia and the same part that saw her stand beside Se'Saera. She needed the definition – that sense of purpose, that meaning to her long,

long life – that Se'Saera gave her, just as Ren and Sela and all the others who had once been the servants of gods needed their deities.

'They are out there,' the Innocent said to Samuel Orlan as the latter approached. 'They will be upon us before the day is over.'

'We don't have to do this,' the cartographer said. 'We needn't be part of this war. We can make a choice here.'

'It has already been made,' Ren replied and began to issue orders.

11.

Heast's blade caught a blow and he shrugged it aside as his horse galloped down the street. He rode into a skirmish between four smoke-stained Leerans and two soldiers of Refuge. Upon seeing the two riders charge into their enemies, the latter pair took advantage of the diversion and ran through a burning house, using it as a dangerous, unstable gateway to the next street. He thought that one of them was the runner, Ralen, but in the smoke, in the frantic fight against the unmounted Leerans, Heast could not be sure.

Oya held to his left. The four Faithful fell quickly, and he was pleased to see that they were not alight with flames, but rather stained by smoke and ash. When the last of the four fell, Heast heard a loud crack from Oya after that caught his attention and he turned to see her pulling her axe out of the burning door frame. Her blow had taken off half the Leeran's head on the ground but slammed into the wood after. The frame, though, was so weak that when she ripped it out, it began to crumple in thick pieces of black wood, bringing the house with it. With a kick, Heast urged his mount down the street, towards the burning buildings ahead. He would have to turn, left or right at the end, and he pulled to the right, in the direction that the two Refuge soldiers had run. There was a good chance, he knew, that the two of them had not known who had thundered down the street, and whether they were friend or foe.

'*Refuge!*' His shout drew the burning air into his lungs. '*Refuge!*'

He wanted to make sure that they knew who it was who came towards them.

'*Refuge!*'

Beside him, Oya echoed his shout.

Then they turned left and rode straight into half a dozen riders.

They were as startled as he and Oya, but Heast's blade caught the first Leeran in the face. She fell back while his and Oya's mounts shouldered through the horses before them. Heast blocked a slash and backhanded another Leeran. Nothing fancy, he knew, but he and Oya emerged on the other side of the riders within moments. Heast took another burning breath and shouted '*Refuge!*' again, and heard the cry returned. It came from ahead of him, but he could not tell if it was from one of the Queen's First Guard or from one of the Faaishan members of Refuge. It could even come from a Leeran, Heast knew. He was not concerned if it did, however. The cry would force the Leerans to stop what they were doing, would give him time to pull those he could to relative safety, while also peeling off bits of the Faithful in quick, running attacks. He glanced behind him at the thought: sure enough, the riders he and Oya had burst through were behind them, riding hard.

Beside him, he heard a startling thud, and for a moment, thought that Oya had fallen. Instead, he saw that she had moved her axe to her left arm, and as they rode along the street, was slamming it into the blackened frames. She did it with as much strength as she could muster and, after the third strike, a crack sounded. At the fourth, it grew, and by the time she swung a fifth time, the burning wall on her left had begun to crumble. Stones and wood and flame began to tumble onto the street in a thundering mix. Heast and Oya urged their mounts ahead and, instead of turning, they galloped through the damaged remains of a house from Celp's earlier destruction.

Once they cleared it, however, they rode straight into another group of mounted Leerans.

These were not as unprepared as the previous group. Fortunately, they numbered only three.

Heast leant back in his saddle as the first of the riders rode past him, his slashing blade passing harmlessly. He came back up in time to block a second blade, even as Oya's shielded arm smashed into the face of the last Leeran. But it was the third that was the problem, for he rounded expertly in the burning street and came charging back at Heast before he could turn, or gain the speed to outrun him. It was Oya who saved him: she was half-turned in her saddle from her attack, and she spun back, her axe crunching into the man's face.

They urged their mounts forwards, cutting to the right, then the left. In the distance, Heast could see the burning roof of Celp's town hall. It had been left mostly intact after its first siege and it now burned in high, terrible flames. Heast had no intention of going towards it, but as he and Oya skirted it, riding past two roads that led to the hall, he saw a pair of Leerans run out of each street. His heart sank at the sight: they were unmounted, and their clothes were alight, to such an extent that the flames had turned them into genderless figures of flame. Madness was his first thought. No soldier would willing douse him or herself in flames . . . but even as he thought that, the Captain of Refuge knew it was not entirely true. He had seen the bodies earlier. He had been told what the ghost of Anemone's grandmother saw. Coupled with the sensation of being watched, he was left with the very clear knowledge that all of this had been organized, had been planned, and all happened because another wanted it to.

Heast and Oya burst out onto the main road with nearly two

dozen Leerans behind them. Not one of these was alight, but as the two entered the road, another six of the First Queen's Guard appeared too. Behind them were their own Faithful, and two of those were covered in flames, running in complete silence.

Heast and the others rode hard for the broken, blackened buildings littered with cinders. Behind them, the firelit sky filled the horizon, as if it were a terrible, violent finishing line and, as Heast and his soldiers burst through the broken buildings, arrows flew into the pursuing Leerans.

'*Refuge!*' he cried out with burning lungs as he turned his horse around. '*Fall in for your captain!*'

With a kick, he drove his mount back down the road, over dead soldiers and horses.

The whole battle angered him. Whoever – whatever – watched him did not care about the Leerans in the city. They were being wasted unnecessarily. It was grounds for rebellion, for executing your captain. Even though the soldiers that were being betrayed in this way were not his own – were in fact his enemies – it left the Captain of Refuge furious. Worse, the tactics invited him to do the same, as if he were a fool.

But Heast knew that neither the horses, nor his soldiers, could keep up this pace through the burning city. He knew that they could not remain in Celp much longer. He was drenched in sweat and his lungs burned with each breath he took. He could only imagine how his horse felt. He could not—

A figure suddenly appeared before him, an axe in its hand. At the last moment, Heast pulled back his blow: a smoke-stained, grey-haired Sergeant Qiyala stared at him with startled eyes. She lowered her axe and indicated behind her. There, half a dozen soldiers followed. One of them was being carried by two others. But it was beyond them that Qiyala was pointing.

Thundering down the street was a score of mixed and mounted Leeran soldiers.

Heast and Oya charged. He blocked a slash with his sword, parried another and deflected at least two or three more blows, even as he felt two hits against his armour. Adrenalin kept the pain away, but he would feel it later. Oya remained beside him, but she took the harder route through the line, using her shield as a battering ram. In the centre of the line, he heard her swear, and turned to see her using her black-armoured arm to block a blow, her shield shattered.

Their charge had stuttered and was in danger of stalling in the middle of the Leerans. Heast, swinging his blade, turned towards Oya and, allowing his horse to lash out with its hooves to drive back her attacker, he rode into one of the burning houses.

The smoke choked him, obscured his vision. There was a splintering sound as he thrust his hilt into the wall of the building, and he heard another as, behind him, Oya followed him in, smashing at the frame of the door as she did. The horse, for all its discipline, reared and snorted, wanting to be free, and Heast drove it forwards. A sudden flame rose before him, but his mount didn't slow. He heard a cracking behind him—

And then he was in the street, the house crumbling behind him.

A moment later Oya's mount struggled free without her.

He saw her arm reaching through the smoke in confusion as the house began to cave in. Reaching out, he grabbed her hand and pulled.

She crashed against his mount as the house collapsed in flames and ash, a narrow gash down her forehead. Her dark eyes met his and, with a nod, thanks she did not need to speak, she turned and grabbed the reins of her horse. It stood trembling, its instincts telling it to run while its training said to wait.

Heast could not keep riding through the streets. He could hear no more shouts for Refuge, and he could hear frantic riding, but mostly, he could hear the riding of larger groups who were closing in on him. For some reason, he did not think that whatever watched him had given any indication of where he was to Waalstan, or to any of the other Leerans. He could not explain it, but he was sure of it. It was simply the Faithful's numbers. They were filtering down the burning streets, and if he and the First Queen's Guard remained split, they would soon be overwhelmed by the Leerans.

Grabbing the horn, he lifted the cloth from his mouth, and took a deep, painful breath before he blew a long, hard note.

Then, with Oya beside him, Heast turned back to where Lehana and Anemone waited in the burned remains of the buildings. To where he would gather them and begin his push to the town hall, to finish it, for better or worse.

Heüala

What Aelyn did not know, what she could not have known then, was the price of repairing the world.

I do not speak of her personal loss. Not her lover, her family, her friends, not even her own dreams. No, I speak of the panic that gripped the world when the three suns were merged. I can still remember the absolute darkness that engulfed that day.

Panic gripped Leviathan's End. We were a microcosm for what happened elsewhere in the world. We burned all the fires inside the skull of the old god, but outside, we could see nothing, not even the shape of our own home. Around us the ocean was still, and we quickly realized that, unless the tides returned, we would be able to leave only by our own strength. It grew cold on the second day and on the third we heard cracking. The ocean around us began to freeze.

After two weeks the sun returned. It came with famine and disease.

We continued to suffer when the Leviathan's blood was drawn from the ocean. Great black waterspouts ran from horizon to horizon. They passed over us, cracking the skull of the old god, flooding us within and threatening to break apart our home. After they finished, corpses of the sealife began to rise – sharks and whales and everything larger and smaller. The stench of rotting flesh was inescapable. We lit fires to burn the dead for nearly a year.

It went on and on, but nothing rivalled the birth of Se'Saera's Children. Nothing had such long fingers of dread as those pregnancies.

—Onaedo, *Histories, Year 1029*

1.

Heast and Oya were the first to return to the burned-out buildings where Anemone, Lehana and the First Queen's Guard waited. Beyond them, in tired, blackened clumps, were two dozen members of Refuge who had reached safety. It was there that Heast found Qiyala.

His sergeant was exhausted. Her face was a mask of soot and sweat and she stared ahead with a numb expression, as if she did not see him. She had fallen into a crouch, a canteen in her hand and an axe at her feet. A little behind her lay Sergeant Bliq. She, Heast realized, had been the soldier he had helped out of the burning streets. Her leg was wrapped tightly in a dirty, bloodstained cloth and Anemone was beside her, examining the wound. Heast expected that the sergeant would be hobbling to her feet soon enough, and though he would prefer to send her away, to send her and the other members of Refuge out of the smoke, he knew that he would need her to ride into the centre of the town with him.

'I have never seen anything like this, Captain,' Qiyala said, drawing his attention back to her. She tightened the lid on her canteen and raised her dark, flat gaze to Heast. 'I've seen a lot. I would have said that I had seen damn near anything that you could see, but that was before the Leerans began to set their own soldiers on fire.

It was – they lit up the countryside like torches in the night. Not a single one of them screamed. They just ran towards Celp.'

From behind the sergeant, two of the First Queen's Guard returned. A third rode double with one. Lehana approached them, but Heast knew that one of his soldiers had fallen.

'We saw the Leerans arrive,' Qiyala continued, her fingers flicking the canteen in a sharp but broken beat. 'It happened two nights ago. We watched them circle us. They had about five hundred, I guess, and our first response was to tighten our defences. We had the better ground and the Hollow told us that there weren't any ancestors. I don't know. It was strange, sir. At first it was strange. The Leerans had no siege machines. They had little in supplies. There was no clear way out for us, but it didn't seem to matter, because we had the better field placement, and they didn't have what it took to starve us out, or to come over our walls. We had time to wait for you. We had time to plan. When it turned dark tonight, we started to think that they might not even know that we were here. We never thought that they would set themselves on fire.'

Anemone left Bliq's side and went to one of the soldier who had ridden in. *Jaela.* That was her name, Heast remembered, now. 'How many have we lost?' he asked.

'It's hard to say. The burning, the . . . I don't know what the Leerans want to call what they've done here, but it caught us off-guard.' Qiyala rose, exchanging the canteen for the axe. 'They didn't set fire to everyone. They hammered barrels into trees and poured oil over men and women without mounts. They would stand there as if it was a shower and then step out be lit. The first died before they reached the city, but others . . . others got through. We had blocked the gate but that didn't stop them. They died there. They broke the east first. Bliq had that side and she lost nearly everyone who was with her. About a hundred, I thought. I lost thirty. Maybe thirty-five.'

'The Hollow is still alive.' Bliq rose slowly and stiffly, her leg unable to take her full weight. 'He had the centre of Celp, but he isn't dead. I know that.'

'The fire is worse there,' Qiyala said. 'You can't be sure of that.'

The other sergeant spat to her left. 'Ain't nobody killing that boy with plain old fire,' she said after she had cleared her throat.

Heast called Lehana over. 'How many did not come back?'

'Just the one, sir.' She offered a brief nod to the two women, who nodded in return. 'This is your new lieutenant,' Heast said to his sergeants. 'Anemone, is Taaira still alive?'

'Grandmother said he was.' Blood showed through the ash on the witch's hands but she did not clean it away. 'He is in the south with eighty soldiers. Many of them are wounded, but he is not.'

'The rest?'

'Spread throughout the area. Corporal Isaap is trying to gather them, but they are by and large pinned down.'

'Have her help them.' Heast grabbed the reins of his horse. It, like him, was surely longing to take a breath of cool air. 'Everyone mount up. Double where you have to.' He pulled himself up. 'We're going to break the back of this, get our soldiers, and get out of here.'

'You're going to charge the centre?' Bliq was disbelieving. 'Captain, that is where they have been trying to herd us.'

'Would you prefer to leave?'

She spat again. 'I'm not leaving anyone behind, sir.'

'Then mount up.'

The charge began a short time later.

Oya led it. She had gathered a new shield and rode between Saelo and Zvae, swords drawn. Before the charge began, Heast saw Qiyala grab a black-armoured hand and pull herself on the back of Fenna's mount. Bliq and the other soldiers without mounts followed her lead. In the charge, Heast could see them spread out around him, the horses charging as if they carried one rider, their strength and speed born from their desire to leave the burning town. The main street split into smaller streets towards the centre of Celp. Before them, men and women who had been set on fire emerged. Not one of them got close to the charge: arrows dropped them before the charge divided, breaking evenly behind Saelo, Zvae and Oya as each took a street.

Ahead, the fires grew in intensity, as if one of the broken shards of the sun had been dropped on the town hall.

The town square burned as if exactly that had happened. The tallest of the fires belonged to the town hall, and the flames that lifted high over the blackened roof had a shape that was not yet complete, but it suggested something monstrous. But it was not that undefined horror that drew Heast's attention, no.

What drew the Captain of Refuge's long experienced gaze was the sight of the Leeran soldiers who were entirely aflame.

It was not just those who stood at the front of the line waiting for them, but those behind, and the silent mounts they sat upon. For each of them, it was as if the fires were not real, as if their flesh was not burning, and their bodies not a horror of shifting, moving flesh. It was as if, Heast realized, they were sitting under the gaze of a beloved leader, as if they were wearing their finest, and on parade.

It was as if, he realized, they sat beneath the gaze of their god, Se'Saera. A gaze, Heast realized as Refuge charged forwards, that watched them intently.

2.

Refuge crashed into the Faithful.

It was a battle unlike any Aned Heast had fought before: Refuge's charge met was met by the Leerans in silence, and the first of the burning soldiers that Oya, Zvae and Saelo slammed into did not even raise their weapons. Instead, they tumbled, already dead, a wall of burning flesh for Refuge to ride through, for their mounts to stamp out, for their discipline to be tested.

The fury that he had felt earlier returned to him, even as his own sword flashed out, crashing into the head of a Leeran soldier who struggled, half alive, towards him. From his left, he heard one of his soldiers shout that their arrows had been used up, but by then the Leerans had closed in, and combat had turned to swords and shields. Up close, the Faithful bore serene expressions on their burning faces, and although their eyes were open, Heast suspected that they were not truly awake.

Even in the square, the Leerans had greater numbers than Refuge, and they pressed against front and left flank strongly. Heast's biggest concern was that they would be able to swell around the flanks and surround them. Se'Saera's Leerans – he would not refer to them as Waalstan's, or ascribe any ownership of the soldiers to the general he had fought in Mireea – were kept from doing that by their own numbers, and by the discipline of Refuge. Yet the fear of being encircled was not one that Heast had alone, and when he turned to give the order to shore up the left, he found both Qiyala and Bliq, along with the other soldiers who had ridden double into the square, had already slid off their mounts and moved to strengthen the edge.

A burning woman burst towards Heast while his attention was diverted. Dimly, he was aware that she had leapt from the back of a horse and onto one of the black-and-red-armoured soldiers of Refuge. The soldier she knocked off the horse had lost her weapon and had been forced to grab the Faithful's burning arms to stop her from choking her. As she did that, the burning soldier surged forwards, charging him. Heast's mount met the charge by rearing back on its legs and lashing out at the soldier. She fell, but it was the two who followed, the two who had come through the gap, that proved too much for the horse. Flames scalded its hair, and the sight of the flames and the smell of burning flesh overwhelmed the animal's training. The horse reared back again, causing Heast to lose control, for him to slip from the saddle.

He hit the ground hard, the wind knocked out of him, his sword lost. The two burning Leerans rushed and Heast rolled to avoid the swords that came crashing down where he had fallen. The Captain of Refuge lurched painfully to his feet, grabbing the ugly dagger in his belt, aware that it would not do much against two soldiers – but there was no one who could turn to help him.

He felt Se'Saera's gaze intensify, as if this moment, this instance, was something that she had been waiting for, as if it was of importance to her. Heast saw his death, saw it in flashes of hard steel and burning limbs, his dagger grinding into the neck of the soldier on his left. On instinct, he turned to the one on the right, and as he did, the burning soldier's chest burst open, as if an unseen hand had punched through him. Heast charged the other, his dagger plunged into the stomach of the soldier, the flames on the body threatening to grab him, threatening to leap to him. They forced him to take two steps back, to brush at his arms as he did.

'Captain!' Anemone's bloodstained hand reached out for him, her wet grip with enough strength to help lift him onto the horse behind her. 'My grandmother—'

'Is laughing.' Lehana had closed the gap that his attacker had come through, her bastard sword lashing out in devastating arcs. 'She's supposed to be helping Taaira and Isaap.'

'She has.' At the back of the square, as if on cue, sounds of battle began to emerge. 'Kye Taaira is very angry, she says.'

Heast understood that. 'Where is Waalstan?'

'In the very middle.'

'On Lehana!' It hurt to shout and he knew, soon, that his voice would soon be burned out. 'On her and push!'

The former guards of the First Queen of Ooila did not hesitate to shift into the formation he ordered.

As they did, Se'Saera's gaze fell away and screams filled the air.

They did not emerge from Refuge. All the warriors were horrified to hear the sounds rise from the burning soldiers of Se'Saera.

Their god had held their pain at bay. In leaving, she left them with only their torment, as if it was a punishment for failure, for being unable to stop Heast. The thought confused him, for she could still very well have killed him. But he had survived her attack and she had left. In her place, the agony of her Faithful announced itself. It destroyed the form that they had, caused mounts to throw their riders, for riders to drop their weapons, for them to lift their burning hands in horror, as if, for the first time, they became aware of what had happened.

Only one was spared.

He sat in the middle of the square, untouched by the flames that consumed the soldiers around him. His silver armour had disguised the fact by reflecting the human furnace around him.

General Ekar Waalstan met the Captain of Refuge's pale, furious gaze.

He raised his sword and charged.

He did it clumsily, as if he had only learned to ride recently and had never truly mastered the skills that a soldier needed.

In his path stepped Lieutenant Lehana, who had not only been trained in all the skills the man before her lacked, but who had lived the life that Waalstan had not.

The awareness dawned in Waalstan's face as he rode towards her. He saw the soldier before him, saw the anger in her, saw that it was a response to the atrocity that he rode through, the violation of everything she had been trained in, everything she had been taught, and the rules that she lived by in her soldier's life. General Ekar Waalstan saw in her the horror of what his orders had given rise to, the devastation he had wrought on men and women who had believed in him and his god, and had obeyed without question.

He saw that and, in the moment before Lehana's bastard sword crashed into him, he lowered his own weapon, to let her blow tear the life from him unimpeded.

3.

'I didn't paint it,' the old man said. From his seat at the fire, he twisted to the painting behind him, as if it was the first time he had seen it. 'If you were going to ask, that is.' In his hand, a broken stick twitched back and forth between Ayae, Jae'le, Eidan and Tinh Tu. 'I can't paint,' he admitted, still staring at the painting. 'I make, well, I can't make.'

Ayae was the first to draw her attention from the painting and turned to him. 'Who did paint it?' she asked.

'No, no, you are not meant to ask that.' He looked at her, but his stick continued to bounce between the four. 'You are meant to ask, you are meant to say, "Where is my friend?" Where is your dead friend? That is what you ask. Then the two men beside you threaten and ask and threaten again until I tell them.'

'No one is going to threaten you. We just want to know where Zaifyr is,' Tinh Tu spoke with a strange gentleness in her voice. 'Why don't you help us find him?'

'But he's not here. He's gone. Gone, gone, gone. I gave him to a blind child and a dead woman. They were here, waiting for me. I told them to do that. To wait for me, that is. I said, "I won't be gone long. You won't have to go into the city. You can trust me." They both would have stuck out up there, you see. That's why I had to do it. You will find, you will find . . . well, you won't find either of them now, but you're welcome to look down the passage to my right to see if the two are still there if you want.'

'He isn't there,' Eidan said. 'No one is there. The earth would tell me.' With slow steps, he began to approach the old man. 'But you know that. You know me. You've seen me before. You gave me Lor Jix's name.'

'You looked familiar but I didn't want to assume.' With a sly glance at the others, the man slipped from his seat and drew close. 'You've changed a bit,' he said, his whisper the kind that a stage actor might make of dramatic whisper in a comedy. 'Just between you and me, of course. The scars make you stand out. Leviathan's Blood made them, I know. She got into you, tried to change you, like she did those sharks and squids. But you're smart. I can tell. No, no, don't protest these things. I know you are. You know her blood can't hurt you. Just like you know you can't hurt me. But I'll tell what I know. I'll tell you that Zaifyr is in Ranan. Well, that he will be soon. He'll be with her.'

'With Se—?'

The old man screamed and leapt forwards. He was so loud that Ayae blanched, and Eidan took a step backwards. '*No!*' he shouted. 'No! You can't say her *name*, you can't!' Then, as quickly as his fury had risen, it left, and he held out his hands in apology, patting Eidan's chest. 'Sorry. Sorry, but she hears it. All the gods hear their names. Well, did. Some still do. They hear it spat on each day. But not Ger.' He turned and spat into the fire and then grinned. 'You can spit on Ger all day.'

At the painted wall, Jae'le lowered his hand. While the others were speaking, he had gone to it, running his hand along it, his fingers lingering not on the images, but on the cracks and faults that ran through the bone. 'What is your name?' he asked, turning to the old man.

'Irue Tq,' he said.

'That was the name of the Fifth Philosopher seventeen thousand years ago,' Tinh Tu said. The gentleness in her voice had left, and her tone was hard and blunt. 'What is your name?'

The old man smiled blissfully. 'Jiqana Felune.'

'That is a slave in Gogair,' Tinh Tu said coldly. 'I ask you again: what is your name?'

'High Priest Famendora of Met—'

His voice broke off suddenly as Eidan lifted him into the air. 'I have no time for your games. Not now.' With an easy movement, he flung the old man towards the back of the cave, towards the elaborate painting on one of Ger's bones. Yet, rather than hit the wall, rather than crumple to the ground at Jae'le's feet, the old man controlled the toss and landed on his feet. When he was upright, he offered a small bow to his unreceptive audience. 'A name is power,' he said. 'I am not so foolish as to give any of you a name. If one is needed today, then I am Irue, for Irue – Irue had handwriting to admire in a man. Or a woman.'

An arm's length from him, Jae'le made a disgusted noise. 'God-touched,' he said, the word an insult. 'I should have struck you down in The Pale House.'

Irue offered a second bow of failed dignity. This time, he tilted in mid-dip and almost fell. 'You know it would have done nothing,' he said, after he had straightened. 'You of all the people alive in this world know that.'

'I don't understand,' Ayae said. 'Surely this man is not the same as the Innocent?'

'Poor Aela.' The old man sighed. 'You must realize that the War of the Gods drove him mad. I have – I know what it is to be mad. To be not a little mad, but to be truly, truly mad, and he is mad. The greatest tragedy of his madness is that it is coherent. It is a terrible combination for a man who was once quiet and honest. A man who might have been the best of us. Of course,' he added, with a glance at Jae'le, 'a man he trusted impaled him on a tree for thousands of years. That didn't help, either.'

'Are you Ger's servant, then?' Ayae asked and indicated the painting again. 'Is that yours?'

'I told you I did not paint that.' Irue stood taller, filled with sudden importance. 'Besides, Ger did not have a servant. Well,' he added. 'Not until recently. Though recently is really our invention. It is a view of the world that is unique to us. The gods saw time as a whole, until they didn't see it. So, for Ger, his servant was always here, even if we could not see it. He was only available to us once our perceptions had defined the world adequately and straightened out time to such a point that he was born.' The old man made pulling motions with his hands. 'But still. Still. Ger didn't always have a servant.'

'Did that servant paint this?'

'Well, no. No, I don't think Ger's servant is much of a painter. I mean, I only met him briefly, so he could be a painter. But. Well. You're a painter. He isn't a painter. He is a killer. And this leg is Ger's leg. It is the bone of his leg, I mean. It had flesh on it before. How could anyone paint a scene on it, if they were not the owner of the leg? So, I figure, Ger painted it.'

Ayae turned back to the painting as he talked. She thought of how the Wanderer had appeared over Zaifyr in Asila. She thought about Lor Jix's speech in Yeflam, of how he had been left to wait for the moment he would be called upon out of the black ocean. The gods had plans. That much, she knew, was true. They had seen what would happen when Se'Saera was born, and the painting before her was, like the others, a message left for the mortal men and women they had seen. The problem was that Ayae did not recognize herself in the image before her. Oh, it was her: from the brown of her skin, to the shape of her nose and the dark of her hair: it was all her. But the emotions in her eyes, the suggestion that she had turned away from what was happening around her in fear . . . that was not her.

'Taane was my mistress,' the old man said quietly. 'Taane, the Goddess of Madness. She was a difficult god to serve. She wanted to be defined to the broken, the lost and the mad, and she did not care what she had to do to speak to them. She did not care what she had to do to me, to be more correct. I look at myself and I look at Aela and I think: that could be me if Taane was still alive. She never made any attempt to protect me. She simply made me do the things she wanted. Even doing this for Ger. All he wanted was for me to be in certain places in certain times, but Taane bound me to his command to stop me from wandering. It was after Linae died. She left me no choice but to obey his every command. His first words to me felt like four mouths, and all he said was that he was the warden and he wanted me to help keep guard on his jail until I could not. But. But. *But.* But, it was not what I thought. I thought it would be the wind and the rain and the earth and the fire, but it was not the elements that he kept in his chains. It was not he, it was . . . well, I should show you. I should. Come. Come.'

He beckoned to them and, without turning to see if they followed, walked to the back of the cave, to a tunnel that led beneath the splitting bones of a dead god.

4.

Aela Ren sent Samuel Orlan to meet the combined force of Mireea, Yeflam and the Saan.

The cartographer had mounted his grey without a word after the Innocent gave him the order. With a surprising sense of sadness, Bueralan watched the wide road swallow the old man in the late morning's sun. The Orlan he had known a year ago, who had ridden into Leera with him and Dark, the Orlan who had betrayed him in Dirtwater, remained only in bits and pieces. The confident, famous man who gambled with the lives of his friends in Ranan could still be seen, but only through the damage that threatened now to consume him. In a fashion, he was like a weathered statue, where the sculptor's original work could still be seen but was now defined by blemishes and age.

Bueralan could identify similar damage within himself, as well. After Ille, after Elar was murdered, he had taken Aned Heast's job in Mireea because he thought it would be simple. An army to stop, a city to defend. In such a job, Bueralan could take a moment to breathe, could make simple choices, ones based on morals close to his own. Instead, Kae, Ruk, Liaya and Aerala had all died. Zean had died as well, but Bueralan had reached out for the stone that held his soul and taken it to Ooila when he should have broken it and left.

'Do you know what he is doing?' Joqan appeared on the other side of the thick, twisted tree trunk Bueralan leant against. He had a heavy axe over his back. 'Aela, that is.'

The Innocent stood alone in the centre of the wide road ahead of them, his hands behind his back.

'He is waiting,' Bueralan said.

'But do you know why?'

'He wants to be easily seen.'

'He has offered to duel their champion.'

'I know,' he said. 'I heard him tell Orlan that.'

'Aela first started offering the duels in Sooia.' Joqan said. 'It did not happen in our first battle. It came after. After we had seen what our war would look like. After our first battles. We knew we would become inured to the death that we caused, that what had so horrified us would one day stop doing so. When that happened, our doubts would leave us. Aela said that our horror would become an abstract one. The thought distressed us. After all, we had been the voices of our gods. We had been feared, yes, and we had raised our weapons when we had been asked, but we had been loved, also. People made pilgrimages to us in times of need. They sought us out so that they could ask a god for vengeance, for forgiveness, and for more. We had never been seen as murderers, not even those of us who had served the God of Death.'

'So you decided to test those you fought against?' Bueralan asked. 'To decide what, exactly?'

'The gods have buried our deaths somewhere in time,' he said. 'They are like jewels to be found in the sand. What if this was the sand? What if the gods had seen us here, and had seen what we would become? What if they had buried our deaths here, in the world without them?'

'You didn't think that you shouldn't go to war?' A hint of disgust entered his voice. 'When it was so objectionable, after all?'

'You have not stood in the world with the gods and heard their voices. You have not seen all that is around you defined by them. You have not felt that absence.'

'I have worked for men and women who had as much power as you can have over another,' Bueralan said. 'They had been paid to listen to their ideologies and they paid me to enact it.' He pushed away from the tree and, in doing so, pushed away from the other man's conversation. 'You make a choice,' he said, at the edge of it. 'After they've spoken, you make it, and you live it. No one else carries the burden for you.'

Ahead, riders were emerging from the sunken glare of the morning's sun, shadows drawing up to the shadow of the Innocent. Without a word, Bueralan joined him.

The god-touched soldiers who stood on the sides of the roads, in the trees, or throughout the marshes were different to the man he stood beside. It had not been obvious to Bueralan: he had been guided by Samuel Orlan's impression of them. For him, they were sad figures, tragic in a certain way, men and women who were victims of their gods' actions. It echoed Orlan's view of how the gods acted, but Bueralan saw something different now. He saw how the gods had freed each one of them of responsibility for their actions. In their service, they had become akin to actors who performed a part they had been taught. Their lines had been said, their thoughts organized and their motivations transcribed, and in doing that, they had no longer needed to make their own decisions. When the gods had died, they had handed the responsibility of themselves to Aela Ren, and he, in response, had crafted a horrific path for them to walk.

The approaching force stopped and four riders broke from the front and continued forwards. The morning's sun left them as no more than shadows at first, but as they drew closer, each of the riders began to define him and herself. Orlan sat in the middle, while beside him, on the left, rode the Soldier, Xrie. He was the youngest of the Keepers of the Divine, a man born in the Saan who wore sashes of red through his armour. Bueralan wondered if he knew that he was one of only two surviving Keepers.

Next to Xrie rode a thickset warrior from the Saan. He was past middle age, but the armour he wore was well made, and well worn. When he halted his horse, Bueralan saw the faintest hint of resemblance to the Saan prince who had been brought to Ooila. *Miat Dvir*, the saboteur thought. The Lord of the Saan had left his home, ridden down the tunnels and crossed the ocean.

It was the last rider, the one who rode next to Orlan, who surprised Bueralan. White, grey-haired and wearing simple but solid armour, Lieutenant Mills rode in the position that Aned Heast would have held, had he been part of the force that crossed the Mountains of Ger. She was clearly the captain of the Mireean forces, but Bueralan had expected to find Heast here, had planned on the old mercenary being an active cog in the unfolding war. It had not occurred to him that he would not be. After Muriel Wagan had given him that position, Heast had rebuilt himself not as a soldier, but as a captain on the Spine of Ger, and Bueralan could not imagine him walking away from it. Yet, he was not dead. He knew that. Bueralan would have heard if Heast had died. The information would have found its way to him, whether he had been in Ooila, or in on a ship in the middle of an ocean.

'Aela Ren,' Xrie said, dipping his head in a slight greeting. Beside him, Orlan left the three and rode back to the god-touched soldiers. 'You do not send a friend as a messenger.'

'I send a man who will not lie for me,' the Innocent said evenly. 'I send a man who makes it very clear that to fight me is to die.'

'He said that if you were defeated all your soldiers would leave this war.' The Soldier did not bother with the challenge in Ren's words. 'Is this true?'

'Yes.'

'My soldiers will not do that if I am defeated.'

'I have not asked them to do so.'

'Then I accept.'

5.

Bueralan watched Xrie dismount with a practised ease, while behind him, his soldiers came up the road. The closer they drew, the easier it was for the saboteur to hear the excitement in their voices. He could understand it: the Soldier, the immortal who had been known as the Blade Prince of the Saan before he came to the Floating Cities of Yeflam, would soon fight the Innocent. Neither man had been defeated in battle and the soldiers behind Xrie were confident in their champion.

In his visits to Yeflam, Bueralan had heard soldiers and mercenaries speak of Xrie. They said that he was a fair man, and a man of skill and talent. No one could claim to have heard him raise his voice or lose his temper. As they formed up behind him now, on a road in Leera, that knowledge was contrasted with the man Xrie faced. Aela Ren was said to be filled with rage, was reported to have torn apart his opponents with his hands, feasted on the flesh and drunk the blood. The same soldiers who said that they had never heard Xrie raise his voice were the same men and women who insisted that the Innocent's soldiers feared him more than anything else. It was why they did what they did in Sooia.

'I met a man by the name of Jae'le recently,' Xrie said, while he waited for his soldiers to assemble. 'I am told you were once a friend of his.'

'He did not say that to you.' Along the road behind Aela Ren, his god-touched soldiers began to emerge. 'But I know him,' the Innocent continued, as Bueralan turned to join them. 'What did he tell you about me?'

'He said that you cannot die.'

'Did Samuel not tell you the same thing?'

'He did.'

Ren spread his scarred hands out, the palms empty. 'Both are correct.'

'All things die,' Xrie said, his tone polite and respectful. 'But Jae'le told me that if I wanted to defeat you, I should lie to you.'

'Jae'le.' The name was said with a real disappointment. 'Is he with you? Bring him forth and let him tell his own lies.'

'He is not here.'

The Innocent did not appear to be surprised. 'He was once a man to be feared and respected,' he said, instead. 'It is sad to hear how he has fallen.'

'I will not lie to you. It is not who I am.'

'A wise choice. Lies create a false reality and you can be certain of nothing within it. I have always been surprised by the people who insist on lies. I cannot understand why they wrap their lives in the falseness that they create. They allow it to shape the reality that they share with their children and their friends and they let it breed real consequences that they call just.'

Xrie did not reply and, for a moment, the two stood before each other in silence.

'Will you draw your sword?' Xrie asked, finally.

'In time,' Aela Ren replied.

The Soldier took a step to his left, as if he had begun a dance, and began to walk around the Innocent.

He did so confidently, his hand on the hilt of his sword. The dyed red tips of his hair blended into the morning's light and, as he circled the Innocent, he briefly appeared to wear a crown of fire.

Bueralan had heard the stories of the Blade Prince. It was one of the stories the Saan allowed to be told and retold beyond the borders of their land. In truth, warriors who travelled outside rarely spoke of what happened on the flat, dusty land where they lived. Theirs was an insular culture, built upon the concept of pure bloodlines, and for hundreds of years, the most that countries around the world heard of was an exile, maimed in a ritualistic fashion. The loss of a hand, mostly. Xrie Dvir changed that. He left the Saan because he wished to and, in the years that followed, the Saan left with him. Sketches of a tribal society emerged, one that caged its women in oral and written histories, and let their men roam free without the ability to write their name. When asked about their home, they had one story that they would tell, and only one.

It was the story of how the Blade Prince of the Saan fought to unite the tribes. It persisted long after he had arrived in Yeflam and become known as the Soldier. Yet, not one of them contained details of his family. No version of the story said that he had been a first son, a third, or even a fifth. He was simply a loyal son in a family who had never ruled. A son who changed that. At the age of fourteen, he went to a meeting of the Saan tribes and there he had presented himself and declared war on the other tribes. He was tested, it was said, with sixteen duels, one for each tribe. After he had defeated them all, he returned home, his declaration of war accepted.

The length of the war was never described, but its defining moment was. It was a battle in a village named Jajjar. For most people outside the Saan, it was the only name that they heard. It was spoken so freely that even Saan in positions of power – like the war scout Usa Dvir, who would not name a lake or a piece of land to outsiders – would say the village's name without hesitation. It was in Jajjar that the Blade Prince of the Saan was trapped with one hundred enemy soldiers. He fought them for over a week and he fought them alone. He fought them after his swords had broken and he fought them with broken swords. He fought them until he was the last warrior to stand in the village.

It was the story every warrior from the Saan told to anyone who asked of their home.

It was the story that the soldiers of the Yeflam Guard repeated to anyone who asked about their captain.

In front of the Innocent, Xrie came to a stop. He was an arm's length away. His hand rested on the hilt of his sword.

He waited.

He waited.

He waited.

His fingers shifted around the hilt of his sword and—

He fell, his chest ripped open, as if the armour and flesh had been no more than paper. He fell sideways, his hand slipping from his hilt, hinting at life, until it was clear that it was unable to break his fall.

'Now,' Aela Ren said, lowering his bloodstained sword. 'You will all die.'

6.

The god-touched soldiers charged past Bueralan and the Innocent, but the saboteur remained where he was and stared at Xrie's body.

'I told that boy not to come here,' Samuel Orlan said beside him. There was a sadness in his voice, one ringed by defeat. 'I told him the Keepers were dead. I told him that Ren and his soldiers had killed them. I said that he should turn around, that he should take – that he should. . .' His voice trailed off as the god-touched soldiers crashed into the combined forces of Mireea, Yeflam and the Saan. The line broke apart, smashed like a child's toy. Voices could be heard, some of them raised an attempt to establish order, while others gave in to panic. 'He should save his soldiers,' Orlan finished. 'That's what I told him.'

The Innocent stepped over Xrie. As he did, he revealed the deep wound that had killed him. The wound delivered by a blow so swift that Bueralan had not seen it. With a slow, ominous walk, Aela Ren made his way towards the battle.

'Get away, Orlan,' Bueralan said. 'Find a place to be safe until this is done.'

'There is no place to be safe,' he said. 'Haven't you realized that yet?'

He had.

'You haven't. You're going to go into that.' The cartographer laughed harshly. 'They can't help us.'

'I told you my plan was bad.'

Orlan called out, but Bueralan ignored him.

He ran off the road, into the green-lit world of Leera's trees, skirting to his left in an attempt to beat around the main body of fighting to reach the back of Xrie's force. There would be someone there – a mercenary captain, someone – whom he could convince to organize a retreat. Someone whom he could convince to find Heast.

Bueralan had planned on the Captain of the Spine being with Xrie. His plan, his only plan since leaving Ranan, was to find the old mercenary and give him what he knew about Se'Saera, about her city, and what Ren had said about Onaedo. Heast would have the contacts to reach out to Leviathan's End, to hear what Onaedo had begun to do if, indeed, she was doing something. He was not convinced that Ren was right – stories about the ruler of Leviathan's End reaching beyond her dead domain were rare – but Bueralan had little else in the way of options.

To his right, he heard the sharp clash of swords. It broke through the shouts that he heard, the screams that were coming from the road. It sounded again, drawing closer, and Bueralan paused on the back of a fallen log. The clashes of swords sounded again, and suddenly, like rabbits bursting out of the undergrowth, soldiers spilled out in front of him. They did not rush towards him, but rather stumbled and turned and headed deeper into the green-tinted world, towards the marshes and empty towns. Their flight scattered swamp crows into the air, their caws of protest piercing the screams, the shouts, the sound of swords, but fell silent when a tall figure burst out in pursuit: Ai Sela.

Bueralan shadowed her run. He told himself not to. He told himself that he would not fight her, that he would be no more successful than Xrie, but still he moved through the trees silently, his eyes on her until the trees around him suddenly thickened, and he lost sight of her.

It took but a handful of heartbeats to turn, to backtrack, to find her path, but even as he did, he heard the clash of blades and the shouts of soldiers, and when he reached Ai Sela, he found her standing over four bodies. At the sound of him, she spun around, her bloodied sword in her hand, but Bueralan had stopped before she could reach him.

It was her face that stopped him. In it was a quality he had not seen before, a quality that was awful in its coldness. It was not the bestial quality that overcame the Innocent at times, the rage that showed how the worst of the stories about him could be true. Rather, it was as if all that made her human, all her compassion and intelligence, all her hard despair, was gone, and in its place was a cold absence, a will so without compassion that Bueralan expected her to attack him.

Instead, she lowered her sword and walked past him.

She left him with the dead, a dead that, Bueralan realized, included Captain Mills. She lay against one of the trees, her bloody hands gripping her sword, her empty gaze on him.

Her last sight had been of him and Ai Sela, he knew.

'Don't touch her!' The sword that pierced his stomach arrived with the voice, the two bursting out of the trees. 'Traitor,' the soldier spat, putting his weight behind the thrust.

The sword ran deep into him, but it did so in such a strange fashion that Bueralan was not sure if it was real or not. He had been stabbed before: he could not have lived the life he had without accepting that someone, somewhere, would beat his defences. But this time, as the blade ran up to the hilt, it was different. It was as if the weapon had been expected, as if the length of steel was always going to slide through his stomach, and his body was prepared. He did not feel the strength within him leave, did not feel his bodily functions fail, did not feel anything beside the throat of the soldier in his hand.

'Don't shout,' he said, forcing himself not to crush his throat. 'They will hear if you shout, and you don't want them to hear.'

The young soldier did not let go of his sword. He held tightly to it as fear grew in his eyes.

'What's your name, boy?' When he didn't respond, Bueralan showed him his free hands. 'Your name?' he repeated. 'I know you're from the Spine. You're the baker's apprentice. Now, what's your name?'

'Jaerc.' It was a whisper, given as he tried to step back, as he tried to release the hilt of the blade in the saboteur's stomach.

But Bueralan's hands had clamped around the boy's hands. 'Who is in charge?' The young soldier tried to take another step back. 'Jaerc.' He tightened his grip. 'Jaerc, I know what you are thinking, but you have to put it aside. I am no traitor. If I was, you would be dead. You can see that. But I am not a traitor and if you want to save some of the people here, if you want to help me do that, you need to tell me who was left at the back, who had the job of defending the rear.'

'Essa,' he whispered and tried to break his bloodstained hands free. 'Captain Essa was given it.'

Bueralan released him. 'Show me where he is.'

7.

Before Eilona left Nymar Alahn's estate, she made a mistake.

'Your guard.' Nymar nodded at Caeli. 'You would be best not to bring her.'

'I have my orders,' Caeli replied, her tone one that allowed no argument. 'Your father was one of those people who gave them to me.'

'I know, but.' His hesitation was a breath in length. 'But the Faithful know you. They know you as an enemy. They have branded you as that. You have killed their comrades. Your presence will only displease them.'

'This is a negotiation,' Eilona began, turning to the other woman. 'I am sure I will be in no danger.'

'Eilona.' Caeli said her name softly, but sternly. 'This is not how things are done. Trust me on this.'

She offered a smile that she knew was brittle. 'I'm sure it will be fine,' she said. She wanted to say, *You don't need to protect me. I know you don't want to.* She wanted to say, *I understand. You don't have to put yourself through this.* 'I am sure I will be fine. There's no need to worry.'

Caeli did not protest, not publicly, though Eilona could see that she wanted to. Once she was in the carriage, she waved to the other woman, whose gaze, she was surprised to see, was not chill or indifferent, but concerned. Then, the carriage moved off, and around her, the sunlit streets lined with tents, people and schools passed.

After two closed schools, Nymar's carriage passed a squat building full of people. Out at the front was a handmade sign that said *Se'Saera's Mercy*. Next to it stood two brown-robed Faithful. They had a line before them, one that consisted of poorly dressed men, women and children, each of them waiting to enter the building.

'A soup kitchen?' Eilona asked, as the carriage revealed the long stretch of the queue.

'We can only run them twice a week because demand is so high,' Nymar said.

'So the Faithful do it, instead?'

'As I said, they have been a great saviour to our city.'

'Where do they get their food?' Outside, one of the schools drifted slowly towards them, its towers disappearing into the morning's sun. 'Are they buying it, or is it from donations?'

'A mix of both,' he said. 'At first, people were reluctant to take their food. Many had heard stories of cannibalism by the Leerans, and there were rumours about the Faithful. Some said that they would rather starve. At first, I thought it would drive the Faithful away, but instead they returned with fruit, rice, food like that. It wasn't long until the queues started to form.' He nodded in satisfaction at a crowd outside the window. 'I hate to think of what would have happened without them.'

Soon, the schools, the streets and the people were replaced by a long stone bridge that ran from the Spires of Alati to Rje. At the entrance to the bridge stood a pair of guards, but the carriage passed by without incident. It was the only vehicle on the road, and Nymar, Eilona and the driver the only people on it, while around her, the destruction from three months ago still littered Leviathan's Blood in shards of stone, the wreckage of ships and a broken central pillar.

A nation could lose its identity in war just as easily as it could be defined by it, Eilona knew. The thought rose unbidden, a bubble of air escaping. She remembered how Ooila had torn itself apart in search of a new identity as it moved from elected rule to full democracy, to an uncertain patriarchy and, finally, to a hereditary matriarchy with generations of suffering. People had done terrible things, things that they would not normally have done. It was as if, she remembered reading, all morality had been suspended.

With that thought in her mind, the carriage passed through the gate into Rje.

It was a much smaller city than the Spires of Alati, a piece of connective tissue between Nale and Guranatan. It was a city defined by expensive hotels, lavish restaurants, private coffee houses and other indemnities to ensure visiting diplomats who wished to speak officially – and unofficially, of course – with the Keepers of the Divine were kept happy.

Faje Metura, Aelyn's former steward, met the carriage outside a relatively modest house. At the sight of the tall man and his two guards, Eilona felt herself tense. Her anxiety rose when Nymar opened the carriage door and, with a genuine smile, shook the other man's hand with warmth. For his part, Faje was smoothly restrained, a professional who was used to revealing only the faintest, most benign, emotions. It was an expression that Eilona had seen her mother use, and within it was a suppressed emotion that made Eilona realize her mistake. She should never have left Caeli.

'I thought we might walk around the streets of Rje and talk,' Faje said, after he had greeted Eilona. Up close, the broken nature of his brown skin, which revealed patches of white, appeared startling and pronounced 'There are many things I would like to show you, but mostly, I admit, I am tired of my office.'

Eilona agreed and, pushing aside her anxiety, said, 'I wouldn't mind being able to speak with some of the men and women from the cities that sank, if you don't mind.'

'Our refugees?' Faje offered her a faint smile as they began to walk. 'I am afraid you won't find any here. This is a city for Se'Saera's Faithful only.'

'I have seen the Faithful helping others in the Spires.' Nymar and Faje's two guards fell in behind them. 'Surely you don't turn away those who are in need of help here?'

'Of course not. Se'Saera does not turn her back on those in need.'

'Unless they are not Faithful. That is the implication of your words, isn't it?' Eilona caught herself in mid-sentence. 'My apologies,' she said, forcing a smile. 'Old habits, I am afraid.'

'No, no need to apologize,' Faje said easily. 'I know you are a historian in Zoum. You have not yet written a book, have you?'

'I mostly lecture. My partner publishes more.'

'Perhaps you will write a book on Se'Saera. After all, what she does is no different to what all the gods have done, is it?'

'Generally speaking, but the gods were a long time ago. Most of what we know is more of an educated guess than a fact.'

'You will have to trust me, then. What Se'Saera does is no more than what any of the old gods did. As you can see from Nymar being here, we have made strong ties to other cities. We hope to build such a relationship with Muriel Wagan and Lian Alahn.'

'That is why I am here. Neela will soon be inhabitable, and work on Mesi is proceeding apace. No one wants the relationships between those two cities and the rest of Yeflam to worsen.'

'It will be difficult.' Faje led her out of the street and into a busier lane, filled with the Faithful. 'Muriel Wagan's reputation is not the best, at least not here.'

Eilona's skin prickled in warning. 'My mother and Lian Alahn have worked very hard to create peace on the shore.'

'Only out of selfishness, I fear,' he said. 'After all, if Mireea had not fallen, neither you nor I would be here having this conversation.'

8.

Spirits began to appear along the soggy, burned shoreline well before Heüala did.

One of Meina's soldiers delivered the news to Zaifyr. He had no real idea how much time had passed since he and the others had stepped onto *Glafanr*, but it was long enough that the others had left him alone. Meina, Anguish and Jix had left the captain's cabin hours, days, maybe months ago, each to enter their own timeless world aboard the ship. Zaifyr had left the cabin as well: he had wandered alone through the long corridors, climbed the rigging, stood beside the wheel, and watched for the sight of the dead in the still river they drifted down. He did not sleep and he did not feel hunger, but eventually he returned to the cabin and its chained book. He sat there, tapping against the charm beneath his left wrist in an odd beat. It was there that the soldier Meina sent found him.

Outside, Zaifyr found the Captain of Steel by the rail. The small pitch-black form of Anguish sat on her shoulder, and he, not her, turned towards Zaifyr as he approached.

'Can you see it?' she asked.

He looked across the still water: a man, his body made from pale silvered lines, rode a horse. It was similarly defined, but it was stretched out in a gallop to keep pace with *Glafanr*. 'I do.'

'I have seen his like before in Mireea.' She continued to stare out across the water. 'Anguish tells me that you have seen them before, as well.'

'They were in Yeflam,' the creature murmured.

'Ancestors from the tribes of the Plateau.' Zaifyr remembered the misshapen bodies that they had worn, the awful violence within them. 'They should not be here.'

But they were, of course.

Zaifyr had never liked the Plateau. He had walked across it early in his life, when he heard about pacifist tribes who lived with the spirits of their ancient family members. He had thought that the tribes would be able to help him live beside the dead and even, perhaps, help him find a way to ease their torment. But the haunts he saw every waking moment of his life were not like the dead in the soil of the Plateau. Those spirits had no fear of losing their identity and they had no desperate need of him. They had responded to Zaifyr in a way unlike any other dead man or woman.

It was not long until the lone rider was joined by another and another, until half a dozen spirits had emerged from the still, burned landscape.

They were a patrol, Meina said, and Zaifyr agreed. They came to shadow *Glafanr*, but not to attack it and, with a sinking sensation, the charm-laced man believed that they would find more of them in Heüala. The thought was not one that filled Zaifyr with pleasure. He could remember only bits and pieces about the kind of soldiers the ancestors had been, but he knew that, for all the violence, all the horror, they had been an excellent fighting force.

Ahead, Heüala, the City of the Dead, began to appear.

It was defined at first in slivers of silvered shape: a straight line high in the sky, a hint of a round dome, a long wall. It took a moment for each part of the city to emerge, as if it had no real form of its own, but was instead made in response to the expectations of those who came to it.

What, then, did it say about Zaifyr that Heüala was not built on the barren land around it, but rather that it sat in the middle of the River of the Dead, surrounded by a stillness of water that made it look as if it floated? Zaifyr did not know. It was certainly not an image that he had been told of as a child, or seen before. To get a clearer look at it, he walked to the front of *Glafanr*, where he was joined by Meina, Anguish and Steel. Lor Jix already waited there. He was not pleased to see Heüala, not in the way he had greeted the ship he had stood on. If anything, he appeared confused by what he saw before him.

Up closer, Heüala looked like a walled prison island. There was a single, empty dock, from which paths ran up the barren ground to the gate of Heüala. Despite the actual space between the two being small, the paths looped and turned, disappearing and re-emerging from the ground beneath. There were dozens of paths and not one was like another, not in terms of design, or the material that had been used to construct it. Some were made from dirt, others from stone, and others from gold. As near as Zaifyr could tell, they all ended at the gate of Heüala, but he was not at all confident of that: the path chosen could very well be a choice of divine judgement, or a reflection of the souls that came to it. The gate, likewise, baffled him, for it was not made from any earthly substance that Zaifyr could name. Instead, it had been forced from something solid and dark, and then it had been speckled with white, as if the stars themselves had been captured and warped into the gates, creating a sense of depth in which anyone who gazed at it could be lost.

Yet, it was what was wrapped around the highest building that drew Zaifyr's attention, even before he saw the spirits on the walls, saw the scouts that had followed them leap into the water and begin to ride to the city. It was the sight of a form he had seen before, a horrific, monstrous figure that had pushed through the sky over Yeflam.

It was, as then, a body made from darkness, one bestial, yet unlike any beast Zaifyr had seen in size, and in the spread of the wings that lay against its colossal body. It was different, as well. The body he had seen over Yeflam had not been completely formed: it had been breaking apart, as if it was made from smoke. But that was no longer apparent. The creature appeared whole and, despite its stillness, very much alive.

'Se'Saera,' he whispered.

9.

Eilona realized she was in very real danger long before the tall, elegant building appeared before her.

She was afraid, but she worked to control that fear. At first, she did not know why she should be frightened. A perfectly acceptable response to the situation was to stop, to request that she be taken back to the carriage, to demand that she be returned to Caeli, but she did not. She continued to walk beside Faje, with the building drawing closer, and the Faithful gathering around the small group. At first, Eilona thought her sense of control came from the fact that none of the Faithful threatened her, that it came, she believed, because they had not been called over by Faje. The Faithful had instead simply risen from where they sat reading outside Rje's buildings, or from where they stood, working on an upturned carriage or broken balcony. But it was not until Faje led her alone up the stairs to the tall building that Eilona knew she would see through whatever was before her because she had placed herself in this danger. She would take responsibility for the situation she was in.

Her only problem was that Faje sensed her fear.

'There's no need to be afraid,' he said and offered his hand to her. 'I want to show you our printing press, nothing more.'

Eilona did not take his hand. 'I did not think there was a press on Rje.' Her voice was cool and controlled, much to her satisfaction.

With a faint smile, Faje lowered his hand and turned to open the door for her. 'This one came from Gogair,' he said, after she had entered. 'It was a gift from Se'Saera. But why should it not be in Yeflam? As a nation, we have one of the highest levels of literacy in the world.'

Inside, an expensive, well-furnished but abandoned hotel foyer waited. 'Yeflam's presses are also some of the most politicized in the world.'

'Ah, but isn't all literature political?'

The press was located on the second floor. At first, Eilona thought that there had been a fight there, but no, the walls of three rooms had been knocked out to accommodate the size of the press. The long, black machinery stretched like a mythical creature through the broken brick. There was nobody operating it and, despite Faje's assurance that he had brought Eilona into the building to see it, he did not attempt to show it to her. Instead, he led her up another flight of stairs.

'Tell me, Eilona,' Faje said, 'how did you feel when your father died?'

She stopped halfway up the stairs. 'What kind of question is that?'

'A simple one.' He was a handful of steps above her when he stopped and turned to her. 'I meant nothing by it,' he said.

'If your plan is to intimidate me—'

'It is not my plan.'

'Then do not ask about my father.'

Faje offered a small tilt of his head in an apology Eilona did not believe. 'I mentioned your father not to offend you, but out of mutual interest. I was always greatly moved by the nature of his death.'

'That is private,' she said, a hint of her mother's steel entering her voice now. 'I have no desire to discuss it with you, as I just said.'

'He was "cursed", to use the more popular term.' He resumed walking up the stairs. 'It was, as you said, a private matter, but the Lord of Mireea's death could have only so much privacy. It is the nature of politics, after all. It could have been an assassination by enemies, a family squabble turned bad, or a disease. The nature of his death was important to all of Mireea's neighbours for no other reason than because the Kingdoms of Faaisha wanted to march upon Mireea. All it needed was for a small chink in your mother's armour to appear. In my previous position, in my work for Aelyn Meah, I was given the task of learning what happened. It was one of my sadder duties, I assure you.'

Despite herself, Eilona followed him up the stairs. The memories she had of her father were but a handful and she would not speak them now, to him.

'For weeks, I wondered how he must have felt in his death. How it must have been for him to feel his heart turn heavy, to feel it become an object that he could feel in his chest.' Faje stopped outside a door, but did not open it. 'It was my first thought when I heard that his organs had turned to stone. I thought he must have felt it, piece by piece, as if each part of him was being separated. I imagined him trying to wake your mother, but unable, because his arms were too heavy to lift. I learned that when Muriel Wagan called for help, he had become so heavy that the bed had broken, and he lay in its ruins when he died. The official cause was suffocation, and not the curse of the late gods, but I think we can step outside such unnecessary differences. Indeed, when I reported to Aelyn Meah, she did not bother to pretend it was anything else. She told me that he was not the first to be inflicted by part of Ger's power. She said most died because there was no balance within.'

He pushed the door open.

Inside waited horror. As with the floor below, the walls of the room had been knocked out, but rather than it being limited to three to accommodate the long form of the press, all the walls of the floor before Eilona had been cleared. Painted rubble lay strewn on the ground in chunks and the load-bearing support beams had been left exposed in their long, crude forms. It was from them that the horror began, for at the beams, chains had been attached, and the long chains ran out to the necks of men, women, and children.

Each had been blinded.

'It is a tragedy when someone is cursed,' Faje said from behind Eilona. He stood close to her, blocking her exit from the room, but not touching her. 'For some, I know, it is wished for, and for others, it is not. For some it changes their lives for the best, and for some it does not. But regardless, each have something that is not their own. They have a power that belongs to another.'

The people could hear Faje, and at the sound of his voice began to move, to pull on the chains, and to make noises that Eilona had heard once before, from a man whose tongue had been torn out of his mouth.

'The Keepers of the Divine kept detailed records of every cursed person within Yeflam,' he said. 'I was quite often in charge of those records. I would document a name, and a power. For example, the man directly in front of us, the man whose hands have been removed, had a bit of extra luck in card games. Across from him, the child you see had an ease with animals that went beyond what any mortal could cultivate. None of it was strong enough to grant them entry to the Keepers' world, but it was enough to be noticed and to be watched. That is how I knew where they were when Yeflam broke apart. It is why Se'Saera told me gather them, and hold them for her, for when she came to claim the parts of her that had been stolen by these people.'

Faje touched her, and Eilona flinched, but he held a letter in his hand, folded and sealed. He pressed it into her unresponsive grip.

'If your mother wishes to be part of Yeflam,' he said, his lips close to her ear, 'she will have to give us the people I have listed here. Some, I don't doubt, will have died. Others may have fled. But those on the shore, those men and women cannot step onto Neela or Mesi and remake their life. Their lives are the price for the mortal men and women who wish to return to their own. They are the toll that Se'Saera has said must be paid.'

10.

'Does the abomination sleep?' Lor Jix asked. Ahead, the dark creature shifted its curled body around the roof of the tallest building in the City of the Dead as if it were, indeed, asleep, and a dream had been the cause of its movement. 'I would not have thought it possible.'

'It is not,' Anguish answered from his perch on Meina's shoulder. 'But her attention? That can be drawn away from here by all those who whisper to her.'

'Do those spirits in the water not call to her?'

The spirits thrashed through the water, generating a white spray that looked, at times, as if it sought to devour both mount and rider. 'If they speak, I do not hear them,' the creature said.

'Anguish,' Zaifyr said. 'How many were taken from the Plateau?'

'Forty.'

'We outnumber them at least six to one,' Meina said. 'If that is how many are behind the walls, that is.'

'But where will they go once they have been struck down? Where does a dead soldier go if he or she dies in the City of the Dead?' Lor Jix held out his dark hand. 'And where do we go, for that matter? We do not look like them, not now.'

'The answers will be offered soon enough.' She nodded at the closing docks. 'But which path will we take to get there?'

Zaifyr glanced at each one, and could not see that any would be better than another. The choice was made by the scouts, whose mounts pulled them from the still water and went without hesitation up the road that was paved with gold. 'The pauper's road,' he said, as *Glafanr* nudged against the dock. 'Let them go as kings and queens. We will go as beggars.'

'We will be humble,' Jix corrected, a hint of disapproval in his voice. 'We will go to Heüala as we were born.'

It was easy to forget that the Captain of *Wayfair* had been one of the Leviathan's priests, and that his piety, so alien and ill-conceived to Zaifyr and Meina, had carried him through the long years at the bottom of the ocean. Meina's response to it was different from Zaifyr's, however. The charm-laced man watched her shake her head, dismiss it and call out to her soldiers around her, to prepare them for the path that they would walk to the city. Zaifyr, in comparison, was reminded of what his brother had said to him of the priests who had served of the gods, of their power and their devotion. He had seen none of it: the shaman in the village where he had grown up had been a minor figure, Zaifyr knew: a woman who lost her faith before she died and was punished by a god who had little concern for the people she had served. He had never seen the priests in all their power, all their awful certainty.

Lor Jix was the first to step on the dirt road outside the docks, and he led them along the long, twisting road without hesitation.

It was a path that Zaifyr could not judge the length of, nor how long he and the others spent on it. When he glanced behind him, the huge shape of *Glafanr* was at times close, then far away, on his left, on his right, and close again, and he found it difficult to tell how far he had come from the docks. In contrast, Heüala appeared to be closing in, continually, but in such incremental measurements that more than once Zaifyr convinced himself that his belief that it was closer was foolish.

He could see the other roads around him, as well. They ran at times beside him – the road of gold was most common – but at other times they crossed above or below the road. In each road that he saw, however, there were shapes on it, dark, shadowed figures that would gaze not just at him, but at Meina, Anguish, and the soldiers that followed in a long line.

Then, as if the road had been short, no more than a crossing, Heüala appeared.

The dark star-brushed gate was closed, and none of the spirits who had ridden ahead were at it, or above it. From where he stood, Zaifyr could not even see Se'Saera's body, curled around the tower.

There was no break on the gate, no hinges, nothing to suggest that it swung open at all, and when Zaifyr placed his hand on it, he met a firm, solid gate, no different from any he had seen while alive. He glanced at Jix, who offered him only a shrug, then at Meina and Anguish. The latter made a swinging motion, like a bat, while the former made a spearing motion.

He lifted the staff and, gently, tapped it against the gate.

It was the staff that broke first: the wood fell apart in his hand, the faint slivers of the dead in it breaking free and rushing outwards, into the starred wall of the gate. Once they hit it, it began to split apart, but not in destruction. Instead, it began to slide back, as if it were a giant puzzle that had been used to make an intricate lock which the staff had broken.

Behind it, a street made from simple paved stone appeared. As more and more of the gate slid back, more of Heüala was revealed, including buildings, lamps, all of them in a mash of old, near-forgotten cultures, the kind that Zaifyr had only seen in ruins, or in the restored sites that his brother Eidan had visited. Much as he wanted to gaze at the buildings, he was drawn away from them, and to the thirty-four spirits that sat in the middle of the square, mounted on horses that threatened to dissolve beneath them.

'No,' Lor Jix said, a growing horror in his voice. 'Not my crew, no.'

Free from the staff, free from the gate, the spirits that had spent thousands and thousands of years at the bottom of Leviathan's Blood beside their captain, began to take shape.

At first, Zaifyr did not understand what had caused the ancient dead's concern, until he realized that the new spirits were silvered, and that they did not take their place to protect them from the warriors.

Rather, they took their place beside the warriors.

11.

The tunnel was long, but Irue's pace did not slacken, not even when it began to shake with tremors. At first, they were gentle, not enough to cause Ayae concern, but after the fourth, they had become stronger, as if they were waves, washing up before one larger than all the others. On the sixth, part of the tunnel behind them collapsed, and in its wake, Eidan said, 'That was not the last. Old man, we do not want to be trapped down here when the final quake hits.'

'You don't want to go back that way, anyway,' Irue said as he waved the dust away from his eyes. 'Not that you want to go backwards, of course.' He blew on the dust in front of him. 'You should go forwards because forwards leads you to Leera and Leera is where Zaifyr is.' With a dusty smile, he pushed his way past Jae'le and Tinh Tu to reach Ayae. In the pale, dirty light, he lifted the broken stick in his hand. 'Could you light this, please?' he asked. 'Just a small flame. No need to set the whole thing on fire. Just the end, please.'

'Eidan's light is better,' she said, pointing to the dusty phosphorescent glow that came from the ground, from their footsteps.

He waved the stick. 'Please,' he repeated.

She shrugged, and a flame rose. It was small and would in no way push back the darkness ahead. Yet Irue's smile grew, as if he had been given a toy, and he waved it in the air in a pattern. 'Thank you,' he said and wrapped his free arm around Ayae's. With a gentle, but firm tug, he pulled her ahead of Tinh Tu and Jae'le, leaving them behind her with Eidan. 'Now, I have a question for you. Just for you, not for the others. For you. My question is: why did the elements need a warden?'

The question caught Ayae off-guard. 'Because some were fickle.' She tried to remember what she had read in Yeflam, months ago. 'Some said that they were childish. That they gave in to their emotions. Ger kept them from destroying things.'

'But nothing has been destroyed since he died,' the old man said, a hint of excitement in his voice. 'The sky is not filled with tornadoes, the ground does not break apart with earthquakes – well, not this ground, this ground does – but my point is, if the elements were uncontrollable and we needed a controller, why have we not been destroyed by them?'

'We have storms and cyclones and earthquakes and fires,' she said, but as she spoke, Ayae knew that it sounded simple.

'Zaifyr believed the elements were fine,' Jae'le added from behind her. 'He often said that they never needed to be chained. Occasionally, he would argue that Ger chained them not for their crimes, but for their power, but he had no evidence for that.'

'This is why a god needs a servant,' Irue said in a loud whisper, as if he was confessing to Ayae a deep, dark secret. Ahead, the tunnel opened into a large and undefined darkness. 'With a good servant, a god can define what it is to the mortals like you and me. Ah, I see your look, but think: no one ever accused Taane of wanting the mad for their power. No one thought she wanted them to lock away her enemies. No, no – everyone knew Taane wanted you to look after the mad. If you didn't, Taane would punish you. And by Taane, I mean me. She told me that and she made me do that. Not always, but sometimes. But people, people knew.'

As abruptly as he had taken Ayae's arm, he released it. He did an ugly skip and run to get ahead of her and his tiny flame disappeared into the black.

'When Ger fell, he spoke for years,' he said from the darkness. As he spoke, a second flame emerged, larger than the first. 'Priests wrote it down. All of it. Then people destroyed it and people saved it and people rewrote it and on and on and on.' A third and fourth flame flickered to life and, as they did, a wall of torches was revealed. Ayae saw it when she stepped into the cavern, where Irue waited for her. To her left and right, the torches stretched down the wall of a huge cavern, the one before it lighting the other through a strip of oiled cloth that joined each together. 'But because there was no one to define what he said,' Irue continued, 'no one to say yes and no, everyone said yes, and everyone said no, and nothing was right. They said he was the Warden of *the* Elements, but they did not say he was the Warden *of* the Elements. They did not see that he was both the warden and the elements. Or that the elements were his domain. They did not, they could not, and so we did not understand these.'

In the middle of the cavern lay a huge set of dark, corroded chains.

They were so large that, from the edges of the cavern, Ayae thought that they were boulders, or broken stalagmites. She even thought that they might be another City of Ger, one of such largesse and magnificence that the whole city would have belonged to a society of people with a wealth she could not fully imagine. But, the closer Ayae walked towards the chains, and the more torches that were ignited – there must have been over two, three hundred, each of them painstakingly attached to the cavern wall – the more her understanding of what she saw was challenged. They were chains, the chains Ger had held, the chains that bound the elements, the metal that was so heavy that no mortal hand could ever have lifted or forged it.

'There are no links,' Eidan said, beside her. 'There are no breaks. No hint of a hammer. There is just—'

'Decay,' Jae'le finished.

'There was not always,' Irue said. 'When I first came here, they were pristine. I sneaked past all the Cities of Ger, past all the priests, and all the gold diggers, and I found them here. Ger told me to make sure that no one would find them and I did that. But I would come in here, at times, and just look at them. They were immaculate, then. They had never held anything. They never will now.'

'How do you know the chains never held anything?'

'He told me.'

'In his four voices,' Ayae said softly.

'A voice for the fire, the wind, the earth and the water.' The old man dropped his burning stick to the ground and stamped his foot on it. 'I had heard worse, before. Perhaps that is why he asked my mistress for me.'

'Did he tell you what the chains were for?'

'They were for a god,' Jae'le said, before he could answer. 'For a new god.'

'He did not say,' Irue admitted. 'But maybe. Or maybe not.'

'What did he say?' Ayae was surprised by Tinh Tu's voice when she spoke. In it there was a strange, hard anger. 'What did the Warden of the Elements tell you? What image of the future did he show you when he gave you his orders?'

'Not this one,' the old man said quietly. 'He showed me Mireea, but it was not destroyed in the war. He showed me Yeflam, as well. A Yeflam like the one we can see now. And Leera. *Leera.* He showed me all of it, but when he did, he was not dead. He was not in the state we see him now. His flesh opened and closed with wounds. He lay in the mountains. He waited for us to deny the new god her power.'

'And then what?'

Irue shrugged.

'He returned.' Ayae gazed at the three around her, at the three who had once ruled much of the world with Aelyn and Zaifyr. 'He and the other gods. Why else would they do this, if they did not plan to return?'

'It would not have been for kindness,' the servant of Taane said. 'I have hated my god for all my life, and I have only learned to hate her more in her absence. It may have taken over ten thousand years, but I have regained some measure of myself to do that. I have fought for it. If Taane returned she would not allow me to keep it.' A shudder ran through the ground, but Irue ignored it. As the single tremor turned into a second and then continued to grow, Irue approached the corroded chain and laid his small, weathered hand on it. 'The gods have never cared for us. The plans that they made, they made for themselves. That has been clear to me since I was given my list of tasks. But I was not meant to stand before Ger, not like this. I fear that the futures the gods made are all but gone, now.'

As he finished, the cavern's roof began to collapse.

The Black Lake

'I should have known,' Aelyn Meah said, surprising me when she spoke. She had been silent for nearly five minutes and I, in truth, had been lost in my thoughts. In my horrors. 'I should have fought Se'Saera,' she continued. 'I should have forced her to kill me. I had only to look at the people she surrounded herself with to know what kind of god she would be. Aela Ren was a monster. His soldiers were agents of genocide.'

I almost spoke on behalf of Ren. I almost began, if not a defence, for there was no defence for what he had done in Sooia, then an explanation.

'But Se'Saera freed General Zilt and his soldiers from their prison on the Plateau,' Aelyn said, before I could. 'She returned a man who was more than a monster to life. She returned a fanatic who saw all who were not strong as failures. She returned a man whose whole life had been about the suffering of others. Every moment I spent with him was a moment that I could hear Tinh Tu's voice in my head, telling me of the horrors he was responsible for in the name of the God of War.'

I knew them well.

'It was the stories of the children I would hear first. It was always the stories of the children. My sister had told me how he would cripple them so that they could not walk. He would do it to a group of five or six. He would then put them in a pit or a cage and he would give them a single knife and wait for the hunger to drive them to pick it up and feast on each other.'

—Onaedo, *Histories, Year 1029*

1.

At first, it looked as if the stone simply came apart, as if it could always be detached, and Ayae had never realized.

Later, she would remember the silence that accompanied it. It did not last long: it was as if the noise of the splitting stone was a heartbeat behind the act, as if the two were distinctly different events. Later, when she was at the edge of sleep, when she was still, the silence would return to her. It would be heavy, pregnant with meaning, and Ayae would jerk awake, as if the mountain was but moments from collapsing on her.

'It must be quite the strain to hold a mountain,' Irue said, his voice distorted by the sound of falling earth above him. 'Especially a collapsing one.'

'The effort is not insubstantial.' Eidan's voice revealed nothing of the strain, but Ayae could see the black scars on his left hand twisted like cords around his fist, as if he had something gripped tightly. 'Did your god show you this, as well?'

'No, she did not. Neither did Ger.' A low laugh escaped him, but there was no humour in it. 'But you should follow the cave. It will take you out. The passage we came down will boil with dirt soon. You can't go back the way we came. Ger's bones have shattered. He is nothing. At the end of his chains is a river. If you are lucky, it will see you out before your strength falters.'

'And what of you?' Jae'le asked calmly.

'I have done enough, I think.'

'You—' Ayae stopped suddenly. The stone above her shuddered, as if a new weight had just settled upon it. 'You will die,' she said.

'I do not think so.' Debris was falling through the cracks and he met her gaze with a bitter clarity. 'You'd best go, before the river is blocked.'

She turned to Tinh Tu. 'No,' the old woman said, before Ayae could speak. 'I could not make him come with us. Believe me on this.'

Irue flapped his hands at them, much like a farmer might do with chickens he wanted to round up for the night. 'Go, go.' He scraped a spot on the floor with his foot to clean it, as if the thick streams of dirt falling around him were nothing. After a third motion, he sat down and closed his eyes, as if he was preparing to meditate. Perhaps he was, but Ayae wanted to go over to him, to grab him, to force him forwards, but when she took a step towards him, Jae'le's hand stopped her. 'Leave him,' he said. 'He will only fight you.'

'We cannot stay,' Eidan said, a faint strain sounding in his voice. 'It is not just this part of the mountain that collapses, but all of it.'

Although she went with them, Ayae turned to glance back at the old man three, four times, always with doubt, and always with regret, until the darkness closed around him. By then, the stone above her and the others had begun to shudder anew and the roof had fallen lower. After one last look over her shoulder, Ayae pushed the old man from her thoughts, and ducked her head beneath the stone. Ahead, Jae'le was hunched over in the tunnel. A short while later, the last of the smouldering torches was passed, but rather than the dark enveloping them, a faint phosphorescent light began to shine from the stone above them. The light was not the pale blue of before, but a mix of orange and red. Ayae thought that Eidan was responsible, but on closer inspection, she saw that the light was created by worms, by hundreds of glowing creatures that had crawled through the breaks in the stone. Jae'le's doing, she realized, with a pang of sympathy for the creatures who would surely die once the mountain fell.

'No,' she said suddenly, her voice stopping not just herself, but the others as well. Ahead, the stone dropped again and, to enter the tunnel, they would be forced to crawl. 'No,' she repeated. 'The river is not that way. It's to the right. If you listen you can hear it.'

In front of her, Jae'le nodded, but if he could hear the rushing water as she could, he did not say. He turned to the right, and after a handful of steps, lowered himself to crawl through the barest opening of a slowly disappearing passage.

Dirt rained within it. In places, Ayae found it hard to breathe; the density of the falling earth was choking her. She found herself getting closer to the ground, as well, the stone above her scraping along her back as it came closer and closer to collapsing the passage completely. Her sword began to tangle regularly in her legs and, after she passed Jae'le's own abandoned sword, she awkwardly pulled her own out, scabbard and all, and left it in the dirt.

Behind her, Eidan grunted. Ayae twisted around to see Tinh Tu sliding around him, her staff still in her grasp. She leant close to him, and Ayae, with a startling panic, thought that she was checking his breath, for his scarred face was pressed into the ground, but a moment later, he took hold of her staff. The action had a mechanical quality about it, as if it was order, and as Tinh Tu crawled past him, her staff dragged in the dirt after her, with Eidan holding onto it.

Soon, Ayae was on her stomach, squeezing through the stone, drawn on by the sound of the river. The phosphorescence had faded and could barely be seen through the dirt, but always there was a path made by Jae'le to follow. Behind her, she could hear

Tinh Tu moving loudly, and every time Ayae glanced behind, she found the woman's face set in a determined grimace, one hand locked on her staff and the man she called her brother unceremoniously dragged behind her.

Soon, the sound of the river became deafening, bringing with it the smell of water, and the speed by which the four moved increased with their desperation to reach it.

Yet, when they did, Ayae's heart sank.

Jae'le's bugs gathered around the dirty break in the ground that opened above the water, but what they revealed was not a way to freedom, but a rushing, mud-filled torrent. It was so fast and so awful that Ayae felt despair gather in her stomach. The normal river had been a dangerous enough prospect, but there was no way to ride safely what she was looking at. No way any of them could expect to drop into that and be taken to safely.

'You will have to navigate it for us,' Jae'le whispered, as if he could read her mind. 'You will have to keep us together.'

She shook her head.

'You can. You must.' He offered her a smile she could barely see. 'We have no choice.'

Tinh Tu pulled Eidan up to the hole. The latter looked to be unconscious, yet his hand was still firmly wrapped around the staff, and the dirt on his face was streaked with sweat, his beard matted with both. Silently, Tinh Tu angled him to the hole, getting him, Ayae thought, ready – but ready for what? For her to tell them that yes, she could get them through that? She made fire. She could turn her skin to stone. She had never done anything with water, probably couldn't do anything. Even if she could, she could certainly do nothing with what lay below them. But Tinh Tu was not waiting: she glanced at Ayae and revealed dirty, hard, determined eyes, and then she pushed Eidan through the break. He hit the rushing stream awkwardly, but without so much as a heartbeat between them, Tinh Tu leapt after him. Jae'le followed and Ayae, with no thought whatsoever for her concerns, for all her doubts, threw herself after them.

She hit the rushing violent river of mud a moment before the stone she had been on broke after her. Around her, everything went black. She felt a force, a massive, smothering force, and she panicked. She tried to kick and twist and claw to reach a surface, but there was no surface, there was no place she could rise to, no place she could take a breath. Involuntarily, she tried to do so in the river, but couldn't, couldn't because the force of it was trying to break her spine, to snap her, and she had no strength to draw in air. Mud pushed into her mouth, into her eyes. She felt herself being flattened. Her fingers curled in on her palms and she felt a hardness in them, a stiffness that was not all the force of the river.

Ayae hit a stone, or a stone hit Ayae. She could not tell, but the impact jolted her, turned her over, sent her into a tumble. A wordless scream burst out of her mouth and she grabbed frantically at the muddy water, trying to right herself, trying trying trying for breath trying for grip trying trying feeling her lungs burn trying trying until she *could*. Until the currents around her felt real, felt as if it had lines she could hold onto it. She could see it, even without seeing, her eyes caked with mud, flooded with the debris she was in, her lungs burning burning. But the currents ran. They ran like lines and she could see ahead of them, and she could see the stones and the heavy debris that ran through them. She could turn, push herself out of the way. Her awareness grew with each second. She saw Jae'le, trying his best to ride the wash, who relaxed into the nudge that directed him into the current she was riding down the river, the current that took her past him, to Tinh Tu and her tangle of robes and the determined grip she had on her staff, the staff that led to the barely conscious form of Eidan. The torrent twisted and rolled and she grabbed the pair of them and pulled them into the stream she rode, even as her chest burned, empty, hollow, burning wanting wanting wanting but not able to receive and her consciousness began to slip in and out and she began to turn began to lose herself but no *no* she had to hold to the line had to had to but she hurt she hurt she—

She took a shuddering, desperate breath as she and the others were spat out of the Mountain of Ger.

Water, dirt, mud, air, all of it felt real to Ayae, real enough to grab, but none of it was what she wanted to hold. Her dirt-caked eyes opened to see the empty afternoon sky and the black line of the horizon rising as the lake beneath her came into focus, as the hard water waited for the four of them to smash across it unless she could grab the sky, could find the pockets and draughts she had been able to find when she fell out of the Keep fighting Fo and Bau. If she could but just find them, hook into them, she could guide not just her, but Jae'le, Tinh Tu and Eidan to the ground, to a place of safety away from the horror of a mountain that was crumbling into itself.

The shallow edge of the Black Lake was not the most comfortable of grounds, but it did, in the end, provide a place to land.

2.

Queila Meina shouted an order and Steel pushed through the gate, elbowed past Zaifyr, and began to form a solid line.

Beyond the gate, the spirits of *Wayfair* assembled on the street beside the ancient soldiers from the Plateau. In Zaifyr's hands, the remains of the staff broke away into nothing, the last of Lor Jix's crew leaving it in a twisted shape, as if the spirit was ripped out and forced into shape on the streets of Heüạla.

The streets that the dead stood upon had a strange flatness to them, one that was replicated in the buildings that lined either side. It was not that Heüala was dead, not exactly, but rather that it had become inert, that within its streets and buildings – the streets that spread out, lapping back and forth beneath towers and hotels – within those streets, a lifelessness emerged to grip the entire town. There was no sense of formal decay on any of the buildings, no pieces of rotting wood, or shattered stones, or fungus and dirt, and the sad emptiness that had defined much of the soggy, burned landscape *Glafanr* had drifted past was absent. But there was something wrong about Heüala. Zaifyr was sure of it. A quality he could not describe, a sense that was unique to the city, had been removed.

From the tallest part of the city, Se'Saera's dark form shifted, brought to full awareness by the flow of dead into its streets. With a strange delicateness, she unwrapped herself from the tower. Two large wings unfolded from her back, the blackness of them smooth and fine, the wingspan enough to sweep over all of Heüala. Her head rose and Zaifyr saw the face he had seen over Yeflam, but with more definition, more certainty to it now. Se'Saera's jaws were like a crocodile's, and the same sense of ancient violence that ran through those beasts ran along the god's face, up to her eyes. But there was a surprise in those eyes: he had not seen, not in Yeflam, not even as he approached, the second long-toothed face, or the third, both of which rose as she uncurled from the tower. The three heads differed from each other in dark textures, but were otherwise identical. As she rose, Zaifyr saw more heads curled around her body, a nest of heads, but these, unlike the three that rose high to gaze at him, were smoking and unformed.

'How many?' he whispered. 'How many heads do you have?'

As many as my parents were in number. The voice sounded in his head, but it did not come from Se'Saera's form on the tower. Instead, it emanated from the body of a child who appeared on the street. She appeared to be no older than nine or ten, though Zaifyr knew that she was no such thing, and from her back rose dark wings, similar to the ones that were spread over Heüala. *You have been led astray, Zaifyr. You have been brought here under a false pretence.*

She did not call him Qian, nor did he feel the sensation of tearing teeth against his skin, as he had when he stood near Se'Saera when he had been alive. 'Did you not tell me once that they loved you?'

It was what I thought before I was named, she replied. *I see their fear of me now. I see what they have done to keep themselves whole. I see what they do to stop me.*

'As well they should. Look what you have done with the dead.'

They are mine.

'They belong to no one.'

The child tilted her head. The movement looked as if it belonged to a puppet. *It is true, I kept the dead in the world for myself, but I am divine, and it is my right,* she said. *The dead are not. They are a creation, nothing more, and I treat them no differently from the way my parents before me treated them. The spirit of Lor Jix is an example of this. My mother did not hesitate to chain him to the bottom of the ocean so that he could give you a message. You, indeed, are no different. The captain before you, the soldiers that stand in protection of you. They are all here because of your divine power.*

'You speak of rights, but what of me?' Anguish had climbed onto Meina's shoulder. 'Do you have the right to make a creation of pain, Se'Saera?'

You are not my true creation. You are my parents. And you are mine.

'You did not answer my question!'

I have that right. The child turned her attention back to Zaifyr. *I will recreate this world, once I am complete. Once all of myself is returned to me, I will begin to remake all.*

'And what will happen to Anguish?' he said.

He will be destroyed. He will thank me for that.

'Then will you destroy all of your parents' creations?'

I will make them better. I will make them stronger. I will make their souls pure by rebuilding them into a new entity.

'Abomination,' Lor Jix whispered harshly. 'You are truly an abomination.'

I am a god. Se'Saera did not focus on the Captain of *Wayfair*. *I am absolute. I understand why you do not like what you hear, but that is because you are not my creation. In part, you reject me because my parents reject me, and what you want, you want because they want it. You want to return to the world my parents made. But I wonder – have you ever considered what that is? Lor Jix is the only one of you who knows the world of my parents. The rest of you know only fragments.*

'I want something different,' Zaifyr said. 'I do not want to return the old gods, or bring in a new god. I want for us to make our choices.'

And what would they be? She laughed. *How would a mortal man like to see death? Would he like paradise, and would that paradise be defined by a castle, by a lake? Would a mortal woman want the same castle and the same lake? What if she wanted to be punished for sins she believed she'd committed? What would her punishment look like? It is better that there are no choices given to mortals. It is better that what my parents created ends and something new is made in its place.*

'They do not want that. I do not want that.' Yet, even as Zaifyr spoke, he felt a despair emerge inside him, a realization that part of what Se'Saera said was correct. They were the creations of another. They were chained to rules and functions that had been made by gods. 'You would offer them only oblivion,' he said. He took a step forwards. 'You would—'

I would free you. The child regarded him without emotion, but he thought he heard sympathy in her voice. *You are a toy of my parents. They have woven you through the strands of fate that they broke apart for this moment. They have driven you here over thousands of years, and not just you, but others. Lor Jix. Your brothers and sisters. You have taken the place of their very own servants. In his rage, Aela Ren broke his kind free from the plans of the gods. They were to do what you do now, but they will not.* A hardness entered her voice. *Nor will you. You lack the ability to change the world. You and your kind are but touches of divinity: you are just bits and pieces of the gods. It is all that they have allowed you to have. They do not want you to change their creation. They want you to preserve it for them.*

His power lashed out suddenly. One of the dead from the Plateau, the soldier Kilian – the name flashed through his mind, a collection of horrific images following it – did not have enough time to stop Zaifyr from taking his spirit. With an iron will, he forced the ancient dead to draw his white-lit blade and thrust it into Se'Saera's back. It happened in less than a second, but even as the blade pierced her and her child's body broke apart, Zaifyr screamed. It was a scream born out of thousands of years of frustration, of trying to find peace for the dead, to free them from the horror that they were trapped in, only to be told here that he did not have the power to do that, and that he never would.

High above him, the three complete heads of Se'Saera answered his scream, the roar of all three together was deafening.

She leapt from the roof.

3.

Bueralan took Jaerc into the swampland to the west to avoid the battle. He wanted to find Essa, find him quickly, but he did not want to do so with another god-touched soldier beside him, and so he skirted a wider path than necessary. He used the swamp crows to guide him. The black birds were crying out, flying out of the trees where they perched to scurry frantically through the canopies, and the saboteur took it as a sign that one of Ren's soldiers was close. It would not be a soldier from the Saan, Mireea or Yeflam. No bird, no swamp crow, especially, would react like that to a mortal man—

The terrifying sound of earth breaking apart stopped his thought. It came suddenly, as if a part of the world had broken away from another.

Bueralan and Jaerc stopped, the latter taking hold of a long, slender tree branch next to him. Beneath their feet, the ground trembled, while around him, the sound of stone crashing into stone continued. The trees began to shake. Bueralan took hold of a branch. The young soldier said something, but Bueralan could not hear his voice. He raised his gaze to the thick canopy: there were no crows in it and it shook and shook as the sound of the breaking earth drew closer, as if the ground itself was about to open beneath his feet.

Animals emerged in a panicked rush, tearing through trees, along the soggy edges of the swamp, through the water. A pack bore down on the two men with a fear that overcame any natural aversion to humans and Bueralan heaved himself onto the branch he held. As he did, another tremor shook the ground and Jaerc stumbled, but the saboteur grabbed the young soldier and lifted him, just as darkness fell over them.

It was a darkness made from earth and stone, thick enough to choke away the air, to cut into the skin.

Bueralan squeezed his eyes shut and, on instinct, turned to shield the young Mireean soldier.

The force of the dirt storm rushed onwards, past them. Behind it, the air was left thick with dust, enough to make it difficult to breathe. The sound of stone crumbling, of the earth shaking, continued, and Bueralan released Jaerc. 'You all right?' he asked, after he dropped to the ground.

'Yeah.' Jaerc's white skin and blond hair was gone, lost beneath the mud and dust. He had his hand over his mouth. 'I – thanks.'

The saboteur spat out dirt. 'What happened?'

'There have been earthquakes in the mountains since Mireea fell.' He paused as the rumble of earth breaking apart consumed the air. 'I guess that was the big one. I thought – well, we were told that they had stopped.'

Bueralan thought of the Temple of Ger. He saw the splitting, breaking skin of the giant god Ger after he had killed Se'Saera's priests. Surely, the same must have happened to the rest of his body, throughout the mountain range. 'Come on,' he said, more roughly than he intended. 'We have to find Essa.'

'The Saan.' The young soldier coughed as he sucked in a mouthful of debris. 'The Saan,' he began again, 'called him a coward. They said he had no stomach for battle.'

'Kal Essa?' The clouds of dust revealed a new, awful world of splintered trees, torn bushes and dead crows before him. 'Who said that?'

'The Saan – the Lord of the Saan.'

Miat Dvir. 'He should have known better.'

There was little for Bueralan to take comfort in, but he could not hear any sound of battle. He could hear swamp crows and he could hear voices of men and women calling out. He resisted the urge to respond to any, made sure that Jaerc did not either. Ren and his soldiers would be as confused and shocked as anyone by what had happened, but they would reach an understanding of it quickly. He needed to find Essa before they made a choice about what to do, if they would keep killing or allow the others to fall back. Bueralan could already imagine them picking up their weapons, could see them stalking through the dust and the debris, towards the cries for help. He had to reach Essa before that began, before the Captain of the Brotherhood responded to the cries for help and began meeting the god-touched.

Kal Essa was in the middle of a makeshift camp. He wore his old, dusty plate and chain, and held his ugly spiked mace in his hand as he barked out commands, turning every so often to turn and spit dirt onto the ground. It was in one such motion that he noticed Bueralan approach him, and offered him a sour smile. 'The other trapped rat emerges,' he said. 'I didn't think Orlan would be alone.'

'You have to leave,' Bueralan said. 'You need—'

'I have injured out there, Captain.'

'I know, I've heard them. Pick up those you can on the way out, but leave the others. They're dead soldiers.'

In the distance, stone crashed. 'I don't leave no soldiers behind,' Essa said. 'Not on the word of a man who has been riding with the enemy.'

Bueralan did not have time to argue. In his mind's eye, he could see the Innocent, the scars on his face highlighted by grime, stalking through the swamp, following the sounds of life. He shifted suddenly, grabbed his sword . . . and then released it just before Essa's spiked mace slammed into his side. The spikes hurt, but it was more the force of Essa's strike, rather than the actual weapon itself. As it had with Jaerc's sword, Bueralan's flesh seemed to be ready for the blow, as if it had expected it, but what bothered him more was how his ribs seemed to shift, seemed to brace for the blow, and not crack beneath it. The force of the blow ensured that the saboteur took a step to his left, but he straightened more quickly than a normal man would. From the dust around him, a small crowd emerged. Before them, and before Essa, Bueralan lifted his shirt, bloody from the wound, and revealed the already healing flesh.

'You can't win here,' he said. 'You'll be hunted if you stay here. You'll be killed. You have to leave.' He released his shirt. 'You have to find Aned Heast.'

4.

The force with which Se'Saera landed caused the ground to shudder.

Through the eyes of another, through the eyes of the long-dead Kilian, Zaifyr gazed at the huge form of the god. She appeared to have no centre but the unmade forms of her other heads, the heads of Se'Saera that would take form once she had gathered to her the remaining power of the gods. The three heads that had risen and gazed not just at him, but at Jix, Meina, Anguish and the soldiers of Steel, came from that unformed mass, leaving Zaifyr with the question of what would happen once she had gathered all the gods' power. Would she break apart – was she no more than the first form the gods took when they made the world? He did not know. He could not know. He would never know: he was, for all his power, the spirit of a dead man.

Gripping Kilian's sword tightly, the sword that was an extension of himself, Zaifyr charged Se'Saera.

Her first head snapped down.

It happened quicker than he thought possible, quicker than he certainly realized, and her hard teeth tore into Kilian's spirit.

Zaifyr left the bite.

He appeared behind Se'Saera, in the spirit of another of her ancient soldiers, Nsyan. He had been a hunter, a killer, and while the images of his life flipped past Zaifyr's consciousness, he drew the dead man's sword and thrust it forwards.

It pierced the god's unmade centre, but if the weapon hurt her, Zaifyr could not tell. Her third head roared and speared down towards him, but before it crashed through him, Zaifyr jumped into the spirit of a woman from Lor Jix's crew, Uyr. He saw her on a giant boat, on the green blue ocean, even as he took a step back, even as he drew her sword.

On the other side of Se'Saera, Meina gave the order for Steel to attack.

Zaifyr wanted to shout out to her, to tell her to call her soldiers back, to order them not to attack, but before he could, a blade pierced through Uyr's back. Instinctively, he shifted into the spirit of the attacker, and in doing so, he moved back into Kilian. New images assaulted him – Kilian over a fire, lifting an iron poker, a man tied to a rack – but a deep, profound sense of despair overcame that.

The dead could not die.

Attack a spirit, break it apart, crush it, spear it, stab it – it did not matter. It was already within the City of the Dead. A spirit could not be destroyed. It could be stripped of its identity, could be rendered without self, but it could not be destroyed. If it could be done, it could only be done by a god. With a sense of desperation, Zaifyr turned towards Steel, just as Se'Saera lashed out with her heads, and two of Meina's soldiers disappeared in a burst of colour.

When the god's heads rose, however, the white outline of the spirits remained. They did not pause before they attacked their comrades.

'You cannot stay here.' Queila Meina's voice brought him back to himself, to his own body. He stood in the gateway of Heüala. 'You have to stop her.'

Zaifyr did not know how he would do that. Before him, Steel

was scattered, Se'Saera's huge form and three heads were breaking them apart, pushing them towards her own soldiers. That they were not already broken was a testimony to their skill, but it was only a matter of time.

'The tower,' Lor Jix said beside him. 'She was curled around that, as if she was protecting it. Surely within it we will find a way to defeat her.'

Surely? 'We can't be sure about that,' he said.

'There are few certainties in death, Zaifyr.' Meina lifted Anguish from her shoulder. 'You,' she said to the black-skinned creature, 'you stay with them.'

'But—'

'You can't help here.' She turned back to Zaifyr. 'The three of you make for that tower. We will give you all the time we can to get there.'

'Meina,' he began.

'Perhaps she is right,' the Captain of Steel said, drawing her sword. 'Maybe we were sent here to ensure that everything was kept the same. Maybe, but I only ever gave allegiance to those who could die like me.'

She ignored Anguish's protest. Instead, she shouted an order to her soldiers – 'Fall into lines!' – an order that grabbed the attention of the broken pieces of Steel and pulled them together. The soldiers began to retreat, to push away Se'Saera's soldiers, to step back from the god herself. In response, Se'Saera's massive foot rose and she brought it thundering down, the clawed toes like half a dozen sabres. Zaifyr expected the men and women falling back to be crushed, for the colour to be stripped out of them, but as the foot thundered downwards, heavy shields rose, and the blow was halted. Se'Saera roared, and her left head came spearing down, but she caught nothing as the soldiers broke away.

'She cannot defeat her,' Anguish whispered harshly. 'Qian – Zaifyr, do something!'

He ran to the left, down the inside of Heüala's wall, Lor Jix behind him. On his shoulder, Anguish howled, but the charm-laced man did not stop. Behind him, he heard Meina shout again, but he did not turn around. A roar split the air, not just one, but three, and for reasons he could not identify, Zaifyr knew that Se'Saera's roar came because she had noticed that he and Jix had left the battle, had sneaked down the side of the town, up a street, and begun running towards the tower.

On either side of the street, simple buildings sat. They were the kind Zaifyr had seen in a number of towns throughout his life, built from wood and brick. They had the same lifeless quality as the buildings around the gate, but it was not until towers began to appear between them that he realized that there were no shadows.

To his right, he heard a great rush of wind as Se'Saera lifted into the air.

He turned suddenly and, in doing so, almost lost Anguish. The small figure gripped on to his shirt, while behind him, Zaifyr heard Jix call out, demanding to know what he was doing. 'Godling!' the Captain of *Wayfair* cried out before Zaifyr shouldered one of the doors open. He paused in the doorway, turned and grabbed the ancient dead. As he did, the huge, dark form of Se'Saera rose high above Heüala.

'Run for the back, run for the next street,' he hissed to Jix, thrusting him into the house and following him. 'We can cut across the lanes.'

He fell silent.

Around him, as if it were a giant, grassy lake, was an empty field, while above him a single, solitary sun shone.

5.

Refuge left Celp in a line defined by smoke and exhaustion. It took a day to leave the burned land and return to where they had left the carts.

After they made camp – picket lines for the horses, saddles removed, soot rubbed from their coats, food and water for each and for the soldiers, tents for the wounded – Heast set a small guard and let the rest of Refuge find patches of ground to sleep on. The soldiers from Maosa did so with rolls and blankets that they borrowed. They had left Celp with nothing. They slept in the smoke-stained clothes they wore beneath their armour and slept with their swords close. He didn't blame them: a hundred and forty-three of Refuge's soldiers had died in the burning ruins of Celp. Another half-dozen would die from their wounds, another dozen would not fight again. The numbers hurt Heast, but he did not deny it. He could not. He had lost just under half of his force in Celp: one hundred and fifty-three of the soldiers who had left Maosa walked out of the city. They did so beside soldiers who had been the First Queen's Guard, who had been trained to hold a sword by some of the finest instructors, and who wore armour none of Refuge would have been able to afford, but they walked out as equals. Lehana ensured that. She demonstrated no favouritism, and any familiarity she showed with the soldiers she had known for years, she made sure to share with the soldiers from Maosa. When she told Heast of her own losses, she said that 'three soldiers' died in the battle and named them. She made no mention of the First Queen, of ethnicity, of anything that would begin to build a divide between the two groups.

'Captain.' Kye Taaira's clothes were stained so heavily with soot that the hilt of his old sword appeared coloured by it as well, though Heast knew it was not. 'The prisoner is awake,' the other man said. 'He asked to speak to you.'

'Has Anemone seen him?'

'Briefly,' Taaira replied. 'She doesn't believe he will last until morning. I am surprised he survived the ride here.'

'Gje Dural was born stubborn.'

The Leeran soldier had been found at the edge of Celp. He had been crawling with his hands over the blackened stones, trying to make his way into the burned landscape that lay in front of him in an awful premonition. An arrow had pierced his right leg and shattered the bone, but it was the fire that had done most of the damage to him. Around the blackened arrow, his clothes had melted into his skin, up to his waist, as if he had been dipped into burning liquid, and then removed.

He had not recognized the Captain of Refuge. Dural had been crawling mostly on instinct, and when one of the soldiers from Refuge bent down to lift him on Heast's command, he thought her one of his own. He whispered thanks, whispered that their god hated them.

Dural lay beneath the dark night sky, no tent roof above him, and no blanket beneath him. The arrow in his leg was broken against the wound and he had been cleaned, revealing the burns that ran up his chest and neck, breaking apart a tattoo of a whole sun before reaching his face. He had been a nondescript man before, a man whose face slid easily out of memory, who worked in the background of camps and kept order, a captain's best asset.

But no more.

'Has he said much?' Heast asked Lehana as he approached.

'No.' She sat on a fallen log behind the burned man, her bastard sword laid against it. On her lap she held one of her shirts, a needle and a half-sewn insignia of Refuge. 'He asked for water, and whose command I was under, nothing more.'

'She told me Aned Heast.' Dural's voice was rough, filled with pain. 'I half expected it to be Bueralan Le.'

'I haven't seen him for a long time. He could very well be dead.'

'I doubt it. Rats like him don't die.'

Heast came over to the man, looked down at him, and met his brown eyes. 'I have seen a lot of things in my time, Lieutenant.'

'Nothing like this.' He grimaced. 'Is the General dead?'

'Yes.'

'She said he'd die.'

'Your god?'

'Se'Saera.' His right hand spasmed, almost forming a fist. 'What kind of god tortures a man with the knowledge he'll die for years? Who tells him he'll be glorious, until he – he fails. Until she orders his soldiers to douse themselves in oil to feed her flames.'

'Why would your god give you that order?' Across from him, Taaira asked the question, not with his customary tone of respect, but with a barely concealed anger Heast had not heard before.

'I don't know. I don't know.' He coughed again, the force running through his pain-racked body. 'I don't know,' he repeated. 'She pulled most of us back to Ranan. Gave the order to retreat a week or so after she pulled back those monsters she made. But the General – she told him to ride to Celp. She told him he would die there. But if she knew that, why send him?' His rough voice broke.

'You tell me, Captain, why you'd send a man you knew was going to die to the battle he'd die in.'

Heast could not understand it. 'A god is not like us,' he said. 'Surely that has become evident to you?'

'She – yeah, yeah. It . . . the things we did. The things she asked us to do.' He fell silent and closed his eyes. His chest still moved, however. 'He was a teacher,' Dural said, finally. 'The General. Waalstan. He was a teacher in Ranan. He taught children language. How to write. He had never been a soldier. I don't know if he was a good teacher. I never had kids, but he – she made him different. When she began to speak to us. All of us. When the first priests began to come out. When they started to speak against the old king. She awoke something in him. I thought it was a gift, at first, but now I think maybe she awoke a madness in him. He would do what she said, but he would forget things. He would wake in the morning and you would think he might be horrified by what he had done. But he never – he never questioned her. He was always loyal. Even when she told him to order everyone to douse themselves in oil. To set themselves alight. A lot of us didn't want to do that. We – I mean, it wasn't disloyalty. It was fear. It was – who sets themselves alight, Captain?'

'You didn't,' Heast said gently. 'Why didn't you?'

'My faith was not . . . not that strong.' Dural closed his eyes. 'Waalstan told us to be strong, but not even he could convince all of us. We would fight for him, but – but to set yourself on fire? Some of them died – the screams.' His hand spasmed again. 'I thought she loved us, Captain. Until then, I thought our god preferred us over everyone. I felt her love inside me. It was guiding, but – but when she told us to set ourselves on fire, how can that be love? You burn a man if you hate him. That's what you do. You burn a man because you hate him.' His breath expelled so loudly that Heast half expected it to be filled with smoke. 'What kind of god does that?'

'One we don't need.'

'Yeah.'

'You get some rest, Dural,' Heast said. 'You think of anything else, you tell it to me, or to anyone else. Don't hold it in.'

'She keeps the dead,' he muttered. 'She'll find me. She'll . . .'

He didn't finish his sentence. Instead, the soldier stared up into the night sky, into the stars and moon and darkness, where whatever thought he had extended itself beyond the ears of those who stood around him, carried by lips that moved silently.

6.

The water from the Black Lake stung, but Ayae used a handful of it to wash her face, regardless. It was better than feeling as if she was wearing a mask of mud.

She hurt, but not as much as she should, really. Her hands were cut, her shirt torn and soggy where her armour didn't run, and there was scarring over the leather where it did, but the worst was her back. It felt as if one long single bruise ran along her spine but, considering what she had just been through, Ayae was thankful that it was no more than that. She was not alone in how she had fared: with the exception of Jae'le, the others moved just as stiffly as she did. Jae'le, however, was completely unharmed, and Ayae's first memory after she landed was of him, lifting her out of the shallow water she lay in. He carried her as if she were a child. She remembered seeing Tinh Tu on the shore, first. The old woman stripped off her muddy robe and stood naked in the fading afternoon's light, her body a patchwork of wrinkles and cuts and muscle. Eidan sat not far from her on a broken stump, his clothes a mix of dirt and cuts, and his face a map of scars, mud and matted hair.

It had been he who asked how she was.

'Exhausted,' Jae'le had said. He had knelt and laid her down on a dry patch of ground. 'She has fewer injuries than either of you.'

'We are only alive because of her,' Tinh Tu said.

'Or because of the gods,' Eidan murmured. 'Remember the painting in the cave.'

'It does not diminish what Ayae did.' Jae'le rose, a dark shape above her. 'But yes, what we saw did suggest we would survive,' he said. 'But we are not without our own power to shape what happens next.'

'Are we to be gods again, then?' Tinh Tu asked.

'No, I speak instead of the relationship between the gods and the mortals. It is one in which one creates and one decides.' Jae'le moved and revealed to Ayae the seething mass of the Mountains of Ger, the earth and debris of their collapse rising high into the night air, unformed but signalling destruction. 'It is entirely possible that the gods meant for us to die. I can imagine dozens of fates where we are crushed beneath the mountain. And just as many where one, or more of us, do not escape. But those fates are no more. We have survived that. Our actions have made those fates non-existent.'

'Unless there is only one fate,' Eidan said. 'If that is so, it's a fate none of us will survive.'

Ayae had faded into an exhausted sleep and the sound of their voices, of their discussion, was one that worked its way into her dreams.

When she had awoken, she walked down to the lake. The midday's sun was high in the sky, but it struggled to reveal the entirety of the mountainous ruins across the lake from her. Close to her, Ayae could see broken slabs of stone scattered along the shore and in the water of the Black Lake. Pieces of the Spine of Ger lay in the middle, the smooth stone of the bridge looking like the bones of a mountain, broken and splintered. Beyond the lake, the dust hung heavily, and Ayae could not be sure just how bad the damage was, how much the mountain peaks had collapsed into themselves.

But she knew Mireea was gone.

She could not imagine any series of events where the damaged city had survived. She could envision the holes throughout the city widening, the broken cobbled road coming apart as the mountain sought to devour everything it had not already destroyed, from the half-submerged hotels to the broken barracks and unharmed houses. Her house. She could see it lying in a crevasse, broken like an egg, its contents spilled across the ground around it.

'I owe you a debt. The three of us do.' Eidan had come up behind her silently. 'We would not have been able to escape without you.'

'I didn't hold the mountain, light our way, or ensure that you were not left behind.'

'Still. I thank you.' He nodded to the mountain. 'It can be repaired. Your home, that is.'

Could it? 'Maybe it should be left,' she said. 'Maybe a new history should be allowed to take hold in its place.'

'You cannot make a new world at the expense of another. I know that well.' He turned to the small camp that they had made. 'We have visitors.'

'What kind?'

'Come and see.'

She did not expect to find Miat Dvir and the Saan but, at the sight of them, a heavy sadness rose within her. She could tell they had seen battle, for many of the soldiers were bandaged around their arms, chests and heads. The Lord of the Saan was no different: his right arm was strapped to his chest, clearly broken. Yet, as Ayae drew closer, she saw that not all of the soldiers were from the Saan. Yeflam and Mireean soldiers lingered on the edges of the group, but there was no sense of order in them, of being part of a force. She knew, just by the sight of them, that Xrie was dead.

'He was killed by the Innocent.' It was Vyla Dvir who spoke. She did so in a heavy voice, her eyes haunted. 'My husband saw him fall. He claims that he had never seen a swordsman so quick and so deadly as Aela Ren. The Blade Prince did not even have time to draw his sword.' Beside her, Miat Dvir nodded stiffly and, closer now, Ayae saw the heavy, dark bruising around his jaw. 'But it was not just the Innocent who killed. His soldiers did as well and they are also terrifying figures. We had a larger force, a well-armed force, and yet to them, our soldiers were nothing. They allowed swords to pierce their bodies, would break blades in their hands, before they crushed the bones of their enemies.'

'You should not have fought them,' Tinh Tu said, sitting before Vyla. Jae'le stood behind his sister, unsurprised by anything said. 'The Innocent's soldiers are like him. They cannot die.'

'The cartographer, Samuel Orlan, told us the same,' she said, startling Ayae. 'He was sent to issue a duel, but he urged us to turn around, to ride away. The mercenary captain agreed with him, but my husband and the other captains thought it was cowardice. He accused the mercenary of wanting more gold to be a soldier.'

'Did Samuel die?' Ayae asked.

She shook her head. 'He returned to the Innocent's soldiers. He said that he was a prisoner, but he would not elaborate as to why he was given the task of delivering this message.'

'How much of your force did you lose?' Tinh Tu asked.

'Nearly half,' Vyla said, turning back to her.

'We cannot win.' Miat Dvir's voice was a painful mumble, yet he persisted. 'Not how we are. Not now.'

'You could never win.'

'We appeal to you.' He looked not at Tinh Tu, but Jae'le. 'You were once a great general. We of the Saan know this.'

'I no longer lead armies,' he said.

A loud squawk startled those nearest and, from high up in the sky, a large white raven began to descend. 'I lead our armies,' Tinh Tu said. The bird settled on a grey branch above her. 'If you wish to petition any of us, you must do so to me.'

'You are no general,' Miat said in his painful mumble. 'You are an old woman. You cannot strike fear into an enemy. You cannot lead us to our victory, to our honour.'

'Kneel.'

The Lord of the Saan appeared, briefly, as if he were confused, for Tinh Tu's voice had been soft, but the command was undeniable. The word *kneel* echoed in the minds of everyone who was in hearing distance, the word containing not a simple command, but a power, an urge, a need that had to be responded to. Unable to resist, Miat Dvir stumbled awkwardly from where he sat, and lowered himself to his knee. He began to speak, but Tinh Tu, with a shake of her head, said, 'No.'

Her second command resulted in a look of horror on Dvir. He could not speak and as he realized that, the warriors close to him rose. They drew their swords, but Tinh Tu, who saw them advance, was unconcerned. In her quiet voice, she said, 'You will kneel.' As each of them did, she looked beyond them, out to the Saan, the Mireean and the Yeflam soldiers. 'You will all kneel,' she said, her voice an awful force that the soldiers were unable to deny.

7.

The dust followed Bueralan and the god-touched to Ranan.

It had not been easy to convince Essa to search for Heast. The sight of his wound, mending cleanly despite the dirt that clung to everything, helped what he said, but Essa was a career soldier. He gathered his fallen. He retreated in organized parts. He said to Bueralan, 'You couldn't convince Heast to abandon that, either.'

'Choices matter.' He waved into the dust, towards the Mountains of Ger. 'They just aren't your choices. Trust me. Our new god makes her world, and the old gods make theirs. You die here, you aren't there for the final battle.' His breath caught, but not with earth or debris. 'You won't be in Ranan with Heast.'

'Choices don't matter, except the choice I make right here?' Essa spat onto the ground. 'You cursed?'

'Not in any way you mean.'

In the end, Bueralan was not sure what convinced the Captain of the Brotherhood to give the order to mount up. It had not been his mention of Refuge. Essa had not blinked at that. He did grunt when Bueralan mentioned Onaedo, but he was not convinced it was that, either. It was not until he had gone, until Bueralan had walked back into the dust towards the road and began to find bodies, that he understood. He bent down to the dirt-choked wounds, to the slit throats, the emptied stomachs and the opened eyes. There was no one alive. The Innocent and his soldiers had left only the dead.

Between the waddling dust-stained swamp crows, there were tracks of soldiers who had fled to the south, away from Essa's escape, but Bueralan did not pursue them. He continued through the dead and followed the road back to the camp of the night before. The swamp crows skittered and flapped out of his way but did not rise into the air, as they had done earlier.

After a while, he turned and gazed at the broken shape of the Mountains of Ger. Dust left it hazy, but even through that unclear filter, he could see that the familiar line of peaks was gone, collapsed into a mountain range that resembled a broken spine. Bueralan had heard it said, a long time ago, that the Spine of Ger, the great stone wall that ran through the mountains, had followed the actual spine of the dead god. He had always considered it a detail of poetics, a detail not at all true, but which, when said, added an undefined quality to the mountain range. But now, gazing at it through the dirt, recognizing how the lost ridges appeared to follow the stone wall, he believed it. The spine of Ger had finally broken, the bone rotting until it could no longer support the god's body and his cairn.

Aela Ren and his soldiers were at the camp, grimy and bloody but unharmed. Orlan sat on a log in front of the two greys and Bueralan began to walk towards him. He was stopped, however, by the sight of the hulking pierced creature that Se'Saera had sent from Gtara. It, like the rest of them, was covered in dirt, but the black-eyed boy the god had sent with it was relatively clean. Startled by that, it took Bueralan a moment to realize that, on the ground before the two was the body of a red-haired, charm-laced man.

Zaifyr.

'He is not dead,' Aela Ren said, approaching him. 'He does, however, sail on the River of the Dead. Or thereabouts.'

'How did they find him?'

'They were given him, in the mountains. The child has said that an old man gave him to them. The old man said he knew me but refused to give his name.'

'It is entirely possible that he doesn't know his name.' Orlan had left the two horses. 'We met him in Dirtwater,' he said to Bueralan.

The same old man who had waited for him when he stumbled out of the Mountains of Ger, who had waited with mounts, boots and a sword.

'He always claimed that Taane had given him a set of tasks,' the Innocent said. 'From the end of the war, he said that. But he was mad, and I could never tell if it was true or not.'

'He hates Se'Saera.' The cartographer's use of the god's name did not go unnoticed by either of the men near him. 'Why would he do this?'

'He was never a complete man. In many ways, being Taane's servant left him a collection of parts. In one breath, he would be terribly lucid, and in another, he would want only to harm himself. It is not impossible to imagine that he reaches out to us, even as he pushes us away.' Ren turned away from the lifeless, but healthy body of Zaifyr. 'You will take him back to Ranan,' he said. 'Take him to Se'Saera.'

As if the dust and dirt had settled into his mind, slowing him, Bueralan did not immediately realize that he was being given an order. 'Where will you be?'

'I am to retrieve General Waalstan's body,' Ren said. 'Se'Saera has given me the location of his final battle. It was in a town called Celp, to the north-east.' A strange note entered his voice. 'He was killed by a group of mercenaries who go by the name of Refuge.'

A chill ran through Bueralan. He thought of Essa, of the Brotherhood, riding out of the dust and into Faaisha, shadowing Aela Ren's path.

'I see both of you have heard of it before,' the Innocent said. 'It was a name that we knew in Sooia, as well.'

'There has not been a Refuge for a long time,' Samuel Orlan said, carefully. 'I doubt that it is led by anyone who can claim the name honestly.'

Ren shrugged. 'We will see.'

'I can go with you,' Bueralan began, but Ren shook his head.

'No,' he said. 'You can make no argument that will convince me, either. Both of you will be needed in Ranan, especially now. Taela's time draws close.'

Bueralan caught his next words, swallowed dirt instead. He would not leave Taela, not now, not as she gave birth. He would be there, to apologize, to admit that he had been unable to discover a way out of Se'Saera's grasp, a way for her to be free. He would hold her hand. He would do what he had to do, after she had given birth.

The thought, like the dust, accompanied him to Ranan, a second skin of dirt and grit, one that he would never be able to scrub clean.

8.

Eilona sat on the deck of *The Frozen Shackle* beside Caeli and wished she had a bottle of laq with her. Just one bottle. A glass would not even be necessary.

Her return to the ship had been swift. After Faje had shown her the poor tortured 'cursed', he had led her down the flights of stairs, past the dark, snaking form of the press, and out into the street where Nymar Alahn and the Faithful waited. Not one of them said a word. They simply formed an escort around her and returned her to Nymar's carriage. From there, she was taken to the Spires of Alati. At the midpoint of the bridge, Eilona's hands began to shake, and she folded them in her lap, hiding her weakness from Nymar. He had said nothing to her since Rje, but sat across from her with a new confidence she found repelling. Before the carriage entered the estate, she decided that, when it stopped, she would demand Caeli be brought to her. But, as the gate opened and the carriage drew up to the house, the other woman was already waiting outside. Beside her stood two guards, one of whom held her sword. Wordlessly, Nymar's guards marched her to the carriage. One handed Caeli's sword to Nymar, who laid it across his lap and sat comfortably across from the two women as the carriage left the estate. No one in the carriage spoke until they were in Burata, until the long stone docks that ran out like limbs into Leviathan's Blood presented themselves. There, Nymar gave her a letter for his father, returned Caeli's sword to her and bid the pair of them farewell.

With her mother's guard beside her, Eilona walked out to where the small dinghy was tied. The two women did not speak to each other. When the dinghy touched *The Frozen Shackle*, Eilona said, 'I'm sorry. I should have have listened to you.'

'You should have.' Caeli rose and slung the sword over her shoulder. 'But I expected it.'

'You expected?' she repeated. 'Did you know what they would show me? How they had gouged the eyes out of people? What they would offer my mother? Did you know that as well?'

'No.' The guard began to climb the rope ladder. 'But you were safe, I promise.'

Eilona refused to let the topic go once she reached the deck. Beneath the darkening sky, she followed the guard. 'I don't understand,' she said. 'How could you protect me there? You were not there. I left you.'

'But not me.' Olcea stood at the wheel, her solid bag resting against it. 'Caeli is right, you were never in danger.'

The guard sat on the stairs before the witch. 'I know my job, Eilona. I know when someone is not going to listen to me.' She sounded tired. 'Like it's any surprise that you didn't, right?'

'I don't understand,' she began.

'Hien was with you.' Olcea started to unwind the cloth around her left hand. 'He has been with you since you left here.'

She made an *oh* sound, suppressed a shudder. 'I didn't – I mean, you should have told me.'

'He was meant to protect both of you.' She pulled out a knife and made a quick cut along her palm, then ran the blood across the wheel. 'But when you left Caeli, he went with you,' Olcea said, cleaning the knife and wrapping her hand. 'We decided on that earlier.'

The Frozen Shackle jolted in movement as oars fell into the water. 'I wasn't trying to be difficult,' she said, a sense of exhausted frustration creeping into her. 'I just know that neither of you want to be here. And neither of you need to be here.'

'But we're here,' Caeli said. 'Besides, in the end, that little trip you made told us a lot.'

'What do you mean?'

'There's no negotiation to be had with Nymar, or anyone who had power in Yeflam, not now. There's only the Faithful, and the Faithful, no matter how many of the hungry they feed, will not welcome your mother, not as she is. She has to submit to them first.'

They all knew what Muriel Wagan's response to that would be.

9.

Campfires dotted the shoreline of the Black Lake, but Ayae walked in the opposite direction, to the skeletal crop of trees behind it. There, in the arm of the largest, sat a man sharpening a sword.

'Silence is an awful thing to behold,' Jae'le said to her, as she approached. 'Tinh Tu's is one of the worst.'

'Why do you let her do it?'

'I do not let her do anything. My sister does what she wants because she can. She always has.'

Ayae grabbed one of the thick, empty branches opposite him. She had been unable to remain in the camp the Saan had made, the silence of it becoming more and more oppressive, until she had felt suffocated by it. It was different to the silence in the Mountains of Ger, the nothingness that had been the prelude to an event that Ayae relived when she closed her eyes. Not that she would forget the camp: it would linger in her memory, like the camp of her youth, the one behind scarred walls and heavily fortified gates. In that camp, the Innocent had stripped away the freedom and the lives of the people who lived in it, and the silence of the soldiers who had come to ask for help was much the same. Ayae had twice begun to approach Tinh Tu to tell her that, but she had stopped well before she reached the other woman. She had seen Ayae twice from the stump she sat on, overlooking the camp, and on both times, the old woman had watched her intently. She did not try to wave Ayae away, but instead seemed to invite her protest. But what would she would say to Tinh Tu? Let these people speak? Let them draw their swords on you? Don't be like Aela Ren? She wouldn't say that. Tinh Tu had done nothing like the Innocent's deeds, and Ayae knew, if the roles were reversed, Miat Dvir would exert his power over Tinh Tu and the others no differently.

'My sister was not subtle,' Jae'le said, as Ayae climbed slowly up to the elbow of the branch. 'But it was necessary, I suspect. Dvir will be under no illusions about his position in the world now.'

With only the slightest twinge from her back, she took a seat. 'Any one of you could have made that point.'

'Tinh Tu is the most powerful of us,' he said. 'It was hers to make.'

'That is why you let her do it?'

'Again that word.' He ran the stone along his blade. 'The relationship of my brothers and my sisters is defined by power, Ayae.'

'They look to you for guidance. All of them do that.'

'Sometimes,' he admitted. 'I think it is because of my age. Because I am the oldest. But it is a strange concept for the five of us. What is a hundred years or so if you have lived so long already?'

'You don't think it is as simple as that, do you?' Ayae said. 'You, of all people.'

'I have known my family for a long time.'

'I know I haven't, but when I first met you, you were trying to protect Zaifyr. At the same time, you were trying to help Aelyn. When you heard Eidan was with Se – with *her*, you tried to help him.' She turned to him, twisted so she could look up into the shadows of the tree that hid all but his shape and the blade of his new sword. 'You talk about power, but you gave up part of yours for Zaifyr. That's why they look to you now. Maybe they didn't always, but you have sacrificed and protected each of them because—'

'Of love?' Above him, a shadow shifted, revealing a swamp crow. It was unconcerned by the closeness of the two, by the sound of the whetstone along the blade. 'You sound like Zaifyr,' Jae'le finished.

'He does not talk of love. That's you putting words in his mouth. But you could learn from him.'

'The man he is now, or the man he was before? I do not think you would have liked the lessons the man before gave.'

'He is not that man any more.' Ayae shrugged. 'Truthfully, none of you are who you once were.'

'It is within us all to return to it.'

'Are you trying to convince yourself? I don't know if it has occurred to you yet, Jae'le, but we may not survive this. We probably will not. How are we to defeat the Innocent when they could not? When no one has?'

'We may die,' he said, a strange calmness in his voice. 'We may not. We are all part of much larger events and we can be certain of little, now. We are pieces the gods have moved in their ancient war. It is oddly fitting, really. It is how life with the gods was when I was a child. You would be ignored for so long that you could forget that they existed. You would begin to argue that they had no influence upon you. That you were free of them. Then, one day, they would disrupt your life. They would react to something you had done, an event that a god had planned. An act you had been destined to do. Then, everything would be in turmoil. The gods would respond. They would move their pieces. They would fight for control over fate, for the right to define the world that we lived in.'

'Perhaps we should not go to Ranan.'

'We would abandon Zaifyr, if we did not,' he said, the stone running along the blade in a second, inhuman voice. 'Would you truly do that?'

She thought of the Innocent, of the painting on Ger's leg, of her fear in it. 'If that was the cost of ending the war,' Ayae said, exploring the idea despite herself, feeling a revulsion for it even as she said it. 'What if it led to something better?'

'Who is to define what will be better for the world?'

'Zaifyr would say the price is fair.'

'But I would not pay it,' he said, 'and neither would you. Not even in your fear.'

A tremor ran through the broken mountains, the sound not of a new quake, but of rock and stone settling into a new position. On her branch, Ayae wondered just what fate had been lost, and what fate had been written.

10.

The shoreline welcomed the dinghy that carried Eilona, Caeli and Olcea with indifference. Beneath a faint moon's light, Hien's invisible grip pulled the boat onto the shore and the three women, once out of it, did the rest.

At a distance, an air of disquiet surrounded the camp: fewer fires dotted the landscape and, as they drew closer, the camp began to look ragged, as if it was the carcass of a giant beast that had begun to decay, its ruined skin flapping like torn tents and its bones exposed tents poles. If not for the shadows of people, at times no more than a piece of smoke, Eilona might have thought that the camp had been abandoned. As it was, it became clear that the tents at the top end of the camp had been pulled down. At the dirty stables, Eilona asked the man what had happened.

'There was an earthquake in the mountains,' he said. 'A huge cloud of dust enveloped us. We were lucky it wasn't mud slides.'

It was a sobering thought.

'Do you know where Muriel Wagan's tent has been moved?' Caeli asked.

He gave them directions that led further up the shoreline of the camp. None of the people they passed on the muddy streets greeted them verbally, but a few exhausted, grimy nods were given. The sight of them forced Eilona to reconsider her mother's response to the Faithful offer. If another series of quakes hit the mountain, could she really stay here, on the shore? Surely she would have to move on to Neela. With each step she took along the muddy veins of the camp, Eilona asked herself more and more questions. Did Faje know about the quake? None of them had felt it, that was for sure. Beside her, Caeli and Olcea were silent, and Eilona wondered, as they approached her mother's tent, if they thought the same.

A guard Eilona did not recognize stood outside her mother's tent. Caeli knew him, however, and he wordlessly lifted the flap for them.

Inside, the Lady of the Ghosts was lighting more candles, brightening the room. She had pushed her hair roughly back, and she wore a pair of linen pants and a heavy black shirt, neither of the pieces clothes her mother would wear in public. She wore them, Eilona knew, when she was working late, when she expected to fall asleep at her table. The table before her held a stack of papers and spoke volumes to the state of the camp.

'Take a seat,' Muriel Wagan said, setting the last candle down. 'A lot has happened.'

'We heard there was a quake,' Eilona said.

'A quake?' She laughed without humour. 'The Mountains of Ger have broken apart. We don't know what has happened up there, but' – she waved at the papers – 'we are moving everyone on to Neela. Not a single person thinks the shore is safe any more.'

'What about Mireea?' It surprised her that she asked. 'Is that gone as well?'

Her mother's second laugh was more a huff of frustration. 'I don't know. No one knows what has happened. But what about you?' she asked, changing the topic. 'You're back much earlier than I thought. Did it go about as well as that suggests?'

'We were expected,' Caeli said. 'They had quite the show for us. Well, for Eilona.'

Her mother glanced at her in query and Eilona pulled out her two letters. 'I fear you will be disappointed.'

Muriel Wagan took the two letters and set aside on the table the one that was addressed to Lian Alahn, as if she expected him soon. The other she slit open. 'It's a list of names,' she said and, before either of the others could speak, added, 'I see. Names of people who have been touched by a god's power. Who are "cursed".' She placed the letter before her and reached beneath the table. A moment later, a bottle of laq and four glasses appeared. 'Tell me,' the Lady of the Ghosts said, while she poured the clear liquid into the glasses.

Eilona did: she spoke of their arrival, of the refugees, of the Faithful, of Nymar Alahn, and of Faje. She mentioned her mistake, took blame for it and was surprised her mother did not berate her. Perhaps she had expected it as well. Occasionally, Caeli would break in, or add something, and once, Olcea spoke, but for the most part, the two other women let Eilona tell the story of what they had seen, and what they thought. When she finished, Muriel Wagan pushed a glass to her, the guard and the witch.

'If I had known you were going to give me this,' Olcea said, eyeing the glass, 'I would have asked for gold.'

Her mother picked up her glass. 'What did you teach all those girls from the orphanage in Mireea if you did not teach them how to drink properly?'

'Taste.'

'You had them drink wine, didn't you?'

'It is what civilized women do, Muriel.' Eilona almost choked to hear the witch so casually refer to her mother, while Caeli laughed. 'That I will even drink this speaks to the desperation we are in.'

The two women joined her mother and Olcea in the toast. 'We weren't shown the rest of Yeflam,' Eilona said, after she lowered the glass. 'It is entirely possible that other lords are not so well aligned with Faje and his Faithful.'

'I am sure they are not,' her mother said. She said something else, but outside the tent, a loud male voice broke over her. Before any of the women could raise themselves, the tent flap was thrust back angrily by Lian Alahn, and he pushed himself inside. A step behind him was a white-haired woman, whose arm was heavily bandaged. Oake, Eilona remembered. Captain Oake. She met the soldier's gaze but found it unresponsive.

'Why was I not told of their return?' Lian Alahn demanded, striding towards the table. Caeli, Eilona saw, rose quietly to her feet. 'Lady Wagan, we have an alliance here. I will not be treated like a second in that. You cannot keep things from me.'

'I had faith in your spies, Lord Alahn,' Muriel Wagan replied drily. 'But if it makes you feel better, I was caught off-guard by their return as well. Now, please, sit down. You too, Captain.'

'Thank you, but I am fine,' Oake replied politely while Alahn cleared himself a space at an end of the table where no one sat on, rather like a father at the head.

With a flick of her hand, Eilona's mother slid his son's letter to him. While they waited for him to slit the envelope and read it, Olcea poured herself a new glass of laq, and made a motion to Eilona, to see if she wanted another. She shook her head. She could see through the sheet of paper Alahn held and, though she could not make out the words, she saw that it was no more than a single paragraph long.

'What has happened to my son?' Lord Alahn lowered the letter. 'If this is a joke, I do not find it funny.'

'What did he say?' the Lady of the Ghosts asked.

'Well?' he asked, looking at Eilona. 'Is this yours? Did you write it to cover your failure to speak to people in Yeflam?'

'Your son has found faith,' Caeli said coolly. 'I assume that is what you hold. Did he tell you that he would not speak to you until you have embraced our new god, either?'

'My son,' he replied, 'is responsible for managing my estates and is in control of the family's finances. I find this highly unbelievable.'

The guard shrugged. 'It is in his hand.'

'Lady Wagan,' he began, turning to her, before he stopped.

She held her letter, flames running along it. Eilona had watched her pick it up from the table while Alahn argued with Caeli and dip it into the nearest candle. 'We were both given letters,' she said. 'I find mine equally as offensive as yours, but I believe mine was written by a former steward of Aelyn Meah, Faje Metura.' She dropped the burning paper into her empty glass. 'You are wasting your time suggesting that anyone but your son wrote the letter you hold.'

Lian Alahn's anger, when he entered the tent, had been theatrical. He had planned to use it in the way that a bully uses his size, or her strength, to force people to obey his wishes. Even Eilona had recognized that in him. But when he rose from the table, his son's letter in his hand, there was a coldness about him that spoke of real fury, an emotion that she was sure very few people saw.

After he had left, Muriel Wagan grunted sourly. She picked up a new glass and pushed it over to Olcea. 'I have never met a more exhausting man,' she said as the witch filled it.

11.

Dural lived for five days. On the sixth, Heast buried him. He dug the grave with the help of Kye Taaira, a dozen steps away from where they had buried the dead of Refuge.

For the first two days, Dural had talked, each time a little bit, and after that he had fallen into a coma. Three of Refuge's soldiers were in the same state, but Dural was the last to die. While they waited, the fires in Celp turned to cinders and warm ash. Lehana led a small group through the ruins, to see what could be salvaged. Nothing, was the answer. The only thing the fire did not touch was the body of the Leeran general, Ekar Waalstan. He lay in the middle of the ruined square where he had fallen, with no hint of decay on his body. His split skull, Lehana reported, was still bleeding. She tried to move him, but found it impossible to do so, alone or with thirteen others. The body was cold and heavy. Heast heard the news with Dural's words in the back of his head. Heard again the insistence that his god must hate her faithful soldiers. Anemone made a journey into Celp alone on the third day and reported that she could not move the body, either. More, she said, the coldness Lehana had reported had seeped out of Waalstan and into the square around him. After that, Heast sent no one and put it from his mind: he had other concerns. Birds from the Lord of Faaisha had begun to settle in the camp with messages tied to their legs.

The Leerans had, it seemed, left Faaisha, and Lord Tuael and his marshals were pushing into Leera, to the capital, where they hoped to meet the combined force of Mireea, Yeflam and the Saan. Heast sent him a short letter in reply. It said that General Waalstan was dead, nothing more.

He did not know why it was important to bury Dural, but he worked quietly at it, before the tribesman joined him. Heast supposed that it was one soldier's gift to another. There would be no one else to do it, no family, no comrades, no friends. He briefly considered burning him, a practice he preferred – a practice Dural might have as well, before Celp – but he could not.

'They burn the dead on the Plateau, don't they?' he asked, pausing outside the shallow hole he and Taaira had dug. 'After they are bled?'

'Yes.' The tribesman stood across the grave from him, dirty and soot-stained. His sword lay on the ground to one side. 'A family member makes a journey to the coast afterwards, to scatter the ashes in Leviathan's Blood. But, like you, Captain, I would not have burned this man. I have seen a little too much fire of late.'

'There is rarely such a thing as a clean death,' Heast said, 'but there are better ones than what we have witnessed.'

'It has angered me.' Taaira laid the shovel on the ground and pulled off his gloves, beginning not with the fingers, as he usually did, but with the wrist. He looked as if he was ripping his skin off. 'I am not unfamiliar with anger. No person is, I believe. On the Plateau, you must learn not to deny your anger, but to understand it. It was no different for me, though I had more anger than others. You do not ask to be Hollow, Captain. You are taken by shamans at your birth, and the rituals that bleed you of your blood are done from a young age. There is pain in it, but you do not think that such an event is strange, not at first. Not until you meet others who grew up among the tribes. Until I met those, I thought that all of us were bled. I was angry when I realized that was not the case. I was young and I reacted to the difference, rather than the task I was being trained for. It is not an uncommon story. All children must learn to deal with their rage. It is something that I did learn to do over time. But this.' He motioned to the grave, to Dural's body, his gloves in his hands. 'I am having difficulties with my anger over this.'

'You are not alone with it. Many others share it.'

'But you do not?'

'I feel it,' Heast admitted. 'But for me, it is a coldness. A clarity.'

'I wish for that,' the tribesman said. 'I have a task, Captain, but it is one that has changed the longer I am with you. I no longer feel as I once did. My anger, now, does not want me to hunt my ancestors. It wants me to ride to Ranan with you. It wants me to fight beside you and strike against Se'Saera. It tells me to complete my task afterwards. The strength of my anger concerns me. I have never felt its like before. I did not feel it when Se'Saera rode onto the Plateau and struck down my own people. My anger was tempered by my duty. But here it is not. Here, I feel naught but a desire to stop her. I close my eyes and I see her soldiers, burning without pain, their skin melting, and I find that I cannot find any justification for the abuse of authority that I have seen.' He turned to Dural's body and let out a frustrated sigh. 'But my anger is further stoked by the fact that I do not know how to kill a god. I feel a futility at the idea. My sword is not made for that.'

'What sword is?'

Taaira had no answer, no more than Heast did.

Gently, the two men lowered Dural into the grave they had dug, and filled it. A crow arrived before they finished. It perched on the arm of a tree and watched. Attached to its leg was a message. It was short, an instruction by Lord Tuael to begin riding towards Ranan. The Lord finished with a flourish, claiming that now was the time to seize the momentum, to end this war. Heast shifted the bird to his shoulder and returned to his camp without the energy that was in the letter. *What sword could kill a god?* The question returned. The answer did not present itself, not after he had met with Anemone, Lehana, Qiyala and Bliq. Not by the time he lay on his roll, after he had given the order to break camp in the morning, to begin moving towards Ranan.

It was Lehana who woke him, a few hours later. She did it gently, but he knew immediately that something was wrong.

'What is it?' he asked.

'He is here.' Her voice was strained. 'He surrendered to a guard. He has asked for you.'

Heast did not ask who. He rose stiffly and walked to where a short, scarred man stood. He had brown weathered skin, much like the armour and clothes he wore. They were a collection of styles, of eras, the markings of a man who had lived much longer than his appearance suggested. He had no weapons on him: they had been collected by the guard who had brought him into the camp, by Corporal Isaap. The young man was terrified. The ring of black-and-red-armoured soldiers who stood around him with their weapons drawn did little to calm his fear.

The Innocent did not share it. He stood next to Isaap with ease, as if it did not matter how many people stood around him, or how well-armed and armoured they were. 'Ah, the Captain of Refuge,' he said, offering a slight nod of his head to Heast. 'It is a pleasure to be in your presence.'

The Confessions of an Innocent Man

'I tried to distance myself from Zilt,' Aelyn Meah said. 'I tried to distance myself from the Innocent as well, but it was difficult. When Se'Saera spoke to me, one or the other was present. But for the most part, I could put them from my mind. I could focus instead on the promise Se'Saera had made. I could focus on her.'

She paused. I thought, at first, she was arranging her thoughts, as she was prone to do, but I realized shortly that she was involved in an internal debate, as if she was deciding what she should tell me next, or not.

'There was one exception to my interactions with the god-touched,' she said, finally. 'I was asked to watch over a young, pregnant woman. Her name was Zi Taela. She carried the first of Se'Saera's children.'

I admit that I did not hide my surprise well.

'No one knew, then,' Aelyn said softly. 'She was just a woman in need of help. Her only friends were Samuel Orlan and Bueralan Le. Both men were weighed down by remorse. Until the very end, they tried to find ways to save her, to protect her. I found myself very easily drawn into that. In Taela I saw a little of myself. Helping her was one of the few ways I could help myself. Perhaps all three of us thought that.'

—Onaedo, *Histories, Year 1029*

1.

'I am not here to fight,' Aela Ren said. 'I have come under Onaedo's Peace.'

'You don't think that applies to you, do you?' Heast took the sword and dagger from Isaap, a short nod directing the Corporal backwards, away from the scarred man. 'Her peace is for mercenaries. It lets them negotiate when their employers will not. Do you think Onaedo would hang any of us if we did not recognize her peace with you?'

'No.' The Innocent stood chin height to Heast. He was a man who was forever looking up at his enemies, but he did so calmly, and clear-eyed. 'But you will honour it, regardless.'

'Is that right?'

'Yes.'

Heast turned the sword around and offered it to him hilt-first. 'We'll honour it.'

'Captain,' began Lehana, her shock, outrage, and confusion at what she saw contained in her single word. Around her, others joined in protest: Bliq repeated Lehana's word, while Oya muttered an obscenity in Ooilan; Fenna swore in the traders' tongue and the fuck was echoed by Qiyala at her side. Single words turned into doubles, then triples – Saelo, Zvae and Isaap, standing at the front of the line, called to him – and the conversation only increased when the Innocent slid his sword and dagger into their leather scabbards. Behind him, Kye Taaira appeared, his large sword in his hand, its sheath over the darkness of it. He gazed at Heast silently but made no move to attack, or attempt to speak. Beside the tribesman, Anemone emerged from the crowd. Lehana repeated, 'Captain.' There was a distraught note in her voice. 'Captain, we cannot let him leave here.'

Heast raised his hand for silence. 'Four incarnations of Refuge have ridden into Sooia to fight Aela Ren and his soldiers.' His gaze did not leave the small man as he spoke to the soldiers around him. 'The first was led by Captain Da Xanan, over five hundred years ago. She rode into Sooia with three thousand soldiers. Her force was one of the largest Refuge has ever had, built from the fortune the Emperors of Sooia paid her. After three years of war, three years that saw over two-thirds of her force killed, she met with the man who stands before us. She met him in a small tent, one staked down at the side of a lake. She said that she talked to him for a day. After, she wrote that Aela Ren was a man who would never betray his word, no matter if he spoke of peace or of war. She said that she had never met a more honest man.'

'I have met every Captain of Refuge who has come to Sooia to fight me,' the Innocent said. 'You are the first I have met outside the country.'

Heast lowered his hand. The silence around him was thick, confused. 'Captain Xanan wrote that you cannot die.'

'It is true.' He paused, as if a part of him could pierce Heast's skin, could find the centre of his soul. 'But that does not give you pause, does it?'

'You need not kill a man to win a war.'

Aela Ren was silent, as if Heast's words had struck inside him, as if they were the first time he had heard them spoken. 'What is your name, Captain?'

'Aned Heast.'

'It is often said that a name is power.'

'It is.' Heast had, over his life, met powerful men and women. He had met them old, young, and every year between. He had learned quickly that no one was like another, not in the details of how they drew their power, or how they displayed it. But few of the people he had met were like the scarred man before him. Aela Ren did not express his power, or show it: if he was met on a road by a stranger, he would be seen as an unfortunate soldier. He would be penniless, scarred, broken, until he began to speak. Once he began to speak, the stranger would think differently, for Ren's sense of self would emerge, and the stranger would see his confidence, his knowledge, and he would soon be of the opinion that of those who could stop the Innocent, he was not one. 'But your name means something, as well. You define it by what you do and what you say. No matter what a warlock or a witch does with your name, you own it. I would imagine you know that as well as I do.'

He nodded. 'I have been sent to gather General Ekar Waalstan's body and return it to Ranan. I have been told he is in Celp. I would appreciate your company with me.'

'If I said no?'

'It is your decision. As I said, I am not here to fight. Not unless I must.'

'But if I said yes?' The soldiers of Refuge murmured in protest. Heast held up his hand for silence again. 'If I said yes,' he repeated, 'is it something your god would be party to?'

'My god hears only what is said in her name.' He paused, to let the importance of what he said settle into those around him. 'In this case, no. It would be a private conversation between you and me.'

'What would we have to talk about?'

Again, the Innocent was silent. His silence, this time, stretched out into Refuge, as if he was reading their thoughts, their fears. 'Do you know much about the God of War, Captain?'

'A little,' Heast replied. 'What has survived time.'

'I knew him. Long ago, I was a servant of a god. Baar was not my god, but he was a god, regardless, and at times I was in his company. He loved to create champions, men and women like you, and those around us.' His scarred fingers flickered towards Lehana and the others. 'War was Baar's creation and he made it an intricate one. He did not create it from one moment in history, but rather thousands, each one a tiny spark. He commanded his servant, a woman like myself, to record these moments in the histories she kept. I have not seen her for years, and I do not know if she continues to write these histories, but if she did, our war would be a volume much larger than either of us was aware of in the start. I wish to discuss that with you, until I have the General's body. I will take my leave from you, then.'

The morning's sun bled a thin line of light across the horizon. 'I will ride with you to Celp,' Heast said.

'Thank you.' For the first time, Aela Ren turned from Heast, turned to the men and women who stood around him, to the soldiers who regarded him grimly. 'Refuge,' he said quietly, as if he was drawing out a truth from all of those who met his gaze. 'There is no history quite like the one you serve.'

2.

Light from the morning's sun ran along the flat roofs of Ranan, leaving pools of shadow, much like rainwater, along the road Bueralan and the god-touched rode down.

Over the last week, he had slept in snatches, grabbing what he could when the grey needed rest, when the dirt and debris forced them to stop. Se'Saera's black-eyed slave did not like the stops: he wandered around the god-touched, around the mounts, murmuring to himself, talking about the god, about how she wanted them to return. Zilt's horrific soldier sat at the far end of the camp, watching him, a foil to his restlessness in terms of stillness and silence. In the last week, Bueralan had come to view the creatures as female, though he could not attribute any one feature or act to her that made him sure of it. At her feet lay the body of Zaifyr, and when it came time to move, she would lean down and pick him up, as if he were a little boy. Yet, no matter how much the black-eyed slave tried to hurry them, the debris from the Mountains of Ger slowed them. More than once, they were forced to backtrack because of a piece of swamp that had opened up through a crack in the land, or because a trail had disappeared into mud.

It eased only when Ranan appeared on the horizon. On the last day, as the clouds of dirt began to fade, Leeran soldiers appeared. The first ones Bueralan saw were thin, their teeth filed down, and on foot, but others began to emerge soon after. These figures were lean, but well fed. They rode strangely silent horses that the mounts of the god-touched did not like. More than once, Bueralan had to pull tightly on the grey's reins to stop it kicking a Leeran horse. The soldiers who rode the strange horses were not nearly as silent. Many greeted the god-touched. Quite a few of them talked to the immortals: they spoke of Se'Saera's order to return to Ranan, to prepare for a great battle. Not one of them was surprised by Zilt's monster and, when she and the blind slave rushed off down the streets of Ranan when the god-touched emerged from the tunnels, none of the Leerans in the streets looked twice at either. Very few looked up from the barricades and walls they were making.

Bueralan wanted to rush to Taela, but years of travel, of caring for mounts, of being aware of their cost, saw him stable the grey properly first. Only Orlan did the same. The cartographer stabled his horse next to Bueralan's – the god-touched soldiers put their horses in stalls and removed their saddles, but did little else. After they had seen to water and food for their animals, Bueralan and Orlan entered the crowded streets. The bustle was such a stark contrast to how Ranan had been just over two weeks ago that, even allowing for the fortification the soldiers were involved in – the construction of ballistas, catapults, the positioning of siege towers for archers – the presence of so many people took away some of the city's strangeness. It did not take away all: for that to happen, Bueralan knew, the people on the streets would have to hang up their swords, open markets, inns, forges and all the other businesses and professions that grounded a city both economically and socially.

The crowds thinned at the bottom of the long steps to the cathedral and, by the time the two men reached the top, the only company they had were half a dozen swamp crows. There were hundreds throughout the city now, driven, no doubt, by the crumbling of the Mountains of Ger and their need for a new home. It was something that Bueralan could understand, but the companionship he felt towards the crows was short-lived: the door to the cathedral opened and Kaze stepped out, surprised to see him and Orlan before her.

'How is Taela?' Bueralan asked.

'Tired.' Kaze smiled wanly. Behind the god-touched woman's glasses, her eyes were heavy and dark. 'She – have you stabled your horses?'

He frowned. 'Is something wrong?'

'No. Well, yes.' She took a breath, trying to calm her agitation. 'We are going to have to cut the child out of her. Not tonight, but tomorrow, maybe. It is too big, Bueralan. She cannot give birth to a child of that size. It will kill her.'

He had seen a child cut out of a woman before. It had been in a siege, and food and water had been scarce, and she had died. It would be different here, he knew, especially with Kaze. 'Have you told Taela?' Orlan asked, when Bueralan did not speak.

'She knows,' Kaze said. 'She can feel it inside her. If you place your hand on her stomach, you can feel it as well. It has a hardness to it that I have never felt in a child before.'

'Is it a child?' the cartographer asked.

'It is Se'Saera's child.'

'Have you told Se'Saera?' Bueralan asked, his voice cracking a little. 'Have you asked her for help?'

Kaze laid her hand on his shoulder. 'Go and see Taela,' she said, instead of answering. 'She asks for you, all the time. Go and sit by her. We'll tell her what we plan later.' She paused and her grip tightened slightly. 'I have done this before. I have cut a number of children out of their mother's womb. I have never lost a child or a mother who was not lost before then.'

Bueralan wanted to ask if Taela was already lost, but he did not. Kaze squeezed his shoulder again and then walked down the cathedral's stairs, to the stables, to the horses she cared for. He turned to find Orlan at the door to the cathedral, the darkness inside waiting, and though he did not particularly wish to do so, he followed the cartographer inside. There, at the door, just as it closed, a tall, dark figure emerged. It was misshapen, as if it had a hump, but once Bueralan's eyes adjusted to the stilled dark of the cathedral, he realized that the shadow belonged to Zilt.

Over his shoulder, he carried the body of the black-eyed slave.

'He died after he delivered Zaifyr.' Zilt shouldered past, pushed open the door that had just closed. 'He is free, as Se'Saera promised him.'

'He was a child,' Bueralan said, turning to him. 'He should have—'

The door fell shut.

Been treated better, he finished.

'Come on,' Orlan said quietly. 'We have someone to see.'

The cathedral was lit by the time Bueralan and Orlan reached the stairs at the end, revealing its empty pews, dais and stairwells.

The hallway to Taela's room was silent. At the door to the room, he found Aelyn Meah, standing near the window, her arms folded over her chest, her gaze on the sleeping woman. The Keeper of the Divine was so still that she appeared like a statue, a creation that had been left on guard. At the sound of him and Orlan at the door, she raised her head. Gently, she placed a finger against her mouth, to caution them to be silent, and came over.

'Taela is sleeping,' she whispered, after she had stepped out into the hall. 'She drifts in and out. She's never awake for long, but we should let her sleep. She is in less pain when she sleeps.'

He nodded.

'Have you seen Kaze?'

'Yes,' he replied quietly. 'She told us that the child will need to be cut out.'

'It is about all that can be done.' There was little hope in Aelyn's eyes. 'My brother is here, is he not?'

'His body is.' It was Orlan who answered. He had been gazing into the room, and when he turned to Bueralan, his gaze mirrored Aelyn's. 'You go in and sit with her,' he said. 'I'll grab a little bit of sleep and come back in a few hours. She shouldn't be left alone, I think.'

After the two had left, Bueralan entered the room. He half expected it to be stuffy, to feel closed up, and that a smell of sickness would have come to define it, but instead, he found a gentle breeze moving about the room, as if it had been captured.

Quietly, he pulled a chair next to Taela. He could see the size of her stomach beneath the thin blanket that had been drawn over her, and she was much, much larger than when he had left. He had heard of women who had three children at once, and he imagined that such a pregnancy would equal Taela's size, now. The rapid increase had clearly taken its toll: her face had lost a lot of weight, and she looked gaunt and hollow, as if she was being devoured by what grew inside her.

Taela opened her eyes.

'How are you feeling?' he asked quietly.

'Tired.' Her hand emerged from under the blanket and he took it. 'I feel like I have this awful weight in me. Like metal.' Her hand had little strength in it. 'They want to cut it out of me,' Taela said. 'Kaze and – and the other woman. Aelyn. They say it is the only way. They think they can do it without her knowing.'

'They can,' he said, when she didn't continue. 'They can, I promise. They'll free you from this.'

But she had fallen back asleep.

Gently, he placed her hand back on the bed, beneath the sheets. As he did, she shifted a little, revealing brown stains of dried blood. Unsurprised, he straightened out the sheet, to conceal it from her when she woke next.

3.

For two days, Tinh Tu's forces made camp in the port town of Gtara. There, they dismantled the six ships that had been abandoned, left tied to the dock.

To reach Gtara, the ragged force had marched along the edges of the Black Lake until the Leeran coastline emerged. The route had been forced upon them by the earth that – even now, nearly a week later – rolled from the Mountains of Ger. It was caused by continuing landslides and cave-ins along the range, Ayae thought, and the earthquakes that accompanied the two, along with the bad visibility, left the main roads a dangerous path of sink holes and expanding swamps. It had been a sink hole that forced Tinh Tu to leave the main roads: it was there the morning after she took command, the vanished ground leaving an inky darkness that, if it had grown any larger, would have swallowed the makeshift camp whole. As it was, they were woken by the protesting cries of swamp crows, which continued to complain while Ayae pored over a map to organize a path to Gtara. 'We can reach Ranan from there,' she said. 'As for the town itself, I don't know what kind of condition it will be in. I wouldn't expect anything pretty.'

When she said that, Ayae envisioned Gtara as a series of broken building frames, wire fences and a dock stretching into Leviathan's Blood. She knew that there would be people there, but it did not occur to her that it would be they who were stripped down to a nearly unrecognizable state.

Ayae rode into the town beside Jae'le, driven ahead of the main body of Tinh Tu's army by the demands of the Mireean and Yeflam soldiers rather than by the old woman's harsh command. After she had mapped a path to Gtara three dozen soldiers had waited for Ayae near the small roll she had slept on the night before.

Vune, a middle-aged Mireean soldier, was their spokesperson. 'We don't feel like we have much choice going forward,' he said. 'It isn't like we love Leera or the new god, but, well, we seen a lot of our friends die. Some may survive. We think we ought to go look for them.' When she didn't speak, he rubbed at his dirty cheek. 'The woman who took away our voices, who made us kneel, you're more like her than us,' he said with blunt honesty. 'You got that curse. You could speak to her. Tell her to let us go.'

'I have no control over Tinh Tu.' She glanced at the predominantly male soldiers in front of her. 'You talk to her yourself.'

'We want her to know we've done enough,' Vune said. 'We're not dogs.'

No, she told him, told all of them, you're not, but no matter what she said, they kept trying to pressure her into speaking to Tinh Tu. After Vyla Dvir revealed that the Lord of the Saan was still unable to speak, they began to double their efforts, and by the end of the second day, their list of grievances had grown to include how hard Tinh Tu was driving them and how she was not listening to suggestions. Unfortunately, Ayae could sympathize with their festering resentment, and it left in her a rising frustration, because she knew that she could not address it. By the third and fourth day, she had taken to riding ahead with Jae'le as a scout, knowing that it was a coward's solution, and one that would not last.

When the two entered Gtara, the smell of decay was the first thing that they noticed. Bodies of men, women and children lay on the ground, covered in dirt from the Mountains of Ger. Jae'le had warned her about the bodies before they entered – 'A bird told me,' he said, scratching the chin of the swamp crow on his shoulder, perhaps the same one as the one in the tree or another she did not know – but even though she was prepared, the sheer number of the dead surprised Ayae. She stopped at the first of them, the smell leaving her nauseous, the sight of the crows picking through the remains only adding to the feeling. It took a moment before she realized that the man in dirty white armour was someone she knew.

Paelor.

'Jae'le,' she said, nudging her horse forwards to catch up to him. 'These are the Keepers.'

'Some of them, yes.' He indicated the single dock, the dock where they would soon stand and watch Eidan drag ships onto the shore. 'The rest are slavers from Gogair, I believe.' He slid off his horse. 'Did you notice the condition of the bodies of the Keepers?' Without qualm, he grabbed one by the leg and pulled the body clear, a pair of crows hopping calmly away as he did. The bird on his shoulder glided down and, with the other two, moved back to the body they had been poking at, leaving Ayae and Jae'le to stare at a face that showed no decay, but rather the signs of advanced age, as if its muscle had been removed. 'Mequisa, the Bard,' he said, 'to judge by his clothes. Not that you would notice it from his body. It is as if his very essence has been stripped out.'

'Do you think . . . ?' She stopped, rephrased it so she would not mention Se'Saera's name. 'Is this what the new god does?'

'To those like you and me?' He shrugged. 'I suspect so. We will have to ask Eidan to bury the bodies. We cannot leave them out in the open like this.'

'We are surely not planning to stay here?'

'Soon Faaishan scouts will be upon us, and we'll want to be able to hold a meeting with their marshals. But more immediately, we will need to take those ships apart to build siege equipment. Our soldiers will need it.'

'Our soldiers?' she repeated. 'Jae'le, why do we even need soldiers?'

'You need an army in war.'

'Think about the things we can do,' she said. 'They can't do those things. In many ways we would have more freedom without them.'

'No, not against the god-touched.' The swamp crow squawked and lifted from the ground, to return to his shoulder. 'We will need soldiers,' he said. 'Even those who want to mutiny, but can't.'

It did not sit well with Ayae, not then, not later that day, when the two scouts entered Gtara and were taken to Tinh Tu. By then, the dead had been swallowed by the ground, and the stench of decay was hidden beneath the smell of Leviathan's Blood. Still, Ayae felt a chill when the two men rode into the town, over the freshly churned soil, as if she was seeing an image of the future of all the soldiers around her.

The scouts did not get to speak to Tinh Tu. After they were presented to her, she said, 'Bring me the Lord of Faaisha and his marshals.' She handed them a letter she had written. 'I expect them in two days.'

4.

From the window of her room on Neela, Eilona gazed at the remains of the abandoned shoreline camp, half submerged in the mud that had rolled down from the Mountains of Ger.

'What do you find so fascinating about the sight of that?' Sinae Al'tor asked, unfolding a chair behind her. 'We avoided a catastrophe.'

'I sometimes see Mireea in it.' Eilona turned to him as he opened the second chair. 'Don't you feel a bit sad, now that it is gone?'

'Like you, I was happy to leave it, but unlike you right now, I am not interested in recasting it in my memory. Now, enough of that: we have my prize to drink.' He reached down into the pack he had carried into the small house and began to pull out a kettle and a small brazier. 'You have no idea how rare tea is,' he said. 'I have not been able to get it in the camp. If you hadn't come to ask me for a kettle, I might not have even known you had any.'

'It won't do anything for your image,' she teased. 'You're supposed to live on alcohol and vice.'

'A cliché is only as good as the money it creates, my dear.'

She laughed and he struck a match, lighting the brazier. Eilona had gone in search of Sinae last night, nearly a week after they had moved on to Neela. The move from the shoreline had been orderly, and nothing but a few semi-permanent structures could be seen of the camp now. Most of the people had lodgings on the southern side of the city, away from the broken stone ramp that led to Wila, the empty island where her mother and the Mireean people had been imprisoned when they first came to Yeflam for refuge.

Eilona had been assigned a small house on the south-eastern curve of Neela, near her mother and her stepfather. There were enough houses that no one had to share, unless they wished, and though Eilona had felt decadent taking a whole house, she pushed aside the guilt by telling herself that there were still empty dwellings. Her new home had no furniture, nothing indeed, but for a small box of tea left in a piece of broken brickwork near where she had laid out her roll and blankets. The tin had been the colour of the brick, and when she had opened it, Eilona half expected coins, or letters of an affair, but the tea had been much more welcome. At least, until she realized that she had no kettle, no cups and no fire.

Sinae had solved that, however.

'Mireea is probably gone, now,' she said to him as the fire took hold in the brazier. Sinae had arrived with the chairs and brazier and his beautiful, blonde guard, but the latter had little interest in the tea. Instead, she wandered around Eilona's house, silent as a ghost. 'When you look at the skyline, the whole mountain range has collapsed, as if it was hollow. As if there never was a god in it.'

'I hear enough about gods every night.' He poured some of Eilona's water into the kettle, the tea leaves following. 'It's bad business. I've been able to sleep in the midnight hours because people are having such divine thoughts.'

'Do you?'

'If they've stopped paying, yes.' He set the kettle down and rose. 'Your mother would prefer I keep them all night and listen, but they're not saying anything of importance.'

No one was, anywhere, Eilona had learned.

She had little to do on Neela, now that her mother's plans had been so turned around. She did not have any complaints in regard to that: she did not want anyone planning to kill her. But she had been left at a loose end, to a degree, and she had taken to going to her mother's house and listening in on the meetings she held in the evening with Reila, Olcea and Sinae. Most of what they talked about came from the witch, who had been spying on the leaders of the other cities – or, to be more precise, Hien had been spying – to try and gauge their position in relation to Faje and the Faithful. Two had become converts to Se'Saera, but Olcea was clear that the Faithful could be found in all the cities, and the 'refugee' problem was widespread in all but the furthest cities, Toake and Enilr. She also believed that all the cities had given their 'cursed' over to the Faithful.

'It makes me think of death,' Sinae said, breaking into her thoughts. He stood beside her, his gaze on the new, strangely shaped mountain range. 'What happens to a god when its body turns to dust?'

'I can't believe people come to you seeking pleasure.'

'Prostitutes and philosophy. Empires are built on the back of both.'

Eilona smiled. 'I don't know what happens to a god,' she said. 'There are theories. Most of them based on the "cursed", on the gods' divinity seeping into the world, as if it was always part of that. But others have suggested that they return to their paradises, that they become one with it and maintain it for the rest of eternity with those who were faithful.' She shrugged. 'I don't particularly subscribe to that. It is a theory that has risen in the last century, as more and more is found out about the old gods. A lot that was thought lost in the Five Kingdoms has started to turn up on small islands, and in parts of the world where their rule did not spread. But the people who propose it seem almost to be trying to reach out to the old gods, to believe in what they once represented, to bring them back, in their own way. The work is half research, half wish-fulfilment, half wanting to go back to a simpler age.'

'I would not have thought seventy-eight gods was a simpler age,' Sinae said.

'Controlled is probably a better description,' she said.

He frowned and turned from the broken skyline. 'What happened to the people who wanted to be free of the gods, back then?'

'There weren't many. There's some evidence of people who didn't want an afterlife, and didn't want to be reborn, but not much. It was hard to escape the influence of the gods when they stood around you.'

'So you could not be free?'

The tone of his voice caught Eilona's attention. 'Not really,' she said, slowly, as the kettle on the brazier began to steam. 'People who didn't want anything to do with the gods were not largely accepted by others. They were driven out of villages, stripped of titles and wealth and, in some cases, stoned. There would be a lot more sympathy for them now, I suspect, but not then. When you think about it, it's not terribly surprising. The gods stood around you, then. Ain, the God of Life, creator of the very planet we stand on, left statues through forests and deserts for people to make pilgrimages to. We have found some of those: they're of men and women and children, but they're not carved by any hand – they're made. Even without the god to power them, they resonate, still. It was difficult to be anything but loyal in a world where the gods were so accessible.'

Sinae nodded, but if he had more to say, more that could give substance to Eilona's concern, or push it away, he did not. Instead, his blonde guard silently entered the room, and he asked Eilona if she knew what flavour the tea was that she had found.

5.

Zaifyr walked alone, but for how long, and how far, he did not know.

There was no change in the world around him. The grass spread from horizon to horizon, with no rises into hills, or mountains, or dips into rivers and oceans.

He did not know where Lor Jix and Anguish were. Though he had stepped through the door with both, neither stood on the field. He called out their names, and did so until he realized that there was nothing alive around him. No birds flew, no insects moved, and no animals or people could be seen. Zaifyr was not confident that his voice had even truly emerged in the shout he gave, either. He did not draw a breath and, after he had finished shouting, he felt a heaviness settle on his chest, similar to the weight that had been upon him in Mireea.

He wanted to sit down on the grass, but he did not. Though he did not know why he thought it, he believed that if he did lower himself, he would not rise. The grass would welcome him, unlike any other grass, and he would lie back in it and stare up at the sun. The sun did not move in the clear sky, and it was this stillness, more than anything else, that warned him against sitting on the ground, not to give in to the desire to stop. It would be easy, though. The thought was ever present. He could take a moment to rest. A moment wouldn't hurt. Nothing of importance would happen in a moment, even here, where time was strangely suspended yet accelerated, as if it had taken place, was taking place, and would soon take place.

Suddenly, a figure appeared before him.

He lay on his back in the grass, a young white man, dark-haired, and with a thin, long face that, though Zaifyr had never seen him before, was familiar. He wore loose-fitting, paint-stained clothes and would occasionally lift his hand to the sky, as if he was painting the sun, though he held no brush, had no paint, and no canvas. The only personal item near him was a rusted sword.

'My name,' the man said, after Zaifyr appeared in his line of sight, 'is Sonen Kint.'

The voice was familiar. 'Anguish?'

'No, no.' The man's hand turned into a finger and he wagged it with each pronunciation. 'No, not here. Not now. Not any more. I am not a creation of Se'Saera, not a soldier of a new god. I am a painter. I paint men and women. Even children. Most are prostitutes. I talk to them and I get to know them and I paint them. In each of them there is something beautiful and fragile and raw, but you can only see it when they are naked. When the symbols by which they define themselves are stripped away.'

'Is that how you changed?' Zaifyr asked. 'Was Anguish a symbol?'

'Sonen is a symbol.' He laughed, a strange, dreamy laugh. 'You should listen to this land. We are all symbols. We are all representations. You should sit and let it speak to you. It is—'

'Paradise,' finished Lor Jix. The Captain of *Wayfair* appeared before the two of them, as if he stepped from a world outside the one they were in. 'We are in the paradise of the gods, where we will want for nothing and need for nothing.'

In Zaifyr's youth, in the cold mountains of Kakar, the shaman Meihir had told him that when he was dead, Hienka, the Feral God, would take him to a camp with a huge forest stretching below it. From there, he would be able to hunt, to trap, to fight. 'No god promised this,' Zaifyr said now, indicating the endless field. 'This is no paradise.'

'The Leviathan promised me an ocean, unlike any I had seen before.' There was a note of bitterness in Jix's voice. 'But regardless of what we were promised, this is it.'

'But this . . .' Zaifyr's voice trailed off. Before him, quite clearly, he could see himself. He was laid out on a stone floor. He could feel cold stone against his back, and could feel dirt in his hair, over his face and neck and exposed hands. He could see the shadowed outline of a figure standing over him, but he did not know who it was. The figure was accompanied by two others, though only the first stood close, while the second stood at a distance, like a servant. He could hear words, as well, but he could not understand them. 'Can you see me?' he asked Jix, feeling the weight in his chest grow heavier. 'When you look down, can you?'

'Look at your chest,' Jix said, instead. 'It is as if you have a wound there.'

It came from where he felt heaviest, where his lungs would be, if he was alive, if he had a body. It was much larger than the red smear that had appeared in Mireea, before he had taken the Wanderer's staff, but it was not dissimilar. He remembered what Anguish had said then – that his family had been bringing his body to his soul, that they had been trying to return him to life – but before he could say anything, he began to retch and water burst from his mouth, black like Leviathan's Blood.

He lifted his hand to his mouth as he gagged again, but more water burst from him, the second so fierce, so powerful that he stumbled to his knees.

'Don't fight it, Zaifyr,' Se'Saera said, her face appearing before him in the room, and in the field. 'It will only hurt more.'

6.

Beneath the morning's gentle light, the blackened trees and grey-stained ground had a soft, dream-like quality.

In a voice that seemed to emerge from the landscape, Aela Ren said, 'Your soldiers watch us.'

'Did you expect them to wait politely in the camp after we left?' Heast rode beside him on a steady brown horse. Only an hour before, as he saddled the beast, Lehana had spoken to him in a hushed, urgent voice. *You can't trust him.* She said that he had not seen what Ren had done in Cynama, had not seen the fires that burned from lava that rose from the ground, breaking through the stone canals by cracking the stone. She told him he had not seen the Innocent's soldiers emerge from the night, a series of dark shadows who butchered people in the streets. *You promised the Queen,* she said, holding tightly onto the horse's reins. *You promised* – he laid his hand on her shoulder, on the black metal of her armour, chipped around the edges, and interrupted her. *I know what I promised,* he said. *And I have seen Sooia. I have seen what Aela Ren does.* With a grunt he pulled himself up onto his horse. *But he did not come here to kill us, not today. He wants to tell us something first.* Lehana had stared up at him in disbelief. *What could he tell us that wasn't the promise of death?* she asked him. 'I imagine,' Heast said to the man beside him, 'that my lieutenant has archers on both sides of us. If you make a sudden move, their orders will be to cut your horse down first, to try and trap you beneath it. They will hope to break a leg in the fall. If they don't, they will aim for your legs, to cut down your movement. Once that is done, they will come with axes, to break you apart.'

'Captain Xanan had a similar plan,' the Innocent replied, not bothered by what he heard, not concerned enough to even turn his head left or right to search for the riders. 'She was our first real defeat in Sooia.'

'I heard that she died beneath the mountain she collapsed on you?'

'Yes, she did. But it was a better fate than being trapped beneath stone for close to a decade. I can still remember the sensation of being crushed, of my bones breaking and repairing, of my skin splitting and healing. It is not a pleasant experience.' The morning's light caught his scars, crossing him with shadows. 'I have felt worse,' he said, meeting Heast's gaze, as if he knew that the Captain of Refuge was trying to gauge if his injuries had come from that. 'Physically and emotionally, I have felt worse. But being trapped beneath stone is a fate I am pleased Captain Xanan did not have to experience.'

Heast nodded, but made no reply.

'Does it surprise you?' Ren asked.

'Should it?'

Ahead, the first ravine marked itself in a dark line, as if it were a fissure to another world.

'Perhaps,' the man beside him said. 'I am aware that to many, I am considered a monster. I have done things that are not easily forgivable.'

'Xanan wrote that you did not enjoy what you were doing in Sooia,' he said. 'Captain Ibori, the third Captain of Refuge to meet you, said otherwise.'

'Both are correct. For a long time, I have been a man consumed by anger. When I say a long time, I do not mean a generation, or a few hundred years, but over ten thousand. I was born when the land looked very different from this. The mountain I lived upon for much of my life does not even exist any more. In such a life, in such a length of time, anger can find many a way to manifest itself. Especially my anger. I was the mortal instrument of the God of Truth, Wehwe. I was god-touched, to use our term. I gave my life to him and dedicated myself to his desires but, until recently, I did not know why he and the other gods went to war. Neither I, nor any of the others like me, were told that. Can you imagine what that was like?' Nudging his horse, Ren began to move around the ravine, ash clouding the legs of his white and black speckled horse. 'I had been so certain of my place in the world beside my god. I may not have always liked what I did – to stand beside a god is not to stand beside a being of kindness – but I understood what a divine being gave to the world, how it shaped the land and our lives. When that was gone, I had only my anger.'

'But not now?' Heast asked. 'Now you are free of your anger?'

'My new god has soothed it, but it is still within me. I can feel it, in the edges of my body, as if it were a weight.'

'Your god watched me in Celp. She watched my soldiers and me ride against Waalstan. It was she who gave the order to her soldiers to douse themselves in flames.' He indicated around him. 'It was she who ordered all of this.'

'Yes, she knew her general would die.'

'And her soldiers?'

'No.' Ren's horse stumbled as a fallen log broke into cinders beneath its hooves. It righted and the Innocent shifted in his saddle for balance. As he did, his left hand rearranged his sword, strapped to the side of his mount. 'I can hear your anger, Captain. I recognize it. I can only tell you that it is futile to look for your own morals in a god.'

Heast grunted. 'It sounds like you've done that.'

'No, not exactly. I once heard the morals of a god. I heard them spoken to me. Wehwe would speak to me about the importance of truth, and of certainty, of how they defined the world. Over the thousands of years I stood beside him, my beliefs were shaped by those words. My anger rose from the fact that the War of the Gods betrayed those beliefs. The gods killed each other and left their creation in a state of anarchy. Without them, there were no truths, no paths for a righteous man to follow, no punishments for a deceitful woman to fear. There was only a descent into madness and oblivion. How could a god do that?'

'Surely you can answer that?' he asked. 'After all those years?'

The Innocent offered a faint smile, a bittersweet line in his scarred face. 'Not with any certainty. It is merely a question that I return to again and again. As I said earlier to you, war is not due to one event. Not even the war I have waged in Sooia was a snap of my fingers and a decision made on whim. I chose it because it was the most progressed of our nations, because it alone had weathered the fall of the Five Kingdoms the best, never having been ruled by those five. But what if there was more than that? What if fate had been touched, shifted by a divine hand, and moved to ensure that I was there? That the hatred I felt sent me there, instead of elsewhere? What if it sent me there to do what I have done, so I may come here now to stand beside a new god and act as a reflection to her?'

Ahead, the blackened ruins of Celp appeared, like charcoal markings on a piece of paper.

'I have been used before,' Heast said. 'That's what you're describing, after all. Being used like a tool. You can't be a mercenary and not feel that once or twice. But when you feel it, you have to make a choice. You must decide if you will let that continue, or if you will step aside from it.'

'Yes, you do.' Slowly, conscious of the archers who moved

through the darkened trees, Aela Ren reached into his saddle bag. From it, he removed a book, bent at the spine, the pages warped, as if they had been written upon. 'You have heard,' he said to Heast, 'of *The Eternal Kingdom*?'

'I have,' he replied. 'It is said that only the Faithful can read it.'

'They can write in it, as well.' The Innocent held out the book to him. 'My choice is already made, Captain. I have looked into my new god, and I have seen what is inside her, and I cannot turn from her. I am but a servant, and I have been one, even when I believed I was not. You, however, are not a servant. You are a mortal man born in this world without a god.'

Heast took the book. 'What will I find in this?'

'A choice. A choice between a promised world and' – he turned to the black trees and ash-covered ground – 'the one you know.'

7.

'Mortals are born in pain,' Se'Saera said. 'My parents wanted that for you, for all of you. The pain was to be divine.'

She stood before Zaifyr twice, on a still field and in a dark room. In the latter, she appeared as a young and beautiful woman, but in the former, she was a child whose wings unfolded from her back.

'I have wondered,' the new god continued, speaking both in the field and in the room, one voice echoing the other. 'I have wondered why they made birth painful. It is such a necessary part of mortality that you might think they would make it pleasurable for the mother and the child. But it is not. It is painful, as if it must teach you a lesson, but what, exactly? I travel with a woman who was the servant of Linae, my mother. Do you know what she told me when I asked her that question?'

Zaifyr could not answer her, could not find a voice to speak. In the dark room, the light was growing, as if the still sun of the second world was seeping into the first. He could see the windows and the light – *was it the morning, the midday, or the afternoon's?* – revealed not just the size and shape of the room, but the people in it, as well.

'Zaifyr,' Se'Saera said, standing above him. 'Don't you wish to know?'

A blond man stood beside Se'Saera, black leather strips wrapped around his body. He stared at him with anger, though Zaifyr had never seen him before.

'Zaifyr?'

A deformed woman crouched further back.

'Leave him be, abomination.' Lor Jix stepped in front of Zaifyr, stepped between him and the god in the still world. In the sunlit room, no one moved. 'Why don't you tell us what have you done to the paradises that the gods promised us?'

'I have done nothing,' she replied. 'All the doors of Heüala opened onto this field. They have done so as long as I have existed.'

'Do not lie to me. The Leviathan spoke of a world of endless oceans. A world those loyal to her would share. This is not that promise.'

'No, it is not.' In the bright room, Se'Saera smiled. When she spoke on the still grassland, the humour was not evident. 'I can see more of the world now. More of what was, what is, and what will be. When the Wanderer was here, when the gods left pieces of themselves with him to be put inside the houses of Heüala, you could open a door to what they promised. You would see oceans and another would see castles that rose high into the sky and chariots that took you to the sun, to palaces made of light. But in truth, it was an illusion. You sat as you do now.'

'It was all symbols,' Sonen said, still lying on the ground. 'All metaphor and simile for your soul, for the part of you that cannot die.'

'Even this grass is not real,' the god said. 'But I could not abide the emptiness, so I made the sun shine over a field.'

'You speak in lies,' Lor Jix said, grinding the words out in anger.

'Do you not want to know why they did it?' The Captain of *Wayfair* did not respond. 'There are a finite number of souls in the world,' she said. 'It was the first thing I learned when I became aware. At that time, there were souls stretched throughout paradise, waiting to be reborn. More were being punished beside the River of the Dead. The number of both was greater than you can imagine, but it was still a number. It had a beginning and an end. And each one of them was power, stored for my parents, waiting their return.' In the sunlit room the god laughed in delight. 'The first thing I did was to let everyone go through the turn, to take hold of the wheel and return, to live again. I thought that they had been left for me. I thought that they were my parents' gift. Now, of course – now I see differently.'

'The gods create—' the ancient dead began.

'—and the mortals decide,' Se'Saera finished. 'That is why birth is painful. The lives of mortals must be staggered, no matter if they are human or not. Even after I released them, there was no wave of births. There was the usual trickle, the souls of mortals caught in safeguards and filters my parents made. They are nearly empty now, though. Soon children will become rarer and rarer.'

'But this sedation of the afterlife, this robbing of all desire?' Jix had lost his bitterness. 'Why would they do this to us?'

'Did you not lead an army of the dead to attack Heüala? Ask yourself, at what point do the living become a threat to the gods and their plans?'

He did not reply.

'Step aside for me, Captain,' the god said, a note of kindness in her voice. 'I could make you do it, but I will offer you a choice, instead. I will offer it to you because my parents have lied to you. My mother, the Leviathan, took your soul and trapped it for thousands of years, all because she was afraid of me. My father, the Wanderer, ensured that your crew would be trapped in his staff because he was afraid of what I would become. Their acts are no different to those of all my parents. They have broken their world. They have left it in tatters. They wanted to leave nothing alive but those that had been infected with their power. They sought to keep control of their world by keeping all the dead here, in Heüala. They wanted to keep fate splintered so that they could continue to make the world in the images they so desired. They wanted to deny a single fate. They wanted to deny me and, in doing so, deny you. But it has not worked. I have sent the souls back into the world. I have let them go to grow without them. I have let them make designs that break the plans of my parents. They have given me choices. They have given me the chance to repair the world. That is what is at stake here. If you step aside, I will be able to remake this world. I will create real rewards and real punishments for those who are loyal to me. Let me return Zaifyr to his body and put an end to the horrors my parents have created.'

'No.' Black water burst from Zaifyr's mouth as he struggled to speak, the word incoherent as he tried to deny what Se'Saera said, to tell Jix of the laughter that mingled with her words, to tell him that he could not trust the new god, just as he could not trust the old ones. He opened his mouth to speak again, but in the sunlit room Se'Saera placed her hand on his mouth, and nothing emerged in the still grassland. *No. You must deny her. She has used us. You heard her. She has done just as her parents did. She has left the dead in purgatory after they have done what she wanted. You must not trust her.*

The Captain of *Wayfair*, the priest whose faith in his god saw him accept a curse for over ten thousand years, stepped aside.

8.

After the tea was drunk, after the midday's sun had begun to rise, after Sinae left, Eilona walked the short distance to her mother's house. Her mind turned over what Sinae had said, and she considered her own responses, asking herself if her concern was legitimate. She was probably over-reacting, Eilona told herself. A lot of people had questions about gods, about the old gods, the new god, and Sinae did not have to be any different from them. It was impossible that Sinae would be anything but loyal to her mother, but even as she thought that, approaching the two-storey house Muriel Wagan and her husband were in, Eilona had to admit that how she knew Sinae was through his relationship with her mother. Five years ago, a few years after she had left for Pitak, her mother had brought Sinae into the Keep, bruised and beaten, a young man whose story of being chained in a house and abused by a rich, older man, emerged in whispers when Eilona returned for a visit. He had been the cause of a public argument with her father, after she had heard him announce at a dinner table that the boy was damaged, pointing him out with a fork. Before two dozen people, Eilona had told her father to be quiet, had scolded him in front of diplomats, then left the hall. The outburst had not helped her reputation, but—

'That idiot.' Eilona heard her mother's exasperated voice as a guard opened the door and she stood, momentarily confused, in the doorway. But her mother, stalking around the room, waved her in. 'Lian Alahn,' she said, but after the door closed. 'That idiot.'

The only other person in the room with her was the witch, Olcea. 'What has he done?' Eilona asked.

'He invited his son and Faje to Neela.' An exasperated sigh escaped the Lady of the Ghosts. 'It seems he is concerned that his son is putting the family wealth into the accounts of the Faithful. He has – and I don't know how – he has got word somehow about the state of his finances. Alahn can't command his son to come here, so he has requested that he and the leader of the Faithful come to Neela to discuss their treaty.'

'But you burned his offer.'

'It is possible that he doesn't know what was offered, but at this point, we had best assume that he does.'

'Nymar took his father's letter to Faje,' Olcea said, exhaustion etched onto her every word. 'I was lucky to see it. Hien passes through Faje's office in Rje twice a day. Mostly, he is discussing the deployment of the Faithful through the cities and the importance of supplies. But this morning, Nymar was there with his father's letter. They had quite the discussion. Nymar doesn't believe a word of it, but Faje, it appears, has had a visitation from his new god. Se'Saera has shown him a future where both he and Nymar are on Neela. They are in this house with Alahn and your mother. I am sure nothing good happens, but Faje was not clear on the details.'

It could mean anything. Eilona's mother could agree to a treaty, could agree to send everyone who was even slightly cursed to Rje, or it could be a lie, one Faje told to Nymar to appease him. Or it could be worse. Eilona was about to begin discussing the ways that it could be worse, when the door opened, and Reila entered. Behind her, Sinae and his beautiful, blonde guard walked in. At the sight of them, her mother ushered all three to the table where Olcea sat.

Eilona declined the offer to join them. A chill threaded through her as she lifted her hand and said no, she had nothing to add. Her gaze flicked to Sinae, but it was the brown-eyed gaze of his guard she met, a gaze that only added to Eilona's discomfort. She would speak to her mother later, she told herself, as she walked up the stairs, to where her stepfather was.

The room was bare except for one of the few cots she had seen on Neela, but Elan Wagan was not in it. Instead, he sat in his wheelchair, his empty gaze directed to the half-open window and the dirty breeze that filtered through it. Eilona had been here on the day he was lifted up the stairs and taken to the room, and she had been in the room when he had begun screaming. She, Reila, Caeli and her mother tried to calm him, but it was not until the guard opened the window that they succeeded. After, he even allowed the old healer to tie a cloth around his mouth, to provide small protection against the dust.

'How is he?' she asked Caeli, who sat on the floor, against the back wall of the room. 'I was told he slept well,' she added.

The guard closed her book, folded the orange and black cover of *Malaeska* into her lap. 'Surprisingly. He doesn't like to be taken from the chair, so he has slept sitting. But he's been good. So good that he didn't even start to yell when your mother did.'

Eilona made a motion, to ask if she could sit, and the other woman nodded. 'I didn't think you liked the mercenary novels,' she said, after she had sat. 'Not even the famous ones.'

'I gave Sinae an old kettle and he gave me this.' She smiled ruefully. 'I thought it would be good for a laugh.'

'It is mostly sad. The author – Winters – wrote it as more a cautionary tale. The Malaeska in the book is the author's alter ego and what happens to her is mostly true. She really did fight in the battles she lists, really did lose a child after her husband abandoned her. The last was what made her write the book. Winters wanted to warn young women not to take up the sword, but needed to make money as well. Hence the torrid love affairs in the book.'

'It's probably why my parents didn't give me a copy as a child.' Caeli offered half a shrug. 'Still hard to imagine that it inspired so much.'

'Winters made a fortune,' Eilona said. 'The books the big mercenary groups put out haven't strayed from her basic formula, either. Like *Malaeska*, they're half propaganda, half a cheap thrill, and half a revenue source.'

'You have three halves.'

'I'm working on it.'

It was the most she had spoken to Caeli since her return. She was used to the guard staring at her with her cold blue eyes, with her judgement, her memory of what Eilona had said about her after she had been given the position of guarding her mother. Since her return, however, Caeli's gaze had been different. Cold, still, yes, but different, also.

'I'm giving it a read,' Caeli said, picking up the conversation after a pause. 'Mostly because I never have. I never thought I would. I used to be so sure of everything, but lately, some of what I've thought has been challenged, and I've come up wrong. So I thought I'd try this.' She turned it over in her hands. 'Not all that sure I'll be writing my own life down, but you have to go where the changes in life take you. You can't ignore them.'

Eilona thought of Sinae and nodded, but said nothing.

'In the Spires,' she continued, 'I should have told you Olcea was watching us. She wanted to tell you, but I said it didn't matter. You didn't have to know. I knew then that you would leave me at one point and I wanted you to. If you had got hurt, well, a little hurt would be all right. My parents got a little hurt, after all.'

'I regret that.' Eilona stared ahead, at her father, and not at the other woman. 'I am glad that they were not killed. That they continued to work. That they took on an apprentice. I'm glad that they survived the siege. I can't apologize enough for what happened. I can understand how a little hurt would be okay.'

'You might understand it, but I don't accept it.' Caeli pushed herself up. 'Not so long ago, I thought someone cursed was nothing but that,' she said. 'I don't think I ever thought about what an ugly thought it was, but I did. I'm not afraid to acknowledge that. I didn't go around telling people what I thought, but I acted on it, and I didn't treat people fairly, or honestly. But a friend changed my opinion. Now, you and me, we may never be friends. There is a little too much in our history for that. But people do change, Eilona. I have seen it. I've seen it in me, you, your mother, everyone.'

Everyone, she repeated, after the guard left. *Everyone*.

9.

With the mid-morning's sun behind him, the Lord of Faaisha rode into Gtara, accompanied by three hundred soldiers.

Ayae was not surprised by the number, but she had not expected Jye Tuael himself. She had thought that the likely candidate would be one of the lesser Lords of Faaisha, one of the lords who complained about Mireea and its position on the Spine of Ger. In Samuel Orlan's shop, Ayae had met half a dozen of the lesser Lords of Faaisha and each one of them had complained about *the* Lord of Faaisha. He was rarely described in a flattering light, and instead was spoken of as a man who did not like to get his hands dirty and who, because of that, worked through agents such as warlocks, spies and diplomats. So well established were those representatives that, when he arrived in Gtara, Ayae mistook him at first for a soldier, no more than a captain, or a claw, as the rank was known in the Kingdoms of Faaisha.

Jye Tuael rode his horse well, his body a practised, comfortable sway in well-made and well-worn chain and leather. The sword he carried was a sabre like a hundred other sabres that Ayae had seen, no better or worse a sword than she would expect from a soldier who made his career on the field. The only thing that set him apart from the other soldiers in worn green cloaks – the colours of the Kingdoms of Faaisha had been put aside, it seemed, in the dense green of Leera – was the gold ring he wore. He would, over the next two hours, twist the ring around his finger, back and forth, as if a combination of half-turns and twists would free him from Tinh Tu's influence.

'The compulsion in your letter ensured I came here,' the Lord of Faaisha said, after he had been led to Tinh Tu. She had awaited him inside an abandoned inn, the room cleared of all but one table and two chairs. He sat at a table opposite her while the white raven walked along the table between them. 'My warlocks assure me it could not be broken.' There was a thin film of anger over his words, but he was, Ayae thought, surprisingly calm. 'I do not consider this the beginning of a healthy relationship.'

'I am not concerned by that,' Tinh Tu said. Ayae stood behind her, between Jae'le and Eidan. On the other side of the room, eight marshals stood behind the Lord of Faaisha. 'I am concerned with the siege of Ranan and nothing more,' the old woman finished.

'We have a force of eight thousand,' he began.

'You have thirteen,' she corrected. 'You will find lying to me has very few benefits. But, let us overlook that for the moment. You are the largest force outside the Leerans themselves and you will be responsible for holding the northern side of Ranan. Most important is that your soldiers do not leave the battle. You and your soldiers must fight until we are victorious or until we are dead.'

Tinh Tu's command was undeniable. A murmur went through the marshals. 'There are times when it is advantageous to leave the field and fight another day,' the Lord of Faaisha said.

'Not this battle.' Her voice allowed for no dissent. 'When you return to your camps, you will also issue an order, on the pain of death, for the new god's name not to be said.'

'We have all said Se—' Tuael's voice choked off suddenly. He coughed and cleared his throat. 'I am not a dog to be treated as such.'

'Consider it fortunate that you did not die.' Tinh Tu reached out to the raven, her long, old fingers scratching it chin. 'The new god can hear her name when it is spoken. Not speaking it is a matter of simple survival. Now, in a moment, my brothers will talk to you. My sister may as well. When they speak, you will listen to all three and you will enact their advice. You will do this. You will have no choice.' She paused and let her words echo in those before her. 'When the battle of Ranan is over, you will not see us again, and you will not speak of us, either. You will be free to reconstruct the story of the battle in any way you wish. You can make a hero or a villain out of yourself, Jye Tuael, it does not matter to me, or to my family. All that matters is that no history will record the four of us here, just as it will not record any details of Aelyn Meah or a man named either Qian or Zaifyr.'

Ayae found herself swallowing her own words, her protest against Tinh Tu's power, her commands. She almost spoke when she heard her name mentioned later. At that moment she felt, more than any time before, a culpability in what was taking place before her, and felt it so keenly it could have been a weight in her hand. She heard again the words of the Mireean and Yeflam soldiers and saw the same desperation and resentment in the Lord of Faaisha and his marshals. She felt her hands curl up, but did not say a word.

'Ranan will not be easy to lay siege to,' Eidan said, from beside her. 'Under no circumstances are you to enter the ravines that cut around and through it. You will need bridges that can be moved into position during the battle to cross them. When you leave, you will see that we have dismantled ships to build ours. I would estimate that you will need a hundred for the size of your force, but that number may change. Once the battle begins, the bridges that connect the five parts of Ranan together will be destroyed, and these temporary bridges will be the only way for us to move from section to section. They will need to be mobile and they will need to be protected. The soldiers you assign to them will be under constant fire and will need to be steady hands. You will also be well advised to bring catapults. They will not be able to hit the centre of Ranan, which is marked by the cathedral, but they will be able to help clear the way for an initial landing.'

'Ranan will soon hold close to thirty-four thousand soldiers,' Jae'le said, from the other side of Ayae. 'The majority of these are Leeran and were once the population of Leera itself. They will be joined by Faaishan and Gogari soldiers. You will find that they are aware of our arrival, and that they have prepared by fortifying Ranan, and by placing various weapons such as ballistas, catapults and towers around the city. However, it is not these that will be the most dangerous of the foes you face. In the centre of Ranan, there is a small force. This force is led by the man known as the Innocent. The soldiers who serve under Aela Ren are unique. They cannot be killed by the likes of you and me. They can only be struck down.'

Eidan spoke next. After he had finished, Jae'le spoke, again. They spoke for close to an hour in this manner, outlining what they knew of Ranan, the type of forces within, the resistance that they would face, the things that they were likely to see. For the hour, Ayae said nothing. She listened to the two men and thought of the scarred walls of her youth, but rather than the terror she so often felt when she recalled the Innocent, a strange sadness came over her, instead. It added to the weight that she felt from her part in watching Tinh Tu issue her commands, and it kept her standing in the inn after the Lord of Faaisha and his marshals were led outside by Eidan and Jae'le.

After the door closed, she said, 'This is not the way we should be doing this. It makes us no better than the Innocent or any god.'

'We are no better.' Tinh Tu's voice no longer echoed with her power. She rose from the seat and turned to Ayae. 'But what choice do we have?' she asked. 'It must be this way.'

'This way?' Ayae gave a half-laugh in disbelief. 'You have bent over three hundred people to your will. Eidan held a mountain range while it broke apart. And Jae'le! I listen to him tell me he has no power, but you all defer to him. Why do the three of you – the four of us – need an army?'

'I met the Innocent, long ago,' Tinh Tu said. 'My brother chained him to a tree in the depths of Faer. It was deep in swamps that altered their form like a maze. I knew this intimately because the swamps were part of my kingdom when we ruled. In that time, Aela Ren became a story for children. He was a lost prince. A knight who betrayed his honour. An honourable thief, even. No one knew who he was, so he could be anything. For cartographers, he became a quest connected to mapping the swamps of Faer. For most, it was a quest that went unfulfilled. But one day, a woman returned to me in a state of great fever and illness, claiming she had found him. After she died, I used her notes to make my way deep into the swamps, into the middle of its tangled, ever-changing heart. It took me nearly a year to navigate those paths. For the longest time, I thought that the swamps were the creation of a dead god, but they weren't. They were my brother's creation. I could see that clearly the deeper that I went into the swamps. But I saw it mostly on the evening that I entered a small clearing and found a man who was neither a knight nor a prince nor a thief. When I found Aela Ren.

'My first thought upon seeing him was that he was a monk, for he bore the pain of his prison in a grave silence. The myth my people told was that Aela Ren was in a cage, but that was not true. Rather, a cage was kept inside him. Wood had been coaxed and grown out of a dozen trees and pushed through him. It pierced and tore his skin apart and shattered his bones and burst his eyes and dislocated his limbs. I know the wounds he received because I watched them for a week. I watched as his flesh was torn and broke and healed again and again as every movement and every breath he took, moved the living cage in him.'

Ayae stood, horrified despite herself. She saw the Innocent held against the tree, a solitary, tortured figure, a man who would repeat his horror in her home, hundreds of years later.

'Jae'le did that. He made the prison and the swamp and he never told anyone about it.' Tinh Tu's scarred lips pressed together. 'I have not asked him why he did it, because I know why. I talked to Aela Ren in his prison. I asked him who he was and what he had done and he refused to answer me. I asked him with all my power and he still refused. In fact, he told me he recognized the power. "It is not my master's power," he said to me. "It is not truth, but I recognize it. I can see Aeisha in you. The Goddess of the Word. She would struggle to ask anything of me, just like you."'

'But,' she began. 'But surely he wasn't right?'

'He was. After a week, I realized that, before this man, my power was fleeting, and nothing more. Eventually, I did get answers from him, but not all. Even in that prison, he had enough power to recognize and fight me.' She turned to Ayae. 'Now, ask yourself, how much harder will it be to kill such a man when he is not imprisoned? How much harder when he is surrounded by his kin? You are right about the things we can do, Ayae. We are powerful and we can do truly awful things. But in the battle before us, we will need these people. We will need them to protect us. To answer when our powers falter before those who were empowered by gods, those who understand what it was to be divine before we were born. We will need them because we cannot defeat the god-touched without them. But we cannot trust them to stand by our side by their own free will. How can we, after all that they have seen?'

10.

Orlan woke him after the morning's sun had passed its zenith.

'Use the bed in the room across from here,' the cartographer whispered, guiding him from the chair beside Taela, and out of the room. Exhausted, Bueralan did not resist. His body felt heavy, as if the steel Taela felt within her was part of him, was his bones and his muscles. He realized only after Orlan had pulled a sheet over him that Kaze had not returned to the room. *Have you seen her?* The old man shook his head. 'She's somewhere,' Samuel Orlan said, a note in his voice Bueralan could not make out. 'Just not here.' The cartographer was clean and wore fine clothes, not the old, worn pieces he had lived in since Ooila. The sight gave Bueralan a small satisfaction. Orlan looked like himself, like the man he had met in Mireea, a lifetime ago. The man who had plotted against a new god, the man who had taken a risk and failed.

But in his dreams, Bueralan dreamed of darkness. He could see nothing, not even himself. He was not alone. He could feel another presence around him, almost as if it was smothering him, but he could not name it. It felt familiar, however. His thoughts drifted. He thought that he was in prison. He had been captured. He had been locked in a cell. He had been buried in the ground in that cell. He could reach out and touch both bars and stone, only to find that neither existed. Instead, there waited for him a huge expanse, an existence he had not previously considered, one without definitions or limits. The prison, he realized then, was not a real one but a philosophical one, one of imagination. Its walls were his failings. Were himself. He was trapped in them because he wanted to trapped. Yet, even as he began to explore this idea, the darkness began to define itself. It was taking on a shape, having a beginning and an end. But there was more beyond it, a second creation. When he reached out, he felt the first world contract around him, lock around his hands, hold him tightly. At first, he wanted to draw his hand back, but when he could not, he pushed forwards, to try and break the barrier, to escape the world that was now suffocating him, making him scream again and again as the borders and shapes emerged around him and sought to stop him from gaining freedom.

Bueralan awoke to the sound of fading screams.

He pushed himself from the bed, two steps taking him to the door, into the hall, a third and fourth to the door of Taela's room, and the destruction within it.

He saw Orlan first. The old man lay against the doorframe, his body pointed outwards, as if he had been trying to get into the hallway, to call for help. As Bueralan turned into the room, he saw the blood that soaked Orlan's lower half, the broken shape of his back, snapped as if he were a toy. It had not happened at the door, however. Orlan had crawled to the door after he had been struck down, after his spine was broken, after flesh was dug out of his back.

After he had risen to help Taela.

She had gone into labour. Bueralan took her hand, still warm, and wet with blood. She had screamed, he knew. Her face showed that. She had screamed, but not in the voice he had heard in his dreams. No. Bueralan had heard another scream, the scream of a child being born, of the soul of his blood brother ripping at Taela's stomach, tearing into her flesh, desperate to be free. He could think of nothing else but the words Taela had said when they had been on *Glafanr*, how she had told him of a clawing inside her, as if the child was trying to escape, to break her open, like a chick in an egg. He could see that, even through the blood, through the mess, through the tears he knew were running down his face.

Behind him, Bueralan heard steps.

'Poor old fool.' Aelyn Meah. He did not turn to her. Instead, he held on to Taela's hand, held on to it, though she could not hold on to him. 'Poor child,' Aelyn said, coming up to the bed. She did not reach out to Bueralan. 'She said this would happen. It was one of the few conversations we had. She said this child . . .' She did not finish her sentence. After a moment, she said, 'I do not see Kaze here.'

'I don't think she was here,' he said.

'No, I think – I think she knew what was going to happen.' It surprised him to hear her repeat her words. 'Did you see the child?'

'No.' He cleared his throat. 'Is it with . . . ?'

'It is not in the cathedral.' Aelyn indicated to her right. 'It went out of the window.'

The frame was broken, the glass shattered. There was blood, and the blood was smeared in small, sharp hand prints.

He laid Taela's hand down and went to the window. The midday's sun was on the rise, but the morning's sun had not yet set, and the two broken shards sat at opposite ends of the horizon. Bueralan could see crowds of Leerans, the shapes of catapults, with a smattering of swamp crows perched along the arms, and he could see the small shadow that was running further and further away.

'I would have thought it would have stayed here,' Aelyn said. 'I would have thought that the child would want to meet its mother.'

She did not mean Taela. 'No,' Bueralan said.

'How can you be sure? This is nothing we have seen before.'

'The soul she used to make his child was once my blood brother.' He turned back to Taela, to Orlan, to the violence of their deaths.

'He will be horrified by what he has done. If he knows. If he is there.'

'You don't know,' Aelyn said, a note of sympathy in her voice that surprised him. 'He could be mad. Her creation could have nothing to do with your brother.'

'I know.' Bueralan reached down and closed Taela's eyes, closed them to the horror of the child she had given birth to, closed them even though he knew she would still be looking down at herself, at the flesh she no longer had. 'But he is still my responsibility.'

11.

Celp smouldered.

At the entrance to the town, at the broken wall Refuge had ridden through nearly a week ago, Heast and Aela Ren dismounted. Both horses baulked at entering the ruins. At first, Heast thought it was because of the warmth that lingered in the ground, the heat that was kept alive by the dull orange that threaded through the ruins like worn veins. But after he stepped through the break in the stone, he realized he was mistaken: the two horses had not responded to the warmth, but to the coldness that caused his skin prickle.

There was no wind, but yet it felt as if the cold was swirling around him. His good leg could feel it most strongly, the chill biting through his boot.

'How strange,' the Innocent said from beside him. 'I half expect it to snow.'

He had never seen it snow in this part of the world. 'Is this your god?' Heast asked. He began to walk forwards, leading the other man towards the centre of town. 'Is she watching you?'

'No.' Ren did not hesitate in his reply. 'But this is her doing.'

Ahead, the remains of Celp's buildings lay in broken arrangements on either side of the road: the roofs of houses had fallen in and exposed splintered, blackened framework. The houses built from brick were the ones that remained standing, pieces of the walls like strange maps that threaded up from the ground to the roof. In other buildings, the black framework rose from ruins and ended in sudden, snapped pieces.

The chill increased with each step Heast took and, halfway along the road to the centre of the town, he passed a wide open space of rubble. It was close to where he and Oya had charged through a building, to emerge on the other side. Around the ruins lay blackened bodies and, though they had been dead for nearly a week, Heast could not smell any hint of decay. Yet, gazing at their remains, the Captain of Refuge could not believe how he and Oya had survived the fires and destruction around them. He could not believe any of them had, in truth, and the thought reminded him briefly of the cold haunts in Mireea, the white-lined figures of the dead who had stood around him and the others after the Leeran siege.

'My soldiers have been in here twice since we fought,' he said, pushing the thought from his mind. 'They said the cold was only around Waalstan's body. They said that no decay touched his body and that he still bled from the wound that killed him.'

'Could they lift him?' Aela Ren asked.

'No.'

'He has been made a saint, then.'

'A saint?' Heast could not remember when he had last heard the word. 'Why would a god make a dead man a saint?'

'You look for reason where there may well be none.' The street narrowed: the ruined, burned buildings closed around them. The still-smouldering stone and wood appeared stronger here, but the coldness was more pronounced. 'The gods had saints before the war. They were, by and large, servants such as priests and soldiers. After they died, the gods would trap their souls in the body. In a fashion, they were still alive, though the men and women had no control over their bodies. They could not move, could not speak, could not partake in any of life's joy. I do not know if they could see out of their eyes, or hear, or smell, but the soul being so trapped ensured that the body did not decay. Their bodies could only be moved by the gods' faithful.'

The centre of Celp opened before them, suddenly. The huge square was surrounded by black rubble and dominated by bodies in various states of stalled decay. The cold had stopped that, just as it had stopped the smell of rot. In addition to that, it gave a sheen to the dirty, silver armour that encased Ekar Waalstan's body.

On his chest a faint circle glowed, as if a part of the sun was trying to burst from him.

'Does it bother you that a god would do this to a loyal servant?' Heast asked.

'Ask me instead if I am surprised.' The Innocent walked around Waalstan's body, stopping at the broken shape of his skull. 'The blood still runs free, here.'

'What has she done to win your loyalty?' Heast asked. 'I would not accept this in any man or woman I served.'

'I have done worse, have I not?' When Heast did not reply, Ren shrugged. 'The answer is not a complex one, Captain. She is a god. She will redefine this world. She will take away our anarchy.'

'Our freedom?'

'If you had been alive when the gods had walked this world, you would not compare the two. A god does not take away your freedom, I assure you.'

'What would happen if your gods returned?' The cold had begun to numb Heast's good leg, but he did not move away from Waalstan's body. 'Would you be loyal to your master again?'

'Look around you, Captain. Not just at this city, but at the world. How in this world can any of the old gods return? Their bodies are broken, their divinity scattered, their creation scarred like I am.' The Innocent held out his hands, palm up, to emphasize his point.

'They will not return. They cannot. Time draws to an end for all of them. Ger's tomb has crumbled. The mountains are in ruin. More gods will follow him into nothing. You and I stand in the final acts of their divine existence. We stand in their destruction.'

He bent down, then, and lifted Ekar Waalstan from the ground. Heast was prepared for him to stand again, for him to be unable to lift the body, but Ren raised the General as if he weighed nothing. The coldness that had spread through the square, through all of Celp, broke as he did. A light spread from Waalstan. It poured from his head, from the wound that had been bleeding but a moment ago. It was light, now, a whiteness, and purity, that filtered over Aela Ren, highlighting his scars, the violence that his body embodied.

The Innocent did not say another word to Heast. Quietly, he carried Se'Saera's saint down the street, the light a nimbus surrounded him until he reached his horse.

Refuge waited there. They waited at the edge of Celp, mounted on their horses as if they, like the two horses Heast and Ren rode, had baulked at the entrance of the town. Lieutenant Lehana sat at the head, her bastard sword unsheathed and held across her lap. Heast did not believe that she would attack Ren. He did not know why he thought that: he had no sign from her, or from Taaira, or Anemone, who sat beside her, but he knew that Lehana would not. Instead, she allowed Refuge to part, to create a path for the Innocent to leave.

Aela Ren did not take it immediately. Instead, he laid the saint's body over the saddle of his horse, and took the reins in his scarred hand. For a dozen heartbeats, he met the gazes of Lehana and the soldiers around him, as if he was gauging them, as if he was committing their faces to memory. Then, after a brief nod, Aela Ren walked down the aisle they had made for him.

Heast did not give the order for any to follow the Innocent. He did not need to. He knew where the scarred man was going, knew that he and Refuge would be there, soon enough. He pulled himself onto his horse and, in the silent company of Refuge, rode back to their camp.

He was halfway to the camp when Kal Essa's scouts found him.

Brother Mother
Sister Father

'After.' Aelyn Meah paused. I was surprised to see how much she grieved for a woman she barely knew. 'After, Bueralan and I went in search of the child.

'I knew my family was closing in on Ranan. In a way, that made it easier for me to leave. I think, even then, I knew what was to come.

'Bueralan Le hunted the child. He was not so dissimilar to the god-touched, not really. A lot has been said of him in recent years but, for all that people have spoken about him being so different, so unique, he was a man defined by loss. I think the great difference between Bueralan and the others such as Aela Ren, was that Bueralan could process his loss. Given enough time, he would grieve like us, and move on, after.

'Given enough time.'

—Onaedo, *Histories, Year 1029*

1.

Beneath the midday's sun, the streets beyond the cathedral of Ranan were full. Bueralan would find himself at the end of a bridge, or at a corner, or walking along a street, and his internal map would be broken not by the barricades, or deviations to the streets, but by the sheer number of men and women around him. They spilled out of flat-roofed houses into the streets. They sat on piles of stone for the catapults, missiles ranging from the size of his head to the size of his torso. They sat on the wooden frames of barricades, stood by huge ballistas, and on top of towers that had been pulled into the city, all of them deep in conversation. '—Faa-isha—' 'Se'Saera has said within the week—' 'She has seen—' 'More than one force?' '—victory.' Their voices threaded around him, a mix of the traders' tongue, of Leeran, none of it hidden by silence, or code, as Bueralan passed. That did not surprise him, but the awareness the Faithful had of him did. He had seen it before, in the attention they paid to the god-touched, but he had not thought that it would extend to him. He was continually caught off-guard by men and women who gave him short nods of greeting, stepped out of his way, and even went as far as to greet him by name, referring to him as 'Lord Bueralan'. Aelyn Meah, who walked beside him, was not once greeted by name, despite the fact that many of the Faithful would have known her by sight and by reputation.

It was how the Faithful treated her that made it clear to Bueralan that he was expected to walk down the streets of Ranan. That not only was he was meant to be walking here, but that he was meant to do so with Aelyn Meah beside him. The Faithful's greetings were Se'Saera's way of letting him know that. Aelyn must have noticed, just as he did, but her face was still, and he could not read the emotions on it. He had been unable to do so since they had left the cathedral.

'My brother is upstairs,' she had said, before they left. 'He is on the top floor. Our new god has him laid out on the ground. She is trying to bring him back to life.'

Bueralan had put sheets over Orlan and Taela. Bloodstains had begun to leave an outline of their bodies, of their wounds, through it. 'Why?'

'I don't know,' she said. 'Zilt and the last of his monsters are with her, but they say nothing the wind can repeat to me.'

Bueralan remembered the shifting breezes in her room before he left Ranan and did not ask her what she meant by the last.

'When my brother died,' Aelyn continued, 'when he came back, he did not know who he was, then. In that state, he can perform great horrors. I assume our new god knows this.'

He began to walk to the door. 'There are enough atrocities already. Maybe you ought to try and stop this one.'

'You think I want this to happen?' Her words stopped him, but before he could speak, she continued. 'I would be careful with my words, if I were you, Bueralan. Responsibility for this does not fall onto many. It falls to one. Just one. She is creating everything that is happening here. She may not be fully aware of how she does it, but this is her creation we are standing in. It speaks to us of pain and suffering and I am not immune to that. Do you think your blood brother is anything but the face of this new world she is making?'

'New world?' His laugh was a half a huff of disbelief. 'She isn't making anything new. You are wrong when you say it is just her. Mother, father, son, daughter. It's the same poisonous dynasty around us.'

Aelyn did not disagree, did not say much until Bueralan picked up his sword, and strapped it around his waist. There, she offered to take him out of Ranan, and as she did, the wind shifted on either side of her feet into shapes, hints of beasts. 'I'm getting my horse,' he said. There was no give in his voice and, as the room receded behind him, the stairs to the cathedral passed and the door opened to reveal the warm, midday's sun, Bueralan felt his resolve harden. He would not leave the grey here. He would not return, after he found Zean. He would not come back to Se'Saera, to Aela Ren, to the god-touched, the immortals, the Keepers of the Divine, the Faithful and, more importantly, he would not return to the dead girl whom he had failed to help.

The door to the stables shuddered open beneath the palm of his hand. Inside, shafts of light ran through gaps high in the wall, but darkness defined the space between the stalls. The grey was towards the end, Bueralan knew. The other horses, watered, and brushed, stood in their stalls and watched him pass, the light falling over half their bodies, giving them a strange radiance that, at the end of the stables, fell over Kaze in faint, golden light.

She sat on a wooden stool, her head leant back against the wall, and a bucket and brush beside her. 'It is over, is it not?' Her glasses sat on her knee, faint silver glints. 'Se'Saera's child is born.'

'You knew.' It wasn't an accusation. 'You knew when you saw me.'

Kaze's long fingers picked up her glasses, put them on. 'You got to see Taela before,' she said. 'She spent her final moments with someone she cared about. How many mortals in the service of a god can claim that?'

He was aware that, behind him, Aelyn Meah had taken two steps back, giving him privacy he did not need. 'You could have done more for her,' he said. 'You had a duty.'

'To defy my god?'

'She's not your god.'

'After all this time, you don't understand.' Kaze nodded to Aelyn. 'We're not like her. She is nothing. A fluke. A creation made by fate's whim, fit only to be consumed by Se'Saera. She is chaos. The only reason she hasn't been killed already is because Se'Saera has given orders for us not to kill her. She is supposed to be here, now. But you and I, we are different. Our fates were locked down from before we are born. Everything about us has been decided. We are the servants of a god. We are defined by that. We cannot defy a god, not for love, not for hate, not for kindness, and not for cruelty.' She rose, her slight stoop straightening as she did. 'I did as I was made to do.'

She tried to shoulder past him, but Bueralan held his arm up. 'You and I, we can't kill each other. That's how it works, right?' He met her hazel eyes. 'But I can hurt you.'

'Pain is our life.' She held his gaze. 'I would have thought you understood that by now.'

He did, and it was because of that, that he did not turn to her as she pushed past him. With long, even strides, she walked past Aelyn Meah and into the darkness of the stables. When the door shut, he turned to the grey, who had watched him with his steady dark eyes the entire time.

'Orlan's horse is in the next stall,' the saboteur said. 'We won't leave her, either.'

2.

Before Heast gave the order to ride to Ranan, before Refuge and the Brotherhood left the ash-stained air of Celp, he returned to the camp for one more night.

Heast kept the copy of *The Eternal Kingdom* in his saddlebag and did not remove it until the afternoon's sun began to rise. Before that, he spent his time talking to Essa and his soldiers and watching Lehana's reaction. At least half of the Ooilan soldiers who had served the First Queen would have fought in the war between Ooila and Qaaina. He was unsurprised, then, when the first meeting he held between Essa and Lehana turned out to be tense. Lehana stood silent and still beside Heast while Essa explained what had happened in Leera – Aela Ren's duel with Xrie, the Mountain of Ger breaking, and Bueralan Le's words – and throughout, the Captain of the Brotherhood kept looking at the Ooilan soldier, as if expecting her to attack him.

After Essa had finished, silence fell between the three of them. They stood behind the wagon where Dural had been laid, near where Heast and Taaira had buried him. 'Is there going to be a problem between you two?' he asked, after a moment.

'Qaaina was a long time ago.' The scarred mercenary shrugged. 'It isn't returning. I have no problems letting it go.'

'The Brotherhood might be a problem for some of us,' Lehana

admitted. 'We lost friends on those fields. We lost them fighting Sergeant Essa's division, in truth.'

'I'm a captain now.' He gazed at her. 'I don't remember you.'

'Armour makes it hard to distinguish sometimes.'

'Aye, but even if I did, I've been on the road too long to hold that grudge.' He glanced at Heast. 'I have no problem with your people. I followed the smoke to find you. I know what they're capable of. Me and mine will ride into Ranan beside Refuge without a problem. As for the rest?' He shrugged again and met Lehana's gaze. 'Our road is long and paved with small coins. All that holds it together is blood. My boys and girls are all we got of each other. Qaaina stopped mattering in that equation a long time ago.'

After he had left, Heast said, 'You'll fight beside worse in this life. You'll see some of it in Ranan. The Faaishan Army will not hold a line with you. The Saan will offer you nothing in battle. Indeed, they are just as likely to try and kill you afterwards. But you can trust in Kal Essa. Outside the people you lie and die with, that's a rare thing.'

Lehana nodded, but her face was impassive. 'I will tell the others that, sir.' She saluted him sharply before she left.

She would learn, he thought. Not soon, but in a few years' time, she would answer as Essa did. It would be after Ranan. After she and the other Ooilan soldiers had stood on muddy fields in Illate, after they stood beside men and women who hated them for generations of slavery, but who needed them now. But it would only happen if they survived the upcoming battle in Ranan, where immortals and gods waited beside the swords and arrows of the Faithful. Heast could still hear Ren's words, could still see him pick up Waalstan and walk out of Celp, unafraid of the soldiers who stood around him. It might be that Lieutenant Lehana would never have a chance to learn the lesson of separating a life of coin from state, Heast admitted privately to himself.

'Is it an interesting book, Captain?' Anemone asked, after the suns had risen and set, after the camp had fallen into a light slumber without incident. 'You've been reading it since you returned.'

Heast turned *The Eternal Kingdom* over in his hands. 'I thought it might offer some insights into the battle before us.'

The witch sat next to him on the log, the dark of the Faaishan forest before them, the rustle of the camp behind them. 'But it did not?'

'Not so far,' he admitted. 'It is a strange book, really. I am no scholar by any means, but it is an incomplete book, I think. It talks about a paradise you and I will go to when we die, where we will not want for anything, where we will not know fear and only know love and bliss. For that, however, we must pledge our allegiance to our new god. We must do it to such an extent that we watch our neighbours and convert them and then speak against them if they do not serve. We must not be afraid to lift the sword against them, it says at one point. It goes on like that, but then, every twenty or so pages, there will be a story about the old gods, and how they loved—' Heast stopped himself before he said Se'Saera's name. '—their child,' he said. 'On those pages, it argues that we should honour all the ways of life the old gods promoted, for they live in the new god. Those pages read very much like fragments. It returns to servitude quickly enough.'

'Why does the idea bother you? Our lives are ones of servitude.' Anemone tapped her wrist, where the hint of a tattoo showed. 'I am in the service of my grandmother and those who came before her. We are both in the service of those who pay us.'

'Both of us made those choices.'

'Are we not being offered one?'

'To believe or die is not a choice.' Heast laid the book to one side and stretched out his heavy leg. 'She speaks of one other thing, however.'

'Must I read it myself?' Anemone asked. 'Or will you tell me?'

'It is the promise of renewal, of rebirth.' He indicated the book. 'She promises paradise to those who are Faithful, but it is what she claims she will do to our world once she is complete that fascinates me. She promises to mend what the old gods did. To give us a sun that is whole, to clean the ocean of its poison, to bring back food sources and animals we have lost. She promises to make us stronger and give us longer lives.'

'It is an attractive promise.'

'It is, until you start to pull it apart, to see why a man like Faet Cohn, for example, would be part of it.'

'Oh?'

'A man whose family history is in slavery is a man who sees himself as someone better than another. He believes there are those human and those not,' Heast said. 'If I could, I would have many things returned to us. I would see the species we have lost brought back to life, for example. It is a terrible thing to think that a living creature has stopped existing. For myself, I do not know that one sun or three is preferable, but I would see the ocean free of poison, and the Mad Coast rendered safe. But if those are only achieved by going back to a way of life we have left, then I am not supportive of it. We must go forwards.'

'And so we will go forwards?' Anemone reached over his leg for *The Eternal Kingdom*. 'To Ranan?'

He was surprised by the question in her voice. 'You would rather not?'

'What we saw in Celp bothers me. My grandmother tells me I should simply accept what I saw. I will see its like again, she assures me.' With the book in her hand, she met Heast's gaze, and he saw not Anemone, not the witch of Refuge, but rather the young woman he had met months ago, the woman who had not long ago been a child, and who had not left her town unless it was in the safe presence of her grandmother. 'But I see men and women in my dreams. They are burning. They are the people I know. They are you and Kye and the rest of Refuge. I want to make them stop, but I do not know how to.'

'Time stops them. Nothing else.' He did not reach out to her. 'I will not make you ride to Ranan with us, not if you do not wish. You can return home and forget all this.'

'I do not have a home outside Refuge.'

'I can find you one,' he said gently. 'If it is what you want.'

Later, after the morning's sun broke through the treelines and after Heast gave the order to break camp, Anemone rode out beside the Captain of Refuge towards Ranan.

3.

Nearly four dozen swamp crows sat, or walked, along the wooden bridges Eidan had built from the slavers' ships. When Ayae approached with a pair of horses, the birds turned to stare at her, but did not lift into the air.

'I think they like you,' Jae'le said from behind.

'Which one is yours?' she asked without turning. 'They all look the same to me.'

One of the crows who sat at the edge of the bridge lifted into the air. 'People often say that about each other, as well.' The crow settled on Jae'le's shoulder and he scratched its head. 'It is as wrong then as it is now.'

'That one looks smaller than yesterday's.'

'Does it?'

With a smile, he led not just his horses, but Ayae's, around the bridges and began, quietly and calmly, to attach the harnesses to each that would allow them to pull them to Ranan.

The rest of Tinh Tu's forces were also busy preparing to leave Gtara. The action had, to some extent, given a physical release to the resentment and anger that simmered in the camp, but Ayae knew that it was not gone. Last night, after Lord Tuael and his soldiers had left, she had gone out in search of Vune and the other soldiers from Mireea and Yeflam. She had in mind to talk to them, to help ease their situation. She found them in a small building on the other side of Gtara, but they had not been welcoming. Vune answered her questions shortly and stiffly and, after a while, Ayae left the building.

Her first instinct was to return to Tinh Tu and tell her that it did not matter what the god-touched could do, or could not do, what they were doing to the soldiers was wrong, and it had to stop.

But she didn't.

Instead, she stood in the middle of Gtara, near where she and Jae'le had found the remains of the Keepers and the slavers, near where the wire of the slave pen had been half formed. *We're doing nothing different. We're just like the slavers, just like the gods.* When she closed her eyes, however, she saw the walls of the town in Sooia, and the people living behind it. She saw the small crops, the wells that had gone dry, the others where access was rationed. If Se'Saera and the Innocent were not defeated at Ranan, that would be the fate of any who did not become the god's Faithful. They would live lives of desperation and of withered hopes and opportunities. *Or like this.* Like the soldiers around her, unless she was wrong. After all, Se'Saera was a god and she could do anything she wanted once she was complete.

But Ayae did not believe she was wrong.

She stared at the stars, at the darkness, and imagined the god within that, a force capable of reaching out, of changing the fates of people, of using them as if she owned them, as if they were a tool for a project she worked on.

'How long until the horses are ready?' Tinh Tu asked, breaking Ayae's thoughts. She had stepped out of the hotel, her white raven on the top of her staff. 'We have four days' ride to Ranan and I do not want to delay it.'

'Soon.' Jae'le stood between two docile horses as he attached the harness that would drag the bridges. A swamp crow – one larger than before, Ayae was sure – stood on the back of the first horse. 'Have you decided what we will do with our brother and sister, yet?'

'We will get both back. Or, more precisely, you two will.'

'We don't know where they are,' Ayae said, caught off-guard by the order. 'We do not have scouts, or spies in the city.'

'They are in the cathedral,' Jae'le said. 'Zaifyr is on the top floor. Aelyn is allowed to move freely on the lower floors.'

'How do—?' She stopped herself. 'Birds. The crows tell you?'

He smiled. 'Whispers in the ear.'

'He has a habit of keeping things to himself,' Tinh Tu said, a note of irritation in her voice. 'But you, Ayae, will make sure he does not slip off to deal with old vendettas.'

Jae'le shrugged, unconcerned by either her tone, or what she said. 'It has taken time to learn most of it. At any rate, sister, you have been busy holding our forces together. And you will need to continue doing that in Ranan. Why don't you leave Aelyn and Zaifyr to me? Ayae can help you in the battle.'

'You are not the Animal Lord any more, brother.'

He stopped, a leather strap in his hand. Behind him, one of the crows let out a squawk as if in indignation. 'The last mirror I saw revealed only my reflection,' Jae'le said.

'Did it reveal the man who has not eaten for over a thousand years? These crows do not gather around you in friendship, but because they wait for you to fall over.' Tinh Tu let out a frustrated sigh. 'You and I both know that once he learns you are there, he will hunt you.'

'He will hunt us all.'

'That is why you will need Ayae.'

They meant the Innocent, they meant – 'I think . . .' Ayae took a breath to calm her voice. 'Look, I am happy to avoid Aela Ren.'

'You cannot give her this task,' Jae'le said. 'She has only known him as a figure of fear.'

'Who else is there to give it to? The Saan? Would you like some of Miat Dvir's favourites to shadow you?' Tinh Tu made a dismissive sound. 'They are not worth a thing next to her.'

'It is true: they would just die.' He returned to the harness. 'But do not ask this of her, sister.'

'You cannot do this alone.'

'I'm here, y'know?' Ayae stepped between the two. 'Don't treat me the way you treat the others. I can hear you just fine.'

'Then don't let him out of your sight.' Tinh Tu began to walk away. 'Don't let him fight that man by himself, sister. He isn't what he once was.'

Frustrated, she glanced at Jae'le, who offered a faint shrug. Without a word, he scratched the head of a crow – this one smaller than the previous two – and returned to attaching the harnesses to the horses, who waited with a patience she had rarely seen in an animal.

4.

The swamps turned into marshes, the marshes turned into the coastline, but Zean's trail remained a broken line with no end.

Bueralan tried not to call the creature Zean, but no matter how he tried to replace it – he used Se'Saera's child, Taela's child, creature, and even monster – he returned to Zean. As the trail he and Aelyn Meah followed wound further and further from Ranan, Bueralan told himself that it was not truly his blood brother whom he followed, that it wasn't the man he had known whom he was hunting, and, in truth, there was evidence of that. The tracks, while human, had a long stride to them, longer than any man or woman could make, and the feet that made them were narrow, rather like a child's, further adding to the likelihood that the physiology of a human had been altered by Se'Saera. But, as both Bueralan and Aelyn said at one point or another to each other, that was not a surprise given the length and size of Taela's pregnancy. The remains of feeding – bloody swamp crows torn apart by sharp teeth – did not suggest a human child, either, just as the waste Zean left was likewise not recognizable. But for Bueralan, Zean's name persisted, and after two days, he stopped trying to call him anything different.

On the third day, he and Aelyn came across the first of the Faaishan forces marching upon Leera.

They appeared first as scouts, riders moving in pairs, easy enough to avoid. Bueralan could have killed them, but he had little desire, and little need. Aelyn was no different. The two of them did not even discuss the fact that battle would soon break out. They had both been living with the expectation since Se'Saera had returned to Ranan. It was inevitable. The only question was if he or Aelyn would return to Ranan to take part. That question was not one that they asked each other, not even when the larger bodies of the Faaishan force began to appear. The two simply continued to follow Zean's trail and skirt the forces. The only real moment of interest was when, at the end of the third day, the trail led them to the edge of a logging camp.

There was not much that could be made from the trees in Leera, but from Zean's empty camp, Bueralan and Aelyn watched the Faaishans felling trees. A second group, Bueralan saw, were assembling bridges, binding the wood together with a mix of nails and ropes.

'He watched them as well,' Aelyn said, pointing to a collection of crow remains. 'He was here half a day.'

Hopefully that meant they were closing in on him.

'I think he is growing,' she added. 'His tracks are bigger.'

Bueralan had noticed that, as well. 'The strides get longer, as if he is jumping, rather than running.'

On the fourth day, they came to an abandoned town. Once, it would had been a trader's stop, a single gate in a simple, wooden wall. Beyond it was a single street, a handful of dirty paths and two dozen buildings. It was a town on the way to somewhere else. Bueralan had seen hundreds of its like, but this town, whatever its name, was no longer that: its wall had been torn down, taken over a year ago when Se'Saera's War began, and beyond the gate, the buildings were skeletons, perches to a dwindling population of swamp crows. In the middle of what remained of the town, the strongest collection of birds burst out in angry flight at their approach and revealed the body of a soldier.

'Zean did this,' Aelyn said, crouched over the bloody remains. 'You can smell the scent in the air. Like rotting meat.'

The scent was new. When they had left Ranan, it had been blood, but that scent had not been perfect. It could be anyone's blood, Aelyn said, after the trail disappeared, and reappeared. Bueralan had relied upon the tracks in the ground, but it was clear that the longer their chase continued, the more Zean grew, not just in size, but smell, and appetite. 'He must have dragged this scout here.' The saboteur walked past Aelyn and the body, to the edge of building's frame. The low marshes ran out into the afternoon's setting sun, the dark line of Leviathan's Blood on the horizon. 'The tracks come in this way.'

'He has eaten part of the flesh here.'

He is Se'Saera's child, he wanted to say.

Away from the body, at the edge of the town, they made a small camp. Bueralan could have pushed on, into the night, as he had done after leaving Ranan, but he was reluctant to do that now. He realized that he had slowed, had allowed himself to be diverted. He was unwilling to run down Zean in these last few miles. He was weighed down by grief and anger. He had slept poorly for the last nights, images of Taela and Orlan in his dreams, mixed with Zean, the Zean he had known, clawing out of Taela's stomach, and he would shift between being furious and wracked by grief. Beside him, Aelyn said nothing, though she must have noticed, for she let him set the pace. He suspected that she knew where Zean was, though he did not know why she was reluctant to reach him, as well.

'Years ago,' she said, sitting next to him in the remains of a building, lit by the stars above, 'I was given the present of a book of writings by a scholar called Irue Tq. My sister gave it to me as a birthday present.' Aelyn smiled. 'We don't celebrate birthdays often, really, so it was a surprise. But my sister has never been the most subtle of us and there was a point to it. Irue Tq was born well before the War of the Gods and was known as the Fifth Philosopher. Tq argued that the number was one of balance, one that symbolized humans, both physically, and in relation to their senses. The book my sister sent wasn't complete. I don't think she has been able to compile a complete edition due to its age, but what she had was enough to read. It was about the impact of the gods on the evolution of humanity.'

'How we've changed?' Bueralan asked.

'Bear in mind, this was before the gods died. What Tq argued was that the gods were resistant to change. They were forces that denied evolution. He argued that the gods treated all living creatures as if they were complete. He used the example of a raven, primarily. He said that the bird had been slowly developing the ability to speak but that, on the cusp of it, the gods had taken away the ability. He argued that the gods had done this, not just with ravens, but with all creatures, but primarily with humans. He said our technology, our intellectual pursuits, our ideas of the world, had not changed in thousands and thousands of years, and he claimed that this was a state maintained by the gods. He had a list of examples of experiments sabotaged, of philosophers burned at the stake, but the one that stayed with me related to literature. He had apparently spent some time collating the number of people who could read, and who could not, and argued that the number had remained static for over five thousand years.'

'That's hardly surprising. Even now, there are nations where illiteracy is high because of the poverty they live in.' Bueralan suspected he knew what she was going to argue, however. 'Are you saying our new god is going to take us back to that?'

'As I said before, Zean is her vision of the future. We will see what that is soon enough.' Aelyn shrugged. 'No, what I am talking about is something different. I am talking about the notion of being unable to make a choice, or rather, being forced to make a choice defined by someone more powerful than you. The gods create the outcomes. You and I make a choice, but what choice is that really? Tq argued that the gods kept us blind because of that. He said that we would never be truly free while they existed. It is something that I can feel at this moment. I can feel it through my entire being. No matter what we do when we find Zean, there will be an outcome that serves our new god, or our old gods, but none that serves us.'

Bueralan did not tell her that she had been that figure. He did not need to. Aelyn Meah was not above the self-awareness required to see the hypocritical nature of her concern.

It was enough, however, for her to indulge his reluctance to reach Zean. Enough for her to sit beside him and watch the night stars brighten and lighten until the morning's sun began to rise. They said little to each during the night. Aelyn was lost in her thoughts, just as he was in his. Bueralan had the deaths of enough people to keep him company, and he supposed, if Aelyn's thoughts were like his, then she had her own deaths, and her own regrets.

In the morning, the two of them followed the trail that led down to the coast, followed the fresh smell of blood that rose from the ocean, followed it like a scent.

In the last hours of the day, they found Zean.

5.

Laena

Eilona paused and dipped her quill into a small ink pot. It was the second of two she had carried from Pitak.

I do not know how this letter will find you. I do not know how any of the letters I have written will find you. I tell myself that you do not expect any yet. I tell myself you are back in Faer, back at the dig site, and you know the mail will take a long time to arrive. I tell myself that, even though I know Se'Saera's arrival could have changed everything for you and you could still be in Pitak. You could be waiting. I try not to imagine your concern.

I try.

Once I have finished, I will place this letter with the others in my bag. I hope that, in the event of something terrible happening in the next twenty-four hours, they can be delivered to you. If it is to be granted by anyone who might be reading this, who has found it in my bag, I want it known that the delivery of this letter is my final wish. Consider it payment for sharing my newly found tea with another, not so long ago.

Laena, the afternoon's sun has begun to set. It has turned the sky outside my window a dirty red, like old blood.

As I write this, two men and a small guard are arriving by boat. The two men are named Faje Metura and Nymar Alahn. They will be brought to my mother for a meeting. The man she shares her power with has insisted on this and my mother, who is growing weary, agreed. Just a moment ago, I watched her and half a dozen others walk over to the island where Faje and Nymar and their guard will disembark. Recently, the same island was a prison to my mother and the Mireean people. Its use today, however, is not a calculated insult, but a necessity: it is impossible to land on Yeflam's shoreline. Mud-slides over the last week have made it unsafe. At night, when the shadows are darkest, to look out at the shore is to look at a different world, one freshly made.

When they return from the island, a meeting will be held in my mother and stepfather's house. I will be in attendance for that. I will listen to Faje Metura tell my mother that if she wishes to have a city for the Mireean people in his new Yeflam, she will have to give him the people who are 'cursed'. It is an offer she will not take, and rightly so. I have seen with my own eyes what the Faithful do to the people who have been changed by the divinity of the gods, but it is not even for that reason that it should not be done. You cannot create a haven by denying others sanctuary. My mother sees that very clearly, but she has little support. The man she shares power with, Lian Alahn, will not agree. He will see the price of 'cursed' flesh as a small one.

I have begun to think that my mother and the god Ain share a common trait. Like the god, my mother has spent a lifetime placing representatives of herself in Mireea and Yeflam. They are made flesh, not stone, but still, her enemies have hunted them, much as the gods hunted Ain's statues during the war. With each one that crumbled, a part of him was lost, and with each part of my mother's network gone, so is she diminished. I no longer believe she can rely on any but four people, if I include myself, and I fear she realizes that.

Eilona dipped the quill, tapped the side of the bottle. She did know how many times she had repeated the action during the letter so far, but she was conscious of it now. Each tap marked a second. Outside, a thin layer of the afternoon's dirty light remained.

I do not consider myself a courageous woman, Laena. Of the two of us, it is you who would face this moment more bravely. You would raise your fists. You who would not be cowed. You who would seek to protect me.

But I do not wish you here. Not for this.

Whatever happens in the next few hours will happen. I will do my best, though as yet, I do not know what my best will be. I hope that I am not a bystander. I hope that whatever story emerges from tonight is one that you can be proud of. But as I said, I am not a brave woman.

In life, in death, please know that I loved you, Laena, and that I love you still.

She cleaned the quill with a small rag, wrapped it in a different cloth, screwed the lid on her ink bottle and placed both with the letter in her bag.

Eilona stared around the bare room she was in and took a breath. She had been on the verge of tears at the end of her letter, and she needed to compose herself before she walked outside. A part of her wished she had a knife. The breath she took was dirty, but no breath in Neela was clean. A knife: she could hold a knife. It would have been something to hold as she left the room and stepped into the grimy, dying light of the day.

Outside her house, Eilona could see a line of figures entering her mother's house, and at the end of them walked the shadowed figures of Sinae Al'tor and his blonde guard. In the last few days she had tried to warn her mother about him, to tell her what she thought, but there had been no time to speak to her alone. In the few moments Eilona thought to push the subject, she baulked. What could she say? That Sinae has said he fears death? That the return of a god has changed him? Of course he should fear death, of course Se'Saera should affect him.

She was the last to enter her mother's house. The guard on the outside, a thickset man with his face wrapped to protect him against the dirt, opened the door for her, revealing the packed room inside.

A long table sat in the middle of the room, filled with glasses and water jugs. The other day, Lian Alahn had had it delivered, and it soaked up much of the room. On one side of it – the side closest to the door where Eilona came in – sat Faje Metura and Nymar Alahn. Next to them were six Faithful, two women, four men, and none of them was armed.

'I'm sorry I'm late,' she said to her mother. 'Have I missed much?'

'We haven't begun.' Muriel Wagan sat on the other side of Faje and Nymar. Beside her, Lian Alahn wore sombre finery to match the simple greys and blacks that her mother wore. On the left of the table, closest to the Lady of the Ghosts, sat Reila and Olcea, while Sinae and his guard sat on the right, next to Lian Alahn. Behind them, Caeli and Captain Oake stood patiently, the arms of the first clasped behind her back, while the latter, her arm free of a splint, held them crossed over her chest. 'Now that everyone is here,' her mother said said, turning to Faje, 'I trust we can begin?'

'We can,' he said. 'However, this will be a simple meeting, Lady Wagan. At the end of it, we expect the cursed to be delivered in chains, outside.'

'What makes you think I will agree to that?'

'Because I have already agreed,' Lian Alahn said, irritated. 'I have grown tired of your politics, Lady Wagan. You are but a refugee here, with no claim, either through birth or blood, to any of Yeflam. I will not see you continue to shatter it, when we could, tonight, unify it.'

6.

From where she stood, Eilona saw the tired resignation on her mother's face. 'You're such a fool, Lian,' she said, without surprise. 'The people before you are not interested in unifying Yeflam. They wish to command it. They will use hatred, fear and greed to do that. They will subvert the honest by convincing them they must forgo their independence to protect the lives that they have. In the years after that, they will divide friends and family to ensure no one will rise against them. They will educate new children to believe that the laws they make are right, that anyone who questions them is disloyal, and those who criticize them deserve punishment.' She sighed and turned to him. 'Have you not seen these things before? Have you not read history?'

'I will not be lectured by a stateless woman like yourself,' Alahn said angrily, rising from his seat. 'I have indulged you too long, and it must end now.'

'Please, there is no need for this.' Faje interrupted and held up both his hands for peace. 'Please understand, Lady Wagan, we are here as a courtesy to you. The cursed that are here are your people, and we wish to make this as painless as possible. Your misguided beliefs are not helping the matter.'

Behind her mother, Caeli caught Eilona's eye. The guard's blue-eyed gaze flicked to her left, to the Yeflam Captain who stood calmly in acceptance of what had been said and, Eilona thought, Sinae and his guard.

'Se'Saera has come to us with a promise to rebuild the world we share,' the former steward of the Keepers said. 'I know I am not alone when I look at our world and see only destruction. Our ocean is black and our sun is broken. We have a shoreline where only the mad can walk. A plateau where the barest hint of blood on the ground causes horrors to erupt. A mountain that breaks apart as the bones of a god decay. This is just the continent directly off Yeflam's edge. I could continue to other parts of the world, but it would be the same. Every one of these anomalies is an illness that none of us can cure. Indeed, to a certain degree, we have constructed our lives around these horrors as if they do not need to be changed. We speak instead of managing them. In my role with the Keepers of the Divine, I listened to immortal men and women address this very issue. Each one of them made a promise to repair the world once he or she was a god and I hoped that I would see the day where it was true, but it was not to come. They have not become gods. They will not. I know now that a god cannot be made from human flesh.' He paused to let his words sink in. 'I understand that it is difficult for you to hear this, Lady Wagan. You have lost your home to Se'Saera and her Faithful, but your home was built on the body of her father, and you can surely see the sacrilege involved in building a city on top of him. You have lost friends, and your own husband—'

Elan Wagan began to scream.

The noise from upstairs interrupted Faje's speech, but it was her mother that Eilona focused on. At the sound of her husband, the weariness in her face etched itself deeper. It was as if the last two years had been revealed by her stepfather's screams, exposed for everyone to see the weight she carried. Eilona was not the only one who had noticed her mother's change, either: Sinae had risen at the sound of her stepfather's screams and attempted to guide Alahn back to his seat, to calm him down.

'Eilona,' her mother said, breaking her thoughts. 'Help Reila with your stepfather, please.'

She wanted to reply, but in her hesitation, Elan Wagan screamed again, and she hurried up the stairs with Reila.

Her stepfather's screams grew louder as the two drew closer. When she and the silver-haired healer entered his room, they found him not in his wheelchair, but on the floor, just short of the window. The chair lay on its back, as if her stepfather had leapt from it and thrown it back. He might well have done that, Eilona admitted, but he did not have the strength in his legs to walk. He was now trying to find a grip on the floor, to pull himself forwards, to reach the empty window.

Eilona bent down to her stepfather and whispered to him, but her voice was lost under his yelling.

'Pull him into a sitting position,' Reila instructed as she rummaged through a leather bag in the corner of the room. 'Quickly now.'

Eilona picked up her stepfather as she would a child and carried him to the cot against the wall. She lowered herself, still holding him, as his screams became angry, violent mutters. All his strength was in his voice and, though he squirmed and tried to break her hold, he could not. Reila appeared before him, a glass jar filled with a smoke-coloured liquid in her hand. With no ceremony, the healer tilted her stepfather's head back and poured the liquid into him, causing him to choke, to spit, but she held his mouth shut to force him to swallow most of it. After he did, Reila released his head, and her stepfather sagged against Eilona.

Below, she heard voices, her mother's first, then Faje and Alahn.

'Daughter.' Her stepfather's whisper startled Eilona more than his screams had. 'Daughter,' he whispered, again. 'She's not here.

Se'Saera is not here. She was, but then she wasn't. I was riding towards her and then she wasn't there. I was screaming and then I wasn't. She won't take my eyes out of envy. She won't take what I see and show me battles I won't fight in. She won't show me that all who I love are dead.' Eilona began to speak, to tell him that she was safe, but Reila lifted her hand. *No*, she mouthed. *Listen*. 'Se'Saera can't see us. She can't see our lives. That is why she takes our eyes.' He relaxed into her arms. 'She can't hear us tonight,' he said, his voice slurred. 'She has had to turn her attention away. She has had to stop listening to our screams. To my screams. She has had to leave me. But she'll be back. She'll take my eyes when she comes back.'

'It's okay,' she said quietly, her vision blurred by tears, 'It's okay.'

'Something has happened,' he said, as if he had not heard her. 'Something has begun . . .' His voice faded and Eilona lowered her ear to his mouth. 'Tell your mother she has only this moment, Eilona.'

Voices erupted in argument below, but Elan Wagan had stopped speaking. His head rested on her shoulder, his breath steady, his body curled like an infant's. Yet, driven by her stepfather's lucidity, Eilona laid him on the cot and rose. As she did, she heard footsteps outside the open window. At the sound, she began to run out of the room.

She flew down the staircase, a jumble of limbs, half blind, wiping tears from her face, until she came to the end.

'Your objection is noted, Lady Wagan,' Lian Alahn was saying, rising once again. Beside him, Sinae also stood. 'But you do not speak for Neela. You do not have any authority in Yeflam. Our meeting today was to give you the chance to ease this transition, but since you will not do that, you will be taken into custody after this meeting. Faje, you can tell your god—'

'Eilona?' her mother said, concerned. 'What is the matter?'

'Father.' She had never called him stepfather. She took a breath. 'He said you have only this moment.'

Outside, the guard shouted and the door shuddered, but no one in the room turned towards the sound. Everyone's attention was on Eilona, on her tear-streaked face, on her words.

'Se'Saera can't hear us,' she said. 'He said something has drawn her attention away.'

A hardness settled into her mother's face. 'Sinae,' she said.

The knife appeared in Sinae Al'tor's hand before Eilona could cry out, before the jumble of her emotions could arrange themselves, but she need not have said a word. With a sudden swiftness he grabbed Lian Alahn's hair and wrenched his head backwards, exposing his throat. From the other side of the table, Alahn's son, who until this moment had not said a word, shouted in protest, but his cry was not enough to stop Sinae's dagger cutting deeply across Alahn's throat. As he did, he released the man who had aspired to be the leader of Yeflam, who had ruled the Traders' Union, and who now stumbled backwards, clutching his neck, desperately trying to speak, trying to accuse those around him of treachery as the door burst open and his soldiers spilled into the room.

7.

The guard who had let Eilona into the house lay crumpled on the floor. A dozen soldiers, their faces wrapped in dark cloth, pushed through the doorway over him.

She felt oddly calm, though she knew she should have turned and run back up the stairs, to whatever safety she could find. Instead, Eilona remained still. Whereas before she had been defined by the moment, by her emotional reaction to her stepfather's words, to Sinae dragging his knife over Alahn's throat, she now felt an odd detachment, as if the world had become unreal. The gaze of the first soldier fell on her, but it wavered, as if he was separated from her by a thick pane of glass. It added to the sense of dislocation from what was happening around her. As if she was floating above herself, she saw Caeli drive her elbow into the side of Captain Oake's head, saw her sword spike down, saw Sinae's guard step in front of her master as he took a step backwards, away from Olcea. She saw the witch, still sitting, and appearing to shimmer, and the Faithful rising at the sight of her. She saw Nymar shouting to his father, his father who was lost to her sight by Faje, who rose, throwing back his chair, crying out to his god.

As if in answer, a faint outline began to materialize in the centre of the room, but the sight of it did not cause rejoicing in the Faithful.

They shouted at each other – 'The witch—' '—first this, *first*—'

'—*control*!' – but before any of them could do anything, the figure drove its hand into the back of the closest Faithful.

The figure's hand grabbed the woman's spine and hooked its other hand on her neck. As if her flesh and bone were nothing more than paper, it broke both, shattering the bone in her back, and snapping her neck.

The attack was so brutal that it caused the soldiers in the door to recoil, to stop their advance. The Faithful scattered towards them, but there was no passage out of the door.

Eilona turned towards Olcea. The witch had not moved from the table. Rather, she sat with a stillness that was unnerving, her unbound hands wet with her own blood. Eilona could see no knife, no way that she had cut into her skin, but she did not doubt that the wounds were self-inflicted. She had only to meet the hard, calm eyes of the witch to know that she was in control of the figure in the room, the figure Eilona realized that she knew. The figure who had piloted *The Frozen Shackle* from Zalhan. The figure who had sat inside Olcea's bag from Pitak.

Hien.

The ghost became more and more visible to her as he mercilessly killed the Faithful in the room, his acts of violence so horrific they broke the courage of the soldiers who had come on Lian Alahn's command, and who tried to flee themselves.

Eilona understood why. Hien was not just terrifying in his violence, but his appearance was pure dread. With each death, with each bit of blood that appeared to seep into his being, the ghost's face revealed its decayed and bloated visage. His right eye was a milky white and rolled back, while his left was brown, but focused downwards. Yet, for all the horror of his face, she knew that he was a young man, that he had once been a soldier in the Marble Palaces of Tinalan, a well-to-do youth, to judge by the fine, intricate work on the armour he wore.

That style of armour was not worn much, now, she knew. Thirty years ago, it had been worn by the soldiers of Emperor J'kl, who had built horrific camps to purify the country. Eilona's gaze drifted back to Olcea, imagining the woman thirty or so years ago with children around her, children who would have never grown old.

What kind of witch are you? Unbidden, Eilona recalled Tinh Tu's words in Zalhan. She had said them casually, then, as if the answer did not truly matter, but Eilona saw now that there had been a respect in her tone. *Very few people lie to me.* Eilona knew that. Knew it intimately. But even though she had ridden beside Olcea on *The Frozen Shackle*, had watched her pilot the ship with no one but Hien, she had not understood the kind of power she had. She saw Olcea in the large, rundown house she had kept in Mireea, the house where she had taught orphan girls herbalism, healing and even witchcraft. She remembered her mother telling her stepfather that Olcea was a war witch. At the time, Eilona had been unable to connect the two, but now, she could. She could see how the violence and tragedy of Olcea's youth bled together into her future self, how she became capable of such coldness that she could take the killer of her family and bond him to her, to be used as she saw fit. Saw how in doing so, Olcea isolated herself, drove away the people with whom she could have rebuilt her life, but remained, performing acts of charity for children who would leave her as they made their own lives. She saw how every act of violence, every death Olcea and Hien were part of, created a cycle of violence and repentance binding the two tighter and tighter, until they were the only family each other had.

'Enough!' Faje Metura grabbed Eilona, pressing a knife against her neck. 'Stop this!'

At the door of the room, Hien paused. He was so defined now that the stitches in his armour could be seen. Behind him, the doorway was empty, and the last of the sun was like a thumbprint of dried blood.

Faje's breath was hot on her ear. 'Se'Saera,' he whispered. 'You promised that it would not be this way.'

'You're not important to her.' Eilona still felt detached from what was happening to her. The sharp edge of the blade did not really feel as if it was against her skin. 'You're just another to be used.'

'You don't know!' He tightened his grip. 'You can't know.'

'She is right,' her mother said, walking around the table, leaving Olcea, Caeli, Sinae and his guard. 'Your Faithful are dead. Nymar hides beneath the table. Lian is dead. His soldiers are dead, or gone.'

'It was supposed to be you,' Faje hissed. 'He was supposed to betray you.' He pointed at Sinae with his knife. 'Se'Saera said he would.'

Across the room, Sinae Al'tor looked confused.

'You speak to her, every night. You ask her questions. She told me that!'

'She doesn't answer,' he said. 'I ask her how she can trap the dead, how she can demand so much from humanity yet give so little. I ask her about the War of the Gods. I ask her, just as many others ask her. But if she thought for a moment that I would betray Muriel Wagan, then she was not listening to me. Beatrice?'

Eilona did not even see the hand of Sinae's guard move: she only heard the thin blade of the dagger pierce Faje's left eye, heard it strike deep in his skull with an awful, intimate sound she did not believe she would ever forget.

Faje fell, and as he did, Eilona felt his dagger slice shallowly along her neck – felt herself take a breath as the reality of the room came rushing back to her and she found herself standing in the middle of such violence that the next breath she took was one that choked within her. Her hands began to shake, but as she went to clasp them together, her mother took them and took her. Her mother with her hard hands, with her hard life, her hard thoughts. Her mother, who had never once allowed a gilded cage into a child's fantasy, drew Eilona into an embrace she had not felt in over a decade.

8.

As the afternoon's light started to fade, fires began to burn in Ranan.

At the edge of the treeline, Ayae stood next to Jae'le and watched the lights reveal the city in long and short shadows, of buildings and people and weapons.

None of it surprised her: she had seen Ranan's cathedral first as they left the dense trees and empty roads. It had appeared like a giant's spear thrust into the ground. Around Ayae, soldiers murmured in awe and fear, but she thought only that it looked out of place. It belonged to a different world, an older world, one in ancient books, dusty and dry, with sketches half-blurred by the age of the ink. She could not shake the sensation that she was seeing something archaic as she rode closer and found that, when the long line of steps to the cathedral revealed themselves, a strange calmness had fallen over her. Beyond the flat-roofed houses and the bridges that linked parts of the city together was the Innocent, his soldiers, and Se'Saera, but Ayae could feel none of the emotions that the soldiers around her experienced. Even the siege weapons, barricaded streets and soldiers failed to cause her skin to prickle with warmth, or harden, as it did before danger. Above her, swamp crows drifted around the city, having found a new roost, and it was here that Ayae's gaze was drawn. The birds looked as if they should have been part of a painting of a wicked castle, where the carcasses of heroes had been left to rot on gibbets, and only pain and suffering waited. But even that failed to break her calm.

'The bridges are our only entry into Ranan,' Eidan said, later. He stood in front of the force, his back to the city he spoke about. Tinh Tu stood next to him, her white raven settled on her staff, as if it were a light she carried. 'The roads that lead into the crevasses will be nothing but traps.'

'We have no siege weapons.' It was Vune who spoke. He stood at the front of the force, a belt full of stone spikes around his waist, a long-handled sledge hammer leaning against his right leg. 'You can see theirs. They point them out to us. Our bridges will never reach the other side.'

'They will,' the other man promised. 'You and your men will just have to make sure that it is secured before any horse rides over it.'

'It's suicide,' Vune said desperately. 'You're sending us to our deaths.'

'You may well die,' Tinh Tu said. 'But should we all fail tonight, it will be better to be dead, than to be in the kingdom of the Faithful.'

Her words were not met with cheers.

Over the last few days, more details of Tinh Tu's plan had been told to the soldiers. None of them had been happy. They argued, and Ayae believed that they would have deserted, if not for Tinh Tu's tight control over them. Unable to flee, they petitioned her with different plans, different advice. Vyla Dvir finally succeeded in having Tinh Tu lift her command of silence from her husband, and Miat argued that they should take and hold the paths up to Ranan. Starve them out, his wife said, translating his whispers. Lay siege and wait until they begin to eat each other. The Lord of the Saan was startled when Tinh Tu replied to him in his own language. After, Vyla suggested a group of assassins during the night. One soldier from Yeflam suggested gliders in addition to this. Another said Tinh Tu could order the Leerans not to attack. Ayae heard a dozen more. She thought some of them had merit, but Tinh Tu, who listened to all of them, replied no to every single one. We will storm the city, she said. We will lay the bridges down. We will ride across. We will hold a section, and then another, until we close in on the cathedral. You must trust me on this, she told them, even though she knew that they did not.

'The last sun is down,' Tinh Tu said. 'It is time, brother.'

Eidan nodded. He bent down to the ground and plunged his scarred hand deep into the soil and drew out a hammer made of stone. It was huge, easily the size of him, and though he carried it as if it weighed nothing, not one person believed that they could have held it. Without a word, he turned and began to walk towards Ranan.

With a loud curse, Vune and the Mireean soldiers lifted the bridges, sixteen soldiers to each of the flat, ugly creations, and rushed after him.

'Last chance,' Jae'le said, beside Ayae. 'You need not come with me.'

She tightened her hand on her reins and shook her head. Despite everything, she still felt calm and balanced within herself. 'What happened to your bird?' she asked, instead.

'He's a smart bird,' he said easily. 'He knew better than to be part of this.'

'Smart bird,' Ayae agreed.

Behind her, one of the soldiers sobbed. She had seen a lot of the men and women cry since Gtara, and the sounds had etched themselves inside her. Despite her own calm, she had told herself again that this was what the gods had done to the soldiers, what Se'Saera would do to them. Ayae hated that she was part of it in the now, but it had only strengthened her resolve to ride into Ranan.

Beneath her, the ground began to shake.

At first, Ayae thought that it was an earthquake, that the damage in the Mountains of Ger had run much longer and much further through the ground than she had thought. The ground started to split open before her, and it was with a sudden concern that she realized that she could see it doing so exactly in the path of Eidan and the bridges.

From the cracked ground a hand emerged. It was a giant hand, easily the size of the horse she sat upon. It was joined by a second hand of equal size, though this hand was dark and muddy. A human-shaped head followed and, from the crevasse, as if in obscene birth, a long, slick, muddy giant drew itself from the ground. It heaved itself to a great, awful height and stood for a moment before Ranan, a huge, single creation. Then it began to move, each step causing the ground to shiver, but the shudders did not come from it alone. Turning to her right, Ayae saw another giant emerge, its back covered in the thick green canopy that ran through the centre of Leera. With the ground shaking beneath it, it began to move towards the first, a cousin, a brother, a sister – she did not know. All she did know was that it was not as tall as the first, but more solid, its form more defined, where the mud and water of the first left a centre that constantly moved. As it came to a halt beside the first giant, new tremors began to ran through the ground, and to her left, Ayae saw a third giant emerge, this one appearing to be made from a hard, rocky ground, both larger and much more angled than either of the other two.

'It is awful, is it not?' Jae'le said softly. 'We make war full of terror and horror. Not even the survivors sleep kindly after.'

In her mind's eye, Ayae saw Aelyn's storm giant, the one that had risen above Yeflam in her rage. She saw it loom behind Eidan's giants on a battlefield thousands of years ago, a battlefield lined with the dead and the living, a battlefield so horrific that surely no force would have stood against them.

'Zaifyr told me that when I first met him.'

'It is not the same as seeing it.'

'No,' she admitted.

The ground shuddered again and the giants began to attack Ranan.

9.

A few miles away, on an eastern road, on a rise that broke through the canopy of Leera, Refuge and the Brotherhood watched the giants stride towards Ranan.

Earlier, a bird from the Lord of Faaisha had arrived, the order to attack at dusk written on its leg. Tuael's seal had been put across the message, but still, Heast had thought it written by a different man. A frontal attack was not the kind of battle that the marshals of Faaisha would have suggested. They would have argued for a siege. They would have said that siege engines laid around the city would drive down the morale, would break them over time, and would do it without heavy losses. Heast had not yet decided how he would convince them that it would be a useless act, but the letter meant that he did not need to.

The ground shook as one of the giants, the one made from stone, slammed its fist down on the edge of Ranan.

'They're clearing the edge for bridges.' Beside him, Essa lowered his spyglass. 'There are Mireeans dragging them into position.'

'Could you see the Saan?' he asked.

'Couldn't be sure, but the man in front of them, the one with the beard, I know him. He is called Eidan. He was one of the cursed men in Yeflam. He was said to be Aelyn Meah's lover.'

From deep in Ranan, catapults fired, flinging boulders at the giants. Two caught the one in the centre, only to pass through its body, and slam into the ground behind.

Heast nudged his horse around, to face Refuge and the Brotherhood. Both groups had made good time from Faaisha to Leera. Heast would have preferred a night to rest both the mounts and the soldiers, but he had little say in that now.

He met Lehana's gaze at the front of the group, then Anemone and, lastly, Kye Taaira.

'You can hear what has started down there.' Heast projected his voice to the soldiers before him. No one, not even the swamp crows in the trees, moved. 'We're going to ride into that. We're going to ride down this road and we are going to use the bridges the Mireeans are setting. Once we're across, we will push towards the cathedral of Ranan. When we're there there, Sergeant Bliq will establish a hold for the injured, and myself, Captain Essa and Lieutenant Lehana will begin issuing orders to take the cathedral. Aela Ren and his soldiers will be there. They are our priority. They are our targets.'

From Faaisha to Leera, Heast had drilled the order into Refuge and the Brotherhood. He had made sure that all the soldiers knew not to engage them singly. He had told them that, while the Innocent and his soldiers could not die, they could be hacked apart, chained, and otherwise immobilized.

None of them, he knew, liked the order.

'You leave Refuge by sword, by fire, by will,' he said. 'In the Brotherhood, you leave on your back.'

A loud shudder ran through the ground, followed by screams.

'When dawn breaks over Ranan,' Heast continued, not acknowledging the sound, 'you will either be standing or you will not. That is the battle we ride into.' He tapped his saddlebag, where the battered copy of *The Eternal Kingdom* was kept. 'You have all seen me read a book over the last few days. You all know this is the book of our new god. A book in which she promises us that she will fix the world. That we will want for nothing. All we have to do for this is give ourselves to her. All we have to do is watch our friends and turn on them if they don't believe what we do. She tells us to cut the eyes out of those who do not see the truth.'

Behind him, stone cracked loudly, as if one of the giants had been split open.

'We are not here to accept that.' Heast drew his sword. 'I will not betray the soldiers I stand by. I will not watch my friends from the shadows. I will not report on them to a god who cuts their eyes out because she does not like what they see.

'But more than that, I will not serve the child of the parents who tore apart our world. Who left us to rot in life and rot in death. Who have poisoned our oceans, broken suns and left us with the burdens of their war.

'What lies before us may well be the end for you and me. If so, I go towards it with my sword drawn and I go towards it as the man I am before you, with the values I hold. If I am to die here, then so be it!' Heast raised his sword with his voice. 'Let the gods see how we defy them! How we reject them! How we rise up to tell them that we do not want them! Let them see our judgement of their actions!'

The Captain of Refuge wheeled his horse around and, with his sword slicing down to signal the charge, began to ride towards Ranan.

His soldiers followed him.

10.

Zaifyr was in a room, not a field, when he took a painful, shuddering watery breath.

'He's here.' Se'Saera knelt above him. He could see her beautiful face, her green eyes, and he could feel sharp edges, like teeth against his skin. At the same time, he could see her in Heüala, her massive, multi-headed form engaged in a battle with Queila Meina and Steel. Around her were the colourless souls of ancient killers. And he could see her in the fields of paradise, a young girl with dark wings unfolding from her back. 'Don't suffer for nothing,' the girl in the field said. 'He cannot return to Heüala,' the young woman in the room said. 'All is lost if he does.'

'The battle has begun.' The blond man appeared behind the god. 'Are you sure it is wise to stay here with him? There are stone giants attacking the edges of Ranan. They will be able to reach us here if we do not ride out to them.'

'My Faithful have been warned. They know what to expect in the streets.' Gently, she rolled Zaifyr onto his side. 'But in the end, what happens in the streets of Ranan is a consequence of what happens here, of whether he lives or dies.'

'It is not how I am used to fighting a war.'

Behind them, a door opened.

'General Waalstan has been returned,' a man's voice said. 'He lies below us, before the altar. Do you wish for me to take the field?'

'No, Aela,' Se'Saera said. 'Have your soldiers protect the cathedral. If our enemies reach the centre of Ranan, they will try to take the cathedral, and you will be needed here.'

'Will they reach us?'

'I see that they do and that they do not. Everything rests on these moments.'

In the field, Zaifyr felt a cold hand on his shoulder. He could see Se'Saera's wings spread and could see her mouth move, but he could not hear what she said.

Then, everything was still.

It was as if the world took a breath, held it, and then released it.

Zaifyr felt himself being helped from the floor. His body was weak, his limbs without strength. It was a debilitation he expected after being dead, but his weakness went further, to such an extent that he felt as if he had been hollowed. Around him, the morning's sun lit the room brightly, and along the face of the man who held him, scars burned like hot wires. *Aela Ren,* Zaifyr realized, wanting to pull away, but unable.

Around him, the world took shape with every step the Innocent took. Damaged walls let the sun in fully to shine through the broken floor. In one of the rooms below, amidst shattered furniture, lay the still form of his brother, Jae'le.

'He fought well,' Ren said, a strange note of sadness in his voice. 'But the years had changed him too much.'

A broken sword lay near him, but it was the countless wounds across his thin body that drew Zaifyr's eye. They were concentrated around his chest and his stomach, but they ran up his neck, to his face. No single wound had been fatal, Zaifyr knew. It was the combined wounds that killed him.

Come,' the Innocent said, moving towards to door. 'You are wanted downstairs.'

Darkness engulfed Zaifyr.

It was just the hall. Just the loss of the sun. But he felt as if he was all of existence in the darkness, as if he had been stripped down to his grief. He knew the rest of his family would be revealed to him and he could not let their deaths grow inside him until they consumed him. He had to prepare himself. He took a step, but it was not a step taken with the aid of Aela Ren. It was a step that did not take him forwards. He felt icy water around him. The pain in his chest returned. Salt water spilled from his mouth. There was a pressure on his head. He wanted to swim upwards, but he could not. He could not move. He was on the verge of panic when a light appeared next to him and revealed that he was inside a sphere. It was not a small sphere and he was in the centre of it. Around him colours began to illuminate in vibrant reds, greens and blues. They were like giant waves suspended in the air above him. Within each of them were dozens of variations of colour, each of them a strand, and each of them cross-stitched, hatched and woven back and forth through the suspended waves, binding them together in a whole.

Before his gaze, the waves began to move, to pulse and shift. From waves came canopies, as if he were in a forest, not an ocean. From canopies came twists, as if he was watching someone stitching. As if what he saw could be held. It was then that Zaifyr realized that he was not alone, but his company was not human, or conscious in any way he would have recognized. Instead, they were thoughts, ideas, concepts, each of them personified into a presence that shaped the light, that split it into strands and gave it movement, as if they were a breath. Slowly, Zaifyr drifted towards the colour, his broken boots finding a purchase that he could not see. When he touched the strands, he felt grief, his grief, and he realized how important it was to acknowledge life, to be part of a culture, a society. His grief was not just for him, but for others who had lost as well. Death was not singular, but communal. With that recognition, he saw the consciousness that he had first sensed when he entered the sphere, and he named it: the Wanderer, the God of Death. Beyond him, Zaifyr sensed others, others whose thoughts were kin to the strange and alien thoughts closest to him, the thoughts that belonged to gods who were dead, who were dying, and who were alive.

He stepped out of the stairwell at the bottom of the broken cathedral, still in the grasp of Aela Ren.

Ayae lay there. Her neck was bent at a strange angle, and the ground was black with soot, but it was her eyes, her brown eyes, that appeared to linger on him, to ask him why he hadn't been there with her.

Not far from her lay soldiers. There was no common uniform to suggest that a certain force had attacked, but Zaifyr saw the black-and-red armour of the First Queen of Ooila, and the mix of styles and type, from leather, to plate, to chain, that typified mercenaries. Many he didn't recognize, but the scarred-faced white man next to a black woman was familiar. Captain Kal Essa, of the Brotherhood. He had been at Mireea. His spiked mace was broken, and it appeared that the Ooilan soldier had tried to protect him after it shattered, but to no avail. Just beyond them lay Aned Heast, his head split open. Another man, a man in the clothes of a tribesman from the Plateau, lay dead behind him.

Zaifyr's numbness grew as Aela Ren led him through the carnage of dead soldiers. He carried Zaifyr to a gathering of men and women at the front of the cathedral, where the doors were broken. There, he could hear voices, but the words made little sense to him. He closed his eyes, expecting it to be the voices of the dead, of the people he knew, but he was startled to realized that it was not.

He could no longer hear the dead.

'Se'Saera,' Ren said, as the two drew closer to her. 'He is here.'

Neither could he feel the god's presence digging into his skin.

'It's over,' she said. 'The battle has been won and lost. There are a few loose ends. A witch, a few soldiers. Nothing important.' Behind her, Zaifyr could see his sister, Aelyn. She had fallen to her knees beside Eidan's body. 'All my enemies are dead but for you, Qian. You are all that lives.'

An old Saan warrior carried a body up the stairs and laid it out, next to Eidan. Tinh Tu. The Saan muttered to himself over her, then kicked her. The movement caught Aelyn's attention and she rose, suddenly angry, but was stopped by another man Zaifyr knew, the saboteur Bueralan. His tattooed arm reached out and fell onto her shoulder. Behind him, crouched a tall, thin figure in a hooded cloak. 'Get out of here, Dvir,' Bueralan Le said. 'Before she kills you.'

Aelyn jerked out of his grasp and turned to Se'Saera. 'What are you going do with my last brother?' she asked.

The god smiled. 'I am going to return him to his prison.'

11.

The door did not so much as open as fall off its hinges. Sunlight lanced painfully into Zaifyr's eyes as it did.

He had experienced this before, over a thousand years ago. Jae'le had opened the door and stood in the doorway, but it was not his brother's shadow who stood there now. Over the last five years, Zaifyr had been reacquainted with the crooked tower, the prison that Jae'le had made. The life his brother had given it had leached away, drawn out by Se'Saera. Each time a bird landed on the crude roof, or the scuttle of a lizard ran along the stones, he heard earth break, saw cracks emerge, and he would say his brother's name. He had tried to stop himself. He was in the last of Jae'le's life, trapped in the decay not of a body but of a soul, until the tower finally broke apart to let him stumble out, eyes weeping at the brightness of the sun he had not seen before, a new shadow standing in his path.

Hard hands lifted him. 'Brother,' a woman's voice said.

'Aelyn.' Through the streaks of his vision, he could only make out the shape of her. 'Aelyn,' he repeated.

She led him out of the tower. His feet were bare – he had taken off his shoes years ago – and the rocks dug sharply into him. Soon, he was lowered into a chair. A table was near him and, as his vision took shape, he saw food and drink laid out on it.

'How do you feel?' his sister asked him.

'Weak.' He reached for the jug. 'Is that water?'

'Let me pour it.' He saw the shapes move, felt a cup pressed into his hands. 'Drink slowly. It will make you sick if you don't.'

Aelyn appeared before him as he took it. Her dark hair was cut close to her head, revealing her neck and the shape of her skull. She was pale, but not as pale as she had been when he last saw her. She had, he thought, a drawn look about her, one he was sure that he shared. 'Before, I didn't even feel hunger or thirst,' he said as he sipped the cool water. 'It came and went this time.'

'Se'Saera left us our immortality but little else.' Behind Aelyn, he could see a small farmhouse and a fenced yard. In it were two grey horses. 'We can say her name as much as we wish, now. She took what she wanted.'

Their power. Their divinity. Zaifyr had realized that when he was on a ship, chained in its hold, a prisoner on his way to Eakar, to the tower that lay behind him in a decayed, broken form.

'Here.' Aelyn pushed towards him half a loaf of brown bread. 'Small bites.'

He tore an edge off with his fingers. 'Does no one come to visit you?' he asked.

'Not for years.' She offered him half a smile. 'Bueralan did, for a while. But what we had to share was only despair. In the end, his duty to Se'Saera's children became more and more important to him. I did not mind when he stopped coming.'

He chewed slowly, resisting the urge to devour the loaf. Aelyn had come to the tower shortly after he was delivered by Aela Ren. She had spoken to him through the walls, and they had argued, and fought. He had expected her to leave, but instead, she had built a farmhouse. The ground, she told him, was no longer poisoned, the river clean, and after a while, it stopped mattering what they had said to each other in anger, what they accused each other of. They had both made mistakes. They had both failed.

They were the only family they had left.

'Some news still finds its way to me,' Aelyn said quietly. 'Nothing ever good. Anemone, the Witch of Refuge, was killed a few months back, bringing to an end the Faithless Uprising. There are still pockets of resistance, of course. I don't think Se'Saera will ever be free of it, truthfully, but this was the end of Muriel Wagan's uprising. The last part of it, at any rate.' The Lady of the Ghosts, Aelyn told Zaifyr, had died two years ago. 'She was killed by General Zilt. He has surpassed Aela Ren in favour, of late.'

'Maybe they will go to war.' He tore another piece of bread apart, not believing his own words. 'Have you seen her children?'

'Look up and you will see them yourself.'

The bright sunlight still stung his eyes, but it was not as bad as before. The whole, complete sun would take him time to get used to, but not as much as the dark, winged shapes that marked the sky before it. They were at a distance, and so Zaifyr could not see their faces clearly, but he could see their wings, and could imagine them descending from the sky, taking those that they wanted to feast upon, or those that Se'Saera wanted killed, or brought to her.

The children were remade souls, Aelyn told him. Se'Saera took the souls that the gods had made originally and rebuilt them into her new flesh. The very first, the one he had seen crouched by Bueralan in Ranan, had not been subsumed in this way, however. He had been an old god's soul, like Zaifyr and Aelyn, but those that had been born after, which had been seeded in the wombs of women by the god herself, had been different. They were remade souls and it was through these children that the god influenced fate. Humanity was but chattel, and each year, fewer and fewer natural births were recorded, to the point, Zaifyr was told, that a pregnant woman was now viewed as a tragic figure. In the sky, the dark shapes shifted and glided, a certain cruel elegance in their movements that reminded Zaifyr of Se'Saera in Heüala . . . and, as he thought that, he lost the sense of himself. He was dimly aware of Aelyn speaking, of her asking if he wanted more water, but he was not there.

A chill ran through his body, through his very soul, and he felt a hand on his shoulder. Above him, the sky changed. It turned dark, and then formed into a sphere. Blue strands weaved around his fingers as if they were stems growing from his very soul.

'They are not to be touched,' a familiar voice said. 'They are not real, except when they are, of course. Then they are real and lived in.'

The Children of the Gods

'We found the child on the coast just as the Battle of Ranan began,' Aelyn said. 'We found him on the day my family died.

'I have relived that day so many times in my mind. I have seen myself listen to Bueralan as he talks to the child. I have asked myself why I agreed to take him back to Ranan.' She paused. I believe, had she been a different person, Aelyn Meah would have wept. But the woman before me was over ten thousand years old. She would not weep for her mistakes, no matter what had happened since. 'I believe it came from a desire of hope,' she said, surprising me. 'Certainly, it is what I heard in Bueralan's voice when he spoke. He wanted the child to be of such hope that it would make the suffering he had seen understandable. It would frame the world for him.

'For a while, it did.

'For a while, it did for me, as well. After the Battle of Ranan, Se'Saera gave a speech. I am sure you have heard it. She held up the heads of her enemies and proclaimed a new dawn. I was there. I watched her lift the heads of those I loved. The child made it easier that day. The child gave me hope that the sacrifices I had made were not in vain.'

—Onaedo, *Histories, Year 1029*

1.

'They are possibilities,' Soren said to Zaifyr. 'They are fate. They are all of its potentials, its promises, and its fears.'

'Why can I touch it?' He turned to the man who had been Anguish, the man whose cold, white-skinned hand had brought him back to the sphere he floated in. 'Tell me why if all of time exists together, if there is no past, present and future, why does it look like this?'

'Because that is how you comprehend it.' Soren released him. 'This is your creation. You have made it.'

'And you?'

'I told you that I was a deceit when we first met,' he said. 'But I am not your deceit. I am just one small soul woven into fate by the Wanderer. He saw that I was born and ensured that Se'Saera would make me again. He left me a message to give to you, but it was not until I lay in the field of paradise that I could put aside Anguish and recall that.'

'Why don't they speak, then? Why must they use you?' Zaifyr waved at the shifting colours around him, at the waves that twisted into trees, into waterfalls, into a whole he was only beginning to comprehend. Around his hand, the blue strands from earlier streamed out, as if caught in a wind. 'Or are you telling me that I made them as well?'

'What you sense is all that remains of the gods' divinity. They have given you the ability to create this in their last moments. They have used what remains of their power and left themselves exposed so that you can influence what happens next.'

'That's what the Wanderer told you?'

'Yes.'

'Then he lied to you,' Zaifyr said. He raised his hand with the blue stems. 'I have seen the future. We do not win. It is Se'Saera's.'

'What you saw was just one possibility.' The dead painter reached out for the threads on his hand. They moved from his grasp, twisting away, ballooning, then shrinking. 'It is all a possibility,' he said, looking up at Zaifyr, 'but none of it is real until you leave. All of fate is contained within this sphere. Here, everything is real, and everything is not. Where we stand now there is field that I lie in, but there is also not. There is no tower in Heüala, but there is. There is no Heüala. There is no *Glafanr*. There is no River of the Dead. But there is. There is nothing and there is everything. We stand within creation itself.'

'To do what?'

'To create.'

'A fate?'

'Yes.'

Overwhelmed, Zaifyr glanced around him. 'How could I even begin to do that? When I put my hand against those strands, I felt millions and millions of souls. To create a fate is to ask the impossible. It would take me thousands and thousands of years to make a single moment.'

'You should not be afraid.' Soren looked up into the colours and shapes above him. 'You are creation.'

The sphere was a skull, he understood suddenly. It contained all the colour that Zaifyr saw. He realized that they were not waves, or trees, but thoughts, twisting and merging, blending together, to a single whole. What he saw was a mind.

'It is Se'Saera,' Soren said quietly, staring up into the coloured shapes. 'She is binding fate within her. She is making it singular. She has drawn what is left of the gods here. Soon, they will all be part of her, and cease to exist.'

'Look in the centre,' Zaifyr said. There, dark blue threads etched with red blossomed. Each of the strands he saw was like the ones in his hand. They were, he knew, Se'Saera's future, the future he had seen outside the crooked tower. 'Tell me, is she creating her fate?' he asked. 'Or is fate creating her?'

'All the gods are creations of fate. Se'Saera is no different than those she seeks to replace.' Soren laughed, and in that laugh, Zaifyr heard the pain and bitterness Anguish had laughed with. 'Fate creates. It is all fate does. There is no purpose, no structure. The gods themselves make that. How many thoughts do you think the gods had before this moment? How many thoughts that became threads that split fate into futures that ended differently for both us? Only numbers that don't exist could count it. Se'Saera was meant to end that splitting. She was fate's creation against its creations. It is why the old gods tried to starve her out of existence, but once that failed, it was why they were forced to create possibilities to stop her. It is why they tried to trap our souls. Why the Leviathan kept Lor Jix's crew. Why the Wanderer trapped them in his staff. Why Meina is here. Why I am here. Why you are here as well, Zaifyr.'

He tried to respond, but pain erupted in his chest.

It was not the same as he felt when Se'Saera was returning him to his body. It was not poisoned sea water lodged in his lungs, not air trying to push it out. Instead, it felt as if a part of his soul was being attacked, that the very fabric of his being was under assault.

Zaifyr fell into the middle of the sphere and, as he did, a smoking, unformed head rose up from the darkness beneath, from the unconsciousness of Se'Saera.

Angrily, instinctively, he reached with all his energy for the dead in Heüala. His power flowed from the centre of his being, as pure as it had ever been, and he felt it spread through Queila Meina and Steel, felt it spear through the ancient killers from the Plateau. He felt the exultation as it slipped into the dead that had been in the Wanderer's staff.

Then something grasped not him, but his power. It took hold with a startling ferocity and wrenched it from his control.

The dead did not spear into Se'Saera's form below him, but burst upwards, to the thoughts she had. It was not Zaifyr's command: he felt hollow as if he had become a conduit. As the dead continued to spear into Se'Saera, the sphere around him began to break apart. Against the darkness, they were like stars falling through the night sky. Barely able to move, Zaifyr watched as the combined thoughts of the gods spiked and burst, as if they were a storm, the last of their consciousness bursting in a fury he could not comprehend, a fury that sought to break apart and devour the blue that had been Se'Saera's fate.

The light of their thoughts brightened, turning into a nova that began to fill the sphere, obliterating not just the blue, but the green, the red, the shades of each, the combinations that had birthed so much difference. Zaifyr's own sense of self was breaking apart as it did. He could no longer sense—

Soren thrust him away as he disintegrated into the light.

He pushed him down to the bottom of the sphere, into the darkness of the skull where there were no thoughts of the old gods, where only the new waited.

His action broke the latent command of the Wanderer over Zaifyr's power, over what had once been the god's power, and it broke the control the god had over the dead. The brightness above Zaifyr stilled and, as he fell further and further into the darkness, the smoking head of Se'Saera rose. But it was not him that she wanted, he knew. Not now. She cared not to rend or tear him apart.

She wanted the parts of her fate that still clung to him, the blue strands in his hand. The strands from which she could rebuild her future. The future where he would sit in front of Aelyn outside the crumbling tower of his prison. Where he gazed at the sky. Where the dark shapes of remade souls passed and he could hear his sister speaking.

The dead speared through him in silver shafts, purging the thoughts that were Se'Saera's fate from Zaifyr. His power ran through them, entirely his own, his fury and anger at not just the new god, but at all the gods destroying the command of the Wanderer.

Below him, the unformed head of Se'Saera broke apart. He heard screams, not just around him in the darkness of the sphere, but in the field, where a child with dark wings stumbled backwards, and in the cathedral room, where she dug her fingers into Zaifyr's arms. He could feel the pain of that, but he ordered the dead to rip away what remained of Se'Saera's fate in him again. But this time, as the silver light burst through him, he directed it up into the blue and green and red of the old gods' thoughts. Fuelled by his fury, the dead ripped at the threads of fates. They tore at what had been made. At the thoughts that bound a world together, that shaped it.

Zaifyr would leave them nothing. He would not leave the divine a single thought to force fate into a future, into a past, into a present. He poured more and more of his power into not rebuilding fate, or giving it structure, but into breaking it. He did it not just for himself, but for Anguish, for the people who had been turned into haunts for thousands of years, for Jae'le, Tinh Tu, Eidan, Aelyn, and for Ayae. He did it for all those he had known and loved and hated. He tore at the structures that dictated those relationships.

He ripped at what had built them. He let the dead enact the fury that had been lurking in their hearts for over ten thousand years, let it combine with the anger that had been seething through his veins since he had seen his first man die by a roadside in Kakar.

With all the power and all the emotion he had, Zaifyr tore apart fate until there was no single colour, no skull, no Soren, no old gods, no new.

Until he could sense not even himself.

2.

Zean crouched on the shoreline, just before the black tide of Leviathan's Blood.

The moonlight illuminated him to Bueralan and Aelyn and revealed not just his thinness, but his length, the height that was already that of an average human. His skin was black, but not in any coloration Bueralan recognized: rather, Zean's skin appeared to pull in the darkness of the ocean and of the night sky, both of which left him with a skin tone much closer to a bottle of ink than to flesh. If that was not alien enough, a pair of wings unfolded from his back, not yet the length of him, and not yet fully grown. At the edge of the sand, Bueralan and Aelyn Meah watched them unfold and fold, as if being flexed. Each time they saw a tremble when both stretched out to their full span.

'Wait here,' Bueralan said to Aelyn, sliding off the grey. He rubbed the beast's nose before he passed the reins to her. 'Let me talk to him first.'

Behind her, at the edge of the marsh, a handful of swamp crows stood like guards. 'How do you know he can talk?' she asked, taking the reins.

'I don't.'

What did he want to happen?

Did he want to kill Zean? When he had left the cathedral,

Bueralan believed that he had little choice but to kill him. When Aelyn had said that Zean might be mad, that he might not know who he was, or what he had done, Bueralan accepted that. In truth, he thought it the best outcome of the carnage he stood in. If Se'Saera had created nothing more than a mad dog, then his responsibility was the moral one. Bueralan would end Zean's madness. But what if he wasn't mad? That question grew inside inside Bueralan as he and Aelyn followed Zean's trail. He saw the intelligence in Zean's movements, saw his curiosity about the world around him, even if that curiosity was ultimately expressed violently. The question, then, Bueralan knew as he slowed his chase, was not if Zean was mad, but what if he was not? What if he was but a child, and horrified by what he had done? What if he was simply afraid?

He did not make a sound across the dirty sand. Half a day's ride to the north, the Mad Coast began and, as Bueralan came within a handful of steps of his blood brother, he thought of how fitting that was.

'Zean,' he said.

The wings shivered and pulled in safely against his long back. Slowly – deceptively slowly, Bueralan thought – Zean turned.

He was male, that was at least clear, but it was his face and not his nudity that revealed the horror of what Se'Saera had created. Defined by long, high cheekbones, Zean had a predatory look to him, much like a bird of prey. He had no hair, either, but his skull was defined by a hard, ridged skin, patterned strangely and not entirely unlike the white tattoos that twisted along Bueralan's arms. Yet it was the mouth that he was drawn to, for though it was small, it was dominated by hard, sharp teeth, so much so that the top of the jaw extended past the skin, as if it was too big for Zean's body.

'I know you,' he said in Ooilan.

'We met a long time ago, when we were children.' Zean had never liked to speak in Ooilan. 'My name is Bueralan.'

'And mine?'

'Zean.'

'No.'

'What, then?'

'Not Zean.' Se'Saera's child gave a shallow hiss and Bueralan took a step back. 'I remember you talking to Mother. I could hear you day and night. You told her it would be okay. That nothing would hurt her.' His wings twitched. 'You lied to her and to me.'

He felt a twinge of sympathy, but his hand still settled on his sword. 'I didn't know you could hear,' he said. 'I thought we could keep her safe.'

'And me?'

'It was one or the other.'

'I was being suffocated,' Se'Saera's child said. 'Each day it would get worse and worse. I did not want to hurt Mother, but I must breathe. It was an urge to me. I had to be free.' His wings folded back, as if he was hugging himself. 'Do you think mother forgives me for what I did?'

'I don't know.'

'She was so fragile.' He made a motion to Bueralan. 'You are all so fragile. You break. You bleed. Mother was right when she said that about you.'

He had never heard Taela say that, but she might have, he allowed. She might have said it at the end. Or it may have been that the child heard Se'Saera. 'You speak well for one so young,' Bueralan said, changing the subject.

'You are not born with language?'

'No.'

'I was born with awareness.' With sharp claws, Se'Saera's child – he would never be Taela's – tapped his chest. 'I hear everything in womb. I learn. Mother Se'Saera talks to me in there.'

'Mother . . .' Bueralan's voice trailed off. 'She talked to you, did she?'

'Yes.' He nodded excitedly, like a child who had been given a gift. 'She would tell me about the world. She taught me language. She taught me this tongue first. I would need it. I would need it to talk to the man who would teach me.'

'Did she tell you who that man was?'

'No. She was speaking just before you arrived. She wanted me to go back to Ranan. She said two people were coming for me, but then she stopped talking. Do you know why?'

Bueralan shook his head. 'Did she tell you I would be here?'

'You and the woman.' A claw waved towards Aelyn. 'She said you would help me. She was going to tell me my name. She said I had to tell it to you.'

'But it's not Zean, is it?'

'No.' Se'Saera's child shook his head furiously. 'That name angers me. I have heard it before but it is not mine. It is another's name.' A second hiss escaped him. 'Don't call me it.'

Se'Saera would have named him Zean. For a brief moment, Bueralan saw himself and the child as they were now, but instead of denying the name, the child awkwardly said that his name was Zean. He saw how it tied him to Se'Saera and her child. 'It is the name of a man very dear to me.' As he spoke, that reality broke apart, an old, decayed creation. 'He was my brother. I thought he might be here so I came to help him.'

'But now you help me instead, yes?'

'No.' Bueralan drew his sword. 'No, I am afraid not.'

3.

Zaifyr could see Se'Saera's face, her girl's face, her young woman's face. He could see both crack and split, as if a larger force was breaking her body open.

'*No!*' Lor Jix's voice was a bellow around him. 'What have you done?'

The sky above Heüala was riddled with fractures. Within those fractures, the silver light of the city had lit a shifting mass. At first, Zaifyr thought he saw Se'Saera. He imagined that the multi-headed form of the god had been drawn into the broken sky. But no, he realized it was something that flowed in constant movement, much like a river, and appeared to have its own current. Zaifyr felt his awareness pulled, but only the part of him that was divine, that held a god's power. The river was trying to draw him through the cracks and beyond Heüala, he remained lying on the ground. Above him, the splits began to widen and the impression he had of a river buckled under what he saw. He saw not just movement, but time.

He saw fate, saw it run into itself, flood over its possibilities, its outcomes, saw it submerge and erupt.

He saw choice.

'What have you done?' Jix's voice, again. His hands shook Zaifyr roughly. 'Godling, you must stop what you are doing!'

Zaifyr could not sense the sphere, could not see the thoughts, could not sense the gods. However he had reached the sphere that had contained fate, he could not return to it. Instead, he felt only pain. It was primarily in his chest, but it was of such acuteness his vision swam. The towers of Heüala looked as if they were changing, as if they were both rising and crumbling, the domes and flat roofs breaking and forming. But when the vision of what he saw did not alter, Zaifyr realized that it was not pain that caused Heüala to change, but rather that he was witnessing change. Beneath the new, moving sky, the City of the Dead was rebuilding itself, was fashioning itself on the new thoughts it could sense.

Zaifyr pushed himself away from Lor Jix and rose unsteadily. Beneath the burned soles of his boots, the ground shifted, and he felt paved stone, dirt, grass and even snow. Before him, the walls of buildings warped as stone turned to wood and wood turned to brick. Doors disappeared and reappeared, each time with different designs.

'There must be a god in the holy city!' Jix shouted. 'Se'Saera must be here to focus Heüala! What have you done to her?'

A small town.

No, a trading outpost. That, Zaifyr realized, was what Heüala was shaping itself into. The rough wooden buildings, the dirt streets, the vendors with stalls on the side of the road.

'Answer me!' The Captain of *Wayfair* grabbed him and thrust him against the wall of one of these stalls. 'Tell me what you have done!'

'What do you see?' His words were painfully torn from him, but what startled him most was the arm he lifted to fend off Jix. It was completely red and had, within its depth, a pulse. 'What is happening to me?' he whispered.

'It is life, godling.' The other man shook him. 'Tell me what you have done so I can fix it when you leave!'

The thought jarred him. 'What does the city look like to you?'

'It is a port town.' He spat the words at Zaifyr. 'It looks like a thousand others perched on shorelines throughout the world.'

'I see a trading post.' He tried to take a deep breath, couldn't. 'Jix, we're not meant to stay here. No one need live in the City of the Dead.'

'Are we to live and die only to live and die again?' The Captain slammed him against a wall that appeared differently to each man. 'Our existence is not a carousel. We are not beasts to ride in a carved circle forever.'

'That is the lie the gods created. There are no rewards. There are no punishments. There is only the life we make.'

'Se'Saera would change that!' Jix hurled Zaifyr into the dirt road and kicked him viciously. 'She will give us order and purpose. Do you not see that? Think of how long we have lived. I have spent over ten thousand years waiting for you and your trial. That is what the Leviathan asked of me. I was faithful. I was patient. But my reward would have been an illusion. A lie! Se'Saera offered a chance to change that, not just for me, but for all of us.'

'We should make that choice.' His red hands could not push him up from the ground and he slumped backwards. 'Tell me why we cannot?' he asked, staring up at the man.

'What choice would you make without a god?' Lor Jix loomed over him dangerously. 'How do we create our morals? From each other? What do we take as guidance? We need the divine for that. They are what binds us together as a society. They are what separates us from the animals. We need Se'Saera!'

'Enough.' A bright blade fell flat on Jix's chest. It was held by Queila Meina, and behind her stood Steel, as strong as they had been when they walked into Heüala. 'Not so long ago, you called her an abomination,' she said, walking around him, to push him away from Zaifyr. 'I don't know what happened to change that in your mind, but to me, Se'Saera remains very much that. Her parents are the same to me.'

'You did not live for more than three decades,' he said, pushing the blade aside. 'You are but a babe in existence.'

'Is that why you are so quick to kneel?'

Jix roared in fury, but unlike Zaifyr, Meina was not racked with pain. When the ancient dead threw himself at her, she stepped to her left, and drove her sword through his chest. Zaifyr expected the colour to leave him, for him to be defined by the white lines of a haunt, just as the dead who were struck down by Se'Saera had been changed. But though a ripple ran over his body, it was no more than a blink. Jix's hands curled around the mercenary's neck and Meina, in response, disappeared.

She reappeared behind him and grabbed the back of his clothes. 'You have the will to stay here, do you?' she said, throwing him into her soldiers.

'This is the domain of a god!' he shouted with such anger, such intensity. 'I will not leave Heüala to the likes of you!'

'Take him,' Meina commanded her soldiers. 'Throw him out of the gates. Drive him out into the fields. Show him that there is no river any more, and no ship to sail upon it. Throw him into the new world and see what he makes of it.'

The Captain of *Wayfair* roared in defiance. Zaifyr heard him warn Meina, heard the threat he gave after, but each word rang with less and less conviction as the soldiers of Steel dragged him out of the gates of the City of the Dead and into a world he did not know.

4.

Se'Saera's child watched Bueralan move around him with a curious tilt to his head. 'Why would you do this?' he asked. 'You are not like the man I found earlier. He was afraid of me.'

'I'm not afraid,' the saboteur said, his sword before him. 'But my friend, Zean. You were made from him.'

'I am myself!' The child bared his teeth. 'That is not my name!'

'Is he in there? Do you hear him?'

'Stop!'

'It's a simple question.'

'Only at the start,' he admitted grudgingly. 'But Mother quietened him. He told us that we did not deserve to live.'

Bueralan stopped. 'After that, you never heard him again?'

'Mother said he was an enemy.' The child was agitated, his wings fluttering, hisses escaping at the end of his voices. 'She said I would have lots of enemies. She did not say you were one.'

'I am not your enemy,' the saboteur said, his sword pointed to the ground. 'Your mother is my enemy. Se'Saera took the soul of Zean and made you. But I think you know that. I think you know you are him. I think you know she put you in Taela. Your mother knew that you would kill Taela when you born. She is the one who started this war. She has killed thousands of people just to make a faith. You're simply part of the wreckage.'

Before Se'Saera's child could respond, Bueralan's sword slashed forwards. The child swayed backwards, caught slightly off-guard, but not enough. Bueralan returned with a backhanded slash that pushed the other further back, into the watery edge of Leviathan's Blood, but again, he did so without injury. He cut a horizontal line to his left, forcing the child to the right, pushing him deeper into the rolling surf. He wanted to cut his movement down, to give himself higher ground when the sand suddenly dropped away, and to let the poisoned ocean do what it could to break the child's concentration. But Se'Saera's child understood that and, as Bueralan slashed towards him, his left arm rose and blocked the blade against his inky-black skin, causing a shudder to run along the blade and into Bueralan's arm.

The child leapt forwards and Bueralan turned his shoulder into him to absorb the blow. The force of it surprised him, and pain spiked through him so sharply that it knocked the wind from him. For a brief second, he thought his shoulder had broken, or at least been dislocated. The child thrust forwards, throwing Bueralan to the ground, and he lost his grip on his sword. But his shoulder moved – painfully, but it moved – and he jammed the palm of his hand into the child's hard head hard enough to roll the child off him and scamper away, scooping up his sword as he came to his feet.

He blocked a raking slash of the child's talons, back-pedalled to get his balance, and turned away another slash, followed by another, before a sudden and wild return cut glanced off the child's head and stopped his advance. Bueralan could not see any open wound, but he wasn't surprised: he had hit the child's arm with enough force to cut deep into the bone – maybe through – on a human. A glancing blow would do little to his head. But Bueralan did not panic. Instead, he lowered the tip of his blade and led with his injured shoulder a charge into the child. At the last moment, he stiff-armed the child instead and hit him hard enough to put him off balance. Bueralan's left leg hooked on the child's right and swept him onto the wings on his back, even as the child's talons raked hard and deep along Bueralan's right side.

That stopped him.

He had expected the wound, but he had expected it to be like wounds he had had before, where his body reacted and minimized the damage before it healed.

Instead, the sharp ends of the child's talons cut deep, sliced into skin, muscle, and ran jaggedly along his ribs with such a force that Bueralan's plan to spear his sword down into the mouth of the child broke apart in the pain. He felt the child's foot slam into his right knee, once, twice, enough to bring him down to where the child could reach out with his talons.

Only to find him gone.

'I know you said you wanted to do this yourself,' Aelyn Meah said as she stepped in front of Bueralan. 'But I'd rather you not die.'

You are god-touched and you cannot die, Aela Ren had said to him, months ago. *Not until a god allows you.*

'Aelyn,' Bueralan began.

'I spent some time with your mother,' she said to the child, ignoring him. She stopped before the winged figure, seemingly unarmed. 'Both of them. Did your second mother teach you the word rape, or did she blur that as well?'

'You were supposed to help me,' Se'Saera's child hissed. 'Mother promised.'

'It could have gone that way.' Around her feet, sand began to stir. 'I could almost see it. But in the end, you must be responsible for what you have done, and I have not done enough.'

The sand erupted suddenly and violently around the child as if it were a pair of hands, but his wings flexed—

'Aelyn,' Bueralan said again.

—and Se'Saera's child leapt into the air out of the sand.

In a blink, Bueralan's sword tore itself from his grasp and flew through the air. It appeared in Aelyn's hand in time for her to sweep the blade upwards, using it deflect the child's dive towards her.

She followed the deflection with a thrust, the steel blade matched by another, a blade in her left hand that appeared to be a mix of dark storm clouds and lightning. With a speed that startled the saboteur, she pressed the child, her swords cutting high, then low, then high, a whirlwind of steel and power that saw the child's arms rise and fall to block them. Blood began to seep from his hard skin, but as if the realization of that inspired a fury in him, the child hurled himself forwards. His move caught Aelyn by surprise and her left arm, the arm holding the storm-formed blade, fell across her chest, only to bear the brunt of the child's charge.

She stumbled, her concentration broken, the weapon disappearing. With a swift backhand, the child sent Aelyn sprawling backwards, knocking the steel blade from her grasp. The child reached for it, but was forced to leap back as sand burst from the ground around the Breath of Yeflam. With a roar, Se'Saera's child landed on the ground away from her, his wings folded around him in poor protection.

'You move well.' Aelyn rose, her hand held against her chest. Sand moved around her feet in a small, isolated storm. 'Where did you learn to fight?'

'I fight!' the child hissed through the gap between his wings. 'I was made to fight.'

Bueralan moved next to her, the wound along the side of his chest still bleeding. 'Zean,' he said. 'I've seen Zean fight like that.'

'Stop saying his name!' Se'Saera's child shouted. 'He is dead. He was weak. You are like him! You will die like him soon! Look at yourselves! You are dying before me already!'

'This isn't death,' she said. 'This is just pain.'

5.

'Wait.' Jae'le's hand fell on Ayae's arm. 'Not yet.'

Her hand had just wrapped itself tightly around her reins. 'The bridges are laid,' she said, her mount shifting, ready to ride. 'Eidan is in Ranan. Tinh Tu is crossing. Both need us there.'

'Soon.' He released her arm. 'But first, there is another group of soldiers approaching the battle. Refuge and the Brotherhood. They are led by the former Captain of the Spine.'

'I don't see any crows whispering in your ear,' Ayae said.

'Tonight I have a thousand eyes to see with.'

Before Ayae could ask what he meant, a new force emerged from the treeline to her right. At the head rode soldiers in black-and-red armour. In their hands, they held long spears unlike any Ayae had seen before. Behind them, the armour of the men and women with whom they rode was different. The plate and chain that the first wore became leather, chain, and occasional pieces of plate, the last dull glints. The strange lances were among them too, but more and more of these soldiers were armed with shields and swords, bows and crossbows. They did not ride under a flag and offered nothing to suggest that they were a unified force but for their discipline, and the lines that they rode in. For a brief moment, Ayae thought the mercenaries were going to ride down into the roads that ran beneath the city, but as the first reached that point, they turned and began to loop towards where she and Jae'le sat before turning towards the three bridges that led into the city.

From her vantage point, Ayae could not glimpse Captain Heast, but she could see the night sky break apart, the wings of a dozen swamp crows above the mercenaries.

Eyes indeed, she thought.

'Refuge and the Brotherhood plan to attack the cathedral,' Jae'le said. He did not tell her that the birds flew into Ranan, did not have to, now that she could identify their shadows. 'Captain Heast believes that it is the heart of the battle, rightly so. We will follow in their wake and when he attacks Ren and his soldiers, we will slip past them and inside.'

Ayae followed the path of the mercenaries and swamp crows as they rode and flew over the bridges into Ranan.

Into a city lit with battle.

The three stone giants loomed above it all, violent creatures summoned to make Ranan shudder and break. Already, they were riddled with bolts from ballistas, cracked by heavy stones from catapults. One of them, the one who had emerged with a tree on its back, was on fire. Like a flag, the flames followed it around as it tore the flat roofs off buildings and hurled them onto the soldiers beneath.

It was clear to Ayae that the three giants had drawn the fire of the siege weaponry, and it was from here, in the heart of the violence, that the battle spread.

Further out at the edges of Ranan, the Faaishans' siege engines laid down a cover for their own soldiers in a mixture of burning pitch, rocks and arrows. A din of noise – of shouts, commands and screams – bled the voices of the Leerans, Faaishans, Yeflamese, Saan and Mireean together. It left Ayae with the impression that a part of the world had just woken and its thousands of eyes and mouths had begun to reject what it saw taking place upon it.

'Do you have a path through that?' she asked Jae'le.

'One with a few detours.' He patted his horse's neck. 'Are you ready?'

She turned to him, held his dark gaze. 'Detours?'

His smile was one of filed teeth. 'Trust in your elders.'

Then he rode.

Ayae felt her heart skip, felt her skin prickle with warmth, but her calmness settled back over her as she rode after him.

At the bridges, the noise of the battle seemed to be amplified. Ayae could make out a few words – 'Giant—' 'Sergeant!' 'Hold the—' '*Incoming*!' – but it was so scattered she could not make sense of it. Ahead of her, burning pitch came down on the broken roof of a building, near the muddy giant. A heavy stone followed it, smashing into the ground, a second and third using the pitch to target the giant.

At the edge of the bridge were four of the men whom Tinh Tu had ordered to carry the bridge. They lay near a broken ballista, the siege weapon torn out of its fitting and surrounded by a series of broken buildings. The roofs had been caved in by the stone fists of giants, and bodies mingled with the debris. It was a destruction of blood and mud that continued up the main road, the ground broken apart, buildings crumbled, a wake behind the three stone giants and the soldiers that weaved through the streets behind them.

Jae'le did not ride in the wake of the destruction, however. As soon as he came off the bridge he drove his horse to the left, up and over the debris of one of the houses, down the other side, into a broken street. It was the opposite direction to the one Refuge and the Brotherhood had taken. They, Ayae saw, had used the path of the giants as a shield, and diversion, something that she had hoped that Jae'le would also do. But he was riding away from the ruined, but protected rear that the giants had given. Without pause, he turned down a narrow lane and burst out into a street that ran parallel to the giants' path.

There a small group of Leerans were trying to prop up a fallen ballista.

Before Ayae could call to him, Jae'le was upon them, his sword a blur, the Leerans shouting, falling, and unaware of Ayae until she rode in behind him.

Her sword caught one man in the back of the head, a woman in the face, and then she found herself face-to-face with Jae'le.

'Set this alight.' He pointed to the ballista. Around it lay six soldiers, all of them dead. 'There is a big push coming. We need to make sure that they cannot circle from behind.'

'This is your detour? We're supposed to ride to the cathedral.' Her horse shied as the wood caught fire. 'Jae'le, what have you seen?'

'Our new god knows this battle.' He slipped off his saddle and turned over one of the dead. 'She knows we would come this way. She knows we would lead with Eidan. She knows that Tinh Tu is heading our force.' With his back to her, he sank down on his haunches and began to examine the soldier's face. 'She has organized her response, Ayae, and we dare not leave these stragglers behind when it comes.' Jae'le rose and held out his hand, revealing what he had pulled out of the dead soldier. 'This is not a simple battle. It has been seen and planned for. We must do our best to respond to it in that fashion.'

6.

Heast turned the body before him over: a young white woman, a crossbow bolt buried in her chest, a look of surprise on her face, and dirty wadding in her ears.

Corporal Isaap approached him. 'All of them had their ears blocked,' he said, his face streaked with dirt and sweat. 'I doubt they even heard us attack them.'

There had been a score. As Heast and his soldiers moved through the streets, leaving their horses a few blocks behind as the battle of Ranan turned into a slow grind or inches and position, they had been surprised by the sudden arrival of the Leerans. They had been running, dressed in light armour, carrying swords and knives. 'They weren't looking for us,' Heast said. 'They weren't expecting us, either.'

'At least here they weren't.'

The Captain of Refuge rose stiffly, the ruin of a building protection for him and a dozen of his soldiers, a pause before another push up the damaged street. Ahead, Refuge spread out in small units, securing their advance to the bridges that led to the cathedral. Around them, the dark sky trailed the smoke and light from burning pitch, most of it concentrated in the paths of the three giants that Heast shadowed. The huge silhouettes still led the attack, but they had begun to stumble and break beneath the barrage of siege weapons, and Heast did not think that they would last much longer. Moments before, the one with a burning back had fallen to its knees, its chest split open, the fire a new beacon for the catapults.

Heast believed that the Leerans had known about the giants well before they had risen from the ground. They had been prepared for them, just as they had been for mounted soldiers. The roads had been filled with enough deliberate debris that, after Refuge and the Brotherhood crossed the bridges into Ranan, they had been forced to dismount. For the last half-hour, Heast had watched saddled, but riderless horses canter down the streets and out to safety.

'Sir,' Isaap said, 'why would they fill their ears?'

'I don't know.' He placed a hand on the Corporal's shoulder. 'Sergeant Qiyala has moved up. Our turn.'

Lehana had the lead a street to his right, while two streets further along, Essa and the Brotherhood made their way forwards. Heast had been forced to push wider than he wanted since so much of the siege fire was concentrated on that first force, but he was still able to use the giants as a diversionary shield for his push.

Heast's half of Refuge stretched out ahead of him, divided into small, tight units along the road. Taaira led the point, his huge sword drawn, but Heast could not make him out clearly in the dark and smoke. He slipped in and out of view, the soldiers with him likewise, though they did not appear to be fighting. Four groups back, Anemone moved with Oya. The former First Queen's Guard had her fire lance over her back and an axe and shield in her hand. She had half a dozen soldiers with fire lances: all of them, Heast was pleased to see, were slung over their backs, their shields held in front of them. Half a dozen had been fired when they came into the streets, but most of the resistance had been scattered by the giants and what formal resistance they had fought had required shields at the front.

A whistle sounded behind Heast and he turned, along with his squad, to face the shadow that emerged.

'Sir.' Fenna stepped around the corner, a sword in her hand, a long shield over her other arm. 'The Lieutenant says we will be at the end of the streets in ten, but we have a problem.'

'What kind?'

'The bridges have been collapsed.'

Heast grunted sourly. 'Just that one or all of them?'

'Can't tell yet, sir.'

'Okay. Tell her to keep going forwards. Report what you just told me to Captain Essa as well. We won't be far behind you.'

After she had left, Heast and his unit pushed up another block, the delay lengthening their gap a fraction, but it was that fraction that saved their lives.

The slight whistle and whine through the air from a stone falling towards them gave only enough time for Isaap to yell. Heast did not know what was said, but it was enough warning for the soldiers to turn back, to turn away from where the stone struck the broken building that they were moving to. Stone burst, rubble struck, and Heast felt his head swim from a piece of rubble that glanced off his head, but even through that ringing, he heard a second and third whistle and whine.

'Move!' He was the first on his feet. 'Make them change their trajectory!'

A series of netted rocks burst across the ground behind him as he and the others began to run. Another followed, this time a clay sphere of burning pitch which erupted over the ground in a giant smudge, washing over two of his soldiers. Heast, slower than the others, caught the man whose face was splashed, caught him as he screamed, and Isaap, who had been in the middle of the run, just ahead of the path of the pitch, took the second, whose clothes were on fire. He dropped him to the ground, rolled him, and cut the straps off his leather armour before Heast reached him. A third whine caused both to look up, and then, before Heast knew it, he was on his back, the building he had been standing next to a shower of dirt and rubble.

'Sir!' Isaap stood over him, shouting through his ringing head, blood streaking down from his hairline. 'Sir!'

'I'm fine.' Heast pushed him away. The man he had been holding, the one whose face had been splashed by pitch, had caught the first hit of the stone and disappeared into the rubble behind it in a bloody smear. The other still lay on his back, alive. 'Grab Meikle,' he ordered Isaap, standing. 'Grab him and move.' A fourth whine could be heard. '*Now!*'

The stone hit the ground behind them, but the three of them were moving ahead, and a part of his squad was coming back for them, so they soon outpaced the bombardment. Heast did not relax: he kept his hand on his sword as he jogged forwards, two of his squad slowing their pace to keep up with him, their own swords drawn, an eerie silence beginning to creep down the street that they ran along.

It was broken when a volley of arrows filled the street, moments before Leeran soldiers began to charge.

7.

Meina crouched beside him. 'I don't think you'll be staying here much longer,' she said. 'You look awful, coincidentally. Like someone has stripped you of all your skin.'

Zaifyr could barely move. The pain in his chest had spread throughout him to such an extent that he no longer felt as if his lungs were struggling to breathe through water, but as if the contents of his veins were splintering their solid form and beginning to circulate again. He could feel the dirt beneath him turn to wood and he could hear voices that were not Meina's, but the words were thin. They broke apart before he could understand them, but he knew that he was in the cathedral. Above him, the moving sky was being turned into a ceiling divided by wooden beams. It would not be long until he knew if Aela Ren would lift him to his feet or not.

'What happened to Se'Saera?' His voice was no more than a whisper, but he knew that it could be heard in both Heüala and in the cathedral. 'Meina?'

'The sky broke open.' The mercenary glanced upwards. 'I didn't see how it began. She was beating me, Zaifyr. She was devouring my soldiers. Each one she took reappeared on her side to fight for her. It hurt to see, but I did not order a retreat. I was buying you time. But when there were about three dozen of us left and you hadn't done anything, I had to give the order to scatter into Heüala.

It was after I gave the order that the sky began to split open. I was running down a street when it happened, and I turned back to where Se'Saera was, and I found that the same cracks were appearing in her. It was almost as if she and the sky were made from the same material. She let out this tremendous roar. I thought she was going to begin destroying the city, but then a light burst from her. It was the brightest light I have ever seen.' She turned back to Zaifyr. 'I don't remember much after that. I was pulled into something. I don't remember what. I saw you there, though. You were falling.'

Above him, the sky broke through the cathedral. It was Heüala's sky, one of movement. He thought he could see colour in it now, streaks, but he was not sure.

'After that, I awoke here,' Meina continued. 'Heüala looked like a town to me, the kind I used to ride through all the time. All of my soldiers were here with me. I found you and Jix shortly after. I haven't found Anguish yet.'

'You won't,' he said quietly in two worlds. He saw again the light falling over him, saw Soren push him away, saw him deny the gods that put him there, before his body disappeared. 'He is gone.'

'Is he . . .' She paused. 'Is he safe?'

Could a soul die? 'I don't know,' he whispered. 'I'm sorry. I don't know.' Could a god die? The divinity of a god certainly did not, he knew, but the consciousness could. Was it the divinity or the consciousness that he saw above him? 'Se'Saera could come back, Meina. Or one of the other gods. When the sky is still they will have returned.'

'It is why I plan to stay in Heüala,' she said. 'I will be its guardian. I will ensure that the door is open for all of us to be reborn.' Meina tapped her fingers on her legs, on the leather armour she wore. 'My soldiers are going to stay with me. We would all like to go through that door. We would all like to be reborn. But we've seen souls in the fields. We have to make sure Heüala is safe from them, or whoever else might try to take it.'

Above him, the roof of the cathedral returned. It left only the faintest echo of the moving sky, one that revealed itself only when he felt his body convulse with pain. 'No one will know that you do this,' he said and reached for her hand. 'You will never be thanked.'

'Eventually, another will replace me.' Meina took his hand. Two of Zaifyr's charms pressed against her fingers, but a third passed through her. 'But when you return, can you do something for me?'

'I don't know what the world will be like,' he whispered hoarsely. 'I don't know what I will be able to do.'

'But you'll try?'

'I'll try.'

'Find my daughter,' Meina said, holding his hand tightly, as if she was afraid he would slip away before she finished. 'She will be in the care of my uncles in Kislolc. It is a town in Zoatia. I want you to find her and tell her what her mother did here. What she is doing here. She's young. She won't understand it all, but I want you to tell her I did this, that I held this city, and that I will see her again.'

Zaifyr's fingers were beginning to slip through hers. 'What is her name?' His voice sounded stronger in the cathedral. 'What is her name?' he repeated in Heüala.

'Aino.' Her voice was distant. 'Aino Meina.'

'I'll find her,' he said. 'I'll tell her.'

'Thank you.'

Then she was gone.

8.

Bueralan and Aelyn split, him to the right, her to the left, a circle of two around Se'Saera's child.

His wings flicked in nervous anticipation, but he said nothing. He did not look as assured as his words might have suggested, and that gave Bueralan pause. Another man would be confident. After all, the child had the better of both him and Aelyn and they were both unarmed and injured now. But while he had taken that advantage through Zean's skills, he did not have Zean's experience. Perhaps there was a latent part of Bueralan's blood brother deep inside the child that told him that and urged caution. Zean would have known that Bueralan's attack had been opportunistic, but no matter what his wound meant – *you cannot die,* he repeated to himself, even as he felt his skin try to knit, as if it was trying to remember a skill it had, *not until a god allows you* – his blood brother would not have underestimated Bueralan. He would have expected the saboteur to readjust. Aelyn Meah was the same. She had fought in more battles than Bueralan could conceive, and she would not have survived ten thousand years of them if she had not learned to adapt.

Zean would know that.

But did Se'Saera's child?

'You were all talk before,' Bueralan said. 'Did we hurt your feelings?'

'Mother made me strong.' The child's wings flickered and spread. If he could have flown, Bueralan thought, he would have. 'She did not make me to run.'

'Wouldn't she?' he replied. 'She hides behind armies and followers.'

'She lets them die for her,' Aelyn said, on the other side of the child. 'She doesn't shed a single tear for them. Would she give one for you?'

'I wouldn't hold out for it,' Bueralan added.

Baited, the child roared and leapt at Bueralan, but even as he did, the child knew the mistake he had made.

The sword in the sand swept up, grabbed by invisible hands.

Like a spear, it pierced through the child's left wing and twisted him around. He landed in a controlled tumble, but it was not enough to stop Bueralan charging forwards and grabbing the right wing before the child could straighten. Ignoring the pain in his side, he took the limb in both his hands and twisted as hard as he could. He heard cartilage pop and Se'Saera's child let out an awful scream as he wrenched himself out of Bueralan's grasp.

Quickly, the saboteur took a handful of steps back, his heel tapping the hilt of the sword as he did. He bent to pick it up and when he came up, the child was rushing towards him, his torn wings spread out behind him.

Bueralan came forwards, the blade slicing out. One of the child's bloody arms came up, blocked the cut, and replied by lashing his talons out, only to be met with steel. Bueralan moved quickly, blocking, parrying, pushing the child backwards as if the blade he held weighed nothing, without the wound in his side slowing his attacks. It was only after he spared a glanced towards Aelyn that he saw why the blade weighed nothing and why the strain of his muscles did not bother his wound. He felt the air currents around him a second later: the pushes and pulls that aided his every movement and which built on his strength and speed. Soon, he found himself pressing the child back, chipping into his arms, causing black blood to run down the child's limbs. He offered no room for a counter-attack and, as Bueralan's blows forced the child to his knees, he brought the blade down on the child's upraised arm so violently that the steel broke.

The child's taloned hand speared into Bueralan's already wounded side, slicing further into the flesh.

Bueralan didn't flinch. He grabbed the child by the neck. His left hand encircled the narrow hardness easily, and with strength aided by Aelyn, jammed the toe of his boot into the other's exposed genitals. That caused the child pain, and in that pain, the saboteur worked the hand that was around the child's neck upwards, trapping in in the crook of his arm as he came around him from behind and attempted to choke him.

The child struggled in his grasp, but he went still when he saw the broken parts of the blade rise from the ground, and hover in front of him.

Behind them stood Aelyn Meah.

The child croaked a word, but it was too late: the broken pieces of the blade flew into his deep-set eyes. The child roared in pain in response and Bueralan jammed his knee in the child's back, the cut, bent wings flapping around him as the broken pieces came back out, and then speared back into the child's skull. This time, fluid rushed out, a mix of blood and water from the eyes. The two pieces of blade did not withdraw, however. They pushed further and further into the child until, with a sudden crack, both shards sank deeply into the child's head, leaving a jagged edge and a hilt protruding.

Bueralan released Se'Saera's child and stepped back. He raised his gaze to Aelyn, whose dark eyes met his, a look of resigned satisfaction on her face.

'You're still bleeding,' she said.

'I can feel it trying to heal, but it just can't.' He spat sand out of his mouth. The movement caused him to wince. 'It's like a skill it has forgotten. Something has happened to Se'Saera.'

She nodded. 'We should return to Ranan, then.'

To the battle, to where her family was. 'Yeah,' he said.

She led him up to the edge of the sand, where the two greys stood. The taller of the two gave him a baleful look, a complaint, Bueralan thought, for being kept out of the battle. When the wind began to gather around their feet, and the saboteur took his reins, he could have sworn he saw the horse consider biting him. Instead, he stamped his hooves, while behind them, the swamp crows began to rustle and move and squawk.

'We're on our way, brother.' Aelyn gave the birds a long-suffering look. 'You mothered less when you were younger.'

The crows offered no complaint, not even when the four of them began to rise into the air, and they were forced to hop and flutter away as one.

9.

Heavy stones hit the streets and buildings around Ayae, but she continued to fight across a flat roof, towards the unloaded ballista.

She had lost her horse earlier, before she had to get onto the roof. When the bombardment from the catapults started in force, a series of heavy stones had torn across the broken road towards her and Jae'le. They had escaped the first, but the second series of attacks had caught them both. Ayae was thrown backwards heavily and her body hardened against the stone she crashed into. She was bruised, but she fared better than their mounts. When she stumbled back to them, Jae'le was slicing the neck of his to end the beast's misery, and hers was already dead. The catapults continued to rain stones and pitch around them and, after a pair of huge boulders crashed near them, Ayae found herself on the top of a flat, undamaged roof without Jae'le. She did not know where he was, but the unloaded ballista was pointed at the streets to her right, aimed at the fighting between Leerans and Tinh Tu's force taking place further up, in the shadow of a single unmoving stone giant.

Ayae's arrival interrupted three Leeran soldiers reloading the weapon. The first picked up a heavy crossbow, but the bolt flew wide, and as he dropped it, Ayae was there. With her free hand, she caught the crossbow, slammed it back up and into the soldier's face. She came around the stunned man, using him as a shield while her sword sliced out in an arc, to catch the second Leeran beneath his chin. The blade bit deep, caught on the bone, and she released it as she fell. She grabbed hard on the front end of the crossbow to turn it into a club, one she swung painfully into the head of the soldier who had shot at her. The man staggered to the side and Ayae swung it again to block the blow of the third soldier. The axe blade splintered the stock, but Ayae's hand jammed into the chest of the third with force, stopping her short, giving her enough room so that she could draw her second blade and cut up, across the soldier's chest, setting her staggering—

A large stone smashed into the side of the building.

Ayae stumbled, but it was the Leeran soldier who fared worse, for she fell backwards into Jae'le's sharp blade.

He pushed the soldier off his sword. 'There are not many left.'

'The catapults are more of a danger to the Leerans than we are.' The ballista began to smoke. 'Do they know that?'

'Faith stops them thinking.' Jae'le turned towards the distant cathedral, defined by the light of the fires around it. 'We need to push forwards.'

As he spoke, another stone crashed onto a roof near the motionless giant. Ayae saw it skid off and through soldiers fighting around them, before ploughing into the building ahead of them.

She grabbed her first sword from the ground and followed Jae'le off the damaged roof, into the street. Ayae did not want to run into the siege fire, but she was committed. Moving quickly – more quickly than she would have normally, but not quick enough to overtake Jae'le – she ran past the remains of the buildings that had already been hit, careful of where her feet fell, aware that within the debris were spikes and holes. She listened for the whine and whistle of stones through the air, as well, and kept an eye out for any Leerans who might attack. It was a balance of the senses similar to the one she kept inside herself, the one to keep her powers from hardening or burning her skin, the one she was beginning to lose as she ran faster and faster.

Ahead, stones burst across the street in a new volley from the catapults. As before, Ayae saw them skid off the roofs of houses near where the last giant stood. Its body, she saw, was cracked and splintered from attacks and she was surprised that it was still whole, and not broken apart like the other two.

Around the buildings near it were soldiers. It pleased Ayae to see that the dominant force was that of the Saan and that they held a defensive line around the handful of houses that shook off the catapults' attacks with minimal damage. The fighting was slow, carried out between shots from the catapults, and as the Leerans were pushed back by both their own soldiers and Tinh Tu's force, Ayae and Jae'le jogged through the defensive line. To reach it, they had passed bodies of men, women and horses, the flesh mingled into the stone, the blood soaking into the earth.

Past the line, they went through the open door of the first building. Inside, Eidan sat in the centre of the room, his eyes open, his hands flat against the floor. He nodded to Jae'le and Ayae as they entered, but said nothing. Behind him, Vyla Dvir, Vune and a soldier from Yeflam Ayae did not know moved among the two dozen wounded that were lying down or propped against the wall.

'The bridges are down, the Leerans knew I would be here, their siege engines are focused on us, and we have a mercenary company to our right fighting for us.' Tinh Tu sat at a table to the left of the wounded. Her white raven stood across from her and watched her write with an old quill as she spoke. 'But you knew that, didn't you, brother?'

'The mercenaries are two groups, actually. As for the bridges,' Jae'le said, 'I thought Eidan planned to cross the gap with one of his giants?'

'It is partly why I made them.' There was a strain in the stout man's voice as he spoke. 'I just need Ayae to take over here for a moment.'

'Here?' she asked. 'You mean the building?'

'Keep the roofs strong so that we have some cover. Sil's servant is out there and it means I need to focus completely on the bridge I make. If it is imperfect, she will exploit that.'

Despite herself, she was surprised and hesitant. 'I've never done anything to a building.'

'Just feel for the structure of it. Let yourself strengthen what is there.' Rocks hit the roof in a loud, vicious series of smacks and skids. 'I only need a minute or two to make the bridge.'

'You're sure about this?'

He offered her a faint smile. 'It is not something anyone else could do.'

That did not reassure Ayae, but she turned and approached the front wall, regardless. Through the doorway, she could see Leeran soldiers approaching through the rubble, armed with swords and axes. They would reach the Saan line soon, and even as Ayae felt a part of herself reaching out for the stone around her, another part of her thought that she should be out there, fighting. She could make a difference out there, unlike in here. The earth had already been dug up and reshaped and rebuilt. It felt strange to her, though it did not feel unnatural. She could feel the life in the building, a strange presence without sentience, created from the connections of the rock and the soil. It was Eidan's influence, she knew. He had made Ranan. He had made it with honesty, for he made all his buildings with that. He told the earth about where it would go, what it would be used for. He recognized the importance of the relationship between the earth and the creations of humans and he honoured that in his work. He did not seek to dominate, but rather to foster coexistence, to be part of a network that connected the living and the artificial together. In gentle hints and nudges, Ayae felt her awareness sweep through those connections, as if she was being led by Eidan himself, into the body of the building, and those next to it.

'Do not lose yourself, Ayae.' He rose to his feet and walked to the door. He paused there and turned to her. 'Hold it for a minute. I won't be long.'

10.

The collapsed bridges left a wide, dark ring around the centre of Ranan like a moat. It was a comparison the Captain of Refuge did not enjoy.

Once he and the others had secured the ruined end of the street, Heast ordered Lehana and Essa to his position. He pulled in Refuge and the Brotherhood so that they sat on the edge of the Saan defensive line. Both soldiers approached him with a question about the order – it bunched up their force, kept them closer to the concentration of siege fire and allowed the archers at the cathedral to have better luck with their pot shots – but as Lehana and Essa reached him, a collection of heavy rocks ricocheted off the roof and over the Saan position. Though the three of them could not see where they landed, they heard the stones hit other buildings and heard the cries of Leeran soldiers caught in it.

'Miat Dvir didn't organize that.' Essa crouched in front of Heast, beside Lehana. The remains of a shattered wall ran beside him, revealing a street covered in broken stone, boulders and soldiers. Archers from Refuge and the Brotherhood lay spread out like a spray of stones to catch any Leeran who tried to come across. There hadn't been any, however, since Kye Taaira tore through their main charge. 'But it looks like he got his wish,' the Captain of the Brotherhood continued. 'He found the cursed he wanted in Yeflam and got them to help him.'

'I don't know if they're helping,' Heast said, 'or leading.'

'I hope they have a plan to cross over the divide, because if they don't, we need one, and I don't like the idea of running back for the first bridges.' Lehana had a long scrape across her chest plate from a sword that had got too close. 'But we can't sit here. Those catapults will be readjusted to hit around the buildings soon enough.'

Sergeant Qiyala's voice barked out, '*Incoming!*' as a stone rose into the sky and came down long and loud a block away from where Heast and the others crouched.

The ruins of a building burst apart.

'Well,' Essa said. 'Now you've done it.'

Lehana grimaced. 'I hate siege weapons.'

'The Faaishans have got to be reaching them. If not, it won't matter if we're here or over the other side at the cathedral. Those catapults'll get us eventually.'

'Leave it to me.' Heast pushed himself up and made his way towards the far wall, where the injured had been placed. All things considered, the Captain of Refuge considered the push up to this point successful. He had lost thirty-three soldiers and had another half-dozen injured. Only one of them, Heast believed, would not return to this battle. The former First Queen's Guard Jaela had been among the four soldiers caught in one of the catapult bombardments and while she had, miraculously, survived where her companions had not, debris from a building had struck her, broken her collarbone and sword arm, and smashed her head into the ground. She had been unconscious since.

'Anemone.' He interrupted the witch, who was bent over a soldier, mending a leg. 'How're you holding up?'

'We're doing okay.' She lifted her bloody hands from the leg, revealing a jagged wound. 'I can do nothing for Jaela here, but she's the worst. Being unconscious is the best thing for her.' She rose into a crouch and came near him. 'My grandmother says you have a look as if you're going to give me an order I won't like.'

He grunted in acknowledgement. 'Do you see the stone giant?'

'I do—'

A shout went up through Refuge, a cry that there was a man out there, a man approaching the giant.

Heast moved to the broken wall. There, he could see the solid white man in loose and ragged clothes walking calmly to the still giant. As if awakened by the man's presence, the stone began to move, the limbs of the giant grinding together with a sound both raw and horrific, as if parts of the earth had been given bones and muscle. It raised its face and, lit by the fires that burned throughout Ranan, Heast saw that the giant had no facial features. Its smooth head suggested not just a blindness, but rather an emptiness, as if it was nothing more than a construction made by the man who strode beneath its feet.

'*Incoming!*' Essa yelled. 'Soldiers and siege!'

Heast turned to see Leeran soldiers clearing the broken buildings to his right. The first man, wearing tattered leather armour, dropped suddenly, a bolt in his head, but there were more behind him. 'Essa, hold them back!' The ground shuddered as the giant took its first step. 'Lehana! Ready the lances! We go over once the bridge is made!'

A series of loud cracks and the sound of breaking earth followed Heast's orders. The Leeran attack wasn't huge – there was a bigger force surrounding the cathedral – but they were swarming over the rubble, unconcerned by arrow and bolt. Essa, shouting orders, had his spiked mace out, his soldiers falling in around him. Trusting in the man, Heast turned to the stone giant in time to watch both it and the man beneath it begin to fall as a dozen missiles of rock and boulder and pitch from catapults rained down. They hit the ground so hard that it split and began to give way into the darkness beneath Ranan.

Taking both the man and the giant with it.

He called out to Anemone, but she had already climbed over the broken wall she had been standing behind with him. Heast didn't hesitate: he pushed himself up the uneven ground, his sword drawn, acting as a human shield for the witch. Within seconds, he was joined by Oya, Bliq, Fenna and Taaira, each of them carrying shields to link around Anemone as she exposed herself to the Leerans around the cathedral. Behind him, he heard sword and shield hit, heard Essa's voice, but not his command. He heard Lehana as well, but Heast's attention was on what was before him, on the breaking edge of the city, on darkness that had already swallowed the man and had latched onto part of the stone giant.

But before it did, flickering white light filled the cracks along its body. Heast was reminded of the ghosts he had seen in Mireea, of the white outlines of men and women he had known, and he thought that he had been wrong about the giant, that it had not been a simple creation to be moved, but had instead been a living creature. The light surged through the giant's frame, but as more and more of it appeared through the giant's broken body, it became clear to Heast that the light was not part of it, but rather holding it, ensuring that its fall was not stopped, but controlled. Beside him, he heard Oya swear, and when he turned from the giant, he saw Anemone with blood running from her hands.

The sound of splitting stone drew his attention back to the giant. He was just in time to see it topple across the empty expanse to the cathedral, the white light guiding it as it did, the old souls of the witches of Refuge ensuring that it came down to bridge the two parts of Ranan.

'*Refuge!*' Heast shouted. '*Brotherhood!*' He pulled the horn from his belt and blew into it, long and hard. '*We are crossing!*'

11.

Ayae did not see Eidan's fall, but she felt it. It was as if the awareness she had of the building was a series of connections that ran into the darkness where he fell. To her growing horror, she felt herself drawn with him, the body giving way, crumbling into the emptiness, her awareness stretching from where she stood . . . 'Ayae.' A voice. A hand. 'Ayae.' She heard her name, again. She saw her hand pressed against the wall of a building, a black-skinned hand on her arm. 'Ayae,' Jae'le repeated. 'We have to go, now. We cannot stay here.'

'Eidan,' she began.

'I know. I saw.' He tightened his hand around her arm but she barely felt it. 'There is nothing we can do.'

'He isn't dead,' she said. 'He's still alive. Jae'le, we can help him.'

'He must help himself.' As if her hand was attached to the house, he prised her loose. 'You and I must cross the bridge before the catapults are realigned.'

He dragged her out onto the road. Pulling her hand free of his grasp, Ayae stumbled down the broken road after him, her mind still filled with the sensation of breaking and falling. She twisted past Tinh Tu, heard her orders to the Saan – 'Let the mercenaries lead across the bridge, let them use their bodies' – and she saw the white raven rise into the sky. In its mouth and claws were the pieces of paper that Tinh Tu had been writing on. Yet, as she thought how much of a target it made, how easy it would be for an arrow to fly through the sky, black swamp crows circled down and she lost sight of the raven as they made a defensive screen around it. Arrows caught a few, but not the white raven, and Ayae's attention returned to the road as she stumbled over a rock. She felt groggy, unlike herself, her attention still on the darkness beneath Ranan where Eidan had fallen. She wanted to climb down there. She wanted to reach for Eidan. He lay at the bottom, alive but hurt. She passed Vune and Vyla Dvir, pushed past Miat and the Saan, and joined the mercenaries who swarmed across an uneven bridge. Beneath it, the darkness called to her, and the figure she knew was down there—

A sudden roar of noise jolted her back to full awareness.

The sound was unlike any she had heard before. It came from the mercenaries, from the lances they held. It was a portent, a promise of what was to come after printing presses, papers, alchemical flasks and magnifiers. A promise of wars that would be fought without swords, without curses, and without witches.

It devastated the front line of the Leerans like no other weapon Ayae had ever seen. Soldiers lay on their backs and sides, their faces and chests torn open with small pellets of lead, stone and glass. Whatever force the black smoke had created when it exploded, it flung the pieces forwards at such a speed that the armour the Leerans worn had proven useless. The pellets had sunk through the gaps, ripped into the leather and sprayed into the soldiers' faces.

Where others came to a halt in the tremendous noise, Jae'le continued onwards. He moved with such an ease through the soldiers of Refuge and the Brotherhood that Ayae found herself struggling to keep up with him. Just when she thought she had lost him, he stopped suddenly and she nearly crashed into his back.

Black smoke filled her nostrils, obscured her vision, but after a moment, she saw what Jae'le was looking at.

The doors to the cathedral had opened.

Men and women were emerging in a solemn procession. There was no sense of urgency, or fear, or eagerness about them. Even at this distance, Ayae knew that the mismatched soldiers had no concern about what was before them.

'The Innocent's army,' Jae'le said quietly.

Ayae went still. 'Is the Innocent there?'

'No. Joqan is at the head.' He turned to her. 'Let them come down. Let them attack. Let the soldiers of Refuge and the Brotherhood deal with them. Let them try their new weapons of war on the god-touched. What we want is inside.'

At the top of the stairs, the immortal soldiers let out a roar and ran down the cathedral stairs. The sound they made contained such raw emotion that Ayae found herself momentarily stunned. She could only watch as they drew closer.

'*Refuge!*' Captain Heast's voice barked out from her left. 'Second wave of lances. Third be ready, fourth after. Hold your line off the bridge, not on it! *Brotherhood!* Secure those streets to our left and right. Don't let them dig in!'

Ayae saw him when she turned: the weighted stance forced by his steel leg singled him out to her, his close-cropped hair and face covered in dirt, a sword in his hand. At the sight of him, Ayae took a strange confidence, an odd reassurance, as if his presence here, in the middle of this battle, in a city that held the soldiers who had invaded Mireea a year ago, was right. Ayae could not elaborate on the feeling. She could not understand it in terms of the events unfolding around her. She could not explain how some of the weight in her lessened. As Jae'le began to move, she followed, her body not yet moving at its natural speed, but closer to it.

Ahead, the Leerans parted and allowed the Innocent's soldiers a path to Refuge.

On their faces, Ayae saw the anger she had heard, the primal, inhuman emotion, built from such hate that she could not help but think of Sooia.

Explosions burst out from the front line of Refuge. Black smoke billowed in the air. The god-touched soldiers staggered, but continued their advance. The soldiers of Refuge dropped to their knees and lifted their shields. A second line stepped forwards, lances raised, a burning cord at the end carrying a flame up to the base of a small container, up and up and—

The god-touched soldiers went down in the roar of smoke.

Ayae saw the man in the lead – Joqan? – fall, his body ripped open, like the Leeran soldiers before. A dozen others fell with him, and the speed with which they went down broke the charge of the god-touched.

Ayae and Jae'le burst through a gap on their right and came upon flat-roofed buildings and a chaotic street filled with Leerans. Jae'le boosted Ayae up, onto the first roof, and she grabbed his arm and hauled him up, the two above the street's chaos within a heartbeat. Ahead of them, swamp crows dropped down and dived and pecked at soldiers. The two ran along the roofs filled with the crows, jumping gaps, bursting through small clumps of soldiers around ballistas, avoiding the Leerans below them, running above a force that had, until moments ago, been unified. They would be again, Ayae knew. From her height, she could see officers bringing order to the soldiers around them. They did it in silence, not in words, but they were unquestionable. By the time Ayae and Jae'le reached the cathedral's steps, order had been returned. On the stairs, she turned around and saw the battle spilling across the prone form of the stone giant, pouring from its broken head as if the violence around it was a series of dreams that it was having.

Then she was in the cathedral.

Inside, the sound of the battle became a dull echo around her, as if she was inside the beating of a giant heart.

Jae'le walked ahead of her, his sword drawn. On either side of him were empty wooden pews, but it was the altar at the front of them that he was drawn to.

A single body lay there.

Ayae could tell only that it was male and white. She could see nothing of his features, for his head had been split open with a sword.

'Waalstan,' Jae'le said softly. 'Ekar Waalstan.'

'He died only recently,' she said. 'The blood from his wound is not dry yet. Can you imagine the pain he was in?'

'Aela Ren brought him here.' Jae'le left the altar and walked towards the stairs on the left, the stairs that led higher into the heart. 'I didn't realize it at the time. I saw Ren return, but the figure he carried was covered in a cloth and I could not see his face. I thought that he carried a dead man, for the cloth was soaked with blood. But as you said, it has only just begun to dry.'

Ayae hurried after him. 'Is the Innocent in here?' She did not ask about Se'Saera. She could feel the sensation of teeth against her skin, but it was faint, as if the god was a distance away.

At the entrance to the stairs, he turned to her. 'You leave him to me. You leave our new god to me, as well. Take Zaifyr and get him to safety. We don't have much time here. Even now the catapults in Ranan are being turned against the cathedral. Tinh Tu's orders to the Faaishans to destroy them – orders that contain the catapults' locations – have only just been received.' Ayae saw the white raven flying into the sky, papers held in its beak.

'No matter what happens when we reach the top of the cathedral,' Jae'le continued, 'you take my brother to safety, please.'

She nodded, not trusting herself to tell him that no, she would not leave him. Not trusting either her conviction or ability.

The stairs twisted up and around four floors, but Jae'le did not enter any of the hallways. He moved up the stairs quickly, smoothly, not once doubting the path he was on. On the second floor, huge windows revealed the battle of Ranan to Ayae. The nightmare that she had seen spilling from the head of the stone giant before the cathedral was much more complete here. She could see the landscape riddled with pools of fire, siege towers, ballistas, catapults, broken streets, ruined buildings, and thousands of men and women fighting in numbers Ayae had never seen before.

On the fourth floor, the doorway was empty, and the room it led to held a waiting light. Ayae took a breath as she followed Jae'le inside.

Four people waited in the middle of the room. Two of them stood, the first a monster like the ones she had seen in Yeflam, the second a handsome blond man in strange leather armour made from strips that wound around his body. But it was not to them that Ayae's gaze was drawn. No. She stared at the scarred man who knelt in the middle of the floor beside a beautiful blonde young woman.

Beside Se'Saera.

The god was still, as if she was a statue, and the sensation of being devoured that Ayae had come to associate with her was as faint as it had been at the entrance of the cathedral. More startling was that Se'Saera's face was fractured, the skin broken like porcelain that had been dropped. Through the lines in her skin, Ayae could see movement, and she had the sudden, awful realization that a living entity was there, trying to emerge, to break through the god's body. Gazing at it, Ayae felt herself drawn to something other than this world, an existence different to her own, one with an endless amount of possibilities. But, when she blinked, it was no longer there. She saw only darkness beneath the god's skin, and it was a darkness of nothing.

Beside her, the Innocent rose.

'She is not dead, not yet.' He spoke calmly, as if the two who had entered were his friends. 'Fate unfolds around us.'

'We are not above it, Aela.' Jae'le held his sword pointed to the ground. 'You cannot pretend that you are.'

'I know the part I play.' He stepped in front of Se'Saera. 'It is the part I have always played. I am the creator of myth and reason. You are that as well, Jae'le. You are one of the immortals who has strode the earth in the absence of the gods. In thirty thousand years, when these moments are rewritten, we will be seen as villains and heroes, myths and parables. Who we are will not matter.'

He took another step towards the Innocent. 'I have come for my brother.'

'He lies in the corner.' Behind Ren, the blond man spoke. He pointed to where Zaifyr lay on his side. 'I will not give him to you. You are the intruder here and you will be dealt with appropriately.'

Jae'le said nothing.

'Zilt will not die easily,' the Innocent said, his hand falling to his weapons. 'But then, who of us will?'

It was then that siege fire smashed into the cathedral.

The Last Designs

'I wish that we had killed him.' The silence of Leviathan's End was like a shroud around Aelyn Meah. 'Is that not awful?' she asked me. 'To wish that you had killed a child?'

—Onaedo, *Histories, Year 1029*

1.

It was not the first volley of stones from the catapults that ripped through the wall of the cathedral, but the third. The first series of stones hit low on the building, enough to make it shudder, for cracks to run through the walls. The second struck high, almost at the same time, high enough to shatter the tall windows Ayae had passed on the stairwell, and to rip parts of the roof away. The cathedral rocked as both volleys hit and, inside, Ayae struggled for balance. Ahead of her, Jae'le did not move, nor did Aela Ren. The two behind them, however, had spread out. Not one of them showed concern at the attacks on the cathedral. As if to challenge their disregard, a third volley came, and it was this one, the largest of the three attacks, that tore open the cathedral.

The roof shattered inwards, stones the size of her body breaking through the wood and metal on the roof, splintering the windows and smashing into the floor.

Ayae turned instinctively, shielding her eyes as the room burst apart. When she removed her hand from her eyes, she found herself staring at the staircase she had come up. For a moment, it did not register to her that it was no longer there, that the stairwell led to a long drop into spiked wood and shards of glass, but then her stomach lurched, and the sight of Ranan alight with battle came to her in a dizzying, unframed openness.

She turned, but in doing so, found that the broken edge of the cathedral revealed even more of Ranan. A thin half-moon of the room's floor extended out over the sight, with buttresses of glass and wood offering a symbolic protection from the elements and arrows. Ayae heard a creak as she gazed at it, and when she turned, she saw the hulking creature running from the broken, shadowed part of the middle of the room. She grabbed the hilt of her sword, but Jae'le's hand pulled her back and he stepped into the creature's path, his sword drawn.

Jae'le's sword ripped through the armour and skin of the creature, but as it did, the creature dropped to the ground and revealed the slim figure of the strangely armoured Zilt behind it. He led with his knife and barrelled straight into Jae'le, catching him off balance. He lost his sword, but trapped the soldier's arm against his side and smashed his palm into Zilt's face. The other man wrapped his spare arm around him just as the creature Jae'le had slashed rose.

With a roar, she charged, and with her arms spread, picked up both men. With them in her grasp, the creature went over the broken edge of the cathedral, into the wood and debris below.

Ayae threw herself after Jae'le, but she was not close enough, not fast enough to grab part of him, not even the edge of his green-feathered cloak, before he fell.

Gripping the edge of the broken floor, Ayae looked over, but she could see nothing.

Behind her, she heard a step.

She was on her feet, both swords drawn, before she realized that there was only one other person in the room with her.

The Innocent stood in front of her, his weapons still sheathed. Behind him, the smoke-filled moon and firelit sky shone through the broken room, highlighting the scars that mapped his body. There was not a part of him that was untouched: the lines, both jagged and straight, thin and thick, ran across his neck, his face, and beneath the black shorn stubble of his hair. It left him with the appearance of a man who was not so much born, but built. A monster made from an old world. 'I doubt that any of them are dead.' He spoke in a voice that was mild, even polite. 'At least, not yet.'

'Feel free to chase them.' What was it that Jae'le had said about the Innocent? What did he say was important? 'I'll even step aside for you.'

'That won't be necessary.' He regarded her intently. 'You are from Sooia, are you not?'

Hide who you are from him. 'Mireea. I was born in Sooia.' The distinction was important to make, even as she heard Jae'le's voice.

'I was born in Sooia, as well,' Aela Ren replied. 'It was in the southern part of the country, in a village that no longer exists, near a mountain long gone.' He offered her a faint smile. 'It was there that my god found me. I was a loyal servant to Wehwe for thousands and thousands of years, but I never forgot my home. It was why I returned there after the War of the Gods.' The Innocent responded to the horror on her face with a twist in his smile, a deepening of the scars around his face, an acknowledgement of what she felt. 'A god is alien, child. It is not like you or me. Not in substance, not in thought. You cannot explain it in your own words. You must use the language it created. When that is all that remains of the gods, you have only echoes of what once defined the world.'

'Is that how you justify what you have done?' Ayae felt her voice catch. She took a breath and tried to calm herself. 'You sought to kill an entire race of people – your own people!'

'I thought to spare them the emptiness that is the endless silence of their soul. In my despair, it was all that I was capable of.' His scarred hands fell lightly to the hilt of his sword and dagger. 'It was not until recently that I realized I was doing what my master and his kin wished. The fate that we stand in is their creation. It is also the creation of Se'Saera. In both these creations I have been used to define the world without gods.'

'You could have said—'

He was upon her before finished speaking, his sword and dagger drawn.

He moved with such speed, such deadly accuracy, that had Ayae's swords not been drawn, he would have cut through her defences, and into her.

But her swords were drawn. She turned away his first thrust, blocked his stab, parried a third attack, and stepped to her right for the fourth, conscious that each move was a retreat, an attempt to buy time to calm herself, to find the centre she needed within herself, and without. She needed time to position herself, to push aside her fear, to find the divinity that was within her. In her head, she could hear Jae'le's voice, urging her to hold a part of herself back, to hide it, but she could not find a part of herself to present to him, yet.

Her turn to the right, towards the mostly entire wall, presented the Innocent to the night sky, to the world defined by war. A gap appeared in his defence and, without thinking, Ayae pushed it, her hands cold and heavy, her blades not as fast as she needed them to be. He ducked and weaved and continued her turn, so that it was her back, not his, that was against Se'Saera and Zaifyr.

He pressed her, then. He came forwards and she caught his dagger, turned it away, blocked his sword, stepped away from the stomp of his boot. Ayae cut down, was blocked, weaved back. She thrust forwards, parried his sword, and as her left-handed sword came up, felt his dagger punch into her right hip, felt it bite deep into her armour, through to her skin. Panicked, she slashed downwards and pedalled back. As she did, Ren ripped the knife out of her, tearing it through the leather armour as he did.

She dropped her hand to the wound, to staunch the blood, pressing through cloth and leather to find that what was lodged in her was a piece of steel.

'How interesting,' Aela Ren said, examining the broken blade of his knife as she pulled the end out and dropped it, bloodily, to the floor. 'It felt as if I was stabbing stone.' He lowered the blade, met her gaze. 'Still, unless you have other tricks, child, it won't be enough.'

Fire burst along the blade of her sword suddenly. *Hide who you are.* 'I've a few,' she said, ignoring Jae'le's voice.

2.

The stones and pitch hurled by the catapults broke open the crown of the cathedral, crashed into the walls to reveal an empty library and small rooms. Some fires burned in the building, but most were further down, littered across the stairs to the cathedral. The stones and pitch also fell across the flat-roofed buildings below, just as they tore into the streets and soldiers friendly and not, and left the battle beneath the cathedral one of chaos.

Heast's first instinct was to find cover behind him, back in the ruins of Ranan. With one exit, he was confident that he could drain the Leerans from their position around the cathedral. The lines of command in the opposition were, if not broken, then damaged and able to be exploited. But the presence of the single bridge was exactly why he ordered Refuge and the Brotherhood towards the cathedral and did not retreat. He didn't hold the bridge. He couldn't hold it. It was not even a bridge, technically. It was the remains of a fallen giant, an animated figure Heast had no control over. If the giant fell into the crevasse, it fell, no matter what he said. If it rose up, it rose. If it did either, it would leave Heast with no immediate path to return to the centre of Ranan. He would be forced to make a new bridge and, in doing that, he would lose the momentum he had gained from both the fire lances and the Leerans' indiscriminate use of catapults.

He had to press forwards.

He had to spend the soldiers to take the ground.

To his left, Sergeant Qiyala and a squad of six were dragging the bodies of the god-touched behind the battle lines. The fire lances had brought down most of Aela Ren's force and, though they had not risen, some were not dead, and Heast was taking no chances. When the bodies were dragged far enough from the fighting, Qiyala swung a heavy axe over the heads of each of them, while others dropped stakes into their bodies.

The loss of the Innocent's soldiers had blunted the Leeran counter-attack. The silent, ear-blocked soldiers still controlled the centre of Ranan, especially to the left, where Refuge fought in a long line over debris, but Heast did not believe they would take back what they had lost. Before the siege bombardment started, he had not been sure, but after, neither Refuge, the Brotherhood, nor the Saan would give up their hold. Still, Heast had seen Bliq and three others fall two houses up. It had been a combination of bolts and swords. Leerans had swarmed around the corner. Part of the Brotherhood had swung towards Bliq, Essa at its head, and the attack had broken against his wicked mace, but it highlighted what a small part of the Leerans was broken. To his right, a block over from Essa and his soldiers, the Saan fought. A pair of Ren's soldiers had cut through a handful of Heast's soldiers when the bombardment started, heading towards him, and the bridge, but the Saan had flooded into the breach that the god-touched made and pulled down Ren's soldiers. The old woman who led them ordered them into the streets with her strange, compelling voice. When she passed Heast after the barrage of siege fire that damaged the cathedral, she offered him the faintest nod, before she was lost behind some houses. Beside her walked Miat Dvir and his wife. There was something about the Lord of the Saan's stance that bothered Heast, but whatever it was, it would have to wait. The battle line on his left that Refuge and the

Brotherhood made drew his attention. The fighting there was dense hand-to-hand combat and, through a broken buildings, Heast could see Lehana and Oya holding the centre. He could hear Lehana's voice ringing out, again and again, with the command to hold the line. At the end of that line, towards the cathedral, Kye Taaira and a small squad held the flank.

They would need reinforcing.

The question was from where, however. Essa was still fighting further up. The line to his right had no fat in it. Qiyala was still dealing with the god-touched. In the bloodstained ruins around him, Anemone and a pair of soldiers tended to the wounded carried out of combat by a dozen soldiers led by Corporal Isaap.

Heast would not send Anemone. He was not sure how much the witch had left in her since the bridge, and if he wanted those soldiers to be of any use again, he had to keep her with them.

That left the Corporal.

'Isaap,' he cried out, then stopped.

Beneath him, the ground began to shake. In the damaged cathedral, a piece of a window fell out, twisting and turning until it splintered on the ground.

Setting his steel leg to hold his balance, Heast at first thought that an earthquake had begun, but to his surprise, he felt the ground rise, much like a wave on a boat. Ahead of him, he saw his soldiers and the Leerans stumble and struggle to regain their footing as the ground rose again. As Heast caught his balance, he heard a loud crack and turned, just in time to see the bridge break, and the giant's body slide with a loud crash into the chasm.

Beyond it, Ranan disappeared.

Awkwardly, Heast made his way stiff-legged towards the edge of the crevasse, unable to believe what he was seeing, unable to believe what was happening.

The centre of Ranan was rising.

Below him now, he could see the ruins Refuge and the Brotherhood had fought through, but on a much smaller scale, as if he were looking at a theatre set, shrunk to half the actual size for the actors to loom over. From his height, he could see the sprawling frames of the catapults throughout the city. They fired as the city rose, but the stones hit the pillar of earth beneath him: a pillar, Heast realized, that had taken the shape of a face.

He stood over one of its eyes – an eye that was opening – and could clearly see in profile the hugeness of it, the massiveness that led to the rest of its features being mashed together. The ugly face was repeated to his left, and again to his right, revealing three identical faces, three faces defined by eyes of stone and dirt, a thick nose of darkest soil, and lips made from clay.

'*LEERANS*,' it said in a grinding voice. '*YOUR GOD IS DEAD*.'

A dirty hand reached over the edge as it spoke. It was human and it reached onto the broken ground near Heast, bloodied and lined with black scars. A second hand covered in mud followed it. When the man's filthy and bloody head came into view, Heast released the hilt of his sword, and stepped forwards to help the man who had made the bridge to his feet.

Eidan sagged against Heast so heavily that the Captain of Refuge almost stumbled. The blow he had taken across his head appeared to be the worst, but there was no real way to tell, given the dirty state of his clothes. Once Heast adjusted to the weight of the other man, he led him away from the edge, past where Qiyala and the others had staked out the god-touched, to Anemone. At the sight of the god-touched, however, Eidan whispered and the ground spoke again.

'*LEERANS*,' the giant head said. '*YOUR GOD IS DEAD. AELA REN'S SOLDIERS HAVE FALLEN*.'

'You're not going to keep saying that, are you?' Heast asked as he pulled the man along. 'It will disturb the focus of my soldiers as much as it'll demoralize the Leerans.'

Eidan laughed roughly. 'No,' he said, his voice staggered with pain, 'but you have to shout to be heard when the enemy blocks its ears.'

The Captain of Refuge grunted in agreement. Before him, the fighting had resumed and, with a shout, he called out to Anemone. As he did, Heast saw two lines of fire flare within the broken crown of the cathedral, the sudden light illuminating not just the faint shadows of people in the ruins, but a green-cloaked man two floors below.

He was on the left-hand side of the cathedral, the most damaged side. The broken frame was like an exposed ribcage on a body, and the cloak a flickering hint of something emerging. Behind it, Heast saw two shapes, the first larger than the other. They were nothing more than shadows until the first grabbed a piece of the cathedral's frame and used it to swing outwards like a giant gorilla. Its misshapen body – a body Heast had seen the likes of before – landed ahead of the green cloak, but the man it landed in front of ducked and darted forwards, his sword cutting a bright line through the dark of the cathedral.

'Jae'le,' Eidan whispered.

The creature's arm shot out and grabbed the man, but as it dragged him into the night sky, Jae'le drove his sword into the misshapen head. As the creature roared, he grabbed the broken edges of the cathedral above him and swung out into the open. The creature's grip remained tight, but Jae'le's boot slammed down on his sword and the creature's grip failed. A second later, he swung backwards and then inwards and landed in the darkness of the cathedral, unarmed.

Next to Heast, Eidan's breath caught, and he whispered, 'Brother,' but Jae'le appeared to be oblivious to the shadow waiting for him.

He turned towards it and was struck twice, both times in the chest as the shadow bore him to the ground.

Jae'le jammed his knee into the groin of his attacker and, with a burst of strength, flipped him off the cathedral.

Eidan's grip was tight on Heast, but the Captain of Refuge pulled his arm free and pushed him not towards Anemone, but towards Sergeant Qiyala. The ledge Jae'le had lain on was empty, but Heast barely noticed. He shouted again, but this time he shouted for Anemone and Isaap. He ordered them forwards, away from the injured, and towards Kye Taaira's side.

There, the ancestor who had fallen burst through the line of Leerans.

3.

Ayae came forwards, her burning blade leading in arcs, slicing through the air on either side of Aela Ren, forcing him to the left, then the right, to dodge the cuts, rather than raise his own weapons to block. Around her, the broken floor of the cathedral was illuminated by the moon's light, and Ayae was conscious that the two of them moved around a huge hole. To fall through it was to fall to the centre of the earth, where a world of nightmares and horrors awaited on the other side.

Ren's sword caught Ayae's, turned it aside while his broken-tipped dagger cut up, held in a slashing position, tried to slice through her chest, her chin. As she leaned back, his right foot lashed out, kicking her left, forcing her to readjust her stance and put more weight on her wounded right side as she brought her burning sword between them in a wild arc. With her other blade, she pushed Ren's dagger away, then cut back, and pushed him backwards, and pressed forwards on her left leg again. The flames of her swords pushed the Innocent backwards, forced him to back onto the thin strip of the broken floor.

Ayae pressed the attack, but as she did, the cathedral began to shake. It took her a moment to realize that it was not the building breaking apart, but the ground beneath it.

It jolted, and Ayae felt herself rise, suddenly. To her left, she saw the battle of Ranan shrink, the lines of streets turning thin, the fires in them pale, and the soldiers fighting within it nothing but a vague sense of motion. The motion stopped as dramatically as it had begun, and in that pause, she heard an awful voice speak.

'*LEERANS*,' it said. '*YOUR GOD IS DEAD*.'

'Eidan,' she whispered, more to herself than to the scarred man before her.

'Jae'le arrived with the whole family?' Ren shook his head. 'He will die here. Likely they all will, but I know Eidan will. There is no fate that Se'Saera has seen where he does not.'

She could see the painting, hear the god's words in Yeflam. '*LEERANS*,' the awful voice said before she could speak. '*YOUR GOD IS DEAD. AELA REN'S SOLDIERS HAVE FALLEN*.'

'No.' The Innocent sounded startled, the confidence he had just spoken with suddenly gone. 'It cannot—'

Ayae darted forwards. The flames from her swords cut left, then right, illuminating the broken tower of the cathedral as she closed in on him. It was the scars on his face that they caught mostly, illuminating the wounds that, the more Ayae saw them, the more they began to appear as if they held him together, as if all that defined him were the horrors that had been done to him, both physical and mental.

Aela Ren's sword thrust low and forced her to present her right side towards him. With a startling burst of speed, his fist – wrapped around the hilt of his dagger – punched her wounded hip. The Innocent did not try to stab or cut, but rather crowded Ayae's space to work the injury. In response, she cut down with her sword, a short jab without much power, but one that gave her enough time to turn her elbow to his head. Her arm hardened and she hit Ren hard in the temple. The weight of the blow caught him by surprise and it allowed her to shuffle her right hip out of his range and bring both her swords around. But, even stunned, his sword and dagger were there to block. He took two steps to back out of her slashes and on the third, he pressed her, his blades snapping out in tightly controlled thrusts.

The first got through her defence, cut along the edge of her armour, tore it open with an ease that surprised her. The second glanced off her sword, the third slipped through, caught more of her armour, while his dagger turned from a slashing angle to a thrusting position held low in his hand, the broken end aimed with all its ugly violence at her. With it, Ren turned Ayae's thrusts and slashes into blocks and parries and she found herself turned once again. But this time, she was not turned towards the cathedral, but towards the damaged edge of the building, where dim images of battle could be seen. As she was pushed towards it, Ayae heard faint shouts and screams, but not the clash of swords, or sounds of fighting. She tried to slow her push, but every move she made to go forwards was one that Aela Ren rewarded with a cut through her armour, a slice along her arms, none of them deep enough to stop her, each blow feeling as if it scraped against something hard beneath her skin, but nonetheless drew blood—

Ayae's heel slipped over the broken edge of the cathedral, into the emptiness of the sky.

Frantic, Ayae spun, her foot coming up and around, pushed by a current of air, and suddenly weighted like a heavy stone. She slammed into the Innocent's left arm, broke his grip on his dagger, and thrust her swords forwards.

He parried, but she saw surprise in his eyes. Pushing herself towards him, her swords lanced, then turned into a burning arc to push him backwards. Unbalanced from the kick, he twisted and turned, but he was not quick enough to dodge Ayae's attacks, not fast enough to avoid her blades, or the raw burst of speed that pushed her towards him, past his defences, and across the side of his face.

She left two long cuts on his face. The first ran along the left side of his chin, the second above his eye, slicing through the top of his ear.

Before her, Aela Ren reached up to his wounds, as if surprised. First he touched his chin, and then the side of his scalp.

'No.' He lowered his bloody hand and met her gaze. 'No,' he repeated, a fury erupting from his voice. 'What Eidan said cannot be true.'

Ayae took a step backwards.

'You are nothing!' Aela Ren's voice was thick with anger as he rounded on her. 'You are not a design! My master did not make you! You have not been buried in fate to kill me.' He spat to his left, into the broken floor. 'I will not die here.'

'Everyone dies.' She held her burning swords in front of her. 'Even you.'

'*Master!*' His voice was guttural, almost inhumane. '*Wehwe!*' He raised his head and shouted through the broken roof, out into the dark sky. 'I will not be sacrificed here! I do not deserve that!'

Aela Ren's anger, Ayae realized, came from a contradiction within him. Despite what he had said to her, he did not accept what the gods had done.

In the broken crown of the cathedral, she had a vision of him thousands of years ago, a man without scars and without a sword. He was a simple man who had been given the task of speaking the words of a god to people around him. Ren offered himself wholly and fully to the task Wehwe had given him. The words of his god might have been difficult for him to understand, might have made no sense to his mind, and might even have contradicted what had been said before, but Aela Ren accepted that. He stood before those who waited on the words of a god and relayed what was said to them. He did it as precisely as he could, always conscious of his responsibilities. His work was holy, a blessing, and he had lost that during the War of the Gods. Once the war finished, he was left in a newfound loneliness, one that was more than the loneliness of flesh, one which defined the world he lived in.

He would gather to him those who shared his experience. He would forge a bond with them that was based on a despair that no other person could understand, but it would not be a friendship. Ayae could see that clearly. The god-touched would not be friends. They could not be. They would speak to each other in short conversations, would repeat to themselves that the gods could not be understood, an attempt to soothe the pain they felt. Each of them would say it again and again until it had become a polished belief, but it would be one forever tested. They would hold duels. They would tempt fate to kill them. And perhaps, in quiet moments, they told each other that they would be happy to die in such a duel, for it meant that the gods were still alive, that somehow, they were not entirely abandoned. But the truth was otherwise. To learn that Ren could die – to learn that any of them could – was to open the unhealed wounds of abandonment, to rekindle the bitterness in him that stemmed from the fact that Aela Ren believed in one simple and very human emotion. He believed he should have been treated with respect. He had been a loyal servant. He was the first of the Faithful. He deserved to be taken into confidence, not pushed aside, and kept in silence, like a child.

Aela Ren charged her.

He came in anger, but where another swordsman might forget his skill or craft, Ren did not. His old sword sliced through the air in tight, controlled slashes. Ayae's burning blades were forced to block above her head, down by her left side, at her right arm, and then at head height with both her swords. Ren held her swords there, pressing down on them with his considerable strength. She could match him for that, however, and just as Ayae thought she could slide out of the attack, he turned and spun, his sword aimed at Ayae's neck. Her sword deflected the blow, but she resumed moving backwards, fire trailing to her left and to her right, lines of smoke snaking the cathedral to map the path she took to its edge.

A step before the edge, the blade of her left sword snapped, broken by the sheer force of Ren's blow. Her right sword caught his blade as it came towards her, and her broken, burning hilt slashed across the old leather armour that he wore. It was an act of desperation, but it worked. Her full blade came slicing back, forcing Aela Ren to duck beneath it. He cut upwards with his sword. As he did, he caught the wrist of her hand holding the broken blade and twisted violently, aiming to break the bone, but found himself unable to do so, no matter his strength. Realizing that, he released his grip and drove his elbow into her face, into her chin, before bringing his sword around in a blistering arc that she had to block frantically. As she did, his hand hit her in the chest, pushing her back to the edge, to the massive drop into the city below.

Ayae hit out with her own empty hand, striking Ren in the chest hard enough to force him back. In that gap, her burning sword cut an X that he blocked, but which allowed her to leave the edge. Ayae wanted as much room as she could get. She needed as much room as she could get. Her next blow was caught by Ren's blade, however, and he sliced his sword down to the hilt, allowing him to step within her guard and punch her hip. Ayae felt the pain run through her, felt it so badly that she stepped back, but as she did, Ren punched her in the face. His knuckles cut on her teeth. She tasted blood in her mouth. He hit her again, and again, rocking her so hard that she dropped her guard and allowed Ren's sword to come racing down at her head.

Ayae's deflection dragged the Innocent's sword along her left arm and opened a long gash that tore through armour and skin, but she was lucky. She knew that, even as her feet came to the edge, again.

She was lucky.

But her luck could not last.

4.

Heast watched as Kye Taaira was pressed backwards by the misshapen creature who, having torn the sword from its head, swung in it vicious, violent arcs at him. His old sword met each blow, a strange light emanating from it, and on every third or fourth attack, the tribesman would use his defence to press forwards. Each time he did, the creature would dart around the Leerans who fought beside it. With its bloody head a hideous mask of violence, and the haunted a twisted, wretched thing caught inside it, it would further show its disregard for life by throwing the men and women before it as shields. Taaira met these attacks, but as he did, as he was forced to dodge, deflect or strike at the soldiers, the creature would dart out at him, its sword swinging in another wild arc, forcing Taaira to meet the blow.

Two of the soldiers from Refuge who had been fighting beside the tribesman had fallen. As a result, the edge of the line that they and Taaira held had begun to fold inwards.

'Isaap,' Heast ordered as he walked towards the battle, Anemone beside him. 'I need you to hold that side. Don't let the creature start to flank us. Anemone and I will help out the tribesman.'

The young mercenary nodded and, with a sharp whistle to his squad, began to run ahead.

'I can hold the creature,' the witch said, her exhaustion clear in her voice. 'But not for long. Not like I have.'

'We will only need a moment.'

Heast turned his gaze back to Kye Taaira. He was aware, as he did, that he was not the only with one eye on the fight. He heard Lehana – 'Strengthen our right!' – but the battleground Refuge and the Brotherhood were spread over was ugly with debris and bodies. As the creature pushed the Hollow, the Leerans reinforced the back of their line, suggesting that Eidan's words had not demoralized them. There was simply not enough space for Heast's soldiers to change their focus and make a reinforcement without weakening another part. Essa and the Brotherhood could offer little more, either. Beyond Bliq's still body, Heast could see the Brotherhood fighting between two streets. The Leerans had pushed there as well, and they were swarming over the buildings to try and bridge the gap between them and Taaira's side.

Ahead, Kye Taaira continued to be pressed by the creature and the Leerans around him. He held his sword in both hands and cut left and right and moved in both directions before he stepped back and around the creature's wild strikes and the jabbing thrusts of the Leerans' swords. As before, Heast was surprised by the way the tribesman fought. There was no give in him, no desire to retreat, but instead there was a savage joy, an almost primal sense of release that filled him. Yet, Heast could not deny the skill and control with which Taaira fought.

The Captain of Refuge watched as, after a desperate swing by the creature came crashing down to the ground, the Hollow spun on his heel and thrust between two Leerans, catching both their swords. Before they could react, his right hand dropped the blade and grabbed the front of one of the soldiers by their armour. With a surge, Taaira pulled him off balance and darted into the gap he made. He dragged his sword free as he did and, with the creature still of the belief that it was safe behind its human shields, Taaira plunged his sword into its ribcage.

The blade erupted with an old white light, similar to the twisted haunt within the creature's chest, and it burst through the creature as if it were rotten meat, creating a nimbus around Taaira.

With a jerk, the Hollow pulled his sword out of the creature, and as he did, a blond man set upon him.

With startling speed, he darted through the Leerans and leapt onto the tribesman's back, a knife flashing out. Before Heast's gaze, Taaira staggered, and the swords of the Leerans turned on him.

But it was the man on his back, the blond man, Heast could not turn away from.

His knife plunged into Kye Taaira's face, but not one of the attacks resulted in blood. As that became apparent, the man grabbed the tribesman's head and, with an inhuman strength, wrenched it around, snapping it.

Heast drew his sword. Beside him, Anemone began to run forwards.

But it was Isaap and his soldiers who were there first. The Corporal and his unit ran hard into the Leerans, screaming, trying to draw attention to themselves as Taaira fell to the ground. It was in vain, for he fell badly. Fell, Heast knew, dead.

The blond man did not retreat as the creature had in the face of stronger force. Instead, he fell into a fighting stance and met Isaap and those with him.

The man – the creature, Heast corrected – wore black leather wrapped around him, but it had been cut open, revealing a bright, almost burning, haunt in his chest. In contrast to the other twisted haunts that Heast had seen, the one inside the blond man was still, as if asleep. With each movement the blond man made, each block of a sword from a Refuge soldier, each cut and slash, the haunt's limbs moved with him. It was not that the haunt aided the man,

Heast knew that immediately, but rather that it was trapped in a complete state of subjugation, as if the soul of the man had been so subdued that it was now nothing more than a slave to the creature that wore its skin.

He did not fight like any of the other creatures Heast had seen. Where they had all fought with a savagery, a primal violence that was the dark cousin to the joy Kye Taaira showed when he fought, the blond man had an elegance, a deadly simplicity that had been created by years and years of practice. With the Leerans rallying behind him, he tore through the face of the first soldier who reached him, ducked under the swing of the next before he drove his knife into the inner thigh of the same soldier, and blocked the blow of Corporal Isaap. The latter managed to slow the charge of the blond man, but only for one parry, one attempt at a thrust, before the knives of the blond man cut across Isaap's face and he pushed the Corporal back into the Leerans before he broke free of the battle.

On instinct, Heast jammed his free hand into Anemone's back, pushing her to the ground the moment before the blond man's dagger plunged into his arm.

With one knife in his left hand, the man was on the witch before she could recover her balance. He cracked his free hand into the side of her skull, but before his dagger could plunge forwards, Heast drove his steel leg into the blond man. His sword snaked out after him, but it found only air as his opponent rolled backwards.

Heast took a step in front of Anemone as she shook her head and struggled to rise, his sword held in front of him.

The blond man darted forward and Heast blocked his attack and pressed forwards. He could not hope to match the man in skill, nor in speed: he knew his worth as a swordsman, and knew that it had only decayed as he grew older. He knew that he was slower than the other man. No matter the blond man's true age, his body was young, and his skill clear.

Heast heard shouts erupting around him. Over the blond man's shoulders, he saw soldiers from Refuge trying to beat back the Leerans that had charged with the blond man, saw swamp crows falling from the sky to peck and harry. He saw Isaap, as well, suddenly clearly through all the fighting, his face bloody, his body making a slow crawl for the fallen sword of Kye Taaira. Heast wanted to shout a warning, but could not: the blond man snaked forwards again and he was forced to block the blow. He only had to hold out until Anemone was on her feet, until she could issue the command to her kin. He shifted his weight, parried, moved to his left, the blond man's knife still in his arm. When his opponent darted forwards again, Heast swung his sword, blocked the knife, and then suddenly jammed the blade down, hoping to pierce the man's foot.

He missed, but the main gambit was the knife lodged in his arm, the knife he dragged out to jam into the blond man's chest.

For nothing.

Ignoring the injury, the man's dagger came arcing up—

'Stop, Zilt.'

—only to do just that.

The blond man's eyes – Zilt's eyes – were wide with shock.

Heast took a step back, out of his reach, leaving the blade that he had plunged into the man's chest. Around him the Saan were swarming into the street as the swamp crows did, rushing over the Leerans.

'You cannot imagine my delight.' The old woman who led the Saan walked along the street towards Heast, Anemone and Zilt as if she had no concerns. On her shoulder sat a slim but very black swamp crow. 'In this battle I have found soldier after soldier with his and her ears stuffed with wadding to dull my voice out. It does not matter how high or how low they are in the chain. They have all blocked the noise of battle and drunk heavily of blood to gorge themselves. But then I hear that you are here. You, the old, cruel general, given life with the most pitiless of his soldiers. You who don't have one piece of wadding in his ears.'

With a bloody hand, The Captain of Refuge helped Anemone to her feet. The witch moved unsteadily and he asked quietly if she was all right. She nodded, but leant on him, and as she did, Heast searched for Isaap among those who had fallen, hoping, wishing, that the young man had not reached Taaira's sword, that he had given up and lifted his own blade. Unfortunately, he found the Corporal near Kye Taaira's body, his hand wrapped around the hilt of the old, brightly glowing blade. His body looked as if it had been dead for weeks: it would break, Heast knew, when he lifted the young man.

'I don't fear you, Tinh Tu.' Zilt had not moved from his pose, his dagger still held high. 'I know you for the impurity you are.'

'You're a fool.' The old woman flicked a part of his leather armour aside and gazed at the haunt in his chest. 'But in that way, you are no different to any other zealot. You believe there is perfection in the world and you pursue it with such single-mindedness that you cannot see the horror of your vision. Instead, you pick up a sword, or a knife, or a mace, and you try to beat and cut the world into your vision, while never once noticing that change is the world, that to be imperfect is to be whole.' Her hand reached up to his eye and pulled the skin beneath it down. 'Do you see how small a man you are, Zilt?'

'You cannot threaten me,' he hissed. 'You can do nothing to me.'

'Take out your eye.'

With a deliberate and unhesitating hand, Zilt pushed the fingers of his free hand into the eye she had just examined, and scooped it wetly and bloodily out.

Heast took a step, ready to tell the old woman to stop, but

Anemone's hand tightened on his arm. 'Grandmother says that you must not interfere.'

'You should listen to your witch, Captain.' Tinh Tu did not turn to face him, but there was a strange quality in her voice, one both compelling and repellent. 'Now,' she said, her tone focused on the man before her. 'You see the world with one eye. You see it like a true zealot, Zilt.'

'You are a coward.' His voice was rough with pain and rage. 'Release me and face me like a real warrior.'

Tinh Tu's laugh was caustic. 'Like the children you killed when you conquered this land so long ago? Was that the work of a real warrior? Cut the hamstrings in both your legs. Cut them so you fall to the ground.' Before Heast's amazed gaze, the blond man cut deeply into his own body and slumped to the ground. 'Years ago, I found a book that described all the horrific things you did,' she said. 'In it, the author detailed an event outside a conquered city, where you did this to one hundred and fifty-eight children. Do you remember? They prayed to the God of War to be rescued.'

'You have people who pray to Se'Saera,' he spat back. 'Have you not heard that the Lord of the Saan prays to her?'

'And receives no answer.' On her shoulder, the swamp crow fluttered and took off. 'I am not concerned about Miat Dvir.'

'You cannot kill me,' Zilt hissed in response. 'None of you can.'

'You met my brother Jae'le, did you not?' Heast's gaze followed the bird through the battle taking place around him, the battle that he felt strangely disconnected from, though he had known its beats and flow just moments before. 'You chased him through that wreck of a cathedral,' Tinh Tu continued, 'and he threw you down here.'

'I killed him!'

'My brother?' Heast watched as the swamp crow settled upon the shoulder of a dark-skinned man in a green cloak, a man who walked through the lines of battle as if he could not be touched. It was, the Captain of Refuge thought, as if the birds were clearing a path for him, that they swarmed the soldiers before him. 'No, Zilt. Don't speak. Listen to me. My brother tossed both you and your kin down here. He did so because he knew the Hollow and his sword were here.' With a gentle dip, the man with the bird on his shoulder picked up the glowing sword of Kye Taaira, as if it were nothing, as if the white light that flowed from it and onto him was but an illusion. 'You think you killed him because you stabbed him with a knife, but you think that only because you are a fool. My brother is the first of us. The first to be touched by a god's power. Do you know what god his power came from?'

'No,' Zilt replied through gritted teeth, the answer torn from him. 'No, I do not.'

'Ain, the God of Life.'

Around his right hand, the hand that held the old two-handed sword Kye Taaira had been given to return his ancestors to the Plateau, Jae'le's skin peeled and broke, but healed itself again. It happened so quickly that Heast's first thought was that he had imagined it, that it was caused by the light against the other man's skin, but he saw the skin peel and split and heal again, as if the power of the sword, and the power of the man were in conflict.

'You will die,' Tinh Tu said to Zilt. 'You will die as if you were nothing. As if you were but a child outside a city gate, caught in the violence of your betters.'

Taaira's sword went through the blond man's back without resistance.

The body fell apart in rot and Jae'le released the sword. The only sign that holding it had bothered him was the way he rubbed the hand that had gripped the hilt. As he did so, he turned, not to the battle taking place behind him, but to the cathedral. There, a thin line of fire could be seen, the arc of a light that had been trying to flare after the siege fire opened the crown. 'The stairs are broken. I couldn't get up there,' he said, not to Heast, but to Tinh Tu. 'Ayae is up there alone. Alone with Aela Ren.' A sigh escaped him. 'I fear that he will kill her before we can stop him, sister.'

5.

The empty sky around the cathedral waited for Ayae, but she refused to take the last two steps into it. Her burning sword turned away the Innocent's attacks again and again in a desperate attempt to starve his momentum. Yet, as her blade met his again and again, she became aware of a growing realization within her that it was only a matter of time before one of the Innocent's thrusts worked through her defences.

It should be Jae'le here. The fight was his, not hers. The Innocent was the nightmare of her childhood, her parents' killer, the bane of an entire nation, but for all the power within her, Ayae did not believe that she could match Aela Ren. At best, she could test him, and she had done that. But she would not be able to test him for long. Her sword, catching and turning, desperately looking for a moment to slip through his guard, would falter before he did. The pain in her arm would soon run through her. The images bubbled to the surface of Ayae's mind with sudden clarity and she could do nothing to stop them. She could not harden her skin, she could not use the currents of air around her. She had even lost the flame on her sword.

The only thing that kept her alive was Aela Ren's rage. It had consumed him and, in doing so, his skill had been overcome by his raw anger, by his desire to beat her into submission.

He was the figure of Ayae's childhood, now. She could see him approach the scarred walls of the camp she had grown up in. Behind him was his army, dark shadows that she could not properly identify. But she did not need to: on Ren was the fury that Ayae had seen on the faces of the god-touched when they charged from the cathedral.

That anger had not been within the Innocent when she first saw him. It had not been evident, either, after the catapults broke open the crown of the cathedral. Until she had cut him, there had been an almost civil sense to Aela Ren. She had the impression that if she had dropped her sword, or if it had broken, he would have let her pick it up, or gather a new one. He would have done that only because he didn't fear her, she knew that, but it did not change the fact that in those moments, he was not the man who had terrorized a nation.

The man could only be seen in his anger.

His anger that destroyed a nation.

That killed men and women.

Boys and girls.

Mothers.

Fathers.

Ayae yelled suddenly, the sound torn from within her, years of fury and fear rising from a part of her that had been taken away.

She blocked Aela Ren's slash, shouldered forwards, bullied herself and her sword away from the edge. Caught off-guard, the Innocent gave ground and Ayae, seeing that, pressed him as hard as she could, slashing left and right, attacking him with all the angry speed she could find. She felt the steel of his weapon chip with every block and deflection he gave.

Then he caught her blade on his, wedged the cold steel in a crack in the steel of his weapon, twisted and sent her blade skidding across the floor.

Ayae didn't pause. She dropped low, put her weight onto her wounded hip, let the pain fuel her anger, and swept her leg under his. The move was slow and unbalanced and Ren leapt. His sword came crashing down but Ayae had rolled away. The leather across her back split under his second blow, but it was mistimed and did little more. She came to her feet quickly, stepped back for a slash, dodged a left thrust, then she jammed her hand into his wrist to break his grip and grabbed hold of his old armour.

It burst into flames.

Ren slammed both his hands into the sides of Ayae's head. She yelled in response, seeing the scarred walls and the cloudless sky of her childhood. He hit her again, grabbed her hair, pulled at it, wrenching her head back as fire rushed up his armour, over him, over her. She saw the old, barely seaworthy ship that took her from Sooia. Took her to Mireea. Took her to the orphanage. To Faise. She saw Faise, and Ren punched her at the base of the throat, the blow choking off her wordless yell at him, almost choking her.

It allowed the Innocent to hurl her across the floor.

She landed near her sword.

Her burning hand scooped it up and fire burst along it.

Unarmed, Ren ran at her. His clothes burning, his skin burning too, but Ayae met him.

Her sword ploughed into Aela Ren's stomach, up to the hilt. As if it meant nothing, his burning hands closed around her neck, to choke her, to tear at her.

His dark eyes were windows to a life of anger and pain. She saw it through the fire that had wrapped around his head, that was melting his skin. They were the same fires that ran over her, that came from her, that would not end, not until she did. Ren's burning fingers dug into Ayae's neck and she wrenched her sword up into his chest. He did not flinch so she did it again. He tore into her skin as if he was searching for her spine, and she slammed the hilt of the sword up, hearing his skin part, his bones break. 'You don't know what this means,' he whispered harshly as the strength in his fingers failed. 'You don't know.'

Completely covered in fire, Ayae took a step back. In doing so, she dragged her sword out of his stomach and, swinging it back behind her shoulder, hammered it with all the force that she had into the side of his head.

He dropped to the floor.

Ayae took a step backwards, and almost fell. The fire on her sword faded, just as the fire that ran over her did. She dropped the sword as the pain in her leg and in her arm returned with a sudden clarity. Exhausted, she spat blood from her mouth and turned.

The broken floor of the cathedral lay in darkness to Ayae's left, but she circled it, even as the pain in her hip began to intensify and she started to limp. On the back wall, the dark shapes of a pair of crows shifted and moved. At Se'Saera's still form Ayae pulled her arm against her stomach. The sharp sensation, like teeth trying to devour her, spiked as she stood before the god and gazed into her broken face. Se'Saera's lips were moving and there was, Ayae believed, movement behind the fractured skin. But no matter what it was, or what it symbolized, it did not draw Ayae's gaze into it as it had done before.

Beyond the god a charm-laced man lay against a back wall. His green eyes were open and his smile had the same cynical one she had seen a year ago.

'Look at you,' Zaifyr whispered as she drew closer. 'You look like you hurt.'

'You have nothing nice to say.' She sank down next to him. With her warm hand, she reached out for his. 'Your family said you'd be in a bad way. That you'd be not you.'

'I can barely move.' His hand took hers weakly. 'You wouldn't believe the things I have seen. The places I went. I wouldn't believe me.'

'I just killed—' Her voice caught and she swallowed. 'I should be dead.'

'We should all be dead.'

Silence stretched between the two of them and Ayae closed her eyes. Outside, she could hear the battle, the violence defined by shouts, screams and the crash of weapons. For a brief moment, it sounded as if the world was ending.

'Ayae,' Zaifyr said, his hand still in hers. 'Is Se'Saera still alive?'

She opened her eyes and saw the concern on his face. 'No,' she said.

6.

Bueralan arrived in Ranan cradled in the belly of a giant bird. Aelyn Meah had constructed it in the night sky, above the watchful gazes of swamp crows. The bird – a much larger version of the crows – was bound together from currents of wind twisted into hard, pale lines around him, Aelyn and the two horses.

The two greys had reacted to the construction surprisingly well. In fact, they had shown more calm than Bueralan, as if, somehow, they had known that they would not plummet to the ground. After the bird had been completed and the four of them were lifted into the depths of the night sky by its pale wings Bueralan thought he saw the tall grey give him a disgusted look as he clung onto the reins. He wondered if the grey showed the same amount of wearied cynicism about the world when he saw the state of Ranan, hours later.

The outer parts of the city were marked by spot fires, broken buildings and small pockets of fighting, but it was the centre that drew his attention. The ground beneath the cathedral had risen, as if a buried giant had tried to rise from where it had lain. From a distance, it looked to be no more than a hill of dirt, one large enough to lift the centre of Ranan above the rest of city. But as Bueralan drew closer, he saw that it was not a hill, but a head: a great, three-faced head made from dirt and stone. Its eyes watched their approach on the bird made from wind and, though its mouths did not open, Bueralan thought that in the head's expression was a sense of familiarity and pleasure. He did not ask Aelyn if he was right. She had warned him, as the bird had first begun to take shape, that she would need to concentrate to keep it in flight. Images of himself plummeting through the sky were clear in his mind then and now, and he did not ask.

Instead, he turned his gaze to the broken spike of the cathedral, to the people who moved in its crown, and through the broken buildings beneath it.

He saw a small group on top, but could not make out who they were. They were gathered around one person – a body, perhaps – and though a part of Bueralan's mind whispered to him, he could not clearly identify it. The bird began to descend and, on the streets around the cathedral, he saw small groups of Leerans on the ground, captured and unarmed.

He saw the god-touched, then. They lay at the edge of the city, their bodies staked to the ground and their heads severed and rolled away from the remains.

Aelyn landed not far from them, dirt whipping up around them as she did. As the shape of the bird disappeared and the wind's embrace left Bueralan, a bearded man approached Aelyn. With a glance first at Bueralan and the horses to see if they were okay, she gave Bueralan a nod and began to walk towards the man. In response, the two greys stamped their hooves, pleased to be on solid ground. That left Bueralan with the god-touched bodies. At the sight of them, he pressed his hand against his side, at the blood-dried cloth, at the wound that did not heal the way he had known it to do so recently, and did not heal in the way it had known it to once do, either.

Leaving the greys, Bueralan walked down the line of severed heads and named them. It gave him no pleasure to do so, but he wanted to know who was there, and who was not.

Aela Ren was not there.

But Kaze was there. Joqan, Ai Sela, and all the others who had stood with the Innocent.

'Well, if isn't the Baron of Kein,' a voice said from behind him. 'You missed the fighting.'

He turned: the Captain of the First Queen's Guard, Lehana, stood two steps in front of him. She had taken off her black-and-red armour and wore a sweat-stained heavy black shirt and black leather pants. Her bastard sword sat on her hip and her right hand rested on its hilt casually, more for perch than for threat. Very briefly, Bueralan thought the sight of her meant that the First Queen was alive. But on the arm of her shirt was a red-and-black insignia, an empty globe over it, and he knew that she was not.

'I was never much of a baron,' he said and offered her a hand. 'How should I refer to you now, Captain?'

'Lehana will be fine.' She shook his hand and gave him a crooked smile. 'I'm a lieutenant at the moment.'

'There can be only one Captain of Refuge.'

'He would say there were many before him.'

'It's hard to imagine, isn't it?' Bueralan said. 'Where is Heast?'

'In the cathedral. The fighting is almost done here and they're debating what to do with the body of the new god.' She nodded over the edge, where the sounds of battle still could be heard. 'The Lord of Faaisha assures us the fighting will be done by morning. The Captain is keen to leave Ranan shortly afterwards.'

Se'Saera was dead? A part of him didn't believe it. It was as if a soft, nagging voice in his head said to him that it was a lie.

'Since you're here,' Bueralan said, changing the topic. 'Am I right to assume that the Queen survived Cynama?'

'She died in Vaeasa,' Lehana said simply as the two of them left the bodies and walked down the road. 'The loss of her Voice broke something in her, I think. Whatever held her illness at bay could no longer do so.'

The two passed soldiers from Refuge, the Brotherhood and the Saan, each tending to their wounded, or pulling the dead into a long line to be identified. It looked like the aftermath of every battle Bueralan had ever seen and he found it both familiar and sad. He would never forget how hollow it felt to find a friend dead after you had won. As if to further remind him of the point, he saw Kal Essa at the end of the line, before the stairs began. He stood over a body, tears streaking down his face, unashamed.

'How bad were your losses?' Bueralan asked quietly as they walked up the stairs.

'Heavy,' she admitted. 'We lost one hundred and four in Refuge. The Brotherhood – I don't know what their original number was, but about eighty are still standing. Together we might scrape a hundred and fifty to hold a line, now. The Saan might reach a hundred. I heard that they were five hundred strong when they left Yeflam. But for all that, it could have been worse. It could have been all of us.'

Inside the cathedral, a pair of soldiers greeted Lehana. Behind them, beams of wood, broken stone and other debris filled the room, and Bueralan could not see the dais or pews. The first of the soldiers, a muscular woman with short black hair and dark black skin, whom Lehana called Oya, wore the same heavy black clothing. On her shoulder was Refuge's insignia. 'Eidan and another went upstairs,' she said. 'He didn't share her name.'

'Did you ask?'

'Aelyn,' Bueralan said, before the soldier could reply. 'Aelyn Meah.'

The second, an olive-skinned woman with grey hair, and who wore dirty, mismatched leather, laughed. 'I told you.'

'Shut up, Qiyala.'

The soldier laughed harder. 'And you wonder why I outrank you.'

Lehana laughed, but offered them only a wave before she led Bueralan past the debris and to the stairs on the damaged side of the cathedral. The stairs were not all made from wood now: some were made from stone and bled into the broken steps. The stone had the appearance of being drawn from the broken wall that lay around him and, as he climbed towards the top of the building, Bueralan found that he could stare out into the night sky and down into Ranan clearly.

In the broken crown of the cathedral, Bueralan and Lehana saw Aelyn and the bearded man who had met her outside. He looked familiar, and it was not until he turned to him and nodded that Bueralan realized he had been the builder he had seen a year ago in Ranan: the man who had made the city from the ruins of the one that had been stripped by the Leerans. He had grown a beard since then, to hide a series of scars on his face, and he moved slowly, as if he was injured. But what surprised him most was the sight of Aelyn Meah reaching out gently, as if to comfort him, to reassure herself that he was there.

Beyond the two, Bueralan found Heast and a young witch in sweaty, dirty clothes. She was introduced to him as Anemone, but he had already guessed who she was.

They stood beside the body of Aela Ren.

For a moment, Bueralan was not sure he believed what he saw. Ren was heavily burned, and there were wounds across his face and stomach, but the scars that had so heavily defined the Innocent could still be seen.

'Who killed him?' he asked.

'Samuel Orlan's apprentice.' Heast offered him a faint smile that did not reach his blue eyes. 'I guess the apprentices of cartographers do make careers in war.'

'More is the pity,' he said.

'Yes.'

He was surprised to find that he actually felt a certain amount of sadness at the sight of Aela Ren. He had not felt that earlier when he had seen the god-touched. Troubled by it, he turned away from the body, away from Heast, Anemone and Lehana, and to the young, brown-skinned girl he had seen on the Spine of Ger, a lifetime ago.

She stood stiffly, favouring her left leg, a bandage wrapped around her left shoulder, blood soaking through it. Beside her stood Zaifyr, who looked, or so Bueralan thought, as if he would fall over at any minute, but surprisingly he was still alive. Next to him stood a man in a cloak of green feathers, and an old woman who held a staff, on which a large white raven perched.

They stood around Se'Saera.

We are victorious. The god's voice appeared in his head, the faint scratch of a voice he had heard since arriving clear to him now. With a frown, he walked towards her kneeling body. *Today, my loyal Faithful, we have vanquished those who would stand against us. We have stood against those who would say that we do not deserve our fate. They would have chosen to keep the world in its godless state. They would have let the emptiness inside their souls define the world.*

Her beautiful white face was broken. In the fractures, he thought he could see movement, like an ocean, a darkness that pulled at his mind, threatening to sweep him away.

But we have denied them, Se'Saera continued. *They have brought against us the strongest that they have, but it has not been enough. Look at the heads that Aela Ren and his kin hold for you. We will not forget the names of these people. The captains and the immortals who came against us. We shall remember Aned Heast and Kal Essa, we shall remember Ayae and Jae'le, Eidan and Tinh Tu. Without them, there are no more who can stand against us. No more who can force us to keep this dying world as if it were our responsibility. We can remake now. Our sun can be brought to one orb. Our ocean cleaned of poison. Your faith makes a new world possible.*

'You hear her, don't you?' Zaifyr said, as he turned to Bueralan. 'Her lips move, but you are the only one who hears.'

'She is giving a speech to her Faithful,' he said. 'She believes that Aela Ren and others are holding up your heads.'

The other man did not look surprised. 'She is trapped within another fate,' he said. 'It is the fate I saw. The one where she wins today.'

'And we die?' It was Aelyn who spoke, who came up behind Bueralan, with Eidan, Heast, Anemone and Lehana. 'Is that what happens?'

'We don't all die,' Bueralan said.

'No,' Zaifyr agreed. 'Not all. But enough.'

We are victorious, Se'Saera said, again. *Today, my loyal Faithful, we have vanquished those who would stand against us. We have stood against those who would say that we do not deserve our fate. They would have chosen to keep the world in its godless—*

'She is repeating herself,' he said. 'As if she is caught in a moment of time.'

'She is dying like her parents,' the old woman, Tinh Tu, said. 'In bits and pieces. The divinity will escape her, as it has the others.'

'We should take precautions still,' Eidan said. 'At least so that the Faithful cannot move her and create a shrine.'

'That will happen, no matter what,' the green-cloaked man – Jae'le, Bueralan assumed – said with a touch a cynicism. 'It will be two or three generations before the Faithful are no more.'

Bueralan turned, ignoring their voices, ignoring Se'Saera, and walked back to Aela Ren's body. He did not know why. After all that the man had done, after all the pain and suffering he had caused, Bueralan did not know why the sight of him dead bothered him. A monster had died. He had never believed that the Innocent would be redeemed. Even Ren himself had known that death was the only end for him.

After a moment, Ayae came up to stand beside him. 'You doing all right?' she asked.

'Not really.' He glanced at the girl. 'You know about Orlan?'

'They found him and a woman earlier. There are so many dead I don't know who to cry for first.' She looked down at Aela Ren. 'Was he a friend—?'

'No,' Bueralan said. He nodded at the fallen sword, near the body. 'You should take it. It'll be balanced for you.'

'I don't think I want that.'

'If not you, it'll go to some treasure hunter, some swordsman wanting to make a name.' He gave a slight, matter-of-fact shrug. Before he left, he said, 'People won't believe he's dead until they see it on someone.'

The evacuation of Ranan went on well into the hot day, past the morning's sun and its humidity, past the first heavy shower during midday's sun, and the second, and into the afternoon's, when the rain began to fall again, but constantly. The evacuation was done professionally, the soldiers and the prisoners in the outer parts of the city removed first, the horses that waited outside collected, and then those who had been on the upraised centre of the city. Until he left, Bueralan heard Se'Saera's voice, repeating her victory speech, her claim that she could make the world whole.

Outside Ranan, he stood apart from the others, stood beside the two greys. With the two horses, he watched the rain wash the streets clean.

Once the evacuation was complete, Aelyn and Eidan walked down to the edge of Ranan. The combined forces watched silently as the former Keeper of the Divine took the hand of the man next to her. The ground shuddered at their touch and, as if in connection to that, the sky turned dark and the rain began to intensify. With a massive groan, the ground began to tear itself apart and the head that held the cathedral aloft began to rise. Bit by bit, a giant began to pull itself from the ground, its hands revealed as roads broke and houses crumbled. As it did, a figure began to emerge from the thick, storming sky, as well. This one did so in streaks of lightning and with the rain defining its hands and torso. It pulled itself from the clouds in a mirror of the giant's action below it. Bueralan thought that it looked as if two creatures from two different worlds were splitting open the fabric of reality to reach each other. When they did, when their heads were of such a height that they were side by side, but reversed, they reached out to each other, to touch the other through the barriers of their worlds. In doing so, they split each other apart: the storm took the earth, the earth the storm, and the bodies of the giants broke apart and became a single vortex that twisted together.

For a minute, the maelstrom roared as the two were destroyed and reformed, until, in a slowly building silence, the two giants became one, and the Crypt of Se'Saera was revealed.

It took the form of a sexless giant who sat on the ground. It sat on crossed legs, its arms folded together in its lap, and its head lowered, as if in meditation. Yet, for all that its rocky body was sexless, it was awash with storms and winds, each of them allowing for the impression of sex to be granted. As Bueralan watched, the giant went from male to female, to combinations of both, and none, the weather trapped within the space of the body forced into a localized ecology that would act as a barrier to any who tried to search the inside of the giant for the body of the last god.

Epilogue

Postscript to *Histories, Year 1029*

This book was delivered to Leviathan's End two months after the Battle of Ranan. It was given to the Captain of *Jao* by an anonymous courier on the docks of Tnegt in Zoatia. The Captain says only that the bearer was a plain, average man, no different from a thousand other couriers he has seen throughout his life.

The book is bound in leather and printed on the fine paper I have used for all the recent volumes of my *Histories*. The typeset is the same, as well. Yet it was not printed on the press I keep in the hold of this ship, and neither, despite the clear use of my voice, is it written by me.

If this book is a hoax, it is an elaborate one. If it is not, if it is a true account of a history that has not taken place, then the questions about its authorship, printing, and arrival here are ones for which I have no answer.

—Onaedo, *Year 1025*

1.

Beneath the morning's sun, Zaifyr walked through torn grass and broken stone until his legs began to hurt. Gently, he eased himself onto a piece of the Spine of Ger to rest.

Being dead, he had discovered over the last three weeks, left a man weak. A long walk made his legs tremble and his body sweat. He could not lift a sword for long. He fell asleep in the saddle. He did not remember being so weak when he awoke in the crooked tower a thousand years ago, but he did not remember much of those first years. In contrast, the three weeks since he had woken in Ranan were clear to him. He had found a new world and he was keen to experience it all, even if that meant days of building his strength back up.

The full extent of the world's changes had not been fully apparent in Ranan. In the cathedral, Zaifyr had struggled with his weakness and with ensuring that he was not overwhelmed by the dead around him. The latter was no different from any battlefield, but even through that, he had been able to notice the changes in his family. It was as if they had been given a renewed focus, a purpose that had been lacking in the last hundred years. They had also embraced Ayae. She returned it, if awkwardly, and uncomfortably at times, but he had not understood the extent of that embrace until after Ranan, until after the six of them rode to the Plateau.

The trip was made at the request of Aned Heast, who had asked, not of him, or Ayae, but Jae'le, to return an old cloth-wrapped sword to the shamans for him.

Zaifyr had never liked the Plateau. He could see the ancient dead trapped in the ground, and hear their voices, full of anger and threats, each time he walked across it. But he could not see them when he entered the Plateau. At first, Zaifyr thought it was because he had closed down his senses in Ranan, but curious now, he opened himself to all of the dead. He expected his senses to be assaulted by the old, trapped haunts, and those who lingered in cold and hunger, but instead, he saw only a pair of women, walking ahead of him. They were old women – sisters, he knew immediately – but they did not stop for him. Instead, they continued in the direction they were originally walking, until they disappeared.

Zaifyr did not speak a word of what he saw, afraid that talking about it might make it untrue, until he met the shaman. The old white man had a ruddy complexion beneath shaggy white hair. He wore an old brown robe and a faded blue scarf and it was the latter that revealed him to them after he appeared on the flat, empty grasslands. He was on foot and alone, but did not hesitate as he approached the six of them.

After he took the sword from Jae'le, he turned to Zaifyr.

'May I ask you a question, ancient one?' After he nodded, the shaman asked, 'For the last week, we have watched the dead disappear. Do you know where they go?'

'Heüala,' he said, feeling a sense of amazement as he said it. 'They return to the City of the Dead. There they will be reborn.'

'Have you done this for us?'

'Not just me.' He told him the story, then. All of it. He laughed with a sense of relief and ran his hand through his hair every time he thought of the dead returning to Heüala. The charms in his hair brushed his skin heavily and he began to unwind them as he spoke, removing them all by the end. 'There is a guardian in Heüala, now,' he finished. 'A soldier by the name of Queila Meina. She keeps the city open for all of us.'

'It is an enormous thing that has been done, ancient one.' The shaman bowed low. 'The man who wielded this sword will have found peace now, thanks to you,' he said, after he rose. 'We hope that his next life will be one without violence.'

After that, Ayae led his family into the Mountains of Ger. Eidan found trails to ride upon, for the mountains looked nothing like Zaifyr remembered, from either the last time he had physically stood there, or when he had seen them with Meina, Anguish and Lor Jix. Around him, the mountain revealed itself in jagged bare lines, trees stripped from whole sides of the mountain range, while trails would suddenly turn into new lakes and streams. It took them two nights to ride from the base of the mountains to the ruins of Mireea, and more than once, the ground ran like a river with tremors, as if the mountains were still busy recreating themselves.

Once at the ruins, Zaifyr watched as the first steps not to rebuild Mireea, but to recreate it, were begun.

'Are you sure this is what you want?' Zaifyr asked, the first night. He sat beside Ayae on a long piece of the Spine of Ger, the starlit sky spread around them. 'You could find a new home in any part of the world.'

'I could.' She shrugged and winced. Her shoulder, despite Jae'le's care, was not yet fully healed, and Zaifyr suspected she would carry a scar once it finished. 'Mireea was my home. But more than that, it was my sanctuary,' she said. 'It reached across the ocean, to the other side of the world, and offered me safety. I would like to see it represent that again.'

'Do you need sanctuary?'

Before his memory could replay the answer, he heard a footstep behind him and felt a breeze run through his hair. 'Aelyn,' he said without turning.

His sister sat next to him. 'I see you kept one,' she said, pointing to the charm around his wrist. 'I thought you buried most of them.'

The silver disc was attached to a strip of old leather. 'This one is blank. The rest I did bury. It is a new world, after all.'

'Is it?' She pulled one of her legs up to her chest, rested her hands on it. 'We haven't really talked about the other world you saw.'

'What is there to say? Our brothers were dead. Our sister. Ayae. You owned horses.'

That took her by surprise. 'Really?'

'They were grey. I saw them in the pen of the small farmhouse you built near the tower. I didn't see it straight away. The tower had to break apart first. But you would come and talk to me over the years. For a while I was angry, but it didn't last.'

'I know that feeling.' He heard, in her voice, the years of their strained relationship, the end of it above Yeflam. As if she heard it as well, she said, 'I didn't mean to kill you.'

'I know.' He reached out for her hand on her knee. 'I'm sorry I made you.'

He kept it there for a while, her fingers curled round his until she lowered her leg. 'What will we do, Zaifyr? In this new world, I mean.'

'When I am well, I have a child I must visit.' But that was not the answer Aelyn wanted to hear. She had lost so much. She had lost the most out of all of them and it was she, he realised, who needed her family the most right now. 'Ayae is right. We cannot pretend we are not part of this world. We cannot look at it and do nothing for it. We have to ask ourselves what we can do.'

'I have asked that before.'

'This is different.'

'Is it?'

Absently, he flicked the blank charm beneath his wrist. 'We have to make sure it is,' he said. 'If we don't, no one else will.'

2.

Elan Wagan's funeral was a small affair. It was, Heast thought, an audience to acknowledge the death of a man that had happened over a year ago, not two days earlier.

The funeral was held not on Neela, but on the bare, dirty island below it, Wila. A single, steel-framed funeral pyre was built in the centre a day before and Wagan's body was laid on top of it, wrapped in multicoloured cloth, before Heast and the others arrived. Unlike the funeral pyres outside Mireea, the new pyre had no image of the gods on the framework. It was not the shortness of preparation time that had kept it off: the night before, Muriel had told him that she intentionally ordered it to be left blank. 'People have already complained about it,' she said. 'They hear that the dead are leaving, that they are no longer trapped in our world, and they think that it is the work of the gods. Or a god.' Heast thought of that again as she lit the pyre of her husband. He thought of the speech that she could have given to the small group of people who stood on the dirty sand. How she could have said that the gods had kept the dead here, how their war had raged for thousands of years with souls as weapons. How the dead could only return to Heüala now because the gods were gone. It was a story that the shamans out of the Plateau were telling and Muriel Wagan could have repeated it, but she didn't. Instead, she greeted all sixteen men and women as the fire burned her husband and thanked them for their presence.

Heast accompanied her back to her house after they left Wila. People were scattered through the streets that they walked through, some carrying long trestle tables and chairs. Many put down their loads and came to offer their condolences to Muriel and her daughter, Eilona, who was half a dozen steps behind her with her partner. Her daughter looked mostly exhausted, but that was not terribly surprising, Heast thought.

Muriel bid her daughter goodbye at her house, left Caeli at the door to stand guard, and led Heast inside. With the door shut, it was quiet and still, the front room empty but for a few stubborn bloodstains on the ground. A flight of stairs upwards, a narrow hallway and a small back room revealed an old leather couch facing the open window. Against the wall were glasses and two bottles of laq.

'Later today,' Muriel said, as she handed him a glass, 'I have a meeting with Ayae. I am told that she will be asking for the land Mireea was on.'

'Asking?' He took the glass, took a seat on the couch and stretched his steel leg out in front of him. 'You might say no to her, but not to the rest of them.'

She sat beside him, a glass in her hand. 'I don't plan to say no. It will be years before anyone can live in Mireea and it will be longer without her influence.' She took a drink and sighed. For the first time since he had returned to Neela, he saw her relax. 'Besides, I hear she killed the Innocent and carries his sword, now.'

'She carries that burden.' The news had been in Jeil before Heast and Refuge reached the port to catch a ship down to Yeflam. 'She does it to tell people he is dead.'

'Then Mireea is a price she can name,' Muriel Wagan, the former Lady of the Spine, said. 'But what of you, Aned? What is next?'

'Refuge needs to rebuild.' He took a sip of the laq. 'We'll go to

Leviathan's End for that, I think. Once that is done, we have work in Illate.'

'Illate?' He saw her surprise. 'You never struck me as the kind of man who kept unfinished business.'

'It is the second half of Zeala Fe's contract.' He offered her half a smile. 'Maybe I'm getting old, but it doesn't hurt that it is Illate.'

'Next you'll be adopting children.'

He laughed, despite himself. 'I have mercenaries instead.'

She made a noise, part disagreement, part agreement. 'Well, I wasn't going to bring this up, but since you are in the mood for change, my daughter's partner made a request of me the other night. Laena wants me to ask you if you'd consider an authorized biography.'

'The war didn't change me, Muriel,' Heast said. 'That is about the last thing I want.'

'No, the last thing you want is a hack following you and your mercenaries around to write *The Adventures of Refuge*. This would be a very different thing.'

'You can't think this is a good idea.'

'At first, I simply thought you wouldn't be part of it, so I didn't think about it. But the idea has stuck. I've rescued thousands of books from Nale in the last two weeks. I've been in contact with the other lords and ladies of Yeflam – that is what they call themselves now, you know.' Heast had heard. Yeflam, it appeared, was drifting towards being a council of city states. 'They defined the world, Aned,' Muriel continued. 'These books, these histories – they define what has gone before us. But what has been missed? What person, what man or woman, was lost, because he or she was too humble? It shouldn't happen to the Captain of Refuge.'

He did not agree, but the thought stayed with him after he left, after he climbed into the small carriage that took him away from the Lady of Neela, who had not entirely lost her title as the Lady of the Ghosts, not yet. He sat in the empty carriage, his steel leg thrust out before him, and tried to push the thought from his mind. Authors had written about him before, he knew. There had been a pair of books about his tactics, dry works for which academics had sent him letters with questions he never bothered to answer. He had not stopped those books being published, but he had stopped a handful of others, cheap fictions that promised little truth. But a biography? An authorized biography? No, he told himself as the carriage stopped outside The Collapsed City, the inn Refuge were lodged at. No, he did not need anyone to write about him.

Inside, the spacious bar was dotted with soldiers from both Refuge and the Brotherhood. He saw Oya and Qiyala next to Jaerc, the former baker's apprentice who had petitioned him for a place. Kal Essa had vouched for him – 'The boy,' he had said, 'has a good hand with a pot of food and a steady hand on a sword' – and Heast had taken him on as a cook and soldier. The scout Fenna nodded at him as he pressed deeper into the inn. She was practising on a flute, but paused to answer his question, to point towards the back, where a series of long tables looked out over Leviathan's Blood. At the furthest, he found Lehana and Anemone, drawn together by both the chains of command and the dead that were still part of the Witch of Refuge.

'Captain,' the former said, as he approached. 'How was the funeral?'

'Fitting.' He took a seat on the other side of Lehana, placing her in the middle. 'Are most still sleeping?'

'There's not much to do on Neela, but there's enough to drink.'

'We'll start tightening the company purse strings in a few days.' Zeala Fe's gold would go a long, long way, Heast knew, if he used it right. He'd probably have to employ an accountant to help him with that. Before, or after Leviathan's End, he thought, he would visit Tjevi Minala again. 'Have you given thought to what I said?'

'You could have asked Anemone first,' Lehana said. 'She might say no.'

'I said yes,' the witch replied. 'You know that.'

The Lieutenant of Refuge sighed. 'I asked around,' she said. 'No one who served in the First Queen's Guard has any objection to Kal Essa or the Brotherhood. But – well, here's my concern: if we are really going to go to Illate, ex-soldiers from Qaaina are not going to make that easy for us. It's already going to look bad when the Queen's old guard shows up under the Captain of Refuge. If the Queens don't immediately march on us it'll be a miracle.'

'How much worse do you really think soldiers from Qaaina are going to make it? I don't think it'll matter after they see the badge that you're wearing,' Heast said. 'Even if they do march, there's not a thing we can do to make it easier. It's going to be hard, and it isn't going to be won in a day or two, maybe not even in a whole year. We're going to need good soldiers and Essa is a good soldier. But if he joins with us, you'll be sharing rank with him. It won't happen if you don't want it to happen.'

'I know.' She let out a breath, turned to Anemone, then back to Heast. 'Okay, make him an offer. But tonight, sir, we'd like for you to meet with a young woman who came in here yesterday. Her name is Laena.'

Eilona's partner. 'She came to speak to you as well?'

'Actually,' Anemone said, 'she came looking for you, but you weren't here. Grandmother had us talk to her.'

'I don't need a biographer.'

'The witch and the soldier disagree.'

'Soldiers, actually,' Lehana added casually. 'The girl got quite the audience.'

'Grandmother says you should meet with her,' the witch said. 'You can do it before you meet with Bueralan Le tonight.'

The soldier frowned slightly at that. 'You still going to make him an offer?'

The Lieutenant of Refuge did not agree, at least on his matter. 'As I said, he's a friend, and I think he needs a friend, now.'

'I don't disagree with that,' she said. 'But, Captain, I think he might be broken.'

3.

After her stepfather's funeral, Eilona returned to her home and slept. The last three weeks of waiting for Elan Wagan to die had left her exhausted, but she didn't realize that until she saw her mother light the wrappings around him, until the flames took hold. She was grateful that Captain Heast accompanied her mother back home.

Eilona did not even try to put off sleep when she returned home. In her clothes, she curled up on the blankets that made the bed she and Laena shared. She lay there, and thought for a moment that she was still awake, that sleep would not come. Laena pulled a blanket over her and closed the window, then settled in a place against the wall to read. But there were no words on the book she held, and soon, Laena's dark skin began to darken, swell and turn into the witch, Olcea. She had come to Wila for Elan Wagan's funeral. She had stood beside the healer, Reila, her hands wrapped in clean white cloth. She had offered both Eilona and her mother condolences afterwards. 'Is Hien still with you?' Eilona asked, a question she had asked days earlier, after she heard the news that the shamans from the Plateau were spreading. But in her dream, she asked it in her room, from her bed where she lay. 'Yes,' Olcea said. 'The dead will not so easily give up those they are bonded to. To be reincarnated is to be reborn without yourself. But to be dead and given blood is to remain yourself. Blood is the drug of the dead, Eilona.' The witch held a blank book in her hand, but there was blood on the cover. It came from her bandaged hands—

'Hey.' Laena's hand pressed against her. 'You having a bad dream?'

She was tangled and sweat-stained in the blanket. 'I guess,' she murmured as she unwrapped herself. 'Sorry.'

'You had to wake up soon, anyhow.' Her partner's hand pushed back her messy hair and she smiled. 'Your mother's dinner is in an hour.'

Dinner wasn't quite the right word for it. Originally, her mother had invited the two of them and a handful of her friends over for a meal in her father's memory, but as news of her father's death moved around Neela, a larger dinner was born. A party, she had at first thought. *A wake*, Laena had corrected her. *That is what Sinae is calling it.* Her first response had been to sigh. The thought of it now made Eilona want to roll back into the blankets of her makeshift bed and sleep until next week. A wake was an old ritual, one in which the living sat beside the dead, and beside the grieving. It wasn't a party. It wasn't a celebration. Her mother, she was sure, felt the same, or even worse, but she still planned to go, and that was why Eilona would, as well. She could only imagine how exhausting it must have been to care for her father since his return from Leera. A part of her had thought that her mother had become inured to the state of Elan during that time, that she had, in fact, stopped seeing him as a person. It was not a criticism of her, but rather an acknowledgement of what would have been a very natural coping mechanism. A lot of Mireeans shared her opinion, Eilona thought, and she believed that part of the wake was motivated by a desire to support the Lady of the Ghosts, who had done so much to support them.

We should have done more, she said to Laena, later. *We should have stayed after he returned from Leera.*

Her partner had simply said, *Yes.*

'I have been thinking,' Laena said now, pushing her over, pushing onto the blankets. 'Maybe we ought to tell Sinae we do want furniture. I know he runs prostitutes. I know he runs Neela's black market economy. I also know he has no respect for history. But I like him and I bet he could get us a bed.'

'If we get a bed, you'll want a couch.' Eilona wrapped her arm around her partner's waist. 'There'll be no end if we get a couch.'

'Maybe that's okay.'

'What?' She looked out of the window, at the last of the afternoon's light. 'Did I sleep a week? Did you meet Aned Heast already?'

Laena laughed. 'No, that's later tonight, after your mother's dinner. But I was just thinking about what you said earlier. About how we weren't here.'

'Yeah, me too.'

'We're not kids any more,' she continued. 'We can't pretend we don't have responsibilities for what little family we have. Besides, I think your mother wants us here. She made us that offer. That might be worth leaving the university for.'

As she rebuilt Neela, Muriel Wagan recreated the economy of her part of Yeflam. Through bribes, scavenging and hard work, she had brought over most of the library of the Keepers from Nale. In addition to that, Sinae had located a printing press in Gogair that was being shipped over. 'Education, researchers, libraries, printing,' her mother said to her, after she told Eilona. 'We can build an economy here with that. We can't rely on markets and trade as we did in Mireea. We're too isolated for that now. Maybe once the roads through the Mountains of Ger are open we can start to rebuild that with Faaisha, but unless we have a miracle, that's decades away. We need to have something else to trade and we need it soon.'

'We will be competing with the Spires of Alati,' Eilona said. 'They have the reputation in the region.'

'They do. But if we have lecturers and teachers from the University of Zanebien, we can challenge that.'

The offer sat in the air.

It still sat, over a week later, after the funeral of Eilona's father. In the room she shared with Laena, she leant her head back against the wall. 'You would have to give up digs. Give up the statues of Ain that you found.'

'I do love digs,' Laena admitted. 'But I love other things as well.'

'Like Aned Heast?'

'Girl, were you just born looking for compliments, or did you learn it?' She laughed. 'I did not even go back to those digs. I was offered. I stood in the trail. I had my bags packed in our little house. But I chose to ride a pony all the way here, instead.' She got on her knees and kissed the top of Eilona's head. 'It doesn't have to be forever. Maybe in a year we won't like it. Maybe Neela will be Mireea. But Pitak isn't going anywhere, and the university isn't, either. In a year, it'll all be right where we left it, if want.'

'Well,' she said, meeting Laena's dark eyes. 'Maybe we should get a couch.'

4.

'What are we doing, Bueralan?'

'You're the one who agreed to a biographer, not me.' In the nearly empty bar, he pointed at Heast with a pint of watered-down beer. 'Next you'll be telling me you've decided to adopt a child.'

'Did you get notes from Muriel?' With a shake of his head, the Captain of Refuge glanced around the bar. Bueralan knew what he saw: a small, rundown box on the edge of Neela, near the closed bridge to Mesi. The tables were mismatched, items scavenged from the city and the shore, and often stolen. Tables were propped up with small barrels, chairs were casks of home-brewed wine, and if there was a clean mug or glass, it was clean only because the previous drinker had wiped it out. Two men sat at the front eating food they had got from the wake – the noise of it was a dull roar inside – while the woman who stood behind the bar had an eyepatch over one eye. 'What are you doing in here?' Heast asked, turning back to him. 'You're using my coin, you could be where Refuge is.'

'I like it here.' He didn't, not really. 'I thought it would be a place to drink seriously in.'

'This is more water than beer.'

'Yeah.' Bueralan looked at his pint, put it on the table and shrugged. 'I feel run out,' he admitted. 'I don't even know how I got here.'

'By boat,' Heast said drily.

Bueralan had ridden to Jeil with the survivors of the Battle of Ranan. Most took him to be a soldier with Refuge because Heast had given him the order to mount up. The Brotherhood, the Saan and the Faaishans made him a space in the lines, thinking that he had suffered a trauma, that he was gone emotionally. Maybe he was. Zean was dead. Taela, Orlan, Kae, Ruk, Liaya and Aerala. Pueral, the First Queen. Even Aela Ren was dead. Bueralan had seen more than enough death. By the time he reached the port, he realized his entire world had been reduced to two grey horses, one of which, he was fairly sure, was beginning to view him as a liability. By the time Heast had booked a ship to Yeflam, Bueralan was considering giving the horses to him and moving on.

But he had come to Yeflam instead. He had come to Neela, to where the Lady of the Ghosts made her new home, to where her husband was dying, and he found the worst inn he could find and took a room.

'Did I tell you someone tried to steal my horse the other day?' he said, the noise of the wake rising behind him, like a swell, before subsiding. 'It was this thin pale guy. He came up to complain that he had been bitten. The horse had torn his ear off. He just had this bloody mess where it had been. Kept telling me that I had to help him, that it was my fault for having such a bad horse.'

'Bueralan,' Heast began.

'I told him, I said: Did you touch him—?'

'*Bueralan.*'

The saboteur sighed. 'What do you want to hear?' he asked. 'There's nothing left. I feel that. I can't even find it in me to get drunk.'

'I have a job.'

'There are no more jobs.'

'There's always more,' Heast said. 'Or there's a short walk into Leviathan's Blood.'

It would kill him, he was sure of that. He could throw himself off the edge and sink into the darkness, in water tainted by blood.

Instead, he took a drink of his beer.

'You want this job,' the Captain of Refuge said, picking up his pint. 'It is in Illate. Before the First Queen of Ooila died, she had me make two promises. One was to see Aela Ren dead, the other was to finish what Refuge started in Illate. She told me that she had been working towards Illate's independence and she wanted us to finish it.'

Despite himself, Bueralan was surprised. He hadn't heard any rumours of anything remotely tied to Illate despite the weeks he had ridden with Refuge. He had heard about Ayae's duel with Aela Ren, about the dead returning to Heüala, the City of the Dead, and he had heard that the Saan had been led by the rulers of the Five Kingdoms. Jye Tuael was, reportedly, claiming that the entire assault on Ranan was his idea. He even heard that Heast planned to offer Kal Essa and the remains of the Brotherhood positions within Refuge if his new lieutenant agreed.

But he had heard nothing about Illate.

'I need someone to represent Refuge in the courts of the Queens of Ooila,' Heast continued. 'I can't send Lehana. I can't send anyone from the Queen's Guard. The other day they were given a letter, branding them as traitors. They each have bounties on their heads for not returning with their Queen. Rumour has it that they're being blamed for her death. But even if that wasn't the case, I wouldn't send them in. Lehana is a soldier. The court is no place for her. It's not for me, either.'

'You think it's a place for me?'

'I think the Baron of Kein will thrive there.'

Bueralan took another drink of watered beer. He let it run

through him, let Heast's statement run through him. 'You're serious?' he said, after a moment.

'Yes. But it won't happen tomorrow, or next week. Refuge needs to rebuild. We're taking in Essa and his soldiers, but we need more. We're going to sail to Leviathan's End at the end of the week.'

'You *are* serious.'

'It's what Refuge does.'

Bueralan did not lie to himself: the offer did appeal. A part of him responded to it. The part of him, he knew, that had stopped him from drinking himself blind, from walking off the edge of Neela, from staying in Ranan. It was the part of him that Zean, Taela and the rest of Dark sat in. It was maybe even the part that Orlan and Ren sat in. In the near-empty bar, he closed his eyes and saw the dark, winged child Taela had given birth to, the creature that had known it was Zean, even as it rejected the knowledge. 'It's what Refuge does,' he said, quoting the man before him. 'But is that what Aned Heast does, now?'

'Yes.' The Captain of Refuge looked into the mug before him and then pushed it away. 'You and I, we have both worked for people we don't like. We try not to, but sometimes you need what is being offered, and you do the work, regardless. It's no different from what a lot of people do. But the difference for you and me is that when we do something we don't like, someone dies. Mostly they die wrongly. They die because they don't have the coin to pay us. They don't have the status. They don't have the privilege. Well, Refuge is for those people. The Captain of Refuge represents the people who cannot represent themselves. Maybe I forgot about that while I wasn't the captain, but I won't forget now.'

'You didn't forget,' Bueralan said. 'You never chipped away at your soul, selling bits and pieces of it.'

'But you did.' Heast didn't say it politely. 'You did it long before you came to Mireea, though you tried not to.'

'I was never part of Refuge. I was a saboteur. I never had that option.'

'It's here for you now.'

Was it?

It was his choice, and his alone. Bueralan could say no. Heast would finish his drink, stand, and walk out. He'd never see him again. He could sell his two horses, buy a ride somewhere out of Yeflam, find a job that meant little to him and wear away the hours, days, and weeks until he walked into Leviathan's Blood, or died of old age. Bueralan was sure his body would get old, sure that it would begin to fail: sure, but not positive. He didn't know if being god-touched meant that he could no longer die quietly in his sixties or eighties, full of regrets and haunted by memories.

'This beer is awful,' Bueralan said, finally. He put it back on the table. 'I think it might be the worst beer I've ever had.'

'There's better beer where Refuge is staying. Grab your stuff. Get your two mean horses. We can go through the wake on the way there, get some food, then get something real to drink.'

'Yeah,' he said, before he thought otherwise about it, before he talked himself into staying on the cask of wine he was using as a seat. 'Yeah, let's do that, then.'

5.

Ayae walked through the streets of Neela, the wake for Elan Wagan spilling out around her, a city alive with people, with the smells of cooked meats, potatoes, vegetables and breads, drinks in bottles and casks, and fires lighting the night sky.

She held a half-drunk bottle of beer in her hand. It had been pressed on her by a large black woman who promised that it was the best beer Ayae had ever tasted. She wasn't sure about that, but it wasn't bad, and it was a bottle she could raise when another vendor tried to press their wares upon her. There was nothing special about the offers to her: the beer and wine, like the food, was free tonight. Rumour had it that Sinae Al'tor had paid for everything. It was not just to honour Elan Wagan, but to honour all the dead, all of the men, women and children who had died since the War of the Gods. It was a wake for all the dead who were now free. A celebration of life and death. When she heard about it, Ayae had been doubtful, but it was hard to argue with the goodwill she saw around her, the pleasure in people's faces.

Depending on who you asked, the freedom that the dead had was either a gift of the gods, of Se'Saera in particular, or of those who had fought at Ranan. She heard the name Qian mentioned in conversation more than once. Aelyn Meah, Eidan, Captain Heast, and even herself: Ayae had heard enough tales about Ranan that she did not know where to begin unravelling the story for anyone who asked. She hoped the shamans who had come down from the Plateau found it easier – she passed one on the street near her, a bowl of cooked spiced potatoes in his hands, a captive audience around him – but Ayae had seen brown-robed members of Se'Saera's Faithful in Neela and heard self-appointed prophets who told stories about nothing that had happened in Ranan. It would be a long time before the truth began to emerge clearly, she knew.

Yet, despite that, Ayae felt good. Since Ranan, she had felt strangely at peace, as if a balance had found her. Part of it, she knew, was simply survival. She had survived not just Ranan, but Aela Ren. There were still mornings when she woke up sweating, the image of his sword, the sword she carried, coming towards her, his scarred face emerging from the darkness behind it. In fuller dreams, dreams that had narrative, she was on the cathedral, the wind whipping around her. Aela Ren stood before her. But she could live with the dreams. She could see there would be a point in her future where they would fade. She could even live with the moments when sadness weighed her down – when she thought of Faise, of Zineer and of Samuel Orlan. It helped that Zaifyr was back, that his strength was returning. She was surprised that it helped, but it did. For his part, he appeared to be mostly bemused by her plans to rebuild Mireea, but he supported her, as did the rest of his family. Perhaps, she admitted, lifting up her bottle to wave away another offer of free beer, it was her family as well. She was not quite comfortable with that, not yet. But her sense of peace was independent of these factors. It came from inside her, from the balance she had found from the four elements, from the parts of Ger that nestled in her being.

'A room is no longer warm when you're in it,' Muriel Wagan said to her, earlier. The two of them stood beneath the afternoon's sun in the small backyard of the Lady of the Ghosts' home. Potted plants spread around them, a collection of green, purple, red, brown and yellow. 'It was the first thing I noticed when you came in. You're different in other ways, of course. You are more reserved. More confident. The war has changed you, but it has changed everyone, I think.' It had left Wagan thinner and older. 'But for you, I think it has left you with a better understanding of what is inside you.'

'I hope I would have found that without the war,' she said.

'Perhaps.' The other woman picked up a watering can, carried it to a barrel of rain water. 'In another fate, you might have stayed in Mireea as Samuel Orlan's apprentice, might have continued your relationship with Illaan Alahn, and I would have done my best to help you.' She lifted the full can out and offered her half a smile. 'I might have even been able to.'

'Maybe.' She hesitated. 'I came here to talk about Mireea, actually.'

'I know. You came to ask if you could have it.'

'Yes.'

Muriel Wagan began to water the first of her plants. 'But you're not really asking,' she said mildly. 'You came to tell me that you took it.'

From the day she left the Mountains of Ger, Ayae had thought about this exact moment, had run it through her head. Tinh Tu, perhaps sensing that before she left, had offered to come with her, but Ayae had waved her off. *It'll be fine*, she had said. *It shouldn't be a problem.* Her confidence had not lasted. In Neela, people gave her space, treated her with a mixture of fear and respect, and fell silent when she entered rooms. Now standing here, watching the Lady of the Ghosts water her garden, Ayae admitted that it might be a problem. 'Yes,' she said, a breath of nervousness escaping her. 'I have taken it.'

'Because you can.'

'Because I can,' she admitted. 'But I'd rather have your blessing.'

'That is not the nature of power,' Muriel Wagan told her, shifting her can to new plants. 'If you will, take that as a small piece of advice, Ayae. The moment you seek the permission of another, you cede your authority to them. You give your power to them. The great trick of governance is to keep that truth an illusion, to let people think that they have power, when they have none.'

Ayae did not reply. Did not know how to reply.

With a wave of her hand, the Lady of the Ghosts took her can back to the water barrel. 'You are more than welcome to the land Mireea was on,' she said. 'I could do nothing with it. No one but you and your kin could, in its current state. If you plan to make it safe and liveable, then we will all benefit from that.'

'I plan to make it a sanctuary,' she said, trying to hide the relief she felt, relief that later, when she left Lady Wagan's house, she would laugh ruefully at. *Who had the power there?* she would ask herself. 'A place for people without homes, and people like me, who have some divinity in them. A place where people can learn about themselves, if they want. Or just be treated well. Not everyone is well treated by that power. I want to make Mireea a place that will help people, again. A place where they can learn who they are, and learn about the world.'

'You are going to make it a school?' She rested the watering can on the edge of the barrel and looked at Ayae keenly. 'Is that right?'

'No, not really. It'll have part of that, but.' She glanced up at the broken sun. 'Se'Saera kept telling us that she could repair our world. That she could fix what the gods broke in their war.'

'It was one of her best arguments, I thought.'

'Exactly. She would look at what we all saw, what we all lived with, and she would promise to fix it, because she was a god. We only had to be faithful. We only had to believe that she would do it. But there are no gods. No one who can fix what was done with our world. If we want the sun whole, or the ocean to be free of poison, then we have to do that. We have to take responsibility for it.'

'So, not a school, but rather a place of research?'

'Something like that, yes.'

Muriel Wagan lifted her can off the barrel. 'That's very interesting,' she said.

They talked for a while longer, until the Lady of the Ghosts finished watering her garden, but Ayae's plans were not far along enough for in-depth discussion. She told Lady Wagan that Aelyn would help her build upon the research. Tinh Tu would guide the kind of books they needed and the researchers with whom they should be in touch. Eidan would build Mireea. He had already said it would take years to complete, simply because of the instability of the mountains. Ayae suspected that he would also be returning to Yeflam, to finish his work rebuilding the Floating Cities, but she did not say that in case it was not true. Jae'le had already begun to talk of travel, of searching for those with divinity in them, and she half expected him to be gone by the time she returned. She did not yet know what Zaifyr would do, but his world had changed so much in the last three weeks that the only thing she expected from him was for him to take time to reconnect with it.

'That's a nice sword you have there.' Caeli's voice broke through her thoughts. 'You know what they say about it?'

'That I found it in battle?' Ayae said, turning to her. 'That it came from no one of any real importance?'

'That's what I tell people, but they refuse to believe. They say the girl who has it killed the monster that owned it.'

She hugged the blonde guard, felt the other woman's arms around her hard, and for the first time since she had ridden into Neela, felt that she had found a part of her home again.

'I'm sorry about today,' Caeli said, letting her go. 'I had the duty. Did your conversation go well?'

'Yeah,' Ayae said. 'You got a beer?'

'Finest beer in Neela.' She held up a brown bottle with a yellow and green label. 'What about yours?'

She showed her black label with a white boar. 'Competing for the title.'

Caeli laughed and the two of them continued to walk through the streets. Ahead, the soldiers from Refuge spilled out of The Collapsed City. A handful of them had set up a band, a flute, a pair of guitars, a harmonica and a drummer. They had gathered quite the audience around them, people holding bowls of meat and potato, with bottles and mugs in their hands. A pair of children ran with a kite past them, along the well-lit street. At the end of it, Captain Heast and Bueralan Le were leading two horses towards the inn. The two women gave a short greeting before they turned down a street filled with people.

'I like his tattoos,' Caeli said, after a swig from her bottle. 'You know him well?'

'No,' Ayae said. 'Just a few conversations here and there. I heard that the group he was part of are all dead.'

'A lot of us are dead.'

She thought of Faise and Zineer and Samuel Orlan. She thought even of Illaan. 'How're you holding up?'

'About Xrie?' Caeli gave half a shrug. 'I wasn't surprised. He was always going to die with a sword in his hand. But it hurt to hear. I didn't love him or anything, but he deserved better.'

They all did. It was one of the reasons why so many people had embraced Sinae's wake, Ayae knew. 'Did Lady Wagan tell you what we plan to do in Mireea?'

'Yeah.' She glanced out the corner of her eye. 'You know she plans to open schools here in Neela, right?'

'I'm not surprised.'

Caeli grinned and took a swig from her bottle. Ahead, Kal Essa was showing children how to throw dice against a wall. He appeared, Ayae thought, quite drunk.

'You got other plans?' her friend asked, after they had passed him. 'You're not just going to stay on the Mountains of Ger, are you?'

'No.' She hesitated. She hadn't told anyone this, yet, wasn't sure of herself. 'I was thinking of going to Sooia.'

'I could go to Sooia.' It was said casually. 'If you'd like the company.'

'I would.' In silence, the two of them continued down the street, towards the men and women offering brown bottles of beer, towards the centre of the grand wake that had taken hold of a whole city. 'I would never have imagined this,' Ayae said, emptying the last of her bottle. 'I couldn't have ever thought of this a year ago. I couldn't have thought of it a week ago, but – well, that's kind of the way it is, now.' Behind the wake, behind the fires, the people, the food, behind it all, the strange shape of the Mountains of Ger beckoned to her. Within those mountains, five people waited for her. Five ancient men and women who had once believed they were the children of the gods. 'We're orphans,' Ayae said. 'We have to guide ourselves. We have to make our own choices. We have to decide what kind of world we live in. What words mean. What actions define.' She paused. 'We're orphans,' she repeated, and smiled.